JACK RYDER MYSTERY SERIES

VOL 1-3

WILLOW ROSE

BUOY MEDIA

Cover design by Jan Sigetty Boeje
https://www.facebook.com/pages/Sigettys Cover Design

Special thanks to my editor Janell Parque
http://janellparque.blogspot.com/

**To be the first to hear about new releases and bargains—from Willow Rose—
sign up below to be on the VIP List.** (I promise not to share your email with
anyone else, and I won't clutter your inbox.)

- SIGN UP TO BE ON THE VIP LIST HERE :

http://readerlinks.com/l/415254

FOLLOW WILLOW ROSE ON BOOKBUB:
https://www.bookbub.com/authors/willow-rose

Connect with Willow Rose:
willow-rose.net

Books by the Author

MYSTERY/THRILLER/HORROR NOVELS

- IN ONE FELL SWOOP
- UMBRELLA MAN
- BLACKBIRD FLY
- TO HELL IN A HANDBASKET
- EDWINA
- IN COLD BLOOD

7TH STREET CREW SERIES

- WHAT HURTS THE MOST
- YOU CAN RUN
- YOU CAN'T HIDE
- CAREFUL LITTLE EYES

EMMA FROST SERIES

- ITSY BITSY SPIDER
- MISS DOLLY HAD A DOLLY
- RUN, RUN AS FAST AS YOU CAN
- CROSS YOUR HEART AND HOPE TO DIE
- PEEK-A-BOO I SEE YOU
- TWEEDLEDUM AND TWEEDLEDEE
- EASY AS ONE, TWO, THREE
- THERE'S NO PLACE LIKE HOME
- SLENDERMAN
- WHERE THE WILD ROSES GROW
- WALTZING MATHILDA
- DRIP DROP

JACK RYDER SERIES

- HIT THE ROAD JACK
- SLIP OUT THE BACK JACK
- THE HOUSE THAT JACK BUILT
- BLACK JACK
- GIRL NEXT DOOR
- HER FINAL WORD

REBEKKA FRANCK SERIES

- One, Two...He is Coming for You
- Three, Four...Better Lock Your Door
- Five, Six...Grab your Crucifix
- Seven, Eight...Gonna Stay up Late
- Nine, Ten...Never Sleep Again
- Eleven, Twelve...Dig and Delve
- Thirteen, Fourteen...Little Boy Unseen
- Better Not Cry
- Ten Little Girls
- It Ends Here

HORROR SHORT-STORIES

- Mommy Dearest
- The Bird
- Better watch out
- Eenie, Meenie
- Rock-a-Bye Baby
- Nibble, Nibble, Crunch
- Humpty Dumpty
- Chain Letter

SCIENCE FICTION/PARANORMAL ROMANCE/FANTASY NOVELS

- The Surge
- Girl Divided

THE VAMPIRES OF SHADOW HILLS

- Flesh and Blood
- Blood and Fire
- Fire and Beauty
- Beauty and Beasts
- Beasts and Magic
- Magic and Witchcraft
- Witchcraft and War
- War and Order
- Order and Chaos
- Chaos and Courage

AFTERLIFE SERIES

- BEYOND
- SERENITY
- ENDURANCE
- COURAGEOUS

THE WOLFBOY CHRONICLES

- A GYPSY SONG
- I AM WOLF

DAUGHTERS OF THE JAGUAR

- SAVAGE
- BROKEN

Hit the Road Jack

JACK RYDER #1

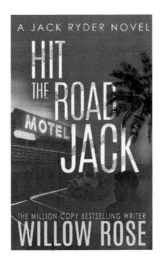

This could be Heaven or this could be Hell

Prologue

DON'T COME BACK NO MORE

ONE

May 2012

SHE HAS no idea who she is or where she is and cares to know neither. For some time, for what seems like forever, she has been in this daze. This haze, in complete darkness with nothing but the sounds. Sounds coming from outside her body, from outside her head. Sometimes, the sounds fade and there is only the darkness.

As time passes, she becomes aware that there are two realities. The one in her mind, filled with darkness and pain and then the one outside of her, where something or someone else is living, acting, smelling and...singing.

Yes, that's it. Someone is singing. Does she know the song?

...What you say?

The darkness is soon replaced by light. Still, her eyes are too heavy to open. Her consciousness returns slowly. Enough to start asking questions. Where is she? How did she end up here? A series of pictures of her at home come to her mind. She is waiting. What is she waiting for?

...I guess if you said so.

Him. She is waiting for him. She is checking her hair in the mirror every five minutes or so. Then correcting the make-up, looking at the clock again. Where is he? She looks out through the window and at the street and the many staring neighboring windows. A feeling of guilt hits her. Somehow, it seems wrong for this kind of thing to take place in broad daylight.

...That's right!

A car drives up. The anticipation. The butterflies in her stomach. The sound of the doorbell. She is straightening her dress and taking a last glance in the mirror. The next second, she is in his embrace. He is holding her so tight she closes her eyes and breathes him in until his lips cover hers and she swims away.

...Whoa, Woman, oh woman, don't treat me so mean.

His breath is pumping against her skin. She feels his hands on her breasts, under her skirt, coming closer, while he presses her up against the wall. She feels him in her hand. He is hard now, moaning in her ear.

7

"Where's your husband?" he whispers.

"Work," she moans back, feeling self-conscious. Why did he have to bring up her husband? The guilt is killing her. "The kids are in school."

"Good," he moans. "No one can ever know. Remember that. No one."

...You're the meanest old woman that I've ever seen.

He pushes himself inside of her and pumps. She lets herself get into the moment, but as soon as it is over, she finds herself regretting it...while he zips up the pants of his suit and kisses her gently on the lips, whispering, *same time next week?* She regrets having started it all. They are both married with children, and this is only an affair. Could never be anything else, even if she dreamt about it. The sex is great, but she wants more than just seeing him on her lunch break. But she can never tell him. She can never explain to him how much she hates this awkward moment that follows the sex.

"They're expecting me at the office...I have a meeting," he says, and puts his tie back on. "I'd better..."

...Hit the road, Jack!

She finally opens her eyes with a loud gasp. The bright light hurts her. Water is being splashed in her face. She can't breathe. The bathtub is slippery when she tries to get up. Her eyes lock with another set of eyes. The eyes of a man. He is staring at her with a twisted smile. She gasps again, suddenly remembering those dark chili eyes.

"I guess if you said so...I'd have to pack my things and go," he sings.

"You," she gasps. Breathing is hard for her. She feels like she is still choking. She is hyperventilating. Panicking.

The man smiles. On his neck crawls a snake. How does that old saying go again? *Red, black, yellow kills a fellow?* This one is all of that, all those colors. It stares at her while moving its tongue back and forth. The man is holding a washcloth in his hand. She looks down at her naked body. The smell of chlorine is strong and makes her eyes water.

"You tried to kill me," she says, while panting with anxiety.

I have to get home. Help me. I have to get home to my children! Oh, God. I can hear their voices! Am I going mad? I think I can hear them!

"I guess I didn't do a very good job, then," he answers. His chillingly calm voice is piercing through every bone in her body.

"I'll try again. *That's right!*"

TWO

May 2012

SHE HAD NEVER BEEN MORE beautiful than in this exact moment. No woman ever had. So fragile, her skin so pale it almost looked bluish. The man who called himself the Snakecharmer stared at her body. It was still in the bathtub. He was still panting from the exertion, his hands shaking and hurting from strangling the girl. He felt so aroused in this moment, staring at the dead body. It was the most fascinating thing in the world. How the body simply ceased to function. And almost as fascinating was what followed next. The human decaying process. It wasn't something new. Fascination with death had occurred all throughout human history, characterized by obsessions with death and all things related to death. The Egyptians mummified their dead. He had always wished he could do the same. Keep his dead forever and ever. He remembered as a child how he would sometimes lie down in front of the mirror and try to lie completely still and look at himself, imagining he was looking at a dead body. He would capture cats and kill them and keep them in his room, just to watch what would happen to them. He wanted so badly to stop the decaying process, he wanted them to remain the same always and never leave.

The Snakecharmer stared at the girl with fascination in his eyes. He caught his breath and calmed down again. He still felt the adrenalin rushing through his veins while he finished washing the girl. He washed away all the dirt, all the smells on her body. He reached down and cleaned her thoroughly between her legs. Scrubbed her to make sure he got all the dirt away, all the filth and impurities.

Then, he dried her with a towel before he pulled her onto the bathroom floor. His companions, his two pet Coral snakes, were sliding across her dead body. He grabbed one and let it slide across his arm while petting it. Then he knelt next to the girl and stroked her gently across her hair, making sure it wasn't in her face. Her blue eyes stared into the ceiling.

"Now, you'll never leave," he whispered.

With his cellphone, he took a picture of her naked body. That was his mummification. His way to always cherish the moment. To always remember. He never wanted to forget how beautiful she was.

He dried her with a towel. He brushed her brown hair with gentle strokes. He took yet another picture before he lifted her up and carried her into the bedroom, where he placed her in a chair, then sat in front of her and placed his head in her lap.

They would stay like this until she started to smell.

Part One

I GUESS IF YOU SAY SO

THREE

January 2015

HE TOOK the dog out in the yard and shut the door carefully behind him, making sure he didn't make a sound to wake up his sleeping parents. It was Monday, but they had been very loud last night. The kitchen counter was still covered with empty bottles.

At first, Ben had waited patiently in the living room, watching a couple of shows on TV, waiting for his parents to wake up. When the clock passed nine, he knew he wouldn't make it to school that day either, and that was too bad because they had a fieldtrip to the zoo today and Ben had been looking forward to it. When they still hadn't shown up at ten o'clock, he decided the dog had to go out. The old Labrador kept sitting by the door and scraping on it. It had to go.

So, Ben took Bobby out in the backyard. He had to go with him. The yard ended at the canal, and Bobby had more than once jumped into the water. Ben had to keep an eye on him to make sure he didn't do it again. It had been such a mess last time, since the dog couldn't climb back up over the seawall on his own, so Ben's dad had to jump into the blurry water and carry the dog out.

The dog quickly gave in to nature and did his business. Ben had a plastic bag that he picked it up with and threw it in the trash can behind the house.

It was a beautiful day out. One of those clear days with a blue sky and not a cloud anywhere on the horizon. The wind was blowing out of the north and had been for two days, making the air drier. For once, Ben's shirt didn't stick to his body.

He threw the ball a few times for the dog to get some exercise. Ben could smell the ocean, even though he lived on the back side of the barrier island. When it was quiet, he could even hear it too. The waves had to be good. If he wasn't too sick from drinking last night, his dad might take him surfing.

Ben really hoped he would.

It had been months since his dad last took him to the beach. He never seemed to have time anymore. Sometimes, Ben would take his bike and ride down there

12

by himself, but it was never as much fun as when the entire family went. They never seemed to do much together anymore. Ben wondered if it had anything to do with what happened to his baby sister a year ago. He never understood exactly what had happened. He just knew she didn't wake up one morning when their mother went to pick her up from her crib. Then his parents cried and cried for days and they held a big funeral. But the crying hadn't stopped for a long time. Not until it was replaced with a lot of sleeping and his parents staying up all night, and all the empty bottles that Ben often cleaned up from the kitchen and put in the recycling bin.

Bobby brought back the ball and placed it at Ben's feet. He picked it up and threw it again. It landed close to the seawall. Luckily, it didn't fall in. Bobby ran to get it, then placed it at Ben's feet again, looking at him expectantly.

"Really? One more time, then we're done," he said, thinking he'd better get back inside and start cleaning up. He picked up the ball and threw it. The dog stormed after it again and disappeared for a second down the hill leading to the canal. Ben couldn't see him.

"Bobby?" he yelled. "Come on, boy. We need to get back inside."

He stared in the direction of the canal. He couldn't see the bottom of the yard. He had no idea if Bobby had jumped in the water again. His heart started to pound. He would have to wake up his dad if he did. He was the only one who could get Bobby out of the water.

Ben stood frozen for a few seconds until he heard the sound of Bobby's collar, and a second later spotted his black dog running towards him with his tongue hanging out of his mouth.

"Bobby!" Ben said. He bent down and petted his dog and best friend. "You scared me, buddy. You forgot the ball. Well, we'll have to get that later. Now, let's go back inside and see if Mom and Dad are awake."

Ben grabbed the handle and opened the door. He let Bobby go in first.

"Mom?" he called.

But there was no answer. They were probably still asleep. Ben found some dog food in the cabinet and pulled the bag out. He spilled on the floor when he filled Bobby's tray. He had no idea how much the dog needed, so he made sure to give him enough, and poured till the bowl overflowed. Ben found a garbage bag under the sink and had removed some of the bottles, when Bobby suddenly started growling. The dog ran to the bottom of the stairs and barked. Ben found this to be strange. It was very unlike Bobby to act this way.

"What's the matter, boy? Are Mom and Dad awake?"

The dog kept barking and growling.

"Stop it!" Ben yelled, knowing how much his dad hated it when Bobby barked. "Bad dog."

But Bobby didn't stop. He moved closer and closer to the stairs and kept barking until the dog finally ran up the stairs.

"No! Bobby!" Ben yelled. "Come back down here!"

Ben stared up the stairs after the dog, wondering if he dared to go up there. His dad always got so mad if he went upstairs when they were sleeping. He wasn't allowed up there until they got out of bed. But, if he found Bobby up there, his dad would get really mad. Probably talk about getting rid of him again.

He's my best friend. Don't take my friend away.

"Bobby," he whispered. "Come back down here."

Ben's heart was racing in his chest. There wasn't a sound coming from upstairs. Ben held his breath, not knowing what to do. The last thing he wanted on a day like today was to make his dad angry. He expected his dad to start yelling any second now.

Oh no, what if he jumps into their bed? Dad is going to get so mad. He's gonna get real mad at Bobby.

"Bobby?" Ben whispered a little louder.

There was movement on the stairs, the black lab peeked his head out, then ran down the stairs.

"There you are," Ben said with relief. Bobby ran past him and sprang up on the couch.

"What do you have in your mouth? Not one of mom's shoes again."

It didn't look like it was big enough to be a shoe. Ben walked closer, thinking if it was a pair of Mommy's panties again, then the dog was dead. He reached down and grabbed the dog's mouth, then opened it and pulled out whatever it was. He looked down with a small shriek at what had come out of the dog's mouth. He felt nauseated, like the time when he had the stomach-bug and spent the entire night in the bathroom. Only this was worse.

It's a finger. A finger wearing Mommy's ring!

FOUR

January 2015

"Hit the road, Jack, and don't you come back no more no more no more."

The children's voices were screaming more than singing on the bus. I preferred *Wheels on the Bus,* but the kids thought it was oh so fun, since my name was Jack and I was actually driving the bus. I had volunteered to drive them to the Brevard Zoo for their field trip today. Two of the children, the pretty blonde twins in the back named Abigail and Austin, were mine. A boy and a girl. Just started Kindergarten six months ago. I could hardly believe how fast time passed. Everybody told me it would, but still. It was hard to believe.

I was thirty-five and a single dad of three children. My wife, Arianna, ran out on us four years ago…when the twins were almost two years old. It was too much, she told me. She couldn't cope with the children or me. She especially had a hard time taking care of Emily. Emily was my ex-partner's daughter. My ex-partner, Lisa, was shot on duty ten years ago during a chase in downtown Miami. The shooter was never captured, and it haunted me daily. I took Emily in after her mother died. What else could I have done? I felt guilty for what had happened to her mother. I was supposed to have protected my partner. Plus, the girl didn't know her father. Lisa never told anyone who he was; she didn't have any of her parents or siblings left, except for a homeless brother who was in no condition to take care of a child. So, I got custody and decided to give Emily the best life I could. She was six when I took her in, sixteen now, and at an age where it was hard for anyone to love you, besides your mom and dad. I tried hard to be both for her. Not always with much success. The fact was, I had no idea what it was like to be a black teenage girl.

Personally, I believed Arianna had depression after the birth of the twins, but she never let me close enough to talk about it. She cried for months after the twins were born, then one day out of the blue, she told me she had to go. That she couldn't stay or it would end up killing me. I cried and begged her to stay, but

15

there was nothing I could do. She had made up her mind. She was going back upstate, and that was all I needed to know. I shouldn't look for her, she said.

"Are you coming back?" I asked, my voice breaking. I couldn't believe anyone would leave her own children.

"I don't know, Jack."

"But...The children? They need you? They need their mother?"

"I can't be the mother you want me to be, Jack. I'm just not cut out for it. I'm sorry."

Then she left. Just like that. I had no idea how to explain it to the kids, but somehow I did. As soon as they started asking questions, I told them their mother had left and that I believed she was coming back one day. Some, maybe a lot of people, including my mother, might have told me it was insane to tell them that she might be coming back, but that's what I did. I couldn't bear the thought of them growing up with the knowledge that their own mother didn't want them. I couldn't bear for Emily to know that she was part of the reason why Arianna had left us, left the twins motherless. I just couldn't. I had to leave them with some sort of hope. And maybe I needed to believe it too. I needed to believe that she hadn't just abandoned us...that she had some stuff she needed to work out and soon she would be back. At least for the twins. They needed their mother and asked for her often. It was getting harder and harder for me to believe she was coming back for them. But I still said she would.

And there they were.

On the back seat of the bus, singing along with their classmates, happier than most of them. Mother or no mother, I had provided a good life for them in our little town of Cocoa Beach. As a detective working for the Brevard County Sheriff's Office, working their homicide unit, I had lots of spare time and they had their grandparents close by. They received all the love in the world from me and their grandparents, who loved them to death (and let them get away with just about anything).

Some might think they were spoiled brats, but to me they were the love of my life, the light, the...the...

What the heck were they doing in the back?

I hit the brakes a little too hard at the red light. All the kids on the bus fell forwards. The teacher, Mrs. Allen, whined and held on to her purse.

"Abigail and Austin!" I thundered through the bus. "Stop that right now!"

The twins grinned and looked at one another, then continued to smear chocolate on each other's faces. Chocolate from those small boxes with Nutella and sticks you dipped in it. Boxes their grandmother had given them for snack, even though I told her it had to be healthy.

"Now!" I yelled.

"Sorry, Dad," they yelled in unison.

"Well...wipe that off or..."

I never made it any further before the phone in my pocket vibrated. I pulled it out and started driving again as the light turned green.

"Ryder. We need you. I spoke with Ron and he told me you would be assisting us. We desperately need your help."

It was the head of the Cocoa Beach Police Department. Weasel, we called her. I didn't know why. Maybe it had to do with the fact that her name was Weslie Seal.

Maybe it was just because she kind of looked like a weasel because her body was long and slender, but her legs very short. Ron Harper was the county sheriff and my boss.

"Yes? When?"

"Now."

"But...I'm..."

"This is big. We need you now."

"If you say so. I'll get there as fast as I can," I said, and turned off towards the entrance to the zoo. The kids all screamed with joy when they saw the sign. Mrs. Allen shushed them.

"What, are you running a day-care now? Not that I have the time to care. Everything is upside down around here. We have a dead body. I'll text you the address. Meet you there."

FIVE

April 1984

ANNIE WAS GETTING READY. She was putting on make-up with her room-mate Julia, while listening to Michael Jackson's *Thriller* and singing into their hair-brushes. They were nineteen, in college, and heading for trouble, as Annie's father always said.

Annie wanted to be a teacher.

"Are you excited?" Julia asked. "You think he's going to be there?"

"He," was Tim. He was the talk of the campus and the guy they all desired. He was tall, blond, and a quarterback. He was perfect. And he had his eye on Annie.

"I hope so," Annie said, and put on her jacket with the shoulder pads. "He asked me to come; he'd better be."

She looked at her friend, wondering why Tim hadn't chosen Julia instead. She was much prettier.

"Shall we?" Julia asked and opened the door. They were both wearing heavy make-up and acid-washed jeans.

Annie was nervous as they walked to the party. She had never been to a party in a fraternity house before. She had been thrilled when Tim came up to her in the library where she hung out most of the time and told her there was a party at the house and asked if she was going to come.

"Sure," she had replied, while blushing.

"This is it," Julia said, as they approached the house. Kids a few years older than them were hanging out on the porch, while loud music spilled out through the open windows. Annie had butterflies in her stomach as they went up the steps to the front of the house and entered, elbowing themselves through the crowd.

The noise was intense. People were drinking and smoking everywhere. Some were already making out on a couch. And it wasn't even nine o'clock yet.

"Let's get something to drink," Julia yelled through the thick clamor. "Have you loosen up a little."

Julia came back with two cups, and…Tim. "Look who I found," she said. "He was asking for you."

Annie grabbed the plastic cup and didn't care what it contained; she gulped it down in such a hurry she forgot to breathe. Tim was staring at her with that handsome smile of his. Then, he leaned over, put his hand on her shoulder, and whispered. "Glad you came."

Annie blushed and felt warmth spread through her entire body from the palm of Tim's hand on her shoulder. She really liked him. She really, really liked him.

"It's very loud in here. Do you want to go somewhere?" he asked.

Annie knew she wasn't the smartest among girls. Her mother had always told her so. She knew Tim, who was pre-med, would never be impressed with her conversational skills or her wits. If she was to dazzle him, it had to be in another way.

"Sure," she said.

"Let me get us some drinks first," Tim said and disappeared.

Julia smiled and grabbed Annie's shoulders. "You got him, girl." Then she corrected Annie's hair and wiped a smear of mascara from under her eyes.

"There. Now you're perfect. Remember. Don't think. You always overthink everything. Just be you. Just go with the flow, all right? Laugh at his jokes, but not too hard. Don't tell him too much about yourself; stay mysterious. And, whatever you do…don't sleep with him. You hear me? He won't respect you if you jump into bed with him right away. You have to play hard to get."

Annie stared at Julia. She had never had sex with anyone before, and she certainly wasn't going to now. Not yet. She had been saving herself for the right guy, and maybe Tim was it, but she wasn't going to decide that tonight. She didn't even want to.

"I'd never do that," she said with a scoff. "I'm not THAT stupid."

SIX

January 2015

WEASEL WAS STANDING outside the house as I drove up and parked the school bus on the street. The house on West Bay Drive was blocked by four police cars and lots of police tape. I saw several of my colleagues walking around in the yard. Weasel spotted me and approached. She was wearing tight black jeans, a belt with a big buckle, a white shirt, and black blazer. She looked to be in her thirties, but I knew she had recently turned forty.

"What the...?" she said with a grin, looking at the bus. She had that raspy rawness to her voice, and I always wondered if she could sing. I pictured her as a country singer. She gave out that tough vibe.

"Don't ask," I said. "What have we got?"

"Homicide," Weasel answered. "Victim is female. Laura Bennett, thirty-two, Mom of Ben, five years old. The husband's name is Brandon Bennett."

My heart dropped. I knew the boy. He was in the twins' class. I couldn't believe it. I had moved to Cocoa Beach from Miami in 2008 and never been called out to a homicide in my own town. Our biggest problems around here were usually tourists on spring break jumping in people's pools and Jacuzzis and leaving beer cans, or the youngsters having bonfires on the beach and burning people's chairs and leaving trash.

But, murder? That was a first for me in Cocoa Beach. I had been called out to drug related homicides in the beachside area before, but that was mostly further down south in Satellite Beach and Indialantic, but never this far up north.

"It's bad," Weasel said. "I have close to no experience with this type of thing, but you do. We need all your Miami-experience now. Show me what you've got."

I nodded and followed her into the house. It was located on a canal leading to the Banana River, like most of the houses on the back side of the island. The house had a big pebble-coated pool area with two waterfalls, a slide, and a spa over-looking the river. The perfect setting for Florida living, the real estate ad would say. With the huge palm trees, it looked like true paradise. Until you stepped inside.

The inside was pure hell.

It was a long time since I had been on a murder scene, but the Weasel was right. I was the only one with lots of experience in this field. I spent eight years in downtown Miami, covering Overtown, the worst neighborhood in the town, as part of the homicide unit. My specialty was the killer's psychology. I was a big deal back then. But when I met Arianna and she became pregnant with the twins, I was done. It was suddenly too dangerous. We left Miami to get away from it. We moved to Cocoa Beach, where my parents lived, to be closer to my family and to get away from murder.

Now, it had followed me here. It made me feel awful. I hated to see the town's innocence go like this.

My colleagues from the Cocoa Beach Police Department greeted me with nods as we walked through the living room, overlooking the yard with the pool. I knew all of them. They seemed a little confused. For most of them, it was a first. Officer Joel Hall looked pale.

"Joel was first man here," Weasel said.

"How are you doing, Joel?" I asked.

"Been better."

"So, tell me what happened."

Joel sniffled and wiped his nose on his sleeve.

"We got a call from the boy. He told us his mother had been killed. He found her finger...well, the dog had it in his mouth. He didn't dare to go upstairs. He called 911 immediately. I was on patrol close by, so I drove down here."

"So, what did you find?"

"The boy and the dog were waiting outside the house. He was hysterical, kept telling me his parents were dead. Then, he showed me the finger. I tried to calm him down and tell him I would go look and to stay outside. I walked up and found the mother..." Joel sniffled again. He took in a deep breath.

"Take your time, Joel," I said, and put my hand on his shoulder. Joel finally caved in and broke down.

"You better see it with your own eyes," Weasel said. "But brace yourself."

I followed her up the stairs of the house, where the medical examiners were already taking samples.

"The kid said his parents were dead. What about the dad?" I asked. "You only said one homicide."

"The dad's fine. But, hear this," Weasel said. "He claims he was asleep the entire time. He's been taken to the hospital to see a doctor. He kept claiming he felt dizzy and had blurred vision. I had to have a doctor look at him before we talk to him. The boy is with him. Didn't want to leave his side. The dog is there too. Jim and Marty took them there. I don't want him to run. He's our main suspect so far."

We walked down the hallway till we reached the bedroom. "Brace yourself," Weasel repeated, right before we walked inside.

I sucked in my breath. Then I froze.

"It looks like he was dismembering her," Weasel said. "He cut off all the fingers on her right hand, one by one, then continued on to the toes on her foot."

I felt disgusted by the sight. I held a hand to cover my mouth, not because it smelled, but because I always became sick to my stomach when facing a dead body. Especially one that was mutilated. I never got used to it. I kneeled next to the woman lying on the floor. I examined her face and eyes, lifted her eyelids, then looked closely at her body.

"There's hardly any blood. No bruises either," I said. "I say she was strangled first, then he did the dismembering. My guess is he was disturbed. He was about to cut her into bits and pieces, but he stopped."

I sniffed the body and looked at the Weasel, who seemed disgusted by my motion. "The kill might have happened in the shower. She has been washed recently. Maybe he drowned her."

I walked into the bathroom and approached the tub. I ran a finger along the sides. "Look." I showed her my finger. "There's still water on the sides. It's been used recently."

"So, you think she was killed in the bathtub? Strangulation, you say? But there are no marks on her neck or throat?"

"Look at her eyes. Petechiae. Tiny red spots due to ruptured capillaries. They are a signature injury of strangulation. She has them under the eyelids. He didn't use his hands. He was being gentle."

Weasel looked appalled. "Gentle? How can you say he was gentle? He cut off her fingers?"

"Yes, but look how methodical he was. All the parts are intact. Not a bruise on any of them. Not a drop of blood. They are all placed neatly next to one another. It's a declaration of love."

Weasel looked confused. She grumbled. "I don't see much love in any of all this, that's for sure. All I see is a dead woman, who someone tried to chop up. And now I want you to find out who did it."

I chuckled. "So, the dad tells us he was sleeping?" I asked.

Weasel shrugged. "Apparently, he was drunk last night. They had friends over. It got a little heavy, according to the neighbors. Loud music and loud voices. But that isn't new with these people."

"On a Sunday night in a nice neighborhood like this?" I asked, surprised.

"Apparently."

"It's a big house. Right on the river. Snug Harbor is one of the most expensive neighborhoods around here. What do the parents do for a living?"

"Nothing, I've been told. They live off the family's money. The deceased's father was a very famous writer. He died ten years ago. The kids have been living off of the inheritance and the royalties for years since."

"Anyone I know, the writer?"

"Probably," she said. "A local hero around here. John Platt."

"John Platt?" I said. "I've certainly heard of him. I didn't know he used to live around here. Wasn't he the guy who wrote all those thriller-novels that were made into movies later on?"

"Yes, that was him. He has sold more than 100 million books worldwide. His books are still topping the bestseller lists."

"Didn't he recently publish a new book or something?"

Weasel nodded. "They found an old unpublished manuscript of his on his computer, which they published. I never understood how those things work, but I figure they think, if he wrote it, then it's worth a lot of money even if he trashed it."

I stared at the dead halfway-dismembered body on the floor, then back at the Weasel.

I sighed. "I guess we better talk to this heavily sleeping dad first."

SEVEN

January 2015

"Who was that guy you talked to last night?"

Joe walked into the kitchen. Shannon was cutting up oranges to make juice. She sensed he was right behind her, but she didn't turn to look at him. Last night was still in her head. The humming noise of the voices, the music, the laughter. Her head was hurting from a little too much alcohol. His question made everything inside of her freeze.

"Who do you mean?" she asked. "I talked to a lot of people. That was kind of the idea with the party after my concert. For me to meet with the press and important people in the business. That's the way it always is. You know how it goes. It's a big part of my job."

He put his hand on her shoulder. A shiver ran up her spine. She closed her eyes. *Not now. Please not now.*

"Look at me when you're talking to me," he said.

She took in a deep breath, then put on a smile; the same smile she used when the press asked her to pose for pictures, the same smile she put on for her manager, her record label, and her friends when they asked her about the bruises on her back, followed by the sentence:

"Just me being clumsy again."

Shannon turned and looked at Joe. His eyes were black with fury. Her body shrunk and her smile froze.

"I saw the way you were looking at that guy. Don't you think I saw that?" Joe asked. "You know what I think? I think you like going to these parties they throw in your honor. I think you enjoy all the men staring at you, wishing you were theirs, wanting to fuck your brains out. I see it in their eyes and I see it in yours as well. You like it."

It was always the same. Joe couldn't stand the fact that Shannon was the famous one...that she was the one everyone wanted to talk to, and after a party like the one yesterday, he always lost his temper with her. Because he felt left out,

24

because there was no one looking at him, talking to him, asking him questions with interest. He hated the fact that Shannon was the one with a career, when all he had ever dreamt of was to be singing in sold out stadiums like she did.

They had started out together. Each with just a guitar under their arm, working small clubs and bars in Texas, then later they moved on to Nashville, where country musicians were made. They played the streets together, and then got small gigs in bars, and later small concert venues around town. But when a record label contacted them one day after a concert, they were only interested in her. They only wanted Shannon King. Since then, Joe had been living in the shadow of his wife, and that didn't become him well. For years, she had made excuses for him, telling herself he was going through a rough time; he was just hurting because he wasn't going anywhere with his music. The only thing Joe had going for him right now was the fact that he was stronger than Shannon.

But as the years had passed, it was getting harder and harder for her to come up with new excuses, new explanations. Especially now that they had a child together. A little girl who was beginning to ask questions.

"Joe…I…I don't know what you're talking about. I talked to a lot of people last night. I'm tired and now I really want to get some breakfast."

"Did you just take a tone with me. Did ya'? Am I so insignificant in your life that you don't even talk to me with respect, huh? You don't even look at me when we're at your precious after party. Nobody cares about me. Everyone just wants to talk to the *biiig* star, Shannon King," he said, mocking her.

"You're being ridiculous."

"Am I? Did you even think about me once last night? Did you? I left at eleven-thirty. You never even noticed. You never even texted me and asked where I was."

Shannon blushed. He was right. She hadn't thought about him even once. She had been busy answering questions from the press and talking about her tour. Everyone had been pulling at her; there simply was no time to think about him. Why couldn't he understand that?

"I thought so," Joe said. Then, he slapped her.

Shannon went stumbling backward against the massive granite counter. She hurt her back in the fall. Shannon whimpered, then got up on her feet again with much effort. Her cheek burned like hell. A little blood ran from the corner of her mouth. She wiped it off.

Careful what you say, Shannon. Careful not to upset him further. Remember what happened last time. He's not well. He is hurting. Careful not to hurt him any more.

But she knew it was too late. She knew once he crossed that line into that area where all thinking ceased to exist, it was too late. She could appeal to his sensitivity as much as she wanted to. She could try and explain herself and tell him she was sorry, but it didn't help. If anything, it only made everything worse.

His eyes were bulging and his jaws clenched. His right eye had that tick in it that only showed when he was angry.

You got to get out of here.

"Joe, please, I…"

A fist throbbed through the air and smashed into her face.

Quick. Run for the phone.

She could see it. It was on the breakfast bar. She would have to spring for it. Shannon jumped to the side and managed to avoid his next fist, then slipped on the small rug on the kitchen floor, got back up in a hurry, and rushed to reach out for the phone.

Call 911. Call the police.

Her legs were in the air and she wasn't running anymore. He had grabbed her by the hair, and now he was pulling her backwards. He yanked her towards him, and she screamed in pain, cursing her long blonde hair that she used to love so much...that the world loved and put on magazine covers.

"You cheating lying bitch!" he screamed, while pulling her across the floor.

He lifted her up, then threw her against the kitchen counter. It blew out the air from her lungs. She couldn't scream anymore. She was panting for air and wheezing for him to stop. She was bleeding from her nose. Joe came closer, then leaned over her and, with his hand, he corrected his hair. His precious hair that had always meant so much to him, that he was always fixing and touching to make sure it was perfect, which it ironically never was.

"No one disrespects me. Do you hear me? Especially not you. You're a nobody. Do you understand? You would be nothing if it wasn't for me," he yelled, then lifted his clenched fist one more time. When it smashed into Shannon's face again and again, she finally let herself drift into a darkness so deep she couldn't feel anything anymore.

EIGHT

January 2015

"Hɪ ᴛʜᴇʀᴇ. Bᴇɴ, ɪs ɪᴛ?" I asked.

The boy was sitting next to his dad in the hospital bed, the dog sleeping by his feet.

"He won't leave his dad's side," Marty said.

Ben looked up at me with fear in his eyes. "It's okay, Ben," I said, and kneeled in front of him. "We can talk here."

"I know you," Ben said. "You're Austin and Abigail's dad."

"That's right. And you're in their class. I remember you. Say, weren't you supposed to be at the zoo today?"

Ben nodded with a sad expression.

"Well, there'll be other times," I said. I paused while Ben looked at his father, who was sleeping.

"He's completely out cold," Marty said. "He was complaining that he couldn't control his arms and legs, had spots before his eyes, and he felt dizzy and nauseated. Guess it was really heavy last night."

I looked at the very pale dad. "Or maybe it was something else," I said.

"What do you mean?"

I looked closer at the dad.

"Did you talk to him?"

"Only a few words. When I asked about last night, he kept saying he didn't remember what happened, that he didn't know where he was. He kept asking me what time it was. Even after I had just told him."

"Hm."

"What?" Marty asked.

"Did they run his blood work?" I asked.

"No. I told them it wasn't necessary. He was just hung over. The doctor looked at him quickly and agreed. We agreed to let him to sleep it off. He seemed like he was still drunk when he talked to us."

27

"Is my dad sick, Mr. Ryder?" Ben asked.

I looked at the boy and smiled. "No, son, but I am afraid your dad has been poisoned."

"Poisoned?" Marty asked. "What on earth do you mean?"

"Dizziness, confusion, blurry vision, difficulty talking, nausea, difficulty controlling your movements all are symptoms of Rohypnol poisoning. Must have been ingested to have this big of an effect. Especially with alcohol."

"Roofied?" Marty laughed. "Who on earth in their right mind would give a grown man a rape drug?"

"Someone who wanted to kill him and his wife," I said.

I walked into the hallway and found a nurse and asked her to make sure they tested Brandon Bennett for the drug in his blood. Then, I called the medical examiner and told them to check the wife's blood as well. Afterwards, I returned to talk to Ben.

"So, Ben, I know this is a difficult time for you, but I would be really happy if you could help me out by talking a little about last night. Can you help me out here?"

Ben wiped his eyes and looked at me. His face was swollen from crying. Then he nodded. I opened my arms. "Come here, buddy. You look like you could use a good bear hug."

Ben hesitated, then looked at his dad, who was still out cold, before he finally gave in and let me hug him. I held him in my arms, the way I held my own children when they were sad. The boy finally cried.

"It's okay," I whispered. "Your dad will be fine."

My words felt vague compared to what the little boy had seen this morning, how his world had been shaken up. His dad was probably going to be fine, but he would never see his mother again, and the real question was whether the boy would ever be fine again?

He wept in my arms for a few minutes, then pulled away and wiped his nose on his sleeve. "Do you promise to catch the guy that killed my mother?" he asked.

I sighed. "I can promise I'll do my best. How about that?"

Ben thought about it for a little while, then nodded with a sniffle.

"Okay. What do you want to know?" he asked.

"Who came to your house last night? I heard your parents had guests. Who were they?"

NINE

April 1984

TIM TOOK Annie down to the lake behind campus, where they sat down. The grass was moist from the sprinklers. Annie felt self-conscious with the way Tim stared at her. It was a hot night out. The cicadas were singing; Annie was sweating in her small dress. Her skin felt clammy.

Tim finally broke the silence.

"Has anyone ever told you how incredibly beautiful you are?"

Annie's head was spinning from her drink. The night was intoxicating, the sounds, the smell, the moist air hugging her. She shook her head. Her eyes stared at the grass. She felt her cheeks blushing.

"No."

"Really?" Tim said. "I find that very hard to believe."

Annie giggled, then sipped her drink. She really liked Tim. She could hardly believe she was really here with him.

"Look at the moon," he said and pointed.

It was a full moon. It was shining almost as bright as daylight. Its light hit the lake. Annie took in a deep breath, taking in the moment.

"It's beautiful," she said with a small still voice. She was afraid of talking too much, since he would only realize she wasn't smart, and then he might regret being with her.

Just go with the flow.

"I loathe Florida," Tim said. "I hate these warm nights. I hate how sweaty I always am. I'm especially sick of Orlando. When I'm done here, I'm getting out of this state. I wanna go up north. Don't you?"

Annie shrugged. She had lived all her life in Florida. Thirty minutes north of Orlando, to be exact. Born and raised in Windermere. Her parents still lived there, and that was where she was planning on going back once she had her degree. Annie had never thought about going anywhere else.

"I guess it's nice up north as well," she said, just to please him.

Tim laughed, then looked at her with those intense eyes once again. It made her uncomfortable. But part of her liked it as well. A big part.

"Can I kiss you?" he asked.

Annie blushed. She really wanted him to. Then she nodded. Tim smiled, then leaned over and put his lips on top of hers. Annie felt the dizziness from the drink. It was buzzing in her head. The kiss made her head spin, and when Tim pressed her down on the moist grass, she let him. He crawled on top of her, and with deep moans kept kissing her lips, then her cheeks, her ears, and her neck. Annie felt like laughing because it tickled so much, but she held it back to not ruin anything. Tim liked her and it made her happy.

"Boy, you're hot," he said, groaning, as he kissed her throat and moved further down her body. He grinned and started to open her dress, taking one button at a time. Annie felt insecure. What was he going to do next?

Tim pulled the dress open and looked at her bra, then he ripped it off.

"Ouch," Annie said. She tried to cover her breasts with her arms, but Tim soon grabbed them and pulled them to her sides. He held her down while kissing her breasts. He groaned while sucking on her nipples. Annie wasn't sure if she liked it or not. He was being a little rough, and she was afraid of going too far with him.

Whatever you do, don't sleep with him. No matter what.

"Stop," she mumbled, when he pulled the dress off completely and grabbed her panties. Tim stopped. He stared at Annie. She felt bad. Had she scared him away? Was he ever going to see her again if she didn't let him?

No matter what.

No. She wasn't ready for this. She had saved herself. This wasn't how it was supposed to happen. Not like this. Not here.

"I want to go home," Annie said.

Tim smiled and tilted his head, then leaned over and whispered in her ear. "Not yet, sweetheart, not yet."

He stroked her face gently and kissed her cheeks, while she fought and tried to get him off her body. In the distance, she heard voices, and soon she felt hands on her body, hands touching her, hands slapping her face. She felt so dizzy and everything became a blur of faces, laughing voices, cheering voices, hands everywhere, groping her, touching her, hurting her. And then the pain followed.

The excruciating pain.

TEN

January 2015

BRANDON BENNETT WAS STILL out cold when I had to leave the hospital. I decided to wait to interrogate him till later. Ben had told me that he had been asleep, so he hadn't seen who was at the house, but there were two of his parents' neighbors who usually came over to drink with his mom and dad. I got the names and called for both of them to come into the station in the afternoon. Meanwhile, I had to drive back to the zoo to pick up the kids and get them back to their school.

"Daddy!" my kids yelled when I opened the doors to the school bus and they stormed in, screaming with joy. Both of them clung to my neck.

"How was the zoo?" I asked.

"So much fun!" Abigail exclaimed. She was the most outgoing of the two, and often the one who spoke for them. I had a feeling Austin was the thinker, the one who would turn out to be a genius some day. Well, maybe not exactly a genius, but there was something about him. Abigail was the one who came up with all their naughty plans, and she always got Austin in on them.

"Good. I'm glad," I said and smooched their cheeks loudly.

"You would have loved it, Dad," Abigail continued. "You should have come. What was so important anyway?"

I exhaled and kissed her again, then let go of her. "Just some work thing. Nothing to worry about."

The twins looked at each other. Abigail placed her hands on her hips and looked at me with her head tilted.

"What?" I asked.

"You only say for us to not worry if there is actually something to worry about," Abigail said. "Am I right?" She looked at Austin, who nodded.

"She's right, Dad."

I smiled. "Well, it is nothing smart little noses like yours should get into, so get in the back of the bus with your friends and sit down. We're leaving now."

Abigail grumbled something, then grabbed her brother's shirt and they walked to the back. The bus gave a deep sigh when I closed the doors and we took off.

The atmosphere on the bus driving back was loud and very cheerful. Loudest of all were my twins, but this time I didn't mind too much. After the morning I had spent with a dead body and a poor kid who had lost his mother, I was just so pleased that my kids were still happy and innocent. They didn't look at me with that empty stare in their eyes, the one where you know they'll never trust the world again. That broken look that made them appear so much older than they were.

"Grandma and Grandpa will pick you up," I said, as I dropped them off at Roosevelt Elementary School.

"Yay!" they both exclaimed.

I told their teacher as well, then parked the bus and gave the keys back to the front office.

"Thank you so much for helping out today," Elaine at the desk said. "It's always wonderful when the parents get involved."

"Anytime," I said.

I walked to my car, a red Jeep Convertible. I got in and drove to the station with the top down. I bought my favorite sandwich at Juice 'N Java Café, called Cienna. It had a Portobello mushroom, yellow tomato, goat cheese arugula, and pesto on Pugliese bread. I figured I had earned it after the morning I had.

The police station was located inside of City Hall, right in the heart of Cocoa Beach. I knew the place well, even though I was usually located at the sheriff's offices in Rockledge. Cocoa Beach was my town, and every time they needed a detective, I was the one they called for. Even if they were cases that didn't involve homicide. As I entered through the glass doors, Weasel came towards me. Two officers flanked her.

"Going out for lunch?" I asked.

"Yes. I see you've already gotten yours," she said, nodding at my bag with my sandwich from the café.

"I'm expecting two of the neighbors in for questioning in a short while. Any news I should know about?" I asked.

Weasel sighed. "The ME has taken the body in for examination. They expect to have the cause of death within a few hours, they say. They're still working on the house."

"Any fingerprints so far?"

"Lots. We asked around a little and heard the same story from most of the neighbors. The Bennetts were a noisy bunch. Nothing that has ever been reported, but the wife and husband fought a lot, one neighbor told us. He said they yelled and screamed at each other when they got drunk. He figured the husband finally had enough. He killed her, then panicked and tried to dismember her body to get rid of it. But the dog interrupted him. He decided to pretend he had been asleep through the whole thing. When we arrived, the dad was asleep when Joel went up, but he might have pretended to be. Joel said he seemed out of it, though. Might just be a good actor."

"It's all a lot of theories so far," I said with a deep exhale. It was going to be a long day for me. I was so grateful I had my parents nearby.

I grew up in Ft. Lauderdale, further down south, but when I left for college, my parents wanted to try something new. They bought a motel by the beach in Cocoa Beach a few years after I left the house. The place was a haven for the kids. They never missed me while they were there. That made it easier for me to work late.

"I've cleared an office for you," Weasel said. "We're glad to have you here to help us."

I put a hand on her broad shoulder. "Likewise. I'll hold down the fort. Enjoy your lunch."

ELEVEN

January 2015

"IT ALL STARTED when they lost their daughter."

It was late in the afternoon at the station. I had interviewed two of the neighbors who usually came to the Bennetts' house to drink with them, but hadn't gotten anything out of them. They didn't even know the Bennetts very well, they told me. They just knew that there was free booze. The Bennetts were loaded, and every drunk in the neighborhood knew that they could always find a party there. Only one of the two, Travis Connor, had been at the Bennett's house the night before. He told us he was the only guest at the time, but he hadn't stayed long. He had left the house at ten o'clock and gone to the Beach Shack to hang out with some buddies. I called, and they confirmed his alibi. The next-door neighbor, Mrs. Jeffries had told my colleagues that she had seen Laura Bennett walk onto the back porch at eleven to smoke a cigarette. So, I let the guy go. His hands were shaking heavily, and I guessed he was in a hurry to find a drink somewhere.

Around three o'clock, a woman had come to the station and asked to talk to someone about the killing of Laura Bennett. Her name was Gabrielle Phillips.

The front desk sent her to me. Now, I was sitting across from her as she explained why she had come.

"They lost their child last year, and that's when it all went wrong," she continued. "I've known Laura since high school," she said. "She never used to drink. But when their daughter died in her bed at night, everything changed."

"Sudden Infant Death Syndrome?" I asked, and wrote it on a notepad.

"Yes. After that, they started drinking. Well, to be honest, Brandon has always drunk a lot, but she never did. Never touched a drop. It wasn't her thing. She didn't like to lose control."

"So, they drank and partied because they lost their child?" I asked.

"Well, Brandon always liked to party. Especially after Laura inherited all that money. He didn't have to work anymore. He had always liked to drink, but it got really bad. She was actually considering leaving him and taking the kids, but then

34

the daughter died in her sleep, and she couldn't take it. She had a drink and then never stopped again. I tried to talk to her, but she shut me out and told me it was none of my business."

Gabrielle looked upset. I could tell she had loved her friend and cared for her. She was choking up, but held back the tears.

"I tried..." she continued. "I really did. But she wouldn't listen to me. I told her that guy was all wrong for her. He was trouble from the beginning."

I reached behind me and grabbed a box of tissues that I handed to her. She grabbed it and wiped her eyes, careful not to smear her make-up. I wrote on my notepad and tried to get all the details down.

"So, you say she inherited a lot of money? From her dad, right?" I asked.

"She inherited ten million dollars from him, and she never even knew him."

I looked up. "Excuse me?"

"She was born outside of marriage. Her mother was an affair that John Platt had once when he was on a book tour. They met in Tampa, where she lived at the time. Nine months later, Laura was born. John Platt refused to have anything to do with the child. He paid a good amount of money to the mother to keep her mouth shut and never tell the child who her real father was. Laura's mother later remarried when Laura was still a baby, and they decided to have the new husband be the father as well. To prevent any awkward questions. And to have Laura grow up with a real family. Her new father loved her, and she still looks at him like her real father. Both of her parents died two years ago in a car accident outside of Orlando."

"Sounds like Laura has suffered a lot of loss the last couple of years," I said.

Gabrielle sniffled and wiped her nose in a ladylike manner.

"So, her husband Brandon, tell me more about him?"

"He is the scum of the earth," Gabrielle hissed. "But, somehow, she loved him."

"How did they meet?"

"At a sports game. Can you believe it? A baseball game. UCF Knights were playing South Florida. Laura went to UCF; Brandon had just come to watch the game with some friends. He was an auto mechanic and smelled like oil and trouble, if you ask me. Smoked and drank too much. Liked to party. I was with her on the night they met outside the stadium. He just walked right up to her and told her she was gorgeous and that he would like to invite her out sometime. I was surprised to hear her accept. I couldn't believe her. But I guess she somehow wanted to rebel against her parents or something. They never liked him either, but she married him anyway. After four months of them dating, he proposed. Four months! I knew she was going to get herself in trouble with this guy. I just knew it."

"So, tell me some more about the inheritance. When did she realize she was going to get all this money?"

"It was right before the pig proposed. Go figure, right? He heard about the money, then wanted to marry her. I couldn't believe she didn't see it, but she told me she loved him, and I really think she did. I think all he loved was her money. Anyway, that's just my opinion."

"How did she learn about the money? From a lawyer?" I asked, thinking it must have been quite a shock...suddenly being a millionaire and suddenly realizing your entire childhood was based on a lie.

Gabrielle shook her head and wiped her nose again. She drank from the glass of water I had placed in front of her. It was hot outside. In the low eighties. She was wearing shorts and flip-flops. The state costume of Florida. Even in January.

"No, it was the strangest thing. He called her."

"Who?"

"John Platt. He called her right before he died. How he got her number, I don't know, but I guess when you're that big you have people working for you. He was sick, he said. Cancer was eating him and he wanted her to come. He didn't tell her why, only that he had something for her. At first, Laura thought it was a joke, but he gave her an address and she looked it up and it turned out to be right. She called me afterwards and told me everything. She was freaking out. Said she had decided she didn't want to go, because it was too weird. But I convinced her to do it. I went with her, so she wouldn't be alone. Together, we were invited into his huge mansion on the beach in Cocoa Beach. He told her he was happy to see her. There were others there. I later learned they were her siblings. Two sisters and a brother. They had all grown up in the house, but were now living on their own, except for the youngest, who hadn't left the house yet, even though he was in his mid-twenties. They weren't very happy to see her, I can tell you that much. They weren't prepared to share their inheritance with some stranger, but they soon learned they had to."

"So, what happened?" I asked "What did John Platt tell her?"

"It was such an awkward scene. He was lying in bed, surrounded by nurses and family. He teared up when he saw Laura. It made her really uncomfortable. He wanted to hold her hand and started to cry. Then, he handed her a piece of paper. *Take this*, he said. *You deserve this more than any of the others.*"

"So, what was written on the paper?"

"It was a will. He had changed his will a few hours before we arrived. His lawyer had signed it and everything. It stated that she was going to inherit everything. All he had. The house, his money, everything."

I leaned back in my chair while the story came together for me. "So, the siblings didn't get anything?"

She shook her head. "Nope. Not a dime. They had grown up in luxury, so their father figured it was time for them to learn how to earn a decent living on their own. That's what he wrote in the letter. Laura had never known who her father was, never had any of his money, now he was giving her everything. I guess he tried to make amends for not letting her know he was her dad all those years. Laura was baffled, to put it mildly. She read the letter, but didn't understand. How could he be her father? She already had a father. She ran out of the house crying, and I ran after her. John Platt died shortly after, we later learned. Good thing for him, I think. Otherwise, the siblings would probably have started a riot. They tried to fight Laura with all their big lawyers afterwards, trying to declare that their dad was dying, and therefore not in his right mind when he made the will. After several months of going back and forth, the judge decided they didn't have a case and closed it. Laura was rich and, in time, came to accept the fact that she had been the result of an affair. Her mother confirmed it was true, and they didn't speak for a long time, but she forgave her eventually. Laura and Brandon bought the house in Snug Harbor and moved here shortly after they were married. She sold John Platt's old house, but wanted to stay in the town. She liked it here, she told me. I didn't see her much after she moved, since I live north of Orlando now, and I work full time, but every now and then, we would meet and catch up. But she was never really happy. She had Ben, and he was the joy of her life, but she kept talking about how Brandon was drinking and gambling her money away on the casino boats, acting like this big shot with her money. She wanted to leave him, but then she was pregnant again and decided to stay for the children. I met with her the week before the baby died. She said she was going to leave him, this time for real. That she was going back to the Tampa area and start over with the kids. Brandon's drinking had gotten worse, and he was still gambling a lot. In a few years, he had spent more than a third of her money. She was still certain he loved her, and maybe he does. I don't know him well enough to say he doesn't. But he also loved the money, and that's what went so wrong. After the baby died, I went to the funeral and Laura had a black eye. She told me in confidence that Brandon had slapped her, that he blamed her for the child's death. They fought about that a lot, she told me. He couldn't believe she hadn't checked on the baby during the night. It was her fault, he told her. And she believed him. She felt so guilty, she told me. So much it hurt. I said she should leave him, that now was the time to go, and she agreed, but she never did. Instead, she lowered herself to his level and took up drinking. The last time I spoke to her was three months ago, and she was so drunk on the phone I could hardly understand what she was saying. Now...I can't believe she's gone. What's to become of Ben?"

I shook my head with a deep exhale. I was starting to wonder that myself.

TWELVE

January 2015

SHANNON HEARD her daughter's voice calling in the distance. Then the door slammed and the voice came closer, even though it was all still drowned in a heavy daze.

"Moom? Moom?" the voice became shrill and clearer.

Shannon tried to blink her eyes to be able to see, but it hurt too much.

She felt a hand in hers, then someone pulling her arm.

"Mom? Please, wake up, Mom, please?"

Shannon growled something, trying to speak, but her lip hurt. She blinked again, and soon an image emerged of her daughter looking at her with terrified eyes.

"Mom, are you all right? Speak to me, Mommy!"

You gotta say something. The girl is scared. Seeing you like this. Say something to calm her down.

Shannon opened her eyes wide and looked at her daughter. Her beautiful Angela. The love of her life. The only beautiful thing in her life. The one thing she had done right.

"Hi, sweetie."

"Mommy. What happened? Are you hurt?"

With much effort, Shannon sat up on the kitchen floor. She leaned her head on the cupboards behind her. So much pain.

"Mommy must have fallen," she said, and felt blood on her fingers when she touched her face.

"Again?" Angela said.

"Yeah. Again."

"You're so clumsy, Mommy," Angela said. She grabbed a towel and wet it. Then she put ice cubes inside of it and handed it to Shannon. She did it with such expertise and experience that it terrified Shannon.

"Thanks, sweetie," she said.

"Where is Daddy?" Angela asked. "Do you want me to call him?"

"No. No. Don't disturb him. I'm fine. Really. I just need to...to rest my head a little bit."

Angela sat down next to her. "I've been thinking," she said with that grown-up voice of hers.

Too grown-up for a six-year-old.

"Maybe you shouldn't be left at home alone anymore. You get hurt all the time. I think it would be best if there was someone with you. Last week it was the stairs, remember?"

Shannon drew in a deep breath. She remembered too well. And so did Angela, apparently. She was getting too old. It wouldn't be long before she figured out what was really going on.

Did you really think you could hide it from her forever?

She didn't. But she had hoped it would get better with time. She had hoped Joe would get better, that it would all blow over and he would stop being so angry with her. For a long time, she had tried to change it by changing herself, by being nicer and staying away from things that made him angry, but now she knew it didn't matter how she behaved. It wasn't going to change.

"You know what? Maybe you're right," she said. "Maybe you and I should take a trip somewhere soon. What do you say?"

Angela's face lit up. "That sounds awesome, Mom."

Shannon sighed and grabbed the edge of the kitchen counter. She pulled herself up, while her daughter tried to help her. She had been thinking about doing this for many months. Now was the time.

"I better go do my homework," Angela said, and jumped for the stairs.

Shannon stopped her halfway up. "Hey, sweetie."

"Yes, Mom?"

"Not a word to Dad, all right? Not a word about the trip, okay?"

She nodded while biting her lip.

She knows. Oh, God, she knows, doesn't she?

"All right, Mom."

THIRTEEN

January 2015

IT WAS dark before I made it back to the motel to pick up the kids. I had missed dinnertime, but my mom had made a plate for me that she heated in the microwave of the small restaurant that was attached to the motel.

The place was called Motel Albert. They had named it after my dad, Albert Ryder, since it was his big dream that had come true. It was located right between A1A and the beach. The rooms were small, but not too shabby. The restaurant at the end of the building had a deck on the beach side where people could sit, have a hotdog or a fish burger, and watch the waves and the dolphins if they were lucky. I loved the place and so did my kids. They could play on the beach for hours and hours nonstop. They were like fish in the water, and I had slowly started to teach them how to surf as well. Abigail was by far the better of them, since she was the daredevil and never afraid of anything, whereas Austin was a lot more careful type. Emily refused to even try, but I kept asking her anyway. At sixteen years of age, everything is lame, apparently. I wasn't giving up on her, though. I had surfed all of my life, and I wanted all of them to have the gift of surfing in their lives as well. I never missed a good swell. The waves in Ft. Lauderdale, where I grew up, weren't as good as they were here in Cocoa Beach. This was heaven for me, and I hoped it would be for my kids as well.

"Tough day, huh?" my mom, Sherri Ryder, asked when I reached for a second portion of fish tacos. She had made them herself, and there was no better on the beach. She knew I couldn't stop eating when I had a lot on my mind. I used to be a lot bigger when I worked back in Miami. Since I moved to Cocoa Beach I had lost around twenty pounds, just because I surfed more and ate healthier. Plus, I rarely stressed, so I didn't overeat. I wasn't in the best shape of my life, but it was getting a lot better. I looked good, I believed. Still had all of my hair, even though my mom thought it was too long and curly for a man in the force.

"Yes," I said. "I mean, I know this stuff happens everywhere; it's just so shocking to see it here in Cocoa Beach."

I sipped my beer, made by the local brewery that my mother had a deal with. I enjoyed the local beers. I had one more. The twins came rushing towards me, closely followed by their granddad, who was skipping to keep up with them. He became such a child around them. It amused me. At the age of seventy-five, he was still very agile. He had always taken very good care of his body. He'd been running for most of his life. I hadn't been good to myself over the years. I hoped to have half of his health in ten years.

"Daaad!" they yelled.

I looked at my dad, who was smiling from ear to ear. There was nothing in this world he enjoyed more than spending time with the twins. "They're too fast," he said panting. "We were playing tag in the back, and I can't catch them."

I laughed and made room for him to sit next to me on the wooden bench. We were sitting outside on the porch, overlooking the dark ocean. The sun had set an hour ago, but I could hear the waves. They were picking up. We were supposed to get a really big swell later in the week. I, for one, hoped I could get time to catch some.

"Where's Emily?" I asked.

"She's in the TV room watching some show I don't understand half of," my mom said. "Why are vampires such a big deal now?"

I chuckled and shook my head. "I don't know, Mom."

"Anyway, she says you let her watch it, but I really don't think young girls should watch things like that."

"It's her thing, Mom. Let her," I said.

My mother didn't look like she wanted to. "I'm just saying it," she said shaking her head. "She needs to know how to be careful what she fills herself with."

"So, you had a tough day, I hear?" My dad interrupted. "We saw it on the news."

I nodded while removing some lettuce from between my teeth. "Yeah, I noticed the choppers earlier. I bet they're all over it."

"What about that poor kid?" my mom asked. "How is he ever going to get through life?"

It was typical of my mother to think about the kid. Kids had been her whole life. She was a kindergarten teacher for twenty-something years and adored all children. A lot more than she adored adults.

I wondered how much they had said about the case on the news. Had they told people that the body was partly dismembered? Weasel had been in charge of making the statements and had called for a press conference the next day. At City Hall, they were terrified that this was going to affect tourism. I couldn't blame them. The tourists meant everything around here. Especially at this time of year. The snowbird season. It meant jobs. It meant security for people. Ever since they stopped the Space Shuttle program, thousands of people had lost their jobs and the real estate market had plummeted. People lost a lot of money on their houses. They recently started a new project out at the Space Center, and they were still launching rockets every now and then, but the area had been bleeding for years. It wasn't only people who had worked on the shuttle that were hurt. Everyone else was too. Hundreds thousands of tourists would usually come to watch a launch, and that meant a lot of money for the hotels, the restaurants, and shops. It helped a little that the cruise ships were booming, but the prices on houses were low, and lots of people were still out of work. My parents had felt it too. They used to have the motel packed several times a year when a shuttle was launched, and now they barely made ends meet.

"I don't know, Mom," I said and finished my beer. "We can only hope for the best."

"You'll catch him," my mom said. "You'll get the guy, and then everything will go back to normal again."

I chuckled. My mother had such great confidence in me; it was sweet. She never did like the fact that I was a detective or on the police force. Especially not when I worked in Miami. She feared for my life every day. I couldn't blame her. I didn't want any of my kids in the force either. But I happened to like my job. Not today, but most days.

FOURTEEN

January 2015

"I THINK we'll head home now," I said, and kissed my mom on the cheek. "Thanks for dinner; it was great, as always."

"We need to change a light bulb in room one-eleven. Could you do that before you leave? You know how your dad is with ladders. I don't like him climbing on them."

"I got it," I said.

I found a new bulb in the cupboard behind the bar, then grabbed the ladder and went into room one-eleven and changed it. I did all I could to help out around the motel. My parents were getting older, and it was harder and harder for them to keep up with the maintenance. It was the least I could do, with all the help they gave me. As my way of saying thanks, I devoted my weekends to helping them out. That way, the kids got to play with their grandparents too, so it was a win-win.

I looked at the twins, who were drawing on one of the tables in the restaurant. They were sitting underneath it and drawing on the bottom. Luckily, my parents hadn't noticed. I cleared my throat.

"Abigail, Austin. We need to go home. Emily?" I called through the window.

"What?" she answered.

"We're going home."

"Finally," she said.

I heard the TV shut off, then the sound of her dragging feet across the ground. She came out. She looked odd with her big army-boots and black outfit in this heat.

I smiled. "How was your day?"

She shrugged indifferently. "Fine, I guess." She grabbed her backpack and put it on. I wanted to give her a hug, but was afraid it would come off as awkward. Instead, I turned to face the twins. "I said we were leaving."

"Aw, we were having so much fun," Abigail said.

Austin crawled out from under the table and walked to me. "It wasn't my idea,"

43

he said, and handed me the crayon. "I know," I said. "Abigail. Get out from under there, now, young lady."

"Wait a second. I just need to finish this."

Was she kidding me?

"Abigail. Now."

She sighed and rolled her eyes. Six years of age and already a teenager. "All right, all right. I'm coming."

We walked to the car and greeted one of the guests of the motel. Harry was his name. He had been a guest for a month or so now. A snowbird. We had a lot of those. They came down from the north and stayed all winter.

"Nice evening?" I said, as we passed him.

He nodded and smiled at the children. "Yes, indeed. Gonna be a beautiful day tomorrow, don't you think?"

"Definitely."

No one discussed the weather as much as snowbirds. They came to keep warm in the winter, while the snow and cold roamed up north and made it miserable for people. Harry petted the children on their heads, then went on towards the beach. An older couple, Mr. and Mrs. Miller, who were also regulars and came every winter, got out of their car and walked towards the rooms. I nodded in greeting as I passed them, and we talked about the weather as well before they disappeared into their room. I was so happy for people like Harry and the Millers. They were the ones who let my parents earn enough money to be able to keep the motel.

I put the kids in the car and drove next door to the place where I had rented a condo. It was also right on the beach, and in walking distance of my parents' place. It was in South Cocoa Beach, in the more secluded part of town. I, for one, loved it here. Arianna hadn't liked it much. She thought it was too small…nothing really happened here, she always said.

That was what I liked about it.

"Can we watch TV before we go to bed, Dad, please?" Abigail asked with big pleading eyes.

"Okay," I said, as we walked towards the complex. I opened the front door and let the munchkins storm in and fight over who should hit the button for the elevator. "But only for half an hour," I said on the way up, when they had finally quieted down. Abigail had naturally won the fight. She always did. She was the big sister and had beat her brother into this world by fifty-eight seconds. She had been beating him ever since.

"Aw," Abigail pleaded. "Can't we say one hour instead?"

I sighed and opened the door to the condo. I looked at my watch. It was going to be late. "Okay." I said. "If you brush your teeth and put on your PJs first."

The kids didn't hear that last part before they stormed inside and threw themselves on the couch and turned the TV on. Emily went to her room and shut the door without a word, while the theme song to SpongeBob filled the living room. Each of the twins grabbed an iPad and started playing while watching TV.

The new generation of multitaskers.

I shook my head and sat next to them, and soon after, the iPads were put away and I had both kids on my lap.

FIFTEEN

September 1984

SHE NEVER TOLD anyone what had happened to her. She was too ashamed, too scared of what would happen if she did. So, Annie kept it to herself. She didn't remember much. She couldn't recall the details, but she believed she had been raped. She just wasn't sure if it had all been a dream. She had woken up in the grass by the lake the next morning, but hadn't been able to remember what had happened. But, as the days passed, little by little, she remembered bits and pieces. She knew she had been with Tim. And she knew she was badly bruised when she woke up. She covered the marks with make-up and stayed away from her friends for weeks afterwards. She even avoided Julia and told her she wasn't feeling well. She didn't want to have to answer her questions. She didn't want anyone to know how stupid she had been.

She was determined to forget everything.

And she had succeeded. After the bruises were gone, no one ever asked questions or wondered what had happened. Except Julia...and Annie simply kept avoiding her. She missed her friendship like crazy, but she had to cut her off. That was the only way she could forget, the only way she could avoid having to talk about that night, that dreadful night when Tim had taken her to the lake.

But, as the fall came, something started to happen to Annie's body. It was like it had gotten a life of its own, like she had no control over it anymore.

She could wake up at night and suddenly be so hungry it felt like she was about to die if she didn't eat. She would keep crackers and candy under her pillow, so her roommate wouldn't wake up when she ate at night. She had a jar of pickles that she ate greedily. And then there was the extra weight. The nightly eating made her gain a lot of weight. And some nights her stomach would hurt. She even started throwing up in the mornings, and wondered if that was due to her strange hours of eating.

Finally, she went to the doctor and was examined. Her mother took her. She had come for a visit, and when Annie had thrown up for the third time while she was there, she suspected something was wrong.

"She's gaining weight rapidly," her mother told the doctor.

"Well, that's not too odd, given her circumstances," he said with a smile. "Congratulations."

Annie's mother shrieked. She went completely pale, then hid her face between her hands. "I feared it might be something like this," she said with a trembling voice.

On the way back to the campus, her mother didn't speak while driving. Not until she parked in front of the dorm. Annie felt sick to her stomach and a thousand thoughts went through her mind.

Was it Tim's? There were others that night. Could it be from one of them?

Her mother turned her head and looked at her. "Listen to me. I don't know who got you into this trouble," she said hissing. "But either you get married, or you have an abortion. You hear me? Or you'll never be able to set foot in our house again. You won't be our daughter anymore."

"But...but..."

Her mother turned her head away. "Fix this," she said. "Or don't come back home."

And just like that, Annie's life was changed forever. Standing in the parking lot, looking after her mother driving away, she knew nothing would ever be the same again. Her plan of becoming a teacher and going back to Windermere to teach at her old school, then marrying a nice guy and having a family was completely broken. Destroyed in a matter of seconds. She had no idea what to do, but she did know one thing. There was no way she was getting rid of the baby. She had heard stories of women not being able to conceive again. She was no killer. She could never kill a child. Born or unborn.

No way.

SIXTEEN

January 2015

THE NEXT MORNING, I watched the sun rise while sitting on my board. Emily had her own car that I had bought for her, and she took care of herself in the morning, so I took just the twins with me to my parents' place to eat breakfast. Meanwhile, I decided to start the day my favorite way, in the ocean. My mother had told me she would take the kids to the school bus, which stopped right outside the motel.

It was one of those unbelievably gorgeous mornings, where the sun was allowed to rise on a cloud free sky. The water was cold at this time of year, the coldest it got in Florida. I know people in other parts of the country would laugh at me thinking sixty-nine degree water was chilly, but to me it was. You get used to it being in the eighties for most parts of the year. So, I had put on my wetsuit and was waiting for the next wave, while wondering about Laura Bennett. I couldn't stop thinking about her and hadn't slept much all night. I kept going back to the way the killer had arranged the fingers after he had separated them from her body. They had all been in a neat row and so carefully cut off, like he didn't want to ruin them any more than necessary.

The waves rolled in in nice straight lines. They weren't big today, but the wind was off-shore, and they were glassy and smooth as I rode them on my longboard. The wind blew the top of the waves off as they broke, and created rainbows in the rays from the sun. I drew in a deep breath and enjoyed every moment of it. To make it perfect, I spotted two dolphins not too far from me. They were chasing fish and making big splashes in the water. I could have stayed like this all day, just surfing and watching nature, but unfortunately, I had to get out and get to work before nine.

I caught one last wave and rode it to the beach, feeling the wind in my face and the thrill of the ride. I usually rode shorter boards, but on small-wave days like this, I enjoyed longboarding. I practiced my cross-steps and made it almost to the tip of the board before I reached the beach. As I came out of the water, I grabbed my board, then turned around and took one last glance at the beautiful scenery, as if to greet the ocean and say thanks before I ran back up and into the shower.

Surfing always made me feel cheerful, and I was still singing when I arrived at the station. A note on my desk told me the medical examiner's office was done with the initial autopsy. I peeked into Weasel's office and let her know where I was going, then grabbed one of the department's cars and drove to Rockledge on the mainland.

The county had recently gotten a new District Medical Examiner, appointed by the Governor, and I hadn't had a chance to meet him yet. It was very rare we needed their help. It was mostly when tourists committed suicide by jumping off cruise ships and ended washed up on our beaches. Or after bar fights when someone was stabbed. I had liked the former District Medical Examiner, Dr. Parker, but unfortunately, he had retired three months ago and they had to appoint a new one.

I parked in front of the office and walked up. I had put on a hoodie. The temperature today would stay in the high sixties, and I found it to be quite chilly. The sun would probably warm up during the day and make it nice, but for now, it felt good wearing a sweater. In January, you never knew what you'd get. It could go from the low sixties and windy out of the North to the low to mid-eighties in a day or two.

"Jack Ryder. I'm here to see Dr. Díez," I said to the secretary behind the counter, while reading the last name from my note.

The secretary smiled. "One moment, please."

I sat down and found my phone. I started going through my emails and answering as many as possible before a door finally opened and someone stepped out.

"Mr. Ryder?" a voice said.

I stood up. In front of me stood a woman in her mid-forties wearing a white coat. Her thick dark brown hair was gathered in a bun on the back of her head. She was short and slightly overweight. Her brown eyes stared at me.

"Mr. Ryder?" she repeated, and reached out her hand. I grabbed it. "I'm Dr. Díez, District Medical Examiner. Shall we take a look?"

SEVENTEEN

January 2015

WE WALKED down a flight of stairs and entered the autopsy suite.

"So, I guess a welcome is in order, Dr. Díez," I said.

She turned her head and smiled "Thank you, Officer. And you can call me Yamilla."

"Yamilla? That sounds Spanish?"

She walked to a table and put on plastic gloves and a mask. I did the same.

"Cuban," she said. "But I was born in Tampa. My father escaped as a child, just before it was too late."

"So, your mother is American?" I asked, as we walked towards the steel table where the covered body was.

Yamilla grabbed the white blanket and lifted it. "Yes and no. She was born on American soil, but has Cuban roots too. Both her parents are Cuban. We have a way of finding each other. Only she's second generation, and like me, she has never been to Cuba." She paused and glanced down. Then she pulled the blanket off.

I swallowed hard at the sight of Laura Bennett once again. Next to her, on another table, lay the cut off parts. Yamilla took in a deep breath.

"We don't see many of these kinds around here."

"We sure don't," I said, and looked closely at the body. "So, what can you tell me about her?"

"She was strangled to death. But not with his hands or anything tied around her neck. You see, there are no marks on her throat. "The Petechiae under her eyelids is a sign of strangulation. He didn't use his hands."

"He's a gentle killer," I said. I looked at the mouth. "There is no sign of aggression. No anger. Any marks under her upper lips?"

Yamilla smiled. "Someone has seen this before," she said. She grabbed the upper lip and lifted it. "As you can see, she has marks here. Her lip was pressed against

49

her teeth, leaving the marks. But there is nothing on the outside to indicate anything was pressed against her lips."

"A pillow," I said. "Leaves no marks."

"Exactly. The killer went to great lengths to not leave any trace."

I leaned in over Laura Bennett's face and studied it closer. "Or, maybe he didn't want to bruise her. He cares about her body, not about her."

"That could be a theory," Yamilla said.

"Anything else? A time of death?" I asked.

Yamilla looked at me from above her mask. "Between one-thirty and two in the morning."

I wrote it on my notepad, thinking that eliminated Travis Connor, who had been seen at the Beach Shack from ten-twenty till it closed at two. The bartender told me he was positive the guy had stayed there till two, since he had trouble getting him to leave.

"Anything else?"

Yamilla paused. There was something.

"She was washed."

"Yes. We determined on the scene that she had been in the shower," I said. "There were still water drops and dirt on the sides of the bathtub. We figured she had been in the shower when the killer surprised her. That's why I'm quite surprised at the time of death. I was certain it had been in the morning hours. I was sure she had gotten out of bed, then was taking a shower when the killer came in."

"No," Yamilla said. "She was washed after death occurred. She was washed with bleach. There is nothing on her body. It's completely clean. No fingerprints. No DNA. Not even a drop of sweat, which there would be if she struggled for her life during strangulation. Her body would have released noradrenaline, a hormone closely related to adrenaline. Yet, I find no trace of anything on her. It has all been washed away."

EIGHTEEN

January 2015

I SAID goodbye to Dr. Yamilla Díez and hit the road again. Across the first bridge that took me to Merritt Island, the island between my beloved Cocoa Beach and the mainland, I couldn't help thinking about this new information. The killer had washed Laura Bennett's body after he strangled her. Who did that? Who washed her with bleach just before starting to cut her up? Was it some kind of weird ritual? Was it to get rid of DNA? Bleach was known to get rid of DNA. Bleach contained sodium hypochlorite, an extremely corrosive chemical that could break the hydrogen bonds between DNA base pairs and degrade a DNA sample. In fact, bleach was so effective that crime labs used it to clean workspaces so that old samples didn't contaminate fresh evidence.

A picture of the killer had started to shape in my mind. The picture of a guy who took his time with his victim. A killer who enjoyed what he did and wanted the moment to last. He was also very controlled. He made no mistakes. This was no ordinary guy. On top of it, he was gentle with the victim's body.

I passed the second bridge and drove into Cocoa Beach shortly after. Tourists and snowbirds were on the roads everywhere, not knowing where to go, cruising down A1A, slowing the traffic down.

At a meeting at the station, I told everyone what I had learned at the medical examiner's office. They didn't seem to buy into my idea of him being a gentle killer much, especially not Weasel, who looked skeptically at me from her seat at the end of the table.

"I still say we take a closer look at the husband. He's the one with the best motive. It was the wife's money. He's getting everything. She was about to leave him. They lost a child, and he blames her for it. Lots of reasons to finish her off in an angry tantrum while drunk, then pretend to pass out."

"But he doesn't remember anything," Joel Hall said. "When we got to the house and talked to him, he was completely out of it. Hardly knew who he was, let alone what had happened the night before."

"How is the guy doing?" Weasel asked. "Can we interrogate him soon?"

"I was with him last night, Marty took the morning shift," Jim Moore said. "I left the hospital at four in the morning, then slept till nine. Brandon Bennett was completely knocked out all the time I was there. But I can go call Marty and see if there is any news."

"Do that," I said.

Jim left the table with his phone in hand. I looked at the others.

"We have to think about who else might have a motive besides the husband," I said. "He might be telling the truth."

The Weasel snorted. "It's him. I just know it is. I can smell it. He's bad news. Besides, there's no sign of breaking and entering on the house. Whoever did this knew Laura Bennett."

"Being bad news doesn't make you a killer," I said.

"True," Weasel said. But she didn't mean it.

"We need to look in other directions as well," I said. "I've ruled out the neighbor who lives down the street, Travis Connor, since he has an alibi, and as far as we know, he was the only one who visited the house on the night of the killing. But there might have been others. He left pretty early. There could have been someone else. Joel, have the other neighbors said anything useful?"

Joel shook his head with a sigh. "Not really. I mean, Mrs. Jeffries told us she saw Mrs. Bennett smoking on the porch at eleven, but that's about it. No one has seen anyone else on the street. But, I'm not done. I still have a couple of houses left on the street that I haven't talked to, since they weren't home."

"You'll continue that today. There might be someone sitting on important information that they don't think is useful," Weasel said.

Joel Hall shrugged. "Sure. But it is a fairly quiet street, and on a Sunday night, most of the people were in bed early."

Weasel smacked her hand on the table. "Come on. This can't be it, people. Someone must have seen something. At least they must have heard her scream. Ask if anyone heard any screams between one and two in the morning."

"There was loud music coming from the Bennett's house," Joel Hall said. "It could have drowned out any screams. Besides, people are so used to hearing them quarrel."

"Plus, she was strangled by a pillow," I said. "She probably couldn't scream."

Weasel growled and leaned back in her chair with a *mommy isn't happy* look on her face.

"I'll ask around anyway," Joel Hall said, to smooth things out.

At the same time, the door opened, and Jim Moore stepped in. "He's awake," he said. "Brandon Bennett is awake."

NINETEEN

January 2015

"I DON'T REMEMBER ANYTHING. I swear. I really don't."

Brandon Bennett was sitting up in his bed at Cape Canaveral Hospital. Marty had taken his son, Ben, and the dog to the cafeteria to get a hot cocoa at my suggestion, while I spoke to the dad. The dog had been allowed to stay overnight, given the circumstances. Everyone felt bad for Ben and wanted him to feel safe. I talked to the doctor before entering the room, and he confirmed that Brandon Bennett had been drugged with Rohypnol, or a Roofie, as it was also called. The date-rape drug. That was why he had been so out of it and why he had been slipping in and out of consciousness for the past twenty-four hours. I had called Yamilla at the medical examiner's office and she told me they had already checked Laura Bennett's blood, and there were no signs of any drugs. Lots of alcohol, but no other drugs. In other words, it was only Brandon Bennett who had been drugged. That told me the killer just wanted to get rid of Brandon, and that Laura had been his real target. That was my theory.

I got up and walked to the window of the third floor. The hospital was situated on a small peninsula and had water on three sides of it. Brandon Bennett's room had views over the Banana River, with Cape Canaveral's huge cruise ships on the horizon waiting to take off later in the day.

"You gotta help me out a little, here, Brandon," I said. "Your wife turns up killed in your bedroom after a night you and she had been drinking heavily. We learn from neighbors and friends that you often fight loudly and violently, especially since the death of your child. People tell me you blame her for it. With her death, you're going to inherit a lot of money. You like to gamble. Convince me that you didn't kill her."

I turned and looked at his face. He was pale and looked ill. He threw out his hands. "I...I don't know what else to say."

I rubbed my forehead, then stared at him, scrutinizing him. Was he a brilliant liar? Or was he telling the truth? He didn't seem to be that bad guy everyone else was so busy making him out to be.

"Did you do it?" I asked. Mostly because I had to. I knew what answer he would give me.

Brandon Bennett looked appalled. "Of course not. Are you kidding me? I loved Laura. I adored her. If she was here, she could tell you. I gave her flowers every week. Ask the local florist. Every freaking Wednesday I had her send my wife flowers. I loved everything about her. I know I was never the model husband or father. I have a problem. I'll admit to that. I drink and I gamble. And I hate myself for that. Believe me. It is destroying me and my marriage."

His voice cracked as he spoke. It made him sound sincere. I cursed it. I really wanted him to be guilty. I wanted him to be the bad news Gabrielle Phillips had talked about. But when I looked at him, that wasn't what I saw. Tears were piling up in his eyes now as he looked at me. His body was shaking from the restraint of holding them back.

He was truly sad that his wife was gone.

"I have no idea how to do this on my own," he said. A tear escaped the corner of his eye and rolled across his cheek.

I handed him a tissue.

"What about Ben? How is he going to get by without his mother?" he asked, choking up.

"All right," I said and nodded. "Let's say I believe you. How much do you remember? Let's start with Sunday evening. What did you do?"

Brandon Bennett sniffled and wiped his nose. "We ordered pizza. Then Laura put Ben to bed. We had a couple of drinks. It was sort of an anniversary for us."

"What were you celebrating?" I asked.

"Not celebrating. Drowning our sorrows while trying to forget. It was a year since our daughter died."

I noted it on my notepad while biting my lip. I couldn't even imagine how devastating it had to be to lose a child. Thinking of any of my three kids, it hurt inside to imagine being without them.

"Okay, so you were drinking. What else?"

Brandon Bennett looked like he was thinking. "It's all a little blurry, but I believe Travis came over and had a drink or two," he said. "He didn't stay long, though. He wanted to hit the Beach Shack when they opened. I guess we weren't such great company either. We were pretty depressed. When he left, we started fighting, as we always did when we had a little too much to drink."

"What were you fighting about?" I asked, studying his face for reactions to what he was saying.

"I actually don't remember," he said. "Probably what we always fight about."

"And what is that?" I asked.

"My gambling. It always starts with her telling me I gamble too much, and that it's her money I'm using. Then, I blame her for losing our child, and after that, there's no turning back."

"I can imagine there isn't," I said with a sigh. I remembered the things Arianna and I could say to one another during a fight. It wasn't pretty. Why did couples do this to one another?

"What else do you remember?"

He shrugged. "That's it. We fought and then we went to bed."

I looked at him with dissatisfaction. "And you can't remember what time you went to bed, I take it?"

He shook his head. "No."

"Did anyone else come over during the night?"

"I...I..."

"You don't remember," I said, and wrote it down.

"There might have been someone else. It's all very blurry."

"So, what else do you remember? Do you remember waking up and the police coming to the house?" I asked.

He shook his head again. "I don't. I remember drinking and fighting, and then waking up here in the hospital a couple of hours ago, and being told what happened."

"That's all?" I asked.

"Yes. I'm sorry, Officer. I seem to have lost a big part of my memory. The doctor told me it was the drug. Mixed with alcohol, it messes with one's memory completely. Again, I'm sorry. I really want to help."

I put my pen away and was ready to leave. "Well, Mr. Bennett. The doctor told me you'll be able to take your son home later today. Don't leave town, all right? We're not done here."

Brandon Bennett shook his head. "I have no intention of doing that. I want this guy as bad as you do, Officer."

"I'm glad. But for now, make sure you take care of your son. He needs you more than ever."

"I will. Thank you, Officer."

I was walking towards the door, when Brandon Bennett suddenly stopped me.

"Wait. There was something." Brandon Bennett looked pensive. "There was someone there. Was it...I think it was."

"Who?"

"Peter," he said, looking directly at me. "Peter stopped by right before midnight. He was angry."

I found my notepad and my pen. Finally, something I could work with.

"Who is Peter?"

"That's her brother. Her older brother."

"The writer's son? Who grew up in her biological father's house?"

Brandon's face cleared up. "Yes. He was the youngest of the three, and the only one we had any contact with."

TWENTY

September 1984

"I'm pregnant and it's yours."

Annie spoke with a quivering voice. She stood in front of Tim in the library, where she had finally found him and approached him. He hadn't responded to her phone calls or her letters, nor had he stopped to talk with her when she approached him on campus. Finally, she had found him sitting in the reading chairs at the library with his friends. It had taken all of her courage to approach him like this, but it had to be done. It was the only way she could get him to listen. At first, she had asked him to step outside with her, told him she had something important and very private to tell him, but he had refused. Laughed to her face and refused.

Now, his face froze in a smile and all his friends stared at her.

"What?" he asked.

"You heard me."

He lifted his pointer. "No, no. You have it all wrong, little missy."

"No, I don't," she said. "It's yours. I'm five months pregnant."

Tim's friends stared at him, waiting for his response. So did Annie. Her legs were shaking, threatening to give in to the rest of her body. She had never been this nervous in her life.

Tim stared at her with big eyes, then shook his head. "I'm not falling for that. Who told you to say this, huh? Was it Chris, huh? Ha ha, Chris. Very funny. You can stop it now."

"It's not a joke," she said. "It happened that night by the lake."

Tim shook his head. "I haven't the faintest idea what you're talking about. I think you've got the wrong person."

Annie stepped forward. "You need to marry me."

The reading room went completely silent. No one was tapping their fingers, no one clearing their throat or coughing. And no one was reading anymore. All eyes were on them.

Tim withered in his leather chair. He looked at her with serious eyes. She could see the fear in them. The fear of his life, as he knew it, being over. Of the anger of his parents. The fear of having to live with someone for the rest of his life that he didn't love or even care for.

Those few minutes of indecision finally mounted into a big smile, followed by loud laughter.

"Marry you? Ha! That's a good one. Very funny. Now get out of here before I make you."

"Tim, it's the right thing to do. For the child's sake. For my sake. My parents are going to renounce me. Without them, I have no money, I have nothing. This child will grow up in the gutter."

Tim scoffed. "What do I care? Don't have the child, then. It's not my child anyway. I wouldn't touch that ugly body of yours, even if you paid me to."

Tim's friends laughed.

Annie felt her anger rise. Tears piled up in her eyes. "It is yours."

He leaned over in his chair. "How do you know?"

"Because I haven't been with anyone else but you…ever." She knew it wasn't the entire truth. They both knew. His friends had been there too that night. They had all raped her. It could be any of them. As they stared into each other's eyes in a power struggle, they both knew she would never have a paternity test taken because that meant she would have to admit to having been with multiple men on that night. It was simply too shameful for her.

"Get out of here," Tim yelled. His face showed real anger now. His nostrils were flaring.

Tears rolling across her cheeks, Annie backed up, frightened of what Tim and his friends might do to her if she stayed. When she reached the front door, she opened it and ran. She ran across campus as fast as she could, the sound of the blood rushing through her veins drowning out everything else. When she couldn't run anymore, she threw herself on the grass, crying heavily, covering her eyes with her hands. Her stomach was in her way constantly now, and she loathed it more than ever. She loathed what had happened to her, and worst of all, she loathed this baby and what it was going to do to her life. Still, she couldn't kill it. She could never do *that*.

"What is to become of me?" she cried out, staring at the stars in the sky, wondering if there was a God and whether he could even hear her. It seemed like he didn't these days.

"I'll take care of you," a voice said.

Annie turned her head with a small gasp and stared into the eyes of Victor. Victor was the campus' biggest nerd. He was strange and awkward and all wrong. But he had always had a thing for Annie. Growing up in the same town and going to the same schools, he had adored her ever since he laid eyes on her for the first time in preschool. And he followed her everywhere. Even to the same college. But Annie couldn't stand the guy. He was always clinging to her in high school, making life miserable for her because none of the cool kids wanted to hang out with her because of him. God, how she had hated him for many years. Even the way he smelled, or the way he said hi and pressed his glasses back on his forehead when he did. The way he dressed, the way his hair was always greasy and falling onto his forehead. In college, she had managed to keep him at a distance, but he still seemed to be everywhere she went. Had he followed her here? Had he heard what she had told Tim?

He reached out his hand towards her.

"I was in the library. I heard everything," he said. "I'll take care of you. That bastard doesn't deserve you. I'll marry you."

TWENTY-ONE

January 2015

PETER WALKER LIVED in a modest two-bedroom condo in Cape Canaveral. I had called in advance and told him I would stop by to make sure he was home. He had the daytime off, he told me when he opened the door and let me in.

"Where do you work?" I asked, as I closed the door behind me.

The condo was a mess. Dogs and cats roamed the living room and were fighting as I entered. It smelled like a pet store.

"At Ron Jon's."

Ron Jon is the biggest surf store in the world, located in Cocoa Beach. It started as a surf shop, but had now evolved into just as much of a souvenir shop for tourists who come to see the store that is open twenty-four hours a day. It has become a landmark for the town and something people talk about. Tourists buy T-shirts with Ron Jon's logo on them and walk around town wearing them. Stickers with their logos are on many of the cars, since they come with every purchase you make. It is a big and booming business, but also causes a struggle for the smaller surf shops around town. I never buy anything in there, since I have all my boards shaped by a local shaper to fit me perfectly. The shop is good for the town and the tourist industry, and they have nice boards, but to be honest, I prefer supporting the smaller local places. That's just the way I am.

"I work the nightshift," he continued, as I sat down on his couch.

"That's a bummer," I said, and took out my notepad and threw it on the table, then found my pen in my pocket.

"So, what can I do for you, Officer?" he asked. "I understood it was about my sister, Laura?"

I nodded, then flipped to a blank page in my pad. "Yes. Your sister Laura. As you probably know by now, she was found killed yesterday morning at her house in Snug Harbor."

Peter sat down as well. "Yes. I heard. Any news about what happened to her?"

I exhaled. "That depends. How well do you know her?"

He shook his head. "She was only my half-sister. I didn't know she existed until my father died."

"So, it's safe to say not very well?" I asked.

"I hardly knew her at all, to be frank," he said. "Even after we knew who she was, I never had the urge to get to know her, if you know what I mean. None of us wanted to know her."

"Why is that? Because she took your inheritance?"

Peter leaned back in his recliner. "Well, yes. Can you blame me? Can you blame us for not wanting her in our lives? She took everything. Came from out of nowhere and took it all. Now, I have to live like this, and I have to work nights at a job I hate. I could have been living the life. I could have been rich."

"To be fair, it was your father's money. He could have given it to a charity. He was entitled to do with the money as he pleased, don't you think? Laura didn't know her real dad growing up. Don't you think it's fair she got a little compensation for being lied to her entire life? After all, you and your sisters had everything growing up, didn't you? She needed that fatherly love, from her real father," I said, deliberately provoking him.

Peter was moving in his seat. What I said struck a chord.

"We had everything, you say? How about, we had nothing? We lived with a father who was never there. We grew up in a house with a father who was never home, and even if he was present, he wasn't there mentally. He would stay in his office and write all his stupid stories about characters that he loved way more than he ever loved any of us. After our mother died, he kept dragging new and younger models home with him from book tours, or wherever he went. They would stay at the house for months and hang by the pool, drinking margaritas at ten in the morning, then he would throw them out once he was tired of them. We never saw him or felt his fatherly love either. None of us did. So, don't come and say she was the one who needed the money the most. At least she grew up in a house with a mother and father that loved her. We didn't. Our dad didn't care about us at all."

Peter was spitting while he talked. I could tell I had upset him.

"So, it is fair to say you're pretty pissed at Laura, right? You and your sisters are all pretty angry with her?"

Peter touched his hair and leaned back. He finally understood why I had come. He calmed down. "I didn't kill her," he said.

"That didn't sound convincing at all," I said.

"Well, it's the truth."

"You were seen in the house," I said. "Someone saw you there on the night she was killed."

Peter exhaled deeply. "I guess I knew you would somehow figure out I was there," he said. "Well, okay. I was there. But I didn't kill her."

"Convince me. Tell me you have an alibi for where you were between one and two in the morning," I said.

Peter swallowed hard. "I…I can't. I was here. I was at home. I went to Laura's house around eleven-thirty, but came back here at one."

"Why did you go to the house? Why were you there if it wasn't to kill her for taking your birthright?"

Peter thought for a long time. I could tell he was debating within himself. I saw that exact same expression on people's faces constantly. He was definitely hiding something.

"I went to ask for money," he almost whispered.

"What was that? Money? Why would she give you money?"

"She gave me money now and then. To help me out."

I leaned back, feeling baffled. "Why? Why would she give you money if you didn't know each other very well?"

He shrugged. He reached over the table, grabbed a cigarette, and lit it. His hands were shaking. He was very nervous.

"I guess she was trying to be nice to me. I am, after all, her brother." He blew smoke in my face. I hated that smell.

"So, you mean to tell me you came to her house right before midnight to get some money that she now and then gave to you as a gift?"

Peter inhaled again. "Yes," he said with a small smirk.

"Do you find this funny?" I asked.

He shrugged. "Not really."

"So, she gave you money now and then. How much are we talking about?" I asked to get the conversation moving. I was already late to pick up Abigail and Austin. I had promised them I'd do it myself today. On top of that, I was starving. I hadn't had any lunch. Not eating made me grumpy.

"A couple of thousand. Once she gave me twenty."

"Twenty thousand dollars. She's a nice sister, huh? Especially for someone you don't know very well or care for."

"She was all right. Guess she felt bad for me."

"What about the others?" I asked.

"What about them?" he said indifferently.

He was starting to annoy me. He thought he was real clever now, trying to pretend he didn't care. He knew I didn't have any evidence to bring him up on yet. It was hardly enough just to have visited the house on the night of the murder.

"Did they receive money like you did? Did Laura give them generous gifts as well?"

Peter shook his head. "I have no idea."

"I guess you don't know them very well either, huh?" I said and got up. I was tired of talking to this guy. It was getting me nowhere. I threw my card on the table before I left.

"Call me in case you remember anything. And don't leave town."

TWENTY-TWO

January 2015

RHONDA HARRIS GLANCED out the window one last time. The yellow police tape across the street was swaying in the wind. Two police cars were still parked outside in the front yard. A small minivan was parked in the driveway. She knew it belonged to the medical examiner's office. They were taking samples, looking for fingerprints, searching the house for anything that could bring them closer to the killer. Rhonda knew the procedure. She had studied them and researched the police's work for years. She had taken classes; she had been on patrol with the police, visited the medical examiner's office, and read tons of books about forensic evidence. Yes, Rhonda Harris was a true expert when it came to police work, and that was what scared her.

She knew they would eventually come for her. She knew it was a matter of days, maybe hours, before they would knock on her front door and confront her.

It was a beautiful day out. As beautiful as they came in January in Cocoa Beach. She had always enjoyed winter far more than she did summer, she thought to herself. She loved the beach at this time of year and would take long walks there. Especially on cooler windier days like this one, when it was nice out, but a little too chilly to actually lie on the beach. Those were the days when the snowbirds and tourists went to the outlets and parks in Orlando or visited Ron Jon's surf shop to get their T-shirts and key chains. Those were the days when she would have the beach all to herself.

Rhonda looked at the cat on her desk next to her computer. He liked to sleep right next to her picture of her daughter and her husband, who lived up in New York now.

What will they think? What will they think of me when they find out what I've done?

The cat stretched and a pen fell to the floor. It rolled across the wooden floor and stopped close to Rhonda's feet. She picked it up. Then she chuckled. The pen was one she had bought when visiting Hemingway's house in the Keys ten years ago.

Why did you do it, Rhonda? Why did you have to do that stupid thing?

Rhonda shivered and forced herself to think about her daughter. She had found all the old photos and gone through them all morning, while tears streamed from her eyes. Pictures of Kate when she was just a child, then of the grandchildren from just a few years ago. So many good memories, so much love.

We had a good run, didn't we? We had fun.

Rhonda sniffled again and wiped her nose on a tissue. Then, she looked at a picture of her belated husband. John had been everything to her.

"I'm sorry for this, John," she whispered. "I never meant for it to go this far. Life was hard after you left. I had nothing. This was my way out. But it ran off with me. I got greedy, I guess. I'm sorry."

She looked at her husband and thought he looked back at her with contempt.

Will they ever forgive me? They're all gonna be angry, aren't they? They'll resent me for this.

The cat purred in his sleep. Rhonda petted his head gently, wondering what was to become of him.

"Hopefully, Kate and the kids will take you to New York with them once all this is over," she said. "You'll like it there. Take good care of the kids for me, will you?"

Rhonda touched the cat's fur again and stroked it gently. The cat purred and rolled to the side. He was still sleeping.

How wonderful it must be to be a cat. Just sleep through everything. Not a care in the world.

She had filled his bowls with water and food, in case it was a long time before they came. It probably wasn't necessary, since they were just across the street and would come quickly when they heard the noise. She put the letter by John's picture on her desk. She leaned over and kissed the cat, before opening the drawer and pulling out the gun.

"I sure hope I'll see you on the other side, John," she whispered through tears.

Without giving herself even a second to think about it twice, she put the cold gun against her temple and pulled the trigger.

TWENTY-THREE

January 2015

ABIGAIL AND AUSTIN were in the front office when I arrived at the school. They were sitting in the chairs looking angrily at me when I entered through the glass doors.

"I'm so, so sorry," I said, feeling awful. "I lost track of time."

"That's okay, Jack," Elaine said from behind the counter. She smiled. "Everybody is late from time to time."

I turned and looked at the two angry faces. They got up, Abigail with a deep annoyed sigh. They walked to the car, giving me the cold shoulder.

"Guys, I said I was sorry," I said.

"You promised you would be on time. School's out at two-thirty, not three-thirty, Dad," Abigail growled reproachfully.

"I said I was sorry," I repeated, and started the car. I turned to check that they both had their seatbelts on before I backed out of the parking lot.

"Where were you anyway?" Austin asked.

"I had to talk to this guy," I said.

"Is he a murderer?" Austin asked with excitement.

"Well…No one is guilty until we prove otherwise, but he did have my interest," I said diplomatically. Truth was, I had a bad feeling about Peter Walker. He was definitely hiding something. I just had no idea what it was. He had been at the scene of the crime shortly before she was killed. He had a motive. A good one. And he had no alibi for where he was at the time of death.

"Wow," Austin exclaimed. "That's so cool. Are you going to lock him away?"

I loved that Austin thought my job was so interesting. It was one of the few things that could get him really excited.

"Maybe," I said, and hit A1A towards my parents' motel. "But you know that first we have to find enough evidence, and so far, we don't have much on this guy."

"But he is your suspect, right?"

"He is one of them, yes."

64

"Cool."

I parked the car in the lot in front of my parents' motel, grabbed the kids' backpacks, and walked inside. I had texted Emily and told her to come here after school. She went to Cocoa Beach High and had band-practice after school today.

Abigail hadn't uttered a word since the school. I put my arm around her and pulled her closer.

"So, how was your day?" I asked.

She shrugged. "Good. Until you forgot about us."

Abigail was always the one I had to work on longer to get her to forgive me. Austin forgot right away when I messed up, but not Abigail.

"I didn't forget you. I was just a little late. And I did say I was sorry. Can you forgive me?"

She stopped and looked into my eyes. She was so strong, I couldn't believe it. At her age. So determined, so willed at heart. She was the type who could amount to something if she set her heart on it. She was going to rule the world one day. Maybe be president. For now, she ruled my heart, and that was more than enough.

"Okay, Dad." She petted me on my arm. "I know you do your best. Just don't do it again. Have Grandma pick us up instead, okay?"

"That's a promise. Now, let's go see if Grandma has something we can eat. I'm starving," I said, and grabbed her hand in mine. Austin had already disappeared into the back.

"Me too," Abigail said. "But, just between you and me, I really don't like the snacks Grandma has."

"Me either," I whispered, thinking of the dry crackers I had the last time I was there in the afternoon. I was hoping she would make me a burger or a fish sandwich. Maybe a crab cake. She was very good at those.

"But, don't tell her," Abigail said. "She'll get sad."

"Oh, and we don't want that, do we?"

"Nope."

TWENTY-FOUR

January 2015

"IS THAT YOU, SON?"

The old man was sitting in the darkness of the living room when the Snakecharmer entered through the front door. He had parked his wheelchair in the corner and the Snakecharmer wondered how long he had been sitting there.

The blind old bat.

"Grandpa!"

The old man smiled as his grandson threw himself in his arms. "It is you," he said with an exhale.

"Yeah, Dad. It's us," the Snakecharmer said. "Who else would it be? Are you expecting company?"

"No," the old man said, chuckling. "Who would want to visit an old blind fool like me?"

"We bought cake," the Snakecharmer said, and placed a grocery bag on the table. He turned on the light in the room. "And beer."

The Snakecharmer opened one for himself, then threw his body on the couch while the boy went into his room. The house was one of those from the fifties, with three bedrooms and two old baths, across the street from the beach, and looked like a bungalow. It was small, but it fit the three of them perfectly.

"Everything all right, Son?" his dad asked.

The Snakecharmer placed a beer in his hand. His dad chuckled again. "Ah, the little things. It's funny how you learn to appreciate them when you don't have much. Like a cold beer on a warm day." He lifted the beer and sipped it. He made a satisfied sound. The area where his eyes used to be was completely disfigured. They had removed his eyes, since there was nothing left from when the acid hit. The skin on his face looked like it was melted. Most people who looked at him felt bad, or discomfort, but not the Snakecharmer. The Snakecharmer liked to stare at his father's disfigured face, and would do so for a long time every now and then. And he was doing so now while drinking his beer. Staring and drinking, while the

66

anger inside of him arose, the anger towards those bitches still out there that he had to rid the world of.

"Cake, you said?" the old man asked.

The Snakecharmer laughed. His dad loved cake. Cake and beer. A strange combination for many people, but not for his father.

"I'll get us some plates," the Snakecharmer said.

"Don't forget to feed the snakes," the old man said, and sipped his beer again. "They seem hungry. Been making a lot of noise today."

The Snakecharmer looked at the glass cage in the corner. He approached it and stared at Mango, his favorite snake. A sixteen-foot Burmese python. One of those that could swallow a child, or that you heard of eating its owner if it wasn't fed. He loved that snake, even though he never took it on the road with him. The snakes he used for that were two Coral snakes that he kept in the cage next to the python. They ate mostly insects and were easy to control, as long as they were fed. Drago and Django were their names.

"I won't," the Snakecharmer said, and stared at the python sleeping on its branch. "I stopped by the pet store on my way here and bought some."

The Snakecharmer had loved snakes ever since he was a small child. He used to catch them and play with them. He would let them bite his hands and arms and look at the blood as it dripped onto the ground. It was mostly black racers that he played with, but he also caught rattlesnakes and skinned them and put their skins up on the wall of his room.

"How about that cake?" his dad asked.

The Snakecharmer chuckled. His eyes still didn't leave the python. He couldn't stop staring at it. Snakes fascinated him. The way they moved so quietly. Then he pulled out two mice in a small container. He caught one by the tail, lifted it above the tank, lifted the lid, and dropped it inside. Then, he waited. Waited with his eyes fixated on the snake who was now waking up and moving towards the mouse. He stared at the mouse, while sensing its fear as it faced the mighty snake. When the snake made his move so fast the mouse hardly realized what happened, and swallowed the mouse in one bite, he laughed.

It was that easy being the predator.

TWENTY-FIVE

January 2015

My mom made a ton of crab cakes for me, and I ate till my stomach hurt. I washed it all down with a sweetened iced tea, homemade naturally. We sat on the deck at the beach and watched the waves while eating. Abigail grabbed a couple of dry crackers and ate them, while smiling.

She was getting to be quite the actress.

After eating, the kids wanted to run down to the beach and fly a kite. I found an old one in the closet inside my parents' living quarters at the very end of the building. While walking along the doors to the many rooms, I thought about how much I loved this place. At first, when my parents had told me their dream of investing in a small motel on the beach, I thought it was the stupidest idea ever. I couldn't believe they would rather spend their pension on this, instead of enjoying the money and relaxing like they were supposed to when growing old.

But not my parents. No, they always had to have something to do. It had always been like that. My mother loved to cook and take care of others, while my dad loved to have guests and be with people. He talked to everyone who arrived at the motel, and some of them ended up becoming their friends. People returned because of him. He created such a warm atmosphere, people were willing to accept old buildings and bad plumbing. The rooms were nicely decorated, my mom had made sure of that. She had a great flair for decorating and made sure all the rooms looked nice and were clean. She didn't clean them herself, but had Jennifer, a small nice Asian woman to take care of it.

Jennifer was like family to all of us, and often joined us for dinner. Her daughter lived in Daytona Beach with her husband, and other than that, Jennifer didn't have anyone around here. We didn't mind being her family.

"You found one!" Austin exclaimed, excited when he saw the kite in my hand as I approached the beach. I took off my shoes and dug my toes into the sand. It felt good. I was a beach boy and never liked to cramp my feet into socks and shoes much. But I had to at work. Even though I preferred to be barefoot or wear flip-flops.

"Yes. Let's put it up," I said, and looked at the trees to determine the wind's direction. I was quite the weather-geek, and at my place at the condo I rented, I had put up a weather station in one of the trees, hoping no one would complain about it. I followed the winds and temperatures closely. The wind was still blowing out of the north. It was supposed to shift later in the day, I had seen in my weather app. I was looking forward to that. If the wind was off-shore all night, it would make perfect conditions for surfing in the morning. And the swell was supposed to build in the coming days, so it could turn out to be epic.

"What do I do, Dad?" Austin asked, as I handed him the kite.

"Let me show you."

I had barely finished my sentence before the phone rang in my pocket. At first, I thought about letting it ring. This was my time with the kids, but then I remembered it might be about the case. When working a big case like this, I couldn't just fall off the surface of the earth.

"One second," I said, and grabbed the phone in my pocket.

"Ryder."

It was Weasel's raspy voice.

"We have another one."

I swallowed hard. "Say what again?"

"Another dead body on West Bay Drive. You won't believe it. It's right across the street from the Bennetts' house."

TWENTY-SIX

October 1984

IT WAS A SMALL WEDDING. Just for the family. Annie's mother wanted it to be that way, since it was obvious to everyone why they were getting married.

Annie never told her family that Victor wasn't the father of the child she was carrying. There was no need to. It would only upset them. Besides, Victor wanted to be the father; he wanted everyone to think he was the father, so they both pretended and kept smiling.

"Victor is such a nice guy," Annie's mother told her after the ceremony, when they were eating appetizers from their plates in the backyard of Victor's childhood home, where his parents insisted the ceremony be held.

They didn't seem as fond of Annie as Victor was. Especially not the circumstances under which the marriage had been arranged.

"And he has money," Annie's Aunt Anita whispered and swallowed one of the salmon appetizers. "Nice score. So what if he isn't among the handsomest of men? At least he's loaded."

Annie couldn't stand hearing her mom and aunt go on about Victor and how perfect he was. As a matter of fact, she had a hard time going through with this wedding at all. The baby was growing rapidly inside of her, and it was very visible now. Victor's mother couldn't stop staring at it in contempt. Annie felt that her white dress was too tight. She felt like she was about to suffocate. And, worst of all, she couldn't stand what was ahead of her. She couldn't stand the thought of having to spend the rest of her life with that geek, Victor, and having a child when she wasn't sure who the father was.

At least you don't have to go through it alone. At least he cares for you. At least he'll make sure you never need anything.

"Are you all right, darling?" Victor whispered, as he rescued her from her mother and aunt. He took her hand and pulled her away from them. They took a stroll in the garden. It felt good to get away from the people and the pretending. Behind the estate was a small park. They found a bench and sat down. Annie didn't care if her white dress got dirty, but could hear her mother's voice tell her to never sit on a dirty bench wearing white. Would that voice ever leave her head? Would she ever be free from her parents?

Part of her couldn't stand the future she had in front of her. Looking at Victor, it felt like she had just married her parents. It was nothing like she had planned. Her life wasn't going to turn out anything like she had planned on those lonely nights in her bedroom as a child.

"You look pale." He kissed her on the cheek.

The kiss made her shiver in disgust. She lifted her eyes and gazed at him. Then, she forced a smile. Just like she had when he had told her he would marry her and make an honest woman of her. Just like she had done when the priest had told him he could kiss the bride and Victor had lifted the veil. She faked it.

"I'm fine, darling. I'm just really tired. That's all."

Victor smiled calmly. "That's the pregnancy." He put a hand on her belly and felt it. His touch made Annie shiver again. She tried to hide it and lowered her eyes.

"You're probably right. I feel so tired all the time lately. My doctor says it's normal. And with all the throwing up, it's only natural to be tired."

"You have a life growing inside of you. It's a big thing, darling. You need your rest. Our baby needs his rest."

Annie gasped lightly and looked into Victor's smiling eyes. It was the first time he had mentioned the baby between them as being his. Annie looked into his eyes, wondering if he really meant it or if he was just acting. Was he really capable of forgetting how this baby had come to the world? Would he really be able to consider it to be his? Never once had he asked about the circumstances. All he knew was, Tim had gotten Annie pregnant and wouldn't take responsibility. It was like he didn't even want to know more.

"There you are," Annie's mother chirped and grabbed Annie's hand. "The photographer is here. You two love birds better get back to the party."

Annie looked tiredly at her smiling mother, who was standing slightly tipsy with a glass of bubbling champagne in one hand and Annie's hand in the other.

Oh, my God. She was enjoying this, wasn't she? She was happy to see her daughter marry a guy she didn't love. A guy that could support her. A guy from a good family. A guy with money to secure her for the rest of her life. This was exactly the kind of man her mother had wanted her to marry, wasn't it? Feeling like the dress was getting tighter, she found it harder to breathe; she pulled out her hand from her mother's.

"Is something wrong?" her mother asked.

Victor chuckled and shook his head. "No, Mrs. Greenfield. Everything is perfect, he said. "It's just the pregnancy. It's wearing her out, poor thing." He stroked her cheek gently, while looking at her with compassion.

Annie felt like throwing up.

"Oh my," her mother said and grabbed Annie's arm. She helped her get back to her feet. Then, she stroked Annie's cheek as well. Annie felt like screaming.

"We can't have widdle Annie-bannie get tooo tired-wired, can we now? No, we can't."

TWENTY-SEVEN

January 2015

I LEFT the kids with my parents, then jumped inside my Jeep and raced to Snug Harbor. Luckily, it was only a three-minute drive from my parents' motel. The medical examiner's van was already parked next to the van from the Sheriff's crime scene unit, an ambulance, and several police cars.

"Hey, Jack," Weasel yelled, as I arrived and parked the car. She seemed tired and her face longer than usual.

"So, what have we got?" I asked, as we walked under the tape and into the house. "Another homicide?"

"It's on the second floor," she said, and we grabbed plastic gloves in the foyer, then walked up the stairs. Through the window on the second floor, I spotted the Bennetts' house that was still blocked by police tape, and wondered if this killer really was so stupid as to strike twice in the same neighborhood.

"Woman, age sixty-seven," Weasel said, as we walked through the hallway and into a big bedroom with bamboo furniture. We stopped at the body on the light carpet. Her face was unrecognizable; blood was sprayed all over the carpet. A gun was lying on the carpet next to her hand.

"Her name was Rhonda Harris," Weasel said.

"Looks like she shot herself?" I asked.

The Weasel nodded. "That's what the ME said."

"Yes, I said that," a voice said behind me.

I turned and spotted Yamilla. She was hard to recognize in all her equipment. I moved and let her get closer to the body.

"I will have to examine her further in my lab, but yes, so far, it's safe to say it was suicide. Shot herself right through the temple."

I got up and looked around. I looked at her computer, her notebooks, and her many books spread all over the floor and tables.

"Looks like she was quite the avid reader," I said.

"Sure does," Weasel said.

"All John Platt books, huh?"

Weasel looked confused. "Well, I hadn't noticed, but I think you might be right. All the open ones are."

I threw a glance out the window at the house across the street.

Weasel rubbed her forehead. "Second death this week in this neighborhood, one of the nicest in town," she sighed. "Gonna be another late nighter for us. If this keeps happening, I'm not going to be so popular around here anymore."

I patted her shoulder while staring at the Bennetts' house. The case had started to haunt me...now more than ever. There was no way these two deaths weren't related somehow.

"What's going on around here?" Weasel asked, wiping her sweaty forehead with a tissue. It was a very moist evening.

"It never used to be like this," she continued. "What do you make of it?"

"Let's just say, I hardly think it's a coincidence that she is a big John Platt fan," I said.

"You think she knew something?" Weasel asked. "You don't think she...she killed Laura?"

I shrugged. "I think she might have known something. Something important. Who was she? What do we know about her?"

"She used to be a reporter for Florida Today, but retired early four years ago," Joel said as he approached us. "Sorry to interrupt, but I just spoke with her daughter up in New York. She's on her way down. Caught a late flight out. Should be here late tonight."

I looked at Joel. He seemed a lot more together than the last time I had seen him. He was still sweating heavily, but we all were.

"Perfect," I said. "Have her come and talk to me tomorrow morning. And I need everything secured from Rhonda Harris' house. Every notebook, her computer, everything she has in those drawers. If she has a knife, I want it checked for blood or Laura Bennett's DNA."

TWENTY-EIGHT

January 2015

THE WAVES WERE CRASHING on the beach when I woke up the next morning. I had slept with my window open to the balcony. They were luring me in. The sound was intoxicating. They were definitely calling for me.

I felt exhausted when I finally sat up. I didn't arrive to pick up the kids from my parents' place till around nine-thirty the night before. Emily had gone back to the condo by herself, but the twins were fast asleep, so my mother suggested they stay for the night. They had decorated a bedroom for them with bunk beds and SpongeBob posters and everything, and the kids loved sleeping over, so I told her all right and went back to spend the rest of the evening with Emily. We watched a movie together and I made popcorn. I got the feeling she enjoyed it, even though she didn't say so. It was just like back in Miami before the twins had come into our lives. Just Emily and me. I couldn't help looking at her when she didn't see it. I saw so much of her mother in her, more and more every day now. I missed Lisa. She had been the best colleague and friend I had ever had. I was happy I got to see her daughter grow up.

When I woke up at six, I put on my wetsuit, but left the upper part hanging from my waist, grabbed my board, and ran with it across the beach to my parents' motel.

"Daaad!" Austin smiled happily when he saw me. They were sitting on the wooden deck eating waffles. I kissed them both.

"Where were you last night?" Abigail asked. "You never came back."

I sat down next to her and grabbed a waffle for myself. My mother brought me orange juice in a glass. It was freshly squeezed. Nothing beats Florida oranges. "I had to work," I said.

"Did you catch the killer?" Austin asked, excited.

I shook my head and took another bite of my waffle. My mom brought me coffee. "Thank you," I said, and gave her a big kiss on the cheek. "Dad's still sleeping?"

She nodded.

"So, did you?" Austin asked again.

"Nope. Not yet."

The Millers came down the stairs and grabbed the table next to us. I smiled and nodded. My mother brought them breakfast while they discussed Blue Springs State Park, where they were going today.

"We hope to see some manatees," Mrs. Miller said.

"You should be able to," my mother replied, while pouring coffee for them. "At this time of year, there are a lot of them up there at the springs. They like that the water stays the same temperature all year around, you know?"

"So, are you going to catch the killer today?" Austin asked with his mouth full.

I chuckled. "I hope so."

"It's not that easy, Austin," Abigail growled, sounding like the true big sister she was with her fifty-eight seconds. "First, they have to gather all the evidence and talk to a lot of people before they can put him away. It's not all like in the movies."

Austin made a grimace at his sister. She threw a waffle at him.

"Hey, hey," I stopped them. "I won't have you fighting. You hear me? We're family. We need to stick together. Now, did you have a good time with Grandma and Grandpa?"

Austin and Abigail both nodded.

"Good. They will pick you up today from school again. It's early release day, and I have asked them to step in, since I'll be busy with the big case. All right?"

They looked at each other, then cheered.

"Yaay!"

I walked them to the school bus and kissed both of them goodbye as Mrs. Sharon opened the doors to the big yellow bus.

"Now, be good today. Don't get in trouble, all right?" I said.

"You too, Dad," Abigail said, and kissed my nose as I bent down to look into her eyes. "Stay out of trouble."

I laughed and waved as the bus disappeared, then I sprang for my board and threw myself into the waves.

TWENTY-NINE

January 2015

"SHE LEFT A NOTE."

I looked at Kate Mueller, sitting across the table from me. From the pictures I had seen of Rhonda Harris, I'd say the daughter took more after her father.

I pushed the note in the small plastic bag across the table so she could see it. She leaned over and put on her glasses.

She read it, then looked up at me.

"What is that supposed to mean?" she asked. "Why would she write this? Why would she write I can't live with myself? I'm sorry? I don't quite understand. What did she do, Officer?"

I leaned forward in my chair. My wet hair fell onto my face. I removed the lock and pulled it all back. I thought for a second about my mother, who always wanted me to cut my hair, and now Abigail had started saying it too. But I liked having long hair, even if the girls in my life didn't think it was suitable for a detective.

My blood was still pumping fast through my veins from the surfing. The exhaustion was gone. I felt more alive than ever and more determined to solve this case than ever. Nothing like a good surf session to clear my brain.

"That's kind of what I was hoping you would clear up for me."

Kate Mueller shook her head. Her blond hair was set in a ponytail. Her face looked terrified.

"I don't believe any of this, Officer. My mother...my mother would never kill herself. She was so happy lately. The last couple of years, she has been so happy. We were going on a cruise next month. She invited us...she was the one who wanted to spend more time with her grandchildren."

"Can you verify it is her handwriting?"

"Yes. That is my mother's handwriting."

"Good. Now, returning to what you just said. I take it you wouldn't say she had been suicidal?"

76

"Not at all, Officer. Not at all. On the contrary." Kate Mueller's blue eyes stared intensely at me. "I have never seen her happier."

I wrote her statement on my notepad, then looked up at her again. "I hate to ask this, but I have to. Do you think she would be capable of committing murder?"

Kate Mueller looked at me, baffled. She put a hand to her chest. "Murder? You think that's what the note meant?"

"Her neighbor from across the street was found killed just two days ago. It does come off a little suspicious."

"I...I have never...no. Not my mother. She was the sweetest old lady. We might have had our differences, but not...that. She couldn't."

I nodded and wrote it down. I wasn't expecting her own daughter to tell me her mother was a murderer anyway, but I had to ask. I moved on with the interview.

"She used to work at Florida Today as a reporter, you say? But she retired early?"

"Yes. My mother was a writer. Always had been. Before she had me, she dreamt about being an author, but as you know, most people can't live off of that, so she had to work as a journalist for a living to support me. She was alone with me. My dad died when I was seven. Up until then, she hadn't worked a day in her life. But then she had to. She was lucky to get the job there, even though she didn't like it much."

"Why didn't she like it?"

Kate Mueller shrugged. "I don't know. She didn't like to have someone telling her what to write and what not to write. She wanted to make up her own stories."

"So, she liked to read as well, I assume. We found all of John Platt's books in her bedroom. Was she especially fond of him?"

Kate Mueller looked surprised. "Not that I know of," she said. "She never liked thrillers or mysteries much."

I showed her a picture of the many books spread on the rug and on her desk. "It seems to me she really enjoyed reading his books, don't you think?"

Kate Mueller stared at the photo, then back at me. "I don't know what to say to that. People change their taste, I guess."

"Okay," I said, and put the picture away. "You say she retired early. How come?"

"I...she was tired of working for the paper, so she told them she wanted to retire. I think it was good for her. She became a much happier person afterwards."

"And that was four years ago?"

"Yes."

"What did she do since?" I asked.

Kate Mueller shrugged again. "I don't know. I never visited her much. To be honest, we never had a real close relationship. I always sensed that she was bitter at me. You know, for making her quit her dream. It was because of me she had to stop writing books and trying to get them published. She had no choice when my dad died. I guess she kind of resented me for that."

"But, she did invite you on a cruise?" I asked.

"The last two years or so she has been trying to get back into my life. Last year, we all went to Paris together. She was the one who invited us and paid for everything, so I could hardly say no, even though my husband isn't that fond of my mother. And I guess I really wanted her to be a part of my children's lives. And, maybe...maybe I was hoping she would forgive me for ruining her life."

Kate Mueller sniffled. I saw tears pile in her eyes. I handed her a pack of tissues and poured her some water.

"How did she get the money for all this?" I asked. "A trip for five people to Paris isn't cheap. Neither is a cruise."

Kate Mueller shrugged again with a sniffle. "She said she had saved a lot of money up. Maybe her pension? I...I never thought to ask."

THIRTY

January 2015

"I THINK I'm going to leave John. I've already contacted a lawyer. I want out."

Melanie Schultz looked at her friends around the table at the restaurant. Sylvia gasped and almost choked on her Chardonnay.

"I thought you were happy with the way things were," she said, her voice trembling slightly.

Melanie shrugged and picked up a tomato with her fork and ate it. Her two-year-old son, Sebastian, was babbling something from his high chair. She gave him a piece of bread to nibble. It had been two hard years with him. She knew she was throwing a bomb on her friends.

"I'm not sure I can live like this anymore," she said. "I mean it's only a matter of time before he finds out about me and Pete, and then it's all over."

"But...but isn't there something we can do? Can't you solve it somehow?" Sylvia said, looking at the others for backup. "I really didn't think it would go this far. Maybe you're just being hasty here. I mean...you have to think it through, don't you? Have you thought about Sebastian?"

Melanie shrugged and ate another tomato from her salad. She really wasn't that fond of salads, and would have preferred to have a sandwich or a taco, but all the other girls always picked salads, and she didn't want to be the only one being unhealthy.

"He'll stay half the time with me and half with John, I guess."

"But, John is always traveling," Molly said. Her face was terrified, her lips tight. "I agree with Sylvia on this. I really think you should think it through."

"I have thought it through. Believe me. He'll just have to stay with me most of the time, then."

"Oh, it's going to crush John. You do realize that, right? It will completely crush him," Molly continued. "He loves Sebastian. And he absolutely adores you. He does everything for you. Do you really want to leave that?"

Melanie felt a pinch of guilt in her heart. Molly was right. That was why she hadn't left him before now. She knew it was going to kill him. He loved her to death. The problem was that she didn't love him back. Never had. She married him because it was the sensible thing to do, because he would take care of her, because that was the way her mother had raised her. All of her teenage years, she had told her how important it was to marry well, to make sure you found a husband that could support you so you didn't have to work. So you could stay home with the children and take care of the house.

But Melanie never really enjoyed staying home with Sebastian. She had liked it when she worked as a secretary at the big law firm in Orlando. She liked staying busy, having colleagues, and having something to do every day...places to be and people to talk to. She never enjoyed just taking care of her baby. She loved Sebastian, of course she did, but it wasn't what she wanted out of her life. She never wanted a loveless marriage and being a staying-at-home mom. She wanted more. She wanted to work. She wanted to go places. To see the world, to meet interesting people and eat exotic food. She wanted to be with grown-up people every day and talk about other things than her child and how to raise him or how to get rid of a rash or how to lose the baby weight while sipping Chardonnay.

There has to be more to adult life than this!

And now she had met a man she really liked. He made her life more interesting. She knew it was wrong, and felt so guilty about seeing him. But it wasn't just about the sex anymore. It was more. They had long talks afterwards. She liked talking to him. He was so interesting. Nothing like John. She was falling for Pete. She was starting to see him as her way out of her suburban boredom. She was going to talk to him about it today. Tonight, she was going to tell John. It was like ripping off a Band-Aid...the faster, the better.

"I know," she told her friends. "I know it's going to be hard, but it's what I want. I want to move on with my life. I hope John will understand. And I hope you will too."

She could tell by the look on her friends' faces that they didn't. They didn't want to. They all enjoyed their lives and didn't like the way she was suddenly questioning hers. It was written all over their faces.

We thought you were one of us.

THIRTY-ONE

January 2015

HE WAS LOOKING at her through the window of his truck. Melanie was her name. She was beautiful. Everything about her was so intoxicating. The Snakecharmer had been observing her for quite a while…months, actually. She and her friends always went to the same place for lunch on Wednesdays with their babies in their strollers. They ate Cobb salads and drank white wine while talking. The same procedure every Wednesday.

Her long painted fingernails were playing with her hair while she spoke to her friends in the parking lot outside the restaurant. They were saying their goodbyes. He rolled down his window and peeked out.

"Hey there," he said. "Can I give you girls a ride anywhere?"

They looked at one another and laughed. "In that thing?" one asked with a shiver.

The three of them shook their heads. The condescending look on their faces was saying, Who does he think he is? Why is he talking to us?

The Snakecharmer laughed. He pulled his arm inside the window.

"All right, ladies. Suit yourselves."

He backed out of the parking lot and drove off with a grin on his face. He watched them shake their heads in his rearview mirror before he drove onto the street, took a right turn, then took a small street down and ended up in front of a big house in a nice neighborhood. He stopped the engine.

Then he waited.

Minutes later, he spotted the woman driving down the street in her brown Audi. She parked the car in the driveway and got out on her high heels. She grabbed the baby from the back seat and placed him on her hip. He smiled and watched her from afar. Such a gorgeous woman with such a perfect life. Such a shame.

"Yes, that's right. I know where you live, little bitch. I know everything about you."

He waited till she walked inside her house before he got out of the car, then he walked into the neighbor's yard, crawled over the wall, and landed in her yard. He knew his way around. He walked up to the back porch with the pool area and watched her through the large windows as she put the baby in a playpen. He hid while watching her open the sliding doors leading to the yard to let the cat out, leaving them open.

It was almost too easy.

He didn't have to wait long before the car drove up. He looked at his watch. It was two o'clock.

"Right on time, as usual, Your Honor," he mumbled, as he watched the judge get out of his black Cadillac Escalade and trot up the driveway wearing his black suit. He was looking over his shoulder to make sure no one saw him. Lucky for him, the driveway was surrounded by big walls, just as the entire house was. People always thought they were protecting themselves by putting up walls around their property, when in reality, they just made it easier for people like the Snakecharmer to act without risk of being seen.

He heard the doorbell ring, then the door open, and soon he saw the judge and the woman cuddled up in a warm embrace against the wall of the foyer.

He watched them through the big windows on the porch. "I guess this court is now in session," he whispered. "The Honorable Judge Martin presiding."

As usual, he could see everything they did. As usual, he could follow their every move when the judge pulled up her skirt and threw her up against the wall. When she pulled down his pants and took him in her mouth. When he lifted her up and threw her on the dining room table and entered her from behind. Yes, everything up until now was just as usual on a Wednesday afternoon in Cocoa Beach.

But after this, nothing would be as usual for the two of them again.

The Snakecharmer picked up his gun, walked towards the sliding door, and walked inside. While he could hear the two of them moaning and groaning in the living room, on the couch, he crept up behind them, placed a gun to the judge's head and fired while yelling.

"All rise!!"

The woman beneath the judge screamed, terrified when the blood spurted into her face, then again when she spotted the familiar face above the lifeless body. The baby had woken up and was crying in his playpen.

"W...what...who...why...?" the woman stuttered, thinking somehow this must be a misunderstanding; somehow, he must have gotten it all wrong. She stared with disbelief at his face, waiting for some kind of explanation, but was struck with terror as she saw the dark chill in his eyes.

"Shhh..." he whispered, then stroked her beautiful face gently with his fingers. A small whimper emerged from her mouth. A tear escaped her eye. He caught it with his finger and looked at it. Then he picked up a pillow. He smiled at her with compassion and excitement, right before he forced it against her lips. She tried to fight him off with all her strength, but with no success. Her painted fingernails pierced through the skin on his arm.

THIRTY-TWO

January 2015

THE SNAKECHARMER WRAPPED the body of Melanie into a blanket, then carried it out to his truck and put her in the back. Drago and Django hissed in their glass tank.

"Easy there, boys," he grinned. "This is Melanie. She will be riding with us today."

He grabbed a gas can, closed the back of the truck, and walked back to the house. He had driven the car into the driveway and closed the gate. No one would ever see him, and even if they did, they wouldn't wonder why he was there.

The Snakecharmer whistled as he walked back to the house with the can in his hand. Today was one of the good days. He had considered leaving something for the detectives to chew on. Something like lipstick painted on a mirror with a message or a note, but had decided that wasn't his thing. It was too risky. He wanted them to know he was the master. He was the one in charge, and if he started leaving little notes behind, then they would just end up tracking him down. And that wasn't part of his plan.

No, he had come up with something much better.

He walked inside and looked at the dead judge on the carpet. Bloodstains had completely ruined the light couch. He poured gasoline on the body of Judge Martin, then saluted him respectfully with a large grin before he grabbed his lighter and set him on fire. Still grinning, he walked to the playpen where the baby was crying. The Snakecharmer smiled at the young child, who was eager to be picked up and reaching his arms in the air. The Snakecharmer tilted his head while the heat from the flames behind him licked at his neck.

"Now, isn't that adorable?" he said.

The baby cried louder, still reaching up his arms. He smiled, then bent down and picked him up, right before he rushed out of the burning house.

He put the child in the passenger seat of the truck and strapped him down, then opened the gate and raced out of the driveway. Once he reached the end of the road, he heard a loud explosion behind him, and with a grin on his face, he watched the house go up in flames in the rearview mirror.

He imitated the sound of the explosion with his mouth, then looked at the child in the back.

"Mama?" the child said with a whimper.

The man shook his head. "No. Not mama. Dada. Can you say that? Dada? Mama is gone. She left us, Son. You know how it is. It's always the children that get hurt."

He stopped at a red light. A police car drove up on his side. The Snakecharmer pretended he didn't notice. Out of the corner of his eye, he watched the officer in the car. He was eating something while looking at the resorts to his right.

He didn't even look at the truck.

The man chuckled to himself, then looked at the baby. "They make it almost too easy."

While waiting for the light to turn, the man could tell the police officer got news over the radio. He looked perplexed, then put on the siren and tried to get out of the line of traffic. The Snakecharmer backed up to make room for the officer and let him drive through.

"Almost too easy," he repeated, as he watched the car disappear in the opposite direction down A1A and heard the many sirens approaching in the distance. "What do you say...Will?"

Yes, that's it. He looks like a Will.

The kid didn't react. He had stopped crying, though. Fire trucks and ambulances were blasting by in the opposite direction.

"Will it is, then."

THIRTY-THREE

January 1985

SHE HAD THE BABY. It took thirty-two hours of labor to get him out, but she had the baby. And Victor was right there all the time, holding her hand, wiping her forehead with a cold cloth, taking her aggressive comments, and loving her when she needed it.

He was there for her through everything.

When he came to take her and their son home, he told her he had a surprise for her.

"You're driving the wrong way," she said. "Our condo is in the opposite part of town."

"I told you I had a surprise," he said with a grin.

Annie really tried to like his smile, but his teeth were so crooked and yellow from too much coffee. His parents were loaded; why didn't he just get them fixed?

Lying in the hospital with her newborn, resting for days, regaining her strength, Annie had decided that if she was going to live with this man for the rest of her life, then she would have to try and make the best of what she had. At least he adored her. Maybe she could change him. People changed. She could get him to have his teeth done, she could get him to stop eating things that smelled bad, maybe use a better cologne. She could change the way he dressed. That was what women did, wasn't it? It had been done before, so of course she could.

They came closer to a gated neighborhood and Victor drove up to the booth. A uniformed man came out. When he saw Victor, he lifted his cap and opened the gate.

"Does he know you?" Annie asked.

Victor couldn't stop grinning. It didn't make him prettier. "He'll get to know you too. Soon."

Annie drew her brows together. What was this? Were they going to visit someone? Was he just showing her and the baby off? Because, if that was the case, then she certainly wasn't up for it.

85

"Victor…I don't think…"

Victor stopped her, then parked the car in front of a big house. Annie looked at it through the window. It was huge. No, it was humongous. And so beautiful. It looked just like a house she had once seen in a magazine.

"Who lives here?" she asked.

"Don't you recognize it?" he asked.

"It looks like…"

Victor pulled out the magazine and showed her. "One and the same," he said, smiling from ear to ear.

"You found the same house? How did you know? Why?" Annie asked, still not understanding what was going on.

"Yes. You showed it to me. Don't you remember? You said it was the most beautiful house you had ever seen."

"But…but that was months ago. How did you…remember?" Annie asked. Her voice was shivering.

"Nothing is too good for my baby," Victor said.

Annie's heart dropped. Could it be? What was he saying? "Do…do you mean…?"

No, it can't be!

Victor nodded, smiling from ear to ear. "Yes, darling. I bought it for you."

Annie found it hard to breathe. She couldn't believe what he was saying. Instead of saying anything, she shrieked and woke up the baby in the back seat.

"Oh, my God, Victor!"

She leaned over and kissed him, and for once, didn't care about his bad teeth or smell. "Oh, my God! Oh, my God! I love you, Victor!"

THIRTY-FOUR

January 2015

IT LOOKED like the end of the world. I could hardly believe my own eyes when I arrived at the scene on Country Club Road. It was late in the afternoon. Flames were still licking the sky. The heat was unbearable. Luckily, the wind carried the smoke out over the Banana River.

It had taken the firefighters hours to get the fire under control and make sure it wasn't threatening the neighboring houses. The fire still wasn't entirely put out, but at least it was contained. Neighbors had gathered in the street, watching the scene with terror in their eyes.

"That poor family," they whispered.

Usually, I was never called out to fires, but Weasel had asked me to come down. I was glad I had asked my mom to pick up the twins.

"So, they got it under control, I hear?" I said.

Weasel nodded. She was wearing her hair in a ponytail today. It looked great. "Took a while, but yes. The entire house burned down, though. They can put it out, they say, but not save it."

I took in a deep breath. The family had lost everything, then. "So, why did you want to talk to me?"

Weasel looked at her shoes, then up at me. "I spoke to the husband. He was on a business trip in Southern Florida. He got here an hour ago. He says his wife and child are missing. He's been calling her. He talked to all of her friends, who she met with for lunch, and they said she went home. With the baby."

My heart stopped. "You think...you think they were in the house?"

Weasel shrugged. "I don't know what I think anymore. But I thought you should know."

I nodded. It was what they would call a suspicious death. That was my field. "Got it. Anything else I should know?"

Weasel looked at me. "No. Go on home to those beautiful kids of yours. Kiss them for me, will you?"

I chuckled. Weasel never had kids of her own. I often wondered if she regretted her decision.

"Sure thing." While I spoke, the firefighters finally managed to put out the last few flames. The spectators clapped, and so did I. They were the true heroes around here. First responders in most situations. They never knew what would await them when they arrived.

"Chief!" I heard the Captain of the fire department yell, addressed to Weasel. He approached her, holding something between his hands. "We found this."

"A gas can," I said. "Where did you find it?"

"In the driveway. Next to that burnt out car over there."

"Was that the wife's car?" I asked. "There seem to be two."

Weasel looked pensive. "The husband said she drove a brown Audi."

"That's not a brown car," I said. "Anyone can see that, even from where we're standing. It might have been burned, but that car was black."

I walked closer and spotted the license plate. It was still sitting in its place. I kneeled next to it, careful not to step on anything. Weasel was behind me.

"Could you run this plate for me, please?" I asked.

"Sure thing." Weasel grabbed her radio and ran the plate. Then she looked at me while shaking her head. "It belongs to Judge Pete Martin." Weasel went pale. "What the...what is Judge Martin's car doing here?"

"Maybe he was visiting?"

"You think he was in there as well? Oh, my God." Weasel clasped her face. I couldn't blame her for being upset. "What the heck is going on around here?" she asked, looking at me like I had an answer for everything.

"I don't know," I said. "But I can tell you one thing. Someone set this house on fire. And that someone wanted us to know it was on purpose."

THIRTY-FIVE

January 2015

WEASEL and I drove in my Jeep together to get to Judge Martin's house. He lived in one of the newer houses in Cocoa Isles, overlooking the Thousand Islands. His wife opened the door.

"Mrs. Martin?" I asked and showed her my badge.

"Yes?" She looked from me to Weasel and back. The terror was in her eyes. It seemed like she already suspected something was wrong. "Weslie? What's going on here?"

"We're looking for Pete," Weasel said.

"He's not here. He was supposed to be home hours ago. I called his cell, but..." she stopped herself. Her eyes were flickering back and forth between us. "Did something happen?"

"We don't know yet, ma'am," I said. "But we did locate his car."

"His car? Where?"

I took in a deep breath. Weslie was personal friends with the judge and his wife. It was best if I told her. I didn't have emotions involved. "It was parked in the driveway of a house that burned down this afternoon. We still don't..."

I didn't get any further before she broke down and cried. "Oh, no!" She clasped her mouth. "I mean, I heard the sirens...I watched it on TV. The news chopper showed everything. I wondered...I knew..."

"Could you tell us what your husband might be doing there?" I asked.

"He...he...he was visiting...he thought I didn't know, but I did. It has been going on for months. I let him. Thought he would figure out that he wasn't really missing out on anything, that he had all he needed at home, if you understand what I mean...It wasn't like it was his first. He always comes back...he always...oh, my...if you'll excuse me, I need to...sit down."

I grabbed her arm before she fell and helped her inside the hallway. I found a chair and helped her sit down.

"Just take it easy, Mrs. Martin," I said. "We don't know that anything has happened to him yet."

Weasel held her hand while Mrs. Martin sobbed, then bit her lip to hold it back. "It's all my fault. I should have stood up to him. I should have told him I knew. Told him to end it as soon as I found out. I even drove over there to see her. She was gorgeous. And so much younger than me. How was I supposed to compete? All I could do was to give him a stable home to come back to and hope he would know not to throw that away, you know?"

I exhaled. "I know," I said. "You did the best you could."

Mrs. Martin choked on a cry. It was hard for her to breathe properly. "You shouldn't be alone," Weasel said. "Do you want me to call your sister to come?"

Mrs. Martin nodded with a sob. "That would be very nice, thank you. I need to call the kids as well. They're upstate. They deserve to know."

"Maybe you should wait with that till we know what happened," Weasel suggested. "The technicians are working the scene right now, and hopefully we'll know more soon."

Mrs. Martin looked up at Weasel. "Technicians? As in crime scene technicians? You think it was arson?"

Weasel nodded. "We're pretty certain. We found a can of gasoline on the scene."

Mrs. Martin gasped and held a hand to her chest. Then, she finally broke down and let the tears roll across her face. Weasel called for the sister while I found a box of tissues in the bathroom and handed it to her. She thanked me and wiped her eyes. "I'm so sorry. I feel horrible that you have to see me like this. It's all just so..."

"Unbelievable. I know," I said.

THIRTY-SIX

January 2015

TWO DAYS LATER, Weasel called me into her office. It was right before lunch and I was planning on hitting the Juice 'N Java within a few minutes when she spoiled my plans.

"Shut the door," she said with a serious face.

"I take it you have news?" I asked and sat down.

She sighed and hid her face between her hands for a second before she looked at me again. "It was him. They finally identified the body found in the burned down house. It was Judge Martin."

"Jeez. Well, at least the family will finally get closure," I said. "Did you tell his wife yet?"

"I'm going over there after this meeting. Just trying to gather myself a little first."

"I understand. What about the mother and child?"

She threw a file on the desk in front of me. "According to this, they found remains of just one body. They used dental records to ID him."

"At least that gives us hope for the mother, Melanie Schultz, and her child," I said and flipped through the pages in the file. Pictures of the carbonized body parts jumped out at me. They had found bullets on the scene too. And then the can of gasoline. They believed it had been poured on the body of the judge. The fire started in the living room.

"Yeah, well. With fires, you never know. But, yes. I have a feeling the mother and child weren't in the house," she said. "I just can't for the life of me...understand what the judge was doing in the house all by himself?"

"It sounds odd. Maybe he was waiting for her to come home. What we know now is they usually met at two o'clock every Wednesday. Her friends have told us and so has Mrs. Martin, who knew all about it. Maybe Melanie Schultz just never made it home?"

Weasel slammed her palm on the table. "But the car, Jack. Her car was right there." She pointed at the file in my hand. "It was in the driveway. She drove home, but then what? She decided to go for a walk? She was picked up by someone? She took a cab out of town and disappeared? What?"

"I don't know. Let's stick to what we do know. The judge. Who do we think would want to kill the judge?" I asked.

Weasel snorted. "Look around. A lot of people. There's an election coming up. His poster is in most people's front yard. He had many supporters around here, but also many opponents. He put criminals in jail. It could be political. It could be revenge. You pick. There's a lot to choose from. There are many people with motives."

"Like his wife," I said.

"Don't get cocky."

"I'm not. I'm serious," I said. "The man was cheating on her repeatedly. That gives her a pretty good motive in my book."

"I've known the woman since we were children. It's not her," Weasel growled.

"We have to at least look into it," I said. "And you know it."

"Good grief. Okay then, but be careful with her, all right? She's in a fragile state of mind."

"I'm always gentle," I said and smiled. "So, are we looking at a connection on the three deaths here?" I asked.

Weasel shook her head. "I talked to Sheriff Ron earlier, and we both agree there is no need to look into that angle. Nothing connects them, apart from the fact that they were committed in our town within a close time frame. I think it's just a coincidence. There is nothing that indicates they're related. One of the deaths is a suicide, so that is certainly not connected to the others."

I wasn't sure I agreed, but didn't say it out loud.

"What about the man Melanie's friends said they saw at the parking lot at the restaurant right after they were done eating?" I asked. "I can't seem to get him out of my mind."

"The Animal Control guy?" Weasel asked.

"Yes. They said he was driving one of the vans from Animal Control and had snakes in a tank inside the van. He offered them a ride, they told us. One of the girls took a look inside and saw the snakes."

Weasel nodded. "Joel called Animal Control, and they told him they didn't have a guy in that area on that date." She looked at me pensively. "You think he might have followed her back to the house?"

I shrugged. "I have no idea at this point. But I think we should have a drawing made and send it to the newspaper and ask the public to help us find this guy. Tell them we'd like to talk to him."

Weasel nodded. "I'll set that in motion. The friends said they got a pretty good look at him. They can help us get a good picture of this Snake-guy. What else? How are we on the suicide and the homicide on West Bay Drive?"

"Nothing much to tell yet," I said. "I'm looking into Rhonda Harris' finances. She made quite a lot of money the last couple of years. I'm trying to figure out where the money came from."

"Good. But don't spend too much time on the West Bay Drive case. The murder of the judge has first priority now, and finding Melanie Schultz and her child. Judge Martin was a high-profile judge around here. People will be demanding justice. I know the Mayor will. It's going to create quite the media-drama once they get the news. I'm not looking forward to that part."

I got up from my chair, holding the file in my hand. "I want to take a closer look at it anyway," I said.

"By all means. It's your case now. Knock yourself out."

"Thanks," I said, and walked towards the door. I grabbed the handle and looked back at Weasel. "And don't worry. I think you look great on TV."

I ducked just in time to avoid the stapler hitting me.

THIRTY-SEVEN

April 1990

SHE HAD everything she could ever ask for in life. She had the most beautiful house in a gated area, she had the biggest most expensive car, and the most beautiful jewelry that Victor brought home for her almost every month just to spoil her.

She had everything, her neighbors said, with jealousy in their voices. Even her child was beautiful. Her little baby boy, who was now five years of age, was just so...so perfect.

Why wasn't she happy? Why wasn't Annie enjoying any of it? Why did she constantly feel like she was trapped in a prison and couldn't breathe?

Why?

She asked herself that very question every day when Victor kissed her goodbye with those yellow crooked teeth and bad breath of his, and she was left alone with the child. She never knew what to do with him. To be honest, she found it hard to spend time with him, and often she would leave him downstairs with some toys, then walk upstairs and go back to sleep or just hide. She didn't know what it was about the child, but she just didn't like to be close to him. She feared it was because of how he had come to be. Did she resent him for it? Did she somehow blame him for the rape?

She didn't know. All she knew was that she was counting the days till he would start Kindergarten after the summer. Then, Annie wouldn't have to be with him all day. Finally, she would be able to have some time for herself.

While sitting in her bathrobe in her bedroom, listening to the boy play with his toys downstairs, smashing cars into each other and pretending they exploded, she wondered if she even loved him.

Victor adored the kid. There was no doubt about it. He loved the boy. But Annie found it harder and harder. When she looked at his face, she sometimes thought she saw Tim's eyes, or one of his friend's facial expressions. And that was when she was reminded of what had happened on that dreadful night six years ago.

94

Two years ago, she had confided everything to her mother. She hadn't been able to hold it in anymore, and just told her everything. She asked her if she was a terrible mother because she found it hard to look at her own child.

Hoping her mother would understand her, she had leaned against her shoulder, longing for a comforting hug, but her mother had, instead, moved away and turned her back on her. She had walked to the kitchen sink and started peeling potatoes while saying:

"Well at least everything turned out fine, right? At least you have a good husband now, and you live a great life in that big house. I tell you, I've never had a house like that. You should be very grateful and not dig up all these ugly memories. Make the best of what you've got. That's what I always say. That's how you get by; that's how you live a good life."

Annie had stared at her mother's back while she spoke. While tears streamed across her cheeks and the feeling of abandonment pierced her stomach, she imagined grabbing that potato peeler out of her mother's hand and piercing her in the heart with it. She wondered what it would feel like and closed her eyes to shut out her mother's words. They felt like punches to her stomach.

Since then, Annie had stopped seeking her parents' comfort and understanding. While her discomfort in that big mansion grew day by day, she wondered if anyone would even care if she died.

"Victor would," she mumbled to herself and shivered in disgust. The more the days passed with him, the more she couldn't stand being close to him. She always dreaded having sex with him and tried to get out of it if he suggested or tried to make a move when they went to bed. There was always a headache or a tiredness to blame it on. Every now and then, she gave in to him, simply because she felt she had to, since he had done so much for her, and let his stinking sweaty body on top of hers. She would close her eyes and think of something else while he finished his business. Lately, she had started to gain a lot of weight, trying to make herself less attractive to him, and it seemed to be working. So, she continued. Sitting in her bedroom during the day, she stuffed herself with chocolate, cheesecake, chips, and sodas. Soon Victor stopped making approaches on her at night at all. It was a small victory for her, but it didn't help with the child. She still wasn't happy, and she blamed the boy.

"Soon," she whispered, sitting in her bedroom, while he played wildly downstairs, knocking over furniture and jumping on the couch. "Soon, he'll be gone all day, and then you'll be able to enjoy your life. Then you'll be happy."

THIRTY-EIGHT

January 2015

WE HAD a drawing made of the snake-guy and it was published in all the local papers and shown on TV, along with pictures of Melanie and Sebastian Schultz. According to Melanie's friends, the guy was both long-haired and long-bearded. He wore his hair in a ponytail. It got a lot of immediate response from the public, but unfortunately, nothing we could use.

As Monday morning came and went, I feared more and more for the life of Melanie and her child. I had hoped they had just gone somewhere else, maybe visited family or friends we didn't know about, and then maybe would see this on TV and call us. But nothing came of it.

On Tuesday, I finally had a breakthrough in the suicide of Rhonda Harris. The bank tracked her big payments over the last couple of years and found them to be coming from across the street, from Laura Bennett's bank account. And they were quite large amounts. Hundreds of thousands of dollars several times a year.

"Why was Laura Bennett paying Rhonda Harris?" I asked Weasel, when we went for lunch at Juice N' Java across the street.

"Ask the husband," she said.

So, I did. I called him and asked him to come down to the station. He arrived in the afternoon. I hadn't seen him since I had been at the hospital to interview him. He looked a lot better now. He was dressed nicely in a white shirt and black pants. He had trimmed his moustache and cut his hair nicely, making him look a little like a young Tom Selleck. He didn't look like the drunk everybody was so busy making him into. But some drunks hid it well. I smelled no alcohol on his breath, though.

"Haven't touched a drink since it happened," he said, as if he could read my mind. He sat down. "Haven't gambled either."

"Good to hear. So, how's Ben?" I asked. I knew he was back in school, since Abigail and Austin had told me. They had all tried to be a good friend to him, they said. I liked that.

"He's better," Brandon Bennett said. "It hasn't been easy, but people have been good to us. They're taking real good care of him at the school."

"That's good to know," I said. "That's what I've always liked about this town. We take care of each other here in Cocoa Beach."

"So, how can I help you, Detective?" Brandon asked. "Is there any news about my wife's murder?"

He hit me right in my guilty spot. I had been dealing mostly with the murder of the judge lately, and I had to put the Bennett killing a little to the side. I wasn't proud of it.

"Not much, no, but I do have something I need to ask you about," I said. I placed the bank statement in front of him. I had underlined the big transfers of money to Rhonda Harris's account.

"What am I looking at?" Brandon Bennett said.

"It has come to my attention that your wife paid your neighbor across the street a lot of money several times a year. Do you know why?"

Brandon Bennett shook his head. "This is news to me as well," he said. "Why would she do that?"

"That's what I'm asking you."

He exhaled. "As much as I would love to help, I have no idea. This is a huge surprise to me as well. I'm sorry, Detective. Have you asked Rhonda Harris's daughter? She might know."

"I have. She didn't know either. And you're sure you didn't know about this?" I asked.

"Positive."

"What about her brother?"

"What about him?"

"You said they stayed in contact. How much contact was that?" I asked.

Brandon Bennett shrugged. "I don't know, Detective. Not much. I knew he called every now and then. She visited him a few times. I remember he came on the night of the murder. I remember he was angry and they went outside to discuss something. She didn't want him there. She asked him to leave, but he wouldn't. He told her he needed money. She said he had enough. Then they went outside and I didn't hear any more. I guess she made him leave, because she returned alone. I asked her what it was about, but she told me it was none of my business. That's when we started fighting. She told me I couldn't go out on the casino boats anymore. I had spent too much money lately. I felt like a child when she spoke to me like that. So, I got angry and told her it was all her fault I was drinking and gambling."

"Because of the child."

Brandon Bennett looked at the floor. "Yes. I couldn't stand being at the house. I couldn't stand being close to her when I felt that way. When I felt like she hadn't been able to care enough for our child."

"Sudden Infant Death Syndrome isn't anyone's fault," I said. "No more than an accident usually is, or a heart-attack."

Brandon Bennett shook his head. "I know...I know...It's just..." He looked up.

"It's just what?" I asked. "You needed someone to blame? We all do when bad things happen. It makes it easier to handle. But, it often destroys our relation-ships." I sighed and let it go. How Brandon Bennett chose to deal with his loss was his choice. "So, do you believe Laura might have hidden something from you? Was something going on between her and her brother?"

"He asked for money a lot. I think that was all. I think Laura felt guilty because she had gotten the entire inheritance. He couldn't take care of himself properly, and she believed she needed to help him out. But he never stopped. I guess that's why she got angry with him."

"You think he could have killed her?" I asked.

"Peter? I don't know. I'm not an expert on killers, Detective."

I chatted with Brandon Bennett for a little while longer, but didn't get anything more out of him. I asked him if he remembered any more from the night of the murder, and he told me that he was slowly regaining some memory, but still nothing that would help the investigation. Nothing between midnight Sunday night and waking up at the hospital Tuesday morning. I kept wondering who could have slipped him that drug in his drink and asked him if he had any friends or anyone he suspected could do such a thing.

"I...I really don't, Detective."

I wasn't getting anywhere, so I sent him away, then put the papers aside and grabbed myself another cup of coffee. I wondered about the brother, Peter. He was beginning to look more and more like a suspect in my eyes. I watched the cars go by outside my window, while also wondering what had been going on between the neighbors. Rhonda Harris's suicide note had said I can't live with myself. What did that refer to? Did she kill Laura? Was she blackmailing her or something? Was she demanding money from her, and when she refused to give her more, she killed her? If so, then what was she blackmailing her about?

There was a knock on my door and Joel Hall peeked in. "Detective? I'm sorry to interrupt, but I have something I need to tell you."

"Come on in. Grab a chair."

"It was just something I thought about last night," Joel said and sat. "Last year, there was a woman in here. She was complaining about John Platt's latest book."

I leaned forward in my chair, then sipped some more coffee. "Complaining? About what?"

"I was the one who took her report. She wanted to file a report against the estate after John Platt died," she said.

I frowned. "Why? Had they committed a crime?"

"She claimed the books weren't written by John Platt. She said they weren't right or something. I never really listened. I pretended to file the report, but never did. It didn't make much sense, what she said. To be honest, I thought she was a wacko. But I thought you should know anyway."

THIRTY-NINE

January 2015

"SOMEONE CALLED FOR ANIMAL CONTROL? I understand you had a snake in your garage?"

The Snakecharmer smiled from ear to ear. The woman opening the door was in her early thirties.

"Yes," the woman said with a deep sigh. "Thank you so much for coming this fast. I just got off the phone a few minutes ago. I was going crazy just thinking about it being out there."

She shivered.

The Snakecharmer looked at the goose bumps on her neck. A thrill went through his body. He thought about killing her right there on the spot, in the hallway of her own house. Just for the thrill of it.

"Let me show you the way," she said. "I think we better go through from the inside. I don't want it to run out into the yard and hide there if I open the garage door. I want it off the property, if you know what I mean."

"Of course, ma'am. I understand. And I take it you have children? I saw the bike in the driveway."

"Yes, she said. "We have a girl."

"We don't want her to get scared by one of those bastards while playing in the yard, now do we?"

The woman shivered again. She was so elegant when she moved, so feminine. The Snakecharmer loved that. Like a gazelle in the savannah. And she was his prey. Just like the predator in the wild, he was watching her every move without her noticing it.

"Nice house you have here," he said, and followed her through the kitchen.

"Yes, thank you."

"What does your husband do?"

"He's a lawyer. Well, actually, we're getting a divorce, so…"

The Snakecharmer froze. He forced a smile. "I see. Well, that's too bad. I mean, it seems like you have everything here. It's always so hard on the children."

The woman sighed. The Snakecharmer felt the blood rush rapidly through his veins. He wanted so badly to snap her beautiful long neck. Talking about the divorce made the furor rise in him. Almost to the point where he was afraid he might snap.

Not now, you fool. Not now.

"I know," she said, and opened the door leading to the garage. "It's in here. I saw it over there by the cupboards. It had a lot of colors. That's how I knew it was one of the bad ones. You know how the saying goes."

"Red touch yellow, kills a fellow. Red touch black, friend of Jack," the Snakecharmer said. "People never remember it right."

"I know," she said with a light laugh. "I can never get it right either. But I definitely saw yellow on it."

"I'll take care of it, ma'am, don't worry."

"I'm glad," she said.

"Oh, and I do hope that there isn't another person involved."

"What was that?"

"An affair. I hope there isn't a third party involved," he said with a smirk. "It always gets nastier if there is."

The woman looked baffled. "I...I don't think that is any of your business. Now, if you'll just catch the snake."

"Of course, ma'am," he said.

"Say, haven't I seen you before?" she asked.

"Only if you've had other problems with snakes, ma'am," the Snakecharmer said, then turned his head away.

"I must be confusing you with someone else, then," she said and closed the door.

The Snakecharmer cursed while walking to the cupboards, grabbing the Coral snake by the tail and pulling it out. "Get out of there, Drago. Playtime is over."

He grabbed it by its mouth and petted it gently while talking to it. "Yes, you did a good job in here. Yes, of course, this woman needs to get what she deserves. What all of them deserve for doing what they do. For ruining EVERYTHING! I know she recognized me. Must be more careful now mustn't we? Those ugly pictures on TV are ruining everything, aren't they? Well, maybe a better disguise would help. Maybe another wig? One that isn't longhaired. Lose the fake beard, huh? Maybe another color of contacts. What's that, Drago? Yes, you're right. We need a new mummy now, don't we?" He laughed at his own little word play. Mummy/mommy. It was funny. "Yes, we do. But not now. Not yet. We must be patient, Drago. We must be patient."

FORTY

January 2015

TRACEY BURDEN WAS A BIG WOMAN, who in many ways reminded me of Kathy Bates in Misery. The comparison didn't stop there, unfortunately. As I followed her into the living room of her house in Titusville, I realized she was just as crazy as well. She was wearing a fluttering colorful dress covered with butterflies. Her hair was put up with butterfly clips and the walls of her living room were decorated with pinned up butterflies, roaches, and spiders.

"I just love bugs," she exclaimed, as I walked inside. "Don't you?"

"Don't we all?" I said, and sat on her plastic-covered couch. I lied. If there was one thing I hated, it was bugs. Butterflies were okay, but the rest I could live without.

"I'm sorry about the plastic, but my cats keep scratching the fabric," she said and smiled. "Can I get you some coffee?"

"I'm good. Thank you."

The big woman sat down across from me. "I'm just so glad someone is finally taking my complaints seriously," she said, almost whispering like it was a secret. "I mean, it's been going on for years. And no one seems to want to listen."

"What has been going on?" I asked.

She looked puzzled. "Well, the forgery, of course. What else did you think I was talking about?"

She looked at me with those slightly wacky eyes. I exhaled and tried to focus. Her house was located on the mainland and had a small yard with dozens of garden gnomes that reminded me of that movie I'd seen with the kids, that Gnomeo and Juliet. Strange movie, I thought. Almost as strange as the woman sitting in front of me.

"BOO!"

I jumped in my seat. Tracey Burden laughed loudly and slapped her leg. "You were away in dreamland there, Detective," she said with a shrill voice. "Can't go around daydreaming on the job, can we?"

"I'm sorry. I've been working some long days," I said, beginning to regret having come here. When investigating murder, you often came upon some really strange types. It always brought out the weirdos.

"I bet. You have a lot to do, don't you? Lots of wackos out there. You sure you don't want any of that coffee?"

"No, I'm good. But I would like to know more about this presumed forgery you're talking about."

"Presumed? Now, I have never. Let me tell you something, Detective. There is nothing presumed about it. I can prove that John Platt hasn't written a word in the last three books that were published in his name. I'm his biggest fan. You might even say I'm his number one fan."

She laughed.

"Really? And how can you prove that he didn't write them?" I asked.

Tracey Burden got up. She picked two books from a shelf. Then she opened them and sat down. She placed the books in front of us. "This is one of the new books; this is one of the old ones. Look at them," she said.

I was wasting my time, but tried to look at the pages anyway.

"It jumps right out at ya', doesn't it?" she asked with a scoff. "They must think we're stupid. It was so obvious; I knew right away. I even created a Facebook-group for others like me who have detected it."

"I...I'm not sure I can see what it is," I said. "Could you help me out here? I'm not that big a John Platt fan."

Tracey Burden scoffed again and shook her head. "Look here and here," she said and pointed. "Look at that description right there. John Platt could never have written that. He actually describes this woman nicely. She is a nice person."

"And?"

"Everyone knows John Platt hates women, and that he always describes them as awful people. Especially since, the older he got, the meaner he was towards women. Someone must have hurt him badly in his life. But, suddenly, after his death, three more books came along where the women suddenly are heroes. That's not something John Platt would write. He was known to hate women. No, hate is too nice a word for it. He loathed them. That was all part of the fun. That's what made his books special."

"So, you're saying he didn't write these books? Then, who did?"

Tracey Burden lit up in a big smile. "Well, I guess that's your job to find out, isn't it, Detective?"

FORTY-ONE

January 2015

I HAD no idea what to do with the information that Tracey Burden had given me. At first, I was simply glad to get out of there. She was a nutcase, and my first instinct was to just forget what she had said and move on. She had hardly provided proof of anything. Yet, it had still aroused my interest. I made some phone calls and tried to look into the matter, but was only met by a wall of silence from the publishing house and lawyers. That wasn't the way to approach this. I let it go for a while and went home to my family. My friends, Eliza and Tom, had invited us over for dinner. They had a child in the twins' class. I had told Emily she could stay home if she wanted.

"So, how are things?" Eliza asked, when she put the bowl of mashed potatoes on the table. "How are you holding up?"

Tom brought me a beer, while the twins scooped mashed potatoes onto their plates and started making volcanoes with the gravy, using their fingers as cars driving down the sides. I was too tired to ask them to stop playing with their food.

"I'm fine. Busy week, but I'm good."

"That's good, Jack. Being busy is good," Eliza said with a compassionate smile. She worried about the kids and me. I always spent most of our dinners together assuring her we were all surviving. It could be exhausting, since she didn't seem to believe me. Or maybe she just saw right through me. The fact was, I still loved Arianna. I still thought about her every hour of the day and wondered if I would ever hear from her again. I still jumped when the phone rang and a small voice inside of me said it could be her. It could be.

Even after four years.

Eliza and Tom had been my friends since we moved here. Well, actually they were our friends, since they went all the way back to when Arianna was still part of my life. Our kids went to preschool together. Eliza was friends with Arianna before she decided to leave. We used to live in the same condominium, and they were pregnant at the same time. She was in shock when Arianna left me. Maybe even more than I was, I sometimes thought.

"Still no word from her?" she asked me every time we saw each other, even now, four years later. We were done eating and moved to the living room, where Tom and I finished our beers. Tom's longboard was leaned up against the wall. I knew it had been a while since he last used it. Between his job at the bank and the family, it was hard for him to find time to hit the waves. Plus, Eliza didn't like it. She thought he spent too much time on the water. Time he could spend on doing things around the house they had just bought.

I shook my head. "No. And, frankly, I don't care anymore, Eliza," I lied.

"But, it's just so odd. So unlike her to just leave and not even check in on you every now and then. I mean, she cared about the twins. I just know she did. What kind of woman leaves her children when they're less than two years old?"

"She was depressed," I said and sipped my beer. I hated always having to defend Arianna.

"She didn't know what she was doing."

"I think she knew very well…" Eliza mumbled.

"What was that?" I asked.

Eliza annoyed me a little. She was always on Arianna's case. I was angry with Arianna for leaving us, of course I was, but I had stopped blaming her a long time ago. I had decided she simply wasn't well.

Eliza received a look from Tom. She shook her head with a sigh. "I know, I know," she said, and leaned back on the leather couch. "We can't say anything."

She paused and looked angrily at Tom. "I just think he deserves to know."

Tom gesticulated. "Why? Eliza? Why now?"

"Because he deserves to know the truth. It has been long enough, don't you think?"

I was starting to get alarmed over their little quarrel. Something was going on here. Exactly what was it I didn't know?

"Could you please just tell me what's going on here?" I asked.

Tom sighed and ran a hand through his hair. "Now see what you've done. Now we have to tell him."

"Tell me what?" I was holding the beer bottle tightly between my hands. "Tell me what, God dammit!"

Eliza looked at me. She took in a deep breath. "She was cheating on you," she said. "There, I said it. Arianna was seeing another guy behind your back. It went on for months. That's why she left. She needed time to think. She told me about it on the day before she left you. I always thought she'd come back. She told me she believed she would come back as soon as she had the time to figure things out. If not for you, then for the kids. She loved those kids, Jack, she really did. She was just so confused."

I put my beer down, then got to my feet. Abigail and Austin were playing in Amy's room. I called them and grabbed my leather jacket without another word. The kids came running out into the hallway.

Tom and Eliza came out to us. "Jack…I…" Tom said, then stopped.

"Not now, Tom," I said. "I'm not quite in the mood for this right now."

I felt so many things I couldn't put words to them. Anger, betrayal, abandonment. How could they have kept this a secret for this long? My best friends?

"We were trying to protect you," Tom said, like he was reading my mind. "We thought you'd been through enough…"

I shook my head in disbelief. I was about to leave when it struck me. I turned and looked at Eliza. "I do have one question."

"Yes?"

"Who was he? Who was the bastard seeing my wife?"

FORTY-TWO

March 1995

"I NEED TO SEE MY SON."

Victor's mother barely looked at Annie as she stormed past her in the foyer of their house. Annie stared after her.

"He's in the study, working," Annie yelled, then decided she didn't care if she found him or not. She returned to the living room, where she put her feet back up and turned on the TV. She grabbed the container of ice cream and returned to her binging. Her sweats had gotten tight around the waist again. Soon, she would have to move up yet another size.

The boy was in his room doing whatever he wanted to do, and this was Saturday, her day of watching reruns of ER. No one, not even Victor's dramatic mother should ruin that. Watching that George Clooney as Dr. Ross nonstop was her treat; it was her drug from the reality of her life being so boring she could hardly bear it.

The voices coming from the study were getting louder. Annie could hear Victor's mom yelling, and suddenly, her interest was aroused. Victor's mother never yelled. She hardly ever showed any emotions except for contempt.

Something was going on.

Annie turned down the volume. She didn't have to hear to watch George Clooney. She had seen every episode anyway; the storyline wasn't important.

"I'm telling you, Victor. You will do this, or I swear..." She heard Victor's mother say.

"You swear to do what, exactly, Mother?" Victor yelled back.

Uh-oh. This was bad. Victor never yelled either. What on earth was going on?

"I swear...I'll...we'll...and your father and I agree on this," she said.

Annie could only imagine how she was spitting and hissing. It sounded like it. This was better than any soap.

"What do you agree on?" Victor yelled.

"We'll take everything, Victor. The company. The house. Everything. You know we can. It's all in our names."

Annie almost dropped the ice cream bucket. Her heart started racing in her chest. What the heck was this? Annie got up from the couch and walked towards the study. The boy was so quiet in his room. She never knew what he did in there. To be honest, she didn't care. She cared less and less about the boy and never spent any time with him, if she could avoid it. He seemed to be fine without her.

"You won't do that," Victor said. "You can't do that to us. To me? I have a family here? We love the house?"

"Oh, you better believe we can and will do that, Victor. You lied to us all these years. Your entire marriage is based on a lie. Believe me when I say that if you don't divorce that...that tramp out there, then we're done with you. You are no longer our son."

Annie stopped breathing. A lump in her throat started to grow, and she felt like crying. Victor's mother was right, wasn't she? Annie was nothing but a tramp. Their marriage was a lie.

"Well, I don't care what you say, Mother. I love her. I love Annie. I love our son, and I love our life together. If you can't handle that, then...well then, take your money, your house, your company, and leave!"

Victor's mother gasped. "Victor!"

"That's right, Mother. I chose my family. I chose my wife. Even if that means we have to be poor. That's how much I love them."

Annie had to find a chair to sit down. She waddled backwards and stumbled into one and sat just as Victor's mother yelled.

"Fine. Have it your way." The door opened and she stormed out of the study. She took one glance at Annie, then stuck up her nose and disappeared.

Victor came out a second later. "Sweetie," he said to Annie. "You're all pale. Are you all right?"

"I...I..." she stuttered.

"You heard it? Well, don't worry. She found out about the boy not being mine. She wanted me to divorce you, but I would never do that."

Annie looked into Victor's eyes. It was hard to breathe. "But...but does that mean we have to be poor now, Victor?"

Victor laughed. "Yes. For a little while. They own the company; you know that. I was supposed to take over eventually, but we don't need that. I'll get another job. I'll start my own company."

"But...but the house? I love our house."

"I do too. But we'll get another one. I'll work hard to keep my baby happy. Don't worry, my love. We have each other and that's all I need."

Then he leaned over and kissed her, flashing his crooked teeth. She was repulsed by his breath.

"Our love is all we need," he said.

She wasn't so sure it was enough.

FORTY-THREE

January 2015

Steven Williams! Steven freaking Williams! Of all people. Her boss. Arianna's boss. She had worked at an advertising agency after the twins had started preschool. She had enjoyed getting out of the condo and talking to grown up people, she had told me. I thought it had been good for her. I thought it had been a good idea, a way to get over her growing depression and sense of meaninglessness in her life. She needed to work; she had always worked, even before I met her, and needed it, I told myself. Needed a sense of purpose, a reason to get out of bed in the morning, a way to stay busy.

And then it turned out she had just been screwing around behind my back? I couldn't believe it. Here I had been busy making excuses for her, telling people she couldn't help herself, defending her, telling them she was sick and needed to get away to overcome this depression.

I couldn't sleep at all that night, and the following day I called the station and told them I would be late. I had no idea where I was going, but suddenly, I found myself parking the Jeep outside the agency's office. I sat in the car for maybe an hour, just staring at the building, feeling the anger rise in me, but still restraining myself from going in. I had no idea how I would react if I did.

Suddenly, I spotted Steven Williams in the parking lot. He had just walked out of the building, flanked by two other suit-wearing men with perfect hair. I watched them while they spoke, all carrying briefcases.

"What the heck did you see in this guy, Arianna?" I asked myself. Was it just the fact that he was everything I'm not? Was it because he had a stable life, a desk-job with no danger, good income, wore a tie to work, didn't have a crumple in his pants, not a spot on his shirt? Was that why? Or was it the excitement? Did she love him? Or was it just sex?

"Goddammit, Arianna. Why would you do this to your family? Didn't you know how much we loved you?"

I felt tears of anger press behind my eyes, thinking about all the wonderful weekends we spent together on the beach playing in the sand, throwing the Frisbee, flying kites, and picnicking in the sand. All the while, she was seeing this guy behind my back. I knew it was self-torture, but I couldn't stop wondering. Where had they done it? At his house? No, he probably wasn't stupid enough to risk that. Had they taken a room at a motel?

While thinking about it, the demon of anger got the better of me. I simply couldn't just stay in my car. I got out and stormed across the street without even looking for cars. Steven Williams was laughing and chatting with his business partners, playing the big guy, when his smirk suddenly froze as he spotted me coming towards him. I wanted to draw my gun, but knew that would be a reason for suspension, so instead I simply approached him, raised my fist, and planted it in his face.

"You bastard!" I yelled, and stood over him, ready to punch again.

My punch had split his lip and he was bleeding.

"Was it good, huh? Did you enjoy fucking my wife?"

Steven Williams stared at me and at my fist, terrified I would hit him again. But I'd never hit a man who was lying down.

"Just tell me you at least loved her," I said, and stared into his face to see if I could detect any kind of emotion besides fear.

But there was none. He had never loved Arianna. He had used her.

"Where did you do it, huh? Did you take her to a motel, huh? Some sleazy place where you could pay per the hour?"

Steven Williams shook his head.

"Then, where? Tell me. I want to know." I lifted the fist higher and more threateningly in the air. Steven Williams whimpered.

"What was that? I didn't hear you properly."

"At yyyour place. We met at your apartment!"

FORTY-FOUR

January 2015

I LET HIM GO. He wasn't even worth my anger. I drove back to the station, then walked to my office, where I closed the door and sat down. I hid my face in my hands. A picture of Arianna showed up on my laptop. She was holding the twins in her arms, smiling. One of the good days, when she was happy with her family, happy with me. Now I started to doubt everything about our relationship. Had it all just been an act? Had I been betrayed all this time? Why had I even kept the picture? I didn't know. Maybe I still loved her. Maybe I had still hoped, till this day, that she would suddenly change her mind and come back. Maybe I had clung to that hope and thought that if just...if she just had time and space, then she would remember what she had loved about our life; she would come back, at least for the children.

"Why do you keep hurting me, Arianna?" I asked the empty room. "Even when you're not here? Were you ever happy with us?"

They had sex at your place! You fool! They slept together in your apartment, your furniture, your bed. How could you not have known this? How did you not see it? How did you not smell it on her?

There was a knock and Joel Hall peeked inside. "Hey there. Is everything all right?" he asked. "You look a little pale."

I nodded. "It will be. Some day. What's up?"

He stepped in. "I just wanted to talk to you about those books. The Platt books?" he said.

"Oh, yeah, come on in."

"I talked to some linguistic-experts and had them take a close look at the books, and I'm afraid they agree with Tracey Burden."

"Really?"

"Yes. They say John Platt's language changed drastically three books ago," Joe Hall said.

I leaned back in my chair. "I'll be..."

"They can't say he didn't write them, since they are very similar in style, but especially the last one, the one that was published three months ago, that the family claims they found on his computer by coincidence, is very different. I wrote it all in this report. I thought you might want to take a look at it."

"Thanks," I said, and grabbed the file as Joel Hall left. I read it thoroughly, wondering what this could mean. Had someone else written the books? Maybe the son? Or, could it be...?

I had a feeling, a hunch, but needed more than that, so I grabbed the phone and called for Peter Walker to come in for some questioning. He was sleeping, he told me, after a night shift, but would be able to make it in around noon. I accepted that and hung up. Then I found the files from the killing of the judge on my computer and went through the details once again. I kept returning to the interview with Melanie Schultz's friends and the details about that guy from Animal Control. Where was he? Why couldn't we find him? Animal Control said they didn't know him. Who was he?

I knew it was a high-priority case, and my superiors were screaming for results they could present to the press. The story was still all over the media, who hadn't taken long to figure out exactly what the good judge was doing at Melanie Schultz's house. Meanwhile, the husband, John Schultz, who had been named the true victim in this case, was being interviewed over and over again, asking the question we all wondered about.

"Where are my wife and son? Where are Melanie and Sebastian?"

The whole story stank of betrayal, just like my own life did.

FORTY-FIVE

January 2015

I PLACED two books in front of Peter Walker.

"What am I looking at here?" he asked.

"Two books that are supposed to be written by your father."

"I can see that much. But why am I looking at them?" he asked. He looked at his watch.

"Busy?" I asked. "I thought you worked the night shift."

"I have a life outside of work too," Peter answered.

"I'll make this short, then," I said. I leaned over my desk and pointed at the books. "Here's my little theory. I don't think these two books were written by the same author. And I think you know it. I think your sister Laura had her neighbor from across the street, Rhonda Harris, write three books for her, pretending they were written by John Platt. I think you noticed right away when you read the first book and you confronted your sister about it. Then, I think she offered you money to shut up about it. I think that's why you were there on the night of her murder. You wanted more money. I think Rhonda Harris believed their scam would be revealed once Laura Bennett was killed, and therefore, she killed herself. To not have to live with the shame." I paused for effect. Peter tightened his lips. That's when I knew I was on to the right path. "Am I right?"

Peter Walker looked at me for a long time without speaking. His hands were shaking and he tried to hide them.

"Take your time." I slurped my coffee while Peter fought within himself to determine whether to lie to me or tell the truth. Finally, he opened his mouth. He exhaled.

"All right. But...I...I...I didn't come up with the idea. Laura did. I spotted it right away when I read the first one. There was no way my dad had written that. I confronted her and told her I would reveal it. That she was an imposter and everyone would know. She begged me not to, then offered me money to shut up. I took it. I didn't want my family's name getting dirty either."

"Plus, you could really use the money. With the lifestyle you had been used to growing up, living in a small condo in Cape Canaveral and working the night shift at Ron Jon's wasn't exactly attractive to you."

Peter stared at me. "So, am I in trouble?" he asked.

"That's not for me to decide. I'm in homicide; I usually don't deal with fraud or extortion. But, tell me one thing. Why did Laura Bennett do this? She had enough money, didn't she?"

Peter shook his head. "She made a series of very bad investments. Plus, they were spending like crazy. She needed more money. They say it's the worst thing that can happen to anyone. To suddenly get money. It's like those lottery winners who take home three hundred million, and then two years later they tell the media they are now in debt up to their ears and that winning the money was the worst thing that could have happened to them. Laura and Brandon were like that. They had no idea what they were doing, and she fell for one scam after another. Like I said, I didn't come up with the idea. She did. Laura did. She knew her neighbor across the street wanted to write and made a deal with her. I had nothing to do with it."

No, you only blackmailed them. No harm in that, right?

God, how I loathed sleaze-balls like this guy. So busy washing his hands afterwards, thinking he didn't do anything wrong.

"What about Brandon Bennett? Was he in on it as well?" I asked.

"No. She was afraid he might find out, and I used that against her. Told her I would tell him if she didn't pay up. It worked."

"How wonderful for you." I cleared my throat. "So, tell me. Did you get angry with her for not wanting to pay up?"

Peter Walker smiled. "I know where you're going with this, Detective."

No shit, Sherlock.

"No, I didn't get angry with her, and I didn't kill her. Why would I? First of all, she did promise me more money that night; second of all, it would be stupid of me to kill the hand that feeds me, don't you think?"

He made a strong point. I let him off the hook for now. None of this indicated that he had killed his sister, and that was all I cared about right now. Somewhere out there in my town, someone would be getting away with murder if I didn't get a breakthrough in this case soon.

Part Two

I'D HAVE TO PACK MY THINGS AND GO

FORTY-SIX

February 2015

"WELCOME TO MOTEL ALBERT, a historic Cocoa Beach hotel."

The man behind the counter was tall and well-muscled, even though he did have a little stomach poking out. His hair was brown, but had been lightened by the sun. His skin was tanned, his eyes gentle and blue. He was wearing shorts and a blue T-shirt that was tight over his chest and showed his muscles. It had stains on it, looked like tomato sauce, but could have been something else. He wasn't shaved. He looked like one of those surfers Shannon had seen out the window of her rental car driving through Cocoa Beach. They were everywhere with their long blond messy hair, riding their skateboards, some even while carrying surfboards under their arms. Next to him stood an old woman. Shannon pulled her daughter closer and pulled her hoodie over her head.

"No, Mom. It's too hot," Angela proclaimed angrily and pulled it off.

Shannon growled and pulled it back on. "Just leave it on, okay?"

"Name?" the man behind the counter asked.

Shannon looked around the lobby. It wasn't quite the type of hotel she was used to staying in, but that was the entire point to it all.

The man behind the counter stared at her, waiting for her reply.

Don't let him see your eyes. Don't let him see your face.

"Name?" she repeated. "Well...Schmidt. I have a reservation booked under the name Schmidt."

"Schmidt, yes," the man said. He turned and pulled out a key. "If you'll just sign here."

He pointed at a piece of paper and Shannon signed it using the alias.

"Okay," the man said and put the paper away without looking at her signature. "Mrs. Schmidt. You'll be in number one-fifteen. Has a nice view of the beach, that one." He handed her the key, then walked around the counter. "My name is Jack. My parents own this place. I help out on the weekends. Let me help you with your suitcases."

"There's no need to," Shannon said, and grabbed the suitcases herself. She turned her head to make sure he didn't see her face, even though it was covered by her scarf. Joe had provided a very rough beating the day before and Shannon was determined this was his last.

Never again.

Angela smiled and stuck out her hand to shake his. "Hello there, Mr. Jack," she said with a grin. "I'm Angela. I am six years old. You can take my suitcase if you like."

"Angela…" Shannon said. "There's really no need to…"

"Ah, but I don't mind," Jack said. "Let me carry it for the young lady. It's right up on the second floor to the right."

Shannon and Angela followed Jack up the stairs and down the long carpeted corridors. He stopped in front of a door, then opened it with the key. It was an old fashioned key, not a card like other hotels had. Everything about this motel was old and seemed like it hadn't been updated since the seventies.

"Here you go," Jack said, and let them inside.

"Thank you," Shannon said, hoping he would leave them alone. She found a twenty-dollar bill and handed it to him.

He chuckled and shook his head. "No need for that."

"Please, I insist," she said. "I'd also appreciate my privacy while I'm here, if you understand."

Jack took the bill, then put it in his pocket. "I'll put this in the tip jar in the bar then. They work hard for their tips down there."

"Whatever," Shannon said.

Jack stayed in the doorway. Shannon wondered why he didn't just leave. He didn't seem like a bellboy, but a lot in this place wasn't like in other hotels. Shannon, who was used to a life of extreme luxury, couldn't remember ever staying in a place like this. Not that it wasn't nice; it was. The dark wood everywhere made it a little somber, though. The floors creaked when she walked on them. The carpets were nice and soft and the beds neatly made. The view was spectacular…sandy beach as far as the eye could see. And the almost green ocean right outside her window. There was a small balcony she could sit on. There were chairs to sit in everywhere, especially on the wooden deck. There didn't seem to be many guests in the motel, which suited her perfectly. You could say the place was charming in its own way. It wasn't massive and big like the hotels she usually stayed in on her tours.

She looked at Jack, wondering why he was still there.

"I'm supposed to tell you about the place. There's a story of a house-ghost that wanders the hallways at night. The story goes she killed herself in one of the rooms downstairs. She was last seen in the bar at the restaurant downstairs. They say she likes to move things around in there."

Jack looked at Angela, like he wondered if those stories would frighten her.

"Don't worry about her," Shannon said. "She loves creepy stuff like that. She has loads of imaginary friends herself. Some of them are dead, she says."

"Have you seen any ghosts?" Angela asked.

Jack chuckled and shook his head. "Not yet. I have two children the same age as you. They're down at the beach now playing with their granddad if you want to come down later?"

Angela made a joyful shriek. Shannon shook her head and saw the disappointment in her daughter's face. But she couldn't be too careful. She had chosen this place because no one would find her here. They wouldn't even think of looking for her here. That would buy her time. Time to figure out…things. Time to find out what she was going to do. If she had to stay in the motel for months before she figured out what to do, then so be it.

"I see you brought a guitar?" Jack asked. "You play?"

"I get by," Shannon said, sensing he was getting a little too nosy now. "Now, if you'll excuse me, we need to get settled in."

"Yes, yes of course. I'm sorry. I didn't mean to impose. I just always wanted to learn how to play. Must be great to have music in your life."

Shannon scoffed. Music was her entire life, and had been for as long as she could remember. It was still her passion, even though it had also made her life complicated over the years, and sometimes she wished she could go back to the time when music was just something she did for fun.

"Anyway," Jack said. He paused and looked at her. "Mrs. Schmidt, I'll see you around. Let me know if there is anything you need. If you have any questions, I'll be glad to be of assistance. I'm here all weekend helping out. I live in a condo right next door. My parents are here 24-7, in case you need anything."

He looked at Angela and reached out his hand. "It was a pleasure to meet you, Angela. I'm sure you and your mom are going to have a great time here at Motel Albert."

He made a funny face and Angela laughed. Shannon smiled, but hid it behind her scarf. He seemed like a nice guy. Not the type to alert the media if he found out who she was, but she could not be too careful.

"The restaurant is always open," he said, looking at Shannon. He had a nice smile.

"I prefer room service," she said.

"That, we don't do. I'm sorry."

"All right. I need to find a pharmacy. Where is the closest?" she asked.

"Right up A1A on the other side of downtown Cocoa Beach."

"Great. Thank you."

"It might be a small town, but they have everything here. We also arrange guided tours, in case you'd like to see what the city has to offer. I bet you'd want to see Kennedy Space Center and maybe take one of the boat rides to see alligators and manatees."

"Alligators!" Angela exclaimed. "I wanna go, Mom. Can we, please?"

"Let's look into it," Shannon said, to keep her daughter from begging more. Truth was, Shannon had hoped they could stay in the room for most of the time, but she knew it would be impossible.

"You can read all about it in our folders in the lobby," Jack said. "There's a lot to choose from. And there are also trips to Disney and SeaWorld in Orlando, of course. Anyway. Welcome."

"Thank you."

FORTY-SEVEN

February 2015

I COULDN'T BELIEVE a month had passed and I was still not closer to cracking any of the cases. I had interrogated Brandon Bennett over and over again, but he still didn't remember much from that night. I was getting nowhere.

I had gone through the Bennett's entire social circle, but no one had a motive, and all had alibis that checked out fine. Including both of her sisters, who were also deprived of their inheritance.

The case of Rhonda Harris's suicide was closed, so that was some good news. But it wasn't good enough. By far. The worst part was the judge. I couldn't believe I had gotten nowhere on his case. I had interviewed tons of criminals that he put away, his family, his political opponents, and still it led me nowhere.

It was driving me crazy.

My dad hadn't been well lately. Not after a bad case of the flu hit him at the end of January. So, I was trying to help out a lot more at the motel. This weekend, I was taking care of everything, so my mom could rest a little as well. It wasn't very busy, so I took my time with the guests and hung out on the deck with some of the snowbirds, telling them where it would be best to fish and where to go to see dolphins. The motel was located on the thinnest part of the barrier island, and we had water on both sides. They could just cross the road to get to the Intracoastal where they could see manatees and tons of stingrays and dolphins. I really enjoyed hanging out at the motel and realized why my dad had wanted this his entire life. People who came here were happy and cheerful. They were looking to have a great time and enjoy the area, and I got to help them with that. It was so much more rewarding than chasing down a killer, I thought.

I had just shown a new guest to her room, when I went down to the beach to find my kids and tell them it was time for lunch. They were building a humongous sandcastle with their granddad. He was smiling from ear to ear.

"Hey, Son," he said and patted me on the shoulder. "Pretty impressive, huh?"

I chuckled. "I bet I could build one that was bigger," I said, teasing. "But decent work there, Dad. The twins need to eat, though. Grandma is serving mahi-mahi burgers on the deck."

The twins looked at each other, then sprang towards the motel with loud shrieks. Emily was sitting on a towel, listening to music on her phone.

"Aren't you warm in all those black clothes?" My dad asked.

Emily shrugged without looking up. That was her answer to everything lately. It was getting worse. She was shutting all of us out. It made me worry about her.

"Let's eat," I said. "Are you coming?"

"I'm not hungry."

"Come on," I said. "Grandma made mahi-mahi burgers?"

"I don't eat anything with eyes," she said.

That was a new one.

"Since when?" I asked.

"Since now. I just watched a video about how they treat animals. It's cruel, Jack. I don't want to be a part of it. You can't make me."

She was looking for a fight. I wasn't. I shrugged. "Well, just eat the bread and the lettuce then. Come on. They're all waiting."

"I'll pass," she said.

I felt a pinch in my heart. I hated when she shut me out and when she refused to be a part of the family. "Come on," I said again. "Grandma is going to be so sad if you don't come."

Emily looked up at me. "She's not my grandmother and you know it. Don't pretend it's something when it's not."

"Ouch," I said. I pretended to have been shot. "That. Hurt. Must. Have. Burger. To. Survive."

Emily rolled her eyes at me, but I detected a small smile on her lips as well. Finally, with a deep sigh, she decided to come with me.

FORTY-EIGHT

May 1998

LIFE WITHOUT MONEY wasn't a lot of fun, Annie soon realized. Eight years after they had said goodbye to the wealth of Victor's family, she found herself sitting in a small two-bedroom condo in a bad part of town. Her son was now a teenager and she loathed him more than ever. Everything about him made her skin crawl. His eyes, the way he looked, the way he spoke. Everything. When he came home from school, she always hoped he would walk straight into his room without a word and play his computer games. She didn't care what he did in there, in his room, as long as he didn't bother her.

Victor hadn't become more attractive in her eyes either. He no longer wore those expensive suits that he used to, nor did he drive a big car. He had lost everything that was just the slightest bit appealing to her. Annie hated every day of her life, and every day when Victor went off to work and the boy was in school she sat at home and watched soaps, eating ice cream and chocolate, feeling sorry for herself that her life had ended up such a mess. She hated having to clean the house on her own now and do the grocery shopping, and all the laundry piling up every day. It just wasn't the life she had pictured for herself growing up. Not at all.

"It's just all wrong," she said to herself.

But she didn't know what to do to change things around. How to get out of this life. She had no money, and even if she got a divorce, she wasn't even getting any. Still, she couldn't stand this condo, nor could she stand her husband or her son. It was all just miserable.

One day, there was a knock on her front door, and outside stood a detective. He was tall and handsome. He even still had most of his hair, she noticed, when he lifted his cap with a "Ma'am" and showed her his badge.

Annie smiled. It had been years since she had looked at a man and thought he was attractive. Not since Tim, and that didn't end well. She suddenly felt self-conscious in her sweats and carrying the extra weight.

"Yes? What can I do for you, Officer?"

He smiled. "Well, I'm here because I have to ask you some questions. "You are Annie Greenfield, right?"

She shook her head. "I used to be. Now I'm married. Come on in."

Annie let the man in, then excused herself and ran into her bedroom to change. She found a pair of jeans that she couldn't fit into anymore, then found a pair of nice black pants that fit her nicely still, and a purple shirt to go with them. She took her hair down, brushed it and put on some make-up, then returned to the living room, where the detective sat on the couch. His face lit up when he saw her.

"Now. What do you say I make us some coffee?" she asked.

"That sounds really nice."

She ran to the kitchen and came back with coffee and cookies. She placed it all on the table, then sat down across from him.

"So, what did you want to question me about?"

The detective cleared his throat, then opened a file he pulled out of his brief-case. Annie touched a lock of her hair and blushed when he looked at her.

"Well, you see. It's an old matter, but it has come to our attention that back in the mid-eighties there were some students at SFU who used the date rape drug Rohypnol to rape girls. We believe you might be one of their victims. The drug was fairly new back then, so it wasn't something that there was a focus on, but there is now. A man we recently arrested on another rape charge told us you were one of his victims back then."

"Tim?" Annie's voice shivered at the awful memories coming back to her. Images from the night by the lake kept flashing before her eyes.

"Yes. Tim Harrold. He's been arrested in another case here in my district, but he admitted to this as well. We're looking for witnesses. Would you be willing to testify, if it came to it? I would need you to tell me your entire story."

Many thoughts flowed through Annie's mind. Pictures of that terrible night so many years ago, the anger that led to her resentment of her own son, the anger that led her to hate all men. Well, most men. Not the handsome detective. It all made sense. That was why she couldn't remember much from what happened. She had heard about this drug numerous times, but never made the connection. It spiked the anger in her once again. She was tired of being the victim.

"Yes," she said. "I would be delighted to."

FORTY-NINE

February 2015

Officer Mike Wagner had been on patrol for three hours. The Cocoa Beach Police Department's car was messy. Mike hadn't cleaned it. He knew he would have to soon, but he hadn't bothered yet.

He opened the window and pulled out a cigar from the pocket of his shirt. He lit it and blew out smoke while looking at the house next to him. He had parked the car on the side of A1A, where the road split into two. He didn't really want to go after people speeding, but hoped they would slow down when they saw him. Officer Mike smoked his cigar. It made him look like Winston Churchill, his colleagues often said. He liked that. Mike had always felt like a big man. Even though he lived in a town where nothing much happened, he still felt important. His work was important. He kept the population safe and was very well-liked among his citizens. As Sergeant, he kept track of all the young kids coming to the force and made sure they understood that they were here to serve the people, not to get off on some big power trip or ego that they might have.

A car drove past him speeding excessively. Officer Mike sighed. He couldn't let that go. The cigar ended in the ashtray and he drove onto the road, soon catching up to the white SUV. He put the siren on and the car slowed down, then stopped. Officer Mike exited his car and walked with big heavy steps up to the SUV. The dreaded walk. He hated the walk. You never knew who might be in the car you had just pulled over. You never knew how they would react to being stopped. Did they have a gun in the car? A colleague of Mike's in Melbourne was shot, not even two months ago, when stopping a speeding car.

You never knew.

Mike spotted the hands on the wheel and noticed they belonged to a woman. That made him relax a little. He usually didn't have anything to fear. Not out on the barrier island, where everything was calm and people usually were respectable. Cocoa Beach was a sleepy town, but had many tourists coming from all over. Mike was always on alert.

"Do you know why I stopped you today, Ma'am?" he asked, as he approached the window. The woman was wearing a hat and sunglasses and a scarf covering her face.

Mike looked inside the car and spotted a young girl in the back seat. His shoulders came down. Nothing but a mom in a hurry.

"No, Officer, I don't," she said.

"You were speeding, Ma'am. A lot."

"I'm sorry, Officer." The woman seemed in distress. "License and registration, please."

The woman leaned over and opened the glove compartment. When she returned and handed him the papers, the scarf fell down and revealed big bruises. It bothered Officer Mike. There were few things that could make him really angry, but a wife beater was one of them.

He looked at the driver's license. Then he froze, immediately star struck.

Shannon King, the famous country singer!

He could hardly speak. His lips were trembling. "I'm sorry, Miss King. I didn't know it was you. Are you having a concert nearby, or...?"

She shook her head and re-covered her face with the scarf. "No. I'm visiting. I would appreciate keeping my visit private, though. If possible, Officer?"

Mike nodded and handed her back her driver's license. He pulled out his notepad. "Naturally. Do you mind?" he said. "I'm a big fan."

Shannon King sighed, then grabbed the pad and pen. She signed it and handed it back.

"Was that all, Officer? I need to get to the pharmacy."

"Well, of course. Just remember, only 35 here on this part of A1A."

"I must have missed the sign. I'm sorry, Officer."

"No problem, Miss King. We're happy to have you in town. May I ask what brings you here?"

"I'm visiting some old friends. Trying to stay away from the media, though. So, if you'd please..."

"Naturally, Ma'am. My lips are sealed. Enjoy your stay."

FIFTY

February 2015

"I miss Mommy!"

The Snakecharmer looked at his son, then slapped him across the face. "Don't say that, Son. She was nothing but a cheating bitch. All women are!"

"Leave the kid alone." The Snakecharmer's dad sat across from him at the kitchen table. "It's not his fault. You just stay away from women, Son. You hear me?"

"Y-yes, Grandpa," the kid whimpered, then ran to his room.

"Now, what are you planning on doing with that one over there?" his dad asked, as he nodded towards Will in the playpen.

The Snakecharmer drank from his beer. "I don't know."

"Don't you think people will start asking questions at some point?"

"I just couldn't leave him there, you know?" The Snakecharmer said, and looked at the kid. He liked him.

"Well, you should have. Kids are trouble. Where did you find him anyway?"

The Snakecharmer looked at the TV in the corner. Luckily, it didn't work. His dad couldn't see anything anyway, but he might hear something. Fortunately, he never left the house, so there was no way he would ever know where the kid had come from. Even though his picture was everywhere.

"I told you. I found him in a dumpster behind the Publix grocery store."

His dad grunted. "You should have given him to the cops. Now we're stuck with him."

"They would just put him in some foster home, and what good would that do him? I like the kid. I can raise him right."

"Don't you think you've got enough on your plate with that one in there?" he said.

"I'll manage. I got it covered, Dad, don't worry."

The Snakecharmer had gotten rid of Melanie. She hadn't lasted more than a week before the smell became too bad. It annoyed him. The Snakecharmer was starting to miss the action. He knew the ground was burning underneath him, but still he felt an itch, a strong desire pulling him. He wanted more. He had already spotted his next victim, and visited her last month down in Satellite Beach. He had kept an eye on her for weeks now and knew her everyday routine to the smallest detail. That was the way he worked. Stayed in complete control. Murderers were caught because they made mistakes. Because they got too eager or thought they were safe; they got stupid or suddenly impulsive. He wasn't going to do that. He was smarter than any of them, and he was going to show them.

"What's wrong, Son?" His dad asked.

The Snakecharmer drank his beer. "Nothing's wrong."

"You seem so tense lately."

The Snakecharmer finished his beer, then went to the fridge and got himself another one. "I just need to get laid. It's been awhile."

His dad laughed. "Yeah, well, as long as you don't marry them. That's when trouble begins."

"I know," he said and thought about his ex-wife. The bitch had been seeing someone else. He had smelled it on her and asked her, but, oh no, it was just from hugging one of her friends. Yeah, right. As soon as he suspected something was going on, he had followed her. And, sure enough. He had seen her with another man. He had been all over her.

Lying, cheating bitch.

FIFTY-ONE

February 2015

_____

THE FOLLOWING MONDAY, I had a small breakthrough in the case of Laura Bennett. For weeks, I had gone through old cases of women being killed in the area, and suddenly I found one that caught my attention.

A young girl of only seventeen had been killed thirteen years ago, in 2002, in her own home in Melbourne Beach. Her parents had been out with friends, and when they returned they found the daughter on the floor, strangled to death. The case was considered a breaking and entering and it was believed she must have surprised the burglar with the result that he killed her in a panic.

It all seemed like the right conclusion, given the evidence. There had been stolen jewelry and a window in the back had been forced open, and there were visible marks from the use of a crowbar. There was just one thing that didn't add up.

The ME had concluded that she had been washed afterwards.

I couldn't believe it. The police report concluded she had to have been taking a shower before the burglar broke into her house, even though it clearly stated in the ME's autopsy report that she had been washed after death had occurred. Washed with bleach.

Just like they had in the case of Laura Bennett.

I called Sheriff Ron and told him what I had found, and then went to Weasel's office to tell her as well.

"I'll be..." she said. "So, you're telling me this is not his first?"

"That's what I'm saying."

"But, in that case, he used his hands and not a pillow?" she asked.

"He learned from his mistakes. He was younger back then and less careful. It might have been his first kill. He doesn't want to bruise the body, especially not the face. That's why he uses the pillow now."

"Good work, Detective," Weasel said. "I'm impressed."

After work, I drove to my parents' motel, feeling a little better for once. I wasn't closer to catching this guy, but now I was getting to know him a little. All I needed was for him to make a mistake.

"They all do at some point," the chief of my old homicide unit in Miami used to say to me. I was hoping he was right.

I parked the Jeep outside the motel, then walked up to the deck where I found Abigail and Austin playing with the little girl Angela. They had been hanging out all weekend, even though I got the feeling the mother wasn't too fond of her doing so. I took it she was just one of those overly protective women, but I knew something else was going on. The way she kept covering her face told a different story. I had seen it a lot of times before, and it pissed me off every time.

"They play well together, don't they?" Mrs. Schmidt had walked up behind me and stopped.

"They really do. It's been awhile since my twins played like this without fighting," I said, and looked at the woman next to me. She was attractive. Everyone could tell she was somebody, even though she covered her face with a scarf and wore sunglasses all the time. It was in the way she moved. She constantly attracted her surroundings' attention, even though she didn't want to. People simply couldn't take their eyes off of her. I couldn't blame them. I felt the same way.

"So, when are you going to tell me your real name?" I asked.

The woman looked at me. "I'm sorry, what?"

"I don't know why you have a made-up reservation in a false name, and it's none of my business," I said. "But, Mrs. Schmidt?"

She chuckled. "I guess it was a little thick."

"It's okay with me if you want to hide. I'm a detective around here. I can keep a secret."

She nodded. I sensed she blushed underneath the scarf. "Well, okay then, Detective Ryder. You can call me Shannon."

I turned and shook her hand. She took off her sunglasses and looked me in the eye. That was when I realized who she was, and understood why she had to hide herself. It took me quite by surprise.

"Nice to meet you, Shannon."

FIFTY-TWO

February 2015

OFFICER MIKE WAGNER'S shift was almost over, and he sat at the station eating his sandwich with one of his colleagues, John.

"So, how was your shift?" John asked.

Mike took another bite and chewed, then shrugged. "Quiet, as usual."

Some of the guys were playing darts at the other end of the room and were cheering loudly.

"Had a couple of speeding mamas and a drunk hobo annoying the tourists on the beach."

"I hate the hobos," John said, and drank from his Big Gulp. "Especially the drunk ones."

"I know. It's Friday, so there will be lots of teenagers on the beach tonight drinking and making bonfires. Make sure they don't burn stuff that isn't theirs, if you know what I mean."

He swallowed the last bite of his sandwich. He could have waited till he got back to the condo to eat, but he liked to have the company. He would probably still munch on a bag of chips in the recliner while watching CSI, once he got home. He needed to grocery shop, but didn't feel like it today. He still had enough chips and sodas for a couple of days. He'd get by. Then he'd hit Wal-Mart at the beginning of next week.

"Working next weekend, I hear?" John said.

"Yes," Mike said. "Both days. But, it's all good. I like work."

John chuckled. "I'd rather be home with the wife and kiddos."

Mike nodded. He didn't want to talk about other people's families. He didn't like to hear about them or how happy they were. He had never had a family of his own and after reaching forty, he had stopped thinking it would come. Not that he hadn't had girlfriends, he did, but they never wanted him long enough. They all split after just a few weeks. He'd never quite figured out why.

"Say, what's that on your notepad?" John asked.

Mike looked at the table where he had put his things down. His phone, his radio, and his notepad.

His notepad with Shannon King's autograph!

"Does it say Shannon King?" John asked, and pulled it to better see.

Mike put a hand to cover it. "Leave it," he said.

"How did you get Shannon King's autograph? John asked loudly. Too loudly. Now the dart-playing colleagues turned to look.

"What's going on here?" George said, approaching them.

"Tell them, Sergeant," John said. "Tell us how you got Shannon King's autograph?"

"What?" George said. "The singer? Damn, she's hot. You meet her somewhere?"

Mike still didn't answer. "Come on, guys," he said. "It's private."

"She's here, isn't she?" John asked with a grin. "Oh, my God. Shannon King is in Cocoa Beach!"

"Is it true, Sergeant?" George said. "Come on, tell us."

Mike sighed. How was he supposed to lie to his buddies? He couldn't. They were his family, his friends, and his entire life. Besides, he really wanted to tell someone about his meeting with the most famous country singer on the planet.

"Yes," he said. "Yes, she was here. I pulled her over for speeding. She had her daughter with her. So, I asked for her autograph."

His colleagues burst into a loud roar. Mike got up, trying to leave. He'd said too much. It made him feel bad.

"Hey, wait a minute there, tiger," George said. "Tell us some more. What did she look like in real life? She is gorgeous, isn't she? What is she doing in Cocoa Beach? Did she have bodyguards with her or anything?"

Mike shook his head. "No. It was just her and the kid. And she told me she wanted this to stay private. She wanted to keep it a secret from the press. And, we keep it that way, you hear me?"

"She can't keep that a secret for long," John said. "Someone will see her and tell the press."

Mike looked at his boys. John was right. The place would soon be crawling with journalists looking for her.

"That might be, but it won't come from any of us, you hear me?"

John saluted him with a grin. "Loud and clear, Sir!"

FIFTY-THREE

February 2015

HAPPY HOUR OYSTERS ARE BACK!

I put the small sign up outside of the restaurant like my mom had asked me to. Today's special was Mahi-Mahi and Grouper, she had written in chalk on the small blackboard.

That was the special every day, it seemed.

The kids had been playing so well, I had been able to go surfing for an hour. When I got back out of the water, I felt refreshed and new and helped my mother change the menu before the guests arrived for dinner...the few of them that chose to eat at the motel. It had actually been a slow winter for my parents, and as we were getting closer to the spring, it had my mother worried. Even though she tried to hide it.

"It'll pick up," she kept saying. "Snowbirds will come. They always do."

But the season for snowbirds was almost over. My dad's health still wasn't too well, and he needed a lot of rest. There was another chance. Springer-breakers came in March, and even though they were often loud and caused trouble with their excessive drinking, they meant business. They liked to stay in cheap motels on the beach.

I helped my mother cook for the guests and for our family. I made a salad for Emily, who had been very into eating healthy lately, and I didn't want to discourage her from that, even though my mother thought it was nonsense.

"Who doesn't like meat?"

"Just let her be herself. She's trying to figure out who she is, and we should let her," I said.

We served burgers for everyone—except Emily—and sat down to eat all together. I loved these family dinners. We even had two extras sitting with us today, since Shannon King and Angela had agreed to have dinner with us. I really liked her, so I hoped we would all be on our best behavior.

It was a success, and while the kids ran onto the beach afterwards, playing ball,

Shannon and I took a stroll with our feet in the water. I pointed out a pod of dolphins for her that were playing in the waves and she gasped in awe.

"I see them all the time out there, when I surf," I said.

"That sounds amazing," she said. "You have quite the life here, Detective. A true paradise."

"Maybe I should teach you how to surf while you're here?" I asked.

Shannon chuckled. "Me? Oh no. I'm not cut out for that. Water isn't my thing. Give me a horse and I can show you a trick or two."

I laughed. "I forgot. You're from Texas."

She laughed lightly. It felt good to walk with her. I enjoyed spending time with her, but I also knew she was married. She never talked about her husband, but she didn't have to.

"So, did he do that to you?" I asked, and pointed at her face where the scarf had fallen down slightly on the side and a bruise showed.

She went quiet.

I went too far.

Then, she nodded. "I had to get away. Mostly for Angela's sake. She started to ask questions. I can't let her grow up like this."

I exhaled, then reached out a hand and touched her bruise gently. I hated men who beat their wives more than anything I could think of. Only cowards would do such a thing. I had seen so much of this when living in Miami.

She grabbed my wrist and held on to it. She looked me in the eyes. I held my breath. I hadn't felt like this for a very long time.

"I..." she said. She removed her eyes from mine. "I should go."

She turned around and went back to the motel.

I stared after her, feeling frustrated. I couldn't fall for this woman. Could I? No, she was too complicated. She was married. She was a celebrity. It couldn't be. I had just met her. No, it was just a crush. It was nothing, I told myself. But I knew I was wrong.

I was already in deep...in over my head.

FIFTY-FOUR

February 2015

SHANNON RUSHED BACK to the room, holding her phone in her hand. She found the key and locked herself in. She ran to the balcony, where she could see Angela playing on the beach with the twins. She could see Jack. He was still standing on the beach where she had left him.

This isn't good, Shannon.

She couldn't fall for him. This was no time to start a romance. She felt so frustrated. She really liked the guy and they had just shared something. Was that a moment? Had they shared something on the beach just now?

No, she couldn't let anyone into her life now. Not the way it was.

She looked at the display on her phone. Her manager, Bruce, had called and left a message. He was the only one who knew this number. She hadn't told him where she was going, only that he could reach her at this number in case it was important. She listened to the message.

"Joe is looking everywhere for you, Shannon," he said. "He was here earlier this morning, trying to force me to tell him where you were. I told him you had left… that you weren't coming back. He went crazy. He trashed the mirror in my hallway, you know the beautiful one you love so much. He's angry. Stay hidden and stay safe. Don't let anyone know where you are. Not until we get the restraining order through. Shit, he scared me. He wants Angela, he said. Please don't take your eyes off of her, promise me that. Well, I gotta go. I hope y'all are still safe. Don't worry about the press. I got it covered, and I managed to cancel the rest of your tour. I told them you were sick. They will start to ask questions soon, though, so we need to figure out what to tell them."

Shannon put the phone down with a sigh, then went to the window and spotted Angela again. She was still playing with Jack's kids. They had been so sweet to Angela. Shannon found an old address book and a number. She stared at the number for a long time before she found the courage to call it.

"Hello?" a woman said.

"Hello. Is this Kristi?" Shannon asked.

"It is. Who am I speaking to?"

Shannon felt tears fill her eyes and tried to hold them back. She choked on her own sobs. "It's me, Kristi. It's Shannon."

Silence for a little while, an awful silence, while Shannon wondered if she had made a mistake, if she should just hang up again. Then there was a shriek.

"Shannon? Is it really you?"

"Yes. It is me," she said, crying.

She could hear Kristi was crying too. "I...I thought I'd never hear from you again."

"I know. I'm sorry. It's all been a little..." she paused and cried. She pulled away the scarf and took off the hat, then looked at herself in the mirror while crying. "It's just been so awful. You know how you want to do everything for your kid, everything you can to make sure she grows up in a real home with a mom and a dad. It's just...life is just not always like in the movies, you know?"

"Oh, dear sis. I'm sorry to hear that. Is it Joe? I had a feeling he was the one keeping you away from us."

"He never thought my family was good enough. And then there were the drugs, and I couldn't...I couldn't stop it, not until we had Angela."

Kristi was crying heavily at the other end. "I read about your daughter. I always wanted to meet her. I can't believe I've never met my niece."

"I'm so sorry you haven't. You have no idea how many times I've wanted to call you or just drive to Florida to visit you, but I was afraid of how Joe would react. And then you moved all the way to Cocoa Beach. I mean, when you lived in the Panhandle, I felt you were closer; this is just so far away."

"We moved because of Jimmy's job. He works at the Space Center now. He was one of those that survived the layoffs when the shuttle program stopped. We lucked out. Now he's working on the Orion rocket."

"That sounds really good. I'm so glad you guys are happy," Shannon sobbed.

"So, why are you calling all of a sudden?" Kristi asked. "Did something happen?"

"I left him, Kristi. I left Joe."

Saying the words made her cry again. It had been the hardest decision she ever had to make. For years, she had stayed with Joe because she didn't dare to do anything else. For years, he beat the crap out of her whenever he wanted to, so she had to cancel concerts and lie to everyone about how she got her bruises. Before Angela came along, she had taken a lot of drugs just to put up with his abuse, but when she became pregnant, she had stopped. Finally, she had started seeing things clearly and realized she had to leave him. Especially now that Angela was older and suddenly understood what was going on.

"So, where are you now?" Kristi asked. "Do you want me to come up? I can catch a flight out of Orlando later today if you need me to."

Shannon wept again. She hadn't dared to hope that her sister would greet her with open arms after so many years. But, of course she would. They had been so close up until the day she had met Joe and Joe had told her that her sister was jealous of her and that she should stay away.

All those lies. All that deceit.

"You don't need to," Shannon said. "I'm here. I'm in Cocoa Beach."

FIFTY-FIVE

February 2015

HE WAS DISGUSTED. The Snakecharmer felt nauseated by what he had just seen. He had been observing Detective Ryder from afar, like he often did, and what was that he had seen? Had the dear detective had a moment with another woman?

With a married woman?

He couldn't believe his own eyes. He knew perfectly well who the woman was, even though she did everything she could to keep it a secret. The Snakecharmer knew everything that went on in his town, and when a celebrity showed herself, rumors spread fast. He had always liked the dear Mrs. King's music, but he certainly wasn't going to anymore. Not after what he had just witnessed. She was coming on to another man? When she was still married? How despicable!

The Snakecharmer wondered for a little while what to do next. He was supposed to go to Satellite Beach and make the last arrangements for his abduction of the woman down there, the one he had been planning on taking for a long time. But, now he was suddenly not so sure anymore. A new plan was shaping in his head. One that was suddenly a lot more urgent than the original one.

But, would it work? Would it really work? It had to. Besides, everything he had done lately had been a success. He had punished all these women for their cheating ways. They had paid their dues. He wouldn't be surprised if someday people would be grateful to him. He had, after all, rid the world of some of its worst scum. Once they figured out what he had done, why he had done it, they would understand; they would even applaud him for his accomplishments. Men would praise him all over the world.

Of course they would.

But, for now, he had to settle for being considered a simple murderer. It was okay. Most artists weren't appreciated in their time.

The Snakecharmer chuckled to himself when thinking about the woman Detective Ryder hadn't found out about yet. The Snakecharmer knew he had found out about the girl back in '02. She had been the Snakecharmer's first girlfriend. A lying cheating bitch like the rest of them. He had gotten away with it almost too easily. He still remembered her pale skin and how fragile she had felt when he had washed her to clean off all her impurity. To think she had slept with that Alex-guy from her class. Someone had told the Snakecharmer about it, and he had broken it off with her right away. Pretended he didn't care. He had spent a year planning everything. Making it look like a burglary. He had read how to do that in one of John Platt's books. How ironic, he thought to himself. But because he had waited so long, no one ever thought about him as a suspect in the case, and soon they ruled it out as a breaking and entering gone wrong.

Too easy.

To be fair, the Snakecharmer admitted that he knew that not all women were lying and cheating. Some were good women. They were out there. He had thought Shannon King was one of them. Until today. But that just showed that you never knew.

Even with your own damn wife, you never knew.

Detective Ryder was finally moving up towards the motel now, after the moment. He was walking right towards the Snakecharmer now. He felt so excited as Detective Ryder came closer and closer.

The detective smiled and nodded. "How are you, Ma'am?"

"Hello, Detective," the Snakecharmer said with a big grin, as Jack Ryder walked past him. He could almost not hold back his resentment. What he had seen repulsed him to a degree where he knew he had to do something to solve this situation. Action had to be taken in this matter. And he knew exactly what to do.

FIFTY-SIX

February 2015

"What are we doing here, Mom?"

Angela had been asking questions all the way in the car. She had been playing with Jack's twins all morning, and had started whining when Shannon told her they had lunch plans and had to go. "I told you. We're here to see someone Mommy knows. They would like to meet you."

The neighborhood her sister had bought a house in was called Snug Harbor. It was an area located next to the canals and the Intracoastal River on the backside of the barrier island. All the houses were waterfront and had a seawall with docks and boats or jet skis. You could still walk or bike to the beach. It was very nice, Shannon thought to herself.

You did well for yourself in life, dear sister.

"But who lives here?" Angela asked. "Who are these people? Do they have children?"

"No. They don't."

"Aw."

Kristi was Shannon's older sister by three years. She hadn't been able to have children, something she figured out very early in her teens when she accidentally became pregnant and their mother forced her to have an abortion, something Kristi had never forgiven her mother for. The abortion destroyed her ability to become pregnant again, the doctors told her.

Shannon took in a deep breath before she rang the doorbell. Her stomach was tossing and turning, and she was about to turn around and run away several times before the door was opened.

She looks just like I remember her. Older, but still the same.

Tears piled up in her sister's eyes. She cupped her mouth. "Oh, my God, Shannon. Is that really you?"

Shannon swallowed hard, then nodded with a sob.

Kristi's eyes turned to Angela. "And this is…?"

137

Shannon nodded, still biting her lip to not burst into tears.

Angela reached out her hand. "Hi. I'm Angela. I'm six years old."

Kristi smiled widely, then sobbed heavily. "Oh, my God. It's really you? Well, hello there, Angela. Welcome to our home. We are so happy you're here."

Angela looked at her mother.

"Well, don't stay out there," Kristi said, and grabbed Shannon's arm right where it was bruised.

Shannon pulled back in pain. "Ouch."

"Mommy fell," Angela said. "Hurt her arm and face. She does this all the time. Stupid stairs."

Kristi looked at Shannon with a worried expression. "Well, good thing we don't have stairs in our house, then," she said. "Come on in."

Inside the living room waited Jimmy. He too had tears in his eyes. He had always loved Shannon, and had been the one to tell Kristi she needed to address Shannon's drug abuse before it was too late. He was the one who told Kristi to intervene, to not let go, even when Kristi wanted to because Shannon treated her badly. That was when Joe started to tell Shannon that Kristi and Jimmy were bad for Shannon, that they were jealous and only wanted to hurt her, to destroy her career. Shannon hadn't liked what he said, but she hadn't cared about anyone either. All she had cared about back then was getting her next fix. The drugs had made her a killer performer on stage, no doubt about it, and her record label hadn't tried to stop it. It had made her even more creative in her songwriting, but it had also destroyed her life. She could see that now. And she had missed out on so much.

"It's so good to see you, Shannon," he said and hugged her. She closed her eyes and enjoyed the embrace. This was exactly what she needed right now. Family.

"Hi, I'm Angela, I'm six," Angela said, and reached out her hand.

Jimmy grabbed her in his arms and held her tight. "I'm so happy to meet you, Angela, who is six years old."

"I hope y'all like shrimp," Kristi said, wiping her tears on her sleeve.

FIFTY-SEVEN

February 2015

"HOW HARD CAN it be to find a woman and a child? A world famous woman and her child!"

Joe Harrison was screaming at the top of his lungs. He grabbed a pile of magazines and threw them at the private investigator he had hired to find Shannon and Angela. He had told him to find Shannon, the most famous singer on the face of the Goddamn planet, whose face was plastered on the cover of all of the magazines, but still he came up with nothing?

Even his buddies at the police station hadn't been able to help him. How the hell could this happen?

"Did you try her sister's place?" he asked the PI.

"Yes. She doesn't live there anymore. Neighbors say they moved six years ago, but they don't know where to."

"And her drunk mother?"

"Still lives in the trailer park in St. Pete, but she hasn't seen her or heard from her in years. I spoke to her on the phone earlier," the PI said.

"How can people just vanish?" Joe yelled. "I don't understand. I want her found. I want her found now! Go down there and talk to the old hag. Tell her I'll freaking kill her if she doesn't tell me where her daughter is."

"Yes, Sir," the PI said, then left.

Joe threw himself on the couch. What had she done? He couldn't believe it had come to this. After all they had gone through? How could she just leave him like this? Well, she wasn't getting away with it. That was certain. She wasn't taking Angela from him…that was for sure. He wanted his daughter back, no matter how much it would cost.

Joe hit his fist into the wall and left a hole. It hurt like crazy. He yelled and picked up some African sculpture that Shannon had paid thousands of dollars for. Joe had always believed it was ugly as hell, and now he threw it to the marble tiles and it scattered into bits and pieces. He growled, then fell to his knees and cried, while picking up the pieces.

"How could you do this to me, Shannon? Don't you know I'm nothing without you? Don't you realize I can't live without you and Angela in my life? How could you just leave like this?"

When he picked up a piece of the sculpture, he cut his finger and it started to bleed. Joe stared at the blood as it dripped to the floor. It was as red as the rage inside of him.

There is no way she is going to get away with this. No way.

Joe screamed. It echoed in the empty million dollar house. His phone rang, and he picked it up.

"Yes?"

"It's me. I have news."

Joe got up from the floor with the phone to his ear. "Sergeant. How wonderful to hear from you."

"I heard from colleagues in Florida that Shannon was spotted in Cocoa Beach. You didn't hear it from me. Now we're even," he said and hung up.

"We're even when I say we are," Joe said, and put the phone in his pocket. There were small drops of his blood on the floor. He found a tissue and wiped the blood off of his finger. He approached a framed picture of Shannon from one of her tours.

"So, Cocoa Beach, huh? That's where you're hiding. Well, not for long, my dear. Not for long."

FIFTY-EIGHT

February 2015

_____

TOM CAME over Sunday afternoon with his board under his arm. I grinned when I saw him.

"Seriously? She's letting you surf?" I asked.

"I couldn't believe it either," Tom said. He had brought his 9.2 foot yellow Robert August longboard. A sheer beauty for the eye. I had always been jealous of that board and asked him numerous times if he would sell it. I was glad to see that he was going to use it for what it was meant for, and not just as a decoration in his living room.

"Are you coming?" he asked.

"Give me a sec to suit up."

I looked at my mother, who was sweeping the wooden deck. She smiled. "Go ahead. I'll look after the kids."

"Great. Thanks. Emily is watching TV. She can help if there is anything you need," I said, rushing towards my condo next door. In less than two minutes, I had put on my wetsuit and waxed the board. When I came down to the water, Tom had already paddled out. I hurried after him. I paddled out, enjoying the occasional splash of water in my face. It was getting warmer now, ready for spring that was right around the corner, when the suits came off and we surfed in nothing but shorts. I looked forward to that. I hated wearing my suit. I always felt so trapped.

"You hear that Katherine is back?" Tom asked, when I had paddled out to the back where he waited for the next set. A flock of pelicans flew past him. One dove into the ocean and caught fish that it gulped down immediately.

Katherine was a great white shark that liked to roam the East Coast. Usually, she stayed up north in North Carolina or outside Jacksonville, but every now and then, she swam all the way down to the Space Coast. Last year, she had been all the way to the Gulf and then back. On her way, she had been very close to the beach in Sebastian Inlet, just a few miles south of us. She was wearing a tracker, and we followed her on an app. It was mostly for fun. I wasn't scared of any sharks. We saw them constantly in the water, and often very close to our boards, but those were smaller, not great whites like Katherine.

"Yeah, Florida Today wrote about it yesterday. But she's still far out in the Atlantic," I said, and spotted a set coming through in the back. I got ready, paddled, and caught one. It was smooth and beautiful. Open faced almost all the way to the beach. I did a couple of turns and walked to the tip and tried to do a hang-five, but I fell off. I got back up on the board and paddled back out, just as Tom caught a wave, and I watched him ride it. Tom was an excellent surfer. A whole lot better than I was. It was a shame he didn't surf much anymore.

When he came back, the ocean was quiet for a while. I took in a couple of deep breaths of the fresh air. Tom was very quiet. I got a feeling something was wrong.

"Are you all right?" I asked.

"Well…" he paused and looked at me.

Uh-oh. Something was really wrong.

"Is it Eliza?" I asked. I had sensed it when I was there. It wasn't just the secret they had kept from me. There was more under the surface.

"It's me. I've done something stupid, Jack. And now I'm paying for it. I had to tell her. I was so scared."

"Whoa, whoa. Let's start from the beginning here. What did you do?"

Tom couldn't look at me when he spoke. "I slept with someone."

"Oh, no, Tom!"

"Oh, yes. I did." He groaned and clenched his fist. "I didn't mean for it to happen. It just did. I…I…There is no excuse."

I felt angry at him for being so stupid. Thinking about how I had felt when they told me about Arianna's betrayal, I suddenly felt for Eliza. Being deceived by someone you loved, someone you believed loved you back, was the worst feeling in the world.

"Who was she?"

"That's the worst part," Tom said. "That's why I had to tell. I was scared the police would come after me. I was afraid you…you would."

"Me? Is that why you didn't return my calls for days?" I asked, thinking about how I couldn't get ahold of my best friend for several days in January.

"Yes. I avoided you. Eliza thought it was important we told you about Arianna. Since she now knew how bad it felt. That's why she invited you over. She wanted a clean slate. I was afraid of losing you."

I frowned. "So, why were you afraid the police would come after you for sleeping with someone…unless…oh, my God, Tom. Please tell me it isn't true."

Tom nodded. "It's true. And it's bad. I slept with Laura Bennett right before she was killed. I thought you would find my DNA all over her. We used a condom, but still."

The news was so shocking that I let several excellent waves go past me. "We didn't. Her body was washed with bleach, leaving no traces of anything on her. How long before she was killed did you sleep with her?"

"In the afternoon of the night she died," he said. "We met on Sunday afternoon at a motel."

"Oh, my goodness, Tom."

"I know. A cliché. At least we didn't choose your motel. We took the Motel 6."

"Well, thanks a lot. So, I take it you had been seeing each other for awhile, then?" I asked, hoping I wouldn't have to put Tom's picture up on the whiteboard as a suspect.

He nodded without looking at me. "A couple of months."

"Poor Eliza," I said.

"I know. I'm not proud of myself. But we were going through some stuff. I fell in. I met Laura through the school. We both volunteered at the multicultural night six months ago. We planned it all together and talked every day for like a week or so. We liked each other. I thought she was sweet and funny, and really good to talk to. We started meeting up for coffee now and then. I kept running into her everywhere all of a sudden. Then, one day, we kissed when we said goodbye. Right in the middle of Minutemen, where everyone could see us. Luckily, no one did. But we wanted more. We decided to meet at the motel. One meeting led to another, and soon we saw each other regularly. Eliza and I were going through some bad stuff. I was feeling awful; I felt like Eliza had stopped loving me. Then, Laura was suddenly there. She liked me. Laura liked me. We talked about me and Eliza and how hard it was for us. She told me about the excruciating loss of her child, and how Brandon blamed her. How he drank and gambled, and how it was getting worse and worse since their daughter died. We both needed a shoulder to cry on. We connected. We could relate. But soon, one thing led to another. I couldn't stop, even though I wanted to. I hated to hurt Eliza like that, but being with Laura made me feel so good, I couldn't stop."

Tom paused and sighed. "I can't believe she's dead."

"So, you got scared when she was found killed and told Eliza everything?" I asked. "She sent you here today, didn't she? She didn't let you surf. She wanted you to come clean to me."

"She's been telling me to talk to you for weeks. I kept avoiding it. Especially since I thought you were mad at us for keeping the secret from you."

"You know me. I don't stay angry that long," I said.

"I feel awful. I've destroyed everything. I had to tell her. I didn't want her to learn from the police or the news when I was arrested," he said, his voice breaking. "That would just be cruel."

Yes that would have been cruel. Just like not telling your best friend his wife was cheating on him until four years later. I couldn't believe it. Was everyone cheating on each other these days? Arianna? Tom? Laura Bennett?

A new set of gorgeous waves were rolling towards me, but I didn't notice. A thought had struck me, and it wouldn't leave.

Melanie Schultz had been cheating too.

FIFTY-NINE

October 1998

SHE ANTICIPATED his visits with great longing. They were the highlight of her entire week. Every Thursday, he had the day off, and that was when he stopped by the condo. It was the happiest time of Annie's life.

She started to dress nicely again. She started wearing make-up and exercising and was quickly losing weight. Victor didn't suspect a thing, but enjoyed this new and joyful Annie. Little did he know, she was dressing nicely and taking care of herself for someone else.

The handsome officer was at her door this Thursday at exactly ten o'clock, like usual. The boy was at the high school, and Victor was working. Since he had lost his job at his parent's company and had to get by on his own, he had started a pool company. He had a shop downtown and visited people's houses and cleaned their pools. Made sure the PH-balance was right and vacuumed them. It was a good job for him. He enjoyed it immensely.

"Lots of fresh air and I'm my own boss," he would say. "Doesn't get much better than that."

But he never made much money. As a matter of fact, they had gotten deep into debt, and creditors called almost every day now. Victor was probably going to lose his shop if things didn't get better.

Annie didn't care one bit about him or what went on with his shop. She wanted out, and now she had found a way. The handsome officer was going to be her way out of this misery. He wasn't rich, but he made a decent living, and he could take proper care of her.

If only he weren't married.

But, then again. So was she. There was a word to solve that. Divorce. She was ready to take that step right now, but she wasn't so sure about him. He seemed more reluctant, and wasn't willing to discuss it with her. She couldn't quite figure him out. He seemed so into her when he was there, but as soon as she brought up the future, he hesitated and didn't want to talk anymore. Annie knew he was going

144

through a rough time at home. They had talked about it, and he often said that he wasn't sure they would make it. Why wasn't he jumping aboard right away? What was he waiting for?

She had considered getting herself pregnant. That way, he would have to choose. But it was a lot of trouble to go through. She had recently lost a lot of weight and looked great. She certainly didn't want to ruin that.

Only if she had to.

She had decided the pregnancy would be her plan B. Plan A was to make him so fond of her, make him love her so much, he would want to marry her and leave that wife of his.

There was a knock on the door and Annie rushed to open it. She stopped at the mirror next to the door and corrected her hair, right before she pulled it open, trying not to seem too eager. There he was. Outside on her doorstep. Looking even more handsome than the last time he was there, it seemed.

"Come on in," she said with a shy smile.

He walked inside and she closed the door. He looked at her with those blue eyes of his. She was breathing heavily now. He turned her on like no other man had ever done. She had never known sex could be like this. Not since Tim Harrold ruined it for her back at the lake fourteen years ago. It was like the officer had opened her eyes. Like she had been asleep all these years, living in a drowsy bubble of nothingness, and now she had finally come to life.

He had made her come alive.

Seconds after he came inside, they were deep in each other's arms. Kissing, touching, feeling. He lifted her up and carried her to the couch, where he ripped off her dress in one smooth movement. Seconds later, he was inside of her, on top of her, panting, breathing. She closed her eyes and let herself get into it with him, secretly wishing she would get pregnant, so he had to take care of her, when suddenly there was a noise behind them. She gasped and opened her eyes, and stared directly into those of her teenage son.

SIXTY

February 2015

"So, what are you doing tomorrow?" Kristi asked, when Shannon was putting on her jacket and getting ready to leave. It had been a great day and evening. Shannon couldn't believe how much she had missed her sister. They had talked for hours and hours, catching up on everything; they had cried and laughed, and even been quiet just to enjoy each other's company again.

"I...I wasn't planning on much," Shannon said.

"I wanna go see the alligators!" Angela exclaimed.

Kristi lit up. "That's a good idea," she said. "It's Monday. I have the day off. We can go with you. We can take one of the airboat rides into the river. They always find something. We might see manatees too." Kristi looked at her husband. "We can take the one up at Lone Cabbage. Oh, it's wonderful. We could do the Lil' Twister...that's a private tour where you go deeper into St. John's River. We did it once. It was a lot of fun."

"Did you see alligators?" Angela asked.

"Yes. Lots of them."

"You've seen alligators before," Shannon said to Angela. "At the zoo, remember?"

"Yeah, but they were so boring. I want to see them in real life."

"I really don't..." Shannon said. "I can't go anywhere where there are too many people."

Her sister nodded, understanding what she meant. She couldn't be recognized, and she certainly couldn't risk anyone seeing her bruised face.

"I understand," Kristi said. "You know what? Why don't we take her? Let me and Jimmy take Angela on this trip. It would be a nice way for us to get to know each other as well, and give you a little time to yourself. I think you need to treat yourself to a day of relaxation."

"I would love that!" Angela said, and looked at her mother with wide eyes. "Can I? Can I go on the boat trip and see the alligators, Mom?"

Shannon exhaled and looked into her daughter's eyes begging for a yes. How she loved her dearly and wanted to see her happy. Besides, her sister was right. It would be great to have a day alone to try and figure out her life. She really needed that. She needed peace and quiet to think.

"Can I, Mom? Please? Pretty please?"

It was funny how her daughter always seemed to think the appearance of the word please was important, but it worked, almost every time.

"Okay, then. But you behave, young lady. You do everything your Aunt Kristi tells you to, all right?"

Angela saluted like a soldier. "Yes, Ma'am."

Shannon smiled and kissed her sister on the cheek. "See you tomorrow then."

"We'll pick her up around nine tomorrow morning. How does that sound?" Kristi asked.

"Perfect," Shannon said, and grabbed Angela's hand. She looked exhausted. It had been a long and eventful day for her daughter. She took her in her arms and carried her to the car, then shut the door. Kristi and Jimmy came outside.

"So, does anyone know you're here?" Kristi asked.

"So far, I've managed to keep it a secret. I hope to continue to keep it that way."

"That's good," Kristi said with a worried face. "We don't want this bastard to find you." She touched Shannon's bruised cheek gently with her finger. "You sure you don't want to stay with us, though? We have room for the both of you."

Shannon shook her head. "No, I'm fine at the motel. They're very nice people. I don't want to impose on you guys. Who knows? We might stay for a long time." Shannon stopped. She thought about the officer that had pulled her over and whether he would be able to keep quiet. He had to. He simply had to. Shannon decided to not tell her sister about it; she would only worry.

"Well, I'd better get going before Angela falls asleep. See you tomorrow."

"Be careful," Kristi said, still with deep worried eyes that Shannon remembered from their childhood, growing up with a drunk mother with a failed career as a singer.

SIXTY-ONE

February 2015

I WAS quiet in the car all the way to Melbourne Beach. I was worn out after a stressful morning of trying to get the twins ready on time. They had been arguing all morning, and it was a nightmare just to get them to get dressed. On top of it, we had overslept, so they missed the bus, and I had to drive them to school myself. Weasel, who had wanted to come with me to talk to the parents of Janelle Jackson, was very focused and pensive as we drove down A1A. We hit the city sign and turned right into a gated community. We showed our badges to the guard and told him they were expecting us.

"Strange to have a breaking and entering in a gated community, don't you think?" I asked, as we were let through.

"It happens," she said.

I had told her my theory at the office as soon as I had come in that morning, but she hadn't quite bought into it yet. She still believed the judge was the target for the fire, and that we should focus on his murder instead of Melanie Schultz's. But, she agreed to look into the angle of the cheating woman, and I arranged for us to meet with Janelle's parents at their house.

"Finally, someone is listening to us," the mother said, as soon as we had sat down in their kitchen. The house was impeccable, so clean I found no dust anywhere, and all surfaces had been wiped down recently. The house smelled of bleach.

Mrs. Jackson looked at her husband, who was sitting next to her holding her hand. They had that air of sadness about them. Their eyes met briefly. I hated to drag them through this, having to tell their story again, but I sensed they wanted to. They wanted us to take up the case again.

"We never believed it was a breaking and entering," Mr. Jackson said.

Mrs. Jackson shook her head. She was small and dark-haired. She looked so fragile, so delicate, like fine china that could break any moment now.

"The reason why we've come today is we believe there might be a connection to a recent murder committed in Cocoa Beach," I said.

"Cocoa Beach?" Mrs. Jackson said.

"Yes. There seem to be similarities with our case and your daughter's, and we want to know if there are others we can use in our investigation. We can't promise you that our investigation will lead to anything, but we'll do everything we can."

Mrs. Jackson nodded again. "Thank you," she said.

"So, tell us what happened," Weasel said.

They looked at each other again, like they were deciding who should do the talking. Mrs. Jackson started out.

"It was in April of 2002. The seventh of April. We had been invited to our friends' house; actually, they were our neighbors back then. Right across the street from us. We asked Janelle if she wanted to come with us, but she said she didn't feel like it. You know how teenagers are. Everything their parents do is lame. So, we let her stay home. The police later explained to us that she was on the computer most of the night, playing Sims. It was her favorite game."

Mrs. Jackson paused at the painful memory.

"The case file also states that she spoke with someone on the phone," I said. I had been reading the file all morning, trying desperately to find something that I could use.

"She called her boyfriend at the time," Mr. Jackson said. "His name was Alex. He was supposed to come over, but his parents had grounded him because he had been caught on the beach drinking beer. He was interrogated by the police, but there was no evidence to lead to his arrest."

"Anyway," Mrs. Jackson continued. "We got back around eleven-thirty and..." she stopped. The words seemed like they were stuck in her throat.

"We found her in the bathroom," Mr. Jackson said. There was a light tremor to his voice as he continued. "Naked...her eyes staring into the ceiling. She was so pale. I knew right away she was dead, still I tried...you know, you've gotta try... can't give up hope."

"So you performed CPR?" I asked.

Mrs. Jackson put a hand on her husband's shoulder. Tears were streaming across her cheeks now.

"You have to try, don't you? I didn't want to accept it...I couldn't..."

The old memories were unpleasant for the couple, and we let them take their time to get through the pain.

"I'm a little interested in Janelle's love life," I said, after a short while of silence. "I know it's not easy for you to talk about. And forgive me for the character of my question, but do you know if Janelle ever cheated on her boyfriend?"

The couple looked at one another, then back at me. "Yes, as a matter of fact she did. She cheated on her old boyfriend, the one before Alex. It was a year before she died. At a dance at the school, she kissed Alex when she was still going out with someone else," Mrs. Jackson said. "How did you know?"

Weasel and I exchanged looks. Finally, something was adding up in this case.

"Where is Alex today?" I asked. "Do you know where we can find him?"

"You can't. He...He was killed in a car accident four months later," Mr. Jackson said.

149

SIXTY-TWO

February 2015

KRISTI LOVED SPENDING the day with her niece. Her husband Jimmy seemed to enjoy it just as much, if not more. It was bittersweet for Kristi to watch that sparkle in Jimmy's eyes when he spoke to Angela. To know that she could never give him what he always wanted most in this world, even though he never said so in front of Kristi.

"Can I get an ice cream?" Angela asked, as they passed a small shop on their way to the airboat.

"Not now," Kristi said. "We can't take it on the boat. When we're done, we can all get one. How does that sound?"

"Yay," Angela said. "I want chocolate."

She was such a pretty girl. She looked so much like her mother when she was that age. Kristi remembered her well. She had always loved her youngest sister the most, even though she always got them in trouble. She was the black sheep of the family, but sometimes the black sheep was also the one that was most loved. Shannon still had that ability. She could get herself into deep trouble and still be the most loved person in the world. Everybody adored her. The great country singer, the world-famous celebrity. Kristi couldn't help being a little jealous of her sister every now and then. Especially when she read about her in the magazines in line at the grocery store. They always made her life seem so glamorous. So out of reach for ordinary people like Kristi. Back when it happened, she hadn't known why Shannon suddenly cut her off. At times, she had thought her sister simply had become too big a name to be around her very ordinary sister. Being idolized by the entire world had to do something to you, didn't it? At least that's what Kristi had thought. But, when her sister suddenly showed up in her town telling her story, Kristi had felt ashamed of how she had been thinking about her. Shannon was nothing like she imagined, like she had read about in the magazines. She was still the same good old Shannon that Kristi loved dearly. She was still her baby sister.

"I'll go buy the tickets," Jimmy said, and left them.

Kristi felt Angela's hand in hers and looked down. "I wish I had a sister," Angela said. "I bet you and my mom had fun when you were kids."

Kristi chuckled. "We did. We were quite the troublemakers, the two of us."

"There were three girls, right?"

"Yes. There's also Liz. She was the middle child. She lives in New York."

"How come I haven't been here to visit you before?" Angela asked.

Kristi exhaled. She spotted Jimmy with the tickets coming out of the shop. She smiled. "I don't know, sweetie. You live very far away."

"I wish I could live here," she said. "It's much more fun here."

"Well, you can come visit anytime you want to. Will that do?" Kristi asked, as Jimmy caught up with them and they got in line for the boat.

"I'd like that," Angela said and walked aboard.

They got earplugs to protect their ears from the noise of the boat, and soon they took off. Their guide was a guy in his thirties wearing a bandana. He found several alligators in the swamps and navigated the boat as close as possible, so they could all take pictures. It was a gorgeous trip, Kristi thought, and Angela was beyond excited.

This is what it feels like to be a real family.

They had thought about adopting, but never really gotten around to it. Kristi wasn't sure she wanted to do it. She didn't want some troubled kid. Who knows what a kid like that had been through?

They had never done anything but talk about adopting, and now it was getting too late for them. She was pushing forty and Jimmy forty-five. Did she regret it? Right now, she did. When holding Angela's hand in hers and looking at the animals from the boat, she regretted it bitterly.

An hour later, they were back on land.

"What a great trip," Jimmy said. "I'm so glad I took the day off for this."

"Me too," Kristi said.

"I need to pee," Angela said.

"There's a restroom right over there," Jimmy said, and pointed at the red building.

"I'll take you," Kristi said, and walked with Angela's hand in hers towards the building. "I'll wait out here," she said, and let Angela go inside.

Jimmy signaled that he would get ice cream for all of them. When he returned, Angela still hadn't come out.

"You think she's all right in there?" he asked.

"I hope so. I'll go in and check."

Kristi opened the door and went inside. There were three stalls. "Angela?" she asked. "Are you all right?"

There was no answer. Kristi's heart stopped. All of the doors were open. A back door to the building was ajar.

Oh, my God. She's not here!

SIXTY-THREE

February 2015

"Angela is missing!"

Shannon was almost screaming on the other end of the line. I looked at Weasel across my desk. There were papers everywhere. We had all the old boxes sent over from the case of Janelle Jackson, and we were going through every little detail.

Weasel caught my alarmed look.

"They don't know where she is. Oh, Jack. You were the only one I could think of to call. Can you help me?"

"Calm down, Shannon. What happened?" I asked.

"My sister Kristi took Angela on an airboat ride. When they were done, she went to the restroom up there, and now they just called and told me they can't find her. They've searched the entire area, but she's not there. Oh, God, Jack. What if Joe has her? What will I do?"

"Where are you now?"

"I'm on my way to Lone Cabbage."

"I'll meet you up there."

I hung up and looked at Weasel.

"What's going on?" she asked.

"Missing child," I said. "By the airboats in Lone Cabbage. "I have to get up there."

Weasel smiled. "Well, what are you waiting for? She obviously means a lot to you. I think we're done here for now anyway."

I rushed to my car and drove towards Lone Cabbage. It was located around thirty miles from Cocoa Beach on the mainland where the river mouthed into a big lake. It took me less than twenty minutes to get there with blaring sirens. I arrived almost at the same time as Shannon.

"Jack. I'm so glad you came," she said, approaching me. "I don't know what to do. This is my sister, Kristi, and her husband, Jimmy." I shook hands with all of them. Anxious eyes followed me as they showed Shannon and me to the restrooms where Angela had disappeared.

"She went in through the door and I waited for her out here. I didn't know there was a back door," Kristi said.

A local officer had been called to the scene. I greeted him and told him who I was. We were still in Brevard County, so I was still within my jurisdiction.

"We walked through the area by the boats, and they even sailed out on the water to look for her. We've been everywhere," Jimmy said.

I looked around. There was a lot of dense forest surrounding the area. If she had run in there, it would be very difficult to find her. I remembered a year ago when a child got lost in woods like these and wasn't found until three days later. It was a terrifying time for everyone. The animals living in there weren't joking around.

"Is there any reason to believe she ran away?" I asked. "How was she before she went inside the restroom?"

Kristi shook her head. The shock on her face was visible. She couldn't grasp how this could have happened. "She was good. She seemed happy. We were about to have ice cream. I...I don't see why..."

"He has her," Shannon said with a trembling voice. "I know he does. This has Joe written all over it."

"I thought he didn't know you were here?" I asked.

She shook her head and bit her lip. "He must have found out somehow. He does stuff like that. He knows people everywhere."

"Have you tried to call him?" I asked.

"Constantly. But he's not picking up," Shannon said. "I'll try again." She pressed her phone frantically. I could tell she was having a hard time holding it together. She had told me about her former drug abuse before she had Angela. I wondered if she craved a drink or a fix right now. I wished I could do more for her.

"Hello? Joe?"

I froze and looked at her. Her eyes sparkled with hope and desperation. "Joe? Joe? You bastard. Where is Angela?"

SIXTY-FOUR

February 2015

"He says he doesn't have her. Where is she, Jack?"

Shannon looked at me like she expected me to have an answer.

"I don't know. I'll start a search," I said. "I'll call in the Sheriff's Department and we'll look for her all night long if we have to. Don't worry."

Shannon put her head on my shoulder. I stroked her hair gently. Suddenly, I missed my kids like crazy.

"I still think he has her," Shannon said. "I think he's lying. It makes sense. Why would he tell me he has her? I would only demand to get her back."

"I guess you're right. But, he's all the way back in Nashville, isn't he?"

"He didn't say. He hung up before I could ask." Shannon sighed. "I have a feeling he's around here somewhere."

I didn't want to say it out loud, but if he had Angela, he would probably be on the road by now...trying to get as far away from here as possible.

"I'll make a few calls," I said. "I'll get the search started, have the dogs come out."

I called Ron, and an hour later, all of my colleagues from the Sheriff's Department arrived and started the search. There were dogs, helicopters, and lots of volunteers, who helped walk through the forest in search of Angela. I felt grateful for every one of them. So did Shannon.

But as nightfall came, they still hadn't found her. Shannon was on the verge of breaking down, and I decided to take her back to the motel.

"But I want to stay here. In case she shows up," she said.

"There are hundreds of people here," I said. "If they find her, I promise you'll be the first to know. You need to get some rest. I'm taking you back now."

Shannon finally agreed to let me drive her back. She was sobbing and crying most of the way. I wanted to comfort her, but it was just so difficult. I was afraid of saying the wrong thing.

"We'll find her. Don't worry," I said for the tenth time, when I drove up in front of the motel. I had asked my mother to take care of the kids, and they were all asleep in their extra bedroom when we arrived. I let them stay in there and closed the door, kissed my mother thank you, then helped Shannon get to her room. I opened the door, and with her leaning on me, I helped her get to the bed. She took one glance at Angela's empty bed and her stuffed animals on top of it, then burst into tears.

"Oh, my baby. Where is she, Jack? Where is she?"

I let her cry in my arms, while I stroked her hair gently. Even when crying she was beautiful. Her hands touched my face and she pulled me closer.

"You need to get some sleep," I said. "Lay down. I'll stay with you till you fall asleep."

"I can't," she said. "I can't sleep without my daughter."

"Listen to me," I said. "You think Joe has her, right?"

She sniffled. "Yes. Yes I do."

"Would he ever hurt Angela?"

She looked pensive for a second, then shook her head. "No, not Angela. Me, he would, but Angela is his diamond. He loves her more than he loves himself."

"So, if we assume she's with Joe, then we must assume she's fine, right? He'll take proper care of her, right?"

Shannon scoffed. A hint of a smile spread across her face. "You make a very good point, Detective Jack Ryder."

"Now, get some sleep. Tomorrow, we'll look for Joe, and then we'll get Angela back to you."

Shannon put her head on the pillow and closed her eyes. "You're a very sweet man, Jack Ryder," she mumbled. "You're very good at saying the right things."

I leaned over and kissed her cheek, like I kissed my children's when tucking them in. It made her smile.

SIXTY-FIVE

February 2015

Shannon woke up with a start.

"Angela?" she cried wearily. "Angela?"

She had dreamt about her daughter. She had dreamt that she had held her in her arms again. Now, there was nothing but the darkness...the vast gloom of the night. Realizing that her daughter was still missing, that it was nothing but a dream, Shannon sobbed. She pulled her legs up underneath her chin and cried. She tried to close her eyes and go back to sleep, but had no success. She turned around and spotted Jack. He was sitting in the chair, his head resting on the wall behind him, his mouth open. His eyes were closed, and he was snoring lightly.

"You're going to wake up with a pain in your neck," she whispered, but couldn't help smiling. Jack was usually so handsome, but right now, he didn't look very attractive. He was drooling slightly.

Shannon tilted her head and looked at him. She couldn't believe he had stayed here for her sake. They had only known each other for a short while, yet she felt so incredibly attracted to him, like they had known each other always.

She stared at him for a long time, wondering if he had planned on staying here, or if he had simply fallen asleep while waiting.

Either way, it was nice to have him here. He made her feel secure, like nothing bad could ever reach her. He had a way of making people feel comfortable when they were around him. It was a very rare quality in a man.

"Who are you, Jack Ryder?" she whispered in the darkness. Outside, the full moon was making it a very bright night. Shannon sat up in the bed, wondering how Angela was doing, if she was all right, if she was scared or even crying? She kind of hoped Joe had her, since she knew she would at least be safe. But, then again. Would she ever see her again? Would Joe let her? Would they have to go through a custody battle? The drug abuse would come up. Shannon traveled all the time. That would be an issue as well. She had no proof that Joe had hit her, she never reported it, and never took pictures of the abuse. They would have to rely on witnesses, and when it came to having friends who would testify on your behalf, Joe by far surpassed her. She had no friends of her own. They were all Joe's.

"Damn you, Joe," she whispered.

Jack grumbled something in his sleep, then moved his head. It fell down, and he started nodding. Shannon chuckled. She longed to feel the warmth of another body close to hers. She longed to have warm arms around her making her feel like she was safe. Shannon cried silently, thinking about all the nights Joe had yelled at her for hours…yelled and slapped her around. The past fifteen years with him had been a living hell. How had she not had the strength to leave him before?

Because she was afraid of him. She was terrified that he would do something like what he had done today. She was so afraid she would never see her daughter again. And now, it had happened. He had taken her, and for all she knew, he could be on his way to Mexico with her in the car.

Shannon sobbed at the thought. She loathed how she had felt angst every day of her life. Anxious about what he would come up with next, what would set him off. The man she was supposed to feel secure with, the one person in the world that was supposed to protect her, had been the source of all her misery. It was all so clear now. But it wasn't over, just because she had decided to leave him. That was very clear to her now. Was it ever going to be over?

Shannon couldn't stop the tears. She tried to wipe them away, but more came as fast as she removed them. Suddenly, she felt someone come up behind her. Warmth spread over her entire body as he leaned in and kissed her on the neck.

"Jack," she whispered. He put his arm around her and pulled her close to him, while kissing her neck and throat. Shannon moaned and leaned her head back. His touches made her tears stop. She whispered his name again, right before she closed her eyes and let herself get into the moment.

SIXTY-SIX

February 2015

I WOKE up in Shannon's arms. It was still early morning. I managed to get myself out of her embrace, then kissed her on the cheek before I reached for my pants and my phone. It was still only a quarter to six. I had fifteen minutes before the kids had to get up and get ready for school.

I looked at the sleeping Shannon. I couldn't believe myself. I never did anything like this. I had taken a chance. I had woken up and found her crying. I couldn't believe I had dared to simply kiss her, but I had wanted to so badly. I wanted to be close to her. She was in such deep pain, and I wanted to simply comfort her, but one thing led to another.

Shannon groaned in her sleep. She looked more beautiful than ever. I felt a pinch of joy in my heart. I really liked her, and I hoped I hadn't ruined everything by sleeping with her. It was beautiful...what we shared. It was so intimate, and even though I did feel guilty, since I was technically still married, and so was she, I couldn't help feeling happy.

I picked up my shirt and got dressed, then leaned over and whispered in her ear. "I need to go, Shannon. The kids are waiting for me. I'll be back once I've put them on the bus, all right?"

Shannon opened her eyes. She smiled. She grabbed my collar and pulled me closer, then kissed me. The kiss was soft and gentle. Kissing her stirred things up inside of me in a way it never had with any other girl. Not even with Arianna.

I just hoped she felt the same way.

"I'll be back," I whispered.

"Okay," she moaned, then went back to sleep. I was glad she finally managed to get some rest. She needed it.

I put on my shoes, then went outside and closed the door carefully, to not wake up Shannon once again, then ran for my condo, where I found new clothes for myself and for the children. I took a very quick shower, then hurried to my parent's quarters at the motel. The kids were still heavily asleep when I entered the bedroom my parents had made for them. Even Emily had crashed there on the futon.

"Guys. It's time to get up," I whispered.

"Dad," Abigail moaned, while slowly coming to life. I leaned in and kissed her. She grabbed me by the neck and hugged me. It felt good. I thought about Shannon. I couldn't imagine not knowing where my kids were. It was unbearable.

"Did you find Angela?" Austin asked. He was sitting up in his bed above Abigail's. I stood up and looked at him. He looked so cute in his little PJs with airplanes on them. Part of me hoped he would never grow out of this stage.

"No, buddy. Not yet. But, we'll find her. We believe she is with her dad."

"Then why don't you just call him and ask?" Abigail asked.

"We did," I said, and threw their clothes on their beds so they could get dressed. Emily went to the bathroom and took a shower. She was always grumpy in the mornings, and I always let her take her time to wake up.

"So, what's the problem, then?" Abigail asked.

"Well, honey, it's not that easy. See, her father says he doesn't have her, but he might not be telling the truth."

"Why wouldn't he tell the truth?" Abigail asked.

I shrugged. "I don't know. Maybe because he doesn't want us to find her."

"That's stupid," Abigail said, and started putting on her clothes. I could hear my mother in the kitchen. I was starving.

"Grown-ups do a lot of stupid things," I said. "Now, get ready. I don't want you to miss the bus again."

SIXTY-SEVEN

February 2015

SHANNON HAD no idea what to do. She took a shower, while wondering if she had made a mistake. It was way too early for her to get involved with someone else, wasn't it? But how could it be wrong if it felt so good? If it felt so right?

The old bathtub was clogged, and soon her feet were in ankle-deep water. She put shampoo in her hair and rubbed it thoroughly, then rinsed, and soon the water in the tub was up to her shins. She turned off the water for a little while to let it run down the drain. It went slowly. As soon as it reached her ankles again, she turned the shower back on and put conditioner in her hair. She shaved her legs while the conditioner sunk in, then rinsed it all out. She closed her eyes and thought about last night with Jack and how wonderful he had made her feel.

What is this? She thought to herself. Did she want to be with him again? Yes. She desperately wanted to feel him close to her again. But, was it right? Was it too early for her? Joe would kill her if he found out. And he'd kill Jack as well. She was terrified of dragging Jack into her complicated life, into something he couldn't get himself out of.

It was all a mess.

Shannon let the water wash over her face, thinking about Angela and how she was the only thing that mattered now. The rest had to wait.

"I miss you, baby girl. Where are you?" she whispered, when turning off the shower. The water was now to her knees.

The plumbing at this motel is awful, she thought to herself, and walked out of the tub, expecting the water to drain. It did a little while she got dressed, but as she turned on the faucet to brush her teeth, something happened. Instead of water running down the drain, water spurted out of it and hit Shannon in the face. The water smelled terrible, like it was rotten, and Shannon shrieked. She looked at her face in the mirror.

What is this?

Shannon looked down at the sink, where murky water was rising from the drain. She turned and looked at the bathtub, where the water had suddenly sucked out, and now it was spurting what looked like muddy water back out of it.

Shannon clasped her face, then ran out of the bathroom while yelling.

"Jaaack!"

She opened the door and ran out to the parking lot. Jack was standing by the road with his kids waiting for the bus. He turned to look at her when he heard his name. The bus came at the same instant, and he helped the kids get inside, then he hurried towards her.

"What's going on?" he asked, terrified. "What's that on you?"

"I...I don't know. It just came out of the drain, it spurted right into my face. It smells disgusting."

"I think we need to call for a plumber. I'm on it. Do you have some other clothes? You can shower at my place. It's a newer condominium; we have better plumbing. My parents constantly have problems down here."

Shannon went back to her room and found a dress she could change into. She felt nauseated by the smell in the room and on her. She hurried out of there and followed Jack to his condo. They met his parents on the way.

"The plumbing is acting up again, Dad," Jack said. "Tell the other guests to not use the showers or flush the toilets until it's fixed."

Jack showed Shannon into his condo, which turned out to be a pleasant surprise. Shannon had expected it to be a real bachelor pad, but it was nicely decorated and, of course, filled with children's toys everywhere and drawings they had made and that he had put on the walls. It was big too. Four bedrooms.

Shannon hurried into the shower, while Jack called the local plumber. She scrubbed herself thoroughly to get the smell away. When she was done, she still felt like it was in her hair, and on her body. What was it? Sewer mud? It smelled so rotten. The mere thought of it made her want to throw up.

Shannon put on her dress, and then returned to Jack in the living room. The condo was located on the third floor and had spectacular views of the Atlantic from every window. Jack hung up the phone just as she walked in.

"The sewer is probably just clogged up again," he said. "The guy will fix it. Now we need to focus on finding Angela. I just got off the phone with one of my colleagues at the station. He tells me Joe has been seen in one of the resorts downtown. He checked in two days ago."

SIXTY-EIGHT

February 2015

"**Where is she?**"

Shannon stared at Joe. He was standing in the door to his room at the International Resort. I stayed a few feet behind her, making sure he knew I was there, in case he tried anything. I made my weapon in my belt visible, to make sure he knew he couldn't do anything.

Joe stared back at Shannon. "You mean to say you haven't found her yet?" he asked. His voice was agitated as he spoke.

"Don't give me that," Shannon said, and pushed him aside. She went inside the room. Joe stepped back and let me walk in as well.

"Angela?" Shannon called. "Angela, sweetie?"

There was no answer. Joe was sizing me up. It made me feel uncomfortable. He was a big guy. Bigger than me.

"Shannon, Goddammit," Joe said. "I told you I don't have her! Do you mean to tell me you don't know where she is?"

I was starting to get an alarming feeling in my body. Something was very wrong here. Joe's voice cracked when he spoke. He was clearly upset about this.

"I thought you found her," Joe said. "Since you didn't call me back last night, I thought she had come back. You mean to tell me our daughter has been missing since yesterday?"

"Why would I call you back, Joe? You hung up on me," Shannon said.

"I hung up because I got so pissed at you. I thought it was some gimmick on your part to pretend like she had gone missing, maybe because you wanted to hide her from me. I don't know."

"Now, why would I do that, Joe?" Shannon asked.

"I don't know. But since I didn't hear from you again, I thought it wasn't important. I figured that if she really had run away from you, she had come back. I expected you to at least let me know."

Shannon approached Joe, her jaws clenched. "You're lying," she said. "You have her somewhere. Where is she, Joe? Tell me!"

"I don't know," he said.

The scene was getting absurd. I was starting to believe him.

"Yes, you do," Shannon continued relentlessly. "You've hidden her somewhere, haven't you? Taken her somewhere else to make sure I never find her again."

"I can't say the thought hasn't crossed my mind more than once," he said. "But, unfortunately, that is not the case. I haven't seen her since you took her away and left without a word."

They stood in front of each other like cocks before a fight. Shannon was growling in anger. Joe had his fist clenched. I was beginning to fear this was going to end badly.

"Shannon," I said. "She's clearly not here. Let's go."

Shannon lifted a finger and pointed at Joe. "This isn't over yet."

"I sure hope not," Joe said. "She's my daughter too. I want to find her as badly as you do."

Shannon growled, then walked past me. I looked at Joe, then gave him my card and told him not to leave town.

"I don't intend to," he said. "Not without my daughter."

I followed Shannon into the hallway. She was grumbling and mumbling and hitting her fist into the walls as we approached the elevator.

"Can you believe that guy?" she asked, when we were in the elevator and I had pushed the button.

"What if he's telling the truth?" I asked. "What if he doesn't have her?"

The realization made my stomach turn. If Joe didn't have Angela, then who the hell did? Had she, after all, run into the forest...maybe to get away from her aunt and uncle? Maybe because she was going through a rough time with her mom and dad splitting up and all? I had spoken to the search team earlier on the phone, and they had searched the forest around the lake all night and found nothing, no trace of Angela, not even a footprint or a piece of clothing. The dogs hadn't even picked up her smell beyond the area surrounding the restroom. It was all very odd.

"He has her," Shannon said. "I know he does."

Maybe it was for the best that Shannon insisted on believing that. At least it was a lot better than the scenarios that were playing out in my head.

SIXTY-NINE

February 2015

HE HAD DONE SOMETHING STUPID. Was this going to be the mistake that would put
him in jail? The Snakecharmer wondered, while staring at the girl on the bed. He
had sedated her. He had stuck a cloth with chloroform in her face and held it there
till she passed out. That way he had been able to get her out of the restroom
without anyone noticing. He had carried her over his shoulder, pretending like she
was asleep and he was her father. No one wondered. It was the easiest thing in the
world.

Now, he had three children to take care of.

"Are you running a day-care now?" the Snakecharmer's father said from his
wheelchair in the corner of the living room. Angela had just woken up and had
started screaming so loudly he had to gag her. Now, she was squirming on the bed,
trying to get out of the duct tape he had bound her hands and feet with.

"What are you going to do with all these kids?" his dad asked.

The Snakecharmer didn't answer...for the simple reason that he had no idea. It
had seemed like such a great idea when he had first thought about it, a perfect way
to punish Shannon King for cheating on her husband, but the Snakecharmer
hadn't thought it through properly.

"I had to help her," he said.

"She was in trouble?" the dad asked.

"Yes," he said, thinking about how glad she should be that he had taken her
away from all the trouble that was about to erupt in her life. She had no idea...of
course she didn't. Children never knew how much it was going to affect them that
their parents messed around. This world was filled with parents, especially
women, who thought they could just fool around and never think about how
much it affected someone else's life. How it destroyed everything for a family.

"It's always the children that get hurt," he said.

"True," his father said.

Earlier in the day, he had been at the motel, dressed in a female fat-suit, a dress

164

and wig, like he always was when going there, but the place had been crawling with police cars, and he had no chance of getting in. He knew then that they would soon be on to him. It was about time he got the hell out of here.

The Snakecharmer found the cloth with chloroform and wet it again, before he placed it over the mouth of the girl. He had packed a couple of suitcases that he placed in the back of the truck while Angela dozed off. He put Will in the back seat and asked the boy to sit next to him, in case he needed anything. He packed his dad's car and put the sleeping Angela in the back seat with the other children. He had colored her hair while she was out and cut it short, so no one would be able to recognize her. These children were going with him, and he was going to take proper care of them. He wasn't going to let them down like their parents had. There was only one thing wrong with this plan.

He couldn't bring his father.

His dad was way too old and sick to travel this far by car. He would only be confused, since he couldn't see anything, and when they moved around, it would be too much for him. The Snakecharmer hadn't told him they were leaving; he simply didn't have the heart to do so. So now, he knelt in front of him and put his father's hand on his head.

"What's wrong, Son?" his dad asked and felt his face.

He wanted to say he was sorry for everything. Sorry for what had happened to him, sorry for bringing him trouble, sorry for leaving him, sorry for stealing his car without asking, but he didn't. He couldn't. Instead, he simply smiled and said, "I'm just going to Publix. I'll take the kids. Give you some quiet time. Do you want me to bring you anything?"

His father smiled. Then he nodded. "Oh, you sweet kid. Yes. Bring me some…"

"Cake and beer," the Snakecharmer said, when a tear escaped the corner of his eye. He sniffled and got up. "I'll bring you cake and beer when I come back."

"Thank you, Son. You're a good boy."

SEVENTY

February 2015

I COULDN'T BELIEVE IT. When we got back to the motel, it was blocked by police cars. Even the ME was there. Weasel was in the parking lot talking to my parents. My colleagues were questioning the guests.

"What the heck is going on?" Shannon asked.

"I have no idea."

I stepped out of the car. Weasel approached me when she saw me. "Jack. Where the hell have you been? I've been calling you like crazy."

I reached into my pocket and pulled out my phone. "The sound's been shut off. I'm sorry. What's going on here?"

"What's going on? I'll tell you what. Hell on earth…that's what." Weasel sighed and rubbed the bridge of her nose. "You called the plumber this morning, right? You called Eric, right?"

"Yes. The sewer was clogged," I said.

"I bet it was," Weasel said. "Eric went in, and you'll never guess what he found." She paused for effect. "That's right. First, he found the drain to be packed with a flesh-like substance. Then he called his supervisor to assess the situation, thinking it looked like chicken meat, maybe from the restaurant. By the time they cleared the drain, they realized, on closer inspection, that it wasn't chicken leftovers. It was small bones and flesh. The pipe leading off from the drain was completely clogged with it. Yamilla is looking at it as we speak, but her first suspicion was that it was of human origin."

I felt sick to my stomach. I looked at Shannon, who was paler than Weasel's white shirt.

"Someone tried to dispose of a body," Weasel continued. "By chopping it up, then flushing it."

"Oh, my God," I said.

"I know," Weasel said. "We are going to have to shut down the motel and your

166

parents and their guests will have to find somewhere else to stay. I will also need your parents to stay in town."

"They didn't do it," I said angrily.

"I know they're probably innocent," Weasel said. "But until I can determine that for certain, they are our main suspects. I'm sorry, Jack. That's just the way it is. You know how these things work."

I did, and that was what scared the crap out of me. My parents had nothing to do with this. I knew they didn't, but I had to find evidence to prove it; otherwise, they would end up paying the price for this.

My mom looked terrified while she was speaking to Sheriff Ron. My dad had put his arm around her shoulder. I approached them.

"We have no idea. You must believe us," my mom said. When she saw me, her face lit up. I hugged her. She was shivering. Ron saw me and nodded.

"I was done here, anyway," he said and put a hand on my shoulder. "We'll figure this out. Don't worry."

"Thanks, Ron."

"Oh, Jack. This is terrible. What do we do?" my mother said. It was terrible to see her in this much distress. My dad looked pale and tired. This was too much commotion for him. For the both of them. I had to get them out of here.

I reached into my pocket and found the keys to my condo. I was so angry my hands were trembling.

"You stay at my place till this blows over. Now, tell me, where do I find a list of all your guests over the last three months?"

"The guestbook in the lobby," my mother said, her voice trembling. "But surely...you can't think that any of our guests could have..."

"Oh, I'm certain they did," I said. "And I'm going to find out who it was and bring them to justice. You trust in that. It just got personal."

Part Three

HIT THE ROAD

SEVENTY-ONE

February 2015

TWO DAYS LATER, we had a clearer picture of what had happened at my parents' motel. I had worked the crime scene with Yamilla for hours and hours and had very little sleep. The kids stayed with their grandparents at my condo, and so did Shannon. It had become a little cramped, but it worked out. Shannon wanted to check into a hotel, but I told her it was a bad idea for her to be alone. I think she agreed. She didn't protest.

So now, we were all living under the same roof. Luckily, my condo was big enough, even though it meant the three kids all had to sleep in the same room, not that they complained about that. On the contrary, they thought it was a party. Well, the twins did. Emily...not so much. But she didn't complain. My parents made sure the children were taken care of and made it to school while I worked.

By the end of the second day, Weasel came down to the motel and we went through what we knew so far.

"There seem to be two bodies," Yamilla said. "We're running the DNA samples to try to compare them with those of Melanie and Sebastian Schultz. They are the two missing persons we have around here, and therefore, the two most likely to be a match."

I took over. "Meanwhile, we have located the room where the body parts were being flushed from. Room one-fifteen. It's the room where Shannon King stayed with her daughter when the sewer clogged, but she hasn't been in it for very long. We believe it was the guest before her, last month, when Melanie and her son disappeared who did this, then vanished afterwards."

"Well, do we have a name?" Weasel asked.

"According to the books my parents kept, it was a Mrs. Hampton who stayed there for the whole month of January."

"A woman?" Weasel said. "What do we know about her?"

"She's been a regular for almost a year. Coming and going. Sometimes, she

170

stays for several weeks at a time. She checked in on January 3rd this year and stayed till January 29th, then came back a week ago on February 23rd and stayed in another room. She hasn't checked out, hasn't paid for her stay this time, but her room is empty."

"Any fingerprints?"

"The room hasn't been cleaned yet, so I'm hoping. So far, they haven't found anything. The techs just started working her room this morning. According to Jennifer, the cleaning lady at the motel, Mrs. Hampton never wanted her room cleaned while she was there, which is always respected. Jennifer remembers when Mrs. Hampton checked out in January from room one-fifteen. It was so clean, she hardly had to clean it. She believed Mrs. Hampton had cleaned it herself. Everything smelled like bleach, she said."

"Bleach, you say?" Weasel said and looked at me.

"I know. It sounds awfully familiar, doesn't it?" I said.

"What else do we know about this Mrs. Hampton?" Weasel asked.

"Not much," I said. "I've seen her around here. I remember helping her with her suitcase last time she checked in. She told my parents she lives up north, outside of Boston, and she comes here as often as she can to get away from the cold. I've tried to locate her, but she hasn't made it easy. Always paid cash. She left no trace. I don't even know which town outside of Boston she is from."

"So, she could basically vanish if she wanted to. I don't like this, Ryder. I really don't." Weasel exhaled.

I looked at Yamilla. "It's all we've got so far," I said. She confirmed it with a nod.

"So, what we believe now is that this woman brought bodies to the motel and dismembered them. She then flushed the body parts into the toilet?" Weasel sighed. "I...Is it really possible?"

"It's been done before," Yamilla said. "Dennis Nilsen was a killer in London who lured men into his apartment, then killed them and dismembered their bodies before he flushed them into the toilet. A lot like what happened here."

"Jeffrey Dahmer did something similar," I said.

"Yes, but he dissolved the body parts in acid first. He was smarter," Yamilla said. "He didn't clog the sewer."

"He also crushed the bones with a sledgehammer, but that's not important for this case," I said. "The point is, it has been done before. Our dear Mrs. Hampton might have gotten the idea from reading about Dennis Nilsen. Maybe that would be a trace worth following."

I had barely finished the sentence before my phone rang. It was Shannon. "I gotta take this," I said and stepped aside.

Weasel and Yamilla exchanged looks. They both smiled. "She's got you on speed-dial now?" Weasel said.

I ignored them.

"Jack?"

Her voice sounded upset.

"What's wrong?"

"I...I just got a call. Some guy told me he has Angela. He's asking for money. What do I do, Jack?"

"What? How did he get your number? I thought no one knew it?"

"He called my manager first. Told him he had Angela and that he would kill her if he said anything. Then, he asked for my number. Bruce gave it to him. Said he didn't dare do anything else. Oh, my God, Jack. This guy has my little girl. What do I do?"

SEVENTY-TWO

February 2015

SHANNON GRABBED a bottle of Xanax from her purse. She looked at herself in the bathroom mirror. Next to her was her phone. Her heart was pounding rapidly in her chest. The guy had sounded so creepy. He had told her he had Angela. She had told him she didn't believe him. Then he had texted her a photo. Angela sitting on a bed. She was still wearing the same dress she had been on the day she had disappeared. Shannon had started crying when she saw it. Angela looked good, though. That had been a comfort. She had a sad look on her face, but she seemed to have been well taken care of. That was a great relief. But after the relief over seeing her alive had settled, unease had rumbled inside of Shannon. The voice on the phone clearly wasn't Joe's. Neither was it one of his friends, none that Shannon knew of at least. It could be someone she had never met, but she was beginning to believe this had nothing to do with Joe anymore. Why would he be asking for money? In a divorce, he would get half of Shannon's money. He would never want for anything.

Angela had been kidnapped by someone else. But, who was he? Was he simply someone who saw an opportunity to score some money? Shannon had been warned about those. When you became a celebrity...that was the price you paid. People would look at you and smell money. Your kids were in constant danger of being abducted for a ransom. Shannon had known about it; she had heard about it and been warned, but never believed it would actually happen to her. Back in Tennessee, they lived a very protected life. Angela went to private school and was never let out of sight. They lived in a gated community with strict security, and they even had security guards of their own patrolling the house to make sure crazy fans didn't somehow come too close. It was the price of being a celebrity.

But, when Shannon had escaped from Joe without leaving a word to anyone else except Bruce, her manager, she had also left that security behind. She had believed she could stay hidden, that she could keep her presence in Cocoa Beach a secret, but now she knew it had been stupid to think so.

You're stupid, Shannon. So incredibly stupid!

Shannon grabbed the bottle of pills and felt it in her hand. She knew it was a bad idea. It was a slippery slope for her to take the pills, but she craved them more than ever. She wanted to make the pain stop, to sedate the voices in her mind that told her she was to blame for this, that it was all her own fault what had happened to Angela. She was going to pay the money. But she needed to calm herself down first.

Shannon opened the top of the bottle and took out a pill. She looked at her face in the mirror, and just as she was about to put it on her tongue, someone knocked on the door.

"Shannon?"

It was Jack. The sound of his voice made her hesitate. She knew very well what would happen to her once she took the pill. She would change. Her personality would alter.

"Shannon? Are you all right?" he said again.

You don't deserve him. He's too good for you.

"I'm fine," she said. "I'll be right out."

She put the pill on her tongue and reached for a glass of water. A strange sound came from behind the door. Someone was tampering with the lock. It clicked, and Jack stood in the doorway.

"Don't do it," he said when he saw the bottle of pills. "Please don't. You know what will happen. You're an addict. One pill will lead to another, and you won't be able to stop. Please, don't do it. I know it's hard right now. But we'll get your daughter home. At least we know she's alive. At least we have a chance now. Don't ruin it. Don't get her back and then neglect her by being an addict again. It might give you comfort now and make the pain go away for a little while, but it's not worth it, Shannon. Please, think of your daughter."

Shannon stared at the glass of water. The pill was still on her tongue. She felt tears piling up. Jack was right. He was so right. But, could she handle this? Could she go through this without easing the pain? Without sedation?

Shannon looked at herself in the mirror again. The bruises were healing nicely, and soon she would be able to walk around without covering her face. The bruises were connected to that old life of hers. Did she really want to go back to that life? Back to the abuse? The life in a constant daze?

Shannon turned her head towards the toilet, then spat out the pill and flushed. Jack approached her, grabbed her face between his hands and kissed her. She cried and threw herself in his arms. He wiped the tears away from her cheeks, then looked into her eyes.

"Now, let's go get her, shall we?"

"What about your case here? You have a lot on your plate?" Shannon asked. "Your parents…The motel?"

"It will have to wait," Jack said. "Angela is what counts now."

SEVENTY-THREE

February 2015

THE KIDNAPPER HAD TOLD Shannon to meet him at Ponce de Leon Landing, a park with a big parking lot close to Sebastian Inlet. He hadn't told her to come alone, so I insisted on coming along. There was no way she should do this alone. Besides, I was armed and she was not. She needed the protection.

We hit the road together.

Shannon transferred the money to the account she had been told to. It was registered in the Cayman Islands, so there was no way we would be able to trace the money afterwards. Two million dollars gone into cyberspace. Just like that.

With the printed out bank-statement as documentation in our hands, we drove to the parking lot. It was right on the beach, and I could smell the ocean as we got out of Shannon's rented SUV. There was a trail between the trees that led to the beach and the crashing waves. She gave me a terrified look, and I took her by the hand, as we walked to the meeting point, by some statue of Ponce de Leon.

We waited for fifteen minutes and nothing happened. Shannon was getting more and more anxious by the minute, and I couldn't blame her. This was nerve racking. I had never done a ransom exchange before and wondered if I should have gotten Ron and my colleagues at the Sheriff's Department in on it. Just to make sure we caught the bastard. But I had decided not to, and I was sticking to that decision. I didn't want to risk ruining it. Shannon didn't care about the money or the guy. She just wanted Angela back.

"You think he might have seen you and blown us off?" she asked.

"I don't know," I said.

"Oh, my God. We already transferred the money. Do you think he might have just taken it and run away?"

"I'm not going to lie to you, Shannon. It's a possibility. You can't trust a guy like that," I said.

Her eyes lost their light. I didn't like being the one doing that to her, but I had to be realistic. Coming here was dangerous for him. He would be seen. And he had no reason to come. Not now that he had already gotten the money. I told Shannon to tell him she wasn't going to transfer the money until she had Angela, but she didn't dare to. She was afraid of scaring him away and never seeing Angela again. She wanted to do everything he told her to, to make sure nothing went wrong. I couldn't blame her, but it left her with very small odds of actually getting what she wanted.

"You don't think he's coming, do you?" she asked nervously. She was biting her lips constantly. I wanted to take her in my arms and just hold her tight. I hated to see her like this.

Suddenly, something happened. A car drove past on the street. We both looked at it in anticipation, our hearts thumping in our chests. But it wasn't what we expected it to be. It wasn't Angela. Instead, whoever was in the truck, rolled down the window and fired a shot at us.

"Get down," I yelled and jumped on top of Shannon. More shots were fired while we hid behind the statue, before the truck's wheels screeched and it disappeared again.

"Oh, my God. What was that?" Shannon shrieked.

I removed myself from her. "Are you all right?" I asked.

"I think so. Are you?"

"Yes. I wasn't hit either."

"You think that was the kidnapper?" Shannon asked.

"Yes. I believe it must have been."

"But…" Shannon was about to cry. "What about Angela? Where is Angela?"

"She's not here, and I have a feeling she's not going to be either. Come, let's get back to the car. I think I got a look at the license plate. I'm not letting this bastard get away."

SEVENTY-FOUR

October 1998

SHE WAS SO FED up with her family. Annie served dinner on the night after the incident where her teenage son accidentally caught her on the couch with the handsome officer. She had yelled at him and told him to go to his room, then gone back to the officer, who had told her it was best if he left. She was disappointed to see him go and so angry with her son for interrupting the one good thing she had in her life. Maybe, possibly, destroying it for her. What if seeing her son made the officer have second thoughts? What if he was scared away and decided never to come again?

"Here's the lasagna," she said, and threw the dish on the table.

Victor was smiling from ear to ear, as always when he came home from work. "Smells delicious," he chirped.

What are you so happy about, you ugly pig?

Their son was sitting at the table, looking at her with his small evil eyes, his nostrils flaring. Annie didn't care about him or what he thought he had seen. She was fed up with him, and with Victor as well. She had wasted so much of her life on them.

"So, how was your day, Son?" Victor asked, obviously not noticing the tension between the boy and his mother. That was Victor for you. He never understood what was going on right beneath his nose. He always believed the best in people, with the result that he was always run over by everyone, the wimp.

"Eventful," their son answered, still with his eyes fixated on Annie.

"Wonderful," Victor said, and scooped up the lasagna with his fork. He even ate ugly. Chewed with his mouth open, smacked his lips, and drank noisily. Their dinners were like torture to Annie.

"And you, dear?" Victor said, addressed to Annie.

She sighed. "Nothing much. The usual stuff."

"Wonderful," Victor said.

That was when the boy dropped his fork onto the plate with a loud sound. Annie jumped in her seat.

"That's it!" the boy yelled. "I've had it. Stop pretending everything is fine. Stop acting like we're a happy little family!"

Victor looked, appalled, at his son. "Son, what has gotten into you?"

"I'll tell you what has gotten into me, Dad. Today, I came home early from school, since some of my classes were suspended, and guess who I found? Yes, that's right. Mommy dear on the couch in the arms of another man." He looked at Annie. "That's right. Mom is cheating on you, Dad, and you don't even have a clue."

Victor's face froze. He stared at Annie without making a sound. Annie felt her heart rate go up. Victor scared her a little. She felt bad that he had to find out about it this way. What would he do? How would he react? Would he throw her out? She would have nothing. He wouldn't do that, would he?

"All we ever wanted was for you to love us, Mom," the son continued. "Don't you think I know? Don't you think I've noticed that you've avoided me all my life? Do you really think I don't know that you only tolerate me and Dad in your life?"

Annie swallowed hard. He was right. That was how she had always felt, but hearing it from his mouth made it sound so awful; it sounded like she was a terrible person.

"Is this true?" Victor asked, his voice trembling. "Did you sleep with someone... here in our home?"

Annie didn't look at him at first. When she did, she saw tears streaming across his cheeks.

"I...Victor...I..."

Victor shook his head. "I can't believe it. I gave you everything. I gave up everything for you. I married you when...when no one else wanted to. I made an honest woman out of you. I bought you that house. I gave up all I had when my mother told me to leave you, when she found out about...that he wasn't my son."

The boy stared at his father, then back at his mother. "Victor is not my real dad?"

It was like the entire ground beneath Annie had opened up and started to swallow her up. She had no idea how to resist falling, how to stay up anymore. There was room for no more lies, no more deceit. She simply couldn't anymore.

"I...I..."

"I can't believe this, Victor said. "You never loved me, did you? You never loved either of us."

Annie had no idea how to answer that, and hesitated just long enough for him to know how she really felt. Victor broke down and cried, then got up and stormed out on the balcony, where he kept all of his chemicals for his pool business. He grabbed a bucket of acid, brought it with him inside, then took one last glance at Annie, and with the words, goodbye, cruel world, he poured the acid over himself.

After that, there was nothing but screaming.

SEVENTY-FIVE

February 2015

HE FELT GOOD ABOUT HIMSELF. The Snakecharmer felt so good about what he had done. He didn't mean to actually kill them, but he had scared them just enough to let them know he was the one in control. They weren't.

And now, he had the money. He never intended to give the girl back to her awful mother. Not after what she did. Not after she slept with Jack Ryder while still married to someone else. It was simply not tolerated.

Just like he hadn't tolerated it when his own mother had done it. It had destroyed everything for him. His dad had tried to commit suicide, but survived, bound to a wheelchair, blind and disfigured for the rest of his life. And she had done all this to him. She was the one who had destroyed the man.

That was why she had to pay for what she had done. Just like every other woman the Snakecharmer encountered who thought it was okay to mess around while married. But, it wasn't okay; it wasn't something that went by easily. It always destroyed the family, and worst of all, it destroyed the children.

After his dad had come back from the hospital, the Snakecharmer's mother was no longer there. The Snakecharmer told his father she had run away, but it was a lie. The fact was, the Snakecharmer had killed her. She was his first. He had strangled her with his bare hands, then dismembered her and thrown her in a dumpster. No one ever found her. Today, the Snakecharmer knew it had been risky back then, since today he knew better how to dispose of a body. But he had been lucky. Later in life, when his girlfriend had cheated on him, he had killed her too, and made it look like a breaking and entering gone wrong.

He now knew why God had put him on this forsaken planet...he knew what his mission was. He had heard God tell him in church one day. He was to rid the earth of these mothers who ruined everything. He was to save those children who were hurt. That was his mission, and he would live up to it.

For years, he hadn't killed anyone. He married well for himself and didn't find any need to do it, not until the bitch cheated on him. And on top of it, she did it

179

while their daughter had been sleeping in the next room. The Snakecharmer had been away; he had been on one of his casino trips to Atlanta with a friend of his when it happened. His wife had been with her lover when the baby in the next room stopped breathing. She hadn't even noticed until the next morning, when lover boy was gone, and she had finally paid attention to her baby.

Sudden Infant Death Syndrome, they had called it. There wasn't anything she could have done, the doctors told them afterwards. But the Snakecharmer didn't believe that. He believed Laura had killed their baby because she was too busy sleeping with someone else to check on her. Laura believed it too. Till the day he killed her. She knew. She was tormented by guilt. She told him it would never happen again. Yet, she continued to see other men, and a year after the death of their child, the Snakecharmer realized she had started seeing a new one. That's when he knew he had to kill her. Her and anyone else cheating. Before he killed her, he started spying on people at the local motels around town, checking in as Mrs. Hampton, wearing a fat suit, a dress, a wig, and sunglasses. He spotted the lying cheating bitches and planned it all out. Often the affairs began at the motels, but later they became more reckless and often started seeing each other in their homes, having sex on the sheets of their marital bed. It was always the same pattern.

The Snakecharmer was good at covering his tracks. And he would have been able to get rid of Laura's body as well, if he hadn't been interrupted by the dog. It was his own fault, though. He knew that much. He had spent too much time on his little ritual, on washing her and sitting with his head in her lap. He liked to do that to his victims, like he had done to his mother after he killed her. He had kept her in his room for days, while his father was in the hospital. He had slept with her in his bed and sat with his head in her lap, pretending she was caressing him like he had always dreamt she would. He had finally been close to his mother like he had longed for all of his childhood. Finally, she was there for him. All of his childhood, he had feared his mother would leave him. Every day he was afraid she would be gone when he came back from school. He knew that was what she wanted. He knew she didn't want to stay with him. He wasn't enough reason for her to stay. But now, he didn't have to be scared anymore.

Finally, she couldn't leave.

SEVENTY-SIX

February 2015

I CALLED Joel at the station and asked him to run the license plate. Meanwhile, Shannon and I drove up A1A, looking for the truck.

We drove across the bridge to the mainland and tried all the motels we could find to see if the truck was there. Shannon was anxious and constantly biting her nails, but another side to her had also shown itself. A determined side that wanted to find Angela and get her home. We had been so close, and Shannon was certain her daughter had to be close by.

I thought she was right.

We had pulled in at a Motel 6 when my phone rang. It was Yamilla.

"I have something I want to run by you," she said. "Something that has been bothering me since the beginning of the case of Laura Bennett's murder."

"Yes. Fire away," I said and shut off the engine. Shannon looked frantically at her phone and found the picture of Angela for the fifteenth time today.

"I was just wondering about the husband. The case file says he was drugged with Rohypnol."

"Yes, they found it in his blood. That's why he didn't see anything or hear anything."

"But, it also says he was out cold for twenty-four hours afterwards. After he was taken to the hospital," Yamilla said.

"Yes. He was still sedated," I said. I had no idea where she was going with this.

"I was just wondering about it because usually you get knocked out like half an hour after you are slipped the drug, and with the amount he had, he would be knocked out cold for twenty-four hours. It just seems a little strange, don't you think? That he was awake and able to talk when the police came, but then out for twenty-four hours afterwards."

And that was when the last piece finally came into place. "You're saying he drugged himself. He knew the police were coming, then slipped himself some

Rohypnol, and half an hour later he was out. The drug in his blood would show in the tests afterwards. That was his way of getting away with murder."

"It's a theory," she said.

"And a very good one," I said.

I hung up and looked at Shannon. This new information was important, but not as important as getting Angela back.

"Shall we take a look?" I asked.

Shannon sniffled and nodded. We got out of the car and walked across the parking lot, looking at all the plates. This new information was flickering through my head. So, Brandon Bennett had killed his own wife? But why? And had he also killed Janelle? And what about Judge Martin and Melanie and her son? I thought about old Mrs. Hampton, who had stayed in room one-fifteen, when suddenly I spotted the truck in front of a room. I grabbed the handle of my gun and approached it to be sure. I double checked the numbers. It was the same.

"He's here," I said to Shannon.

She lit up. "You found it? Does that mean Angela is here as well?"

"That's what we're about to find out."

SEVENTY-SEVEN

February 2015

SHANNON COULD HARDLY CONTAIN her anxiety. Could it really be? Was Angela at the motel? Was she somewhere behind one of those many blue doors with numbers on them? Jack was speaking with the woman behind the counter. She was slightly reluctant in giving him the information, even after seeing Jack's badge and hearing how it was all part of an ongoing investigation.

Kidnapping, he called it.

"I'm not happy about this," she said, as she gave him the number of the room belonging to the owner of the truck outside. "This is a place where our guests can have their privacy."

Jack got the number, then grumbled something Shannon didn't hear before he returned to her. "Got it," he said. "Room 202."

Shannon was biting her nails. She was so scared. Jack was armed, and she watched him as his hand rested on the shaft of the gun in his belt. She'd never liked guns. Shannon had grown up on a farm, where guns were a part of life. Until her brother accidentally shot and killed himself one day. Since then, Shannon had believed guns were the worst thing man ever had created. Next to religion. Shannon loved God, but she hated religion. She never believed God meant for us to have religion. Just like he never meant for us to have guns to kill each other.

But, right now, she was glad Jack had one. There was no telling what this kidnapper was up to. Not after he tried to shoot them down in that parking lot.

Jack stopped and looked at her. "You better stay back," he said. "If this guy starts shooting again..."

"I wanna be there. I want to see my daughter," she said, pressing the tears back. She missed Angela so terribly now it was unbearable. To know that she might be this close now...she didn't want Jack to know how scared she really was. How terrified she was of losing her daughter in this motel.

"Okay. But stay behind me, all right?" Jack said with worried eyes. He too was concerned about how this was going to go down. He had wanted to involve more police and call for back up, but Shannon had begged him not to. It would only make the situation worse, if the kidnapper felt he was up against a wall. He would only harm Angela, she said.

"All I want is to get my daughter back—alive," she had told him.

She could tell by his eyes that he agreed with her. Calling for more police might escalate the situation to an extent where it got out of control. He didn't want that either. If the kidnapper felt like he still had a chance to get away, then he might be more open to negotiations. Shannon would be willing to give him more money, if he wanted. She didn't care about money. He could have everything she owned, for all she cared. She had been poor before. And she had been a whole of a lot happier then than she was now.

"The lady at the desk told me there were three kids in the room, two boys and a girl," Jack said with a low voice. "I don't know who those boys are, but I'm guessing they're not his. But this means we need to be very careful to not hurt any of the children. I will not shoot unless it is entirely necessary, do you understand? So, don't do anything unless I tell you to. All right?"

Shannon bit her lip. It was getting numb from all the biting. She nodded. She was glad he was being careful.

She held her breath as Jack clenched his fist and knocked on the door. A rather heavy woman opened the door. She was wearing a flowery dress and sunglasses. She was holding a baby in her arms. She smiled.

"Yes?"

SEVENTY-EIGHT

February 2015

"WELL, HELLO THERE, OFFICER JACK," the woman said.

I stared at her. She looked like Mrs. Hampton, but how could it be? I had only seen her a few times at the motel, but I was pretty sure it was her. But, who was the baby in her arms? It looked an awful lot like Sebastian Schultz...

What the heck was going on?

I was confused, but one thing I did know for certain. Something was very wrong here. My hand resting on the handle of my gun tightened its grip. I really didn't want to have to pull my gun and endanger the life of the child in her arms and whoever else was in the room behind her.

"I had a feeling you might stop by," she said. The baby in her arms burst into tears. The woman tried to comfort her. As she moved her arm, I spotted a gun underneath her dress. She pulled it out and held it to the child's head. Shannon gasped behind me.

"Lose the gun, Officer, or the kid dies."

I pulled it out and placed it on the ground. Mrs. Hampton picked it up. "Now, get in here," she said. "Hands where I can see them."

We both put our hands behind our necks and walked inside the motel room. Mrs. Hampton closed the door behind us and locked it.

"Mommy!"

Angela ran towards Shannon and threw herself in her arms. Shannon was shaking heavily as she held her daughter in her arms. Tears were streaming across her face. Angela's hair had been colored and cut short.

"Where were you, Mommy? I couldn't find you."

"I was looking for you, sweetie. And now I found you. I'm so happy to have found you."

"Mommy, the man has a gun," she said.

I turned and looked at Mrs. Hampton. She put the baby down, then removed her sunglasses. Looking into her chilly black eyes, I immediately recognized who was hiding behind them.

It was Brandon Bennett.

"You?"

"Yes, me, Officer Jack Ryder. Thanks for all the help with my suitcases, by the way. You sure are helpful to a lady. Especially when the suitcases are as heavy as dead body weight."

I felt sick to my stomach. "You had them in the suitcases, didn't you? Your victims? You had Melanie and Sebastian Schultz in the suitcases?"

"I like my women light," he said with a grin, as the wig came off. "But, no. I would never do that to a child. Will here was always with me."

Brandon Bennett handed the baby a pacifier to make him calm. Sebastian Schultz stopped crying and sucked eagerly on the pacifier. He found a block that he started playing with. He seemed like he was well fed and had been well taken care of. I couldn't believe it.

"What's going on, Dad?" It was Ben. He came out from the restroom.

"We have visitors," Brandon Bennett said. "You remember Detective Jack Ryder, right?"

Ben nodded and sat on the bed. I wondered if he knew what his dad had been up to lately.

Brandon Bennett took off the dress and zipped down his fat suit. "Boy, it gets warm in these things," he said. "Son, could you help me a little?" Ben got up and helped his dad get out of the female body suit. Brandon made sure to still be pointing his gun at us while getting out. Underneath, he was wearing a shirt and pants. His sweat had left marks under the armpits of his light blue shirt. He picked up a fake moustache and put it on. It looked awfully real.

"I must admit," he said. "I was tempted to finish you off at the parking lot, while I had the chance. But I was hoping you would follow me here. You see, Officer, we have a lot to talk about. Now, please sit down."

He pointed the gun at two chairs he had placed in the middle of the room, back to back. Shannon and I looked at one another. There was no way around it. We had to do as he told us. For the children's sake. We sat down with our backs to each other and Brandon Bennett grabbed a roll of duct tape and started taping us to the chairs, then taping my hands in front of me, putting tape on my wrists.

"They always do this in the movies," he said, grinning.

"You watch way too much TV," I said.

"Well, that's what happens when your wife inherits millions. You don't have to work. There isn't much to do when you don't have to work, is there? Well, I could go out and have an affair like so many other men, but my wife beat me to it, didn't she? Ah, you know all about that, Officer Jack."

"I know some," I said, thinking about Tom. Had Brandon Bennett killed his wife because she slept with Tom?

"Yeah, but there is a lot you don't know."

"Like what? Tell me. Explain all this to me," I said.

"Please, sir. Please don't tie up my mother," Angela said. "Don't hurt her. She's a good mother. I promise you."

"NO!" Brandon yelled. "No, she is not a good mother!" His hand was shaking as he pointed the gun at Shannon's head.

Angela cried. "Please. Please, don't hurt her."

"She's about to ruin everything," he yelled so hard spit was flying. "She needs to understand that when you fool around you DESTROY lives. Children's lives. Husband's lives. Everything falls apart. Everything."

I was starting to see a picture. "Your mother cheated, didn't she?" I asked Brandon. "She cheated on you and your father? She hurt you. Both of you. Is that why you hurt Melanie? Is that why you hurt Laura? Because they were cheating? Did you hurt your mother as well?"

Brandon looked at me. His nostrils were flaring rapidly. He looked like a madman. It terrified me.

"I made her stay with me," he said, his voice cracking. "She hurt us, so I hurt her so she couldn't leave us. I made her stay with me. I made her love me."

"Just like you did to Laura and Melanie. You killed your mother, but it didn't satisfy your need, your desire; it didn't make the pain go away. So now, you keep killing her over and over again. Starting with Janelle, your girlfriend."

Brandon Bennett stared at me, pointing the gun at my face. His anger turned into a smile.

"I've been looking forward to having this little chat with you, Officer Jack Ryder," he said. "Or should I say, Detective? Yes, you have come far in your career, haven't you? Homicide detective. Just like your old man. Before he retired and became a motel owner."

I froze. What was this? How did he know about my dad? He had been a detective back in Ft. Lauderdale, but that was many years ago. He had retired early.

"How do you know about my father?" I asked.

"Ah, you don't know, do you? Let's just say I bumped into him once...in my apartment. What was he doing there? Oh, yes, that's right. He was doing MY MOTHER!"

187

SEVENTY-NINE

February 2015

I COULDN'T BELIEVE my own ears. Was he really saying what I thought he was? My dad? My father? Albert Ryder? Cheating on his wife of forty years? No. It couldn't be. I was shocked. My mother and father were so into each other. They loved each other; they would never...he would never.

"Yeah, that's right," Brandon Bennett continued. "Your beloved father slept with my mother and destroyed my entire existence. Why do you think I chose his motel? Why do you think you're sitting here?"

"So, you're doing this to me because of my dad?" I asked. "You want to kill me?"

Brandon Bennett laughed loudly. "Oh, I have something better in mind. You see, I have already done something to you."

My heart dropped. I thought about the children. Abigail, Austin, Emily. Had he hurt them somehow? Then, I thought about my parents. Had he hurt my parents? The blood was rushing through my veins. My anger was rising at the very thought of him being close to anyone in my family.

Brandon Bennett reached into his pocket and pulled out something. He held it between his fingers in front of my face. My heart stopped.

It was a ring. A very special ring.

"How did you get that?" I asked, trying to get out of the chair.

"I took it off her finger," he said, holding it up in the light. "As a souvenir. After I killed her back in 2012."

I went completely numb. Every cell in my body screamed in pain. "You killed her? You killed Arianna?"

Brandon Bennett's eyes shone when he looked at me. "Yes. Isn't it beautiful? Your dad destroyed my family, and now I have destroyed his. You and your kids have been miserable without her. And now you know why she never came back. She was on her way, though. I found her in North Carolina. She wanted to come back to you; she told her friend at the diner where she had worked for a couple of months while figuring her life out. She told her friend she was going back to

Cocoa Beach the following week to be with her husband and children...that she had been thinking it through and realized what she had. That she loved you and the kids, but just needed some time. Isn't it perfect? I grabbed her in her studio, sedated her, and took her to the motel. To your father's motel. I kept her there for a week before I strangled her in the bathtub. I sedated her, then when she woke up, I let her watch her children come and go from the window. The desperation on her face was priceless. She whimpered when she could hear their little voices. Oh, how badly she wanted to be with them again. I sedated her with chloroform and washed her every night. Washed her with bleach to clean the impurity from the other man she had slept with. I even sang to her. You want to know what I sang?"

I couldn't even answer. I wanted to scream; I wanted to yell, but I couldn't. I was too stunned, too torn apart in pain and sorrow. I could hardly breathe.

"You really can't guess it? I sang Hit the Road, Jack, of course," he said, and laughed. "No, seriously. I did you a favor there. She was sleeping around. Would have made you so miserable if she had ever come back to you. Once a cheater always a cheater."

If I hadn't been tied down, I would have killed him on the spot. The cruelty of what he had done felt like a kick in the stomach. I had no more words. Shannon was crying next to me.

"You sick bastard," she yelled at him.

Brandon Bennett walked to her and knelt in front of her. He stroked her cheek. I could sense how she shivered in terror and anger.

"I know Joe didn't treat you right," he said. "But that's not an excuse for sleeping around like some WHORE!"

Shannon jumped when he yelled at her. Angela cried. I tried to gather my thoughts. I kept picturing Arianna. It hurt so badly inside of me, knowing she had been so close, knowing I could have saved her, had I only known she was right there, right in that room where I walked past every day when picking up the children from the school bus. Arianna hadn't left me and stayed away. She had wanted to come back. She had been planning on it. Oh, the terror of knowing this. I didn't know if I would ever be able to live with that knowledge.

"Now," Brandon Bennett said, and looked at us. "I have to figure out what to do with the two of you. The kids and I have to go, you see. We're flying out tonight from Ft. Lauderdale to Grand Cayman, where all this nice money is waiting for us, and where no one can reach us. We might stay there, we might continue to another island, who knows? At least the kids will be safe from their parents and all their crap. But first, I have to get rid of her," he said, and pointed the gun at Shannon. "Jack, I'll let you live. I need you to remember what I did to you for every day for the rest of your life. I need you to tell your father what he did and what I did in return. Otherwise, it will all be in vain, right?"

I had stopped looking at him. Instead, my eyes had locked with those of Ben. Something had stirred inside of him. I looked at my gun on the dresser, where Brandon had put it, then back at Ben, who now saw it too.

EIGHTY

February 2015

"It ends here, Dad."

The gun in Ben's hands was shaking heavily. So was his voice when he spoke.

Brandon Bennett turned around and looked at his son, who was pointing the gun at him. My gun. I had no idea if the kid had ever held one in his hands before, let alone fired one. Would he be able to fire at his dad if he had to? I wasn't so sure. He was, after all, just five years old.

"Ben? What the...? What are you doing, buddy? We're a team, remember? You and me?"

Ben shook his head. He was sweating heavily. "Not any more, Dad. You killed Mom. I can't let this go on anymore. It's not right, Dad. What we're doing is not right."

Brandon Bennett was getting angry now. He took a couple of steps towards his son. Ben walked backwards.

"I will shoot you," Ben said.

Brandon Bennett stopped when he saw the seriousness in his son's eyes. "Give me the gun," he said. "Hand it over. Ben, you listen to me, Son. I don't want to hurt you. Not again, Son."

Ben started crying now. I could tell he was about to cave. He couldn't stand up to his father. At least, I thought he couldn't, but a new strength suddenly showed in him. He was crying, but also snorting in anger.

"You killed Mom," he said. "You told me you were asleep. You told me you didn't see who did it. You lied to me, Dad. You killed her. I just heard you say you did. And other women. You killed them too. They were somebody's mom, Dad. I don't care what Mom did to you. She's still my mom."

"Don't make me shoot you, Ben," Brandon Bennett yelled. "I will if I have to, Son."

The two of them were pointing their guns at each other. This was a bad situation. I feared it would end very badly.

Meanwhile, I had made eye contact with Angela and signaled her to come closer. To get out of the shooting range, in case shots were fired. She walked silently behind Brandon Bennett without him noticing it and hid behind a recliner. I put my hands high above my head and came down past my hips, causing the duct tape to split and my hands to get free.

"You always were an ungrateful kid. A real mommy's boy, huh? Well, I can get by without you."

This was going in the wrong direction.

I reached down and grabbed the duct tape on my feet and ripped it off, then sprang for Brandon's back, just as he fired a shot towards Ben.

Shannon screamed and so did Angela, while Sebastian cried from his play area on the floor. I landed on top of Brandon Bennett. The fall made the gun fly out of his hand. I threw in a couple of punches to his face and knocked him out immediately. Being an amateur boxer in my teen-years, I knew exactly how to do that to make sure he wouldn't get up anytime soon. Then I rushed towards Ben, who was on the floor in a pool of blood. Angela helped her mother get loose. Ben's small body was pulsing and he was shivering with cold already. I took off my T-shirt and tried to stop the blood with it, then screamed for Shannon to call 911.

"Don't leave us, Ben," I cried. "Stay here. Stay with us."

Epilogue

MARCH 2015

IT WAS a beautiful funeral ceremony at Club Zion, our local church, where Ben used to come with his mother. We were singing hymns. Shannon stood by my side, along with all of our kids and my parents. I couldn't believe all that had happened in the past couple of months. I still hadn't recuperated from what Brandon Bennett had told me about my father and Arianna. I hadn't asked my mother about any of it, whether she knew my dad had cheated or not. I decided to let it go. It was, after all, none of my business. They seemed to be doing well now and loved each other dearly. That was all I needed to know. I had decided to leave it all behind me and move on. Even Arianna.

Pastor Daniel took the stage.

"We're gathered here today to say goodbye to Ben..." The pastor paused. All eyes were on him.

"...'s right arm."

I looked at Ben, who was standing in front of the church with his dog on one side and his grandfather in a wheelchair on the other. He had lost his arm, where his dad had shot him. The boy had been depressed for days afterwards while lying in the hospital, even when his grandfather had brought him the dog. Nothing seemed to cheer him up. So, I had come up with the idea of performing a ceremony for his arm in the church, a funeral, where he could say goodbye to it. I got the idea from one of my favorite movies, Fried Green Tomatoes.

Ben had loved it, and luckily, my good friend and surf buddy, Pastor Daniel, liked the idea as well. I was happy to soothe things a little for the poor kid. He was about to leave town to go live with his aunt, the oldest of John Platt's children. She had told us she would take care of him, even though she hadn't known Laura at all.

"Family sticks together no matter what, right?" she had said when we contacted her, telling her Ben had no one else.

I felt reassured she would take good care of him. She had a husband and another kid of her own. She would provide a real family for Ben. And he needed a stable home more than anyone right now.

Brandon Bennett had been taken to a secure prison, while awaiting his trial. I was building a case against him that, hopefully, would end up keeping him in there for the rest of his life. I had, little by little, found out what he had been up to. How he had done it. He had stolen an Animal Control van many years ago, down in Ft. Lauderdale. We found the report from when it was reported stolen. He had used it to spy on the women he planned on attacking. We had found snakes at his father's house, and my theory was that he had used them to get access to these women's houses. He had simply let the snakes into their garages, and then appeared on their doorsteps and told them he was from Animal Control. No one suspected a van from Animal Control when parked in a driveway or on the street. I still didn't know exactly how many women he had killed, but he had taken pictures of his victims with his phone, and that told an entire story of its own.

My first thought was I hoped that he would get the death penalty, but now I hoped he would just suffer for the rest of his life, knowing what he had done. It was a much worse fate than death. Besides, the death penalty was very rarely used in Florida.

Sebastian Schultz had been reunited with his father and so far they stayed with his parents till the insurance came through. He hadn't suffered any abuse or neglect while he was kidnapped according to the doctors. I hoped the boy was too young to remember what had happened to him when he grew older.

To my joy, Shannon had decided to stay in Cocoa Beach for a little longer. To get back on her feet, as she explained to the press, who soon got to hear about the entire kidnapping story and plastered it all over the newspapers and magazines. It was harder for her to avoid the spotlight now, but they still didn't know about her hideout in my apartment, where we were all staying, since my parents' motel wasn't done being examined. So far, we weren't getting on each other's nerves. I actually enjoyed having all of them close to me immensely. Especially after what had happened. Family was my top priority. And Shannon and Angela had quickly become a part of ours. Joe wasn't too happy when she told him she wasn't coming back to Nashville anytime soon, and they were facing a custody battle. It wasn't over yet. Far from it. But, we decided not to worry about it. Now was the time to heal our wounds.

I hadn't told the twins or Emily that Arianna had died yet. I would get to that eventually, and I was waiting for the right moment. First, I needed to come to terms with it myself. Yamilla had already identified the few bone-parts of the other body found at the motel as belonging to Arianna. A DNA-test confirmed it. So, it was official now. I was a widower.

"I have a surprise for you," Shannon said, when we came back to the apartment after the ceremony. She told me to close my eyes while she led me by the hand into the living room.

"Open your eyes," she said.

My eyes landed on the most beautiful orange and black 7.0 foot fun-shaped board I had ever seen in my life.

"What's this?" I asked.

"It's for me," she said. "I found a local shaper to make it for me."

"For you?"

"Yeah. I thought you could teach me how to surf while I'm here."

I laughed and kissed her. The twins made yuck-sounds behind us. They loved Shannon, and liked having her and Angela around, but didn't like it when we kissed publicly. They would have to get used to it.

"On one condition," I said.

"And what's that?"

"You teach me how to play the guitar."

Shannon smiled, then reached out her hand.

"That's a deal, Detective."

THE END

Slip Out the Back Jack

JACK RYDER #2

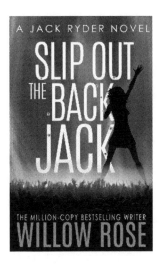

There must be fifty ways to leave your lover

~Paul Simon 1975

Prologue

FOUR BODIES CAST four shadows on the barren walls behind them. The scarce glow from the candle placed on the table in the middle lights up their faces. They take turns with the knife, cutting their thumbs open. A drop of blood lands on the dark wooden table. Eyes meet across the room. Determined eyes. All four thumbs are pressed against each other, one by one. Blood is shared, secrets buried. The pact is made. The four of them know that there is no way back from here.

This is where it begins.

ONE

November 2009

"HURRY UP. We're going to be late."

Maggie Foster's daughter looked impatiently at her mother. Maggie was getting her two year-old out of the Toyota. "I'm doing this as fast as I can," she groaned.

"We'll miss the movie," her daughter continued. "We need to get popcorn too."

"Hey," her father, Dan, said. "You be nice to your mother or we're not going to the movies at all."

Maggie sent her husband a friendly smile. Her oldest daughter had been giving her mother a hard time lately. She was fifteen and acting like a real teenager. Maggie often wondered if it was just due to the fact that her baby sister took up a lot of the attention that she was used to getting or if it was just an age thing.

Her oldest daughter groaned and rolled her eyes at her father.

"Watch it," he said.

Maggie managed to get the baby out and put her on her hip, while Dan took out the stroller from the back. It was late Friday afternoon. The parking lot was already packed behind the mall. There were a lot of people that—like the Fosters—had chosen to spend their Friday night at the mall. Maggie hoped not all of them were going to the movies. A two year-old made a lot of noise and had a hard time sitting still, even if it was *The Princess and the Frog*. Hopefully, there would be other young kids present, so they wouldn't be the only ones destroying it for everyone else.

It was the first time Maggie had taken her youngest to the movie theater. And she did it only to please her oldest daughter, who constantly complained that they never did anything fun anymore—not since *the baby* came into their lives. Maggie wanted to prove to her daughter that they could still do the same things as they used to.

Now, as she walked towards the colorful building housing the mall and movie

201

theater, she wasn't so sure it was a good idea anymore. She had this feeling in the bottom of her stomach that wouldn't leave.

Maggie stopped as they reached the front doors of the mall. The baby was already fussing in her arms. She was sweating from holding her. It was another hot afternoon in Boca Raton, north of Miami. Usually, Maggie loved the heat, but today it had been bothering her. Maybe she was coming down with something.

"Maybe we shouldn't..." she said.

Her oldest daughter growled. "I knew it!"

Dan looked at Maggie. "Are you not feeling alright?"

"But...but, you promised!" their daughter whined.

"I know, sweetie," Maggie said.

"You can't break a promise. You just can't." Their daughter was holding it together, but Maggie could tell she was about to crack. She looked at her husband. Everything inside of her screamed that she didn't want to do this, that she had to get herself back into the car and drive home, but how could she? How could she break her daughter's heart like that?

"I won't," Maggie said, sounding as reassuring as possible. "I'm just tired. It's okay."

Her daughter's eyes lit up. "So, we can go see the movie?"

Dan looked at Maggie. She smiled to convince him it was all right. He would cancel the entire thing if he suspected she wasn't well. The baby was crying. Maggie shushed her to make her calm down, and then gave her the binky. It was going to be hard with her inside the movie theater, but she was going to do it. For her daughter's sake.

"Are you sure?" Dan asked.

Maggie forced a smile and grabbed the door. "I'm sure. Let's go. I can't wait to watch this movie."

TWO

November 2009

THE MALL WAS CROWDED, as always. Teenagers were everywhere, hanging out in the food court and by Claire's. Brad Schmidt remembered when he used to be one of those teenagers, hanging out on a Friday night, looking at the girls. He still liked to look every now and then at the young girls, but made sure his wife didn't notice.

"You want more?" Gabby asked their daughter, Ally.

Ally shook her head.

"Eat the rest," Brad said.

"I'm full," Ally said.

"We paid for this sandwich, so you eat the rest," Brad continued.

"But..." Ally looked at him, but he wasn't going to cave. And she knew it. Brad felt his face turning red in anger.

"Eat it," he said, raising his voice.

Ally looked into her father's eyes and knew there was no way she was winning this. She looked at her mother, who turned her face away, avoiding the glare of the other people in the food court. Brad clenched his fist under the table. He couldn't believe she would defy him like this in public. She would have to hear about this later.

Ally picked up the sandwich and took another bite.

Brad felt the blood calm in his veins. He took in a deep breath and smiled.

"Good girl," he said.

When she was done, Gabby crumbled the Subway wrapper and threw it away. Brad swallowed the rest of his sandwich and washed it down with his Coke. He was looking forward to an evening in the movie theater, just stuffing his face with popcorn and soda. He would probably get a candy bar or two as well, while he was at it, and hopefully without Gabby seeing it. She hated how much weight he had gained over the last couple of years and was always on his case about it. He didn't mind too much. After all, he had nailed the girl, he had a great job where he didn't have to move much, but could stay behind his computer all day, and he had a beautiful daughter. He was happy and wanted to enjoy life. It wasn't like Gabby was that slim anymore either.

They got up and threw away the trash, then walked towards the theater that was already packed with people. They got in line, and when it was their turn, showed the usher their tickets to *The Princess and the Frog*, the movie Ally had been asking to see for several weeks now. Brad didn't care what movie it was, as long as he could sit in the dark and eat without anyone demanding anything of him.

"Anyone need to pee?" Gabby asked, looking at their daughter. Ally nodded. "Good. Come on," Gabby said, and pulled her daughter towards the restrooms.

Brad sat down on a bench to wait. He looked at his watch, wondering if he should just go inside and get some seats while there were still some good ones left. He looked at the popcorn boxes and drinks that Gabby had put down on the bench next to him. He could hardly carry it all on his own, and there was no way he could leave it out here. Someone might take it. No, he had to wait. They would be quick if the line wasn't too long in there.

Brad grabbed his phone and silenced it. Might as well do it right away. A couple walked past him and smiled. He nodded.

"How're you doing?"

A couple of teenagers giggled as they walked past him and disappeared into another movie. Brad wasn't looking forward to his daughter reaching that age. He couldn't bear to think of her as this monster, this erratic creature who would hate her parents and the world they lived in. He hadn't been too good himself, the way he had behaved back then. But she wouldn't be like that. Not his Ally. He had raised her better than that...with tough love, the way his own parents had raised him. It was for her own good. To keep her out of trouble later in life.

Brad's eyes met those of his daughter as she walked out of the restroom. His heart melted. No, Ally wasn't going to be anything like those girls. She was Daddy's girl. She was going to remain that way always.

She bumped into him and almost made him drop his candy. He felt the anger rise in him and was about to yell at her for being so clumsy, but controlled his anger for once. This was not the time or the place.

He looked up and his eyes met with Gabby's. She was always on his case about him being too harsh on Ally, but she knew he loved her.

"Let's go watch the movie," Gabby said, and grabbed the boxes of popcorn in her arms. Ally took her own box and soda, while Brad grabbed the rest. He followed them inside the theater, where Gabby found seats next to a family of four. Brad grumbled a little when he saw the girl in the seat next to him, who could be no more than two years old. The theater was almost empty, why did they have to sit right next to them? Young children were always trouble in a movie theater. Why did people even bring them? They didn't watch much of the movie anyway. It was a waste of money, in his opinion. Now, he just hoped the little girl in the seat next to him wasn't going to ruin it all for him.

"How are you doing?" he said, and nodded to the parents who seemed vaguely familiar. A daughter who looked like she was teenager peeked over as well. He smiled at her. She didn't smile back.

Kids today, Brad thought to himself, and grabbed his first candy bar as the previews came on. Brad smiled and leaned back in his seat as the chocolate melted on his tongue. He felt good at this moment. He had everything under control. He was doing okay for himself, his company was booming, and he had a beautiful family. Life was good.

He had exactly thirty-five minutes left to enjoy it.

THREE

November 2009

As SUSPECTED, the baby couldn't sit still for long. She kept crawling into Maggie's seat and making loud noises. It was exhausting, and Maggie didn't get to watch much of the movie. The man in the seat next to her seemed to be annoyed by the baby crawling up and down in her seat. The theater was almost empty, and Maggie wondered if she should take the baby up to the back row and sit with her there. But she would still make noises. Maggie closed her eyes and wished she were at home, where the baby could be as noisy as she wanted to and she didn't have to shush her constantly.

"Sit down," she whispered.

The baby whined and pushed her hand away, then continued to crawl up on the seat, then down on the floor, then back up. The seat squeaked every time, and people behind them were clearing their throats. The baby crawled up on the seat and jumped in it while laughing loudly. She stared at the people sitting behind them. They shushed her. Maggie felt embarrassed and pulled her down. As she did, she felt her diaper. She turned and looked at her husband.

"I need to change her," she whispered in his ear.

Dan nodded, while stuffing his face with popcorn. He was all into the movie, unlike Maggie, who had hardly seen anything. She was just waiting for this entire thing to be over so she could go home.

Maggie grabbed the bag and swung it over her shoulder, then grabbed the baby, who started crying, since she wanted to keep jumping in her seat.

"Excuse me," she said to the big man next to her. He pulled his leg to the side with an annoyed sigh and let her pass. The baby was crying loudly now, and Maggie hurried as fast as she could to get out of the theater. Once the door shut behind her, she breathed a sigh of relief. Finally, she could relax. Her shoulders came down and she held her daughter tightly in her arms. It would probably have been better if her oldest daughter had gone alone with her father. They would do that next time. There was no way Maggie was doing this again.

She took the baby to the restroom and put her on the changing table. She didn't want to lay down, so she had to hold her with force. It had been like this a lot lately. She had started to get a will of her own and never wanted to do as her mother told her.

"Lay still," she said with sweetness in her voice.

But the girl was still fussing and moving around while she pulled off her diaper. It was heavy with pee. She changed it quickly, then tickled her tummy and kissed her before she put her clothes back on. The baby laughed and grabbed her hair and pulled it. It hurt, but Maggie didn't mind. She enjoyed these moments so much. It was completely different than when she had her first child. Back then, she had been so young, so constantly anxious about doing the wrong thing, it had made everything so hard for her. Plus, she had to deal with a mother-in-law who constantly implied she wasn't doing anything right, with the result that her husband never thought she could do anything right either. Neither could their daughter, come to think of it. Lately, Dan had been on all of their cases, and it was exhausting.

Maggie decided she didn't care about watching the movie and that she would take a stroll with the baby in the mall instead until the movie was done. Maybe the baby would take a nap. Give Maggie a little break.

She grabbed her bag and walked towards the theater. First, she needed to go back in and tell Dan her plans, and then get the stroller, of course.

The baby was laughing and hugging her head, and Maggie felt so cheerful as she opened the door to the theater, where the sounds of pure hell met her. At first, she thought they were laughing. She thought people in the theater were just laughing. Like laughing hysterically, but as she walked up the ramp, she realized the movie hadn't made the audience laugh; it was something else that had made them scream in terror. The deafening sound of shots being fired made her realize the horror that was taking place.

Maggie's heart stopped and she rushed inside, just in time to see her oldest daughter and Dan fall to the floor. By the exit stood the shooter, still firing into the crowd again and again while people tried to escape. Bodies were dropping to the ground like flies. Maggie stared at the shooter and the fire in this person's eyes that seemed to be beyond this life. At first, Maggie couldn't move. She couldn't speak, she couldn't even scream. Instead, she grabbed her youngest daughter and held her tight as she turned around and ran out the same way she had come in.

Part One

MAKE A NEW PLAN

FOUR

March 2015

THE NOISE WAS UNBEARABLE. Stanley Bradley had always hated Disney World more than any place he could think of. But the light in his granddaughter Elyse's eyes when he took her there made it all worth it. Even the waiting in long lines while sweat ran from his forehead and stung his eyes, even the tasteless hotdogs they ate for lunch, even the constant music coming from everywhere and people cheering almost hysterically at the parade in the afternoon.

Just seeing her smile made it worth it.

It wasn't often Stanley got to see his grandchild and spend time with her, since her mother, Stan's only daughter, lived upstate and rarely came to visit.

"You never have time for me anyway," she always grumbled on the phone. "Like you never had time for me while I was growing up."

"It wasn't that bad, was it?" Stan asked.

"Maybe not. But you have always been married to your work. Even when you were home, you always had your nose buried in some research material or some new article published in *The Scientist*. I think I saw the front cover of that magazine more than I saw your eyes, growing up."

Tina always knew how to make him hurt. He hated that she blamed him for not being around enough in her childhood. Especially when the fact was that it was her mother who kept him away from her. Nothing he did was ever good enough for her. It began when she was just a newborn baby. Stan had wanted to change a diaper every now and then, but if he suggested it, Melanie would simply laugh and tell him he was too distracted, that the baby would roll from the changing table while Stanley was lost in some thought or just remembered something he needed to write down.

"You leave this to me," she had told him. "This isn't rocket science." Then she would laugh and take the baby from his hands. Later, when she was older and Stanley wanted to take her places, Melanie would always come up with some excuse for her not to be able to go.

"She needs a nap," she would say or, "no girls are interested in space ships."

"It's a shuttle," Stan would correct her, but it was no use. Twenty-five years Stanley had worked at Kennedy Space Center, and never once had he been able to take his little daughter there. Or the son who came later in life.

"She'll be bored to death," Melanie would say, and take the girl away from him again.

In the end, Stanley finally stopped trying. He immersed himself in his work and his research and let Melanie bring up the children. According to Melanie, it was for their own good. It was what was best for them.

Now, Stanley felt like he had gotten a second chance with his granddaughter. It was all part of his plan to try again. To make up for what he had lost. He only saw Elyse once a year, when Tina came down over spring break. But it had quickly become his favorite time of year, and the visit to Disney his favorite event. Elyse was now four years old and so delightful he caught himself hoping she would never grow older.

"Don't grow up and get angry and mean like your mother and grandmother," he would whisper, when she ran to Mickey Mouse and gave him the biggest hug in the history of hugging, still smiling from ear to ear, even after waiting an hour in line to get inside of his house.

"Look at me, Grandpa!"

Stanley looked and took her picture while Mickey put his arm around her. While looking at her on the screen, he shed a small tear, thinking how he had dreamt of doing something like this with Tina when she was young. Elyse had the exact same smile as her mother. It was captivating.

So much time had been wasted, so much lost.

FIVE

March 2015

THE SUN SHONE through the windows at my condo, cruelly exposing the salt covering the glass on the outside like a filter. It had been blowing from the east for a few days in a row, and the layer of salt in the air from the ocean lay thick on my windows. The salt was like a mist. Now, the wind had finally settled and it was quiet again outside.

Inside my condo, it had become quiet since my parents moved back home when the forensics techs finished their work on the motel, and since Shannon King had decided to move into an apartment I helped her find in the same building as mine. She didn't want to keep imposing on my family and me, even though I told her she could stay for as long as she wanted. She needed time and space to find out what she was going to do. Joe had promised her he would drag her through a custody battle when he left Cocoa Beach to go back to Nashville. I was certain he wasn't bluffing. A guy like him never bluffed.

Meanwhile, the kids and I had gone back to normal. As normal as it gets when you work as a homicide detective. Shannon and I were still seeing each other, and she and Angela often came down to the motel and ate with us. On weekends, we all hung out together at my parents' place while I helped them out.

"Dad?"

It was Abigail. She was standing in the living room rubbing her eyes. It was almost time to get up. I always woke up at sunrise. It was my favorite moment of the day…standing in the living room and watching the sun come up over the quiet Atlantic Ocean. The waves were glassy this morning and I wanted to go surfing as soon as I dropped the kids off at the bus.

I put my arm around her shoulder and pulled her close. "You sleep well?"

She nodded and stretched.

"Are you looking forward to spring break?" I asked. Today was the last day of school before break. I had signed both kids up for surf camp all week.

Abigail nodded. "I can't wait to go surfing."

212

"I don't want to go surfing." Austin had come out of their room too.

I smiled and kissed him. "I'm sure you'll want to once you get there," I said. "It's going to be fun."

Austin groaned. "No, I won't." He crossed his arms in front of his chest and looked at me angrily. He was always grumpy in the mornings and made a big deal out of small things. Mornings were the worst for him. He wasn't a morning person like Abigail and me.

"This is not the time to be discussing this," I said. "Get dressed. Grandma is waiting with breakfast at the deck."

They both sighed, then turned to their room where I had put out clothes for them to wear. Today was a big day at the school. There was an awards ceremony to mark the end of the quarter, and both kids were up for an award. I couldn't be prouder. I had told Sheriff Ron I was going to come in late today. I wanted to be there and take pictures of my babies.

I looked at the clock. It was a quarter till seven. I walked to Emily's door and knocked. "Are you up, sweetheart? I don't want you to miss school."

There was a sound and someone grunting something behind it and I figured it was her. She wasn't a morning person either, but it hadn't always been like that. I guess most sixteen year-olds weren't morning people. When she was younger, Emily would always be the first one up, jumping on my bed. Now, she hardly spoke a word to me till the afternoons. She went quiet behind the door and I knocked again. "Don't fall back asleep, honey." Abigail and Austin came out from their room all dressed and with their backpacks on. "We're leaving for Grandma's now," I said.

"Fine," Emily yelled from behind the door.

"See you this afternoon, sweetheart."

She answered with another grunting sound, and I hoped it meant she was awake enough to get herself into that car of hers and make it to school on time. I had long ago decided she needed to take responsibility for her own life and hoped it was working. I wasn't going to be the kind of dad that checked up on her constantly. I wanted her to know I trusted her.

SIX

December 2002

SHE WAS A CHRISTMAS CHILD. A true blessing for Dottie and James West, as were the three previous girls. But this one was special. Dottie knew she was. Not just because she was born on Christmas night. There was something about her that made Dottie love her more deeply than she had the other three, who were four, six, and nine at the time of little Elizabeth's birth. She knew right from the beginning when she looked into those very blue eyes of her newborn that this one was different than the rest. Just the way she felt while lying in her arms was different. Her body felt different.

When Dottie took her daughter home, she wondered why she hadn't heard her baby cry yet. With the previous three girls, they had cried from the moment they could breathe, but not Elizabeth. She was just lying there, quietly staring at her mother.

"Do you think she's alright?" Dottie asked the next morning, when she woke up and the baby hadn't cried all night. The baby was in her crib staring at her mother without making a sound. "She's so quiet," Dottie said, looking anxiously at her husband.

James shrugged. "I'm sure she's just fine. She's just quieter than the others. That's all." James took a shower, then got dressed. All the while, Dottie tried to feed her baby. But Elizabeth didn't want to suckle. It frustrated Dottie, who kept trying to get her to take the bottle.

"She hasn't eaten at all," she groaned in desperation.

James pulled out a pair of pants from the walk-in closet and put them on. He grabbed a shirt and a tie.

"You think she's alright?" Dottie asked again.

James sighed. "You've asked that seven times since we brought her home. Yes, I believe she is just fine. Just like the three previous were fine."

"She just feels so...so different," Dottie said.

"Different how?" he asked.

"Floppy," Dottie said, and looked at her husband. She kind of liked the way Elizabeth felt in her arms. She was so soft, but she worried that something could be wrong.

James smiled, and then leaned over his wife. He kissed her on the forehead with a light chuckle. "Remember when we had Anna? You thought she had a tumor because of that big birthmark she had on her forehead. And what about Dana? She had little spots all over her body that turned out to be hormones or something. And what was it that was wrong with Tiffany?"

Dottie smiled. "She cried all night two nights in a row and I thought she had colic."

"Now did any of these beautiful girls ever die or have anything wrong with them besides what was going on in your mind?" James smiled and kissed her again.

Dottie drew in a deep breath. He was right. She had felt the exact same way with all of her children. It was only natural for a mother to worry about her baby. The truth was, all four children had been different. No two were alike, so it was silly to compare them in the first place.

"Now, if you'll excuse me, I have to go to work," James said.

"I wish you didn't have to," Dottie said.

James smiled again. "I'll be back tonight. Try not to spend all day worrying. Try to enjoy our newest little family member while I'm gone."

"But, what if she doesn't eat anything?" Dottie said anxiously.

"She will. All children eat when they get hungry enough. Let her settle to this new reality first, then you'll see. It's all a little much right now."

Dottie felt emotional and overwhelmed. She was about to cry. It was the same every time she brought a child home. It was such a sensitive time. She always spent at least one whole day crying afterwards.

James grabbed his briefcase. Dottie could hear the other kids in the hallway now. It was time to get up and get them to school. Luckily, it didn't seem like Elizabeth would demand much of her mother's attention this first day at home. She could still attend to the needs of the others. Was it just this simple? Was Elizabeth simply just an easy child?

James leaned in over Dottie and kissed her again. He looked deep into her eyes. "She'll be fine. Do you hear me? She'll eat when she gets hungry."

SEVEN

March 2015

SHANNON LOOKED at her daughter in the back seat. It was the last day of school before spring break, and they were both looking forward to some time together. Angela had started at Abigail and Austin's school, not in the same class, but they still saw each other every day at recess. But it had been a rough couple of weeks for her daughter. Starting a new school in a strange new place was a lot for a six year-old. But she had handled it well. She was a tough cookie, Shannon was happy to realize.

"See you this afternoon," Shannon said, as they reached the drop-off line and it was their turn. A teacher helped Angela get out of the car. Shannon had been driving her every morning, even though she knew Angela could go on the bus with Jack's kids, but Shannon wasn't ready for that yet. It was hard for Shannon to let her daughter go...ever since she was kidnapped, but life had to go on, and especially Shannon needed her life to move on.

Things were getting harder with Joe, who was building his case against her. Shannon had her lawyer working to build her case, but she was terrified of how this would end. Plus, Angela missed her dad and kept asking when she was going to see him, and that didn't make things easier. All Shannon wanted was for her daughter to have as ordinary a life as possible.

"Love you, Mom," Angela said and slammed the door.

"Love you too," Shannon said, and watched her daughter spring after the other kids inside the yellow brick building. Shannon had come to love Roosevelt Elementary. The entire atmosphere was just what her daughter needed right now. It was a safe environment and there was a lot of warmth. The only thing Shannon worried about was the press. As she drove past the entrance and back onto Minutemen Causeway, she spotted two photographers in the bushes outside of the school. They had been there waiting for their photo-op ever since Angela had started at the school. The school knew about it, and so did the local police, so they made sure they didn't get onto the school's property, but had to stay outside. They still managed to get pictures now and then of her daughter when she was dropped off and picked up, but that was all.

Shannon knew they were trying to get pictures of her and Jack together. They had already succeeded and had plastered the photos all over the magazines. The cover of one of them this week read *Shannon's New Bad Boy* and then they had printed a picture of Jack in his board shorts coming out of the water. It had made Shannon so angry, but Jack had been really cool about it.

"It's the price you pay for dating a celebrity," he had simply said and kissed her. It had been such a relief for Shannon. She was afraid the press would end up destroying the healthiest relationship she had ever had. But Jack was a cool guy. He wasn't so easy to shake. Not even when they teased him at work.

"They'll grow tired of us eventually," he said, the last time photographers had jumped out of the dunes while Shannon and he were walking on the beach together. "I'm hardly that interesting."

He had a way of making Shannon laugh, even when things were bad. She adored him for that. Shannon had decided to stay in Cocoa Beach, to be close to him and his family, who had welcomed her so warmly. Both she and Angela seemed to be thriving here, and except for the photographers, it was as close to paradise as she had ever been. Bruce, her manager, kept asking when she was going back on tour, but she hadn't been able to give him an answer. The papers wrote about her custody battle and divorce and then about her new lover, and she needed time, she kept telling him.

"I can't hold them for much longer," he kept saying. "The label is getting anxious. They're afraid of losing money. But I'll try."

Shannon didn't care much about her career lately, or her label for that matter. Now was the time for her to heal her wounds. And it was time to focus on Angela. Plus, she had started to learn how to surf. Jack had been teaching her and she had to admit it was hard, but she quite enjoyed it. There was nothing like starting the day on the ocean among pelicans and dolphins. She wasn't going anywhere now.

Shannon stopped at a red light in downtown Cocoa Beach. She smiled when she saw two young guys with surfboards under their arms. A sign told her the street would be closed later in the afternoon because of Friday Fest. She was going there with Jack, while his mother had promised to take care of the kids. Sherri was so sweet. She really liked Angela, Shannon could tell.

Shannon picked up her phone and scrolled through her emails. She received hundreds of those daily from her fans. Mostly praise for how much they loved her music; some of them were haters, who asked her to drop off the face of the planet and hoped she realized she was going to hell for living her life in sin. Over the years, Shannon had gotten good at ignoring them and only read the good ones. Those that made her feel good.

Today, one of the emails made her pause and forget about the light that now turned green. In the subject line it said.

I'm sorry for what I have to do.

EIGHT

March 2015

KATIE MUELLER STARED out the window of the mini-van as the countryside passed by. They had almost reached Orlando and were less than an hour from their destination. It was the first time Katie was going to spend spring break without her parents. She was going to Cocoa Beach with some people from her college. She had heard about how everyone went to Florida for spring break since she was a child, but never thought she would actually go there herself. It wasn't exactly her type of thing. She wasn't a party-girl like the others in the mini-van. Not like Leanne or Britney, who were already drinking beers and taking shots up in the front of the car.

As the mini-van hit 520 towards Cape Canaveral and the bridges leading to the island, the girls were singing loudly and laughing, while the three boys that had come along on the trip enjoyed watching them. Katie wondered what she was even doing there.

It was Greg that had convinced her to come. Greg was a history major like Katie. He was the one driving the car. Katie'd had a crush on him since the beginning of the school year. So, naturally, when he asked if she wanted to come, she had said yes. Her parents were thrilled to hear that she was going.

"Finally, you're getting out a little," her dad had said. "I'm glad you're making some friends. College is supposed to be a fun time. I know mine was."

Katie wasn't going to have fun. She couldn't tell her dad that, but that's what she had thought to herself. She was going because she thought she might get to spend some time alone with Greg. She hadn't realized she would also have to endure the perkiness of Leanne and Britney.

"How are you doing back there," he asked, looking at Katie in the rearview mirror.

Leanne and Britney giggled.

Katie smiled. "I'm good, thanks."

Greg smiled. "Good. We're almost there. I booked us all rooms at a small motel.

It's right on the beach. I'm sure we're going to have a lot of fun. Girls stay in one room, boys in another."

They were seven in total. The last girl, Irene, wasn't part of the party-troop either. Still, she wasn't the type Katie saw herself hanging out with either. She couldn't stop staring at her fake mega-boobs. And the fact that she always wore those small tank tops that didn't seem to hold anything inside made her look ridiculous, like a porn-star in some bad movie. She didn't think she had anything in common with this girl, who at the age of twenty-one, insisted on having something altered on her face or body at least once a year, paid for by her parents, naturally.

Katie watched the swampy marshland as they drove towards the water, looking to see if she could spot an alligator somewhere, since everyone said there were alligators in all waterholes in Florida. Until now, she hadn't seen any. A couple of cows were eating grass behind a fence, but that was hardly spectacular. An armadillo had been hit by a car and was lying on the side of the road. Big billboards told her Ron Jon's, the world largest surf shop, wasn't far away. Katie wasn't very fond of the ocean or the beach. She hated to get sandy, and certainly didn't enjoy the way she looked in a bikini. Yet, she had still found herself shopping for a new one for the trip after Greg had asked her to come along. She didn't exactly look forward to showing off her winter-pale pillars of legs. Not when she was going to be next to those long-legged beauties and the Barbie-doll. Katie was short and slightly overweight. She wasn't so sure Greg would enjoy that sight. She had bought a long beach-dress that she could wear to cover herself up until she could lay down in the sand. The worst part was walking or standing. Lying on a towel, she could do.

"We're here!" Greg exclaimed.

Katie looked out the window and spotted the sign. "Motel Albert's?" she mumbled. It sounded like the motel from a horror movie. *Psycho*. What was the name of that motel again?

Bates. That's it Bates Motel.

"A boy's best friend is his mother," she said with a scary pretend-chuckle, as she exited the van and looked at the front of the old motel that looked like it had been built in the sixties, with the red *Motel* sign on top. Greg smiled and looked at her.

"We're going to have so much fun here," he said.

NINE

March 2015

STANLEY BRADLEY FELT sick to his stomach. He sat up in the darkness, leaned to the side, and threw up. He had no idea where it landed, but didn't care either. It was so dark, and all he cared about was the fact that he felt terrible. Not until a lot later, when the worst nausea had subsided, did he start to wonder where he was. The realization hit him like a blow to his face.

"Elyse," he whispered into the darkness. Where was Elyse? She had been with him. They had been at Disney World. Then what? They had walked back to the car in the parking lot. The car had been parked by Pluto, he remembered randomly for some ridiculous reason. They had driven out from there. They had been in the countryside, singing...yes, they had been singing one of Elyse's favorite songs. What was the name of it again? The one from *Frozen*? How did it go again?

The cold never bothered me anyway.

Yes, that was one of the lines, Elyse's favorite line in the song. *Let it go*, was the title of the song.

Then what? What had happened? Where was he now? Where was Elyse?

The car. Something happened to the car. There was something in the road. Something that made the car drive off the road. The tires punctured, he remembered. The car screeched; Elyse was screaming. Then what? Then it all went black.

There was a sound in the room; it sounded like a door opened, the light was turned on, and Stanley covered his eyes.

"Oh, good, you're awake," a voice said.

"Where am I?" Stanley asked with a trembling voice. "Where is Elyse? Where is my granddaughter?"

As his eyes got used to the light, he realized he was looking directly into the barrel of a gun. He gasped and fell back into the bed.

"Now, lay still, Mr. Bradley," the voice said. "It's for your own good. You hurt yourself badly in the accident."

Stanley looked into the barrel with his heart pounding in his chest. "Am...are you holding me prisoner here?"

"You can call it whatever you like," the voice replied. Something was put in his hands. It was a plate of food.

Stanley stared at the steak and potatoes with thick gravy. It looked delicious, but he still felt nauseated.

"I'm not hungry. I demand to know what happened to my granddaughter."

"Eat," the voice said adamantly. The gun was pushed closer to his face. "Eat or your granddaughter dies."

Eat or your granddaughter dies? What kind of an ultimatum was that? How was that threatening?

Stanley shrugged, then grabbed the knife and fork and started eating. As he sunk his teeth into the steak, he realized he was actually quite hungry, and this was good meat. The potatoes were slightly overcooked for his liking, but he ate them anyway, while this strange person kept staring at him while holding the gun.

"It's quite good," he said, still wondering why this person wanted him to eat so badly. Was something in the food? Stanley stopped chewing. What if it was poisoned?

"Finish it."

"What's in the food?" he asked.

"Just eat it."

Thinking he'd better obey this mad personage, he finished the plate. The plate was removed, but only for a few seconds before another one landed in his lap. Spaghetti and meatballs.

"Now, eat this."

"I'm stuffed. I really can't eat any more," Stanley said. "It smells great, but I really can't..."

The cold gun was placed to his temple. "Eat."

TEN

March 2015

I WAS the proudest dad in the entire cafeteria. My twins were both up on the stage holding their recognition awards for hard work. Austin in Math and Abigail in Reading. I knew they had both been struggling in those subjects, and to see them up there so proud for having reached their goals, made my heart overflow with pride. Usually, they mostly got themselves in a lot of trouble at school, and more than once I had been called by the teacher, Mrs. Allen, telling me they weren't behaving well. To see them getting an award, shaking the hand of the principal, almost brought tears to my eyes. Finally, they were doing something right.

I grabbed my camera and took what must have been a thousand photos, while everyone from the class who had received an award was lined up with the teacher. Austin was poking his sister in the side, and then she hit him on the shoulder. Austin squealed and hit her back. Abigail pushed him in return. Meanwhile, the teacher tried hard to smile behind them. I looked at them from above the camera. Austin grabbed Abigail's reward and threw it on the ground. Abigail ran after it and tripped. Now she was crying. The principal looked at Mrs. Allen for help. Mrs. Allen hurriedly got the kids off the stage.

At least it lasted long enough for me to get a picture. It might be a while before they received another, I thought to myself. Their grandparents were going to be so proud.

I was packing the camera away when my phone vibrated in my pocket. I picked it up. It was Shannon. I walked into the hallway, while waving at my kids who were being dragged back to their classroom. I still had water in my ear from this morning's surfing.

"Hi there. I was just thinking about you. I saw Angela in the cafeteria. She seemed happy. I think she already made some friends in her class."

"That's good," Shannon said, distraught. I could tell by the sound of her voice that something was going on.

"What's wrong?"

222

"I...I got this weird email. I think you need to take a look at it."

I looked at my watch. I had told Ron I would be in later today because of the award ceremony. We had a double stabbing last week that we were finishing the investigation of. A girl and her grandfather had been attacked in their apartment by a homeless guy. The grandfather died from his wounds. The guy was in custody and had admitted to doing it, even though he said he couldn't remember much, since he was completely doped up. But the granddaughter that survived was a very strong witness to the events. It was a pretty easy case, but a lot of paperwork. Sheriff Ron had finally assigned me a new partner, Bethany, or Beth, and we had some good teamwork going on. But I was in no rush. I wasn't in a hurry to get to the office, so I guessed I could take a few minutes to meet up with Shannon. I took any chance I could get to see her.

"Sure. Do you want to meet up for coffee at Juice N' Java?"

"I can't deal with photographers or fans taking pictures with their cellphones right now," she said.

She made it sound very serious. I had no coffee at my place, and I didn't have much time.

"All right," I said. "Let's meet at the bar at the motel in five minutes. My mom makes a pretty mean cup of Joe."

"Sounds like a plan."

We hung up. I was thrilled at the prospect of getting to see Shannon and sprang for my Jeep in the school's parking lot. Three minutes later, I was at my parents' motel.

"Aren't you supposed to be at work?" my mom said. She was cleaning the counters in the bar.

"I'm meeting Shannon here," I said. I threw a glance around the room. It was empty. The bar usually didn't open till noon. "Where is Dad?"

"He's taking a nap," my mom said.

I spotted a table in the corner. "We'll just sit over there," I said. "Do you have any coffee?"

She gave me that *are-you-kidding-me* look that only a mother can do. "What do you mean, do I have coffee? Of course I have coffee."

I chuckled. "Good. Could Shannon and I have a cup each? She uses milk, but no sugar..."

"And you like both in yours."

Shannon had entered the bar and walked up to me. My heart skipped a beat from looking at her. I couldn't believe I still got that feeling when looking at her, even this long after we'd started seeing each other. But I couldn't help myself. Being around her made me feel good.

ELEVEN

March 2015

"So, what's going on?"

I looked into Shannon's eyes over the steam of my coffee. She sipped hers and looked away. Something was definitely bothering her.

"You said something about an email?"

Shannon inhaled, and then looked at me. "Don't hate me."

"Hate you? How could I ever hate you?" I asked, shocked at the character of her statement. How could she ever think I could hate her? "I love you," I said. Shannon widened her eyes. My heart stopped. It had just burst out of me. I had never told her I loved her before. I didn't even realize I did.

Was it too soon? Was I going to scare her away?

Shannon smiled. Her eyes hit the table and she blushed. I felt a huge relief.

"Well, there is no beating around the bush with you, Detective, huh?" she said, chuckling lightly.

"I'm sorry. I didn't mean for it to come out like that...I..."

She placed her hand on top of mine. "It's okay, Jack." She looked into my eyes. "I think I love you too."

The words completely blew me away. I felt so happy I could scream.

"But that's not why I told you to meet me," she continued with a serious voice. "You might have to rethink everything after you hear what I have to say."

Uh-oh. That sounded really bad.

"You're scaring me a little here, Shannon," I said and sipped my coffee. "What's going on?"

"There is something I've never told anyone. Something I should have told when it happened...but I was just so..." She stopped. Shannon bit her lip. I could tell this was hard for her. It freaked me out a little.

What could be so bad?

"Nothing you can say will make me feel differently," I said. "Whatever it is, we will figure it out...together. Just tell me everything from the beginning."

Shannon sighed. "I got this email today," she said, and showed me her phone. "I think it's from a fan."

"What does it say?"

Shannon read it out loud to me. Her voice was trembling.

"Dear Shannon King. I am so sorry. I am sorry for what I am about to do. I want you to know how much you inspire me. Your songs make me understand who I really am; they encourage me to follow my dreams. I am sure you had to do bad things too to make it to the top as well. I am just doing what must be done. I hope you understand. Yours truly AM"

I looked at Shannon. She lifted her eyes from the screen and showed me the email, so I could see for myself.

"But, what does it mean? I'm not sure I understand," I said.

"Me either. I didn't understand it either the first time this person wrote to me, so I ignored it. Biggest mistake of my life. I have regretted it ever since."

"So, it's not the first time this person has written to you?"

Shannon shook her head and sipped some coffee. She ran a hand through her hair. Her face was strained.

"Couldn't it just be some lunatic? You must get a lot of those, don't you?"

"I do. But this one is different."

"How is it different? It doesn't even make sense," I said. "I really don't think it's anything to worry about. Why are you freaking out over this?"

Shannon leaned over the table. "Because the last time I got an email from this person, eight people were shot in a movie theater north of Miami. Four of them died."

I leaned back in my chair. I was confused. "You mean to tell me this email came from the Miami movie theater killer six years ago?"

"I believe it does. I received the exact same email six years ago, right before the shooter killed all those people."

"But, couldn't that just be a coincidence?" I asked.

"No. I'm sure about this, Jack. He's about to do it again." Shannon's voice was trembling again.

"As far as I remember, the man was caught. He killed himself," I said.

"I know. I thought it was over too. But now I receive this? What if that was the wrong guy? What if the killer has been on the loose all this time? I'm telling you, Jack. This email is just like the last time. This is exactly how it went down last time. That's what happened six years ago. He sent me all these emails in the days before it happened, telling me how sorry he was, then one email after it was done, telling me it was him. Asking for my forgiveness. I never heard from him again. Until now."

"And, you're telling me you never told anyone about this?" I asked. "Not even the police?"

Shannon shook her head. "I am not proud of it. But I was just starting out. I was at the beginning of my career and terrified it would be the end of it. I had just gotten my breakthrough. I was a hit. I was afraid it would destroy me. I showed it to my manager at the time. It wasn't Bruce. I had another manager back then. I showed it to him afterwards. When I realized it was serious. At first, I thought it was some nutcase writing me, some sick stalker or something. I had been warned that I would get a lot of those and told to just ignore them. But back then, I read everything, all the fan-mail I got, since I was so proud to be getting any. I got so much junk. I didn't know it was connected to the shootings until it was too late. My manager told me to never tell anyone. It wouldn't help the victims or anything, he said. I was young and stupid and I listened to him. Like I said, I'm not proud of this, but now I feel like I need to tell you."

"Well, I'm glad you finally did," I said.

"You're angry. I knew you would be. I'm sorry. I can't change what I did back then, but I can do something about it now."

"I'm not angry. Like I said, I'm pretty sure the guy is dead."

I knew she hadn't meant to harm anyone. As a detective, it was hard for me to swallow this news. But as a boyfriend and someone who loved Shannon, I chose to be understanding. I put my hand on top of hers and smiled.

"I'm glad you came to me with this," I said. "I'm sure it's nothing, but I'll look into it for you, if that will make you more at ease. Now, tell me. Do you still have those old emails?"

Shannon sighed and shook her head. "I deleted them immediately afterwards. My old manager told me to. There was to be no trace of this, he said. If the press ever hacked into my email or someone got access to it somehow, there could be no trace of this, he said."

"And, of course, you listened to him," I said.

This left us with very little to go by.

TWELVE

December 2003

WHEN ELIZABETH TURNED one year old, she still showed no interest in food. She would take the bottle rarely and hadn't started on real food yet. Even though her mother tried to feed her every day, three meals a day, like the pediatrician had told her to. At Elizabeth's first birthday, they threw her a party like they had done for the rest of the girls at that age. Dottie even made a big cake and put one candle in the middle.

She carried it to the table as they sang. Elizabeth clapped her small hands and blew out the candle, and her mother started to cut the cake. They had invited a couple of kids from the playground that they often met when they went there in the afternoons, and then all of her mothers group. All eyes were on the spectacular cake and on Dottie, as she passed the pieces of cake around the table. The kids all dug in, except for Elizabeth. As usual when served food, she merely stared at all the others while they ate without showing any interest whatsoever in her own food.

"Here, let me help you," Dottie said and sunk the fork into the chocolate cake. Her hand was shaking as she brought the fork up to Elizabeth's mouth. She knew in her heart the mouth would remain closed, and so it did. Elizabeth tightened her lips and moved her head away. Dottie felt awful. All of the other moms were looking at her, and she knew what they thought. Elizabeth was so tiny; she knew they all blamed her for not feeding her enough.

"Come on, baby. It's cake. Everyone loves cake. Look at your friends, huh? Just try it, will you?"

But the mouth remained closed. The tiny girl, who was less than half the size of her friends at that age, simply refused to take in solid food. It had started to wear on her parents. Other than with food, Elizabeth was the easiest child Dottie had ever had. She was so sweet, so gentle, and she never cried. But she wasn't developing fast enough. She still hadn't started to crawl, while all of her little friends were constantly all over the place, and their parents after them; Elizabeth simply sat still and watched them. Well, she didn't even sit much, couldn't even sit on her own yet, which worried Dottie a lot. At this age, she should at least be able to sit on her own and roll. Elizabeth could do neither. When sitting in her high chair, they put pillows behind her back to keep her upright. Her body remained this floppy mass that didn't seem to do much. Was she ever going to crawl? Walk? Cry? Eat?

"She doesn't want any," Dottie said, looking up at James, who was standing with his arms crossed.

"Of course she does," James said. "Everybody wants cake. Maybe she just doesn't know what it tastes like. Put some in her mouth and she'll love it."

"Are you sure that's a good idea?"

"I'm positive," James said, but he didn't sound convincing. They had been running to the doctor constantly, asking him what could be wrong with their little girl, and just as constantly they had learned that some kids were just slower developed than others, that there was nothing to worry about, that Elizabeth would catch up eventually; she was just very small and needed more time. She would learn how to eat real food soon enough.

"No grown-ups live only on milk," the doctor said, chuckling. "Just let her take the time she needs."

So they had done so far. But both of them had started to doubt if the doctor was right. James had started to think that they just needed to force Elizabeth into situations where she had to do things she didn't want to. Like put some toy she wanted far away on the floor and tell her to crawl for it, but so far, it hadn't worked. Elizabeth just gave up on getting the toy and found something else to hold in her hand instead. They had even taken away the bottle at one point. Told her there would be no more milk, that now she was supposed to eat real food, but that had only resulted in her simply not eating anything, and after two days, the doctor had told them to bring back the bottle because Elizabeth couldn't bear to lose any more weight. She was too fragile and small.

"Just force the fork into her mouth," James said to Dottie. "Once she tastes the cake, she'll want it." He sounded irritated.

Dottie did as he told her to and forced Elizabeth's mouth open with her fingers, then scooped the cake inside the baby's mouth. She then pulled her fingers out, expecting the baby to start crying, but she didn't. She just looked at her mother with the sweetest little smile, then spat the entire piece of cake out using her tongue. The remains of the chocolate cake ran down her chin and ended up on her shirt.

THIRTEEN

March 2015

Sheriff Ron Harper was on the phone when I knocked on the door to his office.

"Ah, Ryder, come on in," he said, and pointed at a chair. I sat down, holding Shannon's email in my hand. I had printed it out for him to look at. Meanwhile, I had asked Richard, our researcher, to find everything there was about the Miami shootings for me.

"What's up?" Ron asked, when he hung up the phone. "How far are we on the stabbing case?"

"Almost done with that one, sir. But there is something I need you to take a look at. You know Shannon King, right?"

Ron rolled his eyes. "Christ, Jack. Everyone in the country knows about you two. It's on the cover of every damn magazine in Publix."

"Of course." I blushed slightly, thinking about the pictures of me in my board shorts. It was quite intimidating, knowing everyone in the country pretty much had seen the picture. The boys at the office had teased me a lot, placing the magazine on my desk or calling me bad boy whenever they could get away with it. I had told Shannon it didn't bother me, but of course it did a little. I liked to live quietly. But if that was the price I had to pay to be with her, then I did so willingly. She was worth it.

"Shannon received this email today and she handed it over to me," I said and showed it to him.

Ron put on his glasses and looked at it. Then he looked at me with a shrug. "So, what is this? Some stalker or what? Why is this a police matter?"

I explained everything Shannon had told me at my parents' bar, and told him I thought it was an important matter, that we couldn't ignore it.

"As far as I know, they got the guy," he said. "Case is closed, Jack. We're not touching this. A few emails aren't going to change that."

"Listen to me," I said. "Shannon is freaking out. She is certain this is from the killer. Shannon doesn't remember everything from the first emails, but she said he wrote that her song, "Guns and Smoking Barrels" was his favorite song of hers, and that it made him realize what it was he needed to do. She feels awful and has been blaming herself all these years."

"I know that song," Ron said and started to sing out of tune.

"It was her first number one hit, but she told me she hates it because of this, because of what this bastard wrote to her. She thinks he got the inspiration to do the shooting from hearing her song."

"That's awful," Ron said. "But the case is closed, Jack. I feel like I'm repeating myself here. This is just some lunatic writing his favorite singer creepy letters. Nothing new in that. Case's closed. If they don't open it in Miami, we can't do anything about it."

Ron looked at me for a long time, while leaning back in his leather chair. Ron was a good guy. I had always liked him. But he was also a hardhead sometimes.

He shrugged. "We have plenty on our own plates as it is, Jack. Like I said, if they don't open the case in Miami, then there is nothing much we can do."

I growled at Ron, then walked back to my desk and found a stack of papers from Richard. It was all about the shooting in Miami in 2009. I opened the file and started to go through it. Richard spotted me and came over. He was a tall and skinny guy with a nice smile. Why he never got married was beyond me. He was such a nice guy. Used to play pro-baseball in his younger days. Had been a promising pitcher until an injury drastically changed his entire career. After that, he decided to go into the force like his old man had been. He loved to fish in his spare time. I always told him to start surfing instead. There would be plenty of time to fish when he grew old.

"I got what I could find on the computer," he said. "The case is six years old, so the rest is paperwork and probably down in Miami. I can send for it if you'd like, but it'll take a couple of days."

"I am going to need that," I said. "And try to figure out who worked the case back then."

Richard smiled and put a post-it on my desk with a name and a number on it. "Already done. I've also contacted the IT Department and told them to try and track the email address you gave me as well."

"Excellent."

I looked at the post-it and saw a name I recognized well from my past.

FOURTEEN

March 2015

I CALLED my old friend and colleague at Miami Beach Police, Tim. It was his name on the post-it from Richard, I was pleased to know. I had spent many hours with Tim, watching crack-houses and busting drug dealers in downtown Miami. It was a dangerous job, but I loved getting those bastards off the streets. Apparently, he had worked for the homicide division in Boca Raton at the time of the shooting.

"Jack, old buddy! How the heck are you?"

"I'm good, thanks."

"I heard you moved to Cocoa Beach?"

"Yup. Best place in the world. I get to surf every day. Living on the beach."

"Are you staying at your parents' place?"

"Right next door. Got a condo for me and the kids. Right on the beach."

"Sounds good. Maybe I should swing by some day. Stay for a weekend with the girlfriend."

Tim always had a new girlfriend. He was never known to settle down with the same girl for longer than a few months at a time.

"You should do that."

"I hear you got yourself a new girlfriend too," he said.

"Sure have."

"I can't believe you nailed Shannon King. She's like the sexiest woman alive, man. How did you meet her?"

"She stayed at my parents' motel for a little while. I helped her out with some stuff," I said, trying not to get into too many details. I had to be careful what I told people when dating a celebrity. Not that I thought Tim would ever rat me out, but he might tell someone else, who would sell the info for money. Shannon had warned me how fast things spread.

"I'm glad to hear that, buddy. So, when are you coming back? We need you here. I miss you, man."

I inhaled deeply, then looked at the picture of me and the kids taken on the beach in front of my parents' motel. The happiness in their eyes made my heart melt. "I'm not," I said. "I like it here."

"Really? In small town Cocoa Beach? Man. I feel so abandoned down here. You left me in the middle of a case, man."

"I know. Sorry about that."

"That's alright. I got a new partner and we solved it without you. So, what can I do for you?" Tim asked.

"I've stumbled onto something that might interest you."

"Yeah? Like what?" Tim asked.

"It's regarding the movie theater shooting in 2009."

Tim went quiet. I knew him well enough to sense his smile stiffen. "I'll be…The case is closed."

"I know. I just need to know some details. You caught him, right?" I asked.

"He killed himself in his home. I found him there myself. After he shot those poor people in the theater, he slipped out of the emergency exit where he had come in. We have a picture from a surveillance camera of him when he arrived at the mall and parked his car close to the emergency exit. We tracked the plate to a Laurence Herman, and when we stormed his house, we found him dead. He had shot himself. The case is closed, Jack."

"I know it is. I'm just sniffing around a little. Thought maybe you could help me."

"Not going to happen. I am not touching this case again."

"So, let me ask you this. How sure are you that this guy was the shooter?" I asked, looking down at the case files Richard had printed out for me.

Tim paused. "It was him, Jack. No doubt about it."

I knew him well enough to sense his hesitation. He wasn't sure at all. I had gone through the material again and again, and I couldn't get it to fit. It had probably haunted him for years.

"You know just as well as I do that the autopsy concludes that Laurence Herman died between three and three-thirty in the afternoon. The shooting took place at five thirty-five. The guy was already dead, man."

Tim inhaled sharply. "They could be wrong about the time of death," he said. "Happened before. There's always a margin of error. We have the surveillance pictures. They show Laurence parking his car right outside of the emergency exit and him coming out afterwards and driving off."

I grabbed a copy of the surveillance pictures and looked at them while I spoke to Tim.

"First of all, you can't see the person's face on those pictures. He's wearing a hoodie. Second of all, where did you find the car?"

Tim breathed again. "In a ditch in Ft. Lauderdale. It had been set on fire."

"Exactly," I said. "How is Laurence Herman here supposed to make it back to the house in Boca and kill himself if the car is in Ft. Lauderdale?"

"He probably just drove it up there because he knew it had been seen on surveillance photos and wanted to get rid of it."

"Would he really care about that if he was going to kill himself afterwards?" I asked.

Tim sighed, annoyed. I was getting to him. I could tell. I just hoped I was pushing his buttons enough.

"Jack, Goddammit. How am I supposed to know what goes on in the head of a man like that? He's nuts. Insane. He had just shot eight people, women, men, and children. I don't think he was thinking very clearly at that moment, if you want my opinion. Maybe he didn't intend to kill himself afterwards. Maybe he was overwhelmed by guilt. He had, after all, just killed a lot of people. It's bound to get you thinking. Even the worst mass murderers must feel some kind of regret, don't you think?"

"I'm not sure they all do," I said. The killer's psychology was my field of specialty. "Some feel relief. In a true psychopath, the anger has been building for a long time, and when they finally let it loose, when they finally do it, they feel a sense of great relief. Some are even happy, since it has been building for so long. A malignant narcissist feels no guilt afterwards. He feels the weight on his shoulders lifted. Fifty pounds of emotional weight lifted. He feels like he's the master of his own destiny. He doesn't need anything or anyone. The murder isn't over when the victims die. The murder is over when his anger against them recedes. That's why he keeps killing. He is still killing them even after they're dead."

"Okay, Mister Expert. But it's also true that most mass shooters kill themselves afterwards. Who's to know if it's planned? It's not like we can ask them afterwards, right?"

I wasn't getting through to him. I felt frustrated. What more did he need to know? I had to convince him. My gut told me I simply had to.

"True. But I need you to open the case anyway. I have reason to believe it might be worth it. I have reason to believe the killer is about to strike again."

Tim went quiet, then he exhaled. "No way, Jack. This case was the worst I ever worked on. I loathed it. I love you, buddy, you know I do, but I'm not doing it. Sorry. I simply can't."

FIFTEEN

March 2015

I TRIED MY HARDEST. I told Tim about the emails and about Shannon's involvement, and made him promise to keep it from the press, but nothing helped. Tim was not going to reopen the case. Without him reopening it, there was no way I could get Ron or the rest of the team involved either.

It meant I was on my own with this.

What if they were right? What if it was just some lunatic writing the emails and not the killer? It was certainly a possibility. But, then again, it could be him. It could be the killer of four people from that evening six years ago. I couldn't take the risk of not taking this seriously. I didn't dare to. How would this person, this lunatic, know about the emails in the first place? How would he know what to write? If it wasn't him in the first emails either, how did he know the shooting was about to happen? It made no sense. The fact that Shannon had received the emails hadn't been mentioned anywhere in the media. Shannon and her old manager were the only ones who knew. If this was the killer writing her again, then there was no time to waste. I had to stop him. The movie theater shooting was the most ruthless mass shooting in Florida's history. The killer had shot at entire families, even children, while they were watching the newly released movie *The Princess and the Frog*.

The report said the shooter bought a ticket, entered the theater, and sat in the front row. He was wearing a hoodie in the theater, which the usher noticed, but didn't comment upon. It wasn't that unusual. The AC kept the theater very cold and people wore lots of clothes inside. Other than that, he was wearing jeans. The usher had noticed he had seemed to hide his face in the hoodie when handing him the ticket, but just taken him for being some weirdo. He saw weirdos every day. About twenty minutes into the film, it was believed the shooter left the building through an emergency exit door, which he propped open with a plastic tube.

He allegedly then went to his car, which was parked near the exit door, and retrieved his guns. Thirty-five minutes into the film, at five-thirty-five p.m., he reentered the theater through the exit door.

He then fired a 12-gauge Remington 870 Express Tactical shotgun, first at the ceiling and then at the audience. He shot first to the back of the room, and then toward people in the aisles. A bullet passed through the wall and hit someone in the adjacent theater. Witnesses said the fire alarm system began sounding soon after the attack began and staff told people in all theaters to evacuate. One witness, a mother with her child, had been in the restroom, and according to her statement she had heard the shooting and screaming on her way back and never reentered the theater. She had lost her husband, while her daughter had been hit by a bullet that ricocheted from the ceiling, but it only hit her in the arm.

I leaned back in my chair with a deep sigh and looked at Beth across from me. My new partner had this aura about her that made people keep their distance from her. I didn't know her story yet, but I was guessing she was one of those officers who was married to the force. She seldom smiled and I often didn't quite know what to say to her. But now, she looked up and our eyes met. Her eyes were actually pretty. Probably the prettiest feature about her. Otherwise, she was small and plump and hadn't been first in line when God handed out female bodies. But I liked her. Even if she kept everyone, including me, at a safe distance.

"So, what's going on with you, Ryder?" she asked. "You haunting ghosts from the past?" She nodded at the pictures and papers on my desk, all telling the story of the mass shooting. I hadn't told her what I was doing yet.

"Looks like it, doesn't it? I don't know what I'm doing, to be honest," I said. I looked at my computer screen and found the web camera from the pier. The waves looked intriguingly good. I needed to get out of there. Clear my head. There was still an hour before the kids came home on the bus.

"Go ahead, Ryder," Beth said. "I'll cover for you here. Out there is a wave with your name on it."

SIXTEEN

March 2015

STANLEY COULDN'T EAT any more. His stomach was hurting from all the food he had consumed over the last few days. And it kept coming. He kept getting a plate set in front of him, then a gun to his head with the order to eat. He had thought about trying to fight his guardian and get out, but didn't dare to. What would happen to Elyse if he did?

"Is your stomach hurting? Aw, that's too bad," the voice said, as a stack of pancakes landed in front of him. Stanley had gotten a few hours of sleep before he was awakened and told to eat again. He was so fed up with food.

"Please," he said. "Please, no more."

"Eat," the voice said again.

The smell made him nauseous and he felt like throwing up as he took the first bite. He chewed and felt how the pancakes were growing inside of his mouth. His stomach turned at the prospect of having to contain any more food, and when he had swallowed the first two pancakes, his gag reflex tried to send it all back up. Stanley bent over to the side to throw up, but was forcefully pulled back and his mouth held closed. The vomit came up in his mouth and almost choked him.

"No cheating," the voice said. "Now, swallow it all again."

Stanley felt such pain in his throat and stomach. The thought of having to swallow it all again made him cry.

Please, let me go. Please, don't force me to do this.

"Now, swallow," the voice said. "Or your granddaughter dies."

Stanley whimpered, then closed his eyes and swallowed it with much resistance. He gagged again, but this time it only reached as far as his throat before he managed to press it back down. His gastric system had been enlarged over the last couple of days and he felt it happening again. It was excruciatingly painful.

The grip on his mouth was removed and he gasped for air. His guardian grabbed the fork, then cut out a piece of the pancake, dipped it in syrup, and brought it up towards his mouth.

236

"Please," he muttered. "I'm so full. I can't take any more in."

But his guardian didn't listen. The fork was forced into his mouth and then he swallowed the piece whole, without chewing it. Stanley coughed and gasped for air, when another forkful landed in his mouth. Stanley tried to chew this time, but soon after, another forkful was pressed in his mouth and he had to swallow the first in order to not choke. It hurt his throat as it went down. Then followed the pain from his stomach, which was expanding in order to make room for more food.

When will this end? Oh, God, please make this stop.

His guardian clapped his cheek and smiled. "There you go. You ate it all. All the pancakes are gone. They were good, right?"

Stanley looked at the crazy personage in front of him, then nodded. He didn't dare not to.

"Excellent," the voice said. "I bet your stomach is hurting now, right?"

Stanley nodded with a deep moan.

"Good," the guardian said. "Now you know what it feels like."

Stanley closed his eyes and breathed heavily. His stomach hurt so badly he could hardly breathe. Stanley had never been a big eater, and his stomach had gotten quite a shock from all the food it suddenly had to contain. He prayed it was all over. He prayed silently that he'd be allowed to go now, that this person that had kept him there and fed him all this food would somehow be done with him and let him and Elyse go.

Please, dear God. Please, let Elyse be unharmed.

His guardian looked at him and smiled. "Now, I do hope you have room left for dessert."

SEVENTEEN

March 2015

ALL THE GIRLS changed into bikinis as soon as they got to their room at the motel. Katie watched them as they stood in front of the mirror looking at themselves, putting up their long hair in ponytails, putting on more mascara.

You're going to the beach. You're going in the water. You don't need mascara!

Katie didn't feel like showing her winter-pale body off in any small piece of clothing. She didn't want to apply mascara and fix her hair. She grabbed a book and sat on her bed, where she started reading.

"Look at her," Britney said, as she spotted Katie. "Isn't it cute? A fuzzy little bookworm cuddled up in her corner."

The other girls laughed. Katie was used to that. It had always been this way. Nobody ever saw Katie. Nobody cared enough. Only to mock her. But, one day, she would show them. One day she would be famous. One day she would do something big, make a difference in this world. Once she was famous, they would all want to be her friend. They would all look up to her.

"You think she'll ever turn into a butterfly?" she continued. "Nah, she'll probably prefer to stay underground in the dirt and darkness. Unless..." Britney smiled viciously. "Unless, of course, Greg...oh, sweet *dear* Greg...unless he asks her to come with him into the light. That is why you've come, isn't it? It's because of him."

"Oh, Greg," the others moaned and laughed. "Oh, Greg!"

Britney leaned closer to Katie. "You do know the real reason why he brought you here, don't you?"

Katie's heart stopped. She tried hard to not let these girls get to her, but it was difficult. She didn't belong here with any of them and they all knew it.

"He does this every year, you know," Britney said. "He finds some weirdo who has a crush on him, then he fucks her in the dunes and never speaks to her again. That's his thing. That way, he's sure to get laid over spring break."

238

Katie didn't look up from her book. Her heart was pounding in her chest. Could it be? Were they right about him?

"Leave me alone," she whispered.

"Just don't be a fool," Britney said, grabbing her beach towel and sunscreen. "You don't belong here and you know it."

The girls followed Britney out the door and slammed it behind them. Katie stared at the book while tears rolled across her cheeks. It had been a mistake to come on this trip. She had known it from the beginning. How could she have been so stupid to believe Greg could actually be interested in her? Now she was stuck here for an entire week. She couldn't afford to go home on her own. She didn't come from some rich family like the rest of the girls on campus did. She attended Princeton on a scholarship. Originally, she was a foster child, who had lived in six different families, constantly moving while growing up, never finding a place to call home. Not until she reached high school, when Phillip and Eve Monroe had taken her in and loved her like she was the child they never had, even though they had tried for many years. All through her childhood, Katie had buried her nose in books, and because of that she always had good grades, and in high school she did so well for herself that she was accepted to Princeton and able to land a full scholarship. She had always sought comfort in doing well in school, and now she was being rewarded for it. But she had made the mistake of thinking she could be accepted by the other students...that she could be one of them.

Sometimes, it was like they smelled it on her. Smelled the fear on her skin. They knew she didn't belong, even though she didn't tell them. They all knew.

There was a knock on the door and Katie wiped away her tears. Greg peeked inside. Katie's heart started pounding. She'd had a crush on him for what felt like forever. She didn't think people knew, since she had kept it to herself. But, apparently, they did.

"Hi there," he said and entered. He was wearing board shorts and nothing on top. The sight of his torso made Katie blush. He sat on the bed next to her. "Everybody is down at the beach. Aren't you coming? We need an extra man for volleyball."

Greg looked at her with his soft brown eyes. His hair and skin looked like he had been in the sun for weeks rather than cooped up inside of a university, studying. He smiled and put a hand on her arm. "I hope you're not going to sit in here with your nose in a book all week. I was hoping we could have a little fun, the two of us, on this trip."

Katie blushed. She looked at him, scrutinized him. Was he for real? Was he just pretending to be nice to her? She couldn't tell.

Katie closed the book with a slam. It was the first and maybe only time in her life she'd be on spring break in Cocoa Beach. So what if Greg had only brought her there to have sex with her and dump her afterwards. She could enjoy her trip anyway, couldn't she? It was time for her to let her hair down.

"I'll be right out," she said. "Just let me change."

EIGHTEEN

March 2015

THE BEACH WAS CRAWLING with college kids. It was always the same at this time of year. Spring breakers came down and drank their brains out. They probably needed it, I thought. There was a lot of pressure on the young people today, a lot of demands regarding what they wanted to do with their lives. A flock of them had just checked in at the motel and I helped them set up the volleyball net before I went surfing.

"Do you give lessons?" a boy named Greg asked me.

"Not usually," I said. "But I might make an exception if some of you want to try it. I have a couple of soft-top boards out the back. I could give you a few tips, but you have to do the hard work."

The three boys looked at each other. Two of them were athletic and would do fine, but I was more concerned about the third one. He was overweight and might have a hard time getting up on the board.

"We'd love to," Greg said. "Right guys?"

They all nodded.

"Okay. Let me get the boards out."

I found two big soft-top boards and carried them to the beach. I gave the boys a basic lesson on how to do a pop-up right, then how to paddle and how to read a wave. Then I took them out in the ocean and pushed them into some little ones. As expected, Greg and his more athletic friend learned quickly, whereas the third boy, Troy, struggled to even lie on the board. I pushed him into a couple of whitewater-waves to make it easier on him, but he never managed to stand up, much to his frustration. Troy had decided to try again when Greg waved at someone on the beach.

"Katie!"

The girl turned and looked in his direction. Cautiously, she waved back. She didn't seem like she was with them. She was nothing like the other girls they had brought, and somehow, she seemed like she wasn't very comfortable in this situation.

"Katie! Come try this. It's fun," Greg yelled from his board. He turned and told Troy to get off his board.

"Give it to Katie. Let her try," he said. There was something in the way he said it that made my skin crawl. He was the one running the show, no doubt about it. He spoke aggressively and commandingly at his friends.

"What are you waiting for? Go ahead."

Troy looked disappointed, then started to paddle in. I was getting a little tired of these kids and longed to go surfing on my own. A set of big chunky waves rolled in from the back. They were calling for me. I saw my buddy Pastor Daniel paddle out not far from me. He waved.

The young girl approached the water cautiously. She looked like she could crawl into a mouse hole. She was way out of her comfort zone. Two other girls were cheering her on, telling her to get out there to Greg. She decided to do as they told her to. Troy gave her his board and wished her good luck, and then I told her to lie on it and then helped her out. She took a bad beating from one wave that washed her right off the board and she ended up in the whitewater being twirled around. The wave took her right back on the beach. When she came up, her hair was in her face and her bikini top had fallen off on one side, so one of her breasts was showing. Greg burst into loud laughter, as the poor girl tried to catch her breath. The girls on the beach giggled and Katie looked up, disoriented, from the tumbling and the steady pounding roar of the ocean. I was still too far out for her to hear me if I yelled.

Don't turn around, please. Don't turn!

But she did. In those disastrous seconds, Katie turned around to face the beach and let everyone see her one uncovered breast. It was brutal. I felt terrible and jumped up on her board and let a wave take me in, then jumped up next to her. I tried to stand in front of her, so they couldn't see it. The two girls were laughing loudly and yelling. Still, poor Katie hadn't realized what was going on. I pointed to her breast.

"Your...your bikini," I said.

She still looked confused, then lowered her eyes and realized what had happened. Her pale face turned very red. I felt so bad for her. Katie fixed her bikini and looked at me again. I could tell how embarrassed she was...how this small incident would mark her for the rest of the trip.

"Maybe they didn't see it," I said. But we both knew I was lying. If it hadn't been too embarrassing, she would have cried. Her eyes fell to the ground.

"I...I'd better go up."

NINETEEN

November 2005

WHEN ELIZABETH WAS ALMOST three years old, something amazing happened to her. Her mother would never forget this moment that changed her life forever. Dottie was preparing breakfast, making pancakes and scrambled eggs for her family, and she placed the platter of them on the kitchen counter in front of Elizabeth, who was drawing. Since the child had never really shown any interest in food, Dottie didn't expect her to want anything to eat. She grabbed the milk from the fridge and poured the girl a glass like she always did in the morning, since that was the girl's main source of nutrition, but when she turned her head, she saw something truly astounding. The little girl reached out and grabbed a pancake from the stack.

Dottie held her breath.

Could this be? Was Elizabeth finally interested in food? Dottie smiled as she watched her daughter start eating the pancake in her hands. She couldn't believe it. Elizabeth was so tiny from not eating, and it had her mother constantly worrying about her. Dottie herself was a fairly voluptuous woman, all those in the West family were, and they never turned down a meal. Food was everything to them. In the South Georgia town where they lived, elaborate spreads of high-calorie foods were the centerpiece of every social activity. If someone didn't eat, there had to be something wrong with them. And everyone thought something was very wrong with Elizabeth. The neighbors stared at her when they met at church, and even more when they had their usual gathering at the Baptist church afterwards, where all the kids would indulge themselves in sugared doughnuts and cookies. Except for Elizabeth.

Dottie didn't dare to move as she watched her daughter gulp down the pancake...almost without chewing. When it was gone, she approached her and placed the milk in front of her.

"Boy, you've got some appetite this morning," she said, smiling from ear to ear.

Dottie wanted to scream in joy, yell to everyone in the house to get down to the kitchen and watch this.

Elizabeth is eating! Elizabeth is finally eating real food!

But, she didn't. She didn't want to get their hopes up too high…or her own, for that matter. This could be a one-time event. It might not happen again. But still, Dottie tried her luck, looking at Elizabeth's sparkling eyes as she eyeballed the stack of pancakes like she wanted to dig in and eat them all.

"Do you want one more?" she asked.

Elizabeth smiled widely. "Yes!" she exclaimed. "They're good, Mommy."

Dottie's hands shook heavily as she reached over and grabbed another pancake and put it on a plate for Elizabeth. She couldn't believe what was happening. She simply couldn't believe it. All this time, James had told her the girl would eventually start eating, and all this time she had feared he was wrong, but now…now… now she had finally come around.

"Would you like to try some syrup on this one?" Dottie asked, her voice trembling. She feared Elizabeth would lose interest and go back to her old not-eating self.

But she didn't. She looked at her mother with the most endearing smile. "Yes!" she exclaimed and gesticulated with her arms. "I am sooo hungry, Mommy. I am so, so, so hungry!"

"Then you better eat some," Dottie said, and poured syrup on the pancake, then cut it up for her daughter. She watched Elizabeth as she ate. Never had she seen such a beautiful sight. Finally, everything would be all right. Finally, she could stop worrying.

TWENTY

March 2015

SHANNON COULDN'T CONCENTRATE. Her fingers were drumming on the guitar instead of playing the tune of the song she had been working on for days. The words simply wouldn't come to her. She had planned on finishing it today, so she could go on spring break with Angela when she got home from school. But it was almost time to pick her up and she was nowhere near finished.

It would have to wait.

Shannon sighed and looked down at the beach from the balcony of her rented condo, where she was sitting with her guitar in her lap. She spotted Jack in the water. He was pushing in some kids and screaming in joy when they managed to stand up. Shannon chuckled and shook her head. How on earth could he think about surfing with all that was going on? Shannon couldn't even concentrate on her song. It was unbearable how her past had suddenly caught up with her. The mistake she had made so many years ago when deciding to hide the emails from the police had caught up with her and kicked her in the back. She felt like she was lying on the ground and couldn't get up again. And this time, it was worse. This time, she knew this email was from the killer; she had no doubt about it. So, this time, it would be all her fault if the killer wasn't stopped before it was too late. Jack had told her to relax and not beat herself up about it, but she couldn't. She had kept this bottled up inside of her for too long…this guilt…and it had been eating at her. Now, she would give anything in the world to stop this guy.

But how? How was she supposed to do that? There was nothing in the emails that indicated who this person was. AM didn't tell much, did it? Were they initials? Hardly.

Shannon sighed and closed her eyes. She let the breeze hit her face. It was a very hot day out. She liked these warm days, where the wind was your friend.

Someone was laughing loudly on the beach. Shannon opened her eyes and looked. Jack was talking to one of the kids in the shallows. He pointed at her chest. What was that? Had she lost her swimsuit? It was only on one side, but the entire beach could see her breast, and she didn't seem to notice until Jack told her. Some girls were laughing on the beach. Everyone seemed to be staring at her. Shannon felt terrible for the poor girl. That had to be so humiliating. She remembered how it had been at that age. Nothing worse than a public disgrace. Nothing could ruin your life like that.

It was obvious that Jack was trying to cover her till she got it under control. That was Jack for you, always the hero. Shannon loved that about him. Most men would just have looked, or even turned away and acted like they hadn't seen it. But not Jack. He felt responsible.

Shannon had to admit, she was beginning to like him more and more as time passed. She was very fond of him. But she still had her doubts whether it was too soon for her. She feared he was nothing but a rebound for her…an excuse to move on. He had said he loved her, and she believed she loved him too. But, some days, she was unsure. It was all still so new. He made her feel good. That was all she knew, and all she needed right now. But would he still love her with all the demons she carried around and constantly fought? She knew she wasn't an easy person to love. Jack deserved someone much better than her.

As she thought about it, her phone started to ring. She picked it up. It was Joe —again.

"You gotta stop calling me," she said as she answered it. Her first thought was to ignore the call, but he had called at least six times today, and she had a feeling he wasn't going to stop until she picked up.

"Please, Shannon," Joe said. "Just talk to me. I miss you so much. You and Angela. The house is so big and empty without you in it. I'm not sure I can take it. You've gotta come home, Shannon. You've got to."

Shannon closed her eyes and touched the bridge of her nose. When was he going to understand this? "I'm not coming home. I'm never coming back. You have to realize that, Joe."

"But, what about us? Remember how it used to be? How much we used to love each other? Don't tell me you don't love me anymore, because I don't believe it."

Shannon sighed. She spotted Jack on the beach again. He was running towards the water with his own board under his arm. Life with Jack was so easy. Life here in Cocoa Beach had been so easy for her the past month. But, Joe was right. They had a lot of history together.

"I'm the only one who really knows you, Shannon," he said. "Think of all we've been through together. Are you just going to bail on that? Just like that? Throw it all away? We have a daughter together. I helped you build your career. Without me, you would be nothing, and you know it. Angela is mine too. If you don't come back, I'm going to take her away from you. I hope you realize that. I will be forced to reveal everything, Shannon. Don't force me to tell them all your secrets."

"You wouldn't!"

"Of course I would. Not only the judge will know. The entire world will. I'll have a press conference of my own. Tell them the entire story. I'm sure they'll looove that, aren't you?"

Joe laughed. Shannon snorted in anger.

"Go to hell."

Then she hung up.

TWENTY-ONE

March 2015

STANLEY WAS CRYING. It had been many years since he last cried. Stanley didn't believe a real man should cry. He had told his son many times and let him know it wouldn't be accepted. Crying was a weakness.

Nevertheless, Stanley was wailing and howling now. Tears were streaming across his cheeks as his guardian forced food into his mouth. In between swallowing, he pleaded for it to stop.

"Please. Please. I'll do anything."

"If you want that beautiful granddaughter of yours to live, you'll open your mouth and eat," the guardian said.

"I can't. I can't. No more food. Please."

His guardian shook their head with a *tsk*. In one hand was the gun, in the other, the spoon. The dreaded spoon, where potatoes in thick gravy leaned on some undefined chunk of meat. Stanley couldn't stand the sight or the smell. His stomach was so full it was painful to breathe. He was beginning to wonder what this person really wanted from him. To kill him with food?

"Don't give me that. Now, be a good boy. Open up."

Stanley gagged. Food overflowed into his mouth and made him feel sick. His guardian reacted by pushing the potatoes and meat into his mouth and forcing him to swallow it all. Stanley would have bent over in pain if he had been able to move. But he couldn't. It hurt too badly.

Please, God. Help me out of this mess.

The sessions where he was fed were getting longer and longer. This time it had been going on for several hours. Meal after meal was brought into the small room, and spoon after spoon was brought to his mouth. Stanley was so tired and wanted so badly to sleep, but his guardian didn't seem to want to take a break from this strange game. He barely had time to think about escape or how to save his granddaughter from the hands of this crazy person.

He had tried to grab the guardian's wrists once to force the spoon away, but his guardian had let him know that wasn't acceptable behavior by walking out of the room, then coming back with a fire poker that was soon after poked through Stanley's right shin. The pain had made Stanley scream at the top of his lungs. And, then again—even worse this time—when it was pulled out again.

"Don't ever do that again! Do you hear me?" the guardian yelled even louder.

Stanley wasn't going to. He had to think of Elyse. If only he did what this mad person told him to, then maybe he would eventually be able to save her. There were many decisions he had made in his life that he wasn't proud of. So many times he had done what he would later regret. It haunted him daily. But, this time, he was going to make the right decision. And that was to make sure nothing bad happened to Elyse. He would never be able to live with himself if it did.

"Open up, Stanley," his guardian said, and forced yet another spoonful of potatoes into his mouth. He had to swallow in order to not choke. Stanley cried as the wave of pain struck through him. He couldn't stand being in his body anymore. So much pain, so much aching. This time, he was certain he heard his stomach enlarging. He was sure it sounded like a balloon being blown up. Or maybe that was just how it felt.

Stanley moaned and closed his eyes. He tried to dream himself away, to think of something that would make him happy, anything that could take him away from this awful place, even Disney World would be better than this. Ah, yes. Disney World with Elyse seemed like Heaven compared to this. He groaned in sadness, feeling sorry for himself.

Was this nightmare ever going to end?

TWENTY-TWO

March 2015

NEXT MORNING, I woke up with all of my muscles sore from surfing the day before. The waves had been excellent and I had enjoyed myself, even though I couldn't stop thinking about the email. Now, I was awake in my bed, while the waves crashed the beach outside my window. I stared at the ceiling, wondering what to do. Shannon was sleeping next to me, and I enjoyed listening to her deep breaths.

We had eaten dinner at my parents' place the night before, and the kids played so well together. My mom told us to go have some fun without the kids for a change. Even Emily decided to stay at the motel, where my dad promised to teach them all to play pool. I had taken Shannon to Friday Fest downtown. I loved Friday Fest, where they locked down all of downtown for traffic, and there was music and people were everywhere. We had a wonderful evening and ended up letting all the kids sleep at the motel, since it was the weekend and spring break on top of it.

"Good morning, tiger," Shannon said and opened her eyes.

I looked at her, feeling so proud to be with her. She was gorgeous, even after a night out and just waking up. It was unbelievable. My head was spinning. I felt like I was getting in trouble. There was no way out now. I was all in with her.

I leaned over and kissed her. She closed her eyes. "Good morning, gorgeous," I said. "Thank you so much for a great night last night."

"It was quite enjoyable, wasn't it?"

"Sure was."

I tasted her lips once more and forgot everything about the world around us for just a few seconds, then slipped under the covers and pulled her close to me. We made love while the sun rose over the Atlantic Ocean outside my windows. It was beautiful and so intense. I never wanted to let go of her again.

We fell back asleep again and woke up at nine. "What do you say to coffee in bed?" I whispered. "You can stay right here all day. You don't ever have to move again."

Shannon laughed. "If only that was true." She turned and looked into my eyes. "You know very well I have that gig at Runaway Country. I couldn't say no to them when they called. I mean, it's right here."

Runaway Country was a music festival featuring country musicians from all over. It was all the big names, and naturally, the amazing Shannon King had to be one of them. It was a huge event around here and attracted thousands of people.

"I wish you had, though," I said and kissed her again.

"What? You don't want me on stage?" Shannon asked. "You don't want thousands of people adoring the woman you love? What a big surprise, Detective Ryder."

I chuckled. She was right. I never thought much of celebrities and the lifestyle they led. It seemed to me it hurt more people than it helped. I knew Shannon's story of drug abuse and how the pressure of being a celebrity had a part in it. It wasn't a healthy lifestyle and it complicated things. I wasn't the jealous type, but I had thought about how I would feel if she took off on a tour that lasted several months. I knew the temptations and offers were many. She could easily find someone much more handsome and interesting than me. Would I be able to keep her?

I didn't want to think about it. My phone vibrated on the table next to the bed. I groaned, stretched my arm out, and grabbed it. It was Ron. I sighed and rubbed my forehead.

"I gotta take this."

"On a Saturday?"

"If Ron calls on a Saturday, I better take it. That means it's serious. Ron appreciates his weekends more than anyone at the office. Believe me."

"Ryder," I said, with the phone to my ear. I got up and walked to the kitchen to put on a pot of coffee. Shannon whistled behind me as she watched my naked body. I smiled and shook my behind for her. She laughed.

"Ryder, Goddammit. I can't believe I'm saying this, but you need to come in today."

That didn't sound good. "What's going on, Ron?"

"We have a body."

TWENTY-THREE

March 2015

"WHAT DO WE HAVE?"

Ron was waiting for me in the parking lot when I drove up. The place was called The Grapefruit Trail, located on a strip of woods on the south shore of the Tillman Canal in Palm Bay on the mainland. It was a place where cyclists rode their mountain bikes on the hilly trails through the woods.

"A cyclist found something early this morning. He stopped to...well, to take a leak when he spotted something on the ground. He thought it looked strange and called us. We have to walk there."

I followed Ron through the woods for about five minutes and was quickly surrounded by deep dense forest. It was a strange place, with many trails great for biking and hiking. It was also a place that was excellent for hiding a body, I thought.

"It's right in here."

The scene was already packed with crime scene technicians. It was blocked off, and two officers from Palm Bay Police blocked the entrance. We showed them our badges and were let inside. People roamed everywhere among the bushes. The vegetation was heavy.

"Watch where you step," Ron said.

In a place like this, you had to watch for snakes. The area where the body had been found was almost impassable, but as we came closer, I could tell it was almost like a small clearing. Perfect for taking a leak without anyone seeing you, and perfect for hiding something you didn't want to be found.

The remains of what was once a forty-something aged man had been pulled out of the soil. He was still wearing clothes, but by the decomposition, I guessed he had been dead for quite awhile.

"We found his wallet in his pants," Ron said, and showed me a small plastic bag with an old leather wallet and a driver's license in it with the name Daniel Millman. Date of birth told me he was forty-seven years old. At least, he would have been.

"Has the family been notified?" I asked.

Ron smirked.

"Oh, come on," I said. "You want me to do it?"

"Take Beth with you. She can be the compassionate one."

"I have a feeling you don't know Beth very well," I said.

Ron chuckled. Then he shook his head. "So what do you make of it?"

"I don't know," I said, kneeling next to the body. "He's been in the ground for quite some time."

"How long would you guess?"

I shrugged. "You can see how the animals have been eating off him here and here. The body was in the ground, but I'm guessing a fox or something might have tried to dig it out, then the rest of the animals could get to it. Dead things decompose fast here in Florida, but we have to remember, he was in the ground, where the temperature is lower, until the animals dug him out. You can see here and here on the ground where it has been disturbed by digging, and you can tell that his face was scratched when the animals tried to get him out. I'd say maybe three-four months?"

Ron nodded. I could tell the sight of the body moved him. He tried to never show it, but he was a softie. I remembered when I first discovered it. Right after I had moved here and started working at the Sheriff's Office in Rockledge, Ron's dog, the cutest labra-doodle, got sick and had to go through surgery and stay away overnight. Ron had tears in his eyes all day, and even though he tried to hide it, we could all see it. He was devastated and missed the dog like crazy. Ron was a family man. I liked that about him. Three kids and four grandchildren were his accomplishments and pride in life.

"So, what happened to Daniel Millman?" he asked with a sniff.

"There don't seem to be any visual signs of trauma," I said. "No bullet holes, no bleeding. It's hard to tell if he was strangled when the body is decomposed like this, so we'll have to wait till the ME finishes to determine if that's the case."

Ron cleared his throat. "So, are you going to call Beth or should I?"

TWENTY-FOUR

March 2015

I PICKED up Beth at her home in Satellite Beach. She lived in a small house just a few blocks from the beach. In the yard played three kids in a jumpy-jump house, spraying each other with water from a hose. I smiled when I parked the car. I watched as Beth came out, kissed the kids, then sprang for the car. Boy, had I misjudged her.

"Mommy will be home in a few hours," she yelled, as she jumped inside with her plump body into the passenger seat. "You behave, you hear?"

The kids hardly noticed. They were having too much fun. "I got the neighbor to watch them while we're gone," she said as I drove off. "I just hope they don't burn the house down."

I chuckled.

"What?"

"Nothing. I just didn't know you had children."

I continued towards Lansing Island in Indian Harbor Beach, where our victim lived when he was still alive.

"Well, I do," she said with her usual harsh tone, letting me know I wasn't getting any closer to her than this.

"Husband?"

"What's with the questions all of a sudden?"

"Sorry. I just wanted to get to know my partner. That's all." I took a turn and hit the entrance to the island.

Lansing Island was a gated island, where I had been told Bruce Willis owned a house. I didn't know if it was true; there were a lot of rumors about it, as there always were with places only few people were allowed to enter. The island was located in the river and had the most spectacular houses of anywhere around here. I drove up to the gate and a uniformed man came out. I showed him my badge.

"We're here to see Mrs. Millman."

"Is she expecting you?" he asked.

I shook my head. "No."

The guard nodded with a sigh. He understood. "I'll let you in. She's in 219."

He went inside his small guard house, pressed the button, and the gate opened. I drove by and waved to the guard. I drove past many gorgeous houses and could hardly believe anyone lived like this. It was as far from my world as it could possibly be. Not that I would ever trade for anything.

"219, it's here," Beth said.

I looked out the window and spotted a house of about ten-thousand square feet. Maybe even more. It was huge. The gate wasn't closed, so we drove right through. I parked in the enormous driveway, then walked up towards the front door, closely followed by Beth. I found a doorbell and rang it. I took in a deep breath as I heard footsteps approaching behind it. It opened. A woman in her early thirties looked at us, surprised. The look in her eyes made her seem sad. I wondered if she already knew.

"Mrs. Millman?"

"Yes?"

I showed her my badge. "I'm detective Ryder. This is my partner. We're from the Sheriff's office. Can we come in?"

"Of course." The woman stepped aside.

We walked inside the foyer with its marble floors. Mrs. Millman closed the door behind us. She showed us the way into the library, which had the most spectacular views over the river.

"Do you want anything?" she asked. "Coffee?" I detected nervousness in her voice. Her eyes were avoiding ours.

"No, thank you. We're good."

"Do sit down." She pointed at the set of leather chairs and we sat down. She put her hands in her lap. It seemed like she had to pull herself together to focus. I was wondering if she was on something. She didn't smell like alcohol, but something was off.

"I'm afraid we have some bad news," I said.

She nodded, like she was expecting this.

"Your husband...we found his body this morning."

Mrs. Millman didn't seem to react at all. She kept nodding. Beth leaned forward. "Mrs. Millman, do you understand what we're telling you?"

"Yes. Yes. You found Daniel." Mrs. Millman's hands were constantly moving, rubbing against each other in a nervous way.

Beth and I exchanged looks.

"Mrs. Millman. Your husband's body was found in the woods. Buried in the ground. We don't know what caused his death yet, but he seemed to have been in the ground for quite some time. When did he go missing?"

Mrs. Millman shook her head. "November. I reported him missing to Indian Harbor police."

"I am sorry to say this, Mrs. Millman, but you don't seem very surprised that your husband is dead," I said.

She looked at me. She corrected her hair with small fast movements. I couldn't determine if she was in shock or in some kind of denial, or if she already knew her husband was dead.

"Mrs. Millman. Your husband is dead," I repeated. It wasn't uncommon that we had to repeat this kind of information several times before the relatives fully understood what we were telling them. It could be a lot to take in at once. Mrs. Millman was rubbing her hands together while her eyes hit the floor. I detected sadness in her, but couldn't figure out if it was from the information I had just given her or if it was something else.

"I know," she said. "I heard you. It's just...well...He's been gone for a long time now. I wasn't expecting to see him again."

It was like she wanted to tell us something, like we saw the real Mrs. Millman for just a second before she decided to pull back behind the façade protecting her.

"It is, of course, terrible that he's dead," she continued, as emotionless as if she had told us about what she had for breakfast. Her voice sounded blurred.

"We're treating the case as a homicide," I said.

Mrs. Millman looked at me. "Homicide?" she asked.

"Yes. We believed he was killed. We need to know some information about him."

"Like what?"

"Like, what does your husband do?"

"He owns Millman Technologies," she said. "Founded it himself twelve years ago. They make components for the rockets at the Space Center and for Boeing airplanes."

I wrote it on my notepad. I had heard about Millman Technologies. It was one of the biggest and fastest growing companies on the Space Coast.

"So, you reported your husband missing in November, you say. Where was he last seen?"

"Driving home from the office in Cape Canaveral on November eighth," she said. "It was a Saturday. Daniel was supposed to come home for Christopher's sixth birthday party, but he never made it home. His secretary told us he left at five fifteen, and someone saw his car on the A1A driving by the statue of Kelly Slater when entering Downtown Cocoa Beach. It was one of our friends who recognized the car, but no one has seen him since. They found the car in a ditch in Melbourne. No trace of Daniel. I have to admit, I thought he had run off with some twenty year-old."

"And I take it Christopher is your son?" I saw a painting of all three of them over the fireplace.

"Yes. He's in boarding school in Palm Beach Gardens. He comes home every weekend."

"Boarding school in Kindergarten, huh? That is early."

"It's the best school around. Can't compromise with education."

"As I said, we have reason to believe your husband was killed, ma'am," I said. "Do you know if your husband had any enemies? Anyone who would want him dead?"

Mrs. Millman looked indifferent. "You mean, besides me?" Then she chuckled.

"You wanted your husband dead?" I asked.

Mrs. Millman hardly reacted to my question. "Of course I didn't," she answered sharply.

"How was your relationship?" I asked.

"Dead, like him," she answered emotionless. "Has been for years."

I nodded as I wrote it down. I couldn't quite figure out what was going on here. Maybe their marriage had just been so bad that she had stopped caring?

Beth asked for the restroom, then disappeared for a few minutes. I stared at my notes on my pad. Mrs. Millman looked at me.

"Can I get you anything, Officer?"

"Detective," I said. "And, no thank you. I'm still good. Is there anyone you would like us to call for you, ma'am?"

She looked at me like she didn't understand what I said. "Why would that be, Detective?"

"Well, in times of loss, it's often a good idea to…"

"I'm alright," she said.

Beth returned and I got up. I handed Mrs. Millman my card. "Call me if you think of anything that we might need to know."

"Of course, Officer."

"And, don't leave town."

We left the house and got into my Jeep. I started the engine when Beth looked at me. She showed me something in her hand. A small orange bottle of pills.

"Benzos," she said. "It was tucked in between the towels. And this was just in one of the guest bathrooms."

"That explains a lot," I said, and drove out of the driveway.

"The woman probably has them stashed all over the house. Nothing makes you stop caring about things like a benzo. They don't necessarily make you happy, or necessarily make you sad. They just stop your thinking. I once had a depression-induced panic attack and took a benzo. It literally manifested as a vision of a white elephant running through my mind, clearing the negative thoughts and feelings of ultimate doom out. I went to sleep feeling a bit shaken, but not stirred."

It explained why Mrs. Millman hardly reacted when I told her that her husband had been killed and her repeated questions. But it still didn't explain what had happened to Daniel Millman. I had a feeling it wasn't the last time I'd question Mrs. Millman.

TWENTY-FIVE

March 2015

SHANNON STILL FELT happy from spending the night with Jack. She was standing backstage at Runaway Country in Wickham Park in Melbourne, smiling to herself, while Blake Shelton was on. She was going on right after him. She had her stage clothes on, the diamond-covered boots and hat, and she was holding her microphone in her hand, the one she never walked on stage without. It had followed her for years and was covered in diamonds. It was a little much, but that was what a real star had, her manager had told her when buying it for her. It was the first time she'd be going on stage since she left Joe, and she was feeling pretty good about herself for the first time in years. She sensed she was on the right track. Leaving him was the right thing to do.

Wasn't it?

She thought about Angela. The girl missed her dad a lot, especially since Joe went back to Nashville. He was, after, all her father. Shannon hated to do this to her child...to keep her away from her father, but what else could she do? Joe was out of control right now and threatening her with all kinds of things one moment, then pleading with her desperately to come back the next. It was hard. Shannon still had feelings for him. She knew she did, and standing here backstage, where she used to be with Joe for all those years, she missed him. Just a little bit. She didn't miss the yelling and the blaming afterwards or the beating, but she missed what they had before all that started. Before he became jealous of her success. Maybe if she stopped this? Maybe if she dropped her career? Maybe then they could be a real family?

No. It was wrong. Shannon knew it very well. Jack was so right for her. Cocoa Beach was the right place to be. She had never felt better. Angela was happier here too, even though she missed her father.

Blake Shelton finished his last tune and people clapped. The females in the audience screamed. He was good. Shannon had met him on many occasions and liked him. Joe had, naturally, been mad every time she had spoken with him, and that never ended well.

Shannon chuckled and smiled to herself. So many memories she had from her life as a musician. Good and bad. But it all came down to this…it was her dream, her passion. This was what she loved.

She only wished that Jack could be there to see her.

Blake came out and looked at her with a wide smile.

"They're all yours, baby," he said and gave her a kiss on the cheek. "I warmed them up for you."

Shannon smiled while getting ready. The announcer took the microphone. People were already chanting her name.

Shannon King, Shannon King, Shannon King.

Shannon closed her eyes and took in a deep breath. She loved this part. The entrance, the anticipation, the screaming, the fans. Oh, how she loved her fans. They were the reason she could live doing what she loved. It was amazing.

"Please welcome Shannon King!"

Shannon walked onto the stage, holding her microphone in her hand with her guitar around her shoulder. The fans screamed. Shannon stared into the ocean of faces.

"Hello Runaway Country!" she yelled. "How are you out there? Are y'all ready for some music?"

The crowd screamed and Shannon hit the first note of her first song. She sang three songs, then the new one that she had just finished last night, just her and her guitar. The crowd went wild. Shannon enjoyed their applause, thanked them, and went back stage. As she did, she spotted Jack. He was clapping while walking towards her. Shannon smiled and threw herself around his neck.

"You made it!"

"You killed it out there," he said and kissed her. "I'm so proud of you."

"I did, didn't I? I don't think I have ever been better."

They walked back to her dressing trailer and closed the door. Jack poured them some complimentary iced tea and they sat down, Shannon with a deep satisfied sigh.

"It's good to see you smiling again," Jack said. "I'm glad I made it just in time for your set."

"So, what's going on? Did they find a body?" Shannon asked.

"Yes. We don't know much yet. But, let's not talk about that. That's boring depressing stuff."

Shannon smiled and picked up her phone to make a tweet about her set, when she noticed she had received an email. Her heart stopped.

"What's wrong?" Jack asked. "You're completely pale, Shannon."

"It's from him," she said, sensing the panic growing inside her. "It's that guy again."

TWENTY-SIX

March 2015

You were good on stage today, Shannon. You nailed it. Better than any of the other many times I have seen you in concert. I'm guessing this Jack Ryder that we read about in the magazines really does you good. I'm happy for you. It's always good when it works out, isn't it? Unfortunately, it doesn't always work like that, does it? I'm afraid not. That is why I have to do what I must do. Again, you have my apologies. I am so terribly sorry for what I have to do. I hope for your forgiveness.

With love,

AM

Shannon looked at me as I read the email. She was biting her lips. I finished it and gave her the phone back.

"I need you to forward it to my email address. I'll have Richard send it to the IT guys, who will try and track the email address once again. Last time, nothing came of it, he said. The IP address led us to some computer in India. But we'll give it another try. This is another address."

"Do you think he's here?" she asked. "He wrote that I was good on stage. Do you think he was in the crowd?"

"It's definitely a possibility," I said. "He said that he goes to many of your concerts." I paused and looked at Shannon. I wasn't quite sure what to do next. If this person was in the crowd out there, could I find him? I had no idea what he looked like. Even if I blocked all the exits I didn't know what I was looking for. It would only ruin the entire festival and make me very unpopular with Ron. Runaway Country was a huge event around here. I couldn't destroy it without really strong grounds, and so far, an email wasn't quite enough.

"You stay here," I said. "Lock the door when I'm out."

"Where are you going?"

"I have to go look around for a little while. Maybe talk to the officers at the exits, tell them to look for anyone suspicious. Ask them if they've noticed anything. I'll be back for you afterwards."

Shannon nodded and did as I had told her to. I left her trailer, then walked into the festival grounds among the thousands of happy guests with beers in their hands. I walked to the entrance and found Officer Rogers from Melbourne Police.

"Ryder," he said with a nod. "I hear she did good today. I could only hear it from here, but it sounded good."

"Yes. She did really well."

He told me everything had been very calm up until now.

"It's still only the second day of the festival," he said. "There's always tomorrow."

That was one part that worried me. The shooter could strike anytime today or tomorrow. Runaway Country would be the perfect place for this shooter to make his move, if he wanted to repeat what he had done back in '09. There were lots of people gathered in one place, lots he could kill in just a few seconds. But what made me wonder was...how he was planning on escaping? A large fence surrounded the place. Police and security guards were everywhere.

I left Officer Roger and found Officer Taylor inside on the festival grounds close to the Main Stage. Another singer had taken the stage. I talked to Taylor for a little while, but he hadn't seen anything either.

"What exactly are you looking for?" he asked.

I shook my head, while trying to look at every face in the crowd to see if I could spot anything out of the ordinary. Any look in someone's eyes telling me he wasn't there for the music. Any nervous tic that could reveal him.

"That's the damned thing," I said. "I'm not sure I know."

TWENTY-SEVEN

March 2015

THE KILLER WAS WATCHING the show. The singer on the stage was good, but not as good as Shannon King. Shannon was the killer's absolute favorite singer. Everything about her songs just made sense somehow. They were inspirational.

Through the crowd, the killer spotted Jack Ryder, the detective who was known as Shannon King's new boyfriend. He was talking to an officer on duty. The killer smiled. Jack Ryder looked worried.

Guess you got my email.

The killer knew it complicated things that Shannon had started seeing this detective, but the killer wasn't concerned. The killer had prepared this well. Better than last time around. Back in the movie theater, things hadn't turned out exactly like expected, like planned. It had kept the killer from doing anything like this again for all these years. The killer couldn't risk everything going wrong like last time. But that was six years ago. This time, the killer had more experience. This time, everything would be perfect.

I'm so sorry for all this.

The killer imagined lifting the gun and shooting into the crowd. The killer still remembered the feeling from last time. The feeling of complete power. The power of life and death.

So exhilarating. Yet so devastating.

The sensation of the weapon going off, the fear in those faces, the screams, the eyes staring in terror at this mad person with their finger on the trigger. A chill ran across the killer's spine. It was a shame it had to happen again. The killer hated having to do this again, hated to have to feel it again, to see how the victim's chest would explode when it met the bullet from the killer's weapon. It had haunted the killer ever since. It had been all the killer had been able to think of for the last six years. Day and night.

The singer on the main stage stopped and thanked her audience. The killer clapped along with everyone else. Another singer took the stage. People cheered. It was getting dark now. The killer stepped out of the crowd and walked towards a stand.

"A Corona, please."

A woman in a tank top handed the beer over the counter. The killer paid with a ten-dollar bill, asked the woman to keep the change as a tip, save up for college so she didn't have to keep working in places like this, and took the beer.

The killer sipped the beer while glancing at the crowd of happy people. Some were dancing while holding their beers up in the air. Most were singing out loud and recording on their phones. A couple was kissing not far from where the killer stood. None of them knew what was about to happen. None even suspected it coming. The killer felt a deep sense of sadness. They were going to be so surprised. Baffled even. Scared. The killer hated to do this to all these happy people. But it had to be done. There was no one who could prevent this from happening. Not even that detective.

The killer looked at Jack Ryder again. A look of desperation was painted all over his face.

I'm so sorry for this. Sorry for causing you all this distress. But you must understand, there is nothing I can do about it. I am nothing but a means to an end. What I do serves a higher purpose. One you might never understand. And I'm not asking you to. I'm not asking for anyone to understand this.

Detective Jack Ryder was on the move now. He walked behind the crowd and approached the killer. Their eyes met and locked for just a second. The killer's heart started racing.

Has he spotted me? Does he know who I am?

"Could I get a bottle of water, please?" he asked the woman with the ten-dollar bill stuck in her bra. He smiled at the killer with a nod. The killer smiled back.

I'm so sorry, Detective. I'm so terribly sorry.

Part Two

NO NEED TO BE COY

TWENTY-EIGHT

March 2015

STANLEY WAS IN PAIN. His entire body was hurting so badly from overeating for days now. Finally, his guardian left the room and he had a break for a few minutes to go to the bathroom. The door to the hallway was locked. He heard his guardian turn the key. All Stanley wanted was to run to the bathroom and throw up.

He could hardly get out of the bed. His leg hurt too badly, and he had to roll from the bed to the floor and hit the carpet with a thud. Stanley whimpered, then dragged himself by his arms towards the bathroom. The pain was excruciating. He felt like he had gained fifty pounds over the last two days he had been locked up in this room. Barely a moment had passed without him being fed. It was torture. All he had been allowed to do was to go to the bathroom whenever he needed to, but constantly under his guardian's supervision. Finally, they had run out of food, and his guardian had left to get more.

Stanley pulled himself to the toilet, panting and gasping for air. He opened the lid and pulled himself up towards the toilet. He hardly had to put his finger down his throat before food started to pour out of him. Stanley had always hated to throw up more than most things in this world, but now it felt like such a relief. The pressure on his stomach was being relieved slowly as the food sprayed out of him and into the toilet bowl. How on earth could it even contain all this food? He was stumped that he could have this much inside of him. How was it possible?

When Stanley was done, he flushed in a hurry and dragged his body to the sink, where he managed to open the faucet and splash water on his face with one hand, while the other held his body up. He felt so worn out. Completely exhausted. He started to wonder about getting out of this place of hell, but he felt so weary he could hardly think. What was this place anyway? By the look of the decorations, it was a nice house. The curtains were heavy and the carpet was deep and looked expensive. The bed was nice too. King-sized and the sheets made from silk. The room had no other furniture other than a dresser, which he had already looked in the first time he was left alone in there, but found all of the drawers empty. On the walls were paintings of the beach and fish, one of a sea turtle. The air seemed fresh, and he wondered if he was close to the ocean. He hadn't heard any waves, though, but the windows were hurricane-proof, and he knew from his own house that they blocked out all sounds...even from a roaring road. Stanley knew he didn't have much time before his guardian would be back. He had tried to look out the window, but hurricane shutters were closed from the outside, so he couldn't see anything. He did, however, have a feeling that he was on the second floor and the room was facing east, since he could see the light coming through the small holes in the shutters at sunrise and it was gone by midday.

Stanley splashed more water on his face and washed out his mouth, wondering how he had gotten himself into this mess and how he was going to get out of it. What was the idea behind all of this? Why was he being forced to eat all this food? He looked down at his hurting leg, where the fire poker had gone through the pants and the skin. Blood had soaked his pants. The bleeding had stopped. He just hoped it wouldn't get infected. Stanley let his body sink to the cold bathroom floor, where he rested for a few seconds just to get his strength back. He pulled himself up to a sitting position and planted his back against the wall with a sigh. Then, he folded his hands and did something he hadn't done in many years, not since...Not since the time he had started blaming God for making his son what he was. But now wasn't a time to hold a grudge against his Creator. Now was the time to make amends.

Stanley closed his eyes and said a quiet prayer.

"Dear God. I need your help. What do I do? Oh, God, what am I to do? If I try to escape, Elyse might get hurt. If I stay, I am afraid I might die. What do I do? Help me, God," he said, crying.

As he sat there on the floor with his eyes closed not expecting to hear anything from the God he had turned his back on many years ago, he heard an answer in the form of a small knock from the other side of the wall. Stanley doubted it was from God, but it was something. It was hope.

Stanley gasped. He listened to hear it again, and seconds later, it was repeated. A small knock again. Stanley pulled himself to the wall, and then put his ear towards it. There it was again. And again. Three short, three long, then three short again. S-O-S. Stanley knocked back. S-O-S.

"Is there someone in there?" he heard a voice say.

"Yes," he said with tears in his eyes. "Yes, I'm in here. I'm Stanley. Who are you?"

"I'm Roy. Help me. I am being held captive and force-fed for hours non-stop!"

Stanley felt how the blood left his head. He couldn't believe this. He wasn't the only one here. He wasn't the only one being held captive. There were more.

TWENTY-NINE

March 2015

I stayed all night at the festival, until the doors closed at one in the morning. Luckily, nothing happened. There were a lot of frustrating hours, where I kept seeing ghosts everywhere. With every face I looked at, I wondered if that could be the killer. Every loud noise made me jump, thinking this was it. He had struck. It was exhausting.

When the music finally stopped, I couldn't wait to get the people out of there. Soon, the area was emptied completely and I dared to breathe normally again. My two fellow officers went home, and as soon as I had said goodbye to them, I jumped in my Jeep and drove back to my condo. Shannon had decided to go home earlier and was already in her condo when I got back. The kids stayed for one more night at their grandparents' and I knew Angela was with them. I stopped outside of Shannon's door, thinking there was no reason for us to sleep separately when the kids weren't even home. It was funny, but I really missed her when we were away from each other. Even if it was just for a few hours. But, at the same time, I was terrified of smothering her, of scaring her away by coming off too needy and clingy. I knew that was how my ex-wife Arianna had felt when we first met, because I insisted on us being together constantly. I smothered her, she said. She needed her space every now and then. But that was just the way I was. I didn't need any space. Once I found a woman I liked, I didn't see any reason not to be together if it was possible. I didn't know Shannon well enough to know if she felt the same way. Not yet, at least.

I bit my lip, wondering if I should just go up to my own condo. Shannon had a big day tomorrow, with her last concert at the festival. Maybe she needed her sleep. I had to remember who she was. Meeting me and moving here was a big step for her, and she still had her career to consider. She also still had a husband, even though she had filed for a divorce. Joe was resisting it and refusing to sign the papers, which only made everything more complicated.

I sighed and let my hand fall back down. When I was about to turn away from the door and walk towards the stairs, the door opened. Shannon looked at me with a smile.

"Were you seriously going to leave?"

I chuckled and shrugged. "I...I guess."

"I've been watching you through the peephole for the last few minutes. I could hear you on the stairs and you stopping outside my door. To be frank, it freaked me out a little, since I can't stop thinking about that shooter, but then I saw it was just you." She pushed me lovingly. "Don't ever do that to me again. You hear?"

I smiled and pulled her close to me. I leaned down and kissed her soft lips. After a day like this, this was exactly what I needed. "I promise," I whispered.

She pulled my shirt. "Now, come in."

I didn't get much sleep all night, even though I was with her. I kept wondering about Daniel Millman and the shooter's email. I was so relieved that nothing had happened at the festival and started wondering if this person could just be some idiot pulling our legs. Was he just messing around trying to scare us? Or was the threat real? So far, it hadn't turned out to be. The case of the body of Daniel Millman haunted me as well. Something was really off with that wife and that odd place he had been found. It just seemed so wrong. I was still waiting for Yamilla to finish the autopsy and hoping that would provide me with some answers, since the wife couldn't. This coming week, I would have to interview their neighbors at Lansing Island and their friends. It was never easy when it was wealthy people, who, for the most part, thought they were somehow elevated above the law, or at least above suspicion of any kind. They rarely wanted to contribute to any investigation, since they were often too busy for that kind of distraction.

"Go to sleep," Shannon finally whispered, half asleep, and put her arm on my chest. "You're keeping me awake and I have a big day tomorrow. Sunday is the main event of the festival. It's the biggest day with the most people. I have to give them my best."

THIRTY

March 2015

SUNDAY MORNING, I went to check on the kids, since I had hardly seen them in two days. Shannon was getting ready in her apartment while I walked across the beach to the motel. All of our kids were playing beach volleyball with my parents on the sand by the back deck. They were laughing and screaming with joy. Even Emily seemed to be enjoying herself, I was pleased to see. She had a lot of exams right after spring break, and I knew she was worried about them. It was good to see her enjoy herself a little as well. Children's lives had gotten so serious. It was so different from when I grew up. The demands on them were getting too heavy, it seemed. I felt sad that they hardly got to be kids anymore and just goof around like I did.

"Daaad!" Austin yelled and ran towards me.

"Hey, you can't just leave in the middle of the game," Abigail yelled after him.

Austin threw himself in my arms. I grabbed him, lifted him up, and kissed him. "Hi there, buddy. Having fun?"

"You've gotta come play with us, Dad. Can you pleeease?" he asked.

I could feel he had missed me. So, I nodded. "Just a few rounds, then. I have to be at the festival at one when it opens. Shannon is singing again today."

"Can we come, Dad?" Abigail asked.

My veins froze at the very thought. I wasn't very fond of the thought of them being at the festival, when we didn't know if this shooter might show up or not. "That's probably not a very good idea," I said.

"Aw!" Abigail whined. "I really wanted to hear Shannon sing."

I looked at my mother for help. "I have to work, Abigail. Maybe your grandmother has something fun you can do today?"

My mother smiled. "Sure. How about we take a trip to the zoo?"

Austin and Angela cheered. "Yaay!"

But Abigail didn't. "I don't want to go to the zoo. I've been to the zoo before. I have never been to a country festival before. I have never seen Shannon sing. I want to hear Shannon sing."

I looked into her eyes, then played the grown-up card. "The festival is not for children, Abigail. There's beer and there will be drunk people present. I don't want you there with all that. You're too young. I'll ask Shannon if she will sing for you some other time, all right?"

Abigail growled. "That's not the same and you know it, Dad."

"I do. Maybe another time, all right?"

My mom put an arm around Abigail's shoulder. "If you're real nice, then maybe we can go on the zip line? How would you like that?" she asked, knowing very well that Abigail had been pleading me to take her on the zip line above the zoo for ages. I mouthed a thank you to my mother as we returned to the game. I played some rounds and had a lot of fun with my kids, then ate some breakfast that my mother served me on the deck, while the kids decided to go swimming with my dad. I watched the waves and felt horrible that I had to be away all day, since it was a perfect day for surfing. March was always one of the best months. The swell was a reasonable size and often glassy in the morning, as it was today. It was completely wind-still and just plain beautiful. It did look promising for all week, though, and that was great for the kids who were going to surf camp starting Monday.

"So, is there any particular reason why you didn't want the kids present at the festival?" my mother asked.

I shrugged. "We don't know yet. But I have a hunch that it is best they stay home."

"I can tell by your worried face that it is serious. Has it anything to do with that body that was found yesterday at the trails in Palm Bay? It was on all the stations last night. The creator of Millman Technologies? He's a big name around here."

I shook my head. "That's a completely different case. We still don't know much yet."

"Well, it's good you're being careful and protective of your kids," she said and picked up my empty plate. "Just be careful with yourself and Shannon too. Promise me that?"

I smiled reassuringly. The last thing I wanted was for her to worry. "I promise, Mom. There's no need for concern. Nothing will happen to either of us."

THIRTY-ONE

June 2006

DOTTIE WAS WORRIED AGAIN. Ever since Elizabeth had started eating, she hadn't stopped again. At first, it was a thrill and an answer to Dottie's prayers, but watching her now, eating her breakfast seven months and fifteen pounds later, Dottie started to wonder when Elizabeth would take a break. She seemed to be hungry constantly. And if Dottie told her she had to wait till food was on the table, she would respond by throwing a hysterical fit so big Dottie saw no other way than to accommodate her wishes. At first, it seemed like the right thing to do, since she needed the food, but the child had almost doubled her weight in a little more than six months. Before that, she hadn't weighed more than eighteen pounds, the same as an average nine month-old baby, and for a long time it had seemed like she wasn't growing at all, but now she was getting bigger by the day. And it wasn't because she was getting taller.

"I want more," she said, with her mouth still full.

Dottie looked at the kitchen counter. It was filled with empty boxes and bags. Just this morning, Elizabeth had eaten a big bowl of Cheerios with milk, two pieces of toasted bread with Nutella, three breakfast bars, and eight waffles. Dottie felt exhausted. She couldn't keep up with the little girl's demands. It was suddenly like she was bottomless, like she couldn't get full. Where did she put it? How could she hold so much food?

"Maybe I can cut up some fruit for you?" Dottie asked.

Elizabeth looked at her mother, and then let out a deep scream. "I don't like fruit. I want more waffles!"

"I...I'm afraid I don't have anymore," Dottie said, showing Elizabeth the empty package.

Elizabeth burst into tears. "But, Mommy...I'm so hungry! I'm so hungry. I'm so hungry!!"

Elizabeth grabbed her plate and threw it on the floor, where it shattered into pieces.

"Elizabeth!" her mother exclaimed.

Dottie felt confused. She had never seen her usually calm daughter act like this. Was it really the same girl? The same tiny girl who never cried as a baby, who slept through the night and was always content? How could she suddenly act like this? What had happened?

"No!" Dottie said. "You're not having any more food right now. You've had enough," she said.

It was James who had told her she needed to stop the girl; she needed to start saying no. They had discussed it on that same morning before James went off to work. Elizabeth's constant eating was wearing on Dottie and she wanted to share her concern with her husband.

"Just tell her no," he said. "She's at a difficult age, where she needs you to set boundaries for her."

He made it sound so easy. It wasn't. Not when it came to Elizabeth. With all the other girls, Dottie had no problem telling them no or telling them to grab a piece of fruit instead of a doughnut when they came home from school. But, when she did the same to Elizabeth, the child whet into a frenzy, a mania, a tantrum that could go on for hours afterwards. Just like she was doing now.

Elizabeth screamed and started reaching for things that she immediately threw on the floor. She growled and groaned and yelled at Dottie, while screaming for food like she hadn't had any for weeks. In her eyes, Dottie saw a desperation she didn't understand. It was like she was actually hungry. Like she thought she would actually die if she didn't get more to eat. Elizabeth screamed, grabbed a fork, and started to poke herself with it.

"I'm so hungryyyyy!!!"

Frantically, Dottie grabbed the fork and took it from Elizabeth, who stared into her mother's eyes while screaming:

"I want food! Please, Mom. Please!"

Dottie gasped when she saw the desperation in her child. What kind of a mother wouldn't want to feed her child? She felt like crying, then rushed for the freezer, pulling out another pack of waffles.

"Gimme. Gimme!" Elizabeth screamed, and reached out for the frozen package.

Dottie looked puzzled at her daughter, while tears streamed across her cheeks.

"GIMME!!!" her daughter screamed so loud her face turned red.

Dottie handed the frozen waffles to her daughter and watched with anxiety how her three year-old ripped the packaging, and like a wild animal, started eating the frozen waffles, almost swallowing them whole without chewing. When she was done, she licked her fingers, then looked at her mother.

"More. Mommy. MORE!"

THIRTY-TWO

March 2015

I DROVE Shannon to the festival in Melbourne. She seemed to be feeling better than the day before, when she had received the email. I was too. I was getting more and more convinced that this might just be some phony idiot trying to be smart with her. Maybe even get her to pull out of the festival and not perform. I wasn't going to let that happen. I wasn't going to let a fool like that destroy her performance today. For all I knew, that was all he wanted. To make her scared. That was how terrorists like him worked, wasn't it? Filling us with fear so we would change our ways and not live our lives like we wanted to. Well, it wasn't going to work on Shannon or me. We weren't going to live our lives in fear. There were always crazy people out there, and it was always a risk going on stage. Life was a risk. It wasn't going to change the way we lived. And, no matter what, I wasn't going to make her nervous by talking about it. I was determined to protect her, should anything happen, and had brought my gun and badge.

"I'm looking forward to seeing you up there again," I said, as we were let into the festival grounds. I parked in the designated spot reserved for Shannon King. It kind of made me feel important. I had to admit, I was a little proud of having Shannon as my girlfriend. She was such a big star.

She sighed. "I don't know if I can do this, Jack. This thing. It's getting to me. I thought it wasn't, but I can feel myself getting nervous. This email. I keep thinking about it. What if he shows up again today? What does he want from me? Maybe if I didn't go on stage…"

I looked at her. "Don't go there. Listen to me, Shannon. Don't let a guy like that ruin everything for you. You're smarter than that. There are always reasons to be afraid. Even driving here by car could easily have killed you."

"You're not that bad a driver," she said with a smile.

"I'm serious, Shannon. Life is dangerous. There are so many crazy people out there. You can't live your life without running into at least some of them. Just don't let the fear rule your life. You'll end up miserable. This is your passion. This

272

is you. Standing on a stage. Singing your songs for your fans. This is what you love to do. No one should tell you not to. No one should scare you from doing what you love. Think about all the things I see in my line of work. If I didn't have hope, if I didn't believe that what I did made a difference, that there was still goodness in this world, in people, I wouldn't be able to live. I wouldn't be able to do my job. I can't let it get to me. Neither can you. You've got to get this email out of your mind. This is exactly what this guy wants. Now, shake it."

Shannon looked at me and then chuckled. She kissed me and stroked my cheek. "You're so sweet, Jack. Especially when you say things like *shake it*."

"No, I'm not," I said. "I'm a bad-ass cop and you know it. Now get out there and sing."

Shannon chuckled again and opened the door. "As you wish, Detective."

We walked to her trailer, where she was going to change into her stage outfit. I told her I was going to make a couple of rounds and talk to the officers on duty. Make sure everything was running smoothly. Shannon wasn't on until three o'clock. We still had two hours. It gave me plenty of time. Shannon kissed me, standing on the first step of her trailer, holding her guitar in her hand.

"Just make sure you make it back before I go on. I need to know you have my back."

"I will."

THIRTY-THREE

March 2015

SHANNON LOOKED at Jack as he walked away. She liked watching him. He didn't know it himself, but he was so handsome. Girls walking by him stopped and looked when he passed them. He never noticed. Or maybe he didn't care.

Shannon smiled to herself and walked inside of her trailer. She put down the guitar and found the outfit she had picked out for this performance. This was one of her favorite moments. The time when she got herself ready. The anticipation, the butterflies in her stomach, the thrill of it all was always biggest from this moment up until the seconds when she went onto the stage.

Shannon looked at herself in the mirror, then stripped down before she put on her outfit. This wasn't an entire concert, but just four of her most popular numbers, so there wasn't going to be any changing in between songs. She had to choose something that would go with both up-tempo songs and the one ballad she had chosen for this set. She had found this gorgeous dress...just right for the occasion. It wasn't too much or too sparkly, since it was an afternoon performance. Shannon put it on and put on some make-up. That was the part she didn't enjoy too much. Stage make-up was so heavy, but with the light up there, she was going to need it. She was starting to get lines by her eyes and mouth and the light was merciless.

When she was done, she put on her black jacket and favorite hat. She grabbed her guitar and began strumming it, when there was a knock at the door to her trailer. Shannon walked to it and opened the door.

Outside stood Joe.

"What the hell are you doing here?" Shannon asked.

He looked confused. "Well, you invited me."

Shannon shook her head. "No, I didn't. How did you get in here anyway? This is only for performers and their families."

"Well, I am still your husband."

Shannon closed her eyes with a sigh. Of course, he had sweet-talked the

274

guards. Joe could sweet-talk anyone.

"What do you want, Joe?"

"You're the one who asked me to come," he said.

Shannon frowned. "No, I didn't."

Joe pulled out a ticket for the festival. "You sent me this. A ticket just for today. Backstage passes and everything. It came in the mail yesterday. I have to say, I was quite surprised. In a good way. Figured you'd finally come to your senses."

Shannon grabbed the ticket and looked at it. "I never sent you this. Why would you think that?"

"Who else would send me a ticket to a country festival where you're performing?" he asked with a smirk.

"I don't know, Joe. But certainly not me. We're in the middle of a divorce, remember?"

"Well I kind of hoped we would discuss that, since you sent for me and all. I figured you were willing to finally talk about this, to come back to the ol' man. Back where you belong."

Shannon sighed again. "I'm not coming back, Joe. You know it and so do I. It's over. I'm done."

Joe grabbed her arm and held it tight. It hurt. "You're not going anywhere. You hear me? I'm not giving you that divorce and you're not getting Angela. Or else..."

"Or else what, Joe?" Shannon asked, trying to get her arm free from his grip. She tried to see if she could spot a security guard anywhere, but they were too far away, guarding the VIP entrance. The noise from the stage was too loud for them to hear her if she screamed.

"Or else I'll tell your little secret to the entire world."

"You won't do that," Shannon said. "It'll hurt you as much as it'll hurt me. You'll never dare."

"Oh, you better believe I will. I don't mind going down, as long as I take you with me. If I reveal this secret, you know just as well as me that this will all be over. No more screaming fans, no more record label, no more millions."

Shannon's heart raced in her chest. She had no idea what to do or say. He was right. If Joe revealed this secret, it would all be over.

"And, don't try anything," he said. "I've put all the evidence in a safety deposit box, along with a letter explaining everything, and gave the key to my lawyer with the instructions to open it in case something happens to me. He will then reveal everything to the press. So, don't send that boyfriend of yours after me."

"Those are your methods, not mine," Shannon said. She felt like crying. Joe was hurting her arm, and now she was slowly realizing she was never going to get rid of him. He was going to force her to be with him, wasn't he?

"Hey, you let go of her this instant!"

The voice was Jack's. He was running towards them. Joe turned his head and spotted him as well. Shannon smiled.

"Ah, the knight in shining armor, huh?" Joe looked at Shannon. "Enjoy him as much as you can. Tomorrow, you and Angela move back to Nashville with me, or else you know exactly what will happen."

"Let go of her now!"

Joe let go of Shannon's arm and pulled away. "She's all yours," he said with a smirk. "For now."

THIRTY-FOUR

March 2015

"DID HE HURT YOU?"

I stared at Shannon. Her hands were shaking. She was about to cry. I grabbed her in my arms.

"Did he hurt you, Shannon?" I repeated.

She shook her head. "No."

"What the hell is he doing here anyway? I need to talk to those security guards. They're supposed to protect you."

"He had a ticket. Backstage passes. He has a right to be here," Shannon stuttered.

I helped her get back into the trailer, then gave her a bottle of fresh water.

"Here, sweetie. Calm down. My God, you're shaking. God, I hate that guy. I should have punched him right there when I had the chance."

Shannon looked at me, then leaned her head on my shoulder. "No, you shouldn't, Jack. You're a good guy. Don't stoop to his level."

"I'll tell you this much, I really wanted to. Boy, I wanted to. The way he had his hand on you, holding you. I could tell it hurt. Let me have a look, did he leave a bruise, 'cause if he did, you can press charges. We should report this anyway. It would help your case when you fight for Angela. No judge will let a wife beater get the kid."

I felt Shannon's hand on my arm. I looked into her eyes. God, she had beautiful eyes. I felt so protective of her.

"Don't, Jack," she said. "Not now. Let's talk about something else."

I looked into her eyes. Something had changed. Something was different. These weren't the happy warm eyes I was used to. These had a deep sadness to them, a secretive sadness. I didn't understand what was going on, but something was.

"What did he say to you? He said something, didn't he?" I asked, knowing very well I should leave it alone.

"Not now, Jack. I have a show in ten minutes. I can't discuss…"

"Why not? I don't understand."

There was a knock on the door. Shannon jumped.

"Ten minutes," the voice said.

Shannon put a hand to her chest.

"Look at what he is doing to you. You're shaking again. Jumping from someone just knocking on your door. Let me report him for what he did to you today. You can just talk to me. I'll take your statement, so you don't have to face some other officer. That way, you'll get to keep Angela. He can't hurt you anymore."

Shannon's eyes hit the floor.

"There's something you're not telling me," I said.

"Let's talk about it after the set," she said and kissed me. "I need to be backstage now."

I nodded, feeling slightly hurt. I didn't like that she was hiding something from me. It felt so uncomfortable. What could be so bad she felt like she couldn't tell me? She told me about the emails, and I believed I handled that quite well. She knew I would listen and understand, didn't she?

I walked with her backstage and held her hand while she waited for her name to be announced. Then, she leaned over and kissed me and whispered:

"I love you more than you'll ever know," before the crowd demanded her, yelling and screaming her name.

I watched her as she took the stage with the same presence and professionalism as she always did. The audience would never know she was hurting. Like she had done for years, she hid it behind a smile and the performance of a lifetime.

"A rare beauty, isn't she?" a voice said behind me.

I turned and faced Joe. My blood was boiling. I wanted to wipe that smirk off his face.

"Enjoy her while you can," he said, touching his goatee. "She's coming home with me tonight."

My heart stopped. "No, she's not," I said. "She's never going back. At least not to you."

"We'll see about that," he said and disappeared.

What the hell did he mean by that? Was that what Shannon hadn't told me? Had she decided to go back to him? I couldn't believe it. I stared at Shannon as she performed, while I felt like small schoolchild who had just had his lunch money stolen.

I refused to believe it. I simply refused.

THIRTY-FIVE

March 2015

BARBARA ROBERTSON WAS at the concert of her lifetime. She had always wanted to see Shannon King live on stage, and now she finally had her chance. It was something she knew she would never forget.

Barbara clapped and screamed Shannon's name when she came on stage. She had managed to elbow herself all the way up to the front, where she could see Shannon King up close and with no tall guy in front of her blocking her view. Shannon King yelled something and they all yelled back, before she hit the note of the first song on her guitar and the crowd went wild.

No Heart of Mine blasted out from the stage and Barbara screamed, in awe of her favorite singer. She started to sing along, her best friend since they were children, Lindsey, right next to her, trying to dance, even though the space was tight. They were sweating like crazy, salty droplets were running into their eyes and left a stinging sensation. Barbara felt how her hair was getting soaked and slapping onto her forehead. Lindsey laughed and sang along with the crowd.

"No Heart of Mine shall ever be, ever be, ever be yours to break again!"

It was Barbara's favorite song. She knew the lyrics by heart from listening to it over and over again. It had meant so much to her when Sam broke up with her after they finished high school because he "felt like they had grown apart." She didn't understand why he insisted on saying that instead of admitting to her what she already knew, that he had slept with Tracy after prom night, even though he was still going out with Barbara. It was a tough breakup and Barbara had listened to Shannon King's songs over and over again to get through it. It had helped her immensely.

"What a great crowd," Shannon King said when she finished the song. She was sweating too. Barbara was so fortunate to be close enough to notice it. She looked at the woman on stage, who over the last year had become her hero, her idol. Barbara read everything they wrote about her in the magazines and knew that she had left her husband recently and that she was now dating some police guy, who, by the way, was really handsome in all the pictures, but who also had a lot of children. Barbara thought it seemed like a good choice for Shannon, even though the magazines wrote these stories about her destroying her family with her love affair and her cheating on her husband and him being the victim and all. Barbara didn't believe it. And, even if she did, she thought Shannon King was allowed to be with whomever she chose to be with. She was a powerful woman. Barbara had decided to be one too.

"You can either be pitiful or powerful; you can't be both," her mother always told her, quoting Joyce Meyer, her favorite TV preacher.

She liked that saying.

"Y'all ready for some more?" Shannon King yelled out.

"Yeeeeeaaaahh!" the crowd roared back.

"All right, y'all," she said. "I think I might have a little something for ya. A little song called *Break my Heart Again and I'll Put Two Bullets in Yours.*"

The crowd screamed with excitement. Shannon King smiled and started playing, and the band followed along. Barbara screamed with joy. That was one of her favorites too. Lindsey had already started dancing with her beer in her hand. She grabbed Barbara and swung her around. Barbara accidentally bumped into the guy standing next to her. She spilled some beer on his western shirt. He looked at her from under his cowboy hat.

"Watch yourself," he growled.

"Sorry," she giggled, then returned to face Lindsey, who had closed her eyes and was dancing while singing along.

Barbara looked up at her idol on stage, as Shannon approached the crowd and started touching the hands of her fans. Barbara pressed her body towards the fence and reached out her hand as far as she could, as Shannon King approached her and touched it, their eyes locked for just one second, and Barbara screamed in excitement.

"Oh, my God, she touched me!"

Shannon continued down the line of people, not disappointing one single fan, while singing "*If you hurt me, if you break my heart again, I'll put two bullets in yours, and you'll have no more hearts to break,*" when suddenly, a terrifying sound cracked through the air. Barbara went cold all over, recognizing the sound from a drive-by shooting she once witnessed staying at a friend's house. It was the sound of someone shooting into the crowd. The man in the cowboy hat next to her fell to the ground with a loud thud.

After that, there was nothing but panic.

THIRTY-SIX

March 2015

"COVER YOUR HEADS! GET DOWN!"

I was screaming at the top of my lungs, while holding my gun tightly between my hands. Gunfire sounded through the air. It was coming from the other side of the stage. People were screaming. I ran out there and yelled to Shannon to get off the stage. People had started to panic and were trampling on one another.

It was the scene of a living nightmare.

"Help people in the front get onto the stage," I yelled at the security guards. The panic had made the crowd move back and forth in waves, and was crushing the people in front.

"Help people get out of here!"

The guards started pulling people free. Some had fallen and were being trampled on. They risked getting killed. The gunfire had ceased, and I jumped down to help get people out. A girl was screaming from underneath people's feet. I managed to get a hand in and pull her out. She had blood on her face and arms. She looked at me with terror in her eyes.

"Run backstage!" I yelled, while trying to pull another girl out.

"There was a guy," the girl said, as I reached for her friend and she grabbed my hand. "He was shot. The guy next to me got shot."

She was in shock. She was staring at her bloody hands.

"Get inside!" I yelled at her, while pulling out her friend who had been badly trampled upon. Her face was already bruised. I grabbed my phone and called for ambulances and backup, then went back to pulling people free.

The sound of gunfire blasted through the air once again. My heart stopped. It sounded like it came from backstage. People screamed in panic and moved for the exits.

"Shannon," I whispered, jumped up onto the stage, and ran with my gun in hand behind the curtain. Terrified faces and people screaming told me I was right. There had been shooting backstage as well.

"Seek cover!" I yelled at all the faces. "Get down!"

I walked with my gun in hand through the corridor created for the musicians to wait before they went onstage. A woman was screaming not far from me.

It was Shannon. I'd recognize that voice anywhere.

"Shannon!" I yelled and ran to her. I found her on the floor, kneeling next to a body on the ground. I lowered the gun. I was speechless.

It was Joe.

He was lying on the wooden floor, bleeding from the two gunshot wounds right in his heart. Shannon cried and looked up at me.

"He's dead, Jack. Oh, my God. Joe has been shot!"

I couldn't believe it. I grabbed Shannon by the shoulder. "Did you see anything? Did you see who shot him?"

"I was hiding like you told me to. Right behind the stage, when I heard the shot. I thought the shooter had entered this area and I was trying to get away when I saw him. I did see someone in a dark blue hoodie run out of here, but I don't know if it was the shooter or not. I can't believe it, Jack. Joe didn't deserve this."

She looked at me with desperation. I knew she had once loved the guy, just like I had once loved Arianna before she broke my heart.

"Who did this?" Shannon asked, holding a hand to cover her mouth. "Who would do such a terrible thing?"

"I don't know. But we don't know if he's done yet. We need to get you out of here," I said. "You and all the rest of the people. It's not safe here."

THIRTY-SEVEN

March 2015

THE PLACE WAS SOON CRAWLING with police and paramedics and I helped everyone get out from backstage. The scene outside on the festival grounds was like a warzone. People were walking around in a haze, their eyes wide and frantic, crying, looking for each other, asking everyone if they had seen their friends. Some were hurt and getting help from the paramedics. I held on to Shannon as I escorted her out. A paramedic asked her if she needed attention, but she told him she wasn't hurt. We told him about Joe in the backstage area, and he ran to get a stretcher and some more paramedics to help. Shannon was questioned by one of my colleagues for a little while and told him her story before I escorted her to my car.

"Is everyone alright?" she asked me.

Her eyes were flickering in panic and sadness. Just like me, she simply couldn't grasp what had taken place.

"Who...? Why...?" Then she started to cry.

I held her in my arms and told her it was all over now.

"I think I need to take you home," I said.

She sniffled and nodded. I helped her get inside the car, then called Ron, who was by the entrance directing his crew, who were questioning the witnesses, then helping them get home.

"I'm taking Shannon home, then I'll be back," I said.

"Don't take too long. We need all the hands we can get," he said.

I hung up, then started the car and drove off. We drove through crowds of people simply standing in the parking lot, or in the street, talking and crying, asking the same question we all were.

Why?

A news chopper was already circling the scene, and reporters were trying to get through the entrance that had been blocked by the police as soon as they arrived. I hoped it had been before the shooter had managed to get out. I wanted this bastard, and I wanted him to fry for a lifetime.

"I changed my mind," Shannon said, as we hit A1A towards South Cocoa Beach. None of us had spoken a single word since we left the park. I had turned the radio off, since they were all talking about it. On our way, every other car we met was a police car. The entire force was on their way there.

"About what?" I asked.

"I don't want to go back to the condo and be all alone. I know you have to do your duty and help out at the scene, so I think I want to go to your parents' place."

"That's a great idea," I said. "My mom can take good care of you."

"I keep seeing those images, Jack," she said, when I parked the car in front of the motel. "There was a guy. He was right in front of me. I was shaking hands with the audience, like I always do during this song. I was looking at him and giving him a high-five, right when the shots were fired. I looked into his eyes, Jack. I was staring directly into his eyes when he died."

I kissed her and looked into her eyes. I had no words left; nothing I could say would make her feel better. I chose to stay silent and simply kiss her and hold her tight. I was glad to leave her in the hands of my mother.

The kids were playing on the beach, so they didn't notice us coming back. My mother had already heard about the shooting on the news from the TV constantly running in the bar of the motel.

"Oh, my God, I'm so glad you're okay," she exclaimed when we walked inside. She gave me a small slap across the face. "I called you a thousand times. You pick up when a worried momma calls, you hear me? You almost gave me a heart attack, seeing those things on the news and knowing you were both there. I'm an old woman, you know."

"Yes, ma'am," I said, and let her kiss me like she used to when I was a child, holding my face with both her hands. I guessed she needed it.

Then she kissed Shannon.

"Oh, my sweet thing. It must have been terrible for you. They said it happened during your performance?"

Shannon nodded. She bit her lip. I could tell she was holding back her tears.

"I have to get back," I said.

"You go and catch this bastard," my mom said, grabbing Shannon's hands in hers. "I'll do what I do best." She put her arm around Shannon's shoulder. "Come with me, dear. I'll make us all some hot chocolate."

It was with a heavy heart that I left them, since all I really wanted right now was to be with my family. But duty called. At least it felt good to know all my loved ones were in safe hands.

THIRTY-EIGHT

March 2015

"Okay, people. Now that we're all here, let's go through what we have and know." Ron was holding a bagel in one hand and a coffee in the other. It was Monday, before noon, the day after what the media called the Shannon King-inspired shooting at Runaway Country. I had hardly slept all night, since we had been at the scene cleaning up, figuring out what had really taken place.

"Jack. You go first."

"Alright," I said. "We know multiple shots were fired into the crowd at Shannon King's concert yesterday. As we have told the press, two were killed, seventeen hurt by the panic that erupted; one is still in critical condition. Both victims were male. Phillip Hagerty, forty-two, was a captain at Cocoa Beach Fire Department. He leaves behind a wife and two children, a boy and a girl. Second victim was Joe Harrison, thirty-nine, leaves behind a wife and a daughter. His wife was, as many of you know, since it has been all over the media last night and this morning, the singer Shannon King."

There was a silence in the room, and I knew what they were all thinking. The media was relentless when it came to this kind of stuff and had already speculated about whether Shannon had him killed or had even killed him herself. I couldn't believe the insensitivity. They were, after all, in a custody battle, the newspapers had been told by some of Joe's friends. They made him out to be a saint and Shannon to be the bad guy, which made my blood boil. Shannon had made me promise to never tell the real truth. It never helped anyway, she told me. The press believed what they wanted to.

"Both victims were shot twice, directly into their hearts," I continued.

"Someone knows how to shoot," Beth said.

"Yes. Much unlike in the mass-shooting in the cinema in Boca Raton, where it seemed to be very uncontrolled," I continued. "Which is strange, since I had a feeling they were connected, since the shooter sent emails to Shannon King before and after last time, as he did this time."

"Did she receive an email yesterday too?" Ron asked.

I nodded and pulled the printout from my folder. "Yes." I read it out loud for everyone in the room:

"'Dear Shannon, I'm so sorry for what I have done, but I believe you must know by now, I only did what was necessary. Joe deserved to die and we both know it. I did you a favor.' And then, like all the other emails, it is signed AM."

"What the hell is AM?" asked Duncan, another member of our homicide unit. Next to him sat his partner, Ann.

Richard, our researcher and computer expert, leaned over the desk. "As you might guess, it could be a lot of things. It might be the person's initials, but that's hardly realistic. Since the sender of the email goes to great lengths to hide the IP address, we hardly think he would be so stupid as to actually use his real initials. What first comes to mind is naturally AM versus PM. In that context AM stands for *ante meridiem*, which means before noon. But since the shooting in both cases were done in the afternoon, that's not an angle I'm looking into anymore. It could also possibly be Artic Monkeys, the band who called their fifth album simply AM and is called AM by their fans. We do know this killer loves music, so maybe that's an angle…"

"Anything else?" I asked, thinking it sounded all very far-fetched.

"Will.i.am?" he said and shrugged.

"Keep looking into it," I said. "And keep trying to track the email."

"I am," Richard said. "So far, I have been led to India, through Indonesia, to Japan, and now I'm in Africa. Whoever is doing this knows how to cover their tracks in cyberspace. I'm also keeping an eye on social media. I've put a tracker out so I'll be alerted as soon as anyone posts about the shootings in the coming days. There might be witnesses we haven't talked to yet or people with knowledge they haven't told the police."

"Good. What else have we got?" asked Ron, as he finished his bagel.

"According to the techs, the shooter was located somewhere in the stage area when he fired the first two shots into the crowd, the same two shots that hit Phillip Hagerty in the heart and killed him instantly. By the angle, they believe he was actually on the stage when it happened. We'll conduct interviews of the band members later today, but the initial questioning told us they didn't see anyone on the stage with them. Neither did the singer Shannon King," I said. "He must have crept up from behind."

"So, the shooter had a backstage pass?" Beth said. "And, after shooting into the crowd, he ran backstage and killed Shannon King's husband?" Beth paused and looked at me. "Soon to be ex-husband, sorry."

"Exactly right," I said. "How hard are those passes to get ahold of?"

Beth answered. "As far as I know, you can get access to the entire backstage area, if you have enough money."

"Anything else?" Ron asked, as the silence lay upon us in the room again.

"We have multiple videos from the shooting taken with phones," Duncan said. "Ann and I have been going through them. They don't show the shooter's face, though, since he's wearing a hoodie and it's too far away. But you can see a figure up on the stage on two of them, and then the sound of the gun going off twice. The rest is just screaming and panic."

"Okay. Bummer," Ron said.

As the meeting continued, I couldn't stop thinking about Shannon and how hard this had to be for her. She was going to tell Angela about her father's death this morning when my kids were at surf camp and she had her to herself. She knew the girl would see it on TV or hear about it from someone at some point, so she might as well get it done right away, even though she herself was still shaken pretty badly. It was an understatement to say I was worried about her. She was about to face a whole new media-storm of entirely new proportions. She didn't need that. Her fragile mind certainly didn't need that at all.

THIRTY-NINE

March 2015

"WHAT'S THIS?"

Stanley had managed to pull himself back into bed from the bathroom, when his guardian entered with another tray of food. The guardian stuck their nose in the air and sniffed.

"What is that I smell?"

Stanley shrugged and shook his head. "I don't smell anything."

"VOMIT!" the guardian screamed. "VOMIT. FILTHY DISGUSTING VOMIT!"

Stanley's heart was racing. It had felt so good to relieve himself, and he had hoped to be able to hide it. His shin was throbbing from the effort of getting back to bed in time. He was afraid it was getting infected.

"Did you THROW UP?" the guardian yelled and almost dropped the tray of food in dismay.

Stanley cleared his throat. He could feel how his newfound hope was filling him with new energy. He had talked to someone on the other side of that wall. He wasn't alone.

"I...I had to," he said, fearing his guardian's reaction. Last time he had ended up with a fire poker in his leg.

The guardian stormed to the bathroom and opened the toilet lid. "Did you waste all that good food?"

"I...I'm sorry. I couldn't contain any more. It was just too much."

"You didn't like the food?"

"It wasn't that I didn't like it, but it was just too much," he said. "You forced it inside of me."

"So, it was a little too much, now was it?"

Stanley could tell his guardian was mocking him. It was impossible to talk reason to this mad person.

"Listen. I just really want to get my granddaughter and get back home," he said with a deep sigh. "I don't know what this is all about. But, don't you think it's about time to stop? My leg feels wrong. I think I need to get to a hospital."

The guardian made a grimace. "Oh, you think you need to go to the hospital, do ya? Well, that's a completely different matter, then." The last word was followed by hollow laughter.

Stanley looked at the crazy person in front of him. How did someone become like this? How was this person free to walk around, obviously in need of help, endangering other people? How had no one stopped this person? How many like him had been abducted and kept in this house? What was the idea behind it all?

The guardian leaned over. "You think maybe little Timmy might have felt the same way when you beat him with that fire poker for showing up in your living room wearing his mother's dress and shoes, huh? You know what I'm talking about. Don't look so innocent. I'm talking about the time when you beat him senseless and he couldn't walk for days. Yes, now you're getting it. That's right."

Stanley stared at his guardian with wide-open eyes. His first response was—like it had always been in his life—anger. His blood was boiling. How did this... this character know about his son?

"What the hell...?"

His guardian let out some more loud laughter. Stanley imagined what it would feel like to kill this person, to simply place his hands around that broad neck and press till there were no more sounds coming out.

But, before he could react, the fire poker was brought out once again, swung high into the air, and poked through the thigh of his good leg.

"Now, EAT!" his guardian yelled, while snorting and panting in what Stanley could only assume was excitement. The poker was still in his leg when the food was shoveled into his mouth, drowning out his screaming.

FORTY

March 2015

"I HAVE SOMETHING."

Richard came to my desk and sat down. So far, it had been a bad day. I had interviewed all the band members, but none of them had seen the shooter. They had all been facing the crowd, and when panic broke out, they remembered nothing but chaos. I had tried to recreate the concert by drawing on the whiteboard, and with the help from a crime scene technician, had come to the conclusion that the shooter had to have been walking out on stage during the song, on the left side, behind the bass player from Shannon's band. Mark, the bass player told me he had been playing along when he heard the shots coming from behind him. As soon as he saw the person in the crowd get shot, he had thrown himself to the ground, holding the bass over his head. He hadn't dared to turn and look. He had screamed at everyone to get down. When I asked him if he had any idea where the shooter had come on stage, he had said that he was right behind him. It added up well with what the crime scene techs told me, and with the fact that the shooter afterwards sneaked out the back and shot Joe on the way out. The theory was that he was just shooting his way through the crowd, but I kept wondering why no more than two people were killed. It was odd, since the shooter had the possibility of killing a lot more. Maybe we had just lucked out. The fact was, the shooter had gotten out somehow right afterwards, and before we had managed to lock down the area. How or where he had found his way out, we still didn't know. That was as far as we had gotten all day. I needed something to open up this case. I was nowhere near close to catching this guy.

"A witness tells me she saw the killer," Richard said. "She posted in Wake-Up Cocoa Beach, a Facebook group for locals in Cocoa Beach."

"I know the group," I said.

"Alright. Here she is. I printed out her Facebook page. Her name is Barbara Robertson. She wrote in the group that she was up in the front when the shots were fired and that she was standing right next to Phillip Hagerty when he was

289

shot. As a comment to someone else's post, she writes that she is lucky to still be alive."

"Barbara Robertson? Have we questioned her before?" I asked, thinking of the thousands of statements we had right after the incident that I had no idea how to sort through. I had asked Beth to go through them, but didn't think she was even halfway.

"I tried to find her statement in the pile, but her name didn't come up. I'm thinking she might have been one of those that got out of there before we started getting statements, when we still believed the killer was on the loose."

I nodded. We had no idea how many had left while we were trying to get people to safety. My guess was it was at least a couple hundred. I couldn't blame them. At that point, it was all about getting out of there. There had been forty thousand people present. There was no way we could have interviewed all of them. It was all a mess.

"Good work," I said. "Could you please contact her and have her come in for an interview? Any news on tracking that email?"

Richard shook his head as he got up from my desk. "Not yet. But I'll keep on trying."

"You do that."

When he left, I grabbed my phone and called Shannon. Her voice was thick with sadness as she answered.

"Hey. How're you holding up?" I asked. My stomach was hurting from worrying about her.

"Okay, I guess."

"Did you talk to Angela yet?"

"Not yet. It's been quite the morning. The press is camping outside the building and yelling at us from the beach. Bruce is taking care of the calls, but they are relentless. I closed the shutters while Angela and I watched a movie and ate popcorn, just enjoying each other. I've been trying to build up the courage to tell her. I'm about to do it now," she said. "I'll get it done. Just need to…Just need to get it done. Like a Band-Aid, right? She is just so happy right now. She's playing with a cardboard box. She cut holes for her eyes and uses it to dress up like a robot. How am I supposed to break her heart like this? I can't do it, Jack. I simply can't!"

Shannon's voice cracked.

"You have to. She has to hear it from you, remember?" I said, and pushed back my tears, thinking about how hard it had been for me to tell my kids about what had happened to their mother. I couldn't bear the devastation in their eyes while they asked if *she never was coming back, then*? It was agonizing.

"You have to do it, Shannon. Even if it hurts so bad you wonder if life will ever be good again. You have to do it."

FORTY-ONE

March 2015

YOU HAVE TO DO IT.

Jack's words lingered in Shannon's mind as she put the phone down.

"Look at me, Mom. I'm a robot. Beep-beep-booop," Angela said, as she waddled towards her mother dressed in the cardboard box. She had drawn little buttons on the outside of it and made holes for her arms and legs. She was so adorable, Shannon started crying.

"What's wrong, Mommy?"

Shannon sniffled and wiped her nose. "Nothing, nothing sweetie. Mommy's just a little upset."

Angela looked at her mother and tilted her head. Oh, how badly Shannon craved a drink right now. Anything would do.

"Is it those people down on the beach yelling at you that are bothering you? 'Cause if it is, I'll tell them to leave my mommy alone! I hate those people."

Shannon bit her lip. She sat down on the couch and asked Angela to come sit with her. "No, sweetie," she said. "Those people aren't why Mommy is sad. But, they do have something to do with it. See, baby girl, something happened and they want to ask Mommy about it."

Angela frowned. "What do they want to know?"

"They want to know how I'm feeling, how you're feeling, since this thing happened."

"What thing?"

Shannon grabbed Angela's hand in hers. She put it between both of hers and closed her eyes. She pictured the bottle of vodka that she had bought when grocery shopping a few days ago. It was a slip up; she knew it. She had hidden it under the sink in the bathroom, wrapped in a towel, and promised herself to not touch it. Now, all she wanted to do was to run in there and grab it. It was all she could think of.

"What thing, Mommy?" Angela said.

291

Shannon looked into her daughter's eyes. She stroked her cheek gently, wondering if her life would ever be like a normal little girl's, if she would grow up to be a normal girl or if they had completely ruined her chances of that.

"What thing, Mommy?" she was getting impatient now.

"I…" a tear rolled across Shannon's cheek.

"Mommy. You're crying," Angela said. "Why are you crying?"

"Yesterday, something really bad happened," Shannon said.

"Like what?"

"Someone shot some people at one of Mommy's concerts." As she spoke, Shannon relieved the nightmare in her mind. The sound of the gun going off, the screaming, the panic. She felt sick to her stomach. It was all her fault, wasn't it? She could have stopped it. She knew something would happen. The email had told her, and still it happened. People had been killed.

Joe had been killed.

"Are you sick, Mommy? You're all pale," Angela said. "Are you going to throw up?"

Throwing up was the worst thing anyone could do in Angela's eyes. "Maddox threw up in class on Friday. Maybe you caught what she had. It's probably going around."

Shannon shook her head. "No, Mommy's not sick. I'm just really, really sad because of what happened yesterday."

"Did he shoot many people? Did Jack get shot?" she asked with a small gasp.

"No. No. Not Jack. But someone else did. Someone we love very much," Shannon said.

This is it. I'm going to tell her. There is no way back now. God, I could use a drink. Just one.

"Who, Mommy?" she asked with anxiety in her voice.

"Daddy, sweetie. Daddy was shot. He had come to see Mommy, and then…"

Angela let out a small shriek. Shannon grabbed her and held her in her arms. "It's going to be alright," she whispered.

"…Did he…?"

"Yes, sweetie. Daddy died." When the words left her mouth, Shannon felt like she had to throw up. It hurt so badly. She had no idea how much Angela understood of death, but she had once had a cat that died, that they had buried in the yard. But it was so long ago and she had been so young.

"Daddy is not coming back?"

"Remember Milo?" Shannon asked, referring to the cat.

Tears sprang into Angela's eyes. "It's like Milo? He's in heaven waiting for me together with Milo?"

"Yes. They will be waiting for you up there, looking down at you every day, checking to see if you're alright."

"But I'm not going to see him again? I'm not going to visit soon like you told me I would? He's not coming down here anymore?"

Her voice was shrill when she spoke.

"No, honey. It's just the two of us now. And we have to promise each other to be strong. You hear me? We need to take care of each other, now that Daddy is no longer here. You promise to help me with that?"

Angela held back her tears with a sniffle. She nodded while wiping her nose on her sleeve. "Pinky promise."

Shannon swallowed hard and tried to push away her tears. Angela bit her lip, then stroked her mother's cheek gently. "It'll be fine, Mommy," she said, her voice breaking. "We'll take care of each other. Like we always have."

Shannon sighed and closed her eyes. She kissed her daughter's hand, then got up from the couch.

"Do you want to watch another movie?" Angela asked.

Shannon nodded. "I would really enjoy that."

"I saw that *Maleficent* is On Demand now," Angela said. "Could we watch that, please?"

"Of course. Any movie you'd like," Shannon said.

Angela turned on the TV. Shannon could tell she was being brave for her mother's sake. She was holding her tears back. It hurt like crazy to watch. Shannon's stomach was turning. She felt sick.

"Do you think there are movies in Heaven, Mom? Do you think Dad can watch *Maleficent*? I know he wanted to watch it with me."

Shannon swallowed hard to stop herself from crying. "I'm sure he can," she said with a quivering voice. "I'm sure he can watch any movie he'd like."

Angela scrolled through the movies and found *Maleficent*.

"You go ahead and start," Shannon said. "Mommy just needs to go to the bathroom first."

FORTY-TWO

March 2015

"You're the man that saved my life."

Barbara Robertson looked at me before we sat down in Ron's office, which I had borrowed for the interview. The atmosphere in his office was a lot calmer and more comfortable than most places at the station.

"I knew it as soon as I saw your eyes. I knew I had seen you before," she said, grabbing a chair.

I remembered it too. She was the first one I pulled out from the crowd. She and her friend were about to get crushed. Her face was still bruised and she had her arm in a sling.

"You pulled me out and up on the stage. I was about to get trampled. You reached in and pulled me out. Then you pulled Lindsey out as well. She was in bad shape, so I helped her get to our car. I drove the both of us to the hospital afterwards. She's still there. She got a concussion from being kicked in the face when we fell to the ground and people around us panicked and tried to get away. It was awful."

"It was," I said, trying hard to block the memory.

"Well, anyway, thanks for saving my life," she said. "You saved both me and my best friend."

"My pleasure." I cleared my throat. "But the real reason why I called you in today is that it has come to my attention that you were standing right next to Phillip Hagerty when the shots were fired."

Barbara nodded. The expression in her young eyes was gloomy, almost remorseful, like she was blaming herself.

"I...I couldn't believe the bullet hit him and not me. I can't help but feel like I was being protected or something. Maybe I was just really lucky. I heard more than one gunshot. It could easily have struck me instead. I...I feel a little guilty. Why did this guy have to die while I was allowed to live?"

"Survivor's guilt," I said. "It's a very common phenomenon when someone has survived a traumatic event. It's a mental condition that occurs when people perceive themselves to have done wrong by surviving a traumatic event when others did not. It is very common in soldiers surviving combat and after natural disasters."

"Survivor's guilt, huh?" Barbara asked. "Well, that sounds like it. I've felt bad all day. Kind of haven't slept since it happened. I keep hearing the shots, you know?"

"Also very normal," I said and found my wallet. I handed her the card of a psychologist I knew who helped soldiers through PTSD. " She helps private people as well," I told her, as she took the card. "You and your friend should call her. Tell her I sent you. She'll give you a discount."

Barbara nodded and looked at the card. She was very young...in her early twenties. I hated that she had to go through this, and I hated having to rip into the wounds again and again, but I had to get some answers.

"So, tell me," I asked. "You were right next to Phillip Hagerty. Where was the killer?"

Barbara looked at me. I saw anxiety rooted deep in her eyes as she relived the moment in her memories. "He was right in front of us," she said. "On the stage."

"To the left side of the stage from where you were?"

"Yes. I didn't see him as he stepped out, 'cause I was dancing with Lindsey. Then I reached up to touch Shannon King's hand when she walked across the stage, so I didn't look at anything but her. She'd just high-fived the guy next to me, the one that got shot, when I heard the sound. I looked at Shannon; her face was completely frozen and she threw herself to the ground. That was when I saw him. He was standing way back, pointing the gun towards me. It looked like he was shooting at me when he fired the next shot, but it hit the same guy again. I don't know why he hit the same guy twice, but he did, and then the guy fell to the ground. I looked down and screamed, then looked up again, and the shooter was gone."

I noted everything Barbara said, while thinking we had to be dealing with an excellent marksman, since he had hit the same person in the heart twice without hitting Shannon or anyone else in the crowd. Was that a coincidence? Had he maybe really been aiming for Shannon? It seemed so initially, but something told me he wasn't. The email, among other factors, told me he wasn't interested in hurting Shannon. He loved her way too much for that. But why Phillip Hagerty? Was it a coincidence? It seemed less and less likely. In my mind, it was starting to look more like murder. Why else would you shoot the victim twice? Both Joe and Phillip Hagerty had been shot twice in the heart. Something didn't add up.

"Did you see anything...did you get a look at his face?" I asked, thinking we could get a drawing made if she remembered anything.

"He was wearing a green hoodie. I couldn't even see his eyes."

"A green hoodie?" I said and wrote it down. "Was there anything on it? Like words or a picture?"

She shook her head. "There was something written in white, but I can't remember what it was. "Oh, no, wait, that's not true. Now I remember. It said: Angel Girl."

"Angel Girl?"

"Yes. Like the song. Like one of Shannon King's songs. It's the title. *Angel Girl* is the story of a little girl that has to take care of herself. She packs her own lunch, and picks out her own clothes for school. Even though she has bruises, no one dares to think she may be abused until it's too late. It's a very sad song. One of my favorites. Well, all of Shannon's songs are my favorites, but this one is truly special."

"So, the killer was wearing a green hoodie with the title of one of Shannon's songs?" I asked, wondering how much fun the media was going to have with this. It would be obvious to anyone that this killer was heavily inspired by Shannon's songs. It was going to devastate her.

"Yes," Barbara said.

"And you're sure of this?"

"Completely."

I wrote it all down. It wasn't much, since Shannon sold a lot of merchandise all over the country to many of her fans, but it was something.

"Anything else? What kind of pants was he wearing?"

"Jeans."

I noted it. "Good. Anything else you noticed?"

"I saw him leave."

I froze and dropped the pen from my hand. "What did you say?"

"It was the scariest moment of my life, after the first one where he almost shot me. But when I helped Lindsey get to the parking lot and we had just gotten into the car and driven off, we were passed by a big black truck. It accelerated fast past us, but, as it did, I looked through the window and saw that same green hoodie sitting in there. I completely panicked and almost ran us off the road. I didn't touch the gas pedal again until it was out of my sight. I was certain he would be waiting for me somewhere, ready to shoot at me again."

"So, you saw the truck?" I asked. Why on earth had this girl not come forward before?

"Yes. I was terrified he would find me," she said, like she had read my mind. "That's why I didn't report it before. I know I should have. When that Richard guy contacted me and told me to come in, I didn't know what to do. I almost ran away instead."

"You made the right decision," I said. "Can you tell me anything about the truck besides the fact that it was black?"

"The license plate ended with YRJ and it had a large red bumper sticker on the back," she said.

I wrote the information down with great eagerness. She had seen the plate; she knew the last three letters. That was a big breakthrough.

I looked up at Barbara. "What did the sticker say?"

"Shit happens."

FORTY-THREE

December 2008

BY THE TIME Elizabeth turned six, she weighed close to 200 pounds and had diabetes, pulmonary hypertension, asthma, and sleep apnea. Her weight gain was so fast she would wear something twice, then outgrow it. At birthday parties, Dottie caught her stealing cupcakes. When the ice cream truck drove by on their street, it would result in the most outrageous tantrum from Elizabeth, as she screamed to get out of the fenced yard. Once, Dottie even caught her eating the dog's food from the bowl, just shoveling it into her mouth and swallowing it without chewing. Dottie had contacted a nutritionist and tried to limit portion sizes and kept rigidly scheduled mealtimes. She took Elizabeth and her older sister, Anna, walking at a local track for exercise, and she got Elizabeth physical therapy. But she couldn't seem to halt Elizabeth's rapid weight gain. And, more than ever, she couldn't escape her neighbors' constant staring and her relatives blaming her for her daughter's size. Even her husband James made his comments.

"You need to control her," he would say. "It's your job as her mother. She needs to learn self-discipline."

But it was easier said than done. Dottie did what she could to keep Elizabeth out of the kitchen and out of the food and kept the entire kitchen on lock-down. Literally. She had a padlock on the refrigerator, no food in any of the cabinets, and the pantry door was always locked. One day, Dottie had made a pot roast and had turned her back on Elizabeth for a few seconds, and when she turned back, Elizabeth had eaten the pot roast and was choking on it. Dottie grabbed her from behind and managed to get it out, but from that moment on, she knew she had to keep a constant eye on her daughter. Elizabeth didn't chew her food, she swallowed it. On top of that, she constantly acted like she was starving, like she was constantly craving food. It was all she talked about...when they were to eat the next time, how much she would have. It seemed to be constantly on her mind.

"I'm hungry, Mommy," she said this morning on her birthday, like every morning when she opened her eyes.

297

Dottie smiled and kissed her daughter's forehead. "We're going out for breakfast," she said and smiled. "It is, after all, your birthday."

That made Elizabeth smile. She loved going out to eat. Dottie didn't, but it was, after all, the girl's birthday. She deserved it, didn't she? Dottie was an optimist. All her life, food had meant joy and, in times of trouble, comfort. Denying her daughter a treat when it was her birthday felt like denying her the celebration. She feared that she was failing Elizabeth if she wasn't allowed just a little fun. Yet, she was terrified at the way things were heading. With the way her daughter was breathing, she would probably die before next Christmas.

They went to Ihop for pancakes. Elizabeth was panting heavily from walking from the car to the front door. Dottie helped her out and, walking backward and holding both of her hands, led her up the curb. To move forward without falling, Elizabeth rocked from side to side, inching her feet ahead a little at a time. Dottie felt her husband's eyes on them and lifted hers to meet his. She shivered from what she saw…the disgust in his eyes when he stared at his outrageous daughter. It was written all over his face.

He blamed Dottie too.

"Pancakes!" Elizabeth yelled, as they sat down in a booth. Her sisters hid their faces behind the menus when a group of girls their age walked by. It broke Dottie's heart.

"So, you want pancakes?" Dottie asked with a sniffle.

"Yes! Pancakes!" Elizabeth exclaimed. "I'm sooo hungry, Mommy."

The pancakes arrived and the family ate in silence. James kept looking at his watch, like he had somewhere else to be. Dottie got the feeling he would rather be anywhere else than where he was right now. Elizabeth leaned in over her plate with her arms surrounding it, like she was afraid someone would take it away from her. Her older sister Tiffany laughed.

"She's hoarding it," she said.

"No, she's not," Dottie said. "Don't talk like that to your sister."

"Oh, come on," James said. "She's right. It's like she thinks we're going to steal her food…as if she really needs any more."

The revulsion gleamed in his eyes. He wasn't even trying to hide it. He was sitting on the edge of his seat, like he was ready to leave any moment. Dottie wondered how it had come to this. How they had all drifted apart like this. Had she been too busy attending to Elizabeth's needs to notice?

"Okay then," James said. "Let me have an end piece of your pancake, then."

Elizabeth let out a desperate cry. "No!"

"Come on," Dottie said. "Let Daddy have a little piece. You have an entire stack of pancakes. He doesn't have any."

"NO!" she screamed. "If he has a piece, there won't be enough to fill me up! You're not going to touch my food!"

The girl screamed so loud everyone in the diner turned to look. Dottie felt how she blushed. Was she embarrassed of her own daughter?

Elizabeth couldn't stop screaming. "I'm so hungry! I'm starving!"

"That's it," James said and got up. He threw a few bills on the table. "I'm out of here."

"You can't just leave," Dottie said. "It's Elizabeth's birthday."

"I'm done," James said. "I can't take this anymore. Every time we go somewhere with her, she screams like that. It's even at the house. I've told you this for years. You pamper her. You've completely spoiled her. I don't know how many times I've told you to stop feeding her."

"But...but...I've done everything I could, James. You know that. I put locks on the refrigerator and everything. I think something is wrong with her. I really do. I think she really believes she is starving and she is desperate for food. That's why she tries to break the lock to get into the refrigerator. That's why she attacked the fridge with that hammer the other day. Because she genuinely believes she is in desperate need of food. Every minute of her waking day is filled with this intense hunger. I think we need to get her help."

James looked at Dottie and snorted. "Nonsense. It's all just nonsense. You feed her too much, that's it. If she can't understand that, then she needs to be disciplined. No one was ever harmed by a good spanking. That's how my parents taught me what was right and wrong."

"I'm not going to hit her. What are you saying, James? I'm telling you. It's not her fault. She can't help herself."

James shook his head. His eyes glistened in contempt. Dottie had never seen such resentment in her husband's eyes.

"Of course she can. Just like everyone else. She has no self-control. Look at her. She's a whale."

"How can you say such a thing?!" Dottie yelled and got up.

James threw out his arms. "You know what? I give up," he said.

Then, he turned on his heel and left. Back in the restaurant, Elizabeth had attacked Dottie's plate and started shoveling down her food using her fingers, while crying for more.

"I am hungry, Mommy. I'm so HUNGRY!"

FORTY-FOUR

March 2015

WE SENT out a search for a black truck, a Ford with YRJ on the license plate and the bumper sticker saying "Shit happens" to all the TV stations, newspapers, and even radio and had them ask people to look for it. We even posted about it on Twitter and Facebook, in various local groups. Two days later, we had a break-through.

Richard came to my desk in the morning when I had just gotten in and had my first cup of coffee. He leapt towards me and I knew something had happened.

"We caught a break, Ryder," he said. "Finally. We found the truck."

"I'll be...Where?"

"Parked outside a house on Indian Creek Drive in Cocoa Beach. A local patrol spotted it. It had a sticker like described and the license plate ends with YRJ."

I strapped on my Glock and asked Beth to come with me before I rushed out. On the way, I called Weasel, the Head of the Cocoa Beach Police Department, and asked her to send all the men she had to the address.

"We think the truck belongs to the shooter at Runaway Country," I said.

"Already done," she said with her raspy voice. "Joel, Jim, and Marty are almost there. George was the man on patrol. He's waiting for all of you there."

"Who does the house belong to where the truck is parked?"

"A Jennifer and Travis Goodman. That's all I know so far."

"Does the truck belong to them?"

"Yes," Weasel said.

Ten minutes later, I drove through the roadblock into a quiet residential street. George, the officer who had spotted the vehicle during his patrol, pointed towards a truck parked in the driveway of a house from the sixties. It was placed on a canal and had a boat in the driveway next to it.

I walked closer and looked at the sticker on the back and the plate. It all seemed right. "Anyone tried to contact the owner?" I asked, looking at the house.

"They're not home," George said.

"You know them?" I asked.

"Sure. Travis used to be captain at the fire station next to us. We saw him all the time."

"So, he knew Phillip Hagerty?" I asked.

"Sure. They were colleagues. Until Travis was kicked off the force."

"What happened?" I asked.

"Ah, it's an old story," George said.

"Tell it anyway."

"Well, apparently, Travis wore some T-shirts at work that offended some people."

I frowned. "T-shirts? What kind of T-shirts?"

"Racist ones. Some of the shirts included slogans like *MADD—Minorities Against Dumbing Down*, stuff like that. Apparently, it created a hostile environment, according to their supervisor."

"And I'm guessing Travis wasn't too fond of giving his job to Phillip Hagerty?" I asked.

George shrugged. "Probably not. Especially since it was Phillip who reported him for wearing the shirts."

"Let's take a look at this thing," Beth said, as she came up to me. She grabbed her gun and started approaching the car, sliding up its left side. The windows were all closed. It was hard to see from where I was standing, but it looked empty.

"We need to get ahold of this Travis guy before he leaves town," I said and grabbed the phone to call Weasel to ask her to bring him in. It was her town. She knew where the unemployed hid during the day.

While I was dialing the number, Beth grabbed the handle of the car door. I knew somehow, instinctively, at that second I should have stopped her, but it was too late. I looked up just as the truck exploded in an inferno of fire.

FORTY-FIVE

March 2015

THE KILLER WAS WATCHING the scene.

Kabooom!

The bomb went off.

"I'm so sorry," the killer whispered.

The killer put down the binoculars, feeling sorry for what had to be done. The radio played Shannon King's newest album. The killer listened to the lyrics and sang along. The killer felt like sending her another email. The killer needed Shannon to know...needed Shannon to know how sorry the killer was for what had to be done. Shannon hadn't expressed gratitude for the killer ridding her of that bastard, Joe. She had been awfully quiet, even though the media wrote about her constantly, some even claiming she had her husband murdered. That wasn't quite the point to it all. The killer wished they knew the entire truth. If only they knew how he used to beat Shannon up, how he used to mistreat his own family. The pig didn't deserve any better. Once the killer had realized what was going on behind those doors, the killer just knew it was time for action. Shannon couldn't do this all by herself. The guy wasn't going to stop.

It had to be done!

The killer drove off towards the A1A and ended up on Minuteman Causeway. Sirens blared in the distance and several police cars passed the killer's car on the way to the scene. A fire truck emerged from the brand new fire station next to city hall. The killer could still see the pillar of smoke in the rearview mirror.

"Such an awful mess," the killer mumbled and stopped at Simpler Times Market to pick up some groceries. "So sad it has to be this way. But, what's done is done. It had to be this way. It simply had to."

The killer paid for the steak and beers, then left the store. In the distance, the pillar of smoke had disappeared. At least they had managed to put out the fire.

"I'm so sorry," the killer whispered again, then drove off.

The killer stopped the car in front of the house and put it in park. The killer's sister opened the door. "Did you get everything?"

The killer nodded and put the bags down in the kitchen. "First Publix, then Simpler Times."

The sister smiled. "Good. Simpler Times is the best, don't you think? Everything is organic."

The killer never cared much about such things. A steak was a steak, wasn't it? The killer grabbed a beer and opened it.

"Really?" the sister said. "At ten-thirty in the morning?"

The killer lifted it. "Cheers."

The sister rolled her eyes. "You're impossible. Well, at least you got the groceries right."

"Anything for you, sis."

"We do make a good team, the two of us, don't you think?" the sister asked.

"I do."

"I have to say, I'm really happy to have you here," she said. "At first I thought it was a terrible idea, you know, based on how we used to fight as kids, but it has been quite nice to have you around, I must admit."

The killer lifted the beer in the air again. The buzz was already taking off and drowning out the guilt. Life was bearable again. At least for now.

FORTY-SIX

March 2015

"BEEEETH!!"

I didn't believe my eyes. I simply refused to believe it had happened. When the explosion sounded, Beth was thrown backwards into the air and landed in a bush. I ran to her. Her face was covered in blood, her eyes closed. I felt her pulse, while screaming for someone to call for an ambulance. All I could think of while performing CPR on her was the three children playing in her front yard.

"You're not leaving them, Beth," I yelled and prayed in desperation, while pressing her chest down and blowing air into her lungs. "Stay here. Oh, Jesus. Those kids need her. Let her stay, please, please, please."

The ambulance arrived and took her away. Her pulse was weak, but she wasn't dead yet. There was still hope. Luckily, she was the only one who was hurt by the explosion. It hadn't been a very big bomb.

Just enough to kill one person.

It was the killer who had placed it there. I just knew it was. The same guy who had shot Phillip Hagerty and Joe Harrison at the country festival. The same guy who had killed four people in Miami six years ago. Unlike the majority of mass murderers in history, he hadn't committed suicide; it wasn't a planned suicide where he took other lives with him on the way. This was murder. This guy was a serial and serials didn't stop until you made them.

While firefighters came and put out the fire, I grabbed my phone from the ground where it had landed when the explosion sounded, and called Weasel. She already knew what had happened.

"I need to find Travis Goodman, pronto," I said.

"I talked to Jennifer this morning. She works at City Hall as a secretary. Travis moved out a couple of weeks ago, according to her. He lives with his sister in Cape Canaveral. Apparently, it was too much for them that he lost his job."

"Give me the address and I'll take the scumbag in on my own."

"Don't go alone, Jack," she said. "You're upset about Beth, I know, but he could be dangerous. Let me meet you there."

I met Weasel outside the beautiful house overlooking the river in Cape Canaveral. We walked up the driveway and rang the doorbell. A heavily overweight man in his mid-thirties opened the door.

"Weasel?" he asked.

"Travis. We need to talk. Can we come in?" Weasel asked. "This is Jack Ryder from the Sheriff's Office."

"Sure."

Travis moved aside and we walked in. The TV was on in the living room, the coffee table overflowing with chips and empty beer bottles. Weasel looked at it with a sniffle.

"Are you drinking beer before noon now?" she asked.

"What's it to you?" he snarled.

I tried hard to hold back my anger, but it was hard. "Let's cut the BS, shall we? Let's stop playing pretend for a little, can we?"

Travis looked at me. He was wearing one of his racist shirts. It made my skin crawl. I thought about Emily and wanted to rip it off him.

"My partner is on the way to the hospital because of your little homemade bomb," I said. "She has three children. They will be orphaned if she dies. Are you happy about that?"

I felt Weasel's hand on my shoulder to calm me down. Travis stared at me. "What are you talking about?"

"Your truck. You own a black Ford, right? On the back it says, *Shit Happens?*"

"Yeah, but..."

"No buts...we're taking you in."

FORTY-SEVEN

March 2015

"She's alive, but in a coma," the doctor says. "Her skin is badly burned. If she wakes up, she'll need transplantation."

If she wakes up.

Ron was standing in the middle of our room at the station as he told us the news about Beth. It was the end of the day and I had let Travis roast in detention for most of the day. He had resisted his arrest and Weasel and I had to bring him in by force. Now, he was yelling and screaming in his cell, stating he wasn't saying another word without a lawyer. I didn't care. I was upset. Not just because of his shirt, but about everything. I had made sure Beth's kids were able to stay with the neighbor. Luckily, they were. Travis could get himself a lawyer if he wanted to. We had a pretty strong case against him. The truck that blew up was his, it was parked in front of his house, he had a grudge against Phillip Hagerty, and he was a stinking racist. He fit the profile of the psychopath we were looking for. I just needed more evidence.

While going through what I had, my phone rang. It was Yamilla.

"Ryder, I have finally finished the autopsy on Daniel Millman. With all that has been going on, I haven't had the time until now."

"Daniel Millman. I had almost forgot about him," I said, thinking about the trail in the woods where we had found his body. It hadn't been a pretty sight. "So, how did he die?" I sipped my coffee and spat it out when I heard the answer.

"His stomach exploded," Yamilla said.

"What?"

"You heard me. It exploded."

I put my cup down and didn't even bother to dry up what I had spilled. "But how is that possible?"

"I don't know. But it is. It's not the first time it has happened."

"But how?"

"It takes a huge amount of food and liquid. The stomach is capable of

306

extending to quite a massive capacity, but even that has limits. It ruptured. The human stomach can hold up to three liters, and it risks rupture at the five liter point, just for reference. When you eat to the point that you think you might vomit, you're probably at the one to one and a half liter level."

"So, you're telling me that he ate more than five liters of food?"

"It hardly sounds possible, right? I mean, think of it. When you know you're so full you're about to throw up, you have to power through that sensation and up your food intake to the level that will cause your stomach to rupture. At some point during this feast, your gag reflex will kick in. Now, it does happen that some people have such unusual eating habits that their bodies' reflexes no longer respond as they normally would. If the reflexes have been ignored for a long time, the person would no longer vomit at the appropriate time. And then, when the stomach gets to this extremely distended point, the stomach muscles are too stretched out to be strong enough to vomit the food out. That's one scenario."

"What's the other?" I asked.

"The food was forced into him over an extended period of time, causing his body to learn how to ignore its reflexes and let the stomach to expand till it burst. There are signs on his body indicating that might be the case here."

"What signs?" I asked. This had to be one of the strangest cases in my time as a homicide detective.

"Signs of trauma in and around his mouth," Yamilla said.

"Around his mouth? Hm. Given the fact that Daniel Millman was never overweight in any of the previous pictures of him that I've seen, it all seems quite dubious," I said.

"It sure does," Yamilla said. "Now, I have looked into it a little bit and found another case that has similar traits."

"Really?"

"Yes, in 2009, six years ago, the body of a man was found floating in a canal in Boca Raton, north of Miami. His stomach was also ruptured. The ME concluded back then that he had simply overeaten and fallen into the canal, but when I looked into the autopsy report, I noticed the same trauma to the mouth as Daniel Millman had."

"Sounds like we should take a closer look at that," I said.

"I'll send over the details for you to look at. The victim's name was James West."

FORTY-EIGHT

March 2015

KATIE WASN'T FEELING WELL. Ever since the incident in the water, she had stayed away from everyone else as much as possible. She hardly left the room at the motel and didn't talk to any of the girls. All she wanted was for this break to be over so they could go back home. The girls kept laughing and giggling at her. After she had come out of the water on the day it happened, she had been so embarrassed, she had picked her things up, then ran to the room to get dressed. The girls had come in afterwards, while she was still in the shower, and she had heard them talking about her, thinking she couldn't hear them.

"I kind of feel bad for her," Irene said.

"It's her own fault, if you ask me," Britney said. "Her breasts are way too big for her to wear such a small bikini. It was bound to happen."

"Did you see how everyone was looking?" Leanne asked. "It was soooo embarrassing. I'm so glad it wasn't me."

"You would never be so stupid as to go out and try to surf in a bikini," Britney said. "She only did it because Greg told her to. She thinks he likes her. So stupid."

"Don't you think he might like her?" Irene asked. "I mean, he did invite her here, and he seems interested in her."

Britney scoffed. "Nah. Not Greg. Remember Dianna that he brought last year? Same story."

"I'm not sure it's the same," Leanne continued.

Katie could tell that Britney was annoyed with her. She could tell by the tone of her voice.

"Come on. It's exactly the same. Don't you see it?"

"I think it's different with Katie. He seems to really like her. If he hadn't been so far out in the water, I think he would have been the one to help her, not that surfer dude from the motel."

Katie had stepped out of the shower and stood behind the door, listening, while the water was still running to make them believe she couldn't hear them.

She couldn't help smiling at what Leanne had said. Could it be? Could it really be that Greg liked her? It wasn't just an illusion? It wasn't just in her head? She put a towel around her body.

"He just feels sorry for her because she's so pathetic," Britney said. "I mean, how else can you feel for her? She is really sad. I can't see how they could ever be together. Greg is in a completely different league than her."

"You're jealous," Irene said.

Britney snorted again. "As if. I can get any boy I want. I could get Greg without even trying."

Katie pushed the door open. The girls all turned and looked at her. "You stay away from Greg," she said with a courage she had no idea she had. "He's mine."

Britney looked at Katie with a frown. Then she chuckled. "Yours? He'll never be yours. He'll use you for sex and then throw you away like a used towel."

Leanne stepped forward: "Just because it happened to you, doesn't mean he'll do the same to Katie."

Britney threw her a glare. "That was told to you in confidence."

Katie felt her heart race. So, that was what this was all about? Greg had used Britney once, then thrown her away. It made sense.

"Well, I'm going for him," Katie said and looked with confidence at the girls. Britney cupped her mouth and laughed. Leanne and Irene looked at her with compassion. Leanne made a grimace while they all stared at her legs.

"You might want to wipe that blood off your legs first," Britney said with loud laughter.

Katie looked down. Three drops of blood had run down the inside of her thighs and was approaching her knees.

"Guess there isn't going to be any sex for you and Greg this week, after all," Britney said and laughed again.

Katie blushed, then ran back into the bathroom and closed the door, while panting. She put her back up against the door, then slid to the ground while crying.

Why did she have to come on this trip? Why?

FORTY-NINE

March 2015

I'M OKAY. I'm okay. I'm still alive and no one knows!

Shannon felt sick to her stomach as she walked around her condo. She and Angela hadn't been outside the door since Joe had died. They had stayed inside for several days, simply watching movies and talking. Jack had stopped by and brought them groceries, and she had told him she needed time, that Angela needed time. It was, after all, the truth. Angela was watching some cartoon when Shannon finally saw the chance to get into the bathroom and relieve the pain a little.

She found the bottle wrapped up in a towel under the sink and took off the top. Her hands were shaking heavily as she brought it to her mouth. It felt so good when those drops hit her tongue.

She knew it was a slippery slope, but so far, she had managed. No one had known that she had a few sips of vodka every day. It made her calmer and relaxed and a better mother, she believed. Jack hadn't seen it on her or smelled it when he stopped by, and she had made sure to keep his visits short, since she didn't want him to suspect anything. The pain would go away soon, and then she would stop again. It was no problem; it was just the way she would deal with this.

It was what she needed right now.

Shannon gulped down the vodka, then removed the bottle from her lips. She closed her eyes and let the drink do its job inside of her. Her hands soon became steadier, her thinking calmer. She could now focus on just one thing at a time and not have her mind race with the millions of thoughts flickering through her mind.

It's your fault those people died. It's all your fault. Now Angela is fatherless because of you. You should never have taken the stage. Maybe if you hadn't sung that song, maybe if you hadn't touched that guy's hand, maybe...

There were a lot of maybes in her thoughts these days. She couldn't stop them on her own. She kept wondering about that guy that was shot right in front of her, right when she touched him. What if she had touched someone else? Would that person have been killed instead? Was it an accident that he was killed? Was the shooter aiming for her instead? And what about Joe? Why did he have to die?

Shannon grabbed the bottle and took another large sip. She was beginning to feel the alcohol, the delicious warmth it left inside of her body, then the serenity. Finally, her thoughts were numbed enough to quiet down. Finally, she felt at peace. At least for a little while.

She took another sip to make sure she could stay this way before she put the top back on and hid the bottle under the sink wrapped in its towel. She washed out her mouth and brushed her teeth to make sure Angela didn't smell anything, then opened the door.

Angela looked up from the couch. "What took you so long, Mommy?"

Shannon felt the buzz and the earth spun for just a second under her feet. She grabbed the door to not fall.

"Mommy! Are you alright?" Angela shrieked.

"Mommy's fine. Don't worry. Just a little tired, that's all. I'll just lay down for a little while."

Shannon found the couch and put her head down on the soft pillow. She drifted away into a happy dream and soon didn't hear the TV, not even when Angela accidentally zapped onto a news channel and saw her mother's face plastered all over under the headline:

BREAKING NEWS: COUNTRY SUPER-STAR SHANNON KING STOLE LYRICS TO HER FIRST ALBUM AND KILLED THE ORIGINAL CREATOR, HER EX-HUSBAND REVEALS IN LETTER AFTER HIS DEATH

FIFTY

March 2015

I COULDN'T BELIEVE what I was looking at on the screen of my computer. A news-ticker had brought me to CNN's main page, where the story of Shannon was plastered all over the screen in blinking yellow and breaking news signs. According to the news channel, Joe had left a letter with his lawyer telling a story of how Shannon had stolen the lyrics to her first album, *Struck by Love*, the megahit that made her the star she was today, and then allegedly killed the person who originally wrote it. According to the letter, the person's body had been buried in a location that the police in Nashville were now examining.

Now, the news channel was speculating on the theory that maybe Shannon was also behind the killing of her husband, that she hired someone to kill him, since they were facing a custody battle. They had interviewed a friend of Joe's, who was also a police officer, to tell the story of how saint-like Joe was and how he wanted to be there for his child, but Shannon was trying to keep him away from his own daughter and how devastated he was.

"This is bull..." I said and leaned back with a deep sigh. "I don't believe this guy!"

Richard looked at me from across the room. I didn't care what anyone else thought. I grabbed my phone and called Shannon. She didn't pick up. Her phone was turned off and went straight to the answering machine. Of course it was, with all that was going on. She had been in hiding from the world, and especially the press, for days as it was.

It was almost four in the afternoon and I was supposed to pick up Abigail and Austin at surf-camp at four o'clock. So, I decided to call it a day. I drove the Jeep to the camp, which was only a few blocks south of where we lived. I tried hard to not show the kids how I felt and smiled as I grabbed their surfboards and threw them in the back.

"What's wrong, Dad?" Abigail said as soon as she saw me.

I could never hide anything from her.

"Nothing's wrong. I'm happy to see you. Did you have fun today?"

"No," Austin said.

It made me sad. I really wanted him to enjoy surfing as much as I did, but somehow, it didn't seem like he could really get into it.

"I had a lot of fun," Abigail said. "I caught the biggest wave ever. Open-faced, Dad. It was so much fun. I paddled out in the back on my own too. Reached my goal of catching seven waves on my own. No more being pushed into waves for me."

"Wow, that's two more than yesterday," I said impressed.

Catching your own waves and paddling out on your own was a huge step, they were the hardest parts of surfing when starting out.

Abigail got in the car. Austin followed. I looked at him. "I tie-dyed a pillowcase," Austin said. The surf-camp was surfing in the morning and art in the afternoon. "I made a heart."

"That's great too, buddy. But, didn't you surf?" I asked.

Austin sniffled as an answer.

"He did," Abigail answered for him. "But only on the inside."

"That's good," I said. "There is nothing wrong with surfing whitewater."

"No, but he got tumbled really bad," Abigail said. "He cried."

"I got the board in my face!" Austin almost yelled at his sister.

"Hey, let's not fight here. At least you tried," I said and started the car. I felt bad for Austin. He was always beat by his sister, no matter what they did. It wasn't fair.

"I'm gonna drive you to Grandma's and Grandpa's; I have to go see Shannon."

"Yay," Abigail said. "Can I go surfing?"

"If someone watches you."

"I'll get Grandpa to look after me. He loves to watch me surf."

"Sounds good," I said, and drove the four blocks to my parents' place, where I dropped them off.

I tried to call Shannon again as I drove up to our condominium, while cameras flashed and reporters knocked on the windows of the car. I tried to call Emily, but she didn't pick up either. I had no idea what she had done all day. It was spring break for her as well, and I had a feeling she hadn't done anything all day, except sleep in and then play on the computer. I knew she hadn't been at my parents' to eat all day, so I figured she had eaten at the condo if she had eaten at all. She had been so into healthy eating lately, I got a feeling she'd hardly touched anything. I didn't like it.

I left a message on her machine telling her I loved her and I would be at the condo after dinner, and that I hoped she would join us for dinner at the motel. I felt like I had hardly seen her all week, except for in the evenings when we watched *The Tonight Show with Jimmy Fallon* together before bedtime. It had kind of become our thing.

FIFTY-ONE

March 2015

IT WAS a drag getting through the horde of reporters camping in front of our condominium, but somehow I succeeded in elbowing through and avoiding answering questions like:

"Did Shannon King kill Robert Hill?"

"Is your girlfriend a murderer, Detective?"

"Did she kill her ex-husband Joe Harrison too?"

"How can you, as a detective, date a murderer?"

It was Angela who opened the door when I rang the doorbell. She looked sad. "Mommy's all over the news," she said when she saw me.

The TV was on in the living room and Shannon's face was plastered all over it. I walked in and shut it off. "Don't watch that garbage," I said. "And don't believe a word they say, you hear me?"

Angela nodded. I turned and spotted Shannon on the couch. She was heavily asleep.

"She's been sleeping all morning," Angela said.

Looking at her left me with a bad feeling. I felt her forehead; she wasn't warm. I leaned over and smelled her breath. Just as I suspected. It stank of alcohol.

"Goddammit, Shannon," I whispered. "Not in front of your daughter."

"Is Mommy alright?" Angela asked. I could hear the anxiety in her tone of voice. The girl was terrified. She had just lost her father. She had enough on her plate, I thought. I grabbed Angela in my arms and held her.

"Mommy will be fine. She just needs some rest. How about I take you to my parents' place? Abigail and Austin are there. Maybe you can play together? Would you like that? You could go in the motel's pool if you like."

Angela lit up. "Are you kidding? I would love it! But, what about the reporters? Mommy said we had to stay in the condo and close the shutters so the reporters wouldn't see us."

I kissed her cheek. "You let me worry about them," I said, as I grabbed my phone and made a quick call.

"Will you take care of Mommy while I'm gone?" Angela asked when I had hung up.

I glanced at Shannon. She was sleeping heavily still. Probably wouldn't wake up for a few hours.

"Sure thing."

I helped Angela pack a backpack with her swimsuit, goggles, a towel, and her favorite pool toy. I wrote a note for Shannon, in case she woke up while I was gone, then grabbed Angela's hand and we walked to the elevator.

"No," I said, when Angela went to press the button. "I know another way."

I opened the door to the fire escape and we walked down the stairs till we made it to the basement. Every condo had a garage in the basement. I opened mine and saw the impression on Angela's face.

"Woooooww!"

"I know," I said and walked closer to the old red Ducati Streetfighter. I'd had it for many years and spent many hours fixing it up. Until Arianna left us, that was. After that, I had other more important things to attend to. I felt a pinch in my heart as I looked at the old lady. Arianna and I had ridden her together. It had been our thing. She had loved it, loved the feeling of the wind in her hair.

God, I miss you, Arianna.

I missed her and resented her at the same time. It was confusing. I missed what we used to have, but I was so incredibly angry with her for cheating on me and leaving me the way she did.

I pulled the bike out of the garage, then found a helmet for Angela. It was a little too big, but we weren't going very far, so I figured it would do. Her small hands held onto my back really tight.

"Okay, sweetie. Hold on now. Once they spot us, they're going to try and follow us to see where you're going, so I need to lose them, okay? Hold on to me really tight."

"Okay," Angela said.

"Here goes nothing."

I started the engine with a roar, then opened the gate, and the Ducati sprang out of the garage. The entire media corps was focused on something by the front door and didn't notice us at first.

"Look!" Angela yelled through the sound of the engine. "It's Emily!"

I nodded as I swung the bike into the street, and before the reporters realized it was us, we passed the scene. I was the one who had called Emily, and luckily she had picked up this time. I had told her to go down and talk to the reporters. Stall them. Create a diversion. They knew she was my daughter. I knew they would throw themselves at anyone who was vaguely a part of it all, and I would rather it was Emily than Angela, who would only be hurt by their questions. It worked. By the time I had passed all of them, they hadn't even found their car keys yet. Not one of them managed to follow us. I owed Emily big time for this. But it was worth it.

FIFTY-TWO

March 2015

I dropped off Angela at my mom and dad's and told them she couldn't be seen by any reporters, and that she should stay away from the beach area, where they might be lurking. My mom promised to take good care of her, and Abigail and Austin immediately grabbed her and pulled her inside the motel to be a part of some game they had started. Angela laughed as she ran off with my kids. It calmed me down. The poor girl needed a break.

I drove through the garage into my building and parked the bike, then ran up the stairs, opened the door to the front entrance, and pulled Emily inside, out of the claws of the press.

"Thank you!" she moaned. "Those people are awful! How does Shannon put up with them?"

"I'm not sure she does," I said.

"Is it true?" Emily asked, as we took the elevator up to Shannon's floor.

"Is what true?"

"Did she kill some guy and steal his songs to make a career?"

I sighed. The elevator stopped. "I don't know," I said. "I don't think so. It doesn't sound like her. I haven't been able to ask her yet. But I can hardly imagine she could do anything like this."

"Probably that Joe guy was behind it," Emily said. "Figures. Even though he's dead, she still has to deal with him and all his shit."

"Watch the language, young lady," I said, thinking she was so right. Joe was still hurting her, even if it was from beyond the grave.

"Just shows you that you gotta be picky when you chose your man," Emily said. "Can't let yourself be blinded by love or great looks."

I chuckled and kissed her as I left the elevator. "See you at dinner at the motel?" I asked as the doors were about to close.

"Sure," she answered.

I stared at the door as it shut and my smart daughter left for our floor. I had done many things wrong while bringing her up, but it couldn't all have been bad. She was one clever girl.

I walked to Shannon's condo and let myself in. She was still asleep on the couch. I walked inside and kneeled next to her. I kissed her forehead and stroked her thick hair. She was such a beautiful woman. Her features so delicate, her hair long and thick. Why had life decided to be so hard on her?

"How long have you been drinking? Is that why you've been so busy getting me to leave lately when I stopped by? You were afraid I'd find you out, weren't you? You know you can't handle it, dammit Shannon. You know."

I decided I wasn't just going to sit and wait for her to wake up. I walked into the kitchen and started searching. I wanted to remove the bottles of alcohol so she wouldn't fall in again. I went through all the cabinets in the kitchen, in her bedroom, the living room, and finally the bathroom. I found a bottle of vodka wrapped in a towel underneath the sink. My heart dropped. It was almost empty. A tear escaped my eye and I was filled with such an anger I could hardly contain it. I took the bottle into the kitchen and threw it in the garbage can so hard it broke. Then I took the garbage out. When I returned, Shannon was awake. She was sitting up on the couch, her hair all messy on one side of her head. Her eyes were small. She looked terribly pale.

"Jack?"

I closed the door.

"Jack..." she moaned. She forced a smile. "What are you doing here? Where is Angela?"

"I took her to my parents," I said.

I sat next to her on the couch and grabbed her hand in mine. I forced her to look into my eyes.

"We need to talk."

FIFTY-THREE

March 2015

"I NEVER KILLED ANYONE. I swear to God, Jack. I never killed anyone. You have to believe me."

I looked at Shannon. Her eyes had grown wild when I told her what had happened, how the media was all over the story of her apparently killing this Robert Hill and stealing his songs. I told her I needed to know the truth, no matter how hard it was to bear.

"I want to, Shannon. I really, really want to. You need to tell me what happened first. I need to know. I deserve to know."

Shannon tried to avoid looking at me. I could tell she was miserable. All I wanted was the truth from her. Then, we could take it from there.

"It was so long ago," Shannon said. She pulled her legs up on the couch and put her chin on her knees. She suddenly seemed so small, so frail. She was talking slowly and I could tell she was still under the influence of the alcohol. I wondered how far out she had gotten the last couple of days. Was it just a relapse, a setback that she could recover from? Or had she gotten in too deep, so deep she would need professional help?

"Robert Hill was a good friend of mine," she said. "We wrote songs together. We performed together frequently at bars and clubs around Nashville. He didn't enjoy the stage as much as I did, so he mainly hid behind his guitar, while I got to sing the songs. He loved when I sang his songs."

"Did he write the songs for your first album?" I asked.

Shannon looked at me quickly, then at the ground.

"He did, didn't he?" I asked.

"That part is true," Shannon said. "But he wrote them for me. I didn't realize it until it was too late, but he was madly in love with me. I was with Joe. Joe could tell and tried to warn me, but I cut him off and told him he saw ghosts everywhere. I didn't see it, not until it was too late. He wrote the album for me, he told me. He came to the small cottage where we used to live one night and handed me the songs. He told me they were for me. He had been working on them for years, he said. Ever since he met me. He had written them for me to sing. No one else would do them justice, he said. He told me he didn't want his name on them, told me they were mine to keep. I didn't understand until I read the songs. They were a declaration of love to me. At first, I thought I could never sing them, but they were so good. I showed them to Joe, and he told me they were too good to not use. I had to produce an album with them. He knew someone who could help me. But he never liked the idea that it was Robert who had written the songs. He hated him because he was so into me. After Robert gave me the songs, Joe told me to not see Robert again. That it was bad for our relationship...that he was coming between us. In some way, it was true. I was feeling different about Robert since I had found out how he felt about me. But, as soon as I started to avoid Robert, things turned bad. He started following me everywhere I went."

"He was stalking you?" I asked.

Shannon nodded. She bit her lip. "He was everywhere, Jack. If I performed, he was in the audience. If I went to a restaurant, he would stand outside the window and watch me or sit at a table not far away. It was like, the more I avoided him, the more obsessed he got. One day, when Joe and I came home from a performance, a little drunk, since we had celebrated that I had landed my first record deal, he was sitting in our living room. He was angry and had a gun in his hand. I asked him what was wrong and he told me he wanted what was his. I thought he meant the album, the songs, and told him I could try and get him credited for it, but he didn't care about that. He wanted me. He was there because he wanted me. He pointed the gun at Joe. It was so scary, Jack. I was sure he was going to kill him. All his anger was directed at Joe. He was the one who had kept me away from him, he said. I screamed and cried and tried to get him to back down and leave Joe alone, but he wouldn't. His hands were shaking in anger as he spoke. I was terrified, Jack. I was so afraid."

I put my hand on hers. She was in deep distress. "No wonder," I said. "So, what happened?"

"I...We had our instruments at the house. I...I...I had to stop him. He wanted to shoot Joe. I grabbed a microphone stand and slammed it into his back. He fell to the ground and Joe grabbed the stand out of my hand, then slammed it into his back again. He kept going, Jack. He wouldn't stop. He kept hitting Robert, again and again, while yelling and screaming. When he hit the back of his head, it sounded like a watermelon landing on the ground. It split his head open. I told him to stop. I yelled and yelled, but he wouldn't. Joe was so angry. I couldn't stop him."

"So, Joe killed him," I said. "You just knocked him out."

Shannon looked at me and shook her head. "It was a terrible thing we did. It has haunted me ever since. Afterwards, we didn't know what to do. We couldn't call the police; no one would believe us. I had just signed a record deal, the chance of a lifetime. What should I have done? I would lose everything." Shannon paused. A couple of tears escaped her eye. "So, we buried him. In the backyard of the house. The next day, we told the landlord we wanted to move and started looking for a new place. We left the next day and never looked back. We never talked about it again. Not until Joe brought it up a few days ago. He told me he would reveal the secret if I didn't come back to him."

"That's why he was so certain you were going to come back to him," I said. "He told me while you were on stage."

Shannon chuckled lightly then sniffled. "That sounds like him. He told me that day that he had left a letter with his lawyer with the instruction to reveal it all to the press if something happened to him. It was his insurance."

"And it worked. It's all over the media," I said. "In the letter, he claims you were the one who killed Robert Hill. Now, we have to figure out how to avoid having you go to jail for this. It's his word against yours."

FIFTY-FOUR

March 2015

SPRING BREAK WAS ALMOST over when something wonderful happened to Katie. After dragging herself through days of going to the beach with the girls, trying to hide in the room and avoid the others, especially the boys after the incident surfing, she was sitting on her bed on Friday morning, two days before they would go back to school. Katie was counting the minutes and digging her nose into her book to escape reality. She was alone in the motel room when she received a text. She picked up the phone and saw that it was from Greg. Her heart pounded when she opened it.

THERE'S A FULL MOON TONIGHT AT SUNSET. THEY SAY IT'S GOING TO BE BLOOD-RED. DO YOU WANT TO MEET UP AND WATCH IT RISE TOGETHER?

Katie stared at her screen. A smile spread across her face. Could it be? Could it really be? She had avoided Greg ever since the incident in the water, thinking he was probably repulsed by her, and he had left her alone, so Katie had kind of figured he wasn't interested in her anymore. She still liked him and had observed him from afar every day at the beach, while sitting on her towel and reading, but he hadn't spoken to her, so she had almost given up.

He does like me. He wants to meet with me.

Katie texted him back that "Sure, she would love to, what time and where?" He answered right away.

7:30 IN THE DUNES. THERE IS A SMALL BENCH ON THE LEFT OF THE MOTEL. WE CAN BE ALONE THERE.

Katie's heart was racing in her chest.

Oh, my God. He really wants to be alone with me. Oh, my God. He wants to really be with me. Like, really be with me.

Katie took in a deep breath, remembering what Britney had told her earlier on the trip. That Greg brought girls to have sex with them, then tossed them aside afterwards. She had to be careful to not let that happen to her. She still had her period, so that was an excellent excuse for not sleeping with him. She wanted more from him. She wanted them to get to know each other first. She wondered why he hadn't tried to make a move before now. If he was so eager to have sex with her, he could have had her for the entire trip. Had he waited so it wouldn't be awkward afterwards? Or maybe he did really like her for who she was and had taken his time to find the courage to ask. Now that time was running out, he knew he had to act fast before they went back home.

Yes, that was probably it. That had to be it. After all, he had invited her to play volleyball and to go surfing with him. He did want to be with her. The fact that he had left her alone all this time was probably just because she had avoided him; she was the one who hadn't seemed like she wanted to be with him or any of the others.

Katie put her book down, then texted him back.

SURE. SEE YOU THERE.

She wondered if she should add "Looking forward to being alone with you," but decided not to. She didn't want to come off as too eager. If he was the player they said he was, she had to play her cards right. She had to be hard to get. That was the only thing guys like him respected. They liked the chase.

Well, so did she, and she would soon have him in her net. That would show those girls.

Katie got up from the bed, walked to her suitcase, and found the dress she had picked out for the trip. The dress she had bought with the sole intention of wearing it if she ever got the chance to be alone with Greg.

Now was that time. She could hardly wait.

Katie took a shower, then got dressed and looked at herself in the mirror. The other girls had told her they were going to The Lobster Shanty to eat dinner, so they wouldn't be back any time soon. There was an event at the port where girls drank free all night that they would hit afterwards. Katie wouldn't see them until tomorrow.

At least they wouldn't somehow ruin it for Katie. She had decided to skip dinner because she wasn't hungry and felt so nervous about meeting Greg. She put on some make up to make her look really pretty, then sat on the bed and waited. At exactly seven twenty-nine, she got up, corrected her dress, then sighed and looked at her reflection.

"This is it, Katie," she said to herself. "Don't blow it."

She put on lip gloss one last time, then corrected her hair and pulled down the dress again. It was very short and she wasn't too fond of her legs. But, as she pulled it down, her breasts showed too much flesh, so she pulled the dress back up.

There. This was as good as it got.

Katie looked at her watch again and walked out. She had planned on being a couple of minutes late, to make sure he didn't think she was too eager; desperate women were repulsive to men.

Katie closed the door to the room behind her, then walked towards the beach, hoping her tampon would keep her safe for long enough so she didn't have to suddenly run back to the room. She smiled when she felt the evening breeze hit her face. It felt so nice. The ocean was in front of her now and the sun almost set over the Intracoastal on the other side. The moon would rise above the ocean. The light was gorgeous. The moon was already peeking above the horizon. It was big and very red. It looked just like a sunrise. It was spectacular. Katie couldn't wait to enjoy it in the arms of Greg. She walked along the beach to the left, where the bench was placed in front of the big white condominium that was neighbor to the motel.

Katie spotted Greg sitting on the bench as she approached the place they had agreed to meet. He was looking at the moon. Katie waved, but he didn't see her. She walked closer, then waved again, but he still didn't wave back. He didn't seem to see her. She took off her shoes to better be able to walk across the sand and held them in her hand. It felt so nice between her toes. She loved the sand here. It was soft and you could walk with your bare toes in it without ever stepping on a rock or a shell. Katie looked at the moon quickly once again and sighed at the beauty of the scenery. Sandy beach as far as the eye could see, perfect temperature, the moon and the light, and...him. Katie turned her head and looked at Greg again. That was when she realized why he hadn't waved back at her, why he hadn't seen her.

Katie stopped. Everything inside of her froze to ice. It wasn't because he was busy staring at the moon. It wasn't because he didn't notice her. It was because his eyes were closed. He was sitting on the bench with his eyes shut, and Katie realized in that second, as she took the last step towards him, and parts of him were no longer covered by the sand dunes. Now she could see what was going on, and it made everything inside of her turn.

On her knees in front of Greg was Britney, sitting with her back turned to Katie. She had her head bent over his crotch, his pants wide open. Greg was moaning. Britney's head was moving faster and faster. Greg moaned louder and louder until he suddenly arched his body and led out a loud groan.

That was when Britney turned her head and looked directly at Katie. Their eyes locked and Britney licked her lips. Katie bent over and threw up in the sand.

Part Three

GET YOURSELF FREE

FIFTY-FIVE

March 2015

STANLEY HAD LOST count of the days. He guessed he had been in the room for maybe a little more than a week. Maybe it was more, he didn't know. But he hadn't lost hope yet. Both his legs were badly hurt and one was infected and gave him a fever with hallucinations that followed. And then there was the food. He had been forced to eat more food than he had ever imagined he could contain, and his stomach hurt so badly it was almost impossible for him to move.

He kept thinking about Elyse and wondering if she was alright. She was his one thing in life that mattered, his one true pure thing, his second chance.

Things had been bad with Timmy when he was a child. Stanley didn't like to be reminded of it. Stanley hadn't known what to do, what else to do when the boy kept acting so strangely, than to try and beat it out of him. Only, it hadn't helped. Timmy had stayed the same way. He had kept putting on Mommy's dresses and walking in her high heels. He had also brought home a boy as his *partner* when he came back from college to visit at Thanksgiving. Later, he had told his parents that he was going to go through a change and that he would be a woman soon. It was all far too strange for Stanley, and he had told him to never come back again. He simply couldn't cope with it.

Today, he regretted it all. He regretted having beaten the boy so badly he could hardly walk, in pure frustration over the fact that the boy wasn't like others. It was wrong. Stanley knew that. You shouldn't beat a kid. But he hadn't known what else to do. He hadn't known what this was or how to respond to it.

Now, it was too late. Timmy was now Tiana and lived somewhere in California. Stanley hadn't heard from him since the day he told him to leave and never come back. It was Stanley's own fault, and Melanie never hesitated in telling him so. She went to visit their son—or daughter—every now and then, and never told Stanley anything when she returned except *it was a good trip. No delays.*

Stanley had tried to make amends by being a better grandfather than he was a father, but it hadn't changed the fact that he missed his son like crazy, and so badly wanted to get back into his life. Or her life. Or whatever it was. Stanley was confused. It was all so strange and complicated, and he had no idea how to do it. So, for years, he simply hadn't. He hadn't done anything about it. He had pretended it never happened, pretended his son was still his son, only living far away now. At least, that's what he told the neighbors.

"Oh yeah, Timmy is good. Doing great. A lawyer now. Hoping to make partner next year."

The stories got better and better every time. The picture he had created of his perfect son became more and more polished as the years passed.

"Yes, he has two children now. The youngest is adorable. Cute as they get. Yes, it is too bad they live so far away and hardly ever have time to visit. It is a shame. But, what can you do? They got to live their own lives, you know?"

Over and over again he would say things like that and Melanie would shake her head, but she would never correct him or tell on him. She would never embarrass him publicly. It was her way of loving him. He was grateful for that.

Stanley sobbed in his bed, knowing that in a few minutes the crazy person holding him hostage would be back with enough food to feed a small African village for days. He wasn't sure he could take more. It was all so...so miserable.

It was while feeling sorry for himself that Stanley suddenly realized that maybe there was a God after all. Maybe he did hear him when he had cried out his pain and misery in the few moments he had been left alone during the day.

His guardian had forgotten to lock the door. A gust of wind, or maybe it was the air from the AC as it started, now made it open just a little bit, just enough to let the smell of freedom slip inside.

FIFTY-SIX

January 2009

JAMES HAD LEFT THEM. When they returned home from the diner that morning on Elizabeth's birthday, on Christmas Eve, he had packed his things and left them a note telling them he was gone and he wasn't coming back. Dottie was devastated. She cried for days in despair, not knowing what to do next. How was she supposed to support four children and especially one that ate more than the rest of them put together? How?

She asked James that when she called him a few days later, after she had finally gotten ahold of herself just enough to be able to speak to him.

"How are we supposed to get by?"

"I'll send you money."

"What about us? What about the kids?"

"I don't know."

"Come home, James. We'll talk. We'll figure it out. Make some changes. Please, just come home."

"I've met someone else."

The words hit her like arrows to her chest. "Someone else…but…James?"

"We're moving in together. There's nothing you can do about it, Dottie. I'm done. It's over."

"You can't just leave me?"

"I just did."

Then, he had hung up and left Dottie to sob in self-pity for weeks afterwards. He had kept his word and sent her money every week, but it was barely enough to keep Elizabeth satisfied. The rest of them had to eat too. Dottie knew she had to get a job. She found one as a waitress at Denny's and that kept them going for a little while. But it meant a lot of changes for the family, and especially for Elizabeth, who had to go to aftercare at the school, and she didn't take any of the changes well. It was hard enough for her in school, where she was constantly teased about her size, and where she couldn't eat until she was allowed to. But to

328

have to stay at the school's aftercare for three more hours every day was crushing for her. Every day, when Dottie brought her home after a long day at work, she would scream and cry, and the only way Dottie knew to calm her down was to give her food. So, she started bringing home leftovers from the diner, and as long as Elizabeth got those, she kept quiet. It didn't help with her rapid weight gain, but Dottie didn't quite see any other way. She simply couldn't deal with it on top of everything else.

At Elizabeth's annual check-up in January, her doctor looked at Dottie with a deep sigh.

"I know she has gained a lot again, Doctor," Dottie said. "I just can't control it. I've tried everything. I don't know what to do. James tells me to discipline her more, to help her get better self-control, but I don't know how to. I guess I have given up."

The doctor leaned back in his chair and looked at Dottie. "I have come upon something that you might find interesting," he said, much to Dottie's surprise. She was certain she was in for another of his scoldings, which she usually got when visiting with Elizabeth.

"You what?" she asked.

"I think I might know what is wrong with Elizabeth. I read an article about it recently and it just hit me. This is what is happening to Elizabeth West, I said to myself. This is what's wrong with her."

"So, what is it?" Dottie asked, her heart racing. Was there an explanation for her daughter's condition? Was Dottie really not the one responsible for this?

"It's called Prader-Willi Syndrome," he said and leaned forward. "It's a rare genetic disorder in which seven genes on chromosome 15 are deleted or unexpressed on the paternal chromosome."

"I don't think I follow you, Doctor."

"She was born with it," he said. "It's a rare chromosomal abnormality. It causes low muscle tone and impairs signaling between the brain and the stomach. There is no sensation of satiety that tells them to stop eating or alerts their body to throw up when they have eaten too much. Elizabeth feels like she is starving constantly because her brain tells her she is. Patients describe the hunger as a physical pain. To make matters worse, it also causes an especially slow metabolism, predisposing Elizabeth to morbid obesity. Most die from obesity-related diseases later on in life, many from choking because they swallow their food too fast. She does not know when to stop eating. You'll have to keep an eye on her constantly. Food can be a death sentence for patients like her."

FIFTY-SEVEN

March 2015

Travis Goodman wasn't talking. Even after days in jail, he wouldn't say anything. He simply refused to speak a word to any of us. Told us we were all after him, that no matter what he said, he would only harm himself. He knew that much. He wasn't that stupid. Then he started raging on about some conspiracy theory that he had read online about how the police were being run by the blacks and how they had infiltrated the government and put Obama in post. Then he went on to tell me about The Third Reich, about some Nazi leader who was believed to be dead, but allegedly had never died, and was building his empire underground and he knew about how the blacks were planning on taking over the U.S. as a revenge for their slavery.

I stopped listening after a few minutes and knew I would never get anything useful out of him. He couldn't afford a lawyer, so the court appointed one to him. The judge was on our side. He didn't make bail. The guy was suspected of having put an officer in coma and shot into the crowd at the country festival. There was no judge who would let him out, which was good for me. I had time to build his case.

But it wasn't easy. All we had was the truck. His truck that had been blown up in front of his home. His wife, Jennifer, claimed Travis took the truck with him when he moved out of the house. Travis said it had been stolen from his sister's house. There were no reports on the vehicle being stolen anywhere.

Beth was still in a coma, and the doctors feared she would remain that way. They still couldn't tell us if she would get better or not. I feared the worst. I was so mad at this situation. It reminded me of the time with my old partner in Miami, Lisa, who had been killed in the line of duty when I should have protected her. I had taken in her daughter Emily and loved her like my own. I wasn't going to stand and watch while three other children were made orphans. The least I could do was to get justice. I had never found the shooter down in Miami and it haunted me like crazy. This wasn't going to end that way. I was determined to find evidence to put this guy away for the rest of his life. And then some.

The weekend came and Shannon still stayed in her condo, behind closed shutters, while the media speculated about her involvement in the disappearance of Robert Hill. I think she had managed to stay sober. I had removed all alcohol from the condo, and since I was the one shopping for her, she couldn't get ahold of any more. I felt like a prison guard, but if that was the way it had to be to make her well again, then so be it.

The police in Nashville hadn't found the body of Robert Hill yet, to her luck, and so far no charges had been made. We were still holding our breath. On Saturday, she told them everything. I had convinced her it was the only way to get through this properly. They were using radars on the backyard of the house, and if they had buried a body there, it was going to be found sooner or later. I asked them to send a guy down, and he took her entire statement. I told her to use the word self-defense as often as possible, and so she did. With her lawyer at her side, she told him she didn't know where the body was buried, since Joe had taken care of it. But it was somewhere in the backyard. As she spoke to the detective from Nashville PD, I suddenly thought of something.

"Where is the gun?" I asked.

"What gun?"

"You said Robert had a gun. He was threatening you with it when you hit him with the microphone stand. Where is the gun now?"

Shannon shrugged. "I don't know. Joe must have gotten rid of it somehow. I never saw it again."

"Maybe he buried it with the body?" I asked.

"That's definitely a possibility," she said.

The Nashville detective nodded, satisfied. "If that is what happened, then that certainly speaks for your case. We find the gun and it has Robert Hill's fingerprints on it, then we know you're telling the truth, Mrs. King."

All we had to do was to find the smoking gun.

FIFTY-EIGHT

March 2015

"EARLY BIRD GETS THE WORM," was Allan MacGill's favorite saying. And, unlike everyone else in his family, he lived by it. Especially on Sunday mornings when he didn't have to go to work, but could spend the day fishing from the jetty in Cape Canaveral. It was his favorite time of the week. When everyone else in his family went to church at ten, he could be found leaning against the railing at the end of the pier with his fishing line in the water, enjoying God's true church...His creations.

Allan grabbed his bucket and fishing pole from the back of his truck and started walking from the parking lot to the jetty. It was quite a walk, but he enjoyed every moment of it. The freshness in the air before sunrise was indescribable. It had to be experienced.

Allan greeted the other early fishers who were setting up their poles at the jetty, then found a spot by the railing where he could put up his. He took in a deep breath and enjoyed the quiet. In a few hours, it would be spoiled by the many boats coming out of Cape Canaveral Port. Worst were the cruise ships at the end of the day. All those people standing on the deck waving at the people on the pier...the big awful ships with all their waterslides and smell of grease and fried food they brought with them. Boy, how he loathed those. They all left on Sunday afternoon and scared away all the fish. He would usually try and leave before that.

Last Sunday, Allan had lucked out. It had been his best fishing day ever. He had hauled in a bonnet-head...a big bonnet-head shark, at least two feet long. It had been quite the crowd-puller. He had brought it home and cut the meat out and prepared it as steaks on the grill, then invited the neighbors over for a feast and use of bragging rights. It had been perfect. They had all loved it. Allan knew he probably wouldn't be able to do it again, but he was hoping for something as spectacular today as well. He had only one week left on the Space Coast before they went back to Boston, where they lived the rest of the year. Usually, they stayed in

Florida for three months of the year. The three best months of Allan's year. He wished they could stay all year around, but his wife, Angie, wouldn't hear of it.

"I get grumpy when it's hot," she always argued. "And you don't want me grumpy, do you?"

She was right about that. He certainly didn't want her to be grumpier than she already was. No reason for that.

So, Allan had to settle for three months out of the year. And he loved every minute of it. He was already looking forward to January next year. Allan lifted the pole and swung the line through the air and into the canal. He was hoping to see a few dolphins as they swam by, like he usually did here at sunrise.

The sun was peeking over the horizon now and Allan closed his eyes and enjoyed the rays of sun hitting his face. He wasn't looking forward to going back up north to the cold again. Life up there simply wasn't as pleasant as it was down here. This was Allan's small slice of paradise. At least it had been, until this day when his fishing line suddenly tightened and Allan sprang for it to reel in whatever he had caught.

Maybe it's another bonnet-head. It sure is heavy! Maybe it's even bigger than the last time?

As Allan tried to pull the fish in, he became aware of his own weakness and started worrying he might lose his catch. He called for the other fishermen to help. Soon, there were three big heavy men reeling the fish in.

"This is huge!" one of them said with a groan.

Allan smiled, thinking it would be the perfect way to end the season...with the biggest catch of his life. Allan couldn't stop smiling until they pulled again and something came into sight above the wooden railing.

It almost sounded like it was planned, like it had been rehearsed, when all three fishermen gasped in unison at the sight of the long blonde hair.

FIFTY-NINE

March 2015

I GOT the call when I was sitting on the deck of my parents' motel eating breakfast. Shannon still didn't want to leave the condo, so it was just me and the kids. Well, except for Emily, who wanted to sleep in, and, as usual, wasn't hungry. Shannon's sister Kristi had told me she was coming over today to spend time with Shannon and Angela. She had helped out a lot, keeping an eye on Shannon for me when I had to work or couldn't be with her for some other reason.

"Did not," Austin said.

"You did too," Abigail said.

"No, I didn't," Austin said.

"Daaad. Austin's lying," Abigail said.

I sighed with a smile and sipped my coffee. I looked at my beautiful twins. No one could hate each other and no one could love each other as much as those two. Now Austin pulled Abigail's ponytail and she let out a wail.

"Hey, you two," my mom said as she brought out more waffles. She looked at me. "You're just going to let them act like this?"

I chuckled. "They'll figure it out," I said, finishing my coffee.

My mom scoffed. "You're too weak, Jack. You need to be harder on them."

I looked at her. No one spoiled those kids more than she did. She was the last person to say anything. Yet she still was on my case constantly about how I brought them up. I guess she was just worried, since they didn't have a mother, and in her opinion, a mother was by far the most important person in a child's life. I hoped to prove her wrong. I had to believe that a dad could do this alone.

My phone was ringing in my pocket and I got up to take it, kissed my mom on the cheek, and went inside.

"Ryder."

"Ron here. Sorry to disturb you on a Sunday, but we just pulled a corpse out of the canal in Cape Canaveral."

I looked at my family sitting on the deck in the sunlight. I had hoped to spend the day with them for once. The twins had been on my case lately for not being home enough. Even though they loved their grandparents, they still needed to spend time with their dad. At least, that's how Abigail explained it to me. I missed them too. I missed hanging out with them and with my parents as well. I wasn't going to have them around forever. Chances were it was a suicide, a jumper from one of the cruise ships, or a drunkard who fell in last night. It didn't sound like it was my field. Still, I had to be there. Any suspicious death was my area. Sunday or no Sunday.

"I'll be right there," I said.

I hung up and looked at my beautiful family. Abigail stuck her tongue out at her brother. Austin made an ugly face at her in return. I chuckled when Abigail's eyes met mine. I approached them.

"Not again?" she said, reading my face.

"I'm sorry," I said. "Duty calls. You know how it is. It's my job…"

"To catch the bad guys, yes, I know," she said with an angry frown. She crossed her arms in front of her chest. "You promised you'd take me surfing. I wanted to show you how much I have learned at camp."

I sighed. "I know, sweetie. Believe me, I would much rather be out in the water surfing with you than going to Cape Canaveral, but I have to."

"And what about Austin?" she said, pointing at her brother. "You promised you would go fishing with him. You know how much he loves to fish."

I looked at Austin, who avoided my eyes. He never was one to complain. Abigail did that for him.

"I'm sorry, buddy," I said. "Maybe grandpa can help you set the poles up? He's an excellent fisherman, you know."

"I know," Austin said. He forced a smile, trying hard to not let me know how sad he was. I could see it on his face he was disappointed. Sunday was our day together as a family.

"He never spends any time alone with you, Dad," Abigail said. "He needs a father figure. You're his role model."

I looked at my six year-old daughter. Where did she learn stuff like that?

"It's okay," Austin said and patted me on my arm.

"Just go, Jack," my mom said. "We'll take care of it."

I felt awful leaving them all like this. I had promised to fix the sink in one of the rooms at the motel and to paint the upstairs deck as well. There simply weren't enough hours in the day to make everybody happy.

SIXTY

March 2015

"So, WHAT DO WE HAVE?" I asked Ron, as I parked the Jeep at the jetty and walked with him towards the scene. The area had been blocked and a huge crowd of spectators had gathered behind the police tape. It was Sunday, usually the busiest day for the park and the jetty. There was a camping area right out to the canals and a big playground with a picnic area where people grilled and spent their Sunday afternoon with their families.

"A girl. Early twenties. She was pulled out of the water by three fishermen this morning. It looks like she drowned."

We walked under the tape and onto the jetty. I nodded to a couple of technicians that I knew from earlier crime scenes.

"So, why am I here? Sounds like an accident or suicide?"

We approached the body, which was still lying on the jetty where it had been pulled out of the water. Her skin was as pale as her blonde hair. Yamilla Díez was sitting bent over her.

"You're here, Ryder," she answered, "because she was heavily beaten before she fell or was thrown in the water, where she drowned."

I froze when I saw the face of the girl.

"We don't know who she is yet," Ron said. "She didn't have any identification on her body."

"But I do," I said. "I know her."

"You do?"

"She's one of the girls staying at my parents' motel. They're a flock of spring breakers. I gave some of them surf lessons."

I felt sick to my stomach looking at the young girl. I remembered her from the beach when the girl Katie had lost her bikini top. She was one of the girls who had laughed.

"Talk to me about the beating," I said with interest. I kneeled next to the body, while Yamilla went through what she had found so far for me. "She has taken some

336

Slip Out the Back Jack

blows to the body and the right cheek here has a subcutaneous bleed as well in the musculature. You see, here and here there's bleeding under the skin that occurs from broken blood vessels. She also took some blows to the chin and nose. The bruise on the chin looks like she was hit with something hard."

"So, what you're saying is, she was beaten, then thrown into the water?" I asked.

"That's what I believe, yes. Might have been a fight. Maybe the other person took some beating as well, but looking at her fists and knuckles, I hardly believe this girl managed to defend herself much."

I looked down the canal. "If she was thrown in the water, then the current must have brought her down here before the fisherman got his hook in her."

Ron stood beside me. "You're thinking she was attacked while she was at one of those restaurants or bars further down the canal?"

"She's a spring breaker on the last weekend of her vacation. I believe Grill's had open bar for girls last night. She gets drunk and meets her attacker. He rapes her, beats her up, and throws her in the water afterwards." I looked at Ron. "If you visit the bars, then I'll go back to the motel and talk to her friends. I need to contact this girl's family right away."

Ron put a hand on my shoulder. It was tough to look at this girl, the same girl I had seen at my parents' motel so many times the past week. She was not more than a few years older than Emily…killed on a joyful night in town while on spring break. I had a terrible feeling about this.

337

SIXTY-ONE

March 2015

"WHAT DO you mean Britney is dead?"

The three other girls staying in the room were barely awake when I knocked on their door and told them what had happened. Leanne, the tall redhead who I always saw Britney with looked at me like I was lying to her.

"We were just with her last night?" Leanne had tears in her eyes. They all did, except Katie.

"So, you were all out last night?" I asked.

They looked at each other, then at Katie, who was still sitting in her bed under the covers. "Well, we were. Katie stayed here."

"I...I wasn't in the mood for partying," she said.

I noted it on my pad, then looked at the two other girls. "So, the rest of you, Leanne, Irene, and Britney, you all went out? What time did you leave the motel?"

"We..." Leanne looked down. She looked guilty of something. Irene and Katie both avoided looking at me as well. Something was very fishy.

"We left around six to go to dinner at The Lobster Shanty," Irene said.

"And was that all of you?" I asked.

Leanne shed a tear and wiped it off.

"We have to tell him everything," Irene said.

Leanne hissed. "I know. I know." Leanne's face suddenly twisted into an expression of fury as abrupt as a gust of strong wind. "It was just Irene, Britney, and me. Katie stayed at the motel." Leanne stared at Katie, like she was waiting for her to say something.

Katie didn't seem to be feeling well. "Why didn't you go to dinner with the others?" I asked.

"I...I wasn't hungry."

I didn't quite believe her. Something was definitely wrong here.

"She had a date," Irene said. "She was going to meet up with one of the boys, with Greg. They were going to watch the moonrise."

I made notes on my pad.

"How do you know about that?" Katie asked. She sounded angry and hurtful at the same time.

"Because..." Irene looked at Leanne, who didn't seem to want to take part in the conversation. "Because...well, it wasn't exactly Greg who sent you that text and asked you to meet with him."

"Who was it then?" Katie asked. She was the one sounding angry now.

"Britney," Leanne answered.

"She borrowed Greg's phone and sent the text earlier in the afternoon, then deleted the texts afterwards," Irene said. "She asked Greg to meet her there, at the spot where you thought you were going to meet him. She told him she would give him a blowjob, no strings attached. No boy would ever say no to that, right? But it was all a show. A show meant for you to see as you came down there thinking..." Irene stopped. She had made her point.

Katie had tears in her eyes. "So, she did this to me to hurt me?"

I was getting a clearer picture of what was going on now. "So, if I'm getting this right, you came down to meet this Greg and found Britney...found him with her instead?" I asked.

Katie tightened her lips, and then nodded.

"Alright," I said and noted it. "So, Britney was with Greg, then what happened?"

"We stayed at the Lobster Shanty and had some drinks, then Britney came there and told us what she had done," Irene said. "I want you to know, she never told us what she intended to do; we knew nothing until after it was done," she said, addressed to Katie. "If I had known, I wouldn't have been in on it."

"So, Britney came to the restaurant and then what did you do?" I asked.

"We grabbed a taxi and went to the port. We started at Milliken's and ended at Grill's, where we could drink for free all night," Irene continued.

"Who did she talk to during the night?" I asked.

"She talked to a lot of guys. Britney always talks to everyone."

"Why didn't you come home together?" I asked.

"It was getting late," Leanne said. "We wanted to get a taxi home, but Britney wanted to party some more. She was dancing outside on the deck by the water with some guy and told us to just leave. She said she would come home later. We were tired and thought the place was getting boring, so we left."

"So, the last time you saw her, she was dancing on the deck at Grill's?" I asked.

They both nodded. Leanne sniffled and wiped her eyes, not caring that her mascara was smeared. It looked like it was left over from the night before anyway. I turned and looked at Katie. I didn't like this story one bit.

"So, what did you do while they were all out partying?" I asked.

Katie looked at me with wide eyes. "I...I was just here. Asleep."

"Did anyone see you? Were you with anybody?" I asked.

Katie shook her head. The two other girls looked at her. The tension was thick in the room. It didn't take a mind reader to know what the two other girls were thinking. I had no idea what to believe. The girl had a strong motive. What Britney had done to her was really bad, but would she be capable of killing her? I had my doubts. On the other hand, anger and jealousy were hard to control even if you wanted to.

"I need to have Britney's personal information so I can contact her family. What was her last name?"

"Foster," Leanne said. "Her mom lives in North Carolina."

I wrote it down, thinking I had heard that name somewhere before. "Good. Thanks." I got up from the edge of Britney's bed where I had been sitting. "No one touches any of Britney's things. I'll have to have our technicians go through her belongings. I'll ask my parents to give you a new room."

"But, we're going home today anyway?" Katie said.

"Yeah, spring break ends today. We have classes tomorrow," Leanne said. "We're driving home today."

I shook my head. "No, you're not. I'm going to have to ask you to stay for a little longer. We need you here for the investigation. All of you."

SIXTY-TWO

March 2015

STANLEY WAS ON THE MOVE. Both of his legs could hardly move, but he did it anyway. He had to. This was his chance to escape this hellhole once and for all. He stumbled towards the door, left slightly ajar, and then managed to pull his hurting body into the hallway. He couldn't believe it. He was out of the room. As he passed the door next to his, he heard the voice of someone crying behind it. It sounded like Roy, the guy he had spoken to through the walls in the bathroom. He was begging and pleading.

"Please, stop. I can't eat anymore!"

Stanley had wanted to help Roy out, but now realized his guardian was in there feeding Roy right now, so there was no way he could save him. He had to think about himself. He dragged his painful body down the hallway and finally reached a set of stairs. He almost cried when he saw the ray of sunlight coming through the entrance door at the bottom of the stairs. Stanley thought about Elyse and wondered if the girl was somewhere in the house as well, but then decided he would have to come back for her. He couldn't do this on his own. He had to get ahold of the police somehow. The police would be able to help. It was the only way.

Stanley held onto the railing as he dragged his hurting legs down the stairs, resisting the temptation to scream out loud in pain. He panted and used all of his strength and finally managed to get himself to the bottom of the stairs. He was crying in pain as he stopped to catch his breath. In front of him he could see the daylight through the frosted glass of the front doors.

Freedom. Wonderful, beautiful freedom.

Stanley drew in a deep breath. The smell of freshly cooked food filled his nostrils and he felt like throwing up. If he ever made it out of there, he wasn't going to eat again. Never again. Stanley moved as quietly as possible, making sure his guardian wouldn't hear him upstairs. But Roy was making an awful lot of noise up there, so chances were, no one could hear a thing.

At least that's what he thought. Stanley hadn't exactly accounted for the fact that maybe, maybe there were more people in the house.

"Stop right there," a voice said behind his back.

Stanley froze. All hope was sucked right out of him as he turned and looked into the barrel of a gun.

Damn it.

"Where do you think you're going?" the voice said.

Stanley drew in a deep breath. All this pain. All this...for nothing? No. No. No. He wasn't going to take it. Not anymore. He was done.

"You haven't eaten yet," the voice said.

"I can't...I can't..." He looked down the barrel of the gun, then felt the anger rise like a wave in the ocean.

NO MORE!

"I'm afraid I can't stay for dinner," he said. Grabbing an umbrella leaning against the wall next to him, he slammed it into the person with the gun, forcing both the person and the gun to fall to the ground and slide across the tiles. Then, he sprang for the doors. He grabbed the handles and pulled both open at the same time. He limped heavily, but the prospect of feeling freedom again gave him strength and made him push through the pain. The smell of fresh air without a hint of fried chicken in it gave him the last push he needed to make it into the front yard of the house.

SIXTY-THREE

March 2015

BRITNEY'S MOTHER flew down immediately from North Carolina and was at the ME's office in the early afternoon. I made sure two officers from our department picked her up at the airport in Orlando and got her to me in a hurry. I had told her over the phone that we believed something had happened to her daughter and we needed her to come down for identification.

I greeted her as she stepped inside. She was a small delicate woman who looked like she had led a hard life. I could sense she was very fragile, and I tried to break things to her gently.

"Maggie Foster," she said, as I shook her hand. It was at that moment, when she said her name out loud that it occurred to me where I had heard that name before. I stared at her for a few seconds, while trying to get the pieces to fit together. They still didn't.

"Let's go inside," Yamilla said and helped Maggie Foster in.

The identification didn't take long. Maggie Foster took one look at the body and then burst into tears. I grabbed her as she was about to fall when she turned away to cry.

"Yes," she said through tears. "Yes, that's her."

"Thanks, Yamilla," I said, and helped Mrs. Foster get out of the ME's office. There was no reason to stay any longer. I drove Mrs. Foster back to the Sheriff's Office and poured her some water and a cup of coffee. I borrowed Ron's office for our talk. I let her cry for a little while, let the news settle in before I started asking my questions. It was always a delicate moment when interrogating a victim's relatives. It was important to do it as fast as possible while everything was fresh in their memory, but I still had to consider their emotions and the rollercoaster they were going through. It wasn't an easy task. Luckily for me, Mrs. Foster opened the conversation herself.

"Who?" she asked and looked at me for answer. "Who would do such a terrible thing?"

WILLOW ROSE

I shrugged. "We don't know yet, Mrs. Foster. But that's what I am hoping to find out as soon as possible. Now, tell me, I have to ask, your name. I remember it from another investigation that we recently took a look at. It could be a coincidence, since it took place in Boca Raton, north of Miami, but are you the same Maggie Foster that witnessed and gave your statement after the shooting in the cinema in 2009?"

Maggie Foster went pale. "Yes," she said with surprise in her voice. "We used to live in Boca. After the shooting, I went back to my family in North Carolina. I lost my husband that evening. My daughter, Britney was seriously injured when she was shot in the arm. I had to get away. There was no way I could stay."

A million thoughts flickered through my mind as I looked at Mrs. Foster in front of me. This could hardly be a coincidence, could it? But how on earth was this connected? The killing of Britney? Was that connected to the shooting at the country festival?

Maggie Foster suddenly looked at me with wide open eyes. "You don't think... oh, my God," she said. She looked like she remembered something. Then she clasped her mouth.

"What?" I asked.

"She called me last night. I suddenly remember. There is nothing unusual in her calling; we talk almost every day, but she said something."

"What did she say?" I asked.

"She told me she believed she had seen the killer in Cocoa Beach. She had seen the shooter in Publix, she told me. She said she wanted to go to the police and tell them the next day...that is today, before they left town. She was so uneasy, because she knew the guy that was initially called out as the killer, the guy that had killed himself and that all the media said was the shooter...she knew that it wasn't him. She knew because she had looked into the eyes of the killer. Right before she was shot, right before her dad was killed. She never told anyone except me. And I didn't believe her. I told her it was nonsense. I was certain it was him and that it was all over. That's what the police told us. It had to be the truth, right? Maybe I just really wanted to believe it. I couldn't stand the thought of him not being caught, of the shooter possibly still being out there. All those years, I refused to believe her. Even last night. I told her she had to give it up. It was over; it was history. I begged her stop ripping up the past. Still, she kept going on about it. How the police had it all wrong. How they had blamed the wrong guy. She knew it could never be him, because the shooter wasn't a he. It was a she."

344

SIXTY-FOUR

March 2015

COULD OUR SHOOTER BE FEMALE? I found it hard to believe. Usually, shooters in mass shootings were Caucasian males with a death wish. Mass murderers were often characterized as isolated individuals that, over time, had built up aggression towards the society they felt disconnected from.

It did make a lot of sense when I thought it through. Many things about the shootings at the cinema and at the country festival were so different from other mass shootings. There was something about both incidents that rubbed me the wrong way. It didn't seem like the shooter wanted to kill a lot of people. There had been fifteen people in the movie theater; eight were hit and four of them died. With around forty thousand present at the concert, it was quite lucky that only two had been hit. Two certainly weren't many, considering how many people had been there. It was still two too many, but it wasn't a lot.

"Tell me more about the shooting in '09," I said to Maggie Foster. I sensed the memory of what happened back then made her feel very uncomfortable, but I had to know more.

She shrugged. "I don't know if there is much more to tell, other than what I told back then."

I kept thinking about the emails that Shannon had received from the alleged killer. *I'm so sorry. It had to be done,* all of them said. What did this killer mean by that? Why did it have to be done?

"There is one thing that always struck me as odd," Maggie Foster said.

"And what is that?"

"I don't know…maybe it's just silly…" she turned her head away.

I looked at her. "No. Anything will be of help at this point. Please. Continue."

She looked up. Our eyes met. "It's just that…I mean, it may not be important, but we knew all of the others."

"What others?" I asked.

"The three others that were shot in the cinema. I knew them. They weren't our friends, but I knew who they were. It might be a coincidence, but…"

"It might not be. How did you know them?"

"From Britney's school. They all had kids that went to Klein's Jewish Academy. I didn't think about it until afterwards, when Britney told me they had talked about it in class."

"Were all the kids the same age?" I asked.

"No, they were different age groups."

I wrote it all down on my notepad, wondering if we were looking at an anti-Semitic motive.

Maggie Foster looked pensive again. "I wonder…" She paused and looked at me while biting her lip. "It was odd. I don't think we ever mentioned it to the police back then, but…now I wonder if it wasn't only us."

"Only you that what?" I asked.

She tilted her head. "Only us that won those tickets."

"Won the tickets? I don't follow."

"We received a letter in the mail stating we had won tickets to the movie theater to see the newest Disney movie. It was at a lottery at the school. I didn't mention it to the police before, since I didn't think it was important, but now I get the feeling it might be."

I leaned back in Ron's chair and looked at Maggie Foster. There was definitely something there worth moving on with. It felt like we were getting closer now. I still just couldn't quite connect the dots, but I did remember Shannon told me someone had sent a backstage ticket to Joe in the mail and that he thought it was from Shannon, that she had wanted him to be there. It occurred to me the victims might not have been random. I had long had a feeling that neither of the two episodes had been mass shootings. Now it seemed crystal clear to me; they were very thoroughly well-planned killings. This killer liquidated her victims in public, in places she was certain we would see it happen. It was her signature. This killer was making a statement. Like most serial killers, she wanted us to know. And she wanted us to know there were going to be more.

SIXTY-FIVE

April 2009

It DIDN'T TAKE the doctors long to get Elizabeth diagnosed. Through genetic testing, they were able to get the proof that Elizabeth, in fact, had Prader-Willi syndrome, and that was what caused her to eat insatiably and gain weight rapidly, and it explained her behavioral issues as well. It was all very comforting for Dottie to finally be able to put words to her daughter's illness and stop blaming herself. There was no cure for it, the doctors told her, but they did start a treatment with a prescription of daily recombinant growth hormone injections. The growth hormone would support linear growth and increase Elizabeth's muscle mass, and hopefully lessen her food preoccupation and weight gain. At least, that was what the doctors hoped.

And so did Dottie.

It had been years since she felt this relieved, and soon after the treatments started, she could already see an improvement in her daughter. She would still scream for food most hours of the day, but she suddenly seemed to be interested in other things as well. She started reading books while waiting for the next meal to be served, and somehow the books took her away from the constant cravings.

Dottie had learned to keep an eye on her constantly and was better now at limiting her food intake...now that she understood it was a disease and that she wasn't being evil or punishing her when not giving her food whenever she craved it. Dottie started buying healthier food and was very strict with the amount of food her daughter got at each meal, no matter how much her daughter cried. The doctor had helped her find a nutritionist, who knew about the diagnosis, and knew how to handle patients with Prader-Willi Syndrome. Dottie knew if she followed her schedule, it would help her daughter, and that made it easier to be strict about it and endure the screaming fits Elizabeth threw whenever she was denied food.

It was like she had regained some control in her life, and it felt good.

James had moved in with his new girlfriend, and even though Dottie hated the whole situation, and especially this young girl James had chosen in exchange for Dottie, she had decided to accept that this was how things were now...this was their new reality. James had asked to get to see the girls every other weekend, and up until now, Dottie had let him have the three older ones, but kept Elizabeth with her. This weekend was the first time she had agreed to let Elizabeth spend the night at her father's new place, and she was terrified. Dottie had never been away from Elizabeth more than the few hours she was in school every day, and certainly never at night. So, naturally, she was anxious when she packed Elizabeth's overnight bag and made sure her medicine was in there as well.

"Her injections are in the backpack," she said, as she handed over all four girls. "Don't forget to keep an eye on her at all times."

James rolled his eyes. "Take it easy, Dottie. She's my daughter too, you know. I know how to take care of her."

Dottie wasn't so sure he was right. He had refused to acknowledge that Elizabeth had a disease, a syndrome that made her the way she was. When Dottie had told him about the diagnosis, he had laughed out loud on the phone.

"This is what we've come to now? A diagnosis for those who can't control themselves? That is exactly what is wrong with this country. We have a diagnosis for everything. Sometimes people just eat too much, Dottie. That's all there is to it."

His reaction had been part of the reason why Dottie hadn't let Elizabeth spend the night at her father's until now. But he had agreed to give her the injections and make sure she followed her diet. It was, after all, just for a weekend. How much could go wrong in just one weekend?

SIXTY-SIX

March 2015

"WE'RE LOOKING FOR A WOMAN."

I threw a glare around the room. Richard and Ron both looked at me. Ann and Duncan were out.

"Say what again?" Richard asked.

Ron was eating a sandwich while standing by the water cooler. He stopped chewing.

"It looks like the shooting in Miami and the shooting at the festival might have been committed by a woman," I said.

"A female mass shooter?" Ron said. "That's rare."

"That's the other thing," I said. "I'm not sure I believe they were mass shootings anymore. Not the traditional kind, that is. I believe she chose her victims deliberately and killed them, then covered it up as a mass shooting…making it more spectacular."

"So, you're thinking it's a serial killer?" Ron asked. He had started chewing again and washed the bite down with his soda.

"That's exactly what I'm thinking."

"And what about the murder of the young girl this morning?" Richard asked. "I thought that was what we were working on? Am I the only one who is a little bit confused here?"

Ron shook his head. "I was lost long ago."

"I think it might all be connected," I said and sat down at my desk. "See, Britney was at the shooting in '09. She was shot in the arm and her dad was killed. She saw the killer. Her mother told us she spotted her here in Cocoa Beach, at Publix of all places."

"So, you think she was killed because she could identify the shooter?" Richard asked.

I nodded. "All this time, we've been looking for a man, and that made the best cover for this killer. If Britney spilled the beans, she would no longer be able to walk around in public. For six years, she has been able to hide without having to go underground while planning the next attack."

"So, how do we catch her now?" Richard asked.

"I have several things we can check up on. First of all, I want you to call all shooting ranges in the area. There was a distinct difference between the attack in '09 and the one this month. The shooter didn't know how to shoot back then, but she does now. It's my theory that she never meant to hit all the other people, and especially the children present in the movie theater, but she hadn't accounted for the fact that she didn't know how to control a firearm like that, and she didn't think about the fact that a bullet ricochets when it hits a wall or a ceiling. That's why we haven't heard from her for so long. She never meant for this many people to get hurt. She just wanted to shoot the people she had planned, and then get out. But more were hit by bullets and that wasn't the plan. She has spent the last several years getting ready, preparing herself for the next kill by taking shooting lessons. She didn't want anything to go wrong this time. Up until now, I had thought that Joe Harrison was just a coincidental kill, that he got in the shooter's way somehow, but I don't think that anymore. I think she killed him deliberately; it was planned. He was sent a ticket, so she'd be sure where to find him after shooting Phillip Hagerty in the crowd. That's where you come in again, Richard. I need you to take a look at Joe and Phillip. What do they have in common? Can we find a link between those two, and maybe even a link between them and the four that were murdered six years ago in the movie theater, then I believe we'll find our killer. I need background info, everything we have on all the victims."

I stopped to breathe, when suddenly, all the phones rang in the office at once. That was never a good sign. Something was up.

SIXTY-SEVEN

March 2015

SHANNON HADN'T HAD a drink in several days now and she felt terrible. She had been cooped up inside of that condo for so many days it was starting to drive her nuts. Even though Jack and Kristi did come by almost every day to be with her and bring groceries and occasionally cook for her, it just wasn't the same as feeling the fresh air on your skin or breathing in the salty sea breeze. She opened the windows now and then, but then the photographers took pictures, and she didn't want that.

Weren't they getting tired of this by now? Apparently not. The story was still everywhere, and it made Shannon so angry and miserable. Angela was going back to school after spring break tomorrow and Shannon was looking forward to that. She knew her daughter would probably have to hear a lot about her mother and Shannon feared it would be rough for her. But she would have to get by. They all had to.

"Mommy, can you help me?" she said, coming out from her bedroom with a brush stuck in her hair. She looked so adorable with her hair all tangled up, Shannon had to laugh.

"Let me fix it," she said and grabbed the brush.

Angela whined. "Ouch, you're hurting me."

"Sorry, baby, but this is really stuck. How on earth did you get it so stuck in your hair?"

Angela shrugged. "I don't know. I just tried to brush it."

Shannon sighed and tried to untangle the brush. She felt frustrated, and the more she pulled on it, the more Angela whined. Shannon's hands couldn't stop shaking and it bothered her. Why couldn't they simply keep still? Why did she have to feel this unease inside of her constantly, this anxiety, this feeling that something was about to happen, something really bad that would once again crash her entire world? It was like she had stopped trusting the world, like she was constantly expecting terrible things to happen for her. She hated the feeling that

351

she couldn't do anything right in this life. She felt like a child because people had to take care of her the way they did. She hated it. She wanted to take care of herself, of her daughter…she wanted to…she wanted to *get this damn brush out of her daughter's hair!*

"Mom. You're hurting me," Angela screamed. "Mooom."

Shannon let go with a sigh. "I can't do it," she said. "I simply can't do it. I can't do anything right."

Angela stared at her mother. "Yes, you can. You're the best mommy in the world."

Shannon shed a tear, then hugged her daughter. "Thank you, sweetie. I don't feel like I am right now."

"Maybe we should just get the scissors, "Angela said, hugged her mother, and then sprang to get them from the kitchen.

Shannon sighed with relief. Angela was right. There was always a solution to the problems. Always. It didn't have to all be bad. So what if she lost a lock of her hair? It would grow out. So what if the media wrote all those things about her? They would stop when someone else got in trouble. They would forget about Shannon eventually. The fans would forgive her. Wouldn't they? Of course they would. They loved her.

Shannon stared at her computer on the dresser by the wall. She hadn't opened it for many days. She didn't dare to read what they wrote about her on Facebook and Twitter. People could be so mean.

This too shall pass. Like everything else, it will pass.

Angela returned with the scissors and Shannon cut the brush free from her hair, thinking it was all going to get better soon. It had to. She was going to be all right…they were going to be all right, when her phone rang. Shannon looked at the display. She knew the number. It was her lawyer. She let go of her daughter and grabbed it.

"They found it, Shannon," her lawyer said. "They found the body."

Shannon closed her eyes. Her heart was already pounding in her chest. "And the gun? Did they find the gun?"

Her lawyer went quiet.

Uh-Oh. Quiet isn't good. It's definitely not good.

"I'm sorry, Shannon. They didn't."

SIXTY-EIGHT

March 2015

I PUT the siren on as we headed down A1A. Ron was driving. Cars stopped when they heard us and pulled over to let us pass. I was confused as I watched Patrick's Air Force Base go by my window. The call we had received was from the Indian Harbor Police Department. Minutes later, we met Sergeant Bill Gray in front of the gate to Lansing Island. He came out of the small booth as we drove up to the closed boom.

"Where is he?" I asked, as I jumped out of the car.

"He's in here," Bill said and pointed inside of the booth. I looked inside and spotted a man sitting in the chair. The guard stood next to him.

"He keeps saying the same thing over and over again," Bill continued.

"And you're sure he is Stanley Bradley? The same person that was reported missing earlier this month?" Ron asked.

"That's what he tells us," the guard said. "We found him lying in the street inside the community, yelling and screaming. One of the neighbors called for me. I have no idea how he even got inside. He's not on any lists of visitors."

The case had been on Ron's desk for quite some time now. A middle-aged man had gone missing on his way back from Disney World with his granddaughter. The car had been found lying in the ditch off 528 from Orlando by the ramp leading to Cape Canaveral. The two tires on the front wheels had been punctured. When the fire truck arrived, they had only found the granddaughter in the car. She had been unconscious and taken to the hospital. No one knew where the grandfather had disappeared to. Until now.

"Stanley Bradley?" I asked and showed him my badge. "I am Detective Jack Ryder. What happened to you?"

"You need to get my granddaughter," he yelled. "You've got to save her. She's back there."

"As far as I know, your granddaughter is with her mother," Ron said. "She is safe."

353

"She was the only one they found in your car," I said.

Stanley Bradley looked baffled. "But...but...I thought..." Stanley paused as something settled in him. "They lied to me?"

"Who are they?" I asked. "What happened to you?"

Stanley looked at me. His eyes flickered in desperation. "There are more back there. Roy is there. You've got to help Roy. They're going to kill him."

"Who is Roy?" I asked.

"I don't know. But I talked to him through the wall. He is in danger. You've got to get him out of there."

"Slow down a little, Stanley. Please, answer me this. What happened to you?"

"I was taken. Kidnapped. Held prisoner by this awful woman who kept feeding me, forcing food into my mouth. She did this to me," he said and showed me his legs. They were bleeding heavily from deep wounds and one was badly infected. "She hurt me with a fire poker. So I wouldn't leave. She kept me there for a long time."

"You say she was force-feeding you?"

"Yes."

"And, you say she has more kidnapped people she's keeping there?" I said, as my hand landed on the shaft of my gun. If I was right, then we had found Daniel Millman and James West's killer.

"Bill, you stay here with Stanley while Jack and I check this out," Ron said and looked at me.

"Better call for an ambulance," I said. "Stanley here needs medical attention. What house did she keep you in?"

"I...I don't know, to be honest," Stanley said.

"I picked him up outside number 222," the guard said.

"It was a gray house," Stanley said. "That much I saw when I got out. It was big. And had big colored windows on the front."

I wondered if we should just take him with us, but I feared for his safety. Besides, he needed to go to the hospital with those legs as soon as possible. No, we had to find the house on our own. I had a feeling it wouldn't be too hard. I had a very good idea who it was we were looking for. Number 219 was awfully close to 222.

SIXTY-NINE

March 2015

SHE WAS SITTING in the bedroom when she saw him. He wasn't alone. He was with the sheriff. They were running up the street when she found them in the gun's sight.

Bingo!

This time on a Sunday, the streets were usually filled with the children of the gated community, riding their bikes, playing ball, and so it was today as well. As the two officers came running up the street, they told the kids to get inside their houses, and soon the street was cleared.

"I really don't want to have to do this, Detective," she mumbled, as she followed Jack Ryder's every move towards the house. "I am so sorry."

Her eyes drifted across the street towards number 221. The bedroom where they would find the body was the third window to the left. The shooter's heart was starting to pump rapidly now.

One mistake, one wrong move, and it would all be over. She couldn't afford to miss. That's what her teacher at the shooting range in Melbourne had told her over and over again, as she went there every Saturday and practiced her aim.

"If that burglar enters your house and you have him cornered, you only get one chance. You can't miss."

The shooter hadn't missed one shot since that night at the movie theater in Boca Raton. Not one accident. It had been hell for her, knowing all those kids had been hit by bullets. She had realized she had no idea what she was doing. Everything else had been so well planned out. Covering it all up as a mass shooting was brilliant, she thought. It had been her own idea. Inviting the bastards to the same movie theater and getting rid of them all at once, then disappearing. It was the perfect plan. No one would think of her as the suspect. No one would know her motives for doing this before she let them know. She was in control.

But, it hadn't gone as she had planned...all those children that had been hit by stray bullets. It had haunted her for years afterwards. Luckily, none of them died.

Only the ones she had wanted to die had died. In that way, it had been a success. But, she had to make sure it wouldn't go wrong the next time around. She couldn't afford it.

The second time, at the festival, everything had gone as planned. She had killed the two men she came for, and then slipped out easily before they managed to block the exits. And even if she hadn't made it out in time? Well, who would look for a gorgeous blonde woman in the prime of her life?

No one.

Then there was the truck. She had been one step ahead of them all this time. She hated that the female officer had to get hurt, but it had to be done. She had to be punished.

"I'm so terribly sorry," she whispered softly.

The killer cocked the gun and followed the two men as they ran up the driveway towards her house, then stopped, looking confused. The handsome one with curly hair pointed at the house across the street. They spoke for a second, then walked across the street.

The killer watched as the detective took out his gun and knocked on the door to the gray house.

"That's it, my little children," she mumbled. "Follow the trail of bread to find the house of candy. Follow the yellow brick road. See what awaits you on the other side of the rainbow."

She sighed and prepared herself. She really hated that she had to do this. She really did.

SEVENTY

March 2015

I HAD BEEN MISTAKEN. We realized it as we walked up towards number 219 where, Mrs. Millman lived, that it was the wrong house. The only gray house on the street was number 221. I was confused as we made the realization standing in the driveway of Mrs. Millman's house. I had been so certain it was her. I was so sure she was the one we were looking for, that she had killed her husband and maybe James West.

But I had been wrong.

Across the street from her house was the gray house with the big colored windows as Stanley Bradley had described it to us. It was the only one of its kind on this street. There was no doubt about it. It had to be it.

We walked up and I grabbed my gun right before I knocked on the door. There was no answer. I looked at Ron. He nodded. I grabbed the handle and realized the door was open. I walked inside with my gun first.

We had called for backup on our way, and I could hear sirens in the distance, but knew it would take a few minutes before they would be here. I wasn't sure we had minutes if we were going to catch this killer and hopefully save this Roy that Stanley had spoken about.

It was all a very strange story and I didn't like it.

"Hello?" I asked, as I opened the door.

"This is the sheriff," Ron yelled. "Anyone home?"

I walked into the kitchen, but found it empty. Tupperware containers, stacked in towers, with freshly made food inside of them filled the counters. The stove was still hot. A pan with fried chicken was still simmering. It had been turned off recently.

"Someone's expecting company," Ron said, when he looked at all the food.

"Or maybe they're staying over," I said and nodded at the stairs. We walked up with our weapons in front of us, then reached a long hallway with many doors. I opened one door and found a bedroom. It was empty. Then I found another and

357

opened that one as well. Empty too, but someone had been sleeping in there recently. I guessed it might be the owner of the house. It was a big room with views of the river. The bed was a king and the sheets silk. I went through it and into the bathroom that looked big enough to fit my entire living room.

"No one here either."

"How many bedrooms does this place have?" Ron asked.

I walked to the next door, but found it locked. Ron and I exchanged one look before I kicked the door in and we walked inside. There was someone on the bed. The room stank. The air was confined and stuffy. Hardly any light came through the closed hurricane shutters.

"Police!" I yelled and walked up to the bed.

The person lying there didn't move. I hurried towards him. I felt sick. He was lying in his own vomit that had run across his pillow. His eyes stared into the ceiling and his face was frozen in a tortured grimace. It had been a painful death.

"Roy?" Ron asked.

I nodded. "I think so."

"I'll go make sure the rest of the house is secure," Ron said, and left while I looked at the body.

I touched his neck. It felt cold, the way dead people's skin felt when the blood hadn't circulated in it for a while. Livor mortis was starting to show on his skin. The blood had started to pool into the interstitial tissues of the body. It happened between twenty minutes to three hours after death occurred. It wasn't much yet. My guess was he had been dead for about half an hour. My other guess was that his stomach had burst. There were no signs of trauma to his body anywhere. Except for his legs, which were hurt in the same way Stanley Bradley's had been.

To make sure he couldn't leave.

Ron came back and told me we were clear. There was another room next to this where someone had been staying, but it was also empty. Ron called for a second ambulance and asked where *the hell that back up was*, while I opened the shutters to let in the light. I walked back to the bed and looked around, wondering if this was the way Daniel Millman had died, if he had been kept here right across the street from his own home, tortured by being force-fed till his stomach burst. I wondered who would be this sick in their mind, this twisted and brutal, and then I wondered why.

As I threw around a glare that ended at the window, I thought I saw something. Ron was still on the phone, and as he walked towards the window, my eye caught a small yellow spark coming from the window across the street. Before I could react, before I could scream at Ron to get down, the window splintered, and like the snap of a finger, Ron fell to the ground.

SEVENTY-ONE

March 2015

"Officer down. Officer down!"

I screamed into the radio as I grabbed Ron in my arms. He had been hit in the shoulder and it was bleeding heavily. I tried to stop it by pressing my hand on it, then ripped some of the sheets from the bed into pieces and held them against the bleeding. Seconds later, the room was filled with paramedics, and I could let go of him.

I ran outside and towards number 219, where Mrs. Millman lived, where the shots had come from.

I had been right all along!

I kicked the door in and stormed into the hallway.

"Where are you?" I yelled like a mad man. I was a mad man. I was so angry, on the brink of exploding in anger. "Show yourself!"

That was when I heard an engine start. It coughed once or twice, then roared loudly.

The river!

Why hadn't I thought of it before? I ran through the living room out into the back, then passed the pool area, and ended up at the dock. In the distance, I watched as the speedboat disappeared. The sun was setting over the mainland and I wouldn't be able to keep track of it for long. I had to think fast. I couldn't let her get away with this. I couldn't let her disappear.

I looked around, then spotted a jet ski at the neighboring dock. I made a quick decision, as the sirens wailed in the street on the other side of the house. I ran across the yard, climbed the fence, and hoped they didn't have a dog or an alarm system. I jumped onto the Jet Ski and then realized I didn't have the key. I spotted a shed in the back, ran to it and opened it. On the wall inside was a small cupboard with three sets of keys hanging on it.

"Remind me to give these people a theft-precaution course," I mumbled, as I picked the one with Jet Ski written on it.

I jumped on the Jet Ski, put in the key and pushed away from the dock before I turned the engine on. Growing up in Florida, I knew the routine. The ski roared to life and I darted into the river in pursuit of the speedboat. I caught up on it pretty fast. I sped up and reached the back lower side of the speedboat, then realized I had no idea what I should do next.

"Police! Stop the boat!" I screamed through the wind, but the noise from the two engines drowned it out. "Mrs. Millman, stop the boat!"

I came up on the side and managed to yell the words through the noise, and she must have heard something, because the woman driving the boat turned her head and looked at me.

It wasn't Mrs. Millman.

It was a woman I had never seen before. The realization dazzled me, just enough to let down my guard for one second, one crucial second. Just enough for her to make her move. She pulled the wheel and maneuvered the boat in front of my jet ski and bumped into it. There was a loud crash and I was thrown into the air. Next thing I knew, I fell into the water, the deep dark water.

As I resurfaced, spluttering and splashing, I spotted the woman and the speedboat disappearing as darkness surrounded her as the sun finally set on the horizon.

SEVENTY-TWO

March 2015

I COULDN'T BELIEVE I had lost her. The next morning, as I sat in the office and stared at my screen, I felt like such an idiot. It was like I couldn't get anything right lately. Ron and Beth were both in the hospital. Ron was doing better, they said. He had only been shot in the shoulder and would need a few weeks to recover, but he was going to be fine. Beth was another story. She was still unconscious and they didn't know if she was going to make it. I worried about her children. They were still with her neighbor, but I had a feeling they couldn't stay there for much longer. I had asked Richard to try and find Beth's relatives, a grandmother, something, anyone who could take care of the kids until she came back. If she came back. The thought made me sad. She had to get better. I couldn't bear losing another partner.

I had let Travis Goodman go, since I no longer believed he was our man. I had no idea how it was all connected yet, but had a feeling I was really close to figuring it all out.

Close, but no cigar, like my dad always used to say.

The kids had all gone back to school this morning and it felt good to have something go back to normal when everything else was chaotic. I hadn't spoken to Shannon since Sunday morning. The media was still occupying our condominium and I felt bad for her. I had spoken on the phone with her before I went to bed Sunday night and had told her everything. She had sounded tired and sad. It wasn't strange, since she was in a dire situation, now that they had found the body but no gun. I feared all hell could break loose any moment now. It was really bad for her.

I had gotten myself a coffee and sat at my desk, staring at the many files and papers, Richard had placed there. They were all profiles of the victims in the shooting cases. I stared at them without reading them, wondering about Stanley Bradley and the statement I had taken from him the night before. He had explained, in detail, how this woman had stuffed food into his mouth and threatened to kill his granddaughter if he didn't do as he was told. He had also told me something that had been very interesting.

There had been more than one.

He had seen the other one in the kitchen as he had escaped. She was the one who had been cooking the food, while the other was feeding the victims. Stanley had also spent the night at the hospital and I had planned to send over a sketcher to have a drawing made of these two women. I was certain they were still out there in this area. Mrs. Millman had disappeared from the face of the earth and I had sent her picture to the media in the hope she would show up. I had no idea if she was a part of all this or not, but the shots had been fired from her house, so she had to know something.

I looked at the papers, thinking it was so hard dealing with two cases at the same time. I kept getting them mixed up. I took out the file on the four victims from Boca Raton. Their children had all gone to the same school…that was the connection. Then, I picked up Phillip Hagerty's file and went through it. Phillip Hagerty had two children. They both went to Roosevelt like mine did. Then there was Joe Harrison. His daughter went to a private school in Nashville.

No, she didn't.

I frowned, then looked at it again. The information was wrong. It was old. Angela hadn't been at the school in Nashville for the past month. She had changed schools. She went to Roosevelt like most kids in our area did.

Theodore Roosevelt Elementary School.

"Oh, my God," I said.

Richard looked up from his screen. "What?"

"The killer, our female shooter, works at the school. Of course she does. She is a teacher. All we need to do is to find someone who recently transferred to Roosevelt from Klein's in Boca. That's it Richard! That's the connection."

"I'm on it."

SEVENTY-THREE

March 2015

"I GOT A NAME," Richard said and got off the phone.

I lit up. Finally, we were getting somewhere. Richard approached my desk.

"Natalie Monahan. In 2010, she transferred from Klein's to Roosevelt," he said. "But she isn't a teacher. She's a school psychologist. And get this. I ran her name, she owns a house. She owns *the* house on Lansing Island, where Stanley Bradley and Roy Miller were being kept."

"You're kidding me, right? So, the two cases are connected?" I was blown away by this. I mean, the thought had somehow crossed my mind, especially when I found out the suspects were females in both cases, but I just didn't quite see how it was all fitting together. Who was doing what here? And why?

"The school said she didn't check in this morning and that they haven't heard from her, but I found her on Facebook," Richard said.

I walked to him and looked over his shoulder. I looked at the picture. She looked like the woman I had seen on the boat.

"That's her," I said. "She shot Ron. She was on the boat I followed. Print that picture and let's have it out everywhere." Richard was scrolling through her pictures when, suddenly, it dawned on me. "Stop there," I said. "Right there."

Richard stopped at the picture I had seen and made it big so I could see better. Four women standing in each other's arms, smiling, on a boat. The picture was from an older date. I looked down and saw the description.

TBT. MY SISTERS AND ME. THIS WAS TAKEN IN 2000. TRIP TO MIAMI ON A FRIEND'S BOAT. WERE WE EVER THIS YOUNG? LOVE YOU ALL FOREVER.

I pointed at one of the women. "That one right there. That's Mrs. Millman."

Richard looked closer.

"Take away fifteen years," I said, thinking of the picture we had sent out to the media of Mrs. Millman, with her neat dyed blonde hair. In this old picture, she was a brunette...gorgeous and without the bitterness that life had somehow given her later on. Even her eyes were smiling. It was so far from the sedated emotionless woman I had met with at her home.

"So, Mrs. Sarah Millman and Natalie Monahan are sisters?" Richard asked.

"Correct, Detective," I said with a grin. I was feeling uplifted all of a sudden. I hadn't fit the pieces completely yet, but we were getting there. We were on to something.

Richard printed a series of pictures and got busy putting together something we could give to the media. Meanwhile, I went back to my desk. I called the school in Boca Raton and asked them if they had kept the old files for students who visited the school psychologist in 2009. To my surprise, they had. They had them online and could send them to me. I told them the last names of the children I wanted, then waited half an hour before I received the email. I was quite surprised at the school's efficiency down there. I went down to Roosevelt and asked for the files of some of their children as well. It was a hunch, but I sensed I had to follow it. As I got back, I opened the files and went through them, one by one. All were written by the mysterious Natalie Monahan. It didn't take me long to find the connection between all of them. I made two phone calls to clear something up, then put the phone down as the picture became clearer and clearer to me. I didn't get to tell Richard before the phone rang and I had Weasel from Cocoa Beach on the other end.

"We found your woman," she said.

"Sarah Millman? Where?"

"She was speeding on 520 when Officer Hall pulled her over. He took her in. Recognized her right away."

"I'll be right down," I said and slammed the phone down.

"Good news?" Richard asked.

"Yes. Excellent news. Finally."

SEVENTY-FOUR

April 2009

JAMES WEST WAS SO HAPPY. He had all of his daughters over for a visit for the entire weekend. He had missed them all so much, ever since he left the house and his family.

And, this time, Elizabeth had come with them. She had come for the entire weekend for the first time, and James had been so thrilled to see her. Even his new girlfriend, Nicole, had liked her. At least she had pretended to, until Elizabeth threw her first fit and sat down on the floor screaming for food. That was when Nicole had told James he'd better take care of this before the guests arrived.

They were having a party. Nicole was the one who had invited people over, even though James was having the kids for the weekend. She didn't care much; she was only twenty-five and didn't understand what it meant to have kids. James was so in love he didn't care. He let her do whatever she wanted to…as long as she was happy. After all, it wasn't an easy task to have to endure another woman's four children, especially not when one of them was completely out of control like Elizabeth.

James knelt in front of her and tried to comfort her, but Elizabeth still screamed at the top of her lungs.

"I'm HUNGRYYYYY!"

Not knowing what else to do, James slapped her across her face. "Stop that, Elizabeth. You've got to stop that."

Elizabeth cried even louder, acting like a two year-old, hammering her fists into the floor while screaming and yelling that she was so hungry. James slapped her again, thinking this was what his own dad would have done, and it had worked on him as a child. Children shouldn't be in control; they shouldn't be the ones in charge, and Elizabeth had been given way too much liberty to act however she wished. He felt this was his chance to finally make things right with her. This was what should have been done a long time ago. So, he slapped her again.

The girl screamed and the doorbell rang. Nicole sprang for it and opened it for the caterers. When Elizabeth saw the trays of food being carried in, her eyes lit up.

"Food!" she shrieked.

"No!" Nicole yelled and looked at James. "She's not getting anywhere near this food. You hear me? This is for the guests. This is nice food. Expensive food."

James nodded and looked at Elizabeth, who was about to explode in excitement. What was he supposed to do? He couldn't call Dottie, because she would never let him have Elizabeth over again. He couldn't let Elizabeth run around the house on her own. She would only eat the food and Nicole would kill him.

James sighed. It wasn't easy making everyone happy. The three older girls were all getting dressed and were excited about the party that their cool new stepmom was throwing. They wouldn't be anywhere near their younger sister if they could avoid it. He couldn't do that to them. They were finally so happy to be at his place.

"Elizabeth?" he asked.

She looked at him through her tears, but never listened to what he had to say before she stormed into the kitchen and threw herself at the food.

"Noooo!" James yelled and ran after her. He grabbed her by the shoulder, but couldn't pull her almost three hundred pounds off the food.

Meanwhile, Nicole was screaming. "Stop her! James, get her away from the food."

James was yelling at her, hitting her back, trying to get her away, but nothing helped. She was stuffing her face with food.

"Elizabeth, stop! Stop!"

He looked at Nicole's terrified face, while his daughter gulped down the mushroom polenta and shrimps like she was eating popcorn at a movie theater.

"Do something, James!"

So, James had an idea. He knew it wasn't a good one right away, but at least it was something. He lured Elizabeth down to the basement, holding a bucket of ice cream in front of her face, and by promising her she would get it if she followed him. He gave her the bucket and a spoon and let her dig in, while he snuck up the stairs, closed the door, and locked it. He didn't feel good about it, but at least she was happy, now that she had her ice cream, and he would have the entire day with her tomorrow before she went back to her mother's.

"Is she under control?" Nicole asked, when he came back into the kitchen.

James nodded. "Everything is under control." It was hard for him to hide his embarrassment.

Nicole straightened her dress and made sure her hair was perfect. She sighed with relief. "Good. The guests will be here shortly."

James forced a smile. "Great. That's really great."

SEVENTY-FIVE

March 2015

"WHERE IS YOUR SISTER?"

I looked at Sarah Millman in front of me in the interrogation room at the Cocoa Beach Police Department. Sarah Millman looked like answering my questions was beneath her.

"Which one? I have three," she said.

"You know which one I'm looking for. Natalie. The one who shoots people and force-feeds her victims in her house across the street from yours. Or maybe that was you? I'm beginning to think it was you who killed your husband, after all. What about the others? Roy Miller? James West? Why did they have to die? And, what about Stanley Bradley?"

Sarah Millman laughed. "You don't know anything. You have no idea what you're talking about. And you never will."

"Then tell me, Goddammit. Tell me."

"I'm sorry, I can't. I couldn't betray my sisters like that."

"Your sisters? So, now you're saying that they're all in on it?" I asked.

"I didn't say that."

"Well, that's what I'm thinking. Here's how I think it went down. Your sister Natalie worked as a psychologist at the schools. She found the victims. They all had one thing in common. Their children were seeing Natalie on a regular basis because they had trouble at home. They all came from parents who were abusive or neglecting them somehow. It is the same for Don Foster and Brad Schmidt, who were among the four killed in Boca Raton, and it goes for the last two who died here as well. Phillip Hagerty had two children in Roosevelt, who both saw Natalie, and spoke to her about how their dad would come to their bedroom at night and ask them to get undressed. It was her latest case. The case should have been turned over to Social Services so it could be investigated, but it never was. Why? I'll tell you why. Because you and your sisters had a better way of dealing with these things, right?"

367

"Social Services never gets the work done. They have so many cases, they drown in them. They don't have the time to handle all of them," Sarah snorted. "The bastard deserved both of those bullets, and you know it."

I leaned back in the chair. Sarah Millman was finally talking. "When did it start?" I asked. "Who was your first victim?"

I threw a file on the table in front of her that Richard had pulled right before I left the office. I opened the folder. The picture of a man appeared. Sarah Millman looked away.

"He was your father, right? They found him in the canal in Boca Raton fifteen years ago. Stabbed twenty-six times. The killer was never found. Weird, huh? What did he do? Did he beat you up? Was that why you started this vendetta against parents beating up their kids?"

"Any injustice against a defenseless child should be punished," she said.

"I feel the same way, believe me, but you and I are not judges in a court of law. It's not our job to make that decision, and a smart girl like you knows that very well. So, tell me, what did your father do to you girls to make you believe he needed to suffer this fate?"

"He got one of us pregnant," she almost whispered. I could hear the bitterness and anger in her voice.

I sighed. "He raped one of you?"

"Not one. All of us," she said. "Over and over again. Through all of our teenage years. We came from a rich family and lived in an expensive neighborhood, where people had as many boats as they had cars. There is a perception out there, Detective, that child sexual abuse doesn't happen in those neighborhoods to those kids. But, what people need to realize is that child abuse, whether sexual or not, can happen and does happen to any child in any neighborhood. It cuts across all socioeconomic backgrounds, cultural and religious."

"Who was pregnant?"

"That is a secret between the four of us. We swore to never tell anyone. Not even our own mother knew. We never told her anything."

"How did you manage to hide it?" I asked.

"Big dresses, staying out of her sight. She was drunk most of the time anyway. She never knew. When the time came, right before she was about to deliver, we told her we were all going away to France for a couple of weeks over Christmas break to study the language and the art. It wasn't uncommon among our friends. We all left and went to a clinic that took the child and gave it to someone who wished to adopt it. When we found out one of us was pregnant, we made a pact...a blood pact, where we promised we would never look upon any abuse of children without acting on it. See, we believed our mother, the teachers at the school, and most people knew, but chose to turn a blind eye, thinking it was none of their business. Our father was influential. No one dared to touch him."

"Except you and your sisters. You finished him off. And got away with it," I said.

Sarah Millman was smart enough to not answer me. She knew not to say too much. She knew I would never find proof enough to nail her for the death of her father this many years later.

"So, why did your husband have to die?" I asked. "You have a son together. Did he touch him? Did he abuse Christopher?"

"What do you think?"

"I think he did. I think you found out and sent the kid away to boarding school before you arranged to have your husband punished. Your one sister, Natalie, had already bought the house across the street and she was ready to help as soon as you asked her to. Maybe it was even her twisted idea to force-feed him till his stomach burst. It's quite a painful death. Serves good as a punishment, doesn't it?"

"Sounds like you know more about that sort of thing than I do," she said, careful again to not say too much. But I could tell I was right. I could see it in her eyes. I guessed she had started to take the benzos we found in her house after the discovery of what her husband had done to their son, to calm herself down, and that had left her emotionless when they planned his death. It took a calm and cool mind to plan a death like this.

There was a knock on the door and Richard peeked inside. I stepped out.

"You were right, Ryder," he said.

"About what?"

"I just got off the phone with Stanley Bradley's wife. He had beaten his son too. The boy was transgender, and apparently, Stanley had a hard time figuring out how to react to that. So, he beat him up. The boy went to Cocoa Beach High. Graduated two years ago."

"Let me guess. The two schools share the same school psychologist?"

"It's a city thing. It's run from City Hall. She covers both schools in town."

"So, Stanley and Daniel were also punished for abusing their children. I'm guessing Roy was too. It looks like a pattern. Anything else?"

"Two things. First, I think I finally figured out the signature. The AM. It's all explained here," he said and handed me a printout from Wikipedia. "Second, you asked me to look into James West, who was killed in 2009 in Boca Raton by the same manner as Daniel Millman and Roy Miller."

"Yes, you found something?"

"I don't know if it is anything important, but apparently, he was once married and had four children."

"Okay?"

"One of them died in April, 2009."

"Died? How?"

"She burst her stomach."

SEVENTY-SIX

April 2009

JAMES WEST WAS CRYING. For the first time since he was a child, he was crying. He was at his daughter's funeral. A week ago, she had been alive. But now, she wasn't here anymore.

And it was all his fault.

He should have listened to Dottie. He should have taken her word for it when she told him Elizabeth was sick and that she really couldn't control herself, no matter how much she tried.

Why? Why hadn't he listened?

Because he was a fool, that's why. He was a damned fool, and now he had to live with the fact that he had killed his own daughter.

Elizabeth hadn't stayed in the basement. Of course she hadn't. He hadn't been able to hear her because of the music, but at some point during the night, she burst through the door to the basement and broke it into pieces by her forceful weight. James had been drunk at the time. He hadn't thought about her for even a second, he was ashamed to admit. He had completely forgotten she was down there, and as the night progressed, she became more and more desperate. She was screaming for food and finally managed to break through and find her way to the kitchen.

They didn't find her until the next morning, when Nicole screamed from the kitchen and James woke with a start.

"Elizabeth."

Oh, my God. Oh, my God.

He ran downstairs and into the kitchen where Nicole was standing, frozen, holding a hand to her chest. On the tiles lay Elizabeth in a pile of hors d'oeuvres and Spanish Ham with olives and oranges. She had foie grass smeared over her entire face and piles of empty trays next to her. James gasped and knelt next to her. He couldn't believe it. There had been so much food left…big piles of food, and now it was all gone.

"Elizabeth," he said, grabbing her hand. He leaned over her. He could hear her breath and catch her pulse. She was still alive.

He had taken her to the hospital and told them what had happened. They had examined her and told him Elizabeth's stomach had been distended and she was in severe pain. At the emergency room, doctors pumped her stomach, but her condition worsened. A day passed before surgeons discovered that her stomach had been distended long enough to lose blood flow and become septic, and now it had ruptured. Elizabeth died that night in her hospital bed, and now she was lying in her coffin, and he would never see her again. And, as if that wasn't enough, Nicole had left him, and Dottie told him she was going to make sure he never saw any of his children again.

James had pleaded with her, trying to explain to her that it was an accident... that he had tried his best, but he knew it was a lie. He hadn't done his best. He hadn't listened to his ex-wife; he hadn't taken the time to get to really know his daughter and figure out what was wrong with her. He had taken her for being this monster, this person who lacked self-discipline because her mother smothered her.

But it was all too late to change now.

As the funeral was over, James West drove home to his empty house, where his daughter had eaten herself to death in his kitchen, and continued to cry. He cried his heart out, thinking about how stupid he had been, when the doorbell suddenly rang. Outside stood four young women in their twenties. They looked alike, and he guessed they had to be sisters. At first, he thought they were Jehovah's Witnesses and he told them he wasn't interested, when one of them put her high-heeled shoe in the door as he tried to close it on them.

"Oh, but *we* are interested," one of them said.

"We're very interested in you, James West," another said.

"Especially interested in what happened to your daughter," a third said.

"Who are you?" he asked.

"We're the Angel Makers," the fourth said. "I sure hope you're hungry."

SEVENTY-SEVEN

March 2015

"TELL ME ABOUT THE CHILD," I said, as I returned to Sarah Millman.

"What child?" she asked.

"The child you and your sister adopted away to another family."

"What's there to tell?"

I sighed and looked at her. I was getting a little fed up with her tough-girl approach to everything. It was getting old.

"She died, didn't she? How did you find out?" I asked, cutting to the chase.

"It was in the paper," she said. "The story of the girl who ate herself to death. We recognized the name and our daughter in the picture."

"Our daughter? So she was yours?" I asked.

"She was all of ours. We all acted like we were pregnant; we all loved her like she was ours, but none of us could keep her, since we were too young. We thought we were giving her away to a family that would take good care of her, better than what we could. But they didn't. They let her eat herself to death."

"So, you killed James West. You force-fed him till his stomach ruptured, just like had happened to your daughter."

"I never said that I did," she said.

"Was it Natalie who shot those people in the theater? That was her deal, right? She liked to shoot. She learned about the parents through the students at her school, then planned their execution. I'm guessing she's the dramatic one of you, right? After the shooting and the killing of James West, you knew you couldn't stay in Boca. It was too dangerous. So, you all moved up here, to Cocoa Beach, where Natalie got a new job and you got married to Daniel, right? You were pregnant and expecting Christopher at this time."

"I had just given birth," she said. "And we were already married when we moved here."

"Okay, so did you all move up here, or was it just you and Natalie?"

"It was just me and Natalie. She bought the house across the street from me with her money from our inheritance after our mother died."

"And the two others?"

"Angelina and Kelly stayed in Boca. They came up here a year ago."

"Right when they heard you were in trouble, huh?"

"My marriage wasn't doing well, no. That's no secret. They came to help me. There is nothing wrong with that. Besides, Angelina had been laid off from her job and needed a place to stay. Daniel was never home anyway, so she moved in here with me. She never married and never had any children. Kelly married, but was divorced after three years. She never had any children either."

"Tell me about the Angel Makers," I said.

"What?" The way Sarah Millman blushed told me she knew exactly what I was talking about. I put the article from Wikipedia on the table in front of her.

"That's what you call yourselves, isn't it? AM, Angel Makers. According to this article, The Angel Makers were a group of women living in the village of Nagyrév, Hungary, who, between 1914 and 1929 poisoned to death an estimated three hundred people, mostly abusive husbands and family members that had become a burden to them or to get hold of their inheritance. Others poisoned their lovers, some even their sons, as the midwife behind it all allegedly told the poisoners, *Why put up with them?* Is that how you and your sisters think? Why not just rid the world of these abusive people?"

"You must admit, they do make a strong point," she said.

"I do. But this is 2015 America and we have a justice system that is supposed to handle these people."

"Maybe we do and maybe we don't," she said.

"Who wrote the emails to Shannon King?" I asked. "Was it you?"

"I don't know what you are talking about."

"No, it couldn't have been you. You're not the one with the conscience. It has to be one of the other sisters. I'm thinking Natalie. She sounds like she is more emotional. Except, of course, I don't know much about the last two, do I?"

"I don't think you know much about anything, Detective," she said with a smirk.

I leaned back. It was getting annoying. I wasn't getting her to say anything useful. Still, I kept trying.

"So, Angela Harrison told Natalie about her father Joe and how he had beaten her once. Something not even her mother knew. But, a few weeks ago, Angela came to school crying and they sent her to see Natalie, to talk to her. She told her she missed her father, but that she was also afraid of him. I read the files that Natalie wrote. Am I right? That's why Joe had to die, right?"

"I wouldn't know," she said.

"I get that one of you killed Britney Foster because she had seen Natalie in Publix here in Cocoa Beach and knew she posed a threat to you, but what about Beth?" I asked.

Sarah Millman looked at me indifferently.

"Bethany Gruber, my partner? Why did she have to get hurt? At first, I thought it was just a coincidence, that you were trying to scare us off, to try and get us to back off, but then I went through Natalie's files at the school and realized that Beth's youngest daughter had problems too. The little girl told Natalie about how her mother drank, right? That was why you tried to kill her, wasn't it? I just don't understand how you knew that Beth would be the one who would open the truck's door."

"I'm sure I don't know what you're talking about, Detective. However, maybe if someone was trying to kill that little partner of yours, they would have set the bomb up so that it would only go off if someone of her size tried to open the door. You know how short and pudgy she is, not like any of the other officers who would have been called to the scene. That's just a guess, of course; I don't even know whether such a thing is possible," she replied nonchalantly.

"But it was all based on a lie. Beth doesn't drink anymore; she's been in AA for a year and is getting better. See, all I did was to talk a little to her neighbor, who told me everything. If you had done a little research, you would have made the same discovery. The file is two years old when everything went wrong at her household and Beth was drinking...right after her husband left her alone with three children. But, not everything is black and white. That's why we need a justice system. That's why vigilantism is a felony. Now, all I need for you is to tell me where your sisters are. They can explain the rest, but I need to find them. First of all, Natalie, I need to find her. Where is she?"

"She's gone, Detective."

"Where?"

Sarah Millman shrugged. "Who knows? She left last night. Who knows where she might have gone to? Maybe it wasn't just her, maybe it was all three of them that left. Who knows?"

"You've got it all figured out, don't you. Why didn't you leave?"

"I have a son, remember? I can't just leave."

I hit my fist on the table. Mrs. Millman hardly reacted. She was probably still doped.

"Where did she go?" I yelled. "Where is Natalie Monahan?"

Sarah Millman shook her head. "Sorry, Detective. There is no way I'm telling you this. You see, that would blow the entire thing, wouldn't it? We're going to be everywhere, keeping our eyes on you. We'll be your lawyers, your child's teacher, and your policewomen. We'll be everywhere, making sure you behave. You should be thanking us. We're doing society a favor. Do you have any idea how many prisoners on death row right now were beaten by their parents? How many were abused by the very same people that were supposed to protect them? It's a disease. And it is passed down to the next generation. Chances are, if your daddy beat you, then you'll do the same to your child, and so on. We are here to break that cycle. Lord knows, someone has to. Now, if you don't mind, I'm not saying another word till my lawyer is here."

SEVENTY-EIGHT

March 2015

I STOPPED by Shannon's condo on my way home. I had picked the kids up from my parents' place and told them to continue up in the elevator to our apartment with Emily while I checked on Shannon. I felt bad, since I hadn't had any time for her in the past couple of days. At the same time, I felt exhausted after interrogating Sarah Millman all day and not getting much out of her. Her lawyer had arrived and told us everything his client had told us in the initial interviews couldn't be used for anything, since he wasn't present. He was one of those high-paid lawyers that you didn't want to get up against.

I was worried Sarah Millman would get away with everything. I wasn't going to let her. I still had one more card to play, and I was going to do it the next day. Stanley Bradley would identify her in a line-up. If she had been involved in his kidnapping, he could tell me. Meanwhile, I had sent out all kinds of pictures of the three sisters to the media, letting them know we were searching for them, and especially for Natalie Monahan, who I believed to be the shooter at the cinema and at the festival. I also believed she was the one who shot Sheriff Ron before she escaped by boat. Richard had found out that she had been taking shooting lessons at a shooting range in Melbourne. They recognized her picture when he went down there and showed it to them. She had been going there for years.

I rang the doorbell to Shannon's place and waited. I wasn't going to stay the night, since I had promised Emily I would watch *The Tonight Show* with her and I had promised Abigail and Austin that they could sleep in my bed with me, since they had missed me, and Abigail blamed me for never spending any time with them anymore. It was true, I guess, but I had a job to do, I told her.

"You always say that," she said. Then she gave me that look that I can't refuse. She had a way with her daddy.

There was a fumbling behind the door and it was opened. "Shannon?" I said, as her face appeared. My heart started racing when I tried to look into her eyes. She avoided looking directly at me.

"Come on in," she said, and walked to the living room, where she threw herself on the couch.

I sat next to her with a sigh. "Why do you torture yourself like this?" I asked, trying to get her to look at me. "Where is Angela?"

"Sleeping. I put her to bed early. She was getting on my nerves."

"You're drunk," I said. "Again." I tried to hide how emotional I was, but my voice was breaking. So was my heart. I felt so bad for Angela that she had to see her mother like this. Shannon turned into this completely different person when she drank. She was aggressive and angry.

"Do you even want to stop?" I asked.

"I just took a little drink, alright? That's all. Get off my back." She snarled as she spoke. "It's just this damn thing with the police." Shannon closed her eyes. She was swaying. This wasn't just the result of one or two drinks.

I wondered where she got the alcohol from, but decided I didn't even want to ask. There were many ways to get ahold of it. I felt betrayed, like she didn't care about anyone but herself. I knew she was hurting from the case against her and the massive media coverage, but still. I needed her to be stronger. I needed her to want to be strong. An alcoholic would always find her drinks somewhere. It didn't matter if we tried to keep her away from it; she needed to make the decision to stop. That was how my mother had explained it to me when I had spoken to her about Shannon's drinking a few days ago. That was when I had thought I could simply keep her away from the alcohol and then she would get better. But now, I realized my mother was right. It wasn't that easy. It was Shannon's decision to make. I just knew I couldn't watch as she drank herself into misery and dragged all the rest of us with her.

Feeling all kinds of rage, I got up and walked to Angela's bedroom.

"Where are you going?" Shannon said.

I opened the door and found Angela sitting on her bed, crying. Of course she wasn't sleeping. "Come on," I said and picked her up in my arms, still wrapped in her blanket. She put her arms around my neck while she cried helplessly.

"You can't just take her, Jack," Shannon yelled. "She's my daughter, Goddammit."

I walked towards the front door and stopped. I looked at Shannon. Her eyes were glassy and flickering back and forth.

"She won't be much longer if you keep this up," I said, opened the door, and walked out. As the door shut behind me, Angela looked into my eyes.

"Will she be alright? Will Mommy be alright?" she asked.

I walked to the elevator and pushed the button, my blood pumping in my veins. "She's a grown woman. She'll be fine," I said.

SEVENTY-NINE

March 2015

It took a long time for her to calm down, but finally, Angela fell asleep on the couch between Emily and me while we watched Jimmy Fallon talk to Madonna. She sang *Holiday* with Jimmy Fallon and The Roots. It amused me enough to be able to laugh and relax a little. Emily thought it was boring and called Madonna old. She still stayed for the rest of the show, though, and I enjoyed her company. I even managed to get her to talk a little about what was going on in her life and had her tell me she was doing a concert at the school next week, but also said that she didn't want me there.

"What? My daughter is playing a concert and I'm not allowed to be there?" I said.

"Jack," she said through gritted teeth. "I don't want you there. It'll be so embarrassing. You're *durpy*."

"Excuse me? I'm not cool anymore? What happened? And what happened to daddy? You used to call me daddy?"

Emily looked into my eyes and put a hand on my shoulder. "I love you, Jack, but you're not my dad, and you are not very cool. I will kill you if you show up at my concert."

I looked at her, disappointed. "You really mean that?"

"Yes."

"At least tell me what you're doing. Are you playing an instrument?"

"I'm not telling you."

I looked at Emily with a grin. "Then you know what I must do."

"Jack, don't."

I lifted my hands in the air and yelled *Tickle Monster* before I attacked her and tickled her till she pleaded for me to stop.

"Pleeease!"

"Only if you tell me what you're doing in the concert, and only if you call me dad."

"Alright, alright, I give up," she said.

I let her go and sat back down, laughing. She looked at me like she was mad, but I could tell she was about to laugh too.

"So?"

"Okay," she said.

"Okay what?"

"Okay, *Dad*. I'm singing."

"Since when are you singing? You're singing in the concert? Like, in a choir, or what?" I asked. I had never heard Emily sing one tune in her entire life.

"No." She rolled her eyes at me. "It's just me."

My heart was about to melt. "You're singing solo? And you're telling me I can't be there? That's not fair!"

Emily got up from the couch. "But that's the way it's going to be," she said. "I'm too embarrassed about this to want you there. I told my music teacher I didn't want to do it, but she said I had to. I hate it, so that's why I don't want you to see it. Now, it's getting late, *Dad*. I'm going to bed. Goodnight."

I looked after my grown daughter as she walked to her bedroom. I couldn't believe how big she already was. She looked so much like her mother. I wondered if she ever thought about her. Of course she did. She had been six years old when her mother was killed. Lisa was born in the U.S., but her parents came from Bahamas. They moved to Florida before Lisa was born. I often wondered if she had any family over there. Maybe some cousins? I would have to take Emily there some time in search of her roots. It would do her good. She needed to know who she was and where she came from. Her grandparents were both dead now, but surely there had to be other family members?

I grabbed Angela and carried her into the twins' bedroom, where I put her in Abigail's bed. I would make sure she made it to the bus the next morning. I would have to stop by Shannon's to get her backpack, but she could borrow some clothes from Abigail. They were about the same size. I would have to pack her a lunchbox as well and a snack. I guessed Shannon hadn't done any of it. I felt so angry with her for the way she behaved. I knew she was going through a tough time, but still. She had a child. She was responsible for another life.

I stroked Angela's hair, and then kissed her on her forehead, shut off the light, and left the room. I grabbed an apple and ate it while looking out the windows at the dark beach. I walked into the balcony and stood for a little while, listening to the waves. I hadn't had the time to surf much the last week. The waves had been good; I had seen them on Facebook on several of my friend's pictures that they'd posted. I felt like the ocean was mocking me, telling me to come catch some of my own. But this wasn't the time. I had to finish my case first. I looked into the deep darkness and thought about the Bahamas. It was right out there, about three or four hours by boat. It was so close.

So close.

EIGHTY

March 2015

I BOARDED the airplane in Orlando. It was just me. I had made arrangements with a local officer to meet me at the airport in Nassau. It was late Tuesday afternoon. The trip was only one hour and fifteen minutes. I had no idea how long I was going to stay. When I was in the office this morning, I had told Richard to ask our Special Investigative Unit to help him try and trace the emails sent to Shannon once again. Richard had made profiles on all the sisters and found out that one of them, Angelina Monahan, worked in cyber-security. She helped protect big corporations against hackers. She would know exactly how to cover up the email's origins. But one of the IP addresses that came up during their investigation was in the Bahamas, and I thought it was worth a try to look into it. So, I had called the local police in Nassau and had them tell me who owned the house with the address from which it originated. It belonged to an American company called Millman Technologies, they told me.

I hadn't talked to Shannon yet, but my mother had promised to take all of the kids. Emily would help her and my dad out, I told her. Angela wasn't going home to her mother's until I knew she was sober, and so far, she hadn't even called me, so I assumed she was still on a bender. It hurt me like crazy to know she was hurting and there was nothing I could do to help.

"Mr. Ryder?" a smiling man said in his singing English. He had one of those smiles that literally lit up his face.

"Yes," I said and shook his hand.

"I'm Commissioner Ellis, The Royal Bahamas Police Force."

"Nice to meet you."

Commissioner Ellis had a car waiting and we got in. I had told him we believed a person of interest was hiding in the house, and he had agreed to take me there. This was a high-profile case I told him, since it involved two mass shootings and a murder attempt on a sheriff.

"The house is in Lyford Cay," he said. "In Western New Providence. It is one of

The Bahamas' most desirable communities to live in. The biggest properties in the exclusive development sell for twenty million plus, and beachfront homes for ten million and up."

I whistled, impressed.

"It is very exclusive, Mr. Ryder. Only for the über-rich. Gated, naturally. It has a par-72 golf course, twelve tennis courts, a full-service marina, dining facilities, a post office, a private international school, and a mile-long private beach. I do hope you have good reason for us to intrude on this place."

"I do," I said, sincerely hoping I was right about this. I had spoken to Ron about it on the phone to get his permission to follow this lead. He had told me I needed clearance further up. I had spoken to the governor, and he had given me the green light for this. Everyone wanted to nail this shooter more than anything. As long as nothing went wrong, the governor told me.

"Make sure nothing goes wrong, Ryder. This entire case makes me sick to my stomach."

I had promised that. It made me sick too. I hated how these sisters thought they had won this. Sarah Millman was still in our custody, but I had a feeling if I didn't do something, then she wouldn't stay for very long. Her lawyer was that good.

The commissioner had brought along four officers. They were sitting in the small van, looking very serious under their beige hats with the red stripe. The weather was glorious; it was even hotter than Florida, the skies blue, the breeze warm. It wasn't my first time here, but it still amazed me how clear the water was.

"We're entering the gated community now," the commissioner said, and looked at me with a serious look, like he wanted to make sure I still wanted to do this. I nodded and looked out as our car was let through the enormous gate and we entered Disney World for the richest in this world, the über-rich, as the commissioner called them, those that thought nothing of dropping a few hundred thousand at the roulette table, or even millions to buy an island. This was a completely different world. At least for me.

EIGHTY-ONE

March 2015

THE HOUSE WAS EMPTY. I was secondary, since I was operating on British soil, so I wasn't let inside before the Bahamian Police had been inside to make sure it was safe. I walked inside and went through all the ten or more bedrooms, but there were no signs of any of the sisters.

I should've known. They're not that stupid.

I walked through what I believed was the master bedroom and onto the balcony, where I could see the Bahamian officers walking through the yard, searching every corner. I felt so tired. I had been so sure that this was the place... that I would find them here. But it was yet another dead end.

I walked back into the bedroom looked inside the closets and found many dresses, shoes, and suitcases, but there was no telling if that was something new or it was just here so the sisters didn't have to bring much when they arrived. I found jewelry on the dresser and a hairdryer in the bathroom, along with several toothbrushes. It looked like someone was living here, but I couldn't be sure that it was recently. I was about to leave, when I saw something on the floor. I picked it up and looked at it. A tag from a dress. I turned it and looked at the name on the back.

"I'm afraid we don't find them here," the commissioner said, as he walked in. I showed him the tag.

"I know that place," he said. "It's in downtown Nassau." He rubbed his fingertips against each other on one hand. "Pricey place."

"Take me there," I said.

The commissioner told his officers they were done at the house, then drove all of us back to Nassau. We found the small store in the middle of town and I walked in, flanked by two officers. I showed the woman behind the counter the picture of the four sisters and she pointed at one of them, Natalie Monahan.

"This one. She was in here yesterday. Bought three dresses."

"Did she say anything about where she was going?" I asked, almost overflowing

381

with excitement. Finally, I had found her trail. I hadn't been wrong about this. She was here. Somewhere.

The woman shook her head. "No."

I was about to leave when the woman stopped me. "But she did say she wanted to dress nicely for a man."

I stopped and looked at her. "A man?"

"Yes, a man," she said with her strong island accent.

"Do you know anything about this man?"

The lady shook her head. "I just sold her some new dresses."

Once again, I was disillusioned. It was getting late and the sun was about to set. The commissioner drove me to my hotel and I checked in. I lay on the bed of the room, watching the local news and dozing off, when the story of a famous American baseball player named Todd Quentin came on. Apparently, he lived in The Bahamas now, since he had retired, but recently he had been involved in a scandal. Apparently, his ex-wife accused him of having locked their son in the basement because he told his dad he was gay.

"According to the ex-wife, Todd Quentin wouldn't let the son come out again until he admitted he wasn't gay and said that he had just been joking. The ex-wife was out of town when the incident happened, but divorced him as soon as she learned what he had done, and today, she decided to drag him to court and demand full custody of their son," said the reporter in her story filmed outside of a building I recognized as the one marking the entrance of the Lyford Cay community.

I stared at the screen and turned off the sound, while trying to straighten out my thoughts.

Could it be? Could it really be?

I grabbed my phone and called the commissioner.

"I need to get back into Lyford Cay," I said. "Yes it has to be right now. It's a matter of life and death."

EIGHTY-TWO

March 2015

NATALIE MONAHAN WAS ENJOYING her evening with Todd Quentin. Not because of the celebrity company, but more because she was so excited about finally being able to wipe that smirk off of his face. She had been dating him on and off for months now, whenever she visited the island and stayed in her sister's house. It wasn't his money she was after. Lord, no. She had enough for herself. After their parents died, they had all inherited enough money for them to never have to work again. No, just like her job as a school psychologist, this was her charity work; this was her passion; this was her helping out where society had failed.

"More champagne?" Todd asked with his handsome smile.

He was older than her, by fifteen years, give or take. But he liked his women young, she had learned.

Natalie had played it all out with him. Ever since she had heard the story about him and his son. She had approached him at the golf course and he had asked if she wanted a drink in the bar afterwards. Then, she had let him fuck her in the bathroom, just to make sure she had him on the hook. Now he was caressing her hand and it gave Natalie chills all over her back, especially since she knew what was on his mind. His little sex games had become worse and worse, but she had played along...until now, that was. Tonight, she was going to give him what he deserved.

"Yes, please," she said and thought of the nine mm in her purse. She couldn't wait to see his face when she pulled it out. The question was, how far she was willing to let him go?

"I do enjoy these small meetings," he said and looked into her eyes. He had served her dinner on the balcony overlooking the ocean. It was gorgeous with all the lights in the yard beneath them.

She forced a smile. "Me too."

He grabbed her hand and yanked her forward so hard she hurt herself on the table. "Have you been a bad girl, huh?"

She tried not to show she was hurt. She smiled. "So bad."

"Tell me how bad. You've been playing with yourself, huh?"

Natalie felt sick to her stomach. She hated these little games he played. It was terrible, so cliché. And then there was the sex. How this sick bastard could ever have thought any woman would find that pleasing was beyond her understanding. No, this world, and especially the women of this world, would be happy that she removed him from the surface of the earth. It was in everyone's best interest.

Natalie couldn't help thinking about his son. She had met him at the house once. He was twelve and so vulnerable, and yet Todd had yelled at him and called him a fruitcake. He had even slapped him when he didn't answer him correctly.

She had fought the desire to kill the guy right then. She wanted to wait. It had to be done at the right time. And that time was now.

"Oh, yes. A lot."

Todd Quentin laughed loudly and let go of her hand. He continued to shovel down food with his fork. "I like that," he said with his mouth full. He pointed at her with his fork. "I really like that. You sure are something. You're nothing like all those boring housewife bitches you see around here with all their money, charities, and hats. Oh, how I loathe those hats they all wear."

"Well, I'm nothing like that," she said chuckling. "You're right about that."

He stared at her with lust in his eyes and shook his head. "No, lady. You're fine. You are so fine and so damn sexy. I could ride you all night long."

"I bet you could."

EIGHTY-THREE

March 2015

WE HAD JUST PARKED the van in front of Todd Quentin's mansion when we heard the gunshots. Two shots were fired right after one another.

"Break my heart again and I'll put two bullets in yours," I said and looked at the commissioner.

"What does that mean?"

"It's a song. It means we're too late."

I rushed up the driveway, and secondary or not, I ran inside of the house. The commissioner and his officers were right behind me.

"It sounded like it came from upstairs," I yelled and ran up the carpeted stairs. I found myself, seconds later, on the balcony, where I stopped. Right there on the tiles, next to a table with food and champagne in a bucket, stood the famous baseball player Todd Quentin, holding a nine mm gun in his hand. He was naked from the waist down. In front of him lay Natalie Monahan on the floor. She was completely naked, her dress on the floor behind the chair, her panties next to it. She was holding a hand to her stomach, where the blood was streaming out from a big wound.

Todd Quentin looked at me. He was crying. "I...I...she was about to shoot me. She pulled this thing out of her purse while we were...I thought it was a toy. I thought she was playing a game. But then she said she wanted to kill me. She asked me if I knew what it was like to be hated by your own dad, to be abused by the one person who was supposed to love you and protect you. I had no idea what she was talking about. Then, she cocked it and lifted it to pull the trigger. I had to move fast. So, I did. I grabbed the barrel of the gun from her hand and...I got it and turned it at her, told her to not come closer. But she was screaming and yelling, and then she...she leapt towards me and I...I pulled the trigger. I had to."

Three Bahamian officers were soon all over him and got the gun out of his hand. He was cuffed and taken away. I knelt next to Natalie Monahan. She was still conscious, but only barely.

385

"Natalie. Can you hear me?" I asked. "Stay with me. Okay? We have ambulances coming."

Natalie looked at me. I could tell she was holding on to her life with everything she had, all the strength she could find. I felt so desperate.

"Don't go, Natalie. We need you."

I heard ambulances wailing in the distance. They didn't sound like the ones I was used to, but I knew it was them.

"Just hold on for a little while longer. I know everything, Natalie. I know your entire story. I know how your father abused you. I know how one of you was pregnant and gave the child away. I know how the child died. I know that you and your sisters made a pact. I need you to tell me the rest, Natalie. I need you."

Natalie opened her mouth, as if she wanted to say something to me, but no words left her lips. I could tell she was struggling to find the strength. Finally, a word managed to come out of her. A small still word I could barely hear through all the noise coming from down the stairs.

"...sorry..."

I looked directly into her eyes as she went into a cramp. Her eyes died first. Then her body gave in and became limp in my hands.

"No!" I yelled, as a paramedic came rushing in and took her out of my hands. But it didn't matter. There was nothing they could do. She was gone.

EIGHTY-FOUR

March 2015

I CAME HOME three days later and threw myself on the couch with a loud sigh. I was finished in the Bahamas, where I had gone through all the belongings found in The Millmans' big house, and together with the police there, finished the Bahamian side to the case. Todd Quentin was, once again, facing a media frenzy, since everyone was talking about him, both in the Bahamas and back here in the U.S. Finally, it seemed like they had forgotten about Shannon. At least for a little while. I hoped that gave her the peace and quiet she needed. I had noticed the reporters and photographers were all gone from the entrance to our building, so that was a start. I knew my mother had been taking care of all the children, even Angela, for as long as I was gone, but I had no idea how Shannon had been doing. I feared the worst, to be honest.

The case against the Monahan sisters wasn't closed, and it wasn't solved either. I was told Sarah Millman had been released on bail, and now it was up to me to build the case against her. Stanley Bradley had identified her as one of the two keeping him hostage, so that was at least a beginning. We were going for charging her with the murders of her husband and Roy Miller. The two other sisters would be charged with assisting her and the fourth sister, Natalie, in planning her shootings, but it was like they had like sunken into the ground. Their pictures had been shown everywhere, but still there was no trace of them. I hadn't given up on finding them, but prepared myself for the fact that it would take a long time before we did. They would mess up eventually. They all did.

Beth was awake, Richard told me on the phone. She had gone through a severe skin transplant, but was much better now. She had been asking for me. I promised I would go see her the next day. And, Ron was back, Richard said. He was supposed to be on sick leave for at least three weeks, but he couldn't stay away.

"I think the old wife drove him nuts," Richard said. "She is constantly terrified something is going to happen to him again. She wanted him to quit the force, can you imagine?"

"No. I really can't," I said. "The force is his entire life."

It was the truth. He always said we were his second family. And if anyone loved his family, it was Ron. Both of them.

I was sitting on my couch and had opened the windows to listen to the waves, when there was a knock on my door. I got up and opened it. Outside, stood Shannon. Her eyes were clearer, even though she looked very sad.

"I'm so, so sorry," she said.

I smiled and sighed. "Come in."

"I can't blame you for being angry with me. I don't know what got into me. I feel awful, Jack. I really do."

"So, now you're here to tell me you're sober, is that it?" I asked.

"I am sober. I have been for three days now."

I shrugged. "And how am I supposed to believe that? You said that last week too. So what if you're sober now? You'll drink next week or the week after that. This case isn't over; they still haven't found the gun. It will keep going; there will come more bad news, eventually, in the coming months; they'll write bad things about you again. Then what? Then you'll go back to drinking again?"

Shannon shook her head. I saw a light in them I hadn't seen in a long time. Maybe never.

"I won't, Jack. I really won't."

I rubbed my eyes and leaned back in the couch. I really wanted to believe her, but how could I? I didn't want to get hurt again. I didn't want to stand and watch as she hurt herself and her daughter. I simply couldn't.

"Shannon...I...I don't know if I can trust you again. I don't want to live a life where I am constantly afraid you might slip again. I can't watch you all hours of the day. You need to make the decision that you want to get better. You have to make the decision to not drink again."

She nodded. "I know," she said. "And I have."

"So, how can I trust that you won't drink again in, let's say...in a month?"

"Because I won't. I really won't, Jack. Not for the next nine months."

"You say that now, and then you..." I paused and looked at her. "Did you say nine months?"

Shannon bit her lip and then she nodded. "I don't know how this happened..."

I got up from the couch and put both hands in my hair while staring at her, then took them out and sat down again. Seconds later, I got up again and walked back and forth while my thoughts settled. I turned and looked at her, then sat down again. My mouth was open, but no words left my lips. Shannon nodded. She seemed happy, yet anxious.

"I'm terrified too, Jack, but..."

"Terrified?" I finally managed to say. "I wouldn't call it that."

"What would you call it?" she looked at me. "You do want it, don't you?"

"Are you kidding me? Look around. I love kids. The more the merrier, right?"

Shannon chuckled. I put my arm around her and pulled her close. This changed everything. "And, you're sure, right?"

She nodded again. "I took four tests. Today, I went to the doctor and he told me I was six weeks pregnant."

I shook my head. "Wow," I said. "That is really something."

"It sure is," she said and leaned in against me.

"So, what do you say we move in together?" I asked.

She looked up at me, then kissed my lips. "I would like that. I would really love that, Jack."

I looked around the condo that had been my home for seven years, mine and the kids' home. It had been a time of great happiness when the twins were born and of great sadness when their mother left us. I had cried and laughed a lot in this place. I loved that it was right on the water, but now I was beginning to think it was time for a change.

"Maybe we should get a house together," I said. "One that is big enough for us and all of our children."

Shannon smiled again. "That sounds great. I saw that there was a lot for sale two blocks down. We would still be on the ocean and still in walking distance to your parents' place. We could buy that."

"And build our own dream house. I like the sound of that," I said. I had always wanted to build my own house. "But, there is no way I can afford that on my salary. A lot like that is close to a million, and then there's the house…"

"You might not be able to. But I could," Shannon said.

"Oh, Shannon, I couldn't…"

"Of course you can. We're about to be parents. Last time I checked this is 2015. A woman can buy her family a house and provide for them."

I had a tickling sensation in my stomach. I leaned down and kissed Shannon again. I was just so happy to have her back to the woman I loved. Could we do this? Why not?

"Guess I'm building you a house, then," I said.

She chuckled. "We'll all live in the house that Jack built."

Epilogue

HOP ON THE BUS

EIGHTY-FIVE

April 2015

KATIE LOOKED out the window of the bus. Florida's flat landscape raced by as she continued her way back home. At first, the police had asked her to stay until they were done with the investigation of Britney's murder. They had asked all of them to stay, but let the others go a few days before they told Katie she could go back home.

Katie drew in a sigh of relief. It had been scary waiting at the motel for the police to make up their mind if they wanted to charge her with anything. They still hadn't closed the case, Jack Ryder told her, but he didn't believe she had anything to do with it.

"Then, who was it?" Katie had asked.

"That's still under investigation," he answered.

Katie lucked out. She knew she did. She had a pretty good motive. The worst part was that the others believed she had done it. Both Leanne and Irene told her to her face. They were terrified of her, they said. And they had asked for another room at the motel while they waited for the police's verdict. Katie had felt so lonely.

Now, she was looking forward to getting back to the dorm after two weeks in Cocoa Beach. It hadn't quite been the spring break she had dreamt about, but it would still be remembered as something special, she thought to herself.

In the middle of all the chaos, she had somehow found herself. She had realized who she was. She wasn't someone who simply took crap from everyone else...at least not anymore.

Katie smiled when she thought about Britney's face when she had slammed her fist into her pretty nose in the restroom at Grill's restaurant that night. It had hurt like crazy on her knuckles, but it was worth all the pain. Just to get all the anger out that was threatening to burst inside of her. Just to feel the relief of justice being served to the BITCH.

Katie chuckled and spotted a dead armadillo on the side of the road. She had surprised even herself. She didn't know she had it in her. Neither did Britney, apparently. It had been such a thrill just to see the look on her face when Katie attacked her as she came out of her stall in the restroom. Katie had slammed her fist into Britney's porcelain-face again and again, and as she landed, her chin slammed into the toilet. Katie picked her up from the tiles, spat into her face, then slammed her fist into her over and over again till she stopped making sounds.

Katie knew she wasn't dead when she picked her up and carried her outside to the deck on the back side. It was late and there were only a few people left in the bar. No one saw her as she threw Britney over the rail, and no one heard the sound her body made as it plunged into the canal.

But Katie remembered. She remembered every little bit of it. Every sound, every feeling she had felt when giving Britney what she deserved.

Boy, it felt good.

It was even worth going to jail for. But, as it turned out, she didn't even have to do that. She was getting away with it. From now on, no one would ever mess with her again. She looked at her phone and at the picture of Greg she had as the background. Katie knew she had probably lost him. He had been so shaken up by Britney's murder that he hadn't spoken to anyone afterwards. Katie had seen him as he carried his suitcases to the van when the others were let go. He had looked at her with terror in his eyes. That's when she knew she wasn't going to see him again.

Katie opened the phone and deleted the photo. She also deleted Greg from her contacts. He wasn't worth her love anyway. She looked up at the landscape, when suddenly, her phone beeped. She had received a Snapchat. Katie opened it. It was a picture of Katie, taken just as she tossed the body over the railing at Grill's. Katie gasped. So someone had seen her after all? But who?

The picture was gone after a few seconds, and she would never see it again. At least, she hoped. Lucky for her, that's how Snapchat worked. It only lasted for ten seconds, then it was deleted automatically. So was any chat you ever wrote. She wrote back:

WHO IS THIS?

She received an answer and opened it with a pounding heart.

WE SHOULD TALK

Katie stared at the message till it disappeared. Her hands felt warm and clammy. Who was this person? Why hadn't they gone to the police with what they knew? She wrote back.

WHO ARE YOU?

She waited a few seconds before the answer came.

WE ARE THE ANGEL MAKERS. JUST LIKE YOU, WE FIGHT FOR JUSTICE. JOIN US.

Katie stared at her phone till the message was cleared again. She couldn't believe this. Somehow, they knew. Somehow, these people knew what she had done. She realized she didn't feel bad or even afraid. As a matter of fact, she never felt anxious or afraid anymore. Not since that night when she had taken matters into her own hands. She felt strong. Independent. She felt in control. Nothing and no one could touch her now. These people knew her name. They saw her and understood what she had done. She felt like she fit in somewhere. She was famous. Finally.

THE END

The House that Jack Built

JACK RYDER #3

This is the house that Jack built, y'all. Remember this house.

~ Aretha Franklin 1968

Prologue

THERE WAS A ROOM THAT WAS FILLED WITH LOVE

ONE

March 1986

"I'm scared a monster will come and take me, Mommy."

Carrie Kingston looked at her seven-year old son with a smile filled with love. It was the same every night when tucking Scott in for the night. He was afraid of the dark, of monsters in the closets or under the bed. The child had a vivid imagination. Sometimes that was a good thing, an excellent thing, his teacher in first grade told them, but just not when going to bed.

Scott suffered a lot from nightmares and almost every night he would wake up, walk down the hallway and climb into Carrie's bed. It was getting tiresome for Carrie and Scott's father, Jim, since they had to get up and get to work in the morning, and with Scott in the bed, they never slept that well. Carrie was okay with it for the most part. To be perfectly honest, she loved sleeping with her beloved son, but Jim couldn't stand it.

"It'll be fine," Carrie said and kissed her son's forehead, then stroked his red hair gently. How she adored those light blue eyes. Carrie had always wanted a son. She had always imagined having a baby boy. So, when she got pregnant the first time, she was certain it was a boy. It had to be. She was so sure she had bought only boy's clothing and boy's toys. What a disappointment it had been when Joanne came along. It had devastated Carrie, and for years they kept trying to have another child, but without success. Finally, when Joanne was six years old, Carrie had gotten her lifelong wish fulfilled. A little boy. A little adorable baby boy just like the one Carrie had seen in her dreams. And her love for him was so big she could hardly contain it. Carrie didn't mind admitting that Scott was the greatest love of her life. She loved him even more than she loved Joanne, even more than she loved her husband. Even more than she loved herself.

Scott stared at his mother, then at the door to the closet. "Are you sure? I thought I saw something just before."

Carrie chuckled. She tucked the blanket tightly around Scott to make him feel safer. Her mother had told her that's what she used to do when Carrie was afraid of monsters as a child.

"I'm very sure. Remember, monsters aren't real."

"They are to me," Scott said. "Very real. I see them every night, Mommy. They look at me through the window."

Carrie looked at the window. They had left it open because the AC was acting up again. It hadn't been able to cool the rooms down, especially not Scott's bedroom, for a week now. Carrie knew they needed to get it fixed, but she also knew they couldn't afford to have it done right now. Not when they had to have the truck fixed as well, and that was more important, since without the truck Jim couldn't get to work. He needed it. Besides, it was still early spring, so the heat hadn't gotten ahold of them just yet. There was a cooler breeze at night to cool them down. But it wouldn't last long. Soon, they would have to have that AC fixed or it would be unbearable. Living in Florida, you couldn't get by without the AC. It wasn't like Ohio, where Carrie was from originally. This was very different.

"Can we close it, Mom?" Scott asked with fear in his pretty blue eyes.

Carrie shook her head. "I don't think that would be very smart. It will be unbearable in here. You need the air to cool you down."

"But the monsters, Mom. They can crawl through the window."

Carrie sighed again. It was hot in Scott's room and she felt how clammy her son's hands were.

"The screen will stop them," she tried.

"No, it won't, Mommy."

Carrie shook her head. She was getting tired of this. "Stop with the monsters, Scott. There's no such thing."

"But…"

"No buts. They don't exist. They're not real. It's all in your mind," she said, stroking her son's cheek. "Now, go to sleep. You have a big day tomorrow, remember?"

Scott's face lit up. "The play," he said. He had been looking forward to doing the school play for weeks now. Scott loved the stage more than anyone else. He had landed the lead in the play because he was a natural on the stage and had received much praise from his teacher. It wasn't something that happened often.

"I can't wait," Scott said and closed his eyes. After a few seconds, he opened them again. "Could you close the door to the closet?"

Carrie got up from the edge of Scott's bed and walked to the closet door and closed it.

"There. Are you happy? No monsters can come in that way."

Scott nodded. A gust of wind came through the open window and grabbed the curtain. Scott gasped.

"It's just the wind," Carrie said. "Now, go to sleep."

Scott nodded and smiled. "Could you leave a light on, please?"

"If that makes you feel better," Carrie said, and turned on the small lamp in the corner of the room.

"It will. Thank you, Mommy."

Carrie smiled and kissed her son's forehead once again. "Now, sleep tight. There's nothing to be afraid of. This room is filled with nothing but love, and the Bible says love conquers all," she said and left the room.

TWO

March 1986

IT WAS the light that caught his eye and drew him closer. It was shining from the window into the front yard and lit up the night. He had been watching it for several nights in a row. It was always the same. The window was left open and the light shone through the thin curtains.

It was like it was luring him in, telling him to come closer.

So, he did. With his heart pounding in his chest, he walked to the house and peeked in the window through the screen...just like he had done the night before and the night before that.

And just like the other nights, the boy was lying in his bed, sound asleep. He watched the boy for a little while and enjoyed how innocent he looked. It was breathtaking. The man had always been so amazed at how a little boy like that could seem so harmless, so blameless, when they were anything but that.

Just sleeping like he hasn't a care in the world. Doesn't have the faintest idea of the evil lurking right outside his window. But, guess what, little friend? Evil is everywhere. Even in the ones you trust the most.

The boy moaned in his sleep and kicked off his blue blanket. He was feeling hot. His skin was glistering.

There was a rustle from a bush and the man turned to look, but didn't see anything. There wasn't a car in the street. It was all so quiet. He loved the nights. In the nights you could roam free; in the nights, no one watched.

The nights are more alive and more richly colored than the day.

The man thought about the quote by Van Gogh, which had been written on the walls in a toilet booth. He had memorized it because that was exactly how he felt. Come to think of it, that was how he had always felt. Even as a child, he would often wake up at night and stay up for hours. He liked the quietness of the house when everyone else was asleep. As a child, he would go to his brother's room and look at him while he was asleep. He would just stand there and imagine hurting him. He would grab a pillow and pretend to put it over his head and just hold it down till he didn't move anymore. Smother him like Caligula did to Tiberius to succeed him as a Roman Emperor. Stories like that had always fascinated the man. He had devoured everything about the Roman Empire they had taught him in school as a child.

The boy mumbled in his sleep now, and the man turned to look at him again. He turned to the side and groaned. His giraffe toy fell to the floor. The boy didn't notice.

The man looked at him and tilted his head to better see. He was smiling in his sleep now. Seeing him smile made the man lose it. He couldn't hold himself back any longer. He grabbed the screen and pulled it off the window, then he pulled the window up to make it completely open, and climbed inside the bedroom. He walked to the bed and leaned in over the little boy. Then he stroked him gently across the cheek.

"Having a nice dream, are we?" he whispered. "Enjoy. It'll be your last."

The sound of his voice close to his ear made the boy open his eyes. As he spotted the man, he opened his mouth in order to scream, but the man forced his hand over it and covered his nose as well. The small body tossed and turned underneath him. The boy's wild eyes stared at him in desperation. He held on to him till he passed out, then he let go. He waited a few seconds to make sure he was breathing before he lifted him up and carried him out the window and put the screen back on, before he carried the boy to his car.

He started the engine and took one last glance at the window where the light was still shining. He chuckled, thinking how ironic it was that the nightlight was supposed to keep the monsters away.

THREE

March 1986

"Scott? It's time to get up!"

Carrie walked inside her son's room and found the bed empty. She walked to the bed, then to the closet, and checked if Scott was in there getting dressed. But it was also empty.

The bathroom. He's probably in the bathroom. Of course. He's nervous about today and has been up for a long time. Now his stomach is acting up like it always does when he is nervous.

Carrie chuckled then walked to the bathroom door and knocked. "Honey? Are you in there?"

There was no answer. "Scott? Are you okay?"

When there still was no answer, Carrie opened the door that she had always instructed her son to not lock. Her heart dropped as she realized the bathroom was empty. She looked in the shower, just to be sure, but knew in her heart that Scott would never take a shower voluntarily.

"Scott?"

Carrie's voice was starting to tremble. She didn't like this. Unease was spreading through her body like wildfire.

Where is my son?

Carrie walked through the hallway into Joanne's room.

"I'm up, Mom. You don't have to check on me," she snarled.

"I wasn't checking on you, Joanne," she said to her always-angry teenage daughter. "I'm looking for Scott. Have you seen him?"

"He's not in here," she said. "The midget probably hid somewhere. He's so childish. What a dork."

Carrie chuckled. Of course that was just it. Scott loved to play hide and go seek, especially when they were in a hurry.

"Now go, Mom. I have to get ready for school," Joanne said.

Carrie shook her head and scoffed. *Teenage-girls these days.* They were so vain

405

and spent such a long time getting ready. When had that happened? It was just the times, she tried to explain to Jim, who didn't understand anything of his daughter's constant obsession with her own appearance. She was madly in love with Rob Lowe and wanted to look like Demi Moore and sing like that awful Madonna. When you had just turned thirteen like Joanne that was all there was.

"When I was her age, I worked from early in the morning," Jim would say. "At this time of day, I had fed the cows and the chickens and cleaned out the stables before I rode my bike three miles to get to school. And I didn't even have breakfast first."

Those were his stories, and they would grow more and more impressive each time he told them.

Jim was sitting in the kitchen with his coffee when Carrie came out to him. He grunted behind the newspaper.

"Have you seen Scott?" Carrie asked.

"No," Jim answered.

"I think he might be playing hide and go seek with me, and I don't have time for it this morning."

Jim looked at his watch. "Speaking of time," he said. "I gotta go. I'm late for the bus."

Carrie kissed Jim on the cheek, gave him his lunch, and watched as he rushed out the front door. She felt bad that he had to take the bus to work, but she needed the car to buy groceries and had to go to work all the way in Rockledge. She needed it more than him today.

We've got to get that truck fixed.

When he was gone, Carrie continued the search for her son.

"Scott, come on out now!" she yelled. "I give up. You win."

Still, she was met only by silence.

"I don't have time for this. Don't let me get angry with you."

When he still didn't show himself, Carrie started to pour cereal in his bowl, thinking maybe his hunger would lure him out. Joanne came out in the kitchen, grabbed some cereal for herself, and started to eat.

"I don't think he's here," Carrie said anxiously. "He never hides for this long."

Joanne shrugged. "Maybe he already went to school?"

Carrie lit up. "The play. Of course, that's it. He must have been so excited he couldn't wait for the rest of us to wake up. He probably rode his bike to school or something."

"His bike is still in the driveway," Joanne said, glancing out the window.

"Well, maybe he walked," Carrie said and put on her shoes, grabbed her car keys, and stormed out the door.

Part One

THIS WAS THE LAND THAT HE WORKED BY HAND

FOUR

May 2015

"ISN'T IT JUST PERFECT, KIDS?"

Shannon put her arm around my shoulder and looked at the kids. We had taken them to visit the lot where we were going to build our future house.

It had all gone through really fast. Once Shannon and I agreed that we wanted to buy the property, the deal went through within a few days. The lot had been vacant for many years, the real estate agent told us, and that was a shame when you thought about this wonderful oceanfront location.

I couldn't agree more. The lot was perfect for our purpose. There were still the remains of the old house that used to be on the property, but I was going to get that removed as soon as possible, and then start building our new house. The house that was going to belong to us, to our little family.

"What do you say, kids?" I asked and turned to look at the twins.

Abigail looked skeptical. "It doesn't look like much, Dad."

Always so honest. She was right. Right now it didn't look like anything...just the overgrown ruins of an old house that had been torn to pieces by a hurricane in 2005 and never rebuilt. It had been in the hands of the bank for a long time.

Until now. Now it was ours. Well, technically, it was Shannon's, since she had paid for it, but we had put my name on the deed as well, so I would feel like it was just as much mine. She was also going to pay for all the construction of the new house. Meanwhile, I had told her I would make the drawings and design it along with an architect we had hired. I would also supervise the construction as soon as it started.

"You don't have to," Shannon had said. "I can just pay someone to do it."

"No, this is the way I want it," I had argued. "You contribute with money, I with my hours. If this is supposed to feel like my house too, then I need to do this. I need it to be my house too. I want to build the house of my dreams."

She told me she understood and we never discussed it again.

"It might not look like much right now," I said, addressed to Abigail. "But

408

picture a house, a magnificent house with porches facing the beach, with a wooden stairwell that ends in the fine sand right when you step out of the house. Picture a living room with spectacular views, and picture a second floor with bedrooms overlooking the ocean as well."

Abigail closed her eyes. "It's hard to really picture it, Dad."

"I can see it," Austin said.

"So, you really think it's a great idea for all of us to move in together?" Emily grunted.

"We're all going to be a family soon," I said and held a hand to Shannon's stomach.

"What?" Emily asked with a frown.

The twins looked at us as well. We hadn't told them the news yet, and now was as good a time as ever.

"That's right," I said. "Shannon is pregnant. You'll have a new little brother or sister soon."

All four kids stared at us. Angela's eyes widened. "You're having a baby, Mom?" Then she let out a shriek of joy. "I'm going to be a big sister? I always wanted to be a big sister."

"It's not that big a deal," Abigail said and looked victoriously at her younger brother by fifty-eight seconds.

"You might be a big brother instead if it's a boy," Austin said, sounding very clever.

I couldn't hide my laughter. Neither could Shannon. I looked into her eyes, feeling such a deep love for her. For just one moment, while we all looked out on the roaring Atlantic Ocean in front of us, holding each other's hands, we all forgot everything else in our lives. All the troubles, all the worries were gone for just this short moment. I, for one, couldn't wait for all of us to be a family.

FIVE

Cuba 1959

SOME MOMENTS in your life you'll never forget. Hector Suarez had no idea today was one of those when he was sitting in his brother's restaurant in Havana with his girlfriend Veronica.

At the age of only fourteen, Hector didn't know much about politics or what was going on in his country. Born and raised on his parent's farm in Ternimo de Guanajay with nine brothers and one sister, Hector had always lived quietly and happily unaware of the impact a change in the political system could have on him and his family.

All he knew was that he liked Veronica, that he loved the Cuban sandwiches they were eating, and that he was wearing two different colored socks...one yellow and one black.

Hector took a sip of his beer and looked at the girl in front of him. Hector knew it was the woman he wanted to marry one day. He just knew it.

It was while taking the next bite of his sandwich that he heard the screaming. Loud voices in the street as someone ran inside the restaurant and started to yell:

"Castro is taking over! Castro is taking over!"

Not knowing what a life-changing event this was, Hector finished his food, grabbed Veronica by the hand, and escorted her home. He went to bed while his older brothers' loud voices were debating wildly in the living room with their father.

The next day at their Sunday dinner at the farm, where the family always gathered, the voices were still agitated. One of his brothers voiced his support of this new regime. Finally, their father ended the conversation with the single statement that Hector would end up remembering for the rest of his life.

"Government is no good."

That was it. His father had spoken and that ended all discussion and debate, much to his older brother's disappointment.

Just a few weeks later, Hector felt the wrath of this new government that they spoke so much of. His older brother Raul came to his room one night and woke him up. His face was sweating heavily and his eyes pierced with fear.

"Raul? What's going on?"

Raul sprang for the window and looked outside, then closed the curtains. He looked at Hector.

"I'm scared, Hector."

Hector sat up. Fear had not been a part of his life up until this day...only the fear of his father's wrath when he got himself into trouble. But this was different. This was a different kind of fear. It was deeper.

"What are you afraid of, Raul? What's going on?"

Raul sat on Hector's bed. "If I tell you this, will you promise to never ever tell father?"

It was a lot to ask. But with Hector, his loyalty to his brothers was always more important than his loyalty to his parents. It had always been like that for him.

"Of course. What's going on? Talk to me, Raul."

"I'm in trouble. I have done something. I need your help," Raul said.

"What did you do?"

"I helped two men get out of here. I helped them get into the Mexican Embassy," Raul said. "They got arrested. They'll tell them my name. I just know they will. They'll come for me. They'll arrest me too."

Hector didn't know much about politics or government, but he did know what his father thought of this new government and he did know when a brother was in trouble he needed to help him.

The next day, he dressed Raul up in some of his mother's clothing and smuggled him out of Havana in the back of his father's truck. As he left him with his friends in a small town where he could hide in an attic above a pharmacy, Hector shed a tear, wondering if he would ever see him again.

SIX

May 2015

_____

"So, are you excited?"

Kristi looked at Shannon above her steaming cup of coffee. Shannon smiled and nodded. Yes, she was excited about buying this lot and finally settling down in Cocoa Beach. Since Joe was gone now, there wasn't any reason for her to go back to Nashville.

"I am," she said. "I'm very excited about everything. The house, the baby...it's all happening."

"Why do I detect a slight bit of worry in your voice?" Kristi asked.

A guy came out from inside the restaurant and placed their sandwiches in front of them. He looked shyly at Shannon. She was used to that. Cocoa Beach still hadn't gotten used to having her around. It was getting better, though, and lately she had been able to walk around freely in town, especially since the reporters left. She hoped they would stay away. She and Angela needed all the peace and quiet they could get.

"I am worried," she said and took a bite of the sandwich. "How can I not be?"

Kristi sipped her coffee, then emptied it, and started her sandwich. It had become a regular thing for the sisters to meet at Juice N' Java for coffee and sandwiches on Monday mornings when Kristi was off from work. Shannon enjoyed it. She loved having her sister in her life again.

"I'm sure they'll find the gun," Kristi said. "It'll all blow over eventually. Just give it time."

Shannon felt tears pressing behind her eyes. She held them back. She couldn't stand this pressure that was put on her, especially not now that she was hormonal because of the pregnancy and everything. The police in Nashville threatened to charge her with murder of an old friend, Robert Hill. Her ex-husband Joe had left a letter when he died, stating she killed him by beating him to death with a microphone stand, when it was, in fact, him. She had only hit him the first time when he aimed that gun at them and told them he would kill Joe to be with Shannon

412

because he was madly in love with her. Robert Hill had written songs for her first album, songs that had given her a breakthrough as an artist. Now the entire world believed she had stolen the songs, even though Robert Hill told her she could publish them without using his name. Now she risked going to jail over what Joe had done. If only they could find the gun he had held in his hand on that night. The police had told her that would make them believe her story. But they still hadn't, and it ate her up.

"What if they don't?" she asked. "What if they don't find the gun? It's the only evidence I have to let them know it was self-defense...that I didn't mean to kill Robert Hill. They already believe I stole his songs for my first album, when in reality he gave them to me. He didn't want his name on them."

"And, still, you put his name on them now. You did the right thing to change that, to make sure his legacy remains. It pleased his family a lot that you changed it. Nobody wants to see you in jail, Shannon. I mean, who would sing for us? The whole world loves you."

"Not everyone," Shannon said. She hated to feel this emotional, but it was hard not to. The doctor had told her to relax and be sure not to worry. It would affect the child, but it was so hard when facing a murder trial. What was going to become of the baby if she had to do time? She could get life for this. Would she even see her baby grow up? And what about Angela?

Shannon felt her blood pressure elevate quickly. Kristi saw it on her face and put a hand over hers.

"You have to relax. You can't get upset like this anymore," she said. "You have some of the best lawyers in the country working for you. It'll be fine."

"I just wish they would get it over with. I hate the waiting, you know?"

"But you have to go through it. It could take months, maybe even a year before we know what will happen. You have to trust that everything will turn out fine, and then focus on the baby and your new life. Can't you immerse yourself in your music? That used to make you forget about everything else, like the time I graduated and you forgot to show up at my party because you were so caught up in your music, remember?"

Shannon laughed. She did remember. Vividly. Especially how Kristi had yelled at her afterwards. Back then, she hadn't understood why she was so upset. Now, she did. She understood that this was what she had always done to her sisters throughout their lives together. She had taken the spotlight and been too caught up in herself to celebrate their victories.

"I know. I have been writing a lot lately. The hormones have set off the emotional side of me, and the trial too, of course, and maybe the falling in love with Jack. I've said yes to doing a couple of concerts this month. I need to get out there and feel the love of my audience again."

"That sounds good. How does Jack feel about it?" Kristi asked.

"He knows how much my work means to me. He loves his job too and gets caught up in it. In that way, we're much alike. We both have a lot of passion for our work. Luckily, his parents are always there to take the kids if needed."

"Angela is always welcome at my house too, if you ever need it," Kristi said.

"I know," Shannon said.

"So, when do you start building the house?" Kristi asked, finishing the rest of her sandwich.

"As soon as the lot is cleared. There are remains from some old house that was taken down in a hurricane years ago. We need that removed. We should be ready to start in a few weeks. Jack is all excited. He wants this to be perfect."

"I'm sure it will be," Kristi said.

Shannon smiled. Her sister was right. Jack would make it just perfect. If only Shannon could be certain she would be around to enjoy it.

SEVEN

May 2015

We were still trying to track down the last two Monahan sisters, the murderous sisters who called themselves the Angel Makers. They had murdered so many people thinking they were getting the world rid of child molesters and abusers. They had been four in total when they started out, one had died in the Bahamas, and another, Sarah Millman had been arrested, but released on bail. She was being kept under constant observation by us in the hope she would try to contact her two other sisters or they would contact her somehow.

But the trail was getting colder and colder. Meanwhile, Sarah Millman was awaiting her trial. I was trying to get her convicted of killing her husband first. Then her involvement in the other cases would come later. I had given all my evidence to the State's Attorney, Jacquelyn Jones, and hoped she would be able to make a case against her. Sarah Millman and her lawyer had already declared that she was mentally unstable and drugged at the time of the murder, and handed us an evaluation of her mental health. I knew this was going to be a hard nut to crack. But I hadn't lost hope yet. Neither had I lost hope that I would find the two other sisters, Angelina and Kelly Monahan. We had sent out a nationwide search, and so far the trail of Angelina ended in North Carolina, where she was seen two weeks ago at a restaurant. We were almost certain it was her.

I pushed the files aside on my desk and looked at the screen of my computer. I was fed up with this case and couldn't stop thinking about the house. It was all that was on my mind lately. My dream house. I opened an email from the architect and looked at the floor plan he had made so far. I liked it, but had a few changes I wanted to make, so I wrote him back.

When I had sent it, someone entered the room. It was Beth. It was her first day back at the Sheriff's office after the explosion that left her burned on a big part of her body. I smiled when I saw her. Everyone in the room stood up and started clapping. She limped heavily when she walked, but she held her head high.

"Ah, come on," she said as she moved to her desk and saw all the flowers. "I didn't die, you know. This looks like a damn funeral home."

I handed her a card that we had all signed. "From all of us."

Beth snorted and opened it. It was a gift card to a spa treatment. Beth burst into violent laughter. "A spa? Me? That's a good one."

"Well, we thought you could use a day off to treat yourself a little," Ron said. "I am giving you any day off you want to go. Just let me know."

Beth looked at him like she didn't believe him. Then she shook her head. She scoffed, but I could tell she was moved.

"What are you all just standing here for?" she asked. "We got ourselves some female killers to catch, right Ryder? Where are we on that?"

I chuckled and sat down. Everyone returned to their desks. Ron had wanted to buy a cake and everything, but I had told him Beth didn't want any of that. She wanted everything to go back to the way it was. I had visited her every week at the hospital while she was there. That was what she had told me every time I came. I could at least give her that.

"So, how are the kids?" Beth asked.

"Good. They're all good, thanks."

"And the stomach is growing, I take it?"

I smiled at the thought. "Not much yet, but it will be. She is throwing up a lot, though. Not just in the mornings, but all day."

"Then, everything is as it should be," she said.

"It is. And everything is in place with the lot. It is ours and as soon as it is cleared, we start building."

"That sure sounds good, Ryder. Now, where are we on catching the Monahan sisters? Fill me in. I want to nail those murderous women."

I couldn't blame her. The explosion they had caused had burned Beth's face, so the doctors had to transplant skin from her thigh to her face. Beth was never going to look the same again. I fully understood her anger. I think we all did.

EIGHT

May 2015

VERNON WAS BROUGHT into the courtroom wearing his orange suit and handcuffs. His belly-chains rattled as he walked, his heart in his throat like so many times before when he had appealed his case.

The judge looking at him from above her glasses knew him all too well.

"Mr. Johnson," she said, addressed to him, after they had sat down.

A tear left his right eye and rolled across his cheek. This was it. This was the moment of truth.

"Your name and the history of your case have been with me since I started this job. Now, twenty-eight years later, here we are again. New evidence has come to the light of day. A vital testimony has been recanted, and this clearly undermines the confidence the public might have had in the verdict that was previously rendered."

The words leaving judge Brydon's mouth resulted in a loud outburst from the spectators in the seats behind Vernon. He couldn't stop his tears from rolling and turned to look at his mother's face. She too was crying.

Then followed the words he had been waiting to hear for twenty-eight years.

"You're a free man, Mr. Johnson."

Vernon sobbed and looked at his lawyer from the Innocence-Project of Florida. This guy had fought his case since he was an intern. Now, he was a senior partner in the firm. He too shed a few tears and shook Vernon's hand.

"You did it, Vernon."

"No. You did it. Thank you. Thank you for believing in me."

A few hours later, Vernon had gathered his belongings and left the cell that had been his home for the biggest part of his life, since he was only twenty-eight years old. Now he was fifty-six, and one of the few to leave death row alive.

What had gotten him this far? Hope. The undying hope that they would sort it out. He had believed they would. He simply refused to lose confidence that they would. When they had taken him in and asked him all those questions, he knew they had made a mistake and believed they would eventually find out. Even when they had been in the courtroom and the verdict had been stated, he believed it. On the bus ride to the prison, even when they gave him that suit, the one with the rear stripe on it that only inmates on death row wear, even then he had thought: *They'll figure out the truth. They're gonna straighten it all out. Someone will tell them they got it all wrong.* Like they did in the Perry Mason TV shows. Someone would soon yell: *Stop, he didn't do it!*

Even when he walked the long catwalk to his cell with his hands cuffed, he believed there was still hope. It wasn't until they had closed the door and left him alone that it finally occurred to him.

This could be your last stop. This could be where it will all end. They might kill you here. Kill you for nothing.

But still, he had kept the hope. Even if it decreased as time went by. He had appealed his case many times and, finally, after eight years, they had changed it from death row to life in prison, since the body had never been found, but that hadn't been enough for Vernon. He wanted to be cleared of all charges. He wanted to be a free man. He knew he deserved to be. He knew he was innocent and he was determined to prove it.

Now it had happened. It had finally happened, he thought to himself as the glass doors opened and he walked outside in front of the TV cameras and photographers and people with microphones asking him *how he felt.*

"Unbelievable," he said, "It's simply unbelievable." Vernon grabbed his mother and hugged her so tight. Her small body was whimpering and hollering in his arms and he held her, feeling like never letting go again.

"I knew they would realize your innocence sooner or later," she said through the tears. Microphones were pushed in her face as they started to walk out. Vernon's arm was solidly planted on her fragile shoulders, tears gushing across his cheeks.

"Do you feel anger?" a reporter asked.

Vernon shook his head. "Right now, I just want to go home."

All the reporters burst into a laughter, but his mother didn't. She looked into the camera and pointed her finger at it.

"I do have one thing I want to say," she said. "Vernon had twenty-eight years taken from him. An entire lifetime. Meanwhile, the real killer is out there somewhere. He got to live his life, while my Vernon was held in here for something that other person did." She paused for effect. "So, if you're watching this, better get ready. Your time is up. It's time to pay your dues."

NINE

May 2015
———————

ON MY WAY HOME, I stopped by at Swell Surf shop across the street from my parents' motel.

"How's my baby coming along?" I asked as I entered.

The owner smiled. "It's coming along great," he said. "I'm done shaping it and have made an appointment for the glassing. All I need is to do the paint job."

"Ah, I can't wait to take her into the waves. And you'll do the rainbow colors as I asked?"

The owner shrugged. "It's your board."

"Great," I said and smiled. I wanted my new board to be colorful. "So, when do you think it'll be done?"

"Two weeks time."

"Perfect," I said on my way out the door. "If it turns out to be a good board, it might not be the last I buy from you."

The owner smiled. I was glad to be able to help him out a little. I knew his shop was struggling. He had been asking me for months to let him shape a board for me. He surfed with the rest of us at my parents' break often. I thought it was a good idea to support one of the locals.

The entire family met up at my parents' motel for dinner, as usual, sitting out on the deck overlooking the beach. Abigail and Austin told us everything about their day at school, while my parents complained that times were slow at the motel. They were always slow at this time of year, I told them.

Shannon seemed pensive while everyone else was caught up in the talk, and I looked at her for a little while without her noticing it. I liked to look at her. It made me so happy inside. I loved that she had put on a little weight and her cheeks were fuller now. It gave her a cute look. We hadn't told the press the news yet, but it wouldn't be long before they noticed, and then they were going to be all over it. I was enjoying this moment before hell broke loose again. I just hoped they weren't going to occupy our building like they did last time. It would all be better once we had our own house and property that they weren't allowed onto. A big fence surrounding the property would keep their noses out.

I could tell Shannon was worried, and I knew why. I called my colleagues in Nashville almost every day, asking them for news on her case, but so far, no luck. All they needed was to find that damn gun and then it would be all over. But, so far, they had dug out the entire backyard where the body was found and they hadn't found anything yet.

It was driving me crazy.

Shannon was innocent. She wasn't even the one who killed the guy; Joe was. But he was gone, and we had to provide them with something to make them believe what she said. The gun, preferably with Robert Hill's fingerprints all over it, would do just that. It would show them Shannon was telling the truth.

"So, Angela, how was your day today?" I asked, to try and involve her a little in the conversation. My kids always spoke so loudly and dominated the entire conversation so that no one ever heard what Angela had to say. I wanted her to feel at home. This was, after all, her new family.

"Good," she said and blushed a little.

"We saw her at recess," Abigail said.

"Yeah, we played the shark-game," Austin said.

"Did you, now? Well, that sounds like fun," I said, as my eyes met Shannon's. She forced a smile through her worry.

"Did anything exciting happen at your job today, Dad?" Austin asked. He always hoped I had caught some bad guys or maybe been in a car chase. For some reason, he thought that was all I did.

"Not really. Beth came back," I said.

"That's good," my mom said. "She is a fighter, that girl. I tell you. Just like her mom was."

My mother was born and raised in Cocoa Beach and knew about everybody around there.

"She sure is," I said and ate more of my fish taco. A set of waves was rolling in on the beach now, and I couldn't wait to go out after dinner for a little sunset surfing. If I was lucky, I could get a good hour in. The kids were planning on playing volleyball on the beach with my parents. Shannon said she wanted to work on her new song.

They were all good plans for a nice Monday night, but as it often is with plans, they tend to change. And so they did this evening when my phone rang in my pocket. I was inclined to not pick it up, but when I saw whom it was, I knew there was no way I could ignore it. It was Sheriff Ron.

"Ryder. Whatever you're up to, stop it. You're needed down in Sebastian. Pick up Beth on your way."

TEN

May 2015

THE SUN HAD ALMOST SET when we arrived at Sebastian Inlet, thirty-four miles south of Cocoa Beach. Beth seemed tired and I wondered if she had come back to work too early after the procedure. I also wondered if she was all right or if she was afraid. Last time she was called out, she had almost lost her life. I knew she had to be feeling something, but I also knew she would never admit to it. That was just the way she was.

"So, what do we have?" I asked, when we got out and Ron greeted us at the scene. We had been called out to a construction site where they were demolishing an old condominium building to build a new and bigger one.

"Construction workers stumbled over it around four this afternoon. They weren't sure what it was, so they called for their supervisor. He called us right away."

The scene was already packed with police, medical examiners, and technicians combing through the area in their blue suits. Ron led Beth and me to an area where something had been spread on a white sheet. I knew right away what it was. I said hello to Yamilla Díez from the ME's office.

"The workers found this small pile of bones," she said. "Our guys found the skull."

I kneeled next to it and looked at it thoroughly. "Looks old," I said.

"It is," Yamilla said. "There is nothing left except the bone. No clothing, no hair, no nails, nothing."

"Well, the building was built in nineteen ninety-three," Ron said.

"It could have been buried here before that," I said.

Ron nodded and looked around. One of the technicians brought in more bones and put them on the sheet. Yamilla went over to them immediately and began trying to put together the skeleton. It was starting to look like a person.

"It doesn't look like it was an adult," I said, when looking at the femur.

Yamilla shook her head. "No."

421

"A child?" Ron said.

I shook my head. "No. It's too long to be a child. I'm guessing a teenager." I looked at Yamilla, who nodded again.

"That's more likely. But a young one. Not fully grown, so no older than fourteen, I'm guessing. We'll know more once I get him to the lab."

"It's a he?" Ron asked.

"Yes," Yamilla said. "This is, of course, only based on my assumptions. Later examination will determine if I am correct. But a common way in which you might differentiate between male and female is quite simply bone size. This, of course, is not always accurate, but for the most part male bones are larger in size than female bones and are that way because of the additional muscle that may build up on the male body through adolescence and into adulthood. The pelvic area is another good way of differentiating between the sexes. A female will have a larger sub-pubic angle than that of a man, and this is obviously indicative of child bearing requirements in the female that are not required in the male of the species. This difference is noticeable across all species in nature, where birth is from the womb. The male's sub-pubic area is less than ninety degrees whilst the female's is more. The area around the pelvic inlet—in the middle of the pelvic bone—is larger in females than in men, again with relevance to child bearing."

I stared at the human remains that were starting to shape into a real person in front of me. A person who once had a life, a mom and a dad, a school, and friends. It was all just about to begin when it had somehow ended so abruptly. As I looked at the bones on the sheet, something struck me as off.

"What's wrong with the back?" I asked.

Yamilla looked at me. "I've been wondering about that too," she said. "I keep thinking I might have put it together wrong or that some parts are missing."

"What is it?" Beth asked.

"The spine," I said. "It's curved. Like he suffered from spinal stenosis, something you usually see in older people."

ELEVEN

May 2015

IT FELT strange being on the outside. It was nothing like Vernon had expected it to be. It was funny, he thought to himself while sitting on the couch in his mother's small condo in Rockledge; it was funny how many times he had imagined how life would be on the other side, what things would look like, what life would be like, and now that he was out, he had to realize it was nothing like anything he had pictured.

The day after he was released, they had driven back to their old neighborhood, back to where they used to live, and everything was so changed. It used to be old worn-out houses, and some of them you could barely call shacks. Now, it was all brand-new cookie-cutter houses with two car-garages and pools. Even the house Vernon used to live in with his mother had been torn down and another had been built there in its place. Children were playing in the street and all the front yards looked well maintained.

It was nothing like the neighborhood he had grown up in. Nothing.

They had cruised down to the beach at Vernon's request, and they had walked with bare feet in the sand like he had dreamt of so many times while in prison. He had felt the water on his feet and shins and closed his eyes and breathed in the fresh ocean air. The beach looked a lot like it used to, except for the many condominiums that had been built since Vernon was last there. The old motel was still there, though.

"So, what are you going to do today?" his mother asked on her way out. She worked at the Publix, packing grocery bags.

Vernon smoked his cigarette and shrugged. In front of him was a big flat-screen TV that he had bought for his mother the day before. TV he knew from the inside. It was familiar to him. It felt like home.

"I think I'm just going to sit here for a little while," he said.

His mother nodded and sighed, then walked to the front door and left. He knew she didn't want him to just sit there and stare at the TV all day, but right now, it was all he knew how to do. He liked to look out the window at the blue sky, but walking around out there was a little intimidating. It was like it was too overwhelming for him. Like the fact that his space was no longer limited frightened him somehow. It made him feel unsafe and insecure. Inside in the living room in front of the TV with a cigarette in his hand, he felt safe. He felt at home. Out there in the world, there was too much noise, too much turmoil. When he went for a coffee at Starbucks one of the first days out, he had seen nothing but people staring at their phones or computers. Nobody talked anymore. It was like anything you needed to say to someone could be contained in a text message. Vernon didn't like it. He liked looking into people's eyes. He didn't like the coffee either. It was nothing like the coffee he was used to. He had bought himself a burger he really liked, though. That was something he had missed on the inside. A really good burger.

They had paid him a million dollars in replacement for wrongly incarcerating him. That meant Vernon didn't have to work for the rest of his life. Neither did his mom, but she wouldn't hear of it.

"Any honest man or woman should work if they can," she said.

Vernon had a feeling she enjoyed her job too much to let it go. That was the only explanation he could think of for her rejecting his proposal to support her for the rest of her life. He could easily do that with this kind of money. The condo she lived in was cheap, and they didn't have many expenses. But living a life without having anywhere to go every morning after working your entire life wasn't his mother's idea of a great life.

"And do what all day, do you propose? Stay here with you and watch TV? No, thank you."

She liked that she was needed. She liked having a purpose, something to do. He respected that. Now, Vernon had bought the TV he had always wanted, he had eaten the burger, and had put his feet in the ocean. Now, what was he supposed to do with himself? He had no idea.

Except there was one thing he had dreamt about doing for every day of the twenty-eight years in prison. There was one person he had dreamt of seeing again.

TWELVE

Cuba 1969

Ten years after his brother ran away, Hector Suarez still hadn't seen Raul again. The family mourned the loss of one of their sons, and especially Hector's mom took it hard. Two years passed without a word from him until one day when they heard the rumor that he had been moved to another village after having been hidden in the attic while the police searched for him and his face was on matchboxes all over the country.

A year later, Hector heard his brother had been moved to yet another village, and later smuggled out of the country and managed to make it into the U.S. Where he was today was uncertain, but Hector had a feeling he was somewhere safe. And soon after he heard about his brother making it to the U.S., Hector started dreaming about following in his footsteps. He too wanted to get away and provide a better life for his family.

Veronica and he married when they turned eighteen, and soon after she was pregnant with their daughter, Isabella. Isabella was the love of Hector's life, especially after Veronica died. She became sick only a year after the birth of their daughter and never recovered. Now, Hector was alone with his daughter and dreaming of a better life for her. The government had taken his father's farm and their family was poor now. Two more of Hector's older brothers soon did what Raul had done and escaped to the U.S., where they believed a better future awaited them. They all dreamt of the land with streets of gold.

Hector was determined to follow them. Only, he had a daughter, and he was scared of what would happen to her there. He had no idea what life would be like for a little girl, and mostly he was afraid of the trip there. Would it be safe to bring her along? He wasn't sure.

In 1965, Hector decided he was ready to make his own journey to the United States. He forged a birth certificate, since he was only twenty-two years old, and men between the age of fifteen and twenty-five weren't allowed to leave the country. To earn his visa, he was forced by the government to work in the sugar cane fields. There he was, working along with lawyers and doctors, all of them trying to earn their visa to go to the Promised Land. While working the fields, Hector's hatred towards the government and the dreams of a better future increased rapidly. When he lay in his tent at night in the camps where they slept, he would remind himself over and over again that it would come one day, soon. The dream wasn't far away. While working in the fields, Hector only saw his daughter once a month.

As the years passed, he started to wonder if it was worth it...if he would ever get the visa. There was a lot of tension in the country, and the stories of people who tried to get away, but were incarcerated or killed instead were many. Yet, he didn't feel there was any future for him in Cuba anymore, and especially not for his daughter. They weren't told how long they had to work the sugar cane fields in order to gain the visa, and Hector was beginning to wonder if they would ever get it.

Until one morning, after four years in the fields, when his foreman came up to him. Hector was sweating heavily in the heat and his hands were bloody from the hard labor. The foreman looked at him with a disgusted look, then said the words Hector would never forget for the rest of his life.

"Suarez. You're done here. You can leave Cuba."

Hector decided to leave Isabella with her grandmother until Hector had found his brothers and gotten a job to be able to provide for her. She was too young to endure this travel and their future in the U.S. too uncertain. He would have to send for her.

The very next day, Hector was put on an airplane by three of Castro's soldiers. Right when they let him go, one of them stopped him and said:

"If you ever come back to Cuba, we will shoot you."

THIRTEEN

May 2015

"I have an ID."

Yamilla sounded excited on the other end of the line. I shared her enthusiasm. A week had passed, and we still had no idea who this little boy who was found on the construction site in Sebastian was. It had been driving me nuts. I had been going through old cases of missing teenagers in the beginning of the eighties for days, but had come up with no results.

"Finally. Who was he?"

"It was the teeth that gave him away. Dental records show me this is the body of Scott Kingston, who, according to the file, disappeared from his home in Cocoa Beach in 1986."

"1986?" I repeated and noted the name. "That's a lot earlier than we expected."

"And he was a lot younger when he disappeared," Yamilla said. "Only seven, according to our records. His dental records were only a match on the two front teeth. The rest had fallen out and new ones grown in."

"So, you're telling me he wasn't killed in 1986?" I asked.

"No, definitely not. This boy we found was older. I'm guessing thirteen or fourteen years old. He had developed all of his permanent teeth."

"So, he lived several years after he disappeared, then," I said, and wrote everything down.

"That's safe to say, yes," Yamilla said.

"Thank you."

I hung up and went into Ron's office. He was on the phone, but finished his call when he saw me.

"What's up, Ryder?" he asked.

"We got an ID on the boy."

"Finally," he exclaimed.

"His name was Scott Kingston, disappeared from his home in..."

"Scott Kingston?" Ron said very loudly. "*The* Scott Kingston?"

"I take it you know more than I do," I said, and sat in the chair.

Ron drew in air between his teeth. "It's one of the greatest mysteries in our district. The little boy was taken from his house in the early morning hours while he was asleep and simply vanished. Later, a guy was convicted of having kidnapped and killed him, but the body was never found."

"How was he convicted if there wasn't a body?"

"I believe there was a witness or something. Someone saw him, but you might want to look into that. Come to think of it..." Ron went through his pile of papers on his desk and pulled out a newspaper.

"Here." He showed me an article in *Florida Today*. He pointed at the picture of a guy in the arms of his mother under the headline "A Free Man: Vernon Johnson to leave prison 28 years after a lie helped put him behind bars."

I remembered reading about this guy.

"Vernon Johnson here was just released about a week ago, after spending twenty-eight years behind bars for killing Scott Kingston in 1986," Ron said. "He was convicted in 1987."

"But, wrongly? It says here the witness recently admitted to having lied about seeing Vernon Johnson with the boy. The witness was a paperboy and doing his early morning rounds at five o'clock, when he saw Vernon Johnson carrying the boy to his car in front of the Kingston's house. The witness, a boy who was only sixteen at the time he gave his testimony, is now terminally ill, and told a priest recently that he had never been sure that it was Vernon he saw back then, even though he told the police he was certain. The priest then convinced him to tell the police the truth. He told them he had felt coerced by the police to testify that he was certain it was Vernon Johnson he saw, when he had his doubts." I looked at Ron and put the paper down. "So, they based the entire case on a sixteen-year-old's testimony? They took twenty-eight years of a man's life just like that? That's crazy."

"I know. Times were different back then. But, once the boy came forward and told them he wasn't certain and never had been, that was when the Florida Innocence Project took up Johnson's case again and went through the evidence. It was all only based on that one eyewitness testimony. The judge had no other choice than to let the guy go."

I looked up at Ron. "And now we have the body? The body of this boy that apparently was still alive for several years before someone buried him at the construction site of the new condominiums."

"Looks like we just blew the case wide open," Ron said. "And it's all yours."

FOURTEEN

May 2015

Noah loved his new room. It was painted light blue the way he preferred it. Noah was a real boy. His favorite toys had always been trucks and cars and his favorite place to go for his birthday was the airport to watch the planes take off and land.

His mother and father gleamed with pride as they looked at him standing in his new room with pictures of trucks on the walls.

"Do you like it?" his mother asked.

"I looove it!" Noah said, turned, and hugged his mother's legs. "Thank you, thank you, thank you."

Then he threw himself in the beanbag in the middle of the room and just laughed. The bed was the best part, he thought. It was shaped like Lightning McQueen from the movie *Cars* and had a steering wheel and everything.

"We're glad you like it, son," Noah's dad said. "Your mother and I spent many hours painting it, and especially your mother spent a lot of time decorating it. We want you to feel at home in our new house."

"We know it's been hard on you with the move and everything," his mother said, and looked at her husband who nodded. "I mean, with the change of school and everything. Hopefully, this will help make it easier."

Noah grabbed one of his monster trucks. When his parents left, he found another truck and let them smash into each other with a loud noise.

Noah played with his trucks, and soon he was lost in time and space, and forgot everything about the fact that he missed his old friends at his old school on Merritt Island. It was the first time Noah didn't feel sad being in the new house in Cocoa Beach. Since they had moved there two weeks ago, he had hated every moment spent in it and every moment he spent in the new school, where the teachers seemed to correct everything he did.

Noah set up train track and began rolling trains across it. He grabbed a sword and pretended he was a zombie-fighter and started fighting his toy elephant and tiger.

"Ha! Take that, Evil Ely Elephant," he said, stabbing it with the sword.

"And you too, Tiny Tiger!" he yelled and stabbed the tiger in the stomach as well, causing it to fall backwards.

"Ha!"

"Don't you know that zombie-tigers can only be killed with a light saber?" A strange voice asked.

Noah gasped, then turned to face the open sliding door. Behind the screen, a set of brown eyes were staring at him. The man smiled. Noah remembered having seen him before and wondered if he was one of the neighbors.

"You do have a light saber, don't you?" the man asked.

Noah bit his lip, then shook his head.

The man lifted up a black sword, just like the one Robert from his class had. The one he had brought to school once and everyone had admired. The one Robert had never let Noah touch. Noah gasped again.

"May I join you?" the man asked.

Noah looked back at the closed door leading to the hallway and the rest of the house where his parents were. Would they mind? The man did seem awfully nice and he had brought his own sword. Maybe he would even let Noah use the sword?

He turned and looked at the man, then nodded. "Sure."

FIFTEEN

May 2015

"HE REALLY LOVES his new room, huh?"

Steven Kinley looked at his wife, Lauren. "We haven't heard a sound from him in hours. He must be having a great time."

"I'm so happy," Lauren said. "It was all worth it. Did you see his face? It was priceless."

Lauren looked through the hallway at the closed door at the end of it. It was a relief for the both of them to finally see their son with a smile on his face.

The move from Merritt Island to Cocoa Beach had been hard on all of them, but mostly on Noah. He had no siblings, so his friends were his everything, and back at their house on Merritt Island they had lived at a cul-de-sac where both neighbors had kids that he played so well with. Where they lived now, their neighbors were elderly people, who didn't care much about children. The house was much nicer and it was better for Steven to be closer to his job at City Hall in Cocoa Beach. Plus, it was a better school, they believed. It was better for Noah in the long run, but that was hard to see when you were only eight years old and had to leave all of your best friends.

"So, should I start making dinner?" Lauren said and looked at the paperwork in front of her. As the director of Minutemen Preschool, she always had a ton of work to do.

"That would be wonderful," Steven said. "I, for one, am starving."

Lauren put the chicken in the oven, then chopped up some vegetables, and roasted them in the pan. She kept wondering about Noah and how much this move had affected him. She deeply hoped it wasn't a mistake. Noah had seemed a little depressed lately and didn't like his school at all. The teacher had more than once had to call Lauren to let her know Noah wasn't behaving well in class. It wasn't like him to act like this. They did have a lot of tests, Lauren thought, and it made Noah constantly anxious. There had been more than one time he had to stay home from school because of a stomachache. It worried Lauren, while Steven kept telling her it would pass, that Noah simply needed time to adjust to his new reality. He hadn't made any friends in his class yet, and Lauren had started to wonder if he ever would. What if nobody liked him? What if the teacher was mean to him? Was that why he was constantly having nightmares?

Lauren shook the thought and set the table. No, everything was going to settle soon, and then they would be very happy here in their canal-front house. There were so many fun things for them to do here. They could go kayaking or paddle boarding, or he could fish with his father. They even had a pool now, and Lauren knew how much Noah had wanted that while they lived at Merritt Island. He had been begging for one for years. Now that they finally had one, he hardly used it. Well, at least not yet. Maybe he would, later on, when he was more settled in.

It'll come. It'll come. Just give it time.

"Dinner is ready," Lauren said, addressed to Steven, who had his nose buried in his iPad. Probably playing Candy Crush, she thought to herself and walked towards Noah's room.

She knocked on the door. "Noah? Dinner's ready. Come and eat."

There was no answer, and Lauren figured Noah was simply too deeply buried in his playing to answer. She was certain he had heard her and returned to the kitchen to get the chicken out and start cutting it. When Noah still hadn't come out, she looked to Steven, a bad feeling starting to nag at her from the inside. She decided to ignore it. It was silly.

"I'm kind of busy here, could you?" she said.

"I will," he said, slightly annoyed, then walked to the door and knocked. "Noah. Your mom said it was time to eat." He grabbed the handle and walked inside. "Noah?" he called. "Noah!?"

Whether it was the fearful pitch to his voice or simply an awful premonition inside of Lauren that made her drop the plate with the chicken on the tiles, she never knew. But she did know why she started to scream as she entered her son's room to find it empty, then ran into the yard, screaming his name in anguish and terror.

Because that was the only thing she could do. That was the only thing anyone could do when their worst nightmare suddenly was realized.

SIXTEEN

May 2015

WHEN SOMEONE LOSES a child and never knows what happened to him, something happens to them, something indescribable. You can see it in their face, in their glassy eyes. It's like they're in this constant haze, like they're not really living and not really dead. I had seen it before, and now I was staring right at it again.

"Carrie Kingston?" I asked, looking at the woman in the doorway. My first impression was that she didn't look at all like herself, like the woman I had seen in the old newspaper clips from 1986, or in the recent articles written about her when the man who was imprisoned for the kidnapping of her son had been freed a few weeks ago.

"I feel awful about the whole thing," she was quoted saying. "All this time, I thought they caught the guy, and now it turns out that he didn't do it."

Mrs. Carrie Kingston was thinner now, a lot thinner. Her eyes were dark with hollowed sockets. Her skin colorless. Gray wasn't a word that fully covered it.

"Yes?" she asked hardly looking at me.

"Detective Jack Ryder, Brevard County Sheriff's Office. This is my partner Beth. May we come in, please?"

"Naturally," she said and let us in. She moved as if she was in slow motion.

We sat down in the kitchen. The house in Palm Bay was neat and clean, but smelled stuffy and confirmed my suspicion that Carrie Kingston didn't go out much. According to our research, the Kingstons had moved away from Cocoa Beach two years after their son disappeared. They were both retired now, while their oldest daughter lived up north.

"Where is your husband?" I asked when I sat down.

She looked at the clock on the wall. "He's out golfing. He should be here any minute now."

I looked at Beth. "We'll wait for him, then."

"Can I offer you some coffee while you wait?" Carrie asked.

We accepted and she poured each of us a cup. It was late in the afternoon, and I needed a shot of caffeine to keep me awake for the drive back. Luckily, we didn't have to wait long before Mr. Kingston entered the door through the garage. He stared at us, startled, then put down his sports bag.

"What's going on here? Carrie?"

"These nice detectives are here to talk to us, Jim. We've been waiting for you."

Jim looked skeptical. "What about? Is it about that bastard Johnson? 'Cause if you ask me, he should never have been let out."

"It is not about Johnson," I said. "Please, just sit down, Mr. Kingston, and we will get to it."

Reluctantly, Jim Kingston pulled out a chair and sat down.

"You have to excuse my husband," Carrie said. "But we have been through a lot, especially lately with Vernon getting out and everything. The hard part is not knowing. We have no idea what happened to Scott. At least, up until now, we thought we knew who took our son from us; we believed he had received his punishment, but now it turns out, we didn't. It's very frustrating to never get closure."

"I have closure," Jim snorted angrily. "I know that bastard did it, and somehow he fought the system and got out. He was supposed to have been killed. But he managed to work the system. He is clever, you know. Now he is a free man? After all he has put us through? There is not a day where we don't think about our son."

"I understand your anger," I said and looked at both of them. "But that is not why we are here. We are not here to discuss Mr. Johnson."

Carrie Kingston looked into my eyes and gasped. She cupped her mouth. "Oh, my God." Her eyes welled up. "You found him, didn't you?"

I nodded with a sigh. "Yes."

A change went over Jim Kingston's face. He was no longer fuming with anger and despair. Tears were welling up in his eyes as well. It was hard for me to hold mine back.

"Where? How?" Carrie asked, her voice shaking.

"At a construction site," I said. "In Sebastian Inlet. The building has been there since 1993. We believe he was put in the ground before then."

Carrie Kingston didn't move. She simply stared at me, holding a hand to cover her mouth, while years of sorrow and frustration left her body. Her torso was trembling.

Jim Kingston sank in his chair. After years of having his shoulders in this tense position under his ears, he finally let them go with a deep sigh. Tears streamed across his cheeks. "And you're sure, right? You're sure it's him this time...? I mean, so many times we've thought..."

I nodded. "Yes. A few years after Scott disappeared, a body was found in Cocoa Beach that we believed might have been Scott. DNA profiling was the new thing back then, and you were asked to provide us with hair from Scott's brush. We found out it wasn't a match, but we kept his information, and to make a long story short, the ME ran a DNA test again this time. We had the result this morning, and it was a match."

"I can't believe it," Carrie said. "After so many years of not knowing. Of constantly staring at every little boy you see in the street or at the beach or in Wal-Mart. Even later, I kept looking for him everywhere. In crowds. He would have been thirty-seven this year, and just the other day, I stopped myself from staring at this man in his mid-thirties, just because I wondered if it could be him, or what he might look...in case...well, in case he wasn't dead. You keep hoping. That's what hurts the most. I guess I had accepted the fact that he was gone, but there is a part of you that wonders. What if he isn't dead? What if he is out there somewhere... alive? But, I guess...I guess we know for sure now."

"There is something else," I said. "We do believe he was alive for a couple of years after he disappeared. The body we found matching your son's DNA was older. Maybe up to seven years older."

I could have sworn I heard Carrie Kingston's heart stop. Her eyes widened, and she kept staring at me. Then, she burst into tears, and Jim couldn't hold his back anymore either.

"You mean to tell us he was still alive? You mean to tell us we could have found him if we had just looked harder?" he said, his voice trembling with a mixture of furor and unbearable terror.

"There was nothing you could have done differently, Mr. Kingston," Beth said. "Everyone did all they could."

Carrie Kingston was no longer listening to the conversation. She kept shaking her head in disbelief.

"No...No," she said over and over again, her voice breaking. "I knew he was alive. I knew it all this time. I kept looking for him, but you told us it was over. You people told us to let it go. To move on. That the guy who had hurt our son was in prison. That the case was closed and we should leave it alone. I kept telling everyone it wasn't over, that my boy was somewhere, alive, but they wouldn't listen. It was unlikely that he was alive still, they said. Vernon Johnson had killed him and there was a witness. But, there's no body, I kept saying. But still they wouldn't listen. And all this time...all this time, I could have been looking for him. You could have been looking for him. We could have found him. I know we could have." She clenched her fist in desperation. "Seven years, you say? I can't believe it!"

Jim looked at Carrie. I could tell the many years of wondering had taken its toll on their marriage. There was no affection to trace between the two of them. They were simply two people living together in mourning.

"So...so what happens now? Will Vernon Johnson go back to jail?" he asked.

"We don't know," I said. "We're reopening the case."

"How?" Carrie asked.

"Excuse me?" I asked.

"How? How did he die?"

I cleared my throat. "Well, since the body has been in the ground for a very long time, it's hard to determine the cause of death just yet."

Beth and I exchanged looks and both got up from our chairs. It was time for us to go. We had done what we came for. As painful as it was, we had to leave them to their sorrow.

"Again, I am so sorry, Mr. and Mrs. Kingston, for your loss," I said and shook their hands. "We'll be in touch."

SEVENTEEN

May 2015

WE DROVE BACK IN SILENCE. I had an awful taste in my mouth. I couldn't get Carrie Kingston's voice out of my head.

All this time...all this time, I could have been looking for him. You could have been looking for him. We could have found him. I know we could have.

The realization was devastating. To think that the little boy had been somewhere in the area for up to seven years. For seven years, he had been so close they could almost have run into him. But, where had he been? Had he run away and hid somewhere? Or had someone taken him? According to the report, the screen to the window had been taken off. It was put back on so loosely it had fallen off as soon as someone touched it when the police were called. So, there had to have been someone. But who? And where had he kept him all those years? And why?

"A case like that makes you think, huh?" Beth finally said, when we hit the bridges and drove towards the barrier islands where we both lived. It had gotten dark and the lights from the boats on the Intracoastal looked like fireflies in the water.

"Sure does," I said. "Especially when you have kids of your own. How are you holding up, by the way?"

"If you mean am I drinking again, then no."

"Good. I don't mean to pry, but I know that going through hard times can set you back," I said, and thought about Shannon and her falling off the wagon recently. Luckily, the pregnancy had changed all that. I knew that as soon as it was about more than just her own life, she would never do it.

I stopped at the red light.

"But I won't lie to you, Ryder," Beth said. "I have been tempted more than once while being at home all alone waiting to get better. It feels good to be back. Drove me nuts to have to just sit there and rest all the time. Ugh."

I chuckled. It wasn't often Beth ever shared something about herself with me. I liked it. Usually, she kept people at a distance. Usually, that meant people had a lot they weren't too proud of to share. But we all had that. We had all done things we weren't happy about. That was life, right?

I completely understood what she was saying. I liked to stay busy too. Staying at home with nothing to do but rest would drive me nuts. I had thought about it since Shannon suggested I stopped working. She had enough money to provide for the both of us, she said. But that wasn't my thing. What would I do?

Build a house, yes, but once that was done, then what? No. I needed this job and the force just as much as it needed me. It was my second home. But the truth was, at moments like these, when driving back from having given news like this to already suffering people, kicking them when they were already down, in moments like that I did consider leaving the force. Maybe I should just do what my dad had done, retire before I hit fifty and follow my dream. But what was my dream?

I had no clue.

I drove Beth back to her house and dropped her off. "Take it easy, partner," I said and meant every word. Beth needed to rest.

I drove back up A1A and stopped at my parents' motel to pick up the twins. Emily had texted me that she was at home. Angela and Shannon were visiting her sister Kristi for dinner.

The light was still lit on the deck overlooking the beach. I walked up there, thinking my parents were probably sitting outside talking the day through over a beer like they usually did before bedtime. As I came closer, I spotted my mother, but she wasn't sitting with my dad. She was with another man. Someone I didn't know personally, but had only seen in the newspaper. I stopped before they saw me and decided to walk inside the bar instead, where I found my dad behind the counter. He was closing up the bar while looking out at the two of them on the deck outside.

"What's going on, Dad?" I asked.

He drew in a deep breath and looked at me. "An old friend of your mom's showed up today."

I stared at him, startled. "Old friend? Vernon Johnson is my mother's old friend?"

"Not just friend," my dad said and looked into my eyes with a tender yet slightly fearful look. "I never told you this, but your mother once fell in love with someone else. You were six years old when it happened. She was very young when she had you and still was when she met him. That was why we left Cocoa Beach and moved to Ft. Lauderdale back then. Your mother decided to stay with me for your sake, but she loved him. They were deeply in love when he was arrested for having killed that kid. Your mother never got over him."

EIGHTEEN

May 2015

NOAH KINLEY OPENED HIS EYES. At least he thought he had, but it was still as dark as if his eyes were still closed. He blinked a few times. No, they were open. He felt rested, but had a strange unease in his body. He didn't feel like waking up yet. He wanted to sleep more. Maybe it was still night?

He felt hungry. He felt so thirsty, his throat dry as sand. Noah coughed. His body felt almost numb. He blinked his eyes again and again, but the darkness wouldn't go away. Usually, he could see at least something from the light coming from the window, but there was nothing.

Had he gone blind? There was a kid on Noah's old street who was blind. She walked with a stick and had eyes that had rolled back in her head. She was weird and looked scary, Noah thought.

Oh, my God. Am I like her now? Have my eyes rolled back in my head too? Am I going to walk using a stick to find my way too? Oh, God, please, please don't let me be blind.

Noah sobbed and touched his eyes. As he did, his hand slid across something. Noah reached up with both of his hands and felt it. It was like a roof or something, but very close to his face. He tried to lift his head, but it hit the roof with a thud and he put his head back down again. Then he felt around him to the sides and realized it was everywhere. It was surrounding him everywhere. He could hardly move.

What was this?

"Mom? Mooom? MOOOOOM??!" Noah finally screamed while slamming the palms of his hands on the roof. And now he couldn't stop screaming.

He banged on the sides and on the bottom and on the roof. He was scared to death. What had happened? Where was his new blue room? Where was his soft bed with the steering wheel? Where were his pillow and Ely the Evil Elephant?

Where are my mom and dad?

Noah screamed again and cried for hours, then he felt tired and weak and floated out of consciousness for a little while before he woke up again, only to realize nothing had changed. He could still open his eyes, but it felt no different than when he kept them closed. The darkness was still everywhere, enclosing him completely.

"Mooom? Where are you? I'm scared."

Noah was crying again. He felt so confused. Then he remembered something. He remembered having fought zombies in his room. He remembered the nice man who came to play with him with the sword. It was all very foggy. He had played with the nice man; they had been fighting with their swords, then he drank a soda that the man had given him. Noah's had tasted strange and afterwards he had felt sleepy. So incredibly sleepy all of a sudden. He had told the man he needed to take a nap before they could continue the game. He had smiled and tucked him in the bed. He had even caressed his hair till he fell asleep, just like Mommy used to do. He had been so nice to Noah.

But where was the man now? And where was Noah? Was this darkness ever going to end?

Noah banged his fists at the roof again. "MOOOOMMY! HELP! MOMMY. MOMMY! HEEELP!"

He cried and screamed desperately till he wore himself out, then had to stop. Noah felt so weak. So hungry and thirsty. And he had to pee. He had to pee really bad.

NINETEEN

May 2015

SHANNON LEANED over and kissed Jack on the lips. He had been awake most of the night, worrying about the case he was working on. She knew him well enough by now to know what the groaning and constant tossing were all about. He had told her he had visited the parents of the boy whose body they had found just the night before, and after hearing the details, Shannon completely understood why it bothered him so much.

"Let me make you some breakfast," she said and looked deep into his eyes.

His eyes went from worried to relaxed. "Just some coffee would be great," he said and kissed her nose.

Shannon got up and walked into the kitchen. All the kids were still sleeping. In a few minutes, they would be all over the place, looking for shoes and backpacks and fighting. Shannon had learned to enjoy those small moments in the morning before hell broke loose.

From the kitchen, Shannon could hear Jack pull the curtain like he always did first thing in the morning. To check out the waves. It had been very windy lately and a storm system was in the Atlantic, they said on the radio. It was still very far away from Florida. They didn't know yet if it would turn into a hurricane and maybe make landfall. It worried Shannon, but not Jack. He told her it was very rare they made landfall and they hadn't had one since 2005.

"It might get windy for a few days, but after that it'll pass. Don't worry."

Shannon tried hard not to. She had enough to worry about as it was. She was trying to get used to the chaos of being a big family and trying to get past the constant all-day sickness from the pregnancy, while battling the anxiety of possibly going to jail. It was a lot to take at once.

Jack crept up behind her and put his arm around her. He kissed her neck. Shannon closed her eyes.

"So, no surfing today either?" she asked.

"No. Not with that wind. It's nasty out there. Big waves in the back, but it's not worth the effort to try and paddle out. It's all blowing out. But with a little luck, we might get some awesome conditions on the backside of this system. Once it passes us out in the Atlantic, the wind will shift to off-shore and that's when the surf is perfect."

Shannon nodded and handed Jack the coffee. She had heard him talk about off-shore winds being perfect for surfing before. She felt like such a novice when it came to the ocean. She didn't understand why today wasn't a perfect day for surfing when the wind was blowing forcefully onshore and creating all these waves, but according to Jack, wind was a bad thing when it came to wave-surfing. She still didn't fully get it. But she did enjoy surfing with him and had come to the point where she could catch a wave on her own. But now with the pregnancy and all, she wasn't going to be surfing for a long time. She couldn't risk it. She didn't dare to, even though both Jack and the doctor said it was perfectly safe.

There was a noise coming from behind them and they turned to look at Angela, who had come into the kitchen. Shannon smiled and kissed her.

"Good morning, sleepyhead. You want some breakfast?"

She sat down at the table with a sleepy nod. Soon after, Abigail and Austin stormed inside and fought about sitting next to Angela.

"Hey, I wanted to sit there," Abigail whined, when Austin grabbed the chair.

"Sit on the other side of Angela," Jack said and poured cereal into bowls.

"No," Abigail said and crossed her arms in front of her chest. "Austin took my chair."

Jack sighed and looked at her. Then he told Austin to move away. Shannon felt a sting in her heart. She wanted to speak up and tell him Austin hadn't done anything wrong and that it was unfair, but bit her tongue. It wasn't her battle.

Austin refused to move.

"But, Daaad. I was here first."

"No, I wanted to sit there," Abigail claimed victoriously.

Abigail could be quite the handful, and Shannon couldn't help thinking that Jack maybe let her get away with too much. She never said anything, since she didn't want to hurt him. Neither of them ever commented on the other's education of their children. It seemed to work for now. But she wondered how it was going to work out once they started living in the same house. Right now, they lived in separate condos and Shannon and Angela could go downstairs and be on their own every now and then, even though they did hang out at Jack's place most of the time. But what was it going to be like when they were together like this every day? Shannon and Angela were used to it just being them. Shannon wasn't used to all these children and all their conflicts. Would she be able to never say anything? Would it be expected of her to help raise his children as well? Or was she supposed to just stay out of that, even though it affected her life as well. Standing in the kitchen and watching Jack try to solve this little problem, Shannon suddenly wondered how on earth they were going to do this and with a baby on top of it?

Shannon was staring helplessly at the many half-eaten bowls of cereal and screaming children when Jack's phone suddenly rang and he picked it up. He left the room, and Shannon had no idea how to manage the two arguing children.

"You're mean," Austin said to Abigail.

"No, I am not!"

"Yes, you are!"

"Am not!"

"You are. You're a meanie."

"Daaad. Austin called me a meanie!"

Shannon stared at the two of them for what felt like ages with no idea what to do or how to handle them. Finally, Jack returned with the phone in his hand. Shannon drew in a breath of relief. He was back, now he could take care of the two, while she focused on her baby girl, who just like her mother had no idea what to say or do. They simply weren't used to these kinds of conflicts. Shannon smiled when she saw Jack, but then her smile froze. He looked at her seriously.

"It was Ron. I've gotta hurry to the office. Something has come up. Could you please make sure the kids get to the bus on time? Thanks!"

Before she could open her mouth and argue, he had run into the bedroom, put on his uniform, and left, blowing a quick kiss to all of them.

Austin and Abigail had stopped fighting and were eating now, but just for a few minutes before Abigail poked her elbow into Austin's side and Austin wailed, "Abigail hit me!"

"No, I didn't. You were just sitting too close to me. If you had picked the chair over there, then maybe this wouldn't have happened."

"I was here first! Shannon?"

Shannon stared at the three children. She had never had more than one child at a time. This was certainly different. She forced a smile and avoided getting in the middle of their discussion.

"Finish up your food and get ready for the bus. It leaves in ten minutes."

"Yeah, hurry up, doofus," Abigail said to Austin.

"Abigail called me doofus."

"Because you are a doofus, doofus."

Only ten more minutes, Shannon. Only ten.

TWENTY

May 2015

_____

RON PLACED a picture on the whiteboard next to Scott Kingston.

"Noah Kinley," he said and placed his finger at his nose. "Disappeared from his home yesterday. According to his parents, he was playing in his room in their new house, but when they went inside to tell him it was dinnertime, he was gone. The sliding door to the yard was left open to get some of the fresh breeze that we've had lately. The parents had turned off the AC and left the doors open instead. The screen door was shut, but open when the parents came into the room. They looked for him everywhere. We had a team search the canal and the entire neighborhood for most of the night. Not a trace of Noah. It doesn't look good."

"You think he was kidnapped?" Beth asked.

"We don't know yet," Ron said. "He could have just run away. But when children are involved, I don't take chances. I'm putting all my men in to look for him."

We all nodded. No arguing that it was important. I stared at the little boy next to Scott Kingston on the whiteboard. The similarities were obvious. Little boy, almost the same age, disappeared from his room where the window or sliding door was left open. No one in the room wanted to say it out loud, but we were all thinking it.

Vernon Johnson had just been released and now it happened again?

It could be a coincidence. It might not be. We didn't know just yet. When Ron ended the meeting and told us to go to work, I went back to my desk with the pictures of the two little boys flickering for my inner eye. Carrie Kingston's voice was roaming my mind.

All this time...all this time, I could have been looking for him. You could have been looking for him. We could have found him. I know we could.

I couldn't bear it. So many years this boy was still alive after he was kidnapped. We weren't going to make the same mistake again. That was for sure. I was determined not to let that happen.

I looked through the newspaper, where Shannon's upcoming concert in

443

Orlando in two weeks was announced. She had said yes to doing a couple of concerts in the coming months. I hoped it wasn't too much for her. I wanted her to rest. She was, after all, carrying our child. She had been throwing up a lot lately and I wondered if she was up for it. Could it affect the baby? All the loud music, screaming fans, and Shannon straining herself? I wasn't happy about her doing it, but I also knew it was her passion and her entire life, so I hesitated to say anything when she told me about her plans. Now I wished I had. Now that it was too late.

I flipped a couple of pages in the newspaper, then stopped at an article that made my heart pound. I grabbed the paper, then ran into Ron's office without knocking. He looked at me, perplexed.

"What's going on, Ryder?"

I threw the article on the desk. He looked at it.

"Two people were found killed yesterday in Daytona Beach," I said. "These two."

Ron gave the picture an extra glance. "So? It's out of our area."

"Their story. Look at their story. It's a couple. According to the article, they were being charged after their little girl was found locked in basement in *deplorable* conditions. Deplorable conditions. Look at what it says: *a school nurse reported that a nine-year-old student may have been the victim of abuse after the girl was sent to the nurse's office because she smelled strongly of urine. The girl told the nurse that her private parts hurt, so the nurse conducted an examination and found her vaginal area to be red and irritated. The little girl also told the nurse that she wasn't allowed to go to the bathroom in the house and was forced to go to the bathroom outside because her family didn't want to contract the infections she had. When Sheriff's deputies responded, the victim's father and his girlfriend acknowledged they locked her in their unfinished basement with little food and water during the day as punishment for a recent school suspension. The basement door was secured with a lock and chain. He and his live-in girlfriend and her biological son live upstairs, while the little girl lives in the unfinished basement. He said they kept her downstairs because of her lack of bladder control, saying he "cannot afford to keep cleaning up after her."*

I put the paper down and looked at Ron. He looked at me like I had completely lost it. "Where are you going with this?"

"They're dead. They were shot outside of their house yesterday. Both twice in the heart."

Ron's eyes widened. Finally, he understood. "The Monahan sisters?"

"You bet."

TWENTY-ONE

Florida 1969

WHEN HECTOR SPOTTED his brother in the crowd at the train station in Orlando, he started to cry. Raul yelled his name and started to run closer.

"Hector! Hector!"

Seconds later, they were in each other's arms. The trip from Cuba had been long and hard, and finding Raul had taken months. But through other Cubans in Miami, he had heard that Raul had settled on a small island up in Central Florida called Merritt Island. As soon as Raul had polished enough shoes to make enough money for the train ticket, he had written to Raul at the restaurant that he had heard he worked in, and once he was on the train, he could do nothing but hope that Raul would be there. And so he was. Tears were streaming across his cheeks.

"Dear brother. Look at you. You are too skinny!" Raul said and clapped him on the back. He put his arm around his shoulder and pulled him close.

Raul took Hector to the restaurant where he worked. It was a small Cuban place, and the smells and music inside of it made Hector sick with longing for his daughter, Isabella, whom he had left.

At the restaurant, he was also reunited with two of his other brothers who had escaped Cuba the year before. The reunion was tearful, yet joyous.

"We have a job for you here," Raul said. "The owner is Cuban too and he told us you could work with us. You can live with me as long as you want to. After all, I owe you my life, dear brother."

Raul smiled and wiped a tear from his eyes. Then he laughed and patted Hector on the shoulder once again. Hector's other two brothers, Alonzo and Juan, joined in and they all hugged again. Hector's heart was heavy in his chest. He was so happy to finally be there, to finally be in the U.S., but now that he had reached his destination, he was confronted with the fact that he had left everything back in Cuba. Four of the brothers were together, but the rest of the family wasn't. He feared for their lives.

Hector soon started working in the kitchen of the restaurant, and as the days

445

passed, he got used to life in the U.S. without his daughter and parents, even though he missed them every day, every minute. He started to make a decent living and soon was able to get his own place. A condo on Merritt Island soon became a house on Merritt Island, and his job in the kitchen at the restaurant soon led to a job as a butcher in Cocoa Beach, and two years later, he had saved enough money to be able to open his own Cuban restaurant in Cocoa Beach.

Little Havana was the love of Hector's life, after his daughter Isabella, naturally. He wrote her letters every day and hoped they would reach her, but knowing how things worked in his homeland, he also knew it was very unlikely. The political tensions were getting worse, even though Hector didn't understand what it was all about. He knew things were getting worse back home; he heard many stories of people being imprisoned for speaking up for themselves, for defending the right of speech, or if they tried to leave, and he started to wonder how he was going to get his daughter out. He wanted to get his parents to come as well, and the rest of his brothers, but for now he focused only on Isabella. She was the one who deserved a better future. She was the one he was responsible for. She was the one he was being eaten up from the inside with longing for.

Sometimes, he would drive down to the beach after closing up the restaurant or before they opened, and he would simply stare out into the Atlantic Ocean, thinking she was out there somewhere. South of where he was. Breathing in the same air that he did. Maybe swimming in the same ocean. Every day, he wondered if it would be possible to simply take a boat and go get her. But he knew he would be shot if he was caught. They had made themselves very clear. He could never set foot in Cuba again.

TWENTY-TWO

May 2015

I IMMEDIATELY CALLED up my colleagues at Volusia County Sheriff's Office, who covered Daytona Beach. They gave me the details of the case and I told them my concerns.

"I believe it might be connected to a case we're working on down here," I told the detective on the case, and then gave him the details about the sisters.

I hung up and then called Sarah Millman's lawyer and asked him to bring her back in. Two hours later, she was sitting in the interrogation room as Ron and I entered. He wanted to hear what she had to say.

"My client is not saying anything," the lawyer said before I even opened my mouth. "What are the charges?"

"She's not under arrest," I said. "At least not yet."

"So, why are we here?" the lawyer asked. "My client is still only a suspect, as far as I have been informed."

I threw a picture of the couple from Daytona Beach in front of them. "These two were killed outside their home yesterday. It has the scent of the Monahan sisters all over it. They were being charged with child abuse, and they were each shot twice in the heart."

Sarah Millman shook her head. "I don't know anything about this. I was at home yesterday. The guard at the gate can tell you. I haven't been to Daytona for years."

"Have you spoken to your sisters lately?" I asked. "Maybe they're in Daytona?"

"I hardly think so," she said. "It's a very noisy town."

"I wasn't asking if they were there for the speedway," I said.

"I know what you're asking," she said. "But you also know I haven't heard from them. After all, you're tapping my phone, aren't you? You have a tail on me twenty-four-seven. Isn't that what you call it? Don't think I haven't noticed that I'm being followed everywhere."

"Well, it's hardly a secret that we're trying to catch your sisters, so I don't expect you to be surprised," I said.

"I'm not."

"We have a proposition for you," Ron said. "I talked to the State Attorney and they're willing to lower the charges against you if you help us find your sisters."

The lawyer leaned forward. His facial expression told me he believed in her guilt as well. He knew she had a bad case. "What are we talking about?" he asked.

"Assisting murder instead of homicide," Ron said.

It hurt inside of me to know that she might get away with killing her husband, and only being charged with assisting to it, but it was worth it if it meant we would get the two others.

Sarah Millman leaned back and crossed her arms in front of her chest. Her lawyer looked at her. She shook her head.

"It's a good deal," her lawyer said.

Sarah Millman was thinking about it. I could tell this might be a way to get to her. She was afraid of going to jail. She doubted if it was worth it...if it was worth covering for her sisters.

"What about Christopher?" I asked. "If you go in for murder, he'll have to grow up without a mother or a father. You say you fight for the children...against injustice and abuse. But what about your own son? Is he the one who will be lost in all this? 'Cause you're going to jail. I spoke to Jacquelyn Jones this morning, and they're getting ready to press charges. She even believes she has enough evidence to charge you with being an accomplice in the attack on my partner. And that's bad. You know how they get when an officer is involved. They always go for the worst punishment. Even if it was your sister Natalie who set up the bomb, you knew about it. That's what they'll argue. They might even say you planned it along with your other sisters. And then there's the matter of Stanley Bradley, who identified you as one of the women holding him captive and trying to kill him. It doesn't look very good, sweetheart. It's only a matter of days before we'll be taking you in again. And this time, it's for good. It's up to you how badly you want this to end for Christopher."

"Would they agree to us pleading that my client was under the influence of substances while planning or committing the crime?" the lawyer asked.

Ron nodded. "Yes. If she talks."

"I'm not saying anything," she said. "I don't know where they are."

I sighed and got up from my chair. "That's too bad, Sarah. We were just trying to help you out here. Now, we'll just have to settle for whatever we found in your house when our people went through it while you were here talking to us."

"You searched my house again?"

The lawyer was about to speak, but I showed him a copy of the warrant. "Yes, we did," I said.

"This is beginning to look like harassment," the lawyer said.

"You won't find anything this time either," Sarah Millman said.

I got up from the chair and walked to the door. I grabbed the handle, then turned and looked at her. "I guess you have nothing to fear, then."

TWENTY-THREE

May 2015

NOAH KNEW he was in the worst nightmare in his life. As a matter of fact, it was worse than any nightmare he'd ever had. And Noah used to have many. Especially since they moved to the new house. He never liked the house much. There was something about it that made him scared, especially in the dark.

"It was just a nightmare," his mother would whisper when she came to his room after being awakened by Noah's screaming. "Go back to sleep. It was just a bad dream."

But Noah kept having the same dream over and over again; it haunted him even when he was awake.

Where are you, Mommy?

He had no idea if it was night or day. Wherever he was, there was no light. Only walls surrounding him on all sides. Wooden walls that he knocked and knocked on, but had no answer. He had no idea how long he had been lying like this, but he did know he was very, very thirsty.

He had wet his pants and the smell made him sick. The hunger and the thirst ate him up from the inside.

I'm so thirsty, Mommy. I'm so hungry. Where are you? Help me, Mommy!

Did his mom know he was gone by now? She had to know. He had been gone for a very long time. Noah closed his eyes. It didn't matter if he had them closed or open. The darkness surrounded him anyway. Every now and then, he broke into a panic thinking he was never going to get out of this thing. Then he would scream and knock and call for his mommy, but nothing happened. No one came.

Have they forgotten about me?

Sometimes, Noah felt like back when he had been lost at J.C. Penney's at the mall. He had been only five years old, but remembered it vividly. He had been holding his mother's hand, then spotted something, a sweet alligator toy, and let go of his mother's hand for one unforgiving second. When he returned and spotted his mother again, he grabbed her hand and looked up, only to realize it wasn't his mother anymore. It was some other woman wearing the same white pants.

"Hello there," the woman said and knelt next to him.

"You're not my mommy."

"No, I'm not."

Noah had let go of the woman's hand, then run away, getting lost between rows of women's clothing. He had looked and looked but not been able to find his mother anywhere. He had ended up asking a security guard to help him. The guard had found her. Finally, he was back with his mother again and promised to never ever wander off again. It was an easy promise to make, since Noah never ever wanted to feel that feeling again.

But now, it had happened again. He was lost, he was in trouble, and he couldn't get himself out of it. He had no idea how to. There was no nice security guard he could ask; he was all alone, alone in this...this thing.

Noah sobbed and felt sorry for himself, when suddenly, he was interrupted by a sound coming from outside.

Someone was there.

There was a fumbling on the other side, sounds, and then someone saying something, calling his name.

"Noah...Noah..."

Strong light from above blinded him. He held a hand to his face to cover his eyes. But he wanted to see who it was. Was it his mom and dad? Was it the police?

Noah smiled with relief and felt his heart race in his chest. Finally, someone was here. Finally, he was getting out.

A silhouette blocked out the light. Noah couldn't see their face.

"Mommy?" he cried. "Is that you, Mommy?"

A hand reached down and he grabbed it and sat up. Then he was helped up, but it was hard for him to stand, and he kept falling. An arm grabbed him and finally he saw the face of his savior. Only, when he looked into his eyes, he realized with terror that he wasn't here to rescue him. He was the one who had put him there.

TWENTY-FOUR

May 2015

"I HAVE SOMETHING!"

Richard yelled through the room. I looked up from my computer. Outside, the windows the dark gray clouds hung heavily. The storm was still forecasted to stay off the Florida Coast. It was still far away, but it was bringing bad weather to our area already. So far, it wasn't even a tropical storm yet, but it was building. I was keeping a close eye on the radars. The wind gusts made people's clothes and hats fly in the streets. Still, they all wore flip-flops and shorts, since it was very hot.

I walked to Richard and stood behind him, looking over his shoulder. Twenty-four hours had passed since we had searched Sarah Millman's house, and so far, we hadn't come any closer to finding her sisters.

Until now.

"What did you find?"

"I've been through all of the stuff on her computer, and I mean everything. Search history, all her emails, anything she looked at for the last forty-eight hours before we took her computer in. Just now, I was going through her iPad, and I finally came upon something. You are familiar with Snapchat, right?"

I shrugged. "I've never used it myself, but I've heard about it, yes. Emily uses it with her friends."

"Well, basically, it's an app where you send a photo or a video or a text message to someone and users set a time limit for how long recipients can view their Snaps. The time limit ranges from one to ten seconds."

"And afterwards, it's deleted; I know that much," I said.

"Yes, that's how it works. When the ten seconds are up, the pictures are hidden from the recipient's device and deleted from Snapchat's servers."

"Why am I sensing there is a but in here?"

"'Cause there is," Richard said with a smile. "Most people think it's perfectly safe to send their boyfriend a Snapchat of themselves naked because no one else will ever see it and it will be deleted immediately afterwards. But, that is not

451

entirely the case. Snapchat's own documentation states that the company's servers retain a log of the last 200 "snaps" that were sent and received, but no actual content is stored. The documentation further explains that if the file is not viewed by the recipient, it remains on Snapchat's servers for 30 days. Furthermore, a forensics firm in Utah discovered a way to find the so-called deleted pics, and created a way to download them from the 'hidden' location a few years back. Apparently, there's a folder on the device, where all the photos are stored. The team then developed a process of extracting the image data. It takes about six hours, on average, to get the information. Look what I found. This was received in Sarah Millman's Snapchat two days ago."

I stared at his screen. Then a smile spread across my face. In front of me stared Sarah's two sisters back at me. The picture was a selfie taken in front of the house in Daytona where the couple was shot later that same day. The sisters were smiling. The caption read: SHOWTIME!

"You've got to be kidding me," I exclaimed.

"I know. They all make mistakes at some point, right?" Richard said. "I have only seen a little bit, but this is definitely what they have been using to communicate with one another. I'm talking dates, names, everything. It tells us everything they've been up to. I even found a text telling Sarah that they have Stanley Bradley, then a photo, followed by the sisters with his lifeless body in the crashed car before they pulled him out. This is good stuff." Richard opened another picture. "This was taken three days ago."

I looked at the photo and smiled even wider. The picture showed them in front of a resort in Daytona Beach. The caption read:

THE ANGEL MAKERS JUST CHECKING IN

TWENTY-FIVE

May 2015

WE DROVE to Daytona just before sunset. Volusia County Sheriff, Ned Farinella, met us outside the Hotel Tropical Winds. Ron was with me, since Beth was too emotionally involved in this case, and I was afraid of her reaction when facing these women that were responsible for her severe disfigurement.

The sun was setting beautifully into a thick layer of clouds over the mainland, coloring the dark clouds over the Atlantic with its last breath before it disappeared. I stared at the darkness on the horizon, wondering if the storm would make landfall or just come close enough to give us the swell I was longing for. Waves had been picking up all day because of the strong winds. The low-pressure had turned into a regular storm-system now, but it seemed to have stalled. It was still very visible, even this far north of Cocoa Beach. It was a big storm. It now had a sixty percent chance of turning into a hurricane, according to the meteorologists. I just hoped it would stay off the coast. It had been many years since we last had a storm make landfall. Last time it happened, the roof was blown off my parents' motel. This winter had been rough on them financially. They couldn't afford for it to happen again.

"I got all my people here," Ned Farinella said, as we shook hands.

I looked at the many cars parked in the parking lot of the hotel. I just hoped the Monahan sisters hadn't looked out the window of the hotel.

"I spoke to the owner," Ned Farinella said, as we walked up to the front. "They say the sisters are in room 333. They checked in as Amy and Michelle Childs. Told the receptionist they were sisters travelling together. The receptionist recognized them from the picture we sent them. According to the receptionist, they're in their room right now. They came back this afternoon and she hasn't seen them leave."

I felt the handle of my gun while my heart rate went up. We entered the lobby of the hotel and Ned talked shortly with the receptionist before we found the elevator and got in.

"Still there?" I asked.

Ned nodded. "As far as she knows, they're still in the room, yes."

"Good."

I felt the heavy gun between my hands and tried hard to calm my nerves. I hated this stuff; so much could go wrong, and more often than not, someone ended up getting killed. But, at the same time, I was eager to get these women. I wanted them to pay for what they had done to Beth, but I didn't want anyone to die. I wanted them to face justice.

We walked up to the door of the hotel room and I knocked, holding my gun in front of me. "Angelina Monahan? Kelly White?" I yelled, not knowing if the last sister went by her married name or her maiden name since her divorce.

There was no answer, nothing but a loud noise that told me that something was going on behind that door.

"They're trying to escape," Ron yelled.

I kicked the door in, and within seconds, we were both inside the hotel room. My eyes moved slowly across the room, scanning it for any sign of movement. Suddenly, there was something near the balcony. The curtain was blowing. The sliding glass door was open; someone ran through it. It was a woman.

"Stop! Police!" I yelled, then stormed after her. I caught up with her on the balcony, just before she was about to climb the rail and climb down. Her sister was already hanging underneath the balcony and now managed to land on the balcony below, from where she could jump to a grass area next to the building. I threw my arm around the woman's waist and grabbed her. The woman screamed and yelled and tried to fight me off, but I fell backwards with her on top of me.

"The other one is getting away!" Ron yelled.

I spotted her running across the grass, just as the woman on top of me managed to push her elbow into my face so hard I saw nothing but stars for a few seconds, just long enough for her to get out of my grip. She jumped for the rail again and I held up my gun.

"Stop, or I'll shoot," I said.

She froze in the middle of her movement, then turned and looked at me. I recognized her as Angelina Monahan.

"You won't get far. Neither will your sister," I continued. "There are police everywhere down there. It's over, Angelina."

Angelina looked into my eyes, then a smile spread on her face. She shook her head slowly with a scoff.

"It'll never be over, Detective. Don't you realize that by now?"

She turned around with the intention of jumping. Beneath us was pavement. She risked getting killed if she jumped directly down from the third floor without landing on the balcony below first, like her sister had. Either she'd kill herself or she would end up getting away. Neither worked for me. My breathing was getting harder by the second. I felt steadier than ever. Then I pulled the trigger.

Angelina Monahan screamed as the bullet hit her shoulder. It was intentional. I didn't want to kill her, only hinder her escape. Stunned, she turned and looked at me while placing a hand to her shoulder, just as she lost her grip on the railing and fell backwards.

"No!" I yelled and got up to grab her, but my hand just missed hers as she fell into the air. Seconds later, she hit the pavement below, headfirst.

TWENTY-SIX

May 2015

I DIDN'T GET BACK to Cocoa Beach until way past midnight. Angelina Monahan was dead. Her sister Kelly was still on the loose. I was so angry with myself and had a feeling everyone else was going to be too. Especially Emily. She had a spring concert at the school, and for the first time she had told me to come. I had been so excited, since she never wanted me to come to these things, and I had never heard her sing.

My mom was waiting for me on the deck of the hotel. They had closed the bar long ago, but she was still sitting outside with a book and a glass of water. Just like she had when I was young and went out at night. I couldn't help but smile.

"Hey, Ma," I said and sat next to her on the wooden bench.

She put the book down with a sigh. "You missed it," she said.

I closed my eyes. "I know. I feel so bad."

"You should have seen her face when she received your text, telling her you weren't coming, right before she was supposed to go on. I could have killed you right then for doing this to her. She had looked forward to this, you know. It took a lot of courage for her to ask us to come. Especially you. She wanted to impress you."

I inhaled deeply, feeling the guilt eating me up. No one could make me feel like an awful dad like my mother.

"I know," I said. "You don't have to tell me I screwed up."

"I get that your work is important. Believe me, I was married to someone a lot like you once. Until he finally retired and started to live his life with me and not constantly making excuses for not being there. You have to decide how long you think this will work for you and your family. Not all cops have three children to take care of alone, you know."

I looked at my mother and nodded. She was right. I had a huge responsibility on my shoulders. On top of it, I now had a chance to change things radically. Being with Shannon and moving in with her gave me a new opportunity I had

455

never had before. Shannon had told me she wouldn't mind if I didn't work. She could support all of us. It was a huge advantage for me. But I had no idea if that was what I wanted. I loved my job. But I didn't love what it did to my family. I didn't love missing out on nights like this one, where my teenage daughter tried to impress me.

"No one would blame you for choosing your family," my mother said. "The kids, on the other hand, will blame you for the rest of their lives if you miss out on their childhood. One of my dear friends works at a hospice in Orlando and she tells me the thing people there regret the most is not that they didn't work more; what they regret is not spending enough time with their loved ones. Think about it. You have a real chance of starting over and creating a whole new family. Not everyone gets a second chance like that."

I nodded and leaned back against the wall. I kept trying to avoid having to make a decision. I knew if I quit my job at the force, I could never come back to the same position again. Reaching homicide had taken many years for me. If things didn't work out for some reason between me and Shannon and I had to go back to work, I would never get back into homicide easily again. It was a big chance to take. What if I missed it too much?

We sat in silence for a few minutes while I let my mother's words linger on my mind. She had a way of always being right. It was annoying.

"Are the kids here or at the condo?" I asked as I got up.

"Emily and Shannon took them home after the concert. I think they all decided to sleep at your place."

"I better get back there, then, and get some sleep," I said and leaned over and kissed my mother.

I started walking back to the car when my mother turned her head and said, "She was amazing, by the way."

I smiled and nodded. "I had a feeling she would be."

TWENTY-SEVEN

May 2015

BEING outside the walls certainly wasn't all it was cracked up to be, Vernon soon realized. He had no idea what to do with himself. At least while on the inside, they had told him what to do, every day. He had no choice but to do what they told him to. Now, all of a sudden, he had all these choices. He was a free man and could do anything he wanted to.

Nothing frightened him more.

What did people do with themselves all day? Worked? Vernon never had an education. He had tried taking some college courses while on the inside, but never managed to finish them. He had nothing to offer a workplace. Besides, they had given him enough money so he didn't have to work. But, what else was there to do?

He went to the local Wal-Mart a couple of times a week, and to him that was more than enough. Being around people scared him, to be frank. He had no idea what they expected of him or if they knew who he was and feared him. He didn't feel like they even belonged to the same race or era. It was like he was still living in the eighties, where everything was much slower and people actually looked at each other and not into their small screens constantly. It was like the world had stopped communicating.

Vernon liked to take a walk every day. He would go to the park and walk or take the bus to the beach and take a long stroll with his feet in the water. Some-how, the ocean made him calm. It was the one thing that hadn't changed one bit since he went in. He loved the calmness of the ocean. And there was one thing more he loved about the beach, especially Cocoa Beach. He loved the fact that Sherri lived down there. His one and only. The one he had been dreaming of every night while waiting on the inside, waiting for them to finally figure out that they had made a mistake.

Vernon knew she was married, but he just couldn't stay away from her. Now he was standing outside her motel and waiting for her. He had taken the bus there and been there twenty minutes earlier than they had agreed, just to make sure he wouldn't be late. He felt nervous. He was so excited to see her again. Today, she had promised to take him to see Kennedy Space Center. He had dreamt of seeing it for so many years, and she had told him she would take him. For old time's sake, she had said. She felt like she owed him that much.

Vernon didn't know how she felt about him, but to him, she was the only bright thing about being outside again. She was the only one he knew and the only one, except for his mother, who still cared for him after so many years. She had always known he was innocent, she had told him. And it was her great sadness that she had been unable to prove it to the police. She was married to an officer, and now her son was a detective too.

Vernon smiled as his eyes met hers. She was still beautiful, even after so many years, he thought.

"Are you ready?" she asked.

Vernon took his cap between his hands. "You look beautiful," he said.

Sherri blushed. "Vernon," she said with a slight reproach in her voice. "I'm a married woman."

Vernon smiled and bowed his head. "I know, Miss Sherri. I know."

"Now, get in," Sherri said and opened the door to her car.

Vernon nodded and got in. Sherri started the car. Vernon was impressed by how quiet the engine was. A lot had happened to cars. This one even had a back-up camera that made an awful lot of noise when Sherri backed out of the parking lot.

Just as she was about to drive into the street, a police car from the Sheriff's Department drove up and stopped her. A deputy got out and walked up to the car. Sherri rolled the window down.

"What's going on, Officer?" she asked.

He lifted his cap. "I'm sorry Mrs. Ryder, but I need to talk to Mr. Johnson."

Part Two

IT WAS THE DREAM OF AN UPRIGHT MAN

TWENTY-EIGHT

Cuba, April 1st, 1980

ISABELLA SUAREZ WAS WEARING her Sunday best. She knew everything had been carefully planned by her grandfather and her uncle Amador, the only one still left in Cuba. The rest of them had all fled to the U.S., going through Costa Rica or even Spain. But it was getting harder to get out, her grandfather had told her. And they had to try now to get the rest of the family out before everything closed up completely. Being only sixteen years old, Isabella didn't understand much of what was going on, other than what she heard her uncle and grandparents discuss with low voices at the dinner table. But she did know one thing. She desperately wanted to go to her father, who had left her eleven years ago. She had received one letter from him during the many years and knew he was with his brothers in the U.S. She had put his address in the pocket of her dress on this night when her grandfather grabbed her hand and took her suitcase. He put it in the back of their old truck. Isabella grabbed her grandmother's hand and they exchanged one anxious glance before getting in the car.

They drove to downtown Havana, then left the car and got on a bus. The bus driver was a friend of Amador's, and Isabella remembered having seen him at the house several times in the past weeks while they were carefully planning this.

After driving around downtown for a few minutes, the bus driver stopped the bus several blocks from Embassy Row in downtown Havana.

Isabella held on to her grandmother's hand and looked into her eyes. She could tell she was worried. The woman had been the closest Isabella had to having a mother. Isabella knew when she felt anxious. She knew her every movement and recognized any unusual behavior, just like any child did with their mother.

"It'll be fine," Isabella whispered, and held her grandmother's hand tightly in hers. The old woman tried to smile.

"The bus is broken down. Everyone needs to leave the bus immediately," the bus driver said, addressed to the rest of the people on the bus.

It wasn't an unusual event. The old buses driving downtown broke down constantly. So, no one thought of it as being strange or even complained about it. The other passengers left the bus, and as soon as they were gone, the driver closed the doors and looked at Isabella, her grandparents, and Amador.

"You ready?"

Isabella swallowed hard and bit her lip. Her grandparents and Amador all nodded. Isabella hesitated. She wasn't sure what it was she was agreeing to. But she was sure she wanted out of here.

Then she nodded too. The driver smiled. She detected a slight nervousness in his smile. He was trying to hide it.

"Okay," he said, his voice trembling. "Let's do this."

The driver started the bus up. He reached the Peruvian Embassy, then looked in his rearview mirror and looked at Isabella and her grandmother. "Get down now," he said. "Everyone."

They all threw themselves on the floor of the bus. Isabella's body was trembling in fear while her grandmother's arm landed on her back and she felt her creep close to her. She petted her across the hair and whispered in her ear.

"Sh. It'll all be alright."

The bus continued towards the fence of the Peruvian Embassy, and seconds later, the sound of shots being fired at the bus burned themselves into Isabella's memory as she closed her eyes and screamed, drowning out the sound of the bus crashing through the fence.

TWENTY-NINE

May 2015

SHANNON bent over the toilet once again and gagged. Nothing came out. It was the seventh time this morning she had thrown up. There was nothing left. She slid to the floor and caught her breath. The nausea was killing her. She didn't remember it being this way with Angela.

There was a knock on her door. "Ten minutes to showtime," a voice said.

Shannon got up and splashed water on her face. It had been a busy couple of days. Jack had been very occupied with his case and been away in Daytona, leaving her to deal with the kids, and this morning she had flown out to Austin, Texas to do a concert. The stadium was completely sold out. Around thirty thousand people were expecting her to go on stage in ten minutes.

Was it nerves? Could it be that she was simply so nervous it made the nausea worse? Or was this just a different pregnancy than with Angela? She had been throwing up for weeks now. Her doctor told her it would get better...usually, after around three months into the pregnancy, he had said. Well she was more than three months in now, and it didn't seem to have any intentions of calming down.

She also felt so tired every day. Like she was completely drained of energy. She wasn't used to feeling this feeble. Shannon had always been a person with great energy.

She looked at herself in the mirror. She was so pale. She found some make-up and tried to cover up the redness around her eyes and nose. No one knew about the pregnancy yet, and she wasn't ready to tell. Not until it showed. Then she would have to. But she wasn't looking forward to it. The press was already all over the fact that she had bought the property in Cocoa Beach. The covers of the magazines this week told everyone how she was *building her love nest with her hunk-lover, Jack*. Others were really mean and wrote that she had barely buried her ex-husband Joe before she moved on. Some still called her the *murderess country-star*, even though she hadn't even been charged with anything yet, let alone convicted.

Shannon finished putting on her make-up, then smiled her stage-smile, grabbed her hat, and put it on. From afar, no one could see how bad she felt on the inside.

There was another knock on the door and Shannon knew it was time to go out. She went to grab her guitar, but as she leaned down to get it from the box, she felt a pain in her stomach. Like a pinch, but just worse. Shannon leaned against the wall to not fall. She gasped in fear.

It didn't feel right.

She felt her stomach as the pain disappeared. Shannon breathed hard. She felt anxious and looked at her phone. Should she call Jack and let him know?

No, he is busy today. Besides, he'll only worry and tell you not to go on. This is what you love. You need this to not go insane.

It had been a lot lately…taking care of all the children, and Shannon wasn't sure she was made for taking care of children. She loved them, yes, but she needed more in her life.

Shannon opened the door and stepped out. In the distance, she could hear the crowd calling her name. She closed her eyes and smiled. She started walking towards the stage area, deciding to forget everything about the pain in her stomach, children, houses, murder charges, and being a mother and simply do what she did best, what she knew she could do.

Sing.

THIRTY

May 2015

I FINISHED my report on the Daytona shooting and handed it to Ron. There was still no news about the last sister, who seemed to have vanished. Meanwhile, Richard was pulling all kinds of evidence material out of Sarah Millman's Snapchat account, and it was starting to look really good. It was obvious they had thought they were safe using this media to share their pictures, but now it served as excellent evidence. I couldn't have been happier.

After a long day of work, I decided to leave early and go to the lot to see if they had made any progress. They had started to clean it out the same morning and were still at it when I arrived. The bulldozers were cleaning out the yard and tearing down the remains of the old house that had been there since the storm knocked it down in 2005.

I spoke to the workers, who told me it all went according to plan, but that they might need a day or two more than anticipated. I figured they would.

"The old house will be gone in a couple of days, and then you can start to build your own," the foreman said.

I was looking very much forward to that. The architect and I had agreed on the floor plan, and I had asked him to make a bigger deck outside towards the beach, but other than that I was very satisfied. I couldn't wait to see my dream house materialize itself. I couldn't wait for my family to live there. Just me and Shannon and all of our kids. I could imagine all the fun we were going to have. So much joy and happiness.

I had started to dream about the baby and what it was going to be like, holding it in my arms. I couldn't believe I was going to be a father once again. I had thought I was done with that part.

But, with life, you never knew.

I left the lot and drove back the two blocks to my parents' place, where the twins and Angela were putting up a kite on the beach. My dad was helping them

464

and I watched as they got it in the air. I walked up to my dad and stood next to him while watching the kite soar.

"So, where is Mom?" I asked.

My dad didn't look at me. "She's at Kennedy Space Center," he said.

"At the Space Center? What on earth is she doing there?"

"Showing that Vernon character around. Apparently, he's never seen it and really wanted to. After twenty-eight years in jail for something he didn't do, I guess your mother feels like she owes it to him or something."

"Doesn't that upset you?" I asked.

He shrugged. I knew him well enough to know it did bother him.

"After so many years of marriage, you just gotta trust one another, right?" he said, not sounding very convincing.

"Dad. It bothers you. I can tell. Why don't you just say something to her? Tell her you don't want her to see him anymore."

My dad looked at me, then laughed. "I can tell you don't have much experience with the institution of marriage. If I say that, I'll only make things worse. I don't tell your mother what to do and what not to do."

"But, at least, you should be able to tell her it bothers you," I said.

The kite fell to the ground and Abigail ran to fetch it. They all helped each other to get it back up again. A woman walked past with her dog on the beach. It wasn't on a leash. It annoyed me, since dogs weren't allowed on the beach. But many dog owners did it anyway, and now people had started calling the Sheriff's office to complain about it, and Ron had to send some of his deputies to the beach to give them fines. It happened every day now, and took a lot of our resources that we would be happy to use otherwise to maybe, say…solve murders. I understood why people wanted to walk their dogs on the beach. It was a great place to walk, and at this end of the beach, there weren't that many people. But the least they could do was to keep them on leashes so they wouldn't bother people.

I decided not to care, since I was off duty, and turned to spot Emily. She was sitting in the shade on the deck staring at her phone. I left my dad and the kids and walked up to her and sat down. She didn't look at me.

"So, I hear you were pretty amazing last night?" I said.

She didn't look up from her phone, or answer.

"Listen, I understand you're mad at me for not coming. I can't blame you for being mad. But you must believe I really wanted to be there more than anything in this world. Shannon told me all about it. She said you sang so beautifully. I feel so awful for missing it. It's been eating me up all day. You must know I feel bad. I'll be at your next concert. I promise I will."

Emily sniffled and continued to look at her phone. I grabbed it out of her hands and forced her to look at me. I loved her beautiful brown eyes, and looking into them always made me go soft. Teenager or not, she was still my little girl, the same little girl I had taken in and taken care of since she was six years old and her mother died. I loved her like crazy. It was insane.

"Give me that back," she said.

I held it in the air, so she couldn't reach it. "Not till you tell me you forgive me," I said with a grin.

Emily crossed her arms in front of her chest with a sigh. She rolled her eyes. "Okay," she said. "I forgive you."

"You gotta mean it," I said. "Say it like you mean it."

Emily rolled her eyes at me again, but a smile was slowly spreading. "I forgive you, okay? Now just give it back to me. I need my phone."

"Alright," I said and handed it back to her. "I know how you teenagers can't live without your precious phones."

As she reached for the phone, I noticed her collarbone seemed more visible than usual in the opening of her shirt. I looked into her face, feeling suddenly struck by worry.

"Emily? Are you losing weight?"

She stared at me with an angry look. Then she shook her head and pulled up her shirt to fully cover her chest. She was wearing an awful lot of clothing for a day like this with temperatures in the eighties. Come to think of it, it had been a very long time since I last saw her in shorts or even a swimsuit.

"What's going on here, Emily?" I asked.

"Nothing," she said.

That was when I noticed her face had changed as well. Her cheeks had sunken in and her eyes were protruding.

"Are you alright? Are you having trouble in school?"

She looked into my eyes intensely. "Dad, I'm fine." She paused and looked away, then back at me with a smile. "I really am. I'm just tired, is all. School is hard lately. Lots of work." She sighed and rolled her eyes again. "Would you stop with that look? I'm fine. I really am, Dad."

I nodded. "Okay. Just checking."

Emily paused, then looked at me again. "So, Shannon said I was good?"

Seeing her smile made me relax. Maybe I was just overreacting. "Yeah. She said you are a really good singer. She's very hard to impress, so there must be something to it."

THIRTY-ONE

May 2015

MY MOM still hadn't come home when it was dinnertime, so I went in the kitchen and threw together a lasagna that my dad and I ate with the kids. I kept an eye on Emily and noticed that she hardly touched her food.

"You don't like your lasagna?" My dad asked her.

"You know I don't eat meat," she said and put down her fork.

"I'll have it," Abigail said, and grabbed Emily's portion as well.

"I'll just make something else for myself," Emily said, and walked into the kitchen. She didn't return. The kids finished their plates and asked if they could run down to the beach and play ball before sunset. I told them they could, and soon it was just me and my dad left.

"I'm worried about her," I said.

"Who, your mother?" he asked.

I smiled. "Why don't you just call her and ask her when she will be back?" I asked. "No, I meant Emily. She seems to be losing weight."

"Ah, Emily. It's just a phase, son. Teenagers are scrawny. They grow so fast, their bodies can't keep up. You were so skinny you looked like you could snap in two." He looked at my stomach. "Guess you've outgrown that like the rest of us."

"I'm not fat!" I protested.

My dad laughed and tapped my stomach. "No you're not, son, but you're getting older like the rest of us. It happens around forty. The hair recedes, the stomach pops out. It's nothing to be ashamed of. Just shows me you're alive and well."

I couldn't help feeling a little offended. I was still only thirty-five. I had always been skinny, and, yes, I had a little stomach now, but I believed I looked great. I was in great shape and surfed almost every day. Well, almost. Lately, my job had been taking up all of my time.

"Be careful," I said with a smile. "Don't forget you're talking to Shannon King's surfer hunk."

467

My dad laughed and shook his head. "That's right. I forgot. That's what they call you now."

"Well, something like that," I said and sipped my beer.

We sat in silence for a little while and enjoyed the nice breeze from the ocean. The storm was still out there somewhere and created strong winds on shore and choppy waves, but we couldn't complain. It was overcast, but the temperature was very pleasant.

"Any news on the storm, yet?" My dad asked.

I grabbed my phone and looked at my storm-tracker-app. "They have given it a name," I said. "Anna. First tropical storm of the season."

"Anna, huh? Well let's hope Anna stays off shore," my dad said.

A car drove up to the motel. It was my mother. She was alone. I looked at my dad as she approached us on the deck. He avoided looking at her.

"There you both are," she said.

My dad sipped his beer with a grunt.

"You made dinner, Jack?" she asked and looked at the lasagna in the middle of the table and the many empty plates.

"Yeah, lasagna," I said.

"I'm sorry I missed it. I had to drive Vernon back to his condo. I met his mother and she talked my ear off." My mother laughed. "They invited me to eat with them. I couldn't say no. Didn't you get my message?"

My dad shook his head. He never had his phone with him. He never saw any reason to.

"Well, be grumpy if you like. I had a great time," she chirped, then walked inside.

I grabbed a couple of empty plates and followed her. She stood behind the counter and poured herself a glass of water. I placed the plates on the counter, then looked at her.

"Mom. What are you doing?"

"What's that?" she asked.

"What are you doing with this guy? Staying away all day and not showing up for dinner? Dad is very upset. I can't say I blame him."

"Ah, he'll get over it. He's just grumpy because I wasn't there to cook for him. Well, if he's that hungry, he can cook for himself."

I stared at my mother, completely baffled. I had never seen her like this. She had always taken care of all of us. If she ever died, my dad would die right along with her of starvation. There was no way he could ever cook anything.

"But, I need you to do me a favor, son," my mom said and clasped my hand. "I need you to talk to those colleagues of yours. Tell them to back off. They are harassing Vernon. This morning, they stopped us as we were driving out. They asked him all kinds of questions and delayed us. They keep showing up at his mother's condo asking him all kinds of questions or bringing him in for interrogation. They have searched his home several times. And, Vernon, sweet as he is, never even asks them for a warrant. He just lets them walk all over him. They never give him a reason or anything. It's harassment, Jack. The poor guy was in prison for twenty-eight years for something he didn't do. He is so afraid of the police that he'll do anything they tell him to. It's not fair, Jack. You've got to talk to them."

"I can't do that, Mom. We're investigating the possible kidnapping of an eight year old boy. We're pretty desperate. You have to admit, it is kind of odd that just as he is released, another child disappears."

My mother grabbed my arm hard. She forced me to look into her eyes. "He didn't do it, Jack. Just like the first time, he is innocent."

"Why do you keep protecting him?" I asked.

"Because he is innocent. Because he is my friend. Because I let it happen once and I am not going to let it happen to him again. It has been haunting me for twenty-eight years, Jack. I knew he was innocent back then too, but there was no way I could prove it. Now, I feel like it's happening all over again. I can tell he's scared."

"But what if he isn't innocent, Mom? What if he did do it?" I asked.

"What happened to innocent till proven guilty? You and the rest of this small town have him stigmatized. You all believe he's guilty, even though you have no proof to back it up. Tell me this, Jack. You just found the body of the poor boy he allegedly kidnapped and killed back then. I read in the paper he was older than the seven years he was back when he was kidnapped. At least a couple years older when he was killed, right?"

"Right."

"So, who killed and buried him? Can you tell me who did that? 'Cause it wasn't Vernon. He was already in jail."

She was making a strong point. I'd been wondering that myself. Only I didn't want to tell her she was right. I wanted Vernon Johnson to be guilty. I don't know why. I just did. But I couldn't keep ignoring the facts.

"I'll talk to Ron about it," I said, just as the phone in my pocket started to ring.

THIRTY-TWO

May 2015

SHANNON HAD COLLAPSED. It was her manager Bruce that called to tell me. With my heart in my throat, I asked my parents to look after the kids while I got on the last plane to Austin. I arrived right before midnight and was let in through the back door of the hospital to avoid the press. I was met by her doctor outside her room.

"She needs all the rest she can get," Dr. Stanton said. He was her private physician from Nashville that she insisted on keeping, even though he was very far away from Cocoa Beach. He was the best, she insisted, and she never wanted anyone else. He had been called right after it happened.

"What happened?" I asked. "Is she alright? Is the baby alright?"

"Let's sit down," Dr. Stanton said and pointed at the chairs behind us. "She is sleeping now. Which is good. The baby is fine. Shannon will be too. But she can't keep doing what she's doing. She needs more rest. She was severely dehydrated when they brought her in. She had been throwing up all morning, and then with the travelling across the country and going on stage with all the heat from the lights, well she collapsed on the stage."

I breathed a sigh of relief. "Thank God she's alright," I said. "So, it was just dehydration?"

Dr. Stanton paused. It wasn't a nice pause. "Well, there is more. She experienced some pain, she told me when she woke up. Abdominal pain. Now, it might be nothing, but I think it's her body's way of telling her to slow down. I'm not taking any chances with this baby, and I have to order her to stop working for the rest of her pregnancy. She needs rest, she needs to eat better, and make sure she gets enough liquids. She has a history of not being very good at taking care of herself, so it is up to you and me to make sure she does. Now, the press is down the lobby waiting. We need to get them out of her way. She needs her rest and to not have this pressure and stress on her shoulders. How do you suppose we do that?"

Bruce, her manager, was sitting next to me and I looked to him for help. I had no idea how to handle the press.

"I know she wanted to wait to tell them till it showed," I said.

"It would be best if she told them herself," Bruce said. "To show them she's not really ill. If she could do so tomorrow, then we might avoid the ugly headlines. There'll still be a few out there, stating that she's terminally ill or that she has bent under the pressure of being charged with murder. I think it would be best if we avoided too many headlines, for her health."

"I agree," I said. "She gets really upset when they write bad things about her."

"Alright," Dr. Stanton said. "I'll allow her to do one press conference, as soon as she feels up to it, then no more press, no more concerts or anything that is stressful. I want her to take long walks on the beach and play songs on her guitar, spend time with her family, that's it."

I was allowed into her room and spent the rest of the night sleeping in a chair next to her. In the morning, I woke to the sound of her voice.

"Jack?"

I grabbed her hand in mine and got up from the chair. "How are you feeling? Are you hot? Cold? Do you need anything?"

"I'm fine," she said with a smile.

"You scared me, Shannon," I said.

"I know," she said. "I scared myself. I'll be good from now on. I promise."

"No more concerts," I said.

She sighed and the smile disappeared. I knew it was hard on her. She loved to perform.

"No more concerts," she repeated. "No more stress. I promise."

471

THIRTY-THREE

Cuba, April 1980

ONE OF THE Cuban guards in front of the Peruvian Embassy was killed when the bus crashed through the fence. He was shot in the crossfire as the guards tried to stop the bus. Isabella remembered seeing him being removed from the ground and carried away at the same time as she was being helped out of the bus by Peruvian soldiers and brought inside the Embassy. They were met by a Peruvian diplomat. Isabella was still shaking and fought hard not to cry when he spoke to them.

Given the desperate measures the five of them had taken to ask for political asylum, they were granted it by the Peruvian diplomat in charge of the embassy. He promised he would take care of them and make sure Castro's soldiers couldn't reach them.

They could hardly believe they had actually succeeded. Their plan had worked.

The next day, the Cuban government asked the Peruvian government to return them, stating they would need to be prosecuted for the death of the guard. The Peruvian government refused.

"We're protected. The diplomat kept his word to us," Isabella's grandfather said and hugged her when they were told the news.

"Castro won't give up that easily," her grandmother said.

And she was right. Four days later, Castro declared he was going to remove his guards from the Peruvian Embassy. Isabella woke up the next morning to the sound of people screaming and yelling. When she looked outside the windows of the embassy, she saw crowds of people running in the streets towards the embassy's gate. They had temporarily patched the area where the bus had driven through the fence, but hundreds of people now stormed it and broke it down.

"What's going on?" her grandfather asked, coming up next to her.

"This is exactly what we feared," her uncle said. "This is exactly what Castro wanted."

"So, what do we do now, Papa?" Isabella asked anxiously. She spotted women and children among the people outside. It was everyone for himself. They were being pushed and trampled.

"We help them," he said.

That day, seven hundred and fifty Cubans gathered at the embassy in Havana and asked for diplomatic asylum. People were coming in so fast they climbed the walls, since the gate was too full. Isabella, her uncle, and grandparents helped people over the fence one by one as they rushed inside. Outside the fence, news spread by word of mouth and by the second day there were more than ten thousand people crammed into the tiny embassy grounds. People occupied every open space on the grounds, some were even climbing trees and other structures and refusing to abandon the premises. New Cuban guards arrived and now blocked the entrance so no one could get in or out. The embassy grounds were jammed with people. Everything had turned to chaos. Isabella tried to help everyone, and along with her grandmother, she passed out water to the people. At some point, they spotted three trucks pull up outside and dump rocks into the street. They saw everything through the destroyed fence. Isabella looked at her grandmother. Then she felt her uncle pick her up as more people gathered on the outside of the fence and started throwing the rocks at them.

"Traitor! Traitor!" they yelled while the rocks flew everywhere. From atop her uncle's shoulders, Isabella watched the chaos unfold while gasping for breath. She saw a woman with the most beautiful blond hair. Their desperate eyes met, just as her hair went from blond to red.

Isabella screamed as she saw the woman fall to the ground. She was carried away and put on the ground where a wall would protect her. Most of them would sleep there lying close on the floor. She lay all night staring at the stars above, trembling and cursing her own vulnerability. In the street outside, trucks with speakers rolled past and yelled at them, keeping them awake.

"Traitors, Traitors!"

The sound of machine guns being fired in the air caused her grandfather to throw himself at his exhausted family. While lying on the hard ground all night, Isabella heard him murmur a prayer, asking that none of the bullets would rain down on them from this beautiful treacherous sky.

THIRTY-FOUR

May 2015

NOAH WAS TAKEN out of the box once a day. He was given food, and was allowed to go to the bathroom if he hadn't already done so in the box. He was even allowed to walk around a little and move his legs and arms. Every day, he looked forward to the lid being lifted, the light entering, and being let out. Even though it was that creepy man with those piercing eyes that took him out. It was the highlight of his day.

His legs were hurting so badly from lying still in one position all day and night, and he felt how he was getting weaker and weaker as the days passed. There was one small window in the room where he was being kept, and every day when he was let out, he looked to it, to take in as much sunlight as possible from the small window under the ceiling.

It wasn't long that he was allowed outside the box, only enough time for him to eat and drink a little, then go to the bathroom and walk two rounds around the wooden box that he had learned to dread so terribly.

Then, he was put back in and the lid closed again. Those were the terrifying moments, when Noah would cry and plead and beg for the man to not put him back in there, but he showed no mercy. Noah even tried to fight him, but it was no use. He lifted his hand, and with one slap across Noah's face, he let him know just how much stronger he was than Noah.

He didn't give him much food…a few slices of bread and a glass of water every day. It was far from enough for him, and Noah was constantly starving. He felt dizzy even when lying down, and soon he started to sleep a lot. He dreamt about his mother and father and being back at the old house with his old friends and neighbors. He dreamt himself back to where he had last been happy, where he had last felt safe. It didn't take long before he decided he would rather stay in his dreams than be awake in the nightmare he was living.

His guardian never spoke much. He only commanded him to eat, drink, or go to the bathroom. He tried to speak to him to maybe convince him to not put him

474

back in the box, but he wouldn't even look into Noah's eyes. It was like he didn't want to talk to him.

"Please, Sir?" he asked one day when walking around the cold room. As usual, the man was sitting in a chair by the door, watching him as he walked in circles around the box. "Please, tell me your name?"

"Walk. No talk," he said and turned his head away.

"Please, can't I sleep outside on the floor instead of in the box?" he asked.

He didn't answer. He stared at him with his piercing dark eyes.

"I can sleep right over there? I won't bother you. I won't cry or scream. I won't try to escape."

He slapped Noah across his face and Noah fell to the ground. "Walk."

Now, Noah was crying. Tears rolled across his cheeks and he refused to get up. He simply couldn't do this anymore. He refused to.

The man stomped his feet in the ground. "Walk."

"No! I don't want to," Noah said defiantly. "I want to go home. I want to see my mommy!"

The man rose to his feet with an angry movement. He grabbed Noah by the arms, lifted him up, while he was screaming and kicking, then put him inside the box again and closed the lid.

"Please don't. Please don't leave me here!" he screamed.

But he did. And he didn't return until three days later.

THIRTY-FIVE

May 2015

I TOOK Shannon home to Cocoa Beach the next day and put her on my couch with orders to not move. I made her lunch, then kissed her forehead and looked into her eyes.

"Now, promise me you'll take it easy while I'm gone, okay?"

She smiled wearily. She still hadn't regained her strength after the collapse. Dr. Stanton had gone back to Nashville, but promised to come down later in the week to check on her. I, for one, was worried madly about her and the baby.

"What am I supposed to do all day?" she said with a sigh. "Just sit here and watch TV?"

I went to my bookshelf and pulled out five books that I placed on the coffee table.

"Here. Once you've watched all the movies, then read these books. The kids will go to my mother's when they are dropped off till I pick them up this afternoon. We'll have dinner here at the condo, so you can stay put for now. I have to go to work for just a little while, but call at anytime, alright?"

Shannon nodded. She didn't seem too pleased at the prospect of spending the next days on the couch, but I hoped she knew how important it was that she did. For the baby and for her own sake. We couldn't risk any more collapses.

"Will you be alright?" I asked and kissed her again.

"I was just dehydrated, Jack. Will you stop acting like I'm dying? I'll be fine. Go, do your job."

I left, feeling like I'd abandoned her. I wasn't going far, though. I was meeting Beth at the Kinley's house on 4th Street North.

The mother, Lauren, opened the door and let us inside. "Steven," she said, addressed to the husband. He was sitting in a chair in the living room, staring out the window. He didn't react when we came in.

"He's been like this ever since it happened," she said. "I can't get him to do anything. He won't even eat. They keep calling him from the office. They say he is

476

going to lose his job if he doesn't come in, but how can he? None of us can do anything. We keep wondering. Where is he?"

"I understand," I said.

"Please, tell me you have news," she said as we sat down.

"I'm sorry, Ma'am. I don't," I said. "We're here because we need you to tell us more about Noah. It will help the investigation if we know him better."

The disappointment was visible on her face. "Well, I guess no news is better than bad news," she mumbled.

"Have they arrested that Johnson fellow yet?" Steven Kinley suddenly said from his chair. I looked at him. He still stared out the window.

"No, we haven't, Sir," I said.

"But, it must be him," Lauren Kinley said with a slight whimper. "It all fits. He was just released, and then our son disappears, just like that other boy all those years ago. I called the station and told them to look at him, you do have…You have checked him out, right?"

"We have searched his home several times, Ma'am, and we've had him in for questioning more than once. If he has your son, we will find out," Beth said. "Don't you worry."

I could tell she believed Vernon Johnson was guilty as well. It made something turn inside of me. After my talk with my mother, I had realized I had been busy trying to make him guilty as well. But the fact was, he couldn't have kept or buried Scott Kingston, since he was in jail at that time. It would only be possible if he hadn't worked alone. There was nothing placing him at the scene of the crime when Scott Kingston was kidnapped. Only one boy's testimony, which had now been withdrawn, because he wasn't sure it was actually Vernon he saw.

It was my idea to try and have another talk with Noah's parents…to maybe try for another angle on the case. I seemed to be the only one doubting Vernon Johnson's guilt.

"As long as we haven't found your son, there is still hope he is alive," I said. "That's why we need you to tell us everything about him. Even the smallest of details that you think might not be of interest might help us."

THIRTY-SIX

May 2015

"Do you have children, Detective?"

Lauren Kinley looked at me intensely. Her husband Steven had come closer and was sitting with us while we spoke about Noah. It seemed like talking about him made Steven Kinley warm up to us, made him feel better, and got him out of this state of apathy he seemed to be caught in. When speaking of his son, he lit up, and so did his wife. They appeared to be very loving parents and to still have deep affection for one another, even with all they were going through. I couldn't help comparing them to Scott Kingston's parents. Would the Kinleys end up like them in twenty-eight years? I couldn't bear the thought. We had to find this boy. This wasn't going to end like it had back then. I kept wondering if there was anything about the parents or the family that made the kidnapper choose them. Was there anything linking the two cases, other than the fact that the boys were both taken from their own rooms?

"Yes, I do. I have three and one on the way," I said. It felt good to finally be able to tell everyone that Shannon and I were having a baby. Shannon had held a press conference earlier this morning, just before we left the hospital, and now the news was everywhere. I felt very proud.

"Jack is the guy dating the country singer, Shannon King. She's pregnant," Lauren said, addressed to her husband. He didn't look like he cared. "I'm sorry," she said, addressed to me. "I watch a lot of TV. Keeps me from thinking all the time. Steven prefers to sit still and worry. I can't stand the silence in the house these days. I need to have some noise around me."

I could vividly imagine how hard it must be to have to wait for news about your son, not knowing if the next call on the phone would be the police asking you to come down to ID your own child. The very thought made me shiver.

"The teachers at his school tell us Noah had a little trouble," I said, looking at my notepad. I haven't gotten much out of my talk with them so far. Noah seemed to be a very ordinary boy, who had a tendency to get himself in trouble at school, played baseball on Wednesdays, and had guitar lessons on Thursdays. Nothing really struck me as out of the ordinary. Some of my colleagues had already spoken to his best friend's parents, back on Merritt Island, but found nothing suspicious in any of their statements.

"Yes, he did. He was having a hard time adjusting to the new school," Lauren said. "But he is the sweetest of boys. Just missing his old friends, that's all."

I looked at the picture of Noah that the parents had given us and tried to compare it to that of Scott Kingston that we had at the office. The two boys didn't seem very alike. Scott was redheaded, while Noah was blond. Scott was slightly overweight, while Noah was small and skinny. If this was the same guy, then what triggered him about his victims? How did he meet them? Why these two boys of all the boys around here? And why wait twenty-eight years between them?

"Did anything happen in his life up till his disappearance that we might need to know? Did you see anyone suspicious in the street watching your house? A car that was maybe parked close by? Anything?"

Lauren looked at Steven, who looked like he could break down any moment now. The thought that they might have been able to hinder the kidnapping if they had been more alert had to be eating them alive. I knew I would be wondering constantly. Was there anything I could have done differently?

"Not that we can think of, detective," Lauren said.

"Noah did have nightmares a lot," Steven said.

"Well, we had just moved," Lauren said. "The move seemed to affect him a lot. He kept dreaming the same thing over and over again."

I leaned over and looked at both of them. "What did he dream?"

"Just the usual stuff. He believed a man was looking at him through the sliding doors. But it was just a nightmare. I kept telling him it was."

THIRTY-SEVEN

May 2015

I COULDN'T STOP THINKING about the Kinleys when I got home and all the next day. I didn't like that we had no trace of their son whatsoever. As the days passed, the probability of him turning up alive became smaller and smaller.

I was going through my notes and everything on the whiteboard when Ron suddenly stormed in. He looked at me and I knew something was up.

"They found something," I said, while images of the Kinley's horrified faces flickered for my eyes.

Please don't. Please don't let it be Noah, God.

Ron nodded. "A body showed up at another construction site. At the A1A just past Sixteenth Street, where they're building those new condominiums. Let's go!"

We drove there with our hearts in our throats and met with Head of the Cocoa Beach Police Department, the woman we called Weasel, in front of the site. She greeted us as we stepped out of the car. "It was Yamilla who believed this would be of interest to you," she said.

Weasel escorted us to Yamilla. She asked us to come closer and look at what they had found. I was relieved to see it wasn't a recently buried body. It was just bones. It couldn't be Noah.

"It hasn't been in the ground as long as Scott," Yamilla said. "But I'm guessing maybe ten years, give or take some."

I stared at the bones and especially the femur. I swallowed hard. It wasn't very long. "A child?" I asked.

Yamilla nodded. "Looks like it. I don't know much yet. I'll let you know when I know more," she said.

We let her work and drove back to the office. I stared at the whiteboard for a long time, wondering how I was supposed to crack this case open. If it turned out this was another one by the same guy that had killed Scott Kingston, then there was no way this could be Vernon. Everyone had to see that. Were we chasing a killer that had been abducting and killing small children since the eighties? Who the heck was he, and how had he managed to get away with it for this long? How many others were out there? How many more bodies were we going to find?

The thought made me sick to my stomach.

I decided to call it a day and drove back to my parents' motel, grabbed my board, and jumped into the water. Nothing could clear my mind like an hour of surfing. Waves were good. The storm in the Atlantic had moved closer the last twenty-four hours and had given us some very sizable waves. My dad was watching the storm anxiously, while I enjoyed the waves it produced. The forecasters didn't agree on what it was going to do next. Most models kept it off the coast, but a few of them had it hit right on. It was still moving closer very slowly and was threatening The Bahamas now. It was expected to make landfall there tonight. The area it covered over the Atlantic was so big we'd had rain and clouds for days now. It was so rare for Florida to have this kind of weather. I hoped Anna would continue up the coast, so it would continue to produce waves for four or five days still, and then give us off-shore winds as it continued north. That was how we surfers felt about storms. We loved them as long as they stayed in the ocean.

My friend Tom came out to surf with me and we caught waves together for about an hour and a half. It was nice to talk about something else for a change. Noah Kinley was all that had been on my mind all day. Especially his parents. I found it hard to bear that they still hadn't gotten their son back. I couldn't accept the fact that I hadn't been able to help them yet, to bring back the boy. I was so relieved that it wasn't Noah's body we had found on the construction site, but it still ate me up that I had no answers for them. My colleagues were looking for Noah everywhere and had had the dogs out searching the area for the third time, but still with no results. No trace of the boy.

When we were done surfing, Tom and I grabbed a beer on my parents' deck, while the twins threw themselves at him. My kids loved Tom and had known him since they were born.

"So, when are you getting your new board?" he asked.

"I checked on it a week ago," I said. "It's coming along, but still needs the paint job."

"And they're shaping it at Swell? How come? You usually always use the same shaper."

I nodded. Swell was the surf shop across the street from my parent's motel. It was owned by a guy that I had surfed with often. He had talked about shaping a board for me for a very long time.

"I know. I made a nice deal with the owner. He's a surfer himself. I buy so much stuff over there all the time, and a few weeks ago when I was in there, he saw me looking at one of the boards he had shaped. It was very nicely done. He told me he could make me one exactly the way I wanted it for less than four hundred. I had to try."

"That is very cheap," Tom said.

"He makes beautiful boards. Have you seen them over there? He used to be a carpenter or something; he's very crafty with his hands. I'm pretty excited to see how it's going to be."

"Will you stay for dinner, Tom?" Abigail asked and looked at him with pleading eyes.

"Yes, Tom, stay," I said.

THIRTY-EIGHT

April 1980

"Cuba is open."

Hector stared at his brother Raul. He had knocked on the door to Hector's house early in the morning.

"It's true," he said. "We can go get them. We can get our family. They just announced it on the radio. Castro opened the port of Mariel. Anyone can leave if they have someone to pick them up."

Hector couldn't believe it. It had been eleven years since he had left Cuba and left his daughter, Isabella. Every day since, he had dreamt of holding her in his arms again. Could this really be? Was this really happening?

"Pick them up? But how do we do that?" Hector asked.

"We get a boat," Raul said, grinning. "We go down south and get a boat. Then we pick them up."

Hector and Raul jumped in the car and headed to Miami. When they arrived, there were Cubans everywhere—just like them—trying to find a boat.

"It's impossible," Raul said, discouraged by seeing the hundreds of people crowding the harbor. "There aren't enough boats."

"Let's go to Key West," Hector said.

The drive from Miami took six hours. They were driving in long lines all afternoon, every car packed with Cuban exiles with the same mission as Hector and Raul. Hector felt so frustrated and cursed loudly. Raul felt the irritation as well. It was hot in the car, and at the pace they were driving, they weren't going to make it till dark. At the same time, Hector started doubting if they would be even able to find a boat. If everyone in these cars was going to try and get a boat, there wouldn't be any left once they got down there.

"You gotta keep the hope up, brother," Raul said, and pressed the horn on the car for the fifteenth time. The traffic had almost stalled and they were sweating in the car. Hector leaned out the window. They had water on both sides of the car. He could see nothing but cars as far as the eye could reach.

483

"Think about Isabella. Think about seeing her again."

Hector nodded. Raul was right. Seeing her again would be worth all of this. He was just so worried that he wasn't going to succeed.

The car in front of them moved and soon they were back into a little more speed. At least they were moving ahead.

"Everything good comes to he who waits," Raul said. "Trust me. By this time tomorrow, you'll be holding your daughter in your arms. I promise you."

Hector looked at Raul. He felt like throwing up. He was so nervous. Not only because he feared he wouldn't be right, but also because he feared that he was. How was Isabella going to react when seeing her father after this many years? Would she even be able to recognize him? Would she be angry with him for leaving her? Would he be able to become the father he always wanted to be?

It was dark when they reached Key West. Just like in Miami, Cuban exiles were everywhere. They searched for a boat until it was almost midnight before they finally found one. Hector wrote the owner of the boat a check for ten thousand dollars. Just after midnight, they jumped in the boat and took off without having the slightest idea where to find their family members that they hadn't seen in eleven years. They didn't know if it was true—or just a rumor—that Cubans were now allowed to leave the island, or if the two of them would even be able to return to Florida again.

All they had was their undying hope.

THIRTY-NINE

May 2015

SHANNON WAS ALREADY SO bored she had no idea what to do with herself. Dr. Stanton had told her she had to rest as much as possible, and that was all she had done all day. He had been by and checked up on her and told her she was doing much better. But she still had to stay still, probably for the rest of the pregnancy. Everything inside of her had screamed. *Six more months like this!*

It had only been two days.

The good part was, she had written two songs the last two days and played her guitar like crazy. It seemed to be the only thing that would take her mind off of worrying. She seemed to be worrying about everything, but especially the murder case. She couldn't believe they hadn't found that gun yet and started to fear they never would. She was also very concerned about the entire building-a-house-together-and-moving-in-project. She loved Jack's family like crazy, but it was a lot. It was a big change for her and for Angela. And it was going to be an even bigger change once the baby arrived.

Now, she was getting out of Jack's condo for the first time in two days. She was going to have dinner with the rest of the family at the motel. The doctor had told her it was all right to go out and walk a little every day from now on. That was at least something.

Shannon enjoyed letting the warm breeze hit her face when she stepped out into the sand. She walked barefooted with her shoes in her hand to the motel. She breathed in the fresh air and stared at the dark horizon where Anna was roaming. The ocean looked like an angry monster baring its teeth at her. The sky above the water was so dark it looked like it was the end of the world out there, or maybe a scene from *Lord of The Rings*. Maybe she had just been watching too much TV lately.

Jack greeted her on the deck with a kiss and a hand on her stomach. "Is everything well?" he asked.

"Everything is fine," she said.

485

"And does Dr. Stanton agree to that?"

"Yes, Dr. Stanton agrees. He told me I can start taking walks every day now."

Jack smiled. His hair was still wet from being in the ocean. It fell to his face and made him look like a drowned puppy.

"Dinner is served," Jack's mother said and rang the ship bell like she always did to call the children.

Seconds later, they were everywhere. Angela hardly noticed her mother. She was way too busy with the twins. It was amazing to Shannon how fast Angela had adapted to her new family. They acted like they had known each other all their lives. Shannon felt emotional and pressed back her tears. They were coming so easily lately. Probably just the hormones.

Jack grabbed a beer from the bar inside and returned. He brought Shannon a soda. She sat down next to him with a soft sigh. This was all good. Everything was good right at this moment. It amazed her how she didn't even crave a drink anymore. Not since she discovered the pregnancy. Just the thought of alcohol made her feel sick.

Jack's friend Tom was eating with them and Shannon enjoyed having an adult conversation for once. Tom and his wife Eliza had recently decided to separate, and he really needed to talk. Shannon was happy to lend him an ear.

"So, you guys are building a house, huh?" he said, once he had finished pouring his heart out.

Shannon looked at Jack, who nodded. "Yes," he said. "I just approved the floor plan today."

"You did?" Shannon asked, surprised.

Jack nodded while sipping his beer.

"You didn't even let me in on it?" Shannon asked.

"We didn't make any major changes since the first draft," he said. "I figured you had enough on your plate."

"I had nothing to do all day," Shannon said. "I could easily have looked at them."

Jack looked perplexed. Shannon fought her anger. She didn't like to be kept out of things. She felt like she was being treated like a child.

"I'm sorry," Jack said. "I thought I was helping you out."

Shannon inhaled, then drank from her soda. She decided to let it go. Meanwhile, Jack showed Tom the floor plan on his iPad.

"It is going to be truly amazing," Tom said. "I am so glad someone finally bought that old lot and didn't care about that old story."

"What story is that?" Shannon asked.

"Yeah, what story?" Jack said.

Tom looked at their faces.

"You don't know?"

"No," Jack said.

"I thought you knew," Tom said. He looked at Jack. "I mean…with the case and everything."

"What case? What story?" Shannon asked. She felt an unease spreading fast in her body.

"Jack's case," Tom said. "The kidnapping."

Jack frowned. "The Noah Kinley case? What are you talking about?"

"No. The other one. Scott Kingston. It used to be their house on that land. The house that used to be on the lot was where Scott Kingston was kidnapped from. They abandoned the house when they realized he wasn't coming back. They couldn't live there anymore. But they couldn't sell it either. Everyone knew the story. No one dared to buy the house where a kid was stolen in the middle of the night. So, the bank took over and later a hurricane destroyed the house. I thought you knew."

"Well, we didn't," Jack said.

"You didn't see the address on the old case files?" Tom asked.

Jack shook his head. "I guess I didn't notice." He looked at his mother, who was sitting next to Tom. "Did you know about this?" he asked. "You did, didn't you? Of course you did. You know everything around here."

His mother shrugged. "I didn't think it was important," she said.

"Not important? How can it not be important?" Jack asked.

Shannon could tell he was getting himself all worked up now. She herself didn't know how to react. She had heard about the kidnapping from Jack, but to actually live where it happened? She wasn't so sure she wanted that. Not that she usually was superstitious, but still. It just didn't feel right.

"It was so long ago, Jack," Sherri said. "I thought it was such a shame that lot was still empty. It's a great location. Where else in this world do you have water this close on both sides? You said so yourself. You love it here, son. What does it matter that something bad happened there almost thirty years ago?"

Shannon didn't say anything, but to her it mattered. It mattered a great deal.

FORTY

May 2015

SHANNON WAS VISIBLY upset and I tried hard to convince her it didn't mean anything, that it wasn't important for us if a boy had been kidnapped from the property almost thirty years ago. She didn't seem to agree.

"I can't live in a place where kids are not safe," she said, when we got back to the condo. "What if he returns? He hasn't been caught yet and might just have stolen another kid here in Cocoa Beach."

"Exactly," I said. "Don't you see? It doesn't matter what house or property we're in."

"Not an argument that helps a whole lot," she said.

"It has nothing to do with the place or property," I said. I didn't understand why she was freaking out about this so badly. I mean, I was upset that no one had told us, but I had let it go right away. It wasn't that big of a deal. But to Shannon, it was, apparently.

"I just don't like it, Jack. I really don't."

"So, now you don't want to build a house, after all, is that what you're saying?" I asked.

She sighed and threw herself on the couch. I told the kids to get ready for bed. Emily had already gone to her room and closed the door. I hadn't talked to her all day and had planned to do so when we got home. Maybe even watch *The Tonight Show* with her before bedtime.

"I don't know what I'm saying," Shannon said.

I sat down next to her. "You're tired. Maybe we should continue this talk tomorrow when we've had a good night's sleep."

Shannon looked at me angrily.

Uh-oh. What did I do now?

"Please don't talk to me like that, Jack. Please don't patronize me. It's bad enough you make me feel like a child by not including me in decisions. Don't start talking to me like I'm a child too."

488

I sighed and closed my eyes. I felt so tired. Pleasing everybody was a lot of work. Shannon was very emotional right now, and there was no way she was capable of making any important decisions. I had never seen her overreact like this and blamed it on the pregnancy.

We sat in silence for a little while. I had no idea what to say to her to not upset her further and decided to not speak at all. After about ten minutes, I got up.

"Where are you going?" she asked.

"I'm going to Emily's room to watch *The Tonight Show*."

"So, that's it? You're leaving in the middle of an argument?" Shannon asked.

I sighed again. "I don't know what to say to you. I want this house. I have dreamt of building this house all of my life. I want us to be a family. I don't want a stupid thing like this to destroy everything."

"Well, I don't think it is stupid," Shannon said.

"Let's talk about it later," I said.

I walked into Emily's room. She smiled when she saw me. She had already turned on her TV and I guessed she thought I wasn't going to come. This was our tradition and I wanted to honor it for as long as she would let me. After all, I didn't have many years left with her before she would leave the nest. It was all about enjoying every moment.

Naturally, Jimmy Fallon only made it past his monologue before I fell asleep.

FORTY-ONE

May 2015

SHANNON and I didn't discuss the matter further the next morning. The mornings were way too busy with getting the kids fed, dressed, and to the school bus on time. Shannon was nauseated and spent most of the morning in the bathroom throwing up, while I took care of the kids.

As soon as they were off on the bus, I jumped in my car and drove to the office. I wanted to get there as early as possible, since Yamilla had called me yesterday and asked me to come to the ME's office today. I had to finish some paperwork, answer a few emails, and then I was off.

Yamilla greeted me in the lobby and told me to come with her downstairs. I hated going there, the smell alone made me sick to my stomach. I simply didn't understand how Yamilla did it, how she could work in a place like this.

"I have news on Scott Kingston," she said and approached a table where she had put the bones together so it almost looked like a skeleton. A few bones were still missing and hadn't been found...probably taken by animals over the years.

"Great," I said.

"After thorough examination, I have finally found a cause of death. I believe he starved to death."

I stared at Yamilla. "Starved to death?"

"I see serious signs of malnutrition in the bones. They're not developed properly. Around the age of seven, something went wrong. His body stopped developing and his growth slowed down drastically...signs of severe malnutrition or starvation. It also shows in the skeleton's spinal curvature. The bones have rickets and his teeth were affected. There is no trauma to the bones or skull indicating the death could have had another cause."

"How old was he when he died?"

"I believe he was fourteen."

It fit with the fact that the building he was found under was constructed in ninety-three. It had been a construction site at that point. An easy way to dispose of a body.

"So, we know for sure now that the kidnapper kept him alive for seven years?" I asked. It still surprised me. How the heck was this even possible without anyone noticing? Someone must have seen the boy. Neighbors? The kidnapper's family? Where had he been for seven years?

"I think he did. I think he fed him just about enough to keep him alive. For some reason, he didn't want to kill him right away. I believe he kept him in a small place. A place he couldn't stand upright. If you look at the spine, it is so curved, I believe he must have been kept in very small room or something like it. He was crouched for a long time while his body tried to grow."

I drew in a deep breath. Starvation? Kept for seven years in a small room? Who was this creep?

Yamilla cleared her throat and approached another table with a microscope.

"We also found this in the dirt," she said. "Close to the body."

I looked in the microscope and saw tiny splinters.

"Wood?"

"Yes, searchers found pieces of birch bark in the ground next to him. This type of birch bark isn't commonly seen around here. It's very sustainable and takes a long time to decompose. I think the splinters might have been in his body, maybe in his fingers and under his nails."

"From scratching," I said, my heart in my throat.

"Yes. Maybe on a wooden door," she said.

I wrote it down while Yamilla continued to another skeleton. I recognized it as the remains we found on the construction site a couple of days ago.

"We just got a positive ID on this one. Say hello to Jordan Turner," she said. "Jordan was thirteen when he died. Also from starvation. We found the exact same signs in his bones as in Scott Kingston. This one was also kept in a small room and suffered from a severe vitamin D deficiency from the lack of sunlight. He is from Rockledge. He was reported missing in September, 1999."

FORTY-TWO

May 2015

NOAH HAD NO MORE TEARS. He couldn't cry anymore. His legs were hurting from being in the box, his mouth so dry he couldn't swallow. He was so thirsty it made him delirious. Being in constant darkness made him sleep constantly. Now, the lid to the box was opened and he was being pulled out. His body felt so weak he couldn't get up on his own. The light from the window hurt his eyes.

The man placed Noah on the ground. Noah blinked his eyes. A slap across his face woke him up. Noah cried; his cheek was burning. He looked at the man in front of him. His nostrils were flaring; his eyes burning with fire. Noah gasped. He had seen this look in the man's eyes before. The last time he had looked at him like this he had beaten him with a stick. Noah still had stripes on his back.

"Thirsty," Noah whimpered. "I'm so thirsty."

The man laughed loudly. "Thirsty, huh? I bet you're hungry too."

Noah nodded feebly. "Yes."

Violently Noah felt the man grab him by the hair, and soon he was pulled forcefully backwards. Screaming, he was dragged into another room, where he was placed in a shower and stripped of his clothes.

Noah smiled when he saw the showerhead above him, thinking finally he was getting a bath, finally he would get water. He opened his mouth, thinking, hoping, and dreaming of the soft water streaming at him from the showerhead. He closed his eyes and laughed in anticipation of finally getting all the water he could drink, of finally getting rid of this awful smell he was in constantly from his own body rotting inside the box. When he opened his eyes, the man was standing in front of him holding a bucket in his hand. Noah looked surprised at the bucket and managed to think in the split of a second that maybe the showerhead was broken and the man would just give him a bath using water from a bucket, when a second later he was hit in the face with something ice cold. So cold it hurt when it touched his naked skin.

Noah screamed and cried, while the man laughed, lifted another bucket up and threw it at Noah. The ice cold water felt like needles to the skin when it landed all over Noah, who bent to the ground in terror, crying and screaming his heart out.

Water dripped from his nose. His body trembled. He tried to get some in his mouth and cupped his hands to gather a handful and drink it, but he was so cold his hands couldn't be still long enough for him to hold on to the water.

"Please, stop," Noah cried. "Please, stop this. I want to go home. I want to go home to my mom."

He fell to his knees and pleaded while another bucket of ice cold water hit him on the head. He screamed and cried while the man laughed and laughed at him. Seconds later, yet another bucket landed on top of his head. Noah shivered and screamed.

"Help me," he cried. "Please, help me."

"No one can help you, pretty boy. No one can help your rich little ass now. Your mom and dad are gone; they left you to rot in here," the man hissed, then grabbed Noah's ankle and started to pull him across the floor.

Noah felt his body be lifted from the ground and soon he was put back in the small wooden box and the lid closed. Noah cried and screamed for help, fighting the lid so it wouldn't close, but it was no use. The man left without a word, leaving Noah alone again with nothing but the cold as companion.

FORTY-THREE

May 2015

"Jordan Turner," Ron said and hung up an old picture of the boy from the case file, taken in 1998, the year before he disappeared.

"A black kid that disappeared on his way home from school on September tenth 1999. The case was investigated as a runaway, since Jordan had gotten himself in trouble at school and was facing his parents' punishment when he got home. It was believed he simply never wanted to come home. He was nine at the time he disappeared. Friends talked about a car with a man inside of it that had been parked at the school. The driver had asked Jordan for directions outside of the school. Jordan spoke to him shortly, and then walked home alone as usual. Jordan was reported missing the next day to Rockledge Police, but as I said, they believed he had run away and the case was never closed."

"But they didn't do anything to solve it either, I'm guessing," I said, thinking a black kid from a bad neighborhood running away didn't get much attention.

Ron shrugged. "Those are the facts."

"What do we know about the driver of that car?" I asked.

Ron looked at the case file. "Not much. The man was black, the car was an old beat up Ford, uh...that's about it."

"That's not much," I said, leaning back in my chair. "They didn't make a drawing or anything?"

Ron shook his head. "Like I said, they treated it like a runaway. So many kids run away from home every year..."

I knew what he was saying, even though I didn't like it. I wrote the details on my notepad, while Ron closed the meeting. I went back to my desk. I checked the radar. I had been doing that all day. Anna was getting closer and closer to the coast, and the forecasters were getting anxious. It had done a solid amount of damage to The Bahamas when it went through there. If it decided to make landfall, we would have to evacuate the entire coastline. We were all holding our breath.

494

Meanwhile, I had this knot in my stomach from last night. Shannon and I still hadn't talked things out, and I was worried what was going on between us. Was it just the pregnancy? The fear of the future? I could understand if she was worried and nervous about it. So was I. But wasn't it always like that when you were expecting, when big changes came in your life?

I feared she was going to say she didn't want to live on the lot. That would be the worst.

I opened the floor plan from the architect and looked at it. It was truly my dream house. I had even added a sundeck as a surprise to Shannon, since I knew she would love to have one. From up there, you would be able to look over both the ocean and Intracoastal. It didn't get anymore beautiful than that.

I sighed and closed the document, then looked at my phone. She hadn't called yet. Beth approached my desk. She threw me the keys to one of the cars.

"You ready?"

I sighed and looked at her. "Don't think I ever will be."

We got in and drove to the address in Rockledge where Jordan Turner used to live. It was in one of the worst parts of town, the same place we had more than often been called out to drug related shootings. The house was from the fifties, and hadn't been maintained for many years. It was located right next to a road where cars drove past at forty-five miles an hour. Not exactly a safe environment for a kid to grow up, I thought to myself. On the porch sat an old woman on a chair. I approached her.

"Excuse me, Ma'am. We're looking for Mrs. or Mr. Turner. Do they still live here?"

The woman nodded. "That's my daughter," she said. "She's inside."

FORTY-FOUR

May 2015

_____

"THEY'RE CHARGING you with murder. I just got the news."

Shannon stared out the window of the condo, but didn't really see. Instead, images of her in an orange jumper with her hands in cuffs flickered for her inner eye.

"Excuse me?" she asked her lawyer on the phone. "They can't do that!"

He sighed. It wasn't a good sign. "I'm afraid they can," he said. "They have Joe's letter stating you killed Robert Hill with the microphone stand. I don't know what else they have yet, but they seem pretty sure about this, about your guilt."

"But I'm not," Shannon said. "I'm not guilty."

She felt dizzy and sat on one of Jack's chairs. Outside, the storm was moving closer and it was pouring down rain. She saw lightning on the horizon. "I'm not guilty, John. You know I'm innocent. How can they do this to me? I told them everything."

"They think you're lying, Shannon. They believe they have enough material to convict you. That's how these things work," John said.

Shannon had stopped breathing. She felt how the blood was leaving her head. Her stomach turned into a huge knot.

They're going to convict me, aren't they? They're going to put me in jail and I am going to have my baby in jail. Oh, my God, they'll take my baby away from me. I won't get to see my baby grow up, will I?

"Now, Shannon, it's important to take it easy. Nothing is decided yet. There will be a trial, and that's when we'll do everything we can to prove your innocence. I still believe there is hope, and you should too, Shannon. But we need to be smart about this. I need you to try and stay calm and keep your head cool, alright?"

Shannon gasped for air. She was panicking. "I...I...I'm so scared, John. I'm terrified."

"Of course you are," he said. "Now, take it easy and breathe, and when I hang up you call Jack and ask him to come home and help you stay calm. We can't have you collapsing again, Shannon. We have to think of the baby. I might be able to push things back. I'll be pleading that they wait till the baby is born before we go to trial. I'm going to try for that first. That should give us at least six months, if not more, since I will argue that you need time with the baby and physically won't be ready for trial till several weeks after the birth. Plus, you can't breastfeed in court. I think we're looking at trial around Christmas, if all goes well. That gives us a lot of time to figure out our defense strategy."

"Will they arrest me?"

"I have spoken to the State's Attorney and convinced them you are no flight risk. You've already paid a quite huge bail amount, so I think we're good for now. Just don't go out of the country the next couple of months. I need you to stay put."

"That's not going to be a problem," Shannon said.

"Okay. Now, take it easy, then call Jack and I'll be in touch as soon as I know more details. No panicking, you hear me?"

Shannon took in a deep breath. "Alright."

"Talk to you soon."

As soon as Shannon hung up, she felt the tears well up in her eyes. She let them go. She sat for a few seconds and cried while staring at the phone. Then she got up and threw it across the room with a loud scream.

"You bastard, Joe!! You BASTARD!"

FORTY-FIVE

May 2015

BETH and I had finished talking to Mrs. Turner, who had lost her husband five years ago. She had cried a lot when we told her what happened to her son, but at the same time, she was happy to finally get closure. All these years, she had wondered where he was and why he didn't come home.

"It gets so bad, you catch yourself just staring out the window, into the street and expect him to walk around the corner any second," she told us.

It was raining when we stepped out of her house. And when it rained in Florida, it poured. We said our goodbyes and promised to keep her updated if there was any news in the case, then ran towards the car and jumped inside. We closed the doors, then looked at each other and laughed. We were both soaked just from that little run. The rain was still pouring heavily on the windshield.

"That was interesting, huh?" Beth said, when I drove into the street, where the cars had slowed down due to the heavy rain. Our wipers couldn't keep up with the amount of water that was being poured on us.

"It definitely was," I said.

"How come she didn't tell the police what she knew?" Beth asked.

"Probably no one wanted to listen," I said. "A black woman from a poor neighborhood back in the nineties? Not a chance."

"So, what do we do now?" she asked.

"I don't know yet. But we need to go talk to the people at the shop tomorrow," I said. "The fact that she had seen the guy in the Ford parked on the street in front of her house every day for at least a week before her son disappeared is certainly something that should have been investigated back then."

"And that she had seen him before? I can't believe it wasn't investigated," Beth said.

"I know. It's mentioned nowhere in the report, even though she did tell the police that she had seen the guy, that she knew where he worked."

"I can't believe that the same roofing company is still there," I said with a chuckle. "This many years later."

"Well, Mrs. Turner said it was a family business, and that the son had taken over now. But there is always work to do in the roofing business, right?"

I looked out the window at the black clouds covering the horizon. "And there sure will be if Anna gets any closer."

I had just parked the car in front of the Sheriff's Office and run inside through the rain when my phone started to ring. It was Shannon. I picked it up.

"Hi, sweetheart."

"Jack, oh, Jack."

She could hardly speak. I could tell she was tearing up. A million thoughts flickered through my mind. Had something happened to the baby? Had she lost it?

"What's wrong, Shannon? Talk to me. Is it something with the baby? Has something happened?"

"I...I...I need you."

"I'm coming home right away," I said, as I grabbed my car keys from my desk. I signaled to Beth that I had to go home and she understood. I ran to the car and got in. The rain wasn't as heavy as it had been earlier. It would soon be quieting down.

"Talk to me, Shannon. What's going on?"

"They've...my lawyer called. They've decided to charge me with first degree murder," she said, her voice trembling.

My heart dropped. I couldn't believe it. I started the car. "Stay where you are. I'm coming home."

FORTY-SIX

Cuba, April 1980

"ISABELLA SUAREZ? Have you seen a young girl, sixteen years old? She might be with an elderly couple. Their names are Suarez?"

Everything was chaos. When Raul and Hector finally docked in the harbor of Mariel, boats waited everywhere, hundreds of boats…from tiny skiffs to yachts. On the docks, the crowds of people waited, all looking for a way out. Names were being shouted in the crowds, some screamed in joy when they found each other, others cried. In search of their own family, Raul and Hector talked to many of them and soon realized that the rumors had been true. Castro had allowed everyone with a permit to leave Cuba. They could only hope their family was among those that had been granted a permit.

And they could only pray that they would be able to find each other. Until now, they had met nothing but shaking heads, and people telling them: "Sorry, but no."

Still, they kept going. Yelling their family name into the crowds, tapping people's shoulders and asking them personally if they had seen them, met them, or even heard about the Suarez family, about Isabella.

But, after hours of searching, they still hadn't found them.

As the sun set on the horizon and many boats left with their families onboard, Hector felt the panic spread once again. Would he ever find Isabella? Would he ever look into her beautiful eyes again?

He wasn't ready to give up hope.

Hector glared at the many boats leaving the harbor, at people in warm embraces, holding their family members tight, sailing towards the Promised Land, and he could only dream that it would soon be him, holding his daughter in his arms again.

As darkness lay its thick covers over the harbor, the yelling of names was still heard in the distance, and neither Hector nor Raul was ready to give up for the day. They continued to ask their way through the crowds, and finally found someone who recognized their names.

"Suarez? Yeah. I know them," the young man said. "They were the ones who crashed into the Peruvian Embassy in a bus. They were the ones that started all this."

Hector felt the excitement rise inside of him. He had heard about the crash into the embassy on the radio back in the U.S. He had heard how people had stormed the embassy afterwards. This was good news.

"How many were they?"

"I believe it was a young girl, her grandparents, and her uncle."

Hector lit up. They were together, all of them.

"Do you know if they got a permit to leave?" he asked.

"Yeah, they did. Everyone at the embassy did. I know. I was there and I got my permit this morning."

Hector smiled widely. "So, they are here?" he asked.

The man shrugged. "They should be. I'm pretty sure they were among the first to get permits."

"And when was that?"

"Two days ago," he said.

"Two days ago! But that is such a long time ago." Hector sighed and ran a hand through his hair.

The young man shrugged. "Sorry." He placed a hand on Hector's shoulder. "Maybe they're still here, waiting somewhere. We are all just waiting and hoping to find our families. I hope my brother will come."

Hector thanked the young man and wished him good luck in finding his brother, then walked back to the boat that Raul was guarding so no one would steal it. He sat on his chair on the deck, looking hopefully at Hector.

"Any news?"

Hector nodded and told him what the young man had said. He could tell it gave Raul hope.

"They must be here somewhere, then," he said and got up. He walked up to Hector and patted his shoulder with a wide smile. "You're worn out. Let me take the next round."

FORTY-SEVEN

May 2015

I FOUND Shannon sitting on the balcony of my condo overlooking the ocean and the almost black clouds. The rain had ceased, but it still looked like the end of the world closing in on us.

"Shannon. Are you alright?" I asked and hugged her.

She had been crying.

"I don't know, Jack. I am not sure I will ever be. I mean, what am I going to do? I have a baby on the way, but what if I never get to see him or her grow up? We're building this awesome house, but will I ever live in it?"

I pulled her closer to me. My heart was racing in my chest. I was terrified, but I couldn't let her know. I had to be the strong one. But, of course, I was scared. What if I had to raise this child alone? What if I lost Shannon?

I looked into her eyes. "Nothing is decided yet," I said. "You're not convicted yet. You have a very good and very expensive lawyer working your case. You need to keep your head cool and not panic. We'll solve this together."

Shannon sniffled and nodded. I looked into her eyes and moved a lock of hair from her face.

"We can do this," I continued. "You and I can do this together. It's not over yet. But I need you to be strong for me. Can you do that?"

Shannon bit her lip and shook her head. "I don't think I can."

I grabbed her hand and pulled her up from her chair. "Come with me," I said.

I took her to the lot. Our lot. The heavy rain had forced the workers to pause, and their heavy machines stood still on the ground. The rain had turned the soil into mud. We got dirty feet from walking across it in our flip-flops. I pulled Shannon by the hand and escorted her to the middle of the lot. The workers had cleared the ground now and the old remains of the Kingston's house were finally completely gone. There was nothing left to remind us of what had once happened here.

"What are we doing here, Jack?" Shannon asked.

I asked her to stand still, then walked away from her and stopped. "Right here, Shannon," I said, and pointed to the ground beneath me. "Right here is where our bedroom is going to be."

I took ten big steps around to the right, then looked at her again. "And here is where the twins' room is going to be. I know they'll want to keep sharing a room, since they've always loved that."

I took another couple of steps towards her. "And right here is where Angela will be sleeping. I've talked to her about painting her room in a jungle theme with monkeys hanging from the trees."

Shannon chuckled. "She does love monkeys."

"I know she does," I said and walked a lot of steps towards the end of the lot, then stopped. "This is where Emily will be living."

I walked a little back towards her, then pointed again. "All the bedrooms are on the second floor, but on the first, right underneath where I am standing, we have the living room, the dining room, the kitchen, and an office for each of us. Yours will be turned into a studio, so you can make your music at home. I've talked to your producer at your label, and he will be arranging it so it's perfect, with everything you need, since I know nothing about making music, and, as hard as it is for me to admit it, am tone-deaf."

"That's not true!" Shannon said. "I heard you sing in the shower." She chuckled again.

"Anyway," I said, and walked all the way over to her, leaned over, and kissed her. I looked into her eyes. "Right where you're standing, on the second floor, next to our room, will be the best room of all. That's the nursery. I figured we could open the window and let him or her fall asleep to the sound of the crashing waves."

Shannon looked at me, her eyes moist. "Oh, Jack. It's going to be beautiful."

I grabbed her around the waist and pulled her closer. "We're going to be very happy here, Shannon. And you will too. I picture you sitting on the deck in a rocking chair with our baby in your arms, rocking it to sleep while you look at the ocean."

Shannon stared at me, and just as I saw the hint of a smile, a dark cloud seemed to cover her face. She removed my arms and walked away. "But, the thing is, I will never get to experience all that."

"Yes, you will, Shannon. I'm not doing it without you." I took in a deep breath, and then dropped to my knee. Shannon stared at me and clasped her face. I pulled out a small box from my pocket, opened it, and looked up at her.

"Shannon King," I said, my voice breaking. "Will you marry me?"

FORTY-EIGHT

May 2015

I HAD BEEN WAITING for the right time, and no time seemed more right than this moment. It wasn't spectacular. It wasn't perfect in a traditional way. There were no flowers, no band or violinist. Just me kneeling in the mud at the ground of our future house.

I had bought the ring a long time ago. For weeks, I had been warming up to creating the right situation. I had wanted to invite Shannon out for dinner, then put the ring in the dessert, or maybe in her glass. But, until now, the ring had simply been burning a hole in my pocket for almost two weeks.

Now I was kneeling in front of Shannon in the mud, staring at her surprised face, waiting for her answer, when it started to rain again.

Shannon was still looking at me, her hand clasped to her mouth. We were both getting soaked.

"I...I..." Shannon stuttered.

Please say yes, please say you'll marry me?

The hand holding the ring was shaking and my knee was getting tired. My heart was racing in my chest. It felt like an eternity had gone by.

Shannon finally removed her hand from her mouth and smiled. "You really think we have a future together? You really think we can get through this?" she asked.

I nodded, tears rolling across my cheeks. "Of course I think so. I know we will find a way."

She chuckled. "You're such a romantic, Jack. A hopeless romantic. How can I not love you? How can I say anything but yes?"

I stopped breathing. Did I hear her right? Had she said yes?

Shannon grabbed my hand and pulled me up. She leaned over and kissed me, then looked into my eyes while holding my face between her hands. "Yes, crazy romantic, Jack Ryder. Yes, I will marry you. Come what may."

I smiled and kissed her, then placed the ring on her finger. "Come what may," I whispered.

We stood in the rain and kissed for a long time, before we finally both burst into laughter. There was nothing like hearing Shannon laugh. It had been awhile since I had seen her happy. She had that light in her eyes again that I loved so much.

"You're crazy, do you know that?" she said and grabbed my hand in hers. "To take a risk on someone like me."

I smiled. We started to walk across the muddy ground towards the car. We were soaked already, so it was no use hurrying back. Instead, we walked hand in hand, with joy in our hearts and wet hair slapping our foreheads. I chuckled in joy and lifted her hand to see the ring again. It fit her so well. It looked beautiful on her. I knew it would.

As we walked in silence, hand in hand, Shannon suddenly stopped. "What's this?" she asked, and bent down to pick something up from the soil. She rubbed off the dirt and showed it to me. It was a ring. It had a deep reddish brown stone in it.

"Wow," I said.

"I know. It's gorgeous," Shannon said.

She turned it in the scarce light.

"I hope you don't like that ring better than the one I just gave you," I said.

"Are you kidding me?" Shannon said and laughed. "I like this a *lot* better." She placed an elbow in my side while putting the ring in her purse with a small laugh. The rain suddenly increased in strength, and we ran for the car.

FORTY-NINE

May 2015

"Shannon and I have some news!"

I stood up during dinner and looked at everyone around the table. They were all there, even Emily, who hadn't touched her food, as usual. We were eating inside the motel's bar because of the heavy rain.

Everyone looked up at us. I grabbed Shannon's hand and showed them her ring. My mom let out a shriek and clapped her hands.

"Oh, my God!" she said and looked at my dad, then back at us. "You're getting married?"

Shannon and I looked at one another, then back at them. "Yes," I said.

Abigail and Austin looked like they didn't understand anything.

I continued, "Shannon accepted my proposal of marriage earlier today."

Austin looked confused. "But I thought you were already married," he said. "I thought you had to be to make a baby."

All the grown-ups around the table laughed.

"What?" Austin said.

"Don't you think we would have been to their wedding if they got married, doofus?" Abigail said.

Austin looked sad. "How am I supposed to know?"

Abigail rolled her eyes at her brother. "Don't you know anything?"

Austin burst into tears. The moment was ruined. "Abigail," I said.

"What?" she asked.

"Say you're sorry to your brother," I said.

She turned and looked at him indifferently. "Sorry," she said in a tone that clearly let him know that she wasn't.

Shannon and I sat down and everyone returned to their food. Emily left the table. Shannon nodded in her direction and I got up to follow her. Emily hadn't said a word when we told the news. I walked after her into the TV room, where she threw herself on the couch. I sat next to her.

"You don't have to follow me, you know," she said.

"I know," I said and placed my feet on the coffee table.

"Sherri is going to kill you for that. You know that, right?" she asked and pointed at my feet. My mom never allowed feet on the table.

"I know," I said. "So, what's going on with you?"

She shrugged. Some show with vampires was on the TV. I knew she loved the stuff. "Just tired, I guess."

"You do like Shannon, right? Or does it bother you that we're getting married?" I asked.

"I love Shannon," she said. "She's awesome. No it's just...well it's all going a little fast, don't you think?"

I nodded. "True. But it is the right thing to do. Shannon is pregnant and I want to do right by her."

Emily laughed. "You're so old."

I chuckled too. "Guess I can't run from that. I know things are changing rapidly around here, and I guess I forgot to think about how it will affect you."

She looked up at me and smiled. "Are you going for *dad of the year award* here? 'Cause you're in the lead as we speak."

I smiled, leaned over, and kissed her forehead. I put my arms around her, and to my terror, realized she had lost even more weight. I was afraid of scaring her away or making her resent me if I kept asking about it, but at the same time, I was afraid of what would happen if I didn't do anything, if I didn't talk to her about it. In this moment, while holding her small fragile body in my arms, I realized I had no idea what was going on with her, and had no clue how to deal with it either.

I felt lost.

FIFTY

May 2015

NOAH KINLEY HAD FINALLY FALLEN asleep. Inside of his small wooden cell, he laid curled up, naked, and hungry beyond starvation. He hadn't heard from his guardian for what he believed had to be days, but he had lost count. He no longer knew if it was day or night, and had no way to figure out if an hour had gone by or just a few minutes. Noah was so weak from starvation that he drifted in and out of this dreamlike state constantly. It was hard for him to tell what was real and what was the dream.

Now he was dreaming of his mother. She was waiting for him in the kitchen of their old house on Merritt Island, standing by the counter preparing him a snack. Peanut butter and jelly sandwich on white toast. That was his favorite, next to Pop-tarts.

She smiled when she saw him. Her warm and loving smile. Noah had missed her smile so much, and he had missed her kisses and warm embrace.

"Are you hungry?" she asked.

Noah nodded. "Yes. I'm starving!"

"Come, sit," she said and pulled out the chair.

Noah threw himself at the sandwich. His mother laughed. At first, her laughter was hearty and warm, but soon it turned vicious. Like the laughter of his guardian. Now she was speaking with his voice too.

"So, you're hungry, huh? Little spoiled brat is hungry!"

Startled, Noah looked into his mother's wonderful eyes, just to realize it wasn't her eyes looking back at him. It was his. His piercing mad brown eyes. Noah gasped, while his mother started to knock on the kitchen table with a wooden spoon in her hand, still laughing maniacally.

Noah covered his ears from the loud banging noise. "Stop it," he yelled. "Stop the banging."

But, she didn't stop. Noah watched her, startled, while her face turned into that of the man, and soon, Noah was violently ripped out of his childhood home and back into the box, where the banging sound was getting louder and louder.

Noah opened his eyes and let out a loud scream.

"Help!"

Still, the banging continued. On the other side of the box, he could hear the guardian's laughter while he banged on the box with a stick.

"You tired, huh? Little momma's boy is tired, huh?" he yelled between slamming the box. "Well, try and sleep now, you little brat!"

The guard laughed maniacally. Noah cried and tried to cover his ears to block out the sound, but he couldn't make it go away. He was so tired, so incredibly tired. The hunger made him hallucinate, and he kept seeing his mother's face inside of the box, her face with the man's vicious eyes, while slamming the spoon on the table like she had done in the dream.

"Stop it!" Noah screamed in complete and utter desperation. He cried and pleaded.

"Stooooop!"

But the banging didn't stop. It didn't stop for many, many hours. Hours turned into days, and still the banging continued. The man only took a few breaks now and then, just enough for Noah to doze off and get into his dream before it continued again, over and over again.

FIFTY-ONE

May 2015

SHANNON FELT BETTER the next day. Jack had managed to convince her that it would be all right, that they would get through even this, and she was beginning to believe him. After all, it was no use worrying. She got nowhere by worrying.

After Jack and the kids had left the condo the next morning, she decided to treat herself to a day of spoiling herself. She thought she deserved it.

She took the car and drove to the mall on Merritt Island, where she started out getting a manicure, then moved next door to the hairdresser and got a new haircut. It was on her way out of the hairdresser when she was about to pay, that she felt the ring when she stuck her hand inside her purse and pulled it out. She looked at the brown stone and turned it in the light. It was surely beautiful, but very big.

"Thank you so much, Mrs. King," the lady behind the counter at the hairdresser said. She had that smile on her face that Shannon knew so very well. She couldn't wait to tell her friends and family whose hair she cut today. It was always the same.

Shannon gave her a smile, then left the store, thinking she could soon go under the name Shannon Ryder. She wondered if she would take his name. King was, after all, only a stage name.

Shannon turned the ring between her fingers. It was a big ring, and didn't fit any of her fingers. She was on her way to buy herself a new dress, when she found herself stopping in front of the jewelry store. She looked down at the ring, then decided to go in. The woman behind the counter looked at her and smiled.

"Welcome. What can I do for you?" she asked. She looked at Shannon, scrutinizing her. "Say, aren't you…?"

Shannon nodded. "Yes, I am," she said.

The woman behind the counter blushed. "Oh, my. I'm so honored to have you in my store, Mrs. King."

Shannon smiled too. She never knew what to say when people said things like that.

"How may I be of assistance?" the woman asked.

"I...I found this ring. I was just curious as to what kind of stone that it is," she said, putting the ring on the counter.

The lady picked it up and studied it, then froze. She looked up at Shannon with startled eyes. "Where did you get this?"

Shannon felt slightly self-conscious. The way the woman looked at her made her uncomfortable.

"I found it, why?"

"Because it's tortoiseshell. It's illegal here in the U.S. It is banned in most parts of the world as an endangered species."

Shannon looked at the lady. "I'm sorry. I didn't know."

The woman handed back the ring. Shannon took it.

"If I were you, I wouldn't show this to anyone," she said. "It's extremely beautiful, but..."

Shannon put the ring back into her purse, then closed it. "I didn't know. Thank you for your help."

The woman smiled again. "Anytime, Mrs. King. Let me know if there is anything else I can do for you."

Shannon left the store, then drove back to the condo, where she took out the ring once again. She turned it between her fingers, and then decided to put it away. She pulled out a drawer in the hallway and put the ring inside, then closed it.

FIFTY-TWO

May 2015

WE HELD a brief press conference outside of Cocoa Beach City Hall. I was standing next to Ron, who spoke about the search for Noah Kinley and the finds of the two bodies believed to be of Scott Kingston and Jordan Turner.

"Is it the police's theory that this is done by the same guy?" A reporter from *Florida Today* asked.

Ron leaned over the microphone. "That is our theory, yes."

"So, Vernon Johnson is out of the picture?" a female reporter asked.

Ron looked at me. I nodded and took the microphone. "Since Vernon Johnson was in prison at the time both Scott Kingston and Jordan Turner were killed, we don't consider him to be a suspect anymore, no."

"Could he have worked with someone else?" another reporter asked.

"We don't know at this point, but that is not our theory so far," I answered.

"Do you have other suspects?" one of the TV reporters asked.

"The investigation is still ongoing."

They all knew what that meant. *No, we don't.*

Weasel took over and asked the public for help in finding Noah in time.

"The entire city is holding its breath," she finished.

I drove back to the Sheriff's Office with Ron and sandwiches from Juice N' Java in a bag. We ate at our desks, since I had a ton of paperwork to finish. I kept thinking about Shannon and wondering how this was all going to end. I considered calling my colleagues in Nashville and asking them for details in the case, but was afraid I might end up making matters worse instead of helping her. I had to leave it to her lawyer to fight her case. I just felt so damn helpless.

When I finished my sandwich, I received a call from Roosevelt Elementary. It was Abigail.

"Dad, you've gotta come down to the school. I need new shoes."

I sighed and leaned back in my chair. Abigail's shoes had broken that morning when she was about to go out of the door, and I didn't have another pair for her to wear, so I had let her put on flip-flops.

"I know you need new shoes. I'll buy them after work," I said.

"No, I need them now," she said. "I'm not allowed to wear flip-flops to school. The front office will send me home if I don't get new shoes."

I sighed and ran a hand through my hair. "You're kidding me, right? But I wrote a note and everything? I wrote that we didn't have any other shoes for you to wear."

"I know. But I'm not allowed to be in school wearing flip-flops."

I closed my eyes and rubbed my forehead. I knew the rules, but still, it was kind of an emergency. The schools were so strict about these things, it was ridiculous. Abigail had once been sent home from school for wearing a spaghetti-strap shirt. Apparently, that wasn't allowed either.

"Alright. I'll buy some and bring them to you."

"Thanks, Dad."

I told Beth what was going on and drove to the mall in Melbourne, where I found a shoe store and a nice pair of sneakers for my daughter. I rushed to the school and made it inside just before it started to rain again. The front desk didn't allow me to go down to the classroom, so Abigail came to me. She brought Austin with her and they both hugged me and kissed me. I handed her the shoes, then took the flip-flops and said goodbye to them again. I watched both of them as they disappeared down the hallway. They had grown so much lately.

I walked outside to the car and ran to not get soaked. I jumped in, and then drove into the street, when suddenly I spotted Emily's old truck. It passed me in the middle of the street. I felt confused, since I didn't believe she was off from school till three-thirty. The high school was located right next to the elementary school, so it was very possibly her. It looked a lot like it.

I decided to do what every dad would do. I followed her. She drove down Minuteman Causeway, then north on A1A. I kept my distance and spotted her as she stopped at the fitness center. She parked the car in the parking lot. I caught a short glimpse of her as she ran inside, covering her head with a sports bag to not get soaked.

FIFTY-THREE

May 2015

I DECIDED to let it go. After all, skipping school to go exercise was hardly the worst a teenager could do, right? Except, it felt like she was doing something really bad. I knew she had a membership to the fitness club, but didn't know she really used it. Maybe one of her classes was cancelled, I thought, and decided to not go back to the office for the rest of the day. I could do some work from home, and then maybe hit the waves for a little while before the kids came home from school.

Shannon was sitting in the living room with her computer in her lap when I entered. "You're home early," she said as I kissed her.

"I thought I'd work a little from home," I said.

"You mean surfing," she said with a smile.

"I don't know," I said and sat down. "I feel really bummed out about this case. I can't believe we haven't found Noah yet. Not even a trace. The areas around 4th Street North have been searched over and over again. We've talked to all the neighbors. Still, we have nothing."

"What about that roofing company? You said Jordan Turner's mother told you she had recognized the guy waiting in front of their house as someone working at the roofing company in Rockledge?"

"Yeah, we talked to them, but it is now run by the son in the family, and he told us he had no idea who worked there sixteen years ago. He was just a teenager, and there had been so many men working for his dad over the years. They kept no records."

"That's too bad," Shannon said.

"So, what are you up to?" I asked, and looked curiously at her screen. "You looking at rings? Isn't the one I gave you good enough?"

Shannon laughed. "It's perfect, Jack. I love it. No, I just keep thinking about the ring we found in the ground. I took it to the jewelry store today. The woman there told me it was made from tortoiseshell and that it is illegal here in the States."

"Wow," I said. "I didn't know that."

"Me either," Shannon said and looked back at her screen. "But, I couldn't stop thinking about it. Where did it come from? So, I looked up tortoiseshell and jewelry and guess what I found?"

"What? More rings?" I asked.

"No, it is illegal to sell jewelry made with tortoiseshell in most countries around the world, except one place. And that is where I figure this must come from."

"Where is that?"

"Cuba."

"Cuba, huh?"

"Apparently, they don't care about the rules the rest of the world follows or about the fact that the tortoiseshell is endangered." She shrugged. "Anyway, I just thought it was funny. I mean, how do you think a ring like that would end up in the ground on our land?"

"I don't know. Probably would make a great story," I said.

"It is a very rare piece of jewelry," she said and went to the hallway to take the ring out of the drawer. She came back with it and showed it to me. "It might be something that has been handed down as a family tradition," she said. "It looks old and it has this engraving on the inside, look."

I took the ring in my hand and looked at the engraving. A word. A name.

"Armando?" I asked.

Shannon nodded. "Does sound kind of Cuban, right?"

FIFTY-FOUR

Cuba, April 1980

THEY WAITED nine days at the harbor in Mariel. Hector and Raul became more and more frantic in their search for their family. Every day, more and more Cubans came to the harbor, and more and more left on boats. While they waited, thousands of Cubans had left and new boats come to pick them up.

But still they hadn't found Isabella or anyone else from their family. All they knew was that they were on the bus that crashed the embassy and that they were among the first to receive their permits to leave Cuba.

The more the days passed, the more Hector and Raul started to fear that they had been lied to. They feared their family had been incarcerated for their disobedience by the Cuban government. They heard so many stories of people being imprisoned for standing up against the government.

On the ninth day, Hector and Raul were finally allowed inside the Peruvian Embassy. They were greeted by the diplomat, who told them he vividly remembered all five of them...the Suarez family and the bus driver.

"So, what happened to them?" Raul asked, as they sat down in the cold office at the embassy.

"They were allowed to leave," the diplomat said.

"But, we have been here nine days and haven't found them," Hector argued.

"They have already left," the diplomat said. "They were on the first boat out of here. I personally made sure my guards escorted them to the boat. We couldn't risk the Cuban soldiers changing their minds all of a sudden. The boat took them to Miami."

Hector leaned back in the leather chair with a relieved sigh. He looked at his brother, who smiled and laughed too.

"So, you're telling us they're already in Miami?" Hector asked, when suddenly a new worry appeared. Where had they been staying in Miami for nine days? Did they have any money?

516

The diplomat laughed and nodded. "Yes, they should be perfectly safe. But I am sorry you have come this long way in vain."

Hector felt tears in his eyes as he got up and shook the diplomat's hand. "It was worth it, as long as they are safe. Thank you so much!"

"You're very welcome," the diplomat said.

Hector and Raul hurried back to the harbor and the old fishing boat. They couldn't wait to get back. They were laughing and running. But as they approached the boat on the dock, they suddenly realized someone was walking around on the deck. And it wasn't just anybody.

They were soldiers. Cuban soldiers.

"What's going on?" Hector asked and looked at Raul. The soldiers were swarming the boat, searching through it.

With shivering steps, the two brothers approached the boat. As they did, one of the soldiers looked up and his eyes locked with Hector's. Hector gasped when he recognized him. He knew the man was a general in Castro's army. He had looked into his eyes once before, right before getting onto the airplane.

The soldier jumped up from the boat and onto the dock, then looked at Hector with a smile.

"Didn't I tell you I would shoot you if you ever came back to Cuba?"

Hector had no idea what to say. He felt his hands get clammy. His legs were trembling, threatening to give way underneath him. The general stared at Hector, and then burst into loud laughter. He put his hand on Hector's neck, and then forced him to walk with him.

"Now, how do you suggest we resolve this unfortunate situation, huh?"

Part Three

THIS IS MY HEART, IT IS TURNED TO STONE

FIFTY-FIVE

May 2015

I WORKED for a few hours more, then hit the waves to clear my mind a little bit when there was a break in the rain. It was warm out and the water was warm too. Waves were good, overhead high, but quite messy because of the wind. I had fun on my short board and enjoyed not thinking about work or Shannon's case for a little while.

An hour later, I went up and showered at my parents' place before picking up the kids at the bus stop. Abigail and Austin ran into my arms, and I hugged them tight. I felt like they were growing so fast now. Angela came off the bus as well and stayed a little behind while I hugged the twins.

Once I had let them go, I looked at Angela, then walked to her and gave her a warm hug as well. "How was your day?" I asked.

"Great," she said smiling. I could tell she was doing well. She had been very happy lately. I believed she enjoyed having a more normal life now, a life where she went on the school bus and went to a normal public school like all other kids.

I walked up to my parents' place, where the kids threw their bags on the floor, then threw on their swimsuits and ran to the beach. I played beach volley with them for an hour or so, before Emily drove up and parked her old truck in the parking lot of the motel.

I looked at Abigail next to me, then threw the ball at her. "I have to talk to Emily," I said. "Be right back."

Abigail made a disappointed sound.

"Let's play hide and go seek in the dunes instead," Austin exclaimed. It was his favorite game of all.

"Okay," Abigail said. "But no hiding in the motel this time. Only outside hiding places."

They all agreed to that and I ran to Emily who was talking to my mother on the deck. I waved and approached them. I kissed my daughter on the forehead. "How was your day?" I asked.

She shrugged. "Okay, I guess. As usual."

"Nothing interesting happen? Any classes cancelled?"

She looked at me, and then shook her head. "No. Not this close to end of the year. Why?"

It was my turn to shrug. "Oh, I don't know. Maybe because I saw you drive away from the school around lunch time?"

Emily snorted. "Are you spying on me?"

"Nope. Was just at Roosevelt with some shoes for your sister. Where were you going?"

Her eyes avoided mine. "Just getting some lunch. The food in the cafeteria is so nasty. I had a sandwich at the Surfnista."

I sighed. "Emily. We both know that is not true. First of all, you hardly eat anything anymore, second I saw you park at the fitness center. Are you cutting classes now to go work out? Look at you. You're skin and bones. What's going on, Emily?"

Emily looked at me. Her nostrils were flaring. "Well, if you already know everything, then why are you asking me?" she yelled, then stormed to her car and got inside. Before I could reach her, she had driven off.

I went back to the deck, where my mother was still standing. "Guess I handled that really well," I said.

My mom put a hand on my shoulder. "She's been through a lot. A girl her age asks a lot of questions. Where am I from, who am I going to be? What will I look like? She can't get many answers when she doesn't have her parents. Plus, everything around her is changing. You're expanding the family, and that means you have less time for her. Give her time."

"But, the thing is, I don't feel like I have much time," I said. "Every day that passes, she seems to be getting thinner and thinner. I can't stand to look at it. I feel like I need to do something. I just don't know what."

"I have noticed she hasn't been eating and the weight loss," my mom said. "I'll try and talk to her, if you think that would help."

"Thank you," I said and hugged her. "What would I ever do without you?"

FIFTY-SIX

May 2015

SHANNON WALKED ACROSS THE SAND, looking at the dark clouds on the horizon. She had just watched the local news, which was all about Tropical Storm Anna. She spotted Angela playing in the dunes with the twins. Angela saw her, then signaled for her to be quiet. Shannon realized they were playing hide and go seek and decided she could hug her daughter later.

She whistled the tune to the new song she had been working on the past couple of days, when she spotted Jack on the deck of the motel with his mother. They seemed to be in a deep conversation. He looked serious, but his face lit up when he saw her. He waved and she approached them.

Shannon kissed her future mother-in-law on the cheek and her future husband on the mouth. "What's going on?" she asked. "Why the serious faces?"

"It's Emily," Jack said. "I'm worried about her."

"Is she still not eating?"

Jack shook his head. "I saw her today skipping class to go to the gym and work out. I think she is deliberately trying to lose weight."

"That's bad. We need to get her professional help," Shannon said. "Before it goes too far."

Jack went quiet. It seemed like he didn't agree.

"I don't know," he said. "I don't trust those kinds of people much. They'll only give her medicine, and that's not what she needs."

"But this is serious, Jack," Shannon said. "She needs help."

Jack and his mother both went quiet. Shannon knew it was hard for relatives to accept the fact that someone in their family was seriously ill and needed help. She wondered if she had gone too far, if she had somehow overstepped their boundaries. The atmosphere was unpleasant. Shannon felt like she had to say something to make things better. She picked the ring out of her pocket and held it in the air.

"Look what we found at our lot," she said and showed it to Sherri.

522

"It's tortoiseshell," Jack said. "Shannon took it to the jewelry store and they told her it was illegal."

"Isn't it beautiful?" Shannon asked.

Sherri studied it closely. "Armando?" she said, and looked surprised at Shannon.

"Yes. Sounds Spanish right? We thought it might be Cuban, since using tortoiseshell for jewelry is common in Cuba. Interesting, right?"

Sherri frowned. "Armando is Vernon's birth name," she mumbled.

Shannon stared at Jack, then at Sherri.

"What do you mean?" Jack asked.

"Vernon was originally born Armando, so was his father and his father before him. It's a family name."

Jack looked confused. "So, his name is really Armando?"

"Yes. After his father. Armando Jesus Castro García. It was a family name, but his mother changed it when they came to the States."

"So, Vernon Johnson is from Cuba?" Jack asked.

"Yes. He came here during the Mariel boatlift in 1980. But there was so much hatred against the Cubans back then, so his mother decided to change the name to make it easier on them, to be able to get a job and a new life. Say, do you think this may be his ring?"

FIFTY-SEVEN

May 2015

VERNON FELT ANXIOUS. Sherri had called and asked him to come down to the motel and meet her family. She had something she wanted to show him, she'd said. Something important.

Vernon jumped on the bus and sat by the window as it drove over the bridges taking him to the islands, wondering what it could be that was so important. He wasn't too fond of the idea of meeting her son. He was a detective with the Sheriff's Department and it was his colleagues that constantly came knocking and asking him questions about the disappearance of that boy, Noah Kinley.

Vernon had followed the case on TV closely, and every time they talked about it, his name was mentioned in connection to the case and every time they had talked about the similarities to the old case from '86, the one Vernon had been imprisoned for.

It was like it was happening all over again. When Noah had gone missing, it was just like the first time. The police had been at his doorstep the very next day asking him all these nasty questions. Later that same day, they had taken him in. They had cuffed him again and Vernon had cried and pleaded for them to leave him alone. His mother had seen it and she too had feared it was happening all over again. For hours, they had kept him in custody, asking him questions over and over again.

"Where is Noah? What did you do to him?"

Over and over again. He had felt so tired in the end, he had almost told them he had done it, just to make them leave him alone.

But, luckily, they had suddenly released him. He had gone home to his mother, who had been on the couch, crying since he'd been taken in. She hadn't shown up for her job at Publix, and later they called and told her she was fired. Vernon's mother had been devastated. Her job was her everything.

She had looked at him with big tearful eyes.

"Did you do it?"

Vernon looked surprised at his mother. "What do you mean *did I do it?*"

She threw a cushion at him. "Did you do it, damn it? Did you kill that kid? Did you take that second one? Did you kill him too?"

Vernon had stared at his mother in complete shock. He had been so sure his mother believed in his innocence.

"I can't believe you would even ask that."

The next day, he had moved out. He had bought a condo on the water in Titusville with some of his money. His mother kept saying how sorry she was, but Vernon didn't believe her. Just like the rest of the world, she believed he was guilty. Deep down, she believed it, and that was enough for him.

Vernon went to the door as his stop came closer. He got out and walked towards the motel. He looked forward to seeing Sherri again. He enjoyed her company. So far, she was the only one who had stuck by him and kept believing in him through it all. Even when they started to accuse him the second time around.

"Vernon!" Sherri came down the street to meet him. She opened her arms and gave him a big hug. Vernon closed his eyes and enjoyed the closeness. He hadn't been very close to another human being much during his years in jail. It felt strange for him to hold her in his arms. Strangely wonderful.

"I'm so glad you came," she said. "Come, meet my son."

Vernon smiled, then let her drag him towards the deck of the motel. Vernon recognized them both from the magazines. Shannon King was even more beautiful in real life.

"It's an honor to meet you, Mrs. King," he said.

"Vernon, meet my son, Jack. Jack, this is Vernon," Sherri said.

"Nice to meet you," Vernon said and reached out his hand.

Jack Ryder took it a little reluctantly. In his eyes, Vernon saw the same suspicious look that every one else seemed to have. Except Sherri.

"Sit down, Vernon," Sherri said. "I'll get you a beer."

"Oh, I don't drink, Miss Sherri," Vernon said. "Just water will be fine."

Sherri brought water for all of them and they sat down on the wooden furniture. Vernon loved the motel and fully understood why Sherri loved it here. It had such a quiet charm to it.

"So, what did you want to talk to me about?" Vernon asked nervously. He felt like Jack Ryder was supervising his every move.

"Show him," Sherri said, addressed to Shannon King. The famous country singer put her hand in her pocket and pulled something out. She showed it to Vernon. He stopped breathing. Everything inside of him froze to ice. He took it in his hand, then looked at the engraving. He couldn't believe it.

"Where did you get this?"

"You know it?" Jack asked.

"Are you kidding me?" Vernon said, his voice trembling heavily. "It belonged to my father. I haven't seen it since I was fifteen years old."

FIFTY-EIGHT

May 2015

VERNON JOHNSON WAS CRYING. He was sitting on my parent's deck and crying. I had no idea how to cope with it. I didn't like the guy, for some reason, maybe because he had spent so much time with my mother and I felt jealous for my dad.

My mom put her arm around him, and that made everything turn inside of me. My dad was in the back working on the pool pump that had broken, and here she was holding someone else. I knew it was wrong, but I couldn't help feeling upset about it.

"He used to always wear this ring," Vernon said.

"What happened to him?" My mom asked. "You never spoke of him?"

"He was taken away from us," Vernon said. "They took him one day. "

"Who did?" My mom asked.

"Castro's soldiers. They put him in prison. We never heard from him again. When Castro decided to open the harbor of Mariel to anyone who wanted to leave, my mother decided it was time for us to go. We didn't have any relatives come to pick us up, but we paid someone to take us with them. Cost us everything we had, but it was worth it. We had to get away. My dad had been gone for seven years by then, and we knew we would never see him again."

"Why was he taken to jail?" I asked.

Vernon shrugged. "So many were imprisoned because they spoke up against the regime." Vernon paused and looked at the ring. "Where did you find it?"

"Two blocks down there is an empty lot," Shannon said. "We just bought it and we're building a house on the grounds. We found it in the soil where the former house had been."

"You mean the ground where the Kingston's old house was?" Vernon asked. He sounded surprised.

"Yes. Kind of strange, isn't it?" I asked. "So, how do you figure it ended up there?"

526

"I...I...I have absolutely no idea," he said, sounding all of a sudden nervous. "Can I keep it, though? It's my only memory of my dad."

"I think we might need to hold on to it for a little while longer," I said. "While the investigation is still going on. I'll make sure you get it once we're done."

Vernon looked anxious. Small pearls of sweat appeared on his upper lip. He wiped them away with the back of his hand.

"Okay. That's okay," he said and handed it back to me.

"Jack!" My mother said. "It's the man's only memory of his father."

"I'm sorry. But I need to keep it for the investigation."

"Now you're just being a bully."

My mother got up and walked to Vernon. "Come. Let me take you home."

Vernon got up. He looked at me defiantly. I didn't know what it was, but I really didn't like the guy. He looked at me angrily.

"I can find my own way home, thank you, Miss Sherri," he said. "Good day."

He turned around and walked away. My mom looked at me angrily. "Look at what you did. Don't you think he has been through enough? Can't you show a guy some mercy?"

I stared at Vernon as he disappeared around the corner of the building. I started to feel a little guilty. But I only did what I had to, I told myself. Maybe it wasn't nice of me, but something told me this ring was important.

FIFTY-NINE

May 2015

THE CONSTANT BANGING on the lid of the box ceased all of a sudden, and then there was nothing but quiet. At first, Noah enjoyed that he could finally sleep, enjoyed the peace and calm in his mind from days of insomnia because of the noise. But soon, another well-known emotion made its entrance. With the quiet came the fear. Where had his guardian gone? Was he all alone now? Would he come back? Had he grown tired of his games and left him to rot inside the box? Would Noah die in the box?

Noah Kinley tried to accept the fact that death was closing in on him. He was lying silently in the box waiting for his body to simply give up. His tiredness had put a damper on the hunger and thirst, and even though he was still only a child, Noah knew perfectly well that his body wasn't going to take much more of this. His back was hurting constantly from the beatings he had to endure, and his head was throbbing with pain from the lack of sleep and water.

He was cold in the box. Constantly freezing. The lack of nutrition had sucked him dry and he was only skin and bones and couldn't keep his body warm enough.

It had been days since the lid was last lifted and Noah taken out to eat and go to the bathroom. At least he thought it was. He couldn't distinguish between night and day anymore. All there was, was darkness.

"What do you want from me!" he screamed into the darkness when he felt the strength for it. But there would be no answer. Every now and then, he cried. Cried when he thought about his parents, wondering if they were looking for him, if they were worried and sad. Wondering why they hadn't found him yet.

"I want my mommy! I want to go home!"

He had thought his eyes would eventually get used to the darkness, that he would be able to see something like he used to in his bedroom at home, but it never happened. It was like he had gone blind.

He tried to remember his mother's gentle smile, to recall little details that he used to love when looking at her. The mole on her upper lip that moved when she spoke. The vein in her forehead that popped out when she was angry with him. Her ears. Her ears that were uneven on each side of her head.

Noah no longer cared that he peed himself in the box. It had become more and more rare that he had to go anyway, and if he did, he just let it happen. The smell didn't even bother him anymore.

Noah tried to count the seconds and minutes to be able to determine when a day had gone by. But it was in vain. He had lost the will to keep trying to pretend like he was alive.

He had lost hope.

Just as he thought he would never get out of the box again, the lid was opened and light entered. It hurt his eyes and he had to squint. Arms pulled him out of the box and dragged him across the ground. Noah tried to fight, but his guard was too strong.

"Let me go. Let me go home!" he yelled.

He was thrown into another barren room lit up by bright fluorescent lights. He landed on the bare cold floor, his naked body throbbing in pain from being locked in the same position for days. Before he could manage to get up, the door was closed behind him. The light was so bright it felt like an explosion of white suns, and he had to close his eyes and cover them with his hand. It was like the light pierced through his retinas and sent waves of pain into his head. Noah crouched in the corner of the room and pulled his knees up to hide his head in them. His eyes hurt so badly from the bright light.

"Please, turn it off," he whispered feebly.

He felt so tired, all he wanted was to lie down onto the cold floor and fall asleep. But the bright light made it impossible for him to sleep. It pierced painfully through his eyelids and hurt him.

"Please, turn it off," he yelled, even though he knew it wouldn't help. "Please, turn the lights off!"

SIXTY

May 2015

"What's going on?"

My dad had entered the deck and looked at all of us. My mom hadn't spoken a word to me since the incident with Vernon. She was looking at me angrily. My dad stood with a wrench in his hand, his shirt soaked with sweat.

My mom shook her head. "Nothing," she said, walked past my dad into the motel. I felt awful. In less than an hour, I had managed to severely anger two of the women in my life.

"Jack?" my dad asked.

"It's nothing, Dad."

I didn't want him to know what had happened. He felt threatened by this Vernon enough as it was. He looked confused, then wiped sweat from his forehead. "Well, then, if it's nothing, then I think I'll jump in the ocean. Tell your mom the pool is up and running again when she gets back out here."

I looked at Shannon. I could tell she felt uncomfortable. I sat next to her and put my arm around her. I pulled her closer and kissed her.

"Do you want to go back to the condo and get some take-out instead?" she asked.

"Nah, my mom will be herself in a little while. Don't worry. She can never stay mad at me for very long."

We sat on the bench and looked over the ocean where my dad was soon walking out in the waves.

"She's gaining strength, they say," Shannon said and leaned her back on me.

"Who? Anna?"

"Yes. I watched it on the news before I got here. She's growing."

"I don't think we've ever had a storm stay out there this long," I said. "Usually they pass in a few days...maybe a week, but it has been on its way for at least two weeks now. It has stalled for the past days, moving very slowly while growing bigger and more powerful."

I thought about the storm and then about Noah Kinley, who had disappeared right before the storm had started to build in the Atlantic. I wondered if he was still alive somewhere around here after two weeks. Did the killer keep him alive like he had done to Scott and Jordan? Why? He had the power to kill them whenever he wanted to. Was it because he enjoyed it? Did he get off in some weird satisfaction by keeping them alive? Was it a power trip?

My dad returned with a satisfied look on his face. "That was just what I needed," he said with a deep sigh. Like me, he loved being in the ocean. It didn't matter if I was in the water or on a surfboard or even on a boat. The ocean was my element. It was where I belonged.

"Did you have fun out there this afternoon?" my dad asked and wiped himself with a towel.

"It was okay," I said. "Waves have been building to a good size, but the wind kind of messes it up."

"I figured," my dad said.

My dad used to be a surfer when he was younger. I knew he dreamed about going out there again, but his knees couldn't take it. After two knee surgeries, he was told by his doctor he couldn't surf anymore. I felt bad for him. I dreaded the day I couldn't surf anymore.

My dad sighed with contentment.

"Well, better get dressed before dinnertime."

My dad left us and I smiled and looked at Shannon. I kissed the top of her head and held her body close to mine. It felt good to sit here. To be close to her. I wondered what I would do if she ended up going to jail. I simply couldn't bear the thought.

I reached down and touched her belly and thought about the baby growing in there. I couldn't wait to hold him or her in my arms. It was strange how I, not so long ago, had thought it was over for me, that I wasn't going to have another baby, and didn't feel sad about it at all…how I suddenly longed to hold a baby in my arms again.

Speaking of babies, I spotted Abigail and Angela walking up from the beach, and I waved at them. "Hi guys. Dinner is almost ready. Where is Austin?"

Abigail looked at me with wide eyes. I hadn't noticed before, but now I did. Her eyes were torn in fear.

"We can't find him, Dad. We've looked everywhere."

SIXTY-ONE

Cuba, April 1980

THEY WERE PACKING HIS BOAT, cramming people in it. Hector could do nothing but watch as more than two hundred people were being loaded onto the old 70-foot fishing boat by the soldiers. Hector didn't understand where all those people had come from. They hadn't been among the ones waiting at the harbor. They didn't look like ordinary people. Many of them were toothless and their clothing looked like they were beggars.

There was nothing Hector could do, even though he didn't feel comfortable about this. The general had promised him that he and his brother, who was wanted by the police, would be able to leave the island if they promised to never return and if they took a bunch of refugees with them.

It was either that or Cuban prison, where they would probably die. Hector had accepted the terms, and now they were loading the many people onboard. Hector looked terrified at how deep the boat lay in the water with the heavy load and wondered if they would even be able to make it across the ocean to the coast of Florida.

"We can't take anymore," Raul said, as another batch of people were being lined up. He looked at Hector. "The boat is going to sink."

"I know. But we don't have a choice," Hector said. "This is our only chance to get out of here."

Raul knew he was right and stopped arguing. Soon, the General loaded the last passenger onto the fishing boat, then grinning from ear to ear, told them they could leave Cuba.

"Safe travels," he said with a chuckle.

With their hearts in their throats, they started up the old engine and left the harbor of Mariel. The weather seemed to be with them. Clear blue skies and the ocean as calm as possible. It gave them hope. The boat could sail, and soon they saw the harbor disappear in the distance. They went slowly, but steadily ahead. As soon as the coast of Cuba was far behind them, Hector and Raul breathed in a sigh of relief and looked at each other. They hugged once and laughed.

"We did it. We made it out," Raul said. "Again!"

"Not many can say that," Hector replied.

In front of them was nothing but the endless ocean, and soon behind them as well. They were happy to see Cuba go, more than happy, exalted even, but none of them could escape the anxiety that nagged on the inside.

What if we don't make it to land?

The boat was sailing steadily, but they could tell the engine was struggling with the weight. The people were closely crammed, and soon a fight broke out between two of the men.

Hector and Raul looked at one another, not knowing what to do. The fight continued. The two guys fighting were struggling, and suddenly, one of them was thrown over the railing by the other. Hector gasped and looked to Raul. Raul elbowed through the crowd to the railing and looked down. Hector followed him. The man who had been thrown overboard didn't know how to swim, and seconds later, he disappeared and went straight to the bottom.

"We have to do something! The guy is drowning," Hector yelled and looked at Raul.

Raul turned to stare at their passengers, then he shook his head. Hector turned and looked at them as well. That was when he realized. These weren't ordinary refugees. These weren't people waiting to see their family on the coast of Florida. These weren't families with children and grandparents looking for a new and better life.

These were the unwanted people. The undesirables. These were the ones not even Cuba wanted to keep.

SIXTY-TWO

May 2015

"Austiiin!"

I was yelling his name at the top of my lungs as I ran across the dunes, looking everywhere for my son. In the distance, I could hear my family calling his name as well. We had been everywhere. The beach, the area around my condominium, our condo building, the basement underneath, my parents' motel, the pool-area. Everywhere.

And still, he was nowhere to be seen.

"Austiiiin!"

All kinds of scenarios went across my mind. I pictured him going in the ocean and drowning. But, then again, Austin was an excellent swimmer. He was a surfer, even though he didn't enjoy it much, he still knew the ocean.

I pictured him walking into the street behind my parents' motel and being hit by a car. But when I went down there, there was nothing. I walked up and down the road to see if he had been hit and was lying helpless somewhere, but didn't see anything. I even crossed A1A and walked to the houses on the other side. It was mostly condominiums and townhouses. I walked in and out of their areas yelling his name and down to the Intracoastal River to see if he was hiding anywhere down there or maybe had fallen in the water.

But he wasn't there either.

They had been playing hide and go seek when he disappeared, Abigail had told me. Austin had hid in the dunes close to our condominium, she was certain. But when she went to look for him, he wasn't there. She and Angela had then been looking all over the beach for him, but with no luck.

"Maybe we should call for help," Shannon said, as I returned to the motel where everyone was waiting, looking at me for answers. But I didn't have any. I had no idea what to do. I grabbed my phone and called Ron.

"I'll have a search team at your place within the hour," Ron said. "Dogs and everything."

"Thanks, Ron."

I hung up and looked at my family. My heart was racing in my chest and I found it hard to breathe properly. I was so anxious and angry at the same time. I looked at my mother.

"What's Vernon's number?" I asked.

My mother looked at me and shook her head. "No, Jack. No. It's not him. He didn't take Austin."

"I think I need to be sure first," I said. "Come to think of it. I don't need his number. I'll go directly to his place and search it myself."

"Don't, Jack," my mother said. "You're all worked up. Why would Vernon take Austin, huh?"

"I don't know. To get back at me, maybe? Because he is mad that he never got to be with you, I don't know. I guess I don't care why right now. All I care about is getting Austin back home in one piece."

My mother grabbed my arm and pulled it. "It's not him, Jack. He didn't do it. He is innocent."

"I think I'll be the one to determine that," I said, and pulled myself free. I walked to my Jeep, jumped in, and drove off. I called Beth and asked her to find Vernon's address for me.

"Ron called," she said. "I am so sorry, Jack. I was just on my way down to join the search team. I'll call you back as soon as I have the address. Do you want me to go with you?"

"No, I'll do this alone," I said. "Besides, I'm already leaving Cocoa Beach."

"Just don't do anything you'll regret, Jack. You hear me? Jack?"

I heard her. I just couldn't promise anything.

SIXTY-THREE

May 2015
_____

"WHERE IS HE?"

I looked at Vernon Johnson, who was standing in the door to his apartment. He looked surprised.

"Jack? What's going on?"

"Don't pretend you don't know," I said.

"What do you mean?"

"My son. Where is my son? Where is Austin? I know you have him. Austiin?" I called through the door.

I tried to walk in, but Vernon blocked my way. "You know what? I'm getting pretty tired of you people coming here, constantly accusing me of all these things. I am a free man. I was acquitted, remember? The judge let me go."

"Doesn't mean you're innocent. Just that they don't have enough evidence. I don't know how you did it, but I want my son back."

Vernon shook his head. "I don't have him."

"I want to see for myself. I want to go in and see," I said.

Vernon shook his head. "No can do. I'm done being the nice guy here. If you want in, you go get a warrant."

I felt the blood boil in my veins. I felt like taking my gun out and just shooting him in the leg or shoulder and making up a story later. But that wasn't me. That wasn't who I was.

"How do you believe I would have done it, huh, Detective? I was in jail when Scott Kingston was killed and buried, I was in jail when Jordan Turner was abducted and killed. You know I'm innocent. There's no way I could have done any of these kills. I served my time for something I didn't even do. And now you won't leave me alone? I am still in prison. I am still being a suspect in yours and everyone else's eyes. I can't even go to the store and buy groceries without people whispering behind my back. I am innocent, for crying out loud. You got the wrong guy back then. I have the court's word for it, now please just leave me alone!"

"If you have nothing to hide, then why can't I search your place for my son, huh? Why won't you let me in? I'll tell you why. Because you know I'll find something. Because you're not as clean as you claim to be. You know something. I saw it in your eyes today when I showed you that ring. And now my son is missing? I don't believe in coincidences. If you don't have anything to hide, then let me in."

Vernon Johnson scoffed. "Nice try, Detective. But I'm not letting you inside my apartment. I am sorry your son is missing, but it's really not my problem. Now, if you'll excuse me, my dinner is getting cold."

He closed the door on me with a loud bang. I snorted and hammered on it, yelling Austin's name.

"If you're in there, Austin, just remember I'm not giving up. I will come back for you. Don't worry."

I felt like an idiot standing out there hammering on a door and yelling. I *was* an idiot. I knew I was acting like one. But what else could I do? I felt so helpless, so frustrated. I was certain Vernon knew where my son was. If he wasn't here, then he knew where he was.

I decided to go back to my car, and I sat in the parking lot for a little while, slamming my hand into the steering wheel, when my phone rang. It was Shannon. I picked it up. "Any news? Have you found him?"

"No. I'm sorry. But we have found something else."

My heart dropped. What had they found? A piece of his clothes? What?

"What did you find?" I asked and started the engine.

"You better come home and see for yourself."

SIXTY-FOUR

May 2015

I wasn't happy about leaving Vernon Johnson's place. I was still certain Austin was somewhere inside of his apartment, and I feared what this sick bastard might do to him. At the same time, I knew it was going to take a while before I could get a warrant to search his place. If I could find a judge that would grant it to me. I didn't have much solid ground to base my suspicion on.

I drove over the bridges, cursing and yelling my anger out. It had gotten dark when I reached the island and drove up in front of the motel. Cars were everywhere, and I couldn't find a space, so I had to park next to the neighbor's fence. I hoped they didn't mind. Shannon came towards my car. My parents were standing behind her, my dad holding my mom's shoulders. They all had worried faces.

Uh-oh. This doesn't look good.

I opened the door and jumped out. Shannon looked at me. "What's going on?" I asked.

"We found this," Shannon said and handed me a note.

I took it and looked at it. It was handwritten note where Austin had written his name. Nothing else. I turned the paper to look at the back.

"What does this mean?" I asked.

"We found the note in Austin's shoe. Someone had put it in front of the door to your condo."

Shannon showed me the sneakers. They were Austin's, all right. His favorite sneakers, his Game Kicks, that had buttons on the side and blinked and played music. And he could play some game on them. I never understood what it was for, but I knew he loved them and always wore them. They had been crazy expensive, but I didn't mind buying them for him, since he enjoyed them so much.

I looked at the shoe and then at the note.

"It doesn't tell us anything," Shannon said. "Other than he is alive."

"And that someone has him. Someone who wants to make sure we know they have him," I said.

538

"What do we do now?" Shannon asked.

I sighed and shrugged. "I...I have no idea. Where are Angela and Abigail?" I asked and started walking up towards the motel.

"They insisted on joining the search team," my mother answered. "They're searching the entire beach area. Emily went with them."

"She came back?" I asked.

"I texted her," Shannon said. "Told her what was going on. She came home right away. She was very upset."

I walked to the deck and looked into the darkness that had swallowed my son. A dozen flashlights flickered in the distance. Austin's name was being called from everywhere. A sudden realization struck me like a blow to the face.

I had to go through the night without my son.

"You haven't told the search team about the note?" I asked.

"I wanted to show it to you first," Shannon said.

"I'm glad you did."

She leaned on my shoulder. "Oh, Jack. This is terrible. I am so sorry."

I kissed her on the top of her head. "I know. We'll find him though. I know we will."

"You think he might have been taken by the same person who took Noah Kinley?" she asked.

I didn't answer. I didn't know what to say. I couldn't tell her that was all I was thinking about. I couldn't tell her I was certain it was the same guy. Except for the note. The note and shoe gave me hope. It wasn't something the kidnapper had done before. Either it was someone else, or the kidnapper was escalating, and that often meant making mistakes.

SIXTY-FIVE

May 2015

VERNON WAS UPSET. He kicked a chair in his apartment and caused it to fall over. Then he picked up a vase and threw it against the wall. It shattered to pieces that landed on the carpet. He had bought the place furnished, since he didn't want to have to go out and buy all this crap that people had in their houses; he just wanted a place to live. Some old lady had lived there, and now she was in a home somewhere, and he was staying in all of her old furniture. He hated this place even more than he hated his mother's place, where he had stayed in the beginning.

Why? Because he wasn't free here either. He felt like he was even more in prison than when he was still on the inside. It bothered him, since all he did when he was on the inside was to dream of getting out.

But that wasn't why he was angry. It wasn't because of the constant harassment from the police or the media that always mentioned his name whenever the case about the missing child came up. No, that wasn't why. He was very angry now because of that stupid ring Jack Ryder had found. It stirred something up inside of him, and he couldn't let it go.

The ring had been his father's. He knew it had. He remembered it vividly. It used to sit on the hand that beat Vernon, and it would always leave a mark somewhere. Vernon could never forget that ring. Not even if he wanted to.

But, he didn't. Right now, he didn't want to forget anything. He wanted to remember. He wanted to know what the heck was going on. And there was only one way to find out. Only one person who knew the truth.

His mother.

Vernon ran down the stairs and found his bike that he had bought at Wal-Mart. He had decided he didn't want a car, since it had been so many years since he had last driven one, and he enjoyed the fresh air so much. So, he had bought himself a bike instead, and now he was riding it through the dark night towards his mother's place.

He parked it outside and stormed up to her condo and knocked on the door. It took a while before she opened the door, probably because she was already asleep. She liked to go to bed early.

"Vernon? What are you doing here?" she asked sleepily.

Vernon pushed her to the side and barged in.

"What's going on?" she asked.

"What happened to my father?" he asked breathing heavily from the biking and running up the stairs.

Vernon's mother rubbed her eyes and shut the door behind her. "What do you mean, what happened to your dad?"

"What happened to him?"

"I've told you. He was taken by Castro's soldiers. He was put in jail, where they killed him."

"How do you know he's dead?" Vernon asked.

His mother sighed, then sat on the couch. "I...I guess I just thought he was. Since I never heard from him again."

"So, you never saw his dead body?"

"No. No, I didn't."

"You never buried him? You never held his funeral, right?" Vernon asked.

"True, but..."

"Why was he put in prison?" Vernon asked.

"Why? I don't know why. Castro didn't need a reason to put him in jail. Your father was very outspoken. He might have said something against the regime. He wanted to fight for our rights. Castro took everything."

Vernon sat down and covered his face.

"What's going on, son?" his mother asked. "Why all of these questions all of a sudden?"

Vernon looked up. "Because they found his ring, Mama. Do you remember his ring? The brown one with the big stone? The engraving said Armando. They found it where the kid was taken. The Kingston kid."

Vernon's mother gasped and cupped her mouth. Her eyes grew wide and fearful, then tears streamed across her cheeks.

"But...but how? How did it end up there?" she asked. She looked alarmed. "I don't understand? How?"

"That's what I intend to find out."

Vernon got up from the couch, when his mother grabbed his arm. "There is something you should probably know before you go, son. You better sit down for this."

SIXTY-SIX

May 2015

THE LIGHT WAS NEVER TURNED off. Noah waited for it to be, but it never happened. At some point, the door to his room was opened and a loaf of bread and a cup of water were placed on the floor.

"Eat," said the voice.

Noah, who had no idea when he had last eaten or even drunk anything, rushed to it and gulped down the water, keeping his eyes closed from the bright burning light. He ate greedily while his guardian watched him. Noah no longer cared that he was naked or that the guard stared at him. He was too hungry and thirsty. It was all about survival at this point.

When he had finished the cup of water, he licked the last drops on the sides and finally opened his eyes to look up at his guardian.

"Can I have some more, please?"

The guardian slapped him across the face so the cup fell to the ground. "No!"

"Please?" Noah pleaded. Being this thirsty was the worst feeling in the world. It made him feel so desperate. He suddenly understood those stories he remembered hearing about people drinking their own urine in order to survive being trapped in places without water.

He didn't care if his guardian hit him again. He needed water. "I'm so thirsty. Please, Sir?"

His guardian took the cup from the floor, then left, slamming the door shut. Noah stared at the shut door, wondering how long it would be before it was opened again. He prepared himself for a long wait and lay down in the light. The floor was cold and the light hurt his eyes, even when they were closed.

Suddenly, the door opened again, and the cup was placed in the same spot. "Here," the voice said. "Now, never ask for more again, you hear me?"

Noah nodded and jumped for the cup. He placed it on his lips and let the warm water run inside of his mouth. It felt so good when it touched his tongue. Noah enjoyed every second of it. When he was done, he handed the cup back to the man.

542

He looked up at him and their eyes met. In the bright light, he couldn't see his entire face, but his eyes had something in them he hadn't seen in his guardian before.

"You never told me your name?" Noah asked.

The man didn't answer.

"Please? Could I know your name?"

"Why?"

"Because you're the only one I see."

"My name is not important," he said.

"Then, please, tell me why you're keeping me here," Noah asked bravely. The other times when he had asked, it had resulted in a beating. He had learned to fear the man's stick and bad temper. But, today, he seemed different. Like he was approachable. Maybe there was some humanity in him, after all?

"You don't need to know," he said. "Just know that I will be the last person you'll ever see."

Noah's heart dropped. He was scared. It was strange, because he knew that he would probably be killed by this man, but still he refused to give up hope completely. There was something inside of him, a small still voice that kept telling him all hope wasn't lost yet. Not yet.

Your parents are looking for you. The police, everyone must be searching everywhere for you. They'll find you. I know they will.

"So, if you are certain you will kill me, and you will be the last person I ever see, then why not tell me your name? What's the risk? I won't be able to tell anyone else, right?" Noah argued.

The man sighed. He grabbed the cup from Noah's hand and walked to the door. Just before he left, he turned and looked at Noah, who was sitting on the floor, his body trembling in the windowless room.

"The name is Hector. Hector Suarez."

SIXTY-SEVEN

May 2015

NATURALLY, I couldn't sleep all night. None of us could, except the youngest kids, of course. Abigail and Angela wanted to stay awake, but just before midnight, they caved in and slept on the couch in my living room. Shannon and I sat on the balcony. She held my hand in hers. I couldn't stop the tears from coming.

"You've got to get some rest," she said and wiped a tear from my cheek. "I'm sure we will find him tomorrow."

I stared into the darkness. The beach was empty now. No more flashlights. No more voices yelling my son's name out. Nothing but the sound of the crashing waves. On the horizon, I saw lightning. Anna wasn't far away.

"I just can't bear the thought of him being out there all alone," I said. "He must be so scared. Austin isn't strong like Abigail. He won't survive under much distress for long."

"He might be stronger than you think," Shannon said.

"I sure hope so." I paused and looked at her. My beautiful bride to be. The soon to be mother of my child. I had been so blessed in my life. "The scary part is, if it is the kidnapper that has him," I continued. "He has successfully hidden children from us for many years. He had Scott Kingston for seven years. And no one suspected a thing. They all assumed he was dead. The worst part is not knowing, right? You should have seen Scott's parents, Shannon. They were not alive. They were so dead, so emotionally exhausted. I don't want to end up like them."

"It is a terrible thought, Jack. But you can't do this to yourself. You can't think like that. Yes, Austin is missing right now, but we have no idea what will happen tomorrow."

I stared at her, while a million thoughts flickered through my mind. Something had struck me.

"Wait a minute," I said and got up from the chair.

"What?" Shannon asked.

544

"The note," I said and pulled it out from my pocket. I unfolded it and looked at it. "Look."

"What am I looking at?" Shannon asked.

"The handwriting. Austin's name. He spelled it wrong. If you look closely, you can see, he wrote AUSTEN. He wrote an e instead of an i."

"So? He was in distress?"

"No. He learned how to spell his name when he was three years old. He knows how to do it right. I taught him by drawing in the wet sand when he was very little. He must have done it on purpose," I said.

"Why would he do that?"

"Because he's telling me something," I said.

"What is he telling you?"

I looked at Shannon.

"It's a code. We used to make our own code system. That was the only way we could keep secrets from Abigail. A is one, B is two and so on. It's a boy scout thing."

"So, these are numbers?" Shannon asked.

I leaned over and kissed her. "Yes." I got up and went to my desk and started to look at the note. I tried different things, but couldn't get it to be anything but 1-21-19-20-5-14. I stared at it for a while, not knowing what it could refer to, until I realized it. I got up and looked at Shannon.

"It's a phone number. Shannon, it's a phone number. 121-192-0514. You were right, Shannon. Austin is smarter than I give him credit for. He is a survivor. He must be in a place where the number is written somewhere."

Shannon looked at me with her head tilted. "Are you sure about this? It sounds a little far fetched. As far as I know, the area code here is 321. I don't know of any place that has 121?"

"It's all I've got right now, Shannon. It's all I've got."

SIXTY-EIGHT

May 2015

I DIDN'T WAIT till morning. It was three a.m. when I called Richard and asked him to try and track the number. He was on it right away, and an hour later, he called me back.

"The area code belongs to Birmingham in England," Richard said.

My heart dropped. England? How was this possible?

"But," Richard added. "I made some calls around. I know a guy with the feds who does this and he helped me track it. We traced it to a neighborhood in Daytona Beach. I can't get closer than that. But I can tell you it was last used today at six o'clock to make a phone call. You'll never guess to whom."

"I think I might have an idea. Sarah Millman, right?"

"Right."

Richard gave me the address of the neighborhood in Daytona, and I looked it up on the computer. Then I leaned back in my chair with a deep sigh. Shannon came up behind me.

"I'll be damned…" I said.

"What is it?"

"It's the neighborhood where the couple was killed. The couple that held their child in the basement and was killed by the Angel Makers for it. What the heck is going on here?"

Shannon shrugged and sat down next to me. "I don't know. Do you think the Angel Makers kidnapped Austin?"

"I…I don't know. I'm beginning to think so," I said and grabbed my phone. I got up, kissed her on the forehead, and grabbed my car keys.

"Where are you going?" she asked.

"I have to go get him," I said.

"Jack, don't. It could be an ambush."

I shrugged. "So what if it is? I have to go. I can't leave him up there all alone for any longer."

"Think about it, Jack. Austin is smart, but there is no way he could have come up with that code alone. He wouldn't dare to. Plus, how would he know the number of the phone if it is a cellphone? It's not like the number is written on the outside of a cell. They want you to come for him, Jack."

I sighed and kissed her on the lips. "I know. But I have to go anyway."

"Can't it wait?"

"No. I have to go and get him."

"Alone? How about taking Beth with you?" she asked.

"Beth can't leave her three kids home alone at four in the morning," I said. "It's not like she has a babysitter at hand...or a husband, for that matter."

"What about Ron?" Shannon asked. She sounded desperate. "I'm scared, Jack. Please don't go alone."

"Ron will have to contact the local sheriff, and before they get out of bed, the Angel Makers have left with my son. Shannon. I am a detective. I can defend myself. I will be fine. Don't worry."

She sighed and kissed me twice before I was allowed to leave. I jumped for my Jeep and drove off. I stopped for gas at the local Seven-Eleven on A1A and bought coffee and a Coke to keep me awake.

"Leaving town, huh? Good call. In a few hours, all the roads will be packed," the young guy behind the counter said. "It's going to be complete chaos."

"Excuse me?" I asked.

"Oh, you haven't heard. I just assumed you had and that you had decided to be the first to leave town."

"No, I haven't heard. What's going on?"

"They just announced it on the radio. Breaking news and everything. The National Weather service says Anna is going to make landfall within the next twelve hours."

SIXTY-NINE

May 2015

IT WAS all over the radio as I drove up North towards Daytona. They had all the blaring alarms going and the reports from the National Weather Service, ordering everyone in the coastal areas to evacuate.

I picked up the phone and called Shannon. She sounded tired. "Jack? Is everything alright?"

"Anna is going to make landfall," I said.

"What? When?"

"Within the next twelve hours. I need you to get the children and my parents and prepare to leave first thing in the morning. Make sure to close the hurricane shutters before you leave. My parents know what to do."

"But...but...I have never..."

"It's going to be alright, Shannon," I said. "It's still only a tropical storm. They say it might upgrade to a category one hurricane right before it hits land, but it's not one of the big ones. As long as you go inland, you should be fine. I'm thinking we should find a resort in Orlando and book it for the entire family."

"Sure. That sounds good, Jack. I'll make sure to make the reservations as soon as possible. But, what about you?"

"I'll be back as soon as possible. I have no idea how long it will take me to find Austin or what is waiting for me up there, so that's why I need you and my parents to take care of everything in case I don't make it back in time. Austin and I will just find you in Orlando."

"I have a better idea," Shannon said. "How about we all go to Nashville?"

"Nashville?"

"I still have my house, and it's big enough to house several of our families. Up there, we'll be far away from any storm. And the kids might think it's fun. It's actually more of a ranch. I have horses and everything."

"You don't have to try and convince me, Shannon. You had me at *I have a better idea*. Anything is better than being locked in at a resort while it's pouring outside."

"Good," she said. "I'll reserve the tickets and take everybody with me, hopefully early in the morning."

"And Austin and I will join you later. That sounds like a plan," I said. I liked the idea of my family being far away from the storm. I didn't like it when my loved ones were scared, and a storm raging outside the windows could be very scary.

"Now promise me that," Shannon said. "Promise me you'll be okay and that you'll come with us."

I sighed and turned off towards Daytona Beach. "I promise," I said.

Then we hung up.

The sun would have risen on the horizon by now, if it hadn't been covered in the blackness of the storm threatening us from the ocean. It was pitch dark over the horizon and the winds had picked up. It was shaking the car pretty bad.

I drove over the bridge to the beach shores, towards the neighborhood where the phone had been used last, wondering what I was going to find once I got there. I knew Shannon was right. I knew they wanted me to come. There was a reason for all this, and I was about to walk right into it. But what other choice did I have? The police all along the coast were busy getting people out of their houses and onto the mainland. They had no time to help me out, even if they wanted to. When Anna made landfall, she was so big it would affect the entire coastline of Florida. There would be wind gusts of up to eighty miles an hour and heavy rainfall. It was important to get people out while there was still time. And evacuation took time. It was all that was on their minds right now. A storm was coming, and it could be deadly if you were at the wrong place at the wrong time.

This might turn out to be an ambush, but I had to do it. I feared for Austin if I didn't go and get him. I had to at least try. Even if it cost me my life.

SEVENTY

May 2015

A FEW MINUTES LATER, I was driving through the beach-shore neighborhood. Many had already left. Their houses were left with shutters closed and empty driveways. Others were still packing the cars, getting their belongings, children, and pets into the cars. I could tell on their faces they were worried. It was tough leaving everything behind, not knowing what you would come back to. Especially when you lived beach-side...that was usually hit the hardest. You could come back to a house with no roof and water damage inside, windows broken, a house filled with sand or like most did, a house that no longer had a screen around the pool.

I didn't know exactly where I would find Austin, but I had a pretty good hunch.

It was easy to recognize the house. The entrance was still blocked by police tape. I parked my car and got out, holding a firm hand on my gun.

The house was a shabby blue beach cabin from the fifties. It was still marked in the driveway where the bodies had been found. Bullet holes on a tree and a fence behind were marked with red.

A wind gust grabbed me and almost made me fall. I fought through the wind and walked to the front door and looked in the window next to it. It was dark inside.

What if you are wrong? What if he isn't here? Then you've wasted all this time.

It was pretty far fetched. I knew that much. And it would be devastating if I was wrong. That would mean me leaving Austin somewhere unknown while the storm raged. But my gut told me I was on the right track. I had to be. I had to believe I was.

I walked around the house and looked in all the windows, while clasping the gun between my hands in a tight grip. If these insane women wanted to attack me, I wasn't going down easily. I would fight for my life.

I looked inside the kitchen when a gust of wind grabbed the palm tree next to me and a branch was loosened. It fell towards me like a missile from the sky and landed right next to me.

I gasped and stared at the huge palm tree branch. It had sharp pointy edges that would have cut me severely had it hit right.

Luckily, it didn't. I crept along the house wall towards the next window and looked in. Then I let out a small shriek. Inside, I spotted Austin. He was lying on a bed. He was facing the wall, so I couldn't see his face. My heart rate went up quickly.

He is here! I knew he would be! Is he alive? Oh, my God, what have they done to him?

My eyes were glued to the window while I wondered how to approach this. The Angel Makers were merciless. They had already tried to kill Beth using a bomb. They might do it again. They had also shot Ron from the house across the street. I wondered what their move would be this time?

I decided there was only one way to find out. I had to just go in. I tried to open the window, then used the handle of my gun to break it instead. There was no time to waste. I removed the glass so I wouldn't cut myself, then crawled inside. I landed on the floor with a thud. Austin didn't seem to react. He wasn't moving at all.

Is he asleep? Why isn't he moving? He should have woken up from the sound of me entering? Why isn't he moving?

"Austin?" I said and rushed to him. I grabbed his shoulder and turned him around. When my hand touched his body, he felt warm.

"Austin?"

Austin's eyes met mine. His mouth was covered with duct-tape. His eyes filled with tears. I saw a fear in them I had never seen before. A note was taped to his chest. On the note it said:

WE DON'T HURT CHILDREN. BUT WE WILL IF WE HAVE TO. LEAVE US ALONE!

The note was for me. It was the Angel Makers making a point. They were angry. I had pissed them off by killing one of theirs. I had declared war on them.

"Austin, are you alright?" I asked.

His eyes told me he wasn't. I was about to take off the tape from his mouth, when he groaned and made me look down at his hands. Between them, he was holding a hand-grenade. The pin had been pulled out. The only thing hindering it from exploding was him holding the striker lever down. His hands were shaking with restraint. He was whimpering behind the tape and had tears flooding from his eyes, screaming desperately for my help.

SEVENTY-ONE

May 2015

"I'M GOING to take the tape off your mouth, now, alright?" I said, my voice shaking in fear. "It will hurt a little, but it is important that whatever you do, you don't let go of the grenade, alright? Nod to let me know you understand, Austin."

Austin nodded.

"Good," I said, and grabbed the edge of the tape. I pulled it as fast as I could. Austin screamed. I stared at the grenade and his hands, but they didn't move. I was sweating heavily now. My hands were clammy and drops of sweat rolled from my forehead to my nose. The air was very moist and it was hard to breathe properly.

"Dad," Austin said, his voice trembling in fear. "I'm scared."

I forced a smile to try and calm him down. "I know, son. Me too. But we'll find a solution."

I wiped the sweat off my forehead with my arm and looked at my son. I cursed those women for what they had done to him.

"Now, I'll untie your feet," I said and grabbed the tape used to hold his feet together, making sure he didn't move or try to get out of there. It was so brutal, so cruel to put him in this position. I could hardly restrain my anger.

Why would anyone do this to a child? Why? Just to get back at me? It made them no better than the people they tried to fight, in my opinion. I pulled off the tape carefully, while Austin tried to lie still. He hardly moved.

I looked at my poor son, who was clutching the grenade between his hands. He too was sweating heavily. I kneeled next to him on the bed and stroked his hair.

"You're doing great here, Austin," I said. "You're doing really great." My voice was trembling too. I couldn't hide how scared I was. Austin knew me well enough to be able to tell. "Now, the next thing I am going to ask you to do is to get up on your feet. Do you think you can do that without letting go of the lever?"

Austin looked into my eyes. Never had I seen such an expression on his face before. It was heartbreaking.

"Do you think you can do that?" I asked again.

552

He swallowed hard, then nodded cautiously.

"Okay," I said. "Let's try, then. Remember, if you let go of the lever, it explodes after four seconds, all right? So, don't let go."

Austin nodded again to show me he understood. My heart was pounding in my chest as I watched him swing his legs to the floor and slowly raise his body from the bed. Tears were rolling across his cheeks, and I could tell the fear had a firm grasp on him.

"Look at me, Austin. Look into my eyes," I said, when he managed to sit up. His eyes met mine. His entire upper body was shaking. "You're doing great," I said. "You're doing really great."

Austin gasped for air. I could tell the fear was overpowering him now. I forced him to keep looking at me.

"Now, try and stand up," I said. "I'll help you."

He lifted the hands with the grenade up in front of him, and I grabbed him around the waist. I lifted him up till he was on his feet. Austin whimpered when I let go. I stared at his hands. They were still firmly attached around the grenade.

"Okay," I said. "So far so good. You're standing up now. You're up. I haven't been this excited about you standing up on your own since you were a one-year-old."

My comment made Austin chuckle. I looked into his eyes to make sure he knew I had this under control. I was trying to ease his fear and I believed I succeeded. At least for a few seconds. Up until the first bullet hissed through the air and hit the wall behind me.

SEVENTY-TWO

May 2015

"GET DOWN!"

It was my first reaction as another bullet hit the wall and left a deep hole. It was my instinct to react like this, but Austin didn't throw himself on the ground. Due to the grenade, he didn't dare to. He kept standing on the carpet. He was a sitting duck.

I reacted fast. I grabbed him in my arms and lifted him into the air. Grenade or no grenade, he had to get out of there. But as I grabbed him, the next bullet entered the room and hit me in the shoulder, forcing me to let go of Austin, who fell to the floor. He screamed. I gasped and looked at his hands. They were still in place, holding down the lever.

"You okay?" I asked, while throwing myself next to him with my back against the wall, while bullets were still being fired through the window above my head.

Austin stared at me with wide eyes. "Dad. You're...you're bleeding," he said.

I felt my shoulder. Blood was gushing out of it very fast. My shirt was already soaked. I grabbed the sheet from the bed and ripped it apart. I wrapped my wound with it and tried to stop the bleeding. Austin stared at me, sweat springing from his face. He was clasping the grenade.

"I'll be alright," I said. "It's only a scratch."

I used my gun to fire a few shots out the window, then fell back down next to Austin. He looked tormented.

"I can't hold on to it much longer," Austin whimpered.

I looked at my son and the grenade between his hands. I had an idea, but wasn't so sure it would work. It seemed like the shooting was coming from the house next door. The houses in this neighborhood were pretty close together. Maybe... just maybe. Would he be able to?

"Listen, son," I said. "I need your help."

Austin looked at me. It was risky. What I was going to ask him to do could end up costing him his life. And mine as well. It could also end up saving us both if it worked.

If it worked.

Austin was only six years old…almost seven, he would argue. Would he be able to pull this off? Was it too much responsibility to put on one kid's shoulders? I would have done it myself. But I was hurt now. Austin was my only chance.

"I need you to play a game, alright? Let's say we're at one of your baseball games. You're very good at baseball, right? You love it, right?"

Austin nodded. "Y-y-yes."

"Alright. Now let's pretend this is one of your games. You're pitching. You can win the game if you do this right. I need you to aim for the house next door. Aim for the window, and then throw the grenade towards it. The best throw you have ever done. The throw of a lifetime. Can you do that?"

Austin stared at me. I could tell he was about to cry. "Don't cry, Austin," I said through the throbbing pain. "You're our only chance now. You can do this. You're a big boy."

Austin bit his lip. He looked at me, determined, then rose to his feet, still with the grenade clasped between his hands. He stood with his back against the wall.

"Good boy. Now, count to three, then walk to the window and throw it. Can you do that?"

Austin went quiet. I feared he had lost his courage. "Daad?" he said.

"Yes, Austin, what is it?"

"I don't want to surf anymore. I don't like to surf."

My heart stopped. I stared at him. Where did this come from all of a sudden? I shook my head with a moan. "You never have to surf again. I promise you. Just help us get out of here alive. Throw that damn thing!"

Austin took in a deep breath, took one step, and stood in front of the window, then let go of the lever with one hand and lifted the grenade with the other. I stared at him, my heart racing in my chest. Right when he let go of it and it hissed through the air towards the neighboring house, I heard a shot being fired. I got up on my feet, jumped at Austin, and pulled him down. Seconds later, the explosion sent most of the outer wall of the house down on top of us.

SEVENTY-THREE

May 2015

I ASKED Austin to stay where he was, once we had gotten out of the debris from the fallen wall. I rushed towards the neighboring house, where the grenade had hit and blown the walls down. I walked with the gun in my hand, pressing through the pain with the adrenalin in my body, across the fallen debris.

I spotted her on the floor of what I believed used to be the hallway. She was lying on her back with the rifle on the floor next to her. Her eyes were staring lifeless in the air, blood running from her head. I pointed my gun at Kelly Monahan, the last of the four sisters, then bent to feel for a pulse. But there wasn't any. She was dead.

Relieved, I ran back to Austin, who was sitting in what was left of the room, shaking, with his knees pulled up against his chest. I kneeled next to him. He looked up. "Is it over?" he asked.

I nodded with a relieved sigh. The adrenalin was still pumping inside of me, but finally, I felt like I could relax. She was gone. The last sister was gone.

"Yes, Austin. It's over."

Austin cried and sniffled. "What about you, Dad?" he asked. He looked at my shoulder.

"That? I told you, it's just a scratch," I said to comfort him. "The bullet barely touched me. Now, come on. Let's go home."

I called 911 on my way out of there and told them where they could find the body, then told them I wasn't going to stay there, since it was too dangerous with the storm coming closer. Then I called Ron and told him everything.

"I'll be..." he said. "We'll issue a warrant for Sarah Millman's arrest again," he said. "As soon as everything is back to normal. This time, she won't make bail."

"Is all the beachside evacuated?" I asked, as we hit the bridges leading to the mainland. I felt a big relief to leave the beach behind me for once. Anna was quickly approaching. I could feel her breathing down my neck.

556

"Yes. Everyone is out. We have left the area too. I'm in Orlando with my family. Where are you going now?"

I looked at the clock on my dashboard. It was almost eleven. It was too late to make it to the airport and meet with Shannon and the rest of my family. She had left a message telling me they had booked airplane tickets for ten fifty-five. It was the last plane out of Florida for today. Everything was closing down now. She told me she would wait for me at the airport, but leave if I didn't make it. I had tried to call her before I called Ron, but her phone was shut off. So was Emily's and my mother's. I guessed they had already boarded. My shoulder was hurting like crazy, but I pretended to be fine to not scare Austin.

"I don't know," I said. "I think we might drive to Nashville."

"That's one heck of a long drive," Ron said. "Are you sure it's a good idea. What about your shoulder? You said you were hit?"

"It barely touched me; it doesn't even hurt anymore," I lied. I had my phone on hands free and put the speaker on, so I could focus on driving. Austin was listening in. I didn't want him to worry.

"I'll be fine."

"Maybe you should go to the ER once you hit the mainland," Ron said. "Just in case."

"Nah, I'm fine. But thanks for worrying."

I hung up. I could tell Austin was getting concerned. His eyes didn't leave my wound. It looked worse than it was, I thought. I tried to ignore the pain.

"You have more messages, Dad," Austin said, looking at the phone in the holder. "Don't you want to hear them?"

"Sure," I said, thinking it was probably Shannon or my parents calling to ask me if I would make it in time.

Austin pressed the phone and the message came on. But it wasn't from Shannon or my parents. It wasn't a voice belonging to anyone I loved.

It was Vernon Johnson.

SEVENTY-FOUR

May 2015

I KNOW, I am probably the last person you wish to hear from now. I have nowhere else to turn. I need to cleanse my name once and for all. But I need you to help me. I know where Noah Kinley is. Meet me at Swell.

I stared at the phone, then back at the windshield. It was pouring down outside now. It was hard to see the road. I saw lightning in my rearview mirror. It was followed by a loud clap of thunder. The voice of Vernon Johnson wouldn't leave my head.

I know where Noah Kinley is.

I looked at the display. The message wasn't more than fifteen minutes old. What the heck was he up to now? Cleanse his name? I didn't understand. How did he know about the kid? What did he want from me? Was he trying to ambush me? Or was he trying to help? Why did I have to meet him at the surf shop? It made no sense. But there was one sentence that I couldn't stop repeating in my mind.

I know where Noah Kinley is.

I shook my head and tried to think about something else. I reached I95 and turned off towards Jacksonville.

Austin looked at me. "What are you doing, Dad?"

"Getting you to safety," I said.

"Are you just going to leave that boy?" he asked, startled.

"What else do you want me to do?" I asked. "We don't even know if he is telling the truth. It's way too dangerous to go back there."

"But…but you can't do that! You heard what he said. He knows where the boy is. You've got to go there, Dad. He told you he needed your help. You can help rescue the boy."

I sighed. "I can't think about that now, Austin. Getting you to safety is more important for me right now."

"How can you say that?" Austin asked. He looked at me like I had just told him

Santa wasn't real. I was his hero, I knew that. And right now, his hero was letting him down.

"It might be a trap, Austin. I just found you. Do you have any idea how afraid I was of losing you? I don't want you to be in danger again. I can't let that happen again. I simply can't. Now, stop it. Let it go. I'm driving to Nashville, and that's the end of the discussion."

But Austin wouldn't let it go. He was suddenly as stubborn as his sister could often get.

"I can't believe you, Dad. The boy needs your help. What if he's killed during the storm? How will you be able to live with yourself, knowing you could have helped him? What if it was me?"

Austin was making all the right arguments. It hurt like crazy. I really didn't want to have to go back. I really didn't. All I wanted was to drive north, get far away from the trouble and the storm, and drive till we reached Shannon's ranch and stay there with my family till the storm was over. Just holding everyone I loved tightly in my arms. That was all I dreamt about right now, after all we had been through. But Austin was so right. It hurt to admit it.

There was no way I could leave the kid in Cocoa Beach.

I looked at Austin with a deep sigh. Austin smiled. "Now, let's go back and get him," he said.

SEVENTY-FIVE

May 2015

THE FLUORESCENT LIGHT above Noah was flickering. Something was going on outside of the room. His eyes were still hurting, and he couldn't keep them open for many seconds at a time without covering them to protect them from the bright light.

But something was definitely going on. For the first time since he had been kidnapped, Noah heard voices. They were coming from behind the door, and when he put his ear to it, he could listen to them.

There were two voices. One belonged to Hector, his guardian; the other, he didn't recognize. Noah hoped it was someone who had come to help him, but he wasn't sure. It sounded like this person knew the guardian. Noah didn't want to risk anything, so instead of banging on the door to let this person know of his existence, he put his ear to the door and listened to them. They seemed to be arguing.

"You sick bastard!" the stranger said. "You kept the kid for years. What did you do to him, huh?"

"I only did what a little boy like him deserved," Hector replied.

"An innocent stranger! A little boy! How could he deserve such a fate?" the stranger yelled.

"You know perfectly well, why," Hector replied.

"Just because of that? Just because of what happened to you more than thirty-five years ago?"

Hector didn't say anything. He hissed at the stranger, and Noah knew the stranger had to be careful now. That was exactly the way he always hissed at Noah when he didn't like his behavior. It was usually the sound he would make right before he did something bad to him.

Be careful, stranger!

Noah wanted to yell it, wanted to scream and bang on the door, but something held him back. Fear of Hector's wrath held him back.

"You're sick," the stranger continued. He clearly didn't know Hector the way Noah did. He would know to stop now if he did.

"A sick, sick bastard is what you are."

Hector still didn't say anything. Noah knew how Hector was staring at the stranger right now. He knew the look in his eyes when he was angry. He always became quiet right before he hit. He would stare at Noah with those piercing brown eyes…stare at him with madness in his eyes. Evil madness.

After spending a long time with Hector, Noah had learned to avoid that anger. He knew to please him to keep that look from appearing in his eyes; he knew what to say to soften him up.

But the stranger didn't know. He kept yelling at Hector. And that was a bad idea. That was a very bad idea. Noah could vividly picture how Hector was now grinding his teeth in anger, waiting for the right moment to lash out.

"What do you want?" Hector asked. "Why have you come?"

"I want the kid," the stranger said. "Where is he?"

Noah gasped. It could only be him they were talking about, couldn't it? Had the stranger come to get him? Would he get out of here?

"I don't know where he is," Hector said.

"You're lying. I know you did it. I know you took him and the two others as well. 'Cause that's just how sick you are. And then you made sure it was all blamed on me."

Two others? Noah swallowed hard. There had been others? It wasn't just him that was being punished, that was being kept like this?

Suddenly, Noah felt the tears well up in his eyes. He felt such anger towards Hector and what he had done. He was no longer afraid of what would happen. He removed his hands from his eyes, turned to face the door, and then slammed both his fists into it, while screaming at the top of his lungs:

"HEEEEEELP! I'M IN HERE!!! HEEEEELP ME!"

SEVENTY-SIX

May 2015

I DROVE up in front of Swell about an hour and fifteen minutes later. The streets had been vacant, so I allowed myself to ignore the speed limits to get there faster. The rain was pouring heavily and the wind gusts pulled and tossed the car.

I assumed Hector Suarez had left town long ago, and didn't understand why Vernon wanted to meet me here. As suspected, the shop was closed. Shutters covered all the windows.

I looked at the shop through my windshield, shaking my head.

"There's no one here," I said. "Vernon tricked us."

"Why would he do that?" Austin said.

"I don't know. To get back at us."

I was about to put the car into gear, when I spotted something parked up against the façade of the building.

It was a bike.

I knew from my mother that Vernon hadn't bought a car, since he didn't feel safe driving after all these years, and since he loved being outside feeling the fresh air on his face.

I sighed and put it in park. I looked at Austin. "I better go check to be sure."

Austin smiled. He didn't like the idea of leaving without being certain either. "Okay, Dad."

"You stay here, alright?"

Austin nodded.

"I'll leave the engine running, so you can listen to the radio. I'll be right back, okay? Will you be okay alone out here?"

A thunder clap crackled through the air outside. I could tell Austin was terrified. He never liked thunderstorms, and these were some very severe ones.

I sighed, then opened the door and rushed out. I ran to the door and tried to look inside, but the glass was covered with shutters. I grabbed the handle and realized the door was open. I walked inside and closed the door behind me. The light was on inside the shop, which I found very odd. The lights kept going out, then coming back on. My clothes were soaking and dripping on the floor, leaving a small puddle beneath me. I felt my shoulder. The bleeding seemed to have stopped, but it still hurt like crazy when I moved my arm.

I heard voices coming from the back. I walked to the counter. The door was open behind it. I had never been into the back of Hector's shop. That was where he shaped the boards. He never let anyone in there and always showed us the boards outside in the store.

"Hector?" I asked. "Vernon?"

The voices coming from behind the door were loud and drowned me out. I looked around me, then decided to pass the counter. I pushed the door open and was let into a small hallway with several doors on each side. There was a light coming out from behind one of the doors. I pushed it open.

"Hector?" I asked.

Then, I gasped. Inside the small office stood Vernon. He was holding a gun, pointing it at Hector. It wasn't until I saw them really close to one another that I realized how much the two of them looked alike. Hector had long dreadlocks, making him appear different, but now I saw the similarity.

Behind another door in the room, I could hear the cries of what sounded like a little boy.

"What the hell is going on here?" I said and pulled my own gun.

Hector looked at me, then grinned. He looked at Vernon. "Go ahead," he said. "I know you want to."

He was right. Vernon pulled the trigger before I could stop him. Hector was shot right in the chest, then fell to the ground in a pool of blood.

SEVENTY-SEVEN

April 1980

HECTOR AND RAUL took turns steering the boat and keeping an eye on the passengers. They trusted no one. They had no weapon to defend themselves with if anyone came against them. All they could hope for was that they would leave them alone till they reached Florida, and then they would be someone else's problem.

If only they could keep things calm for that long.

Many eyes were staring at them. The ocean seemed endless. There wasn't a boat in sight. If someone threw them in the water, no one would lift an eyebrow. No one would be able to save them.

Hector started thinking about those swimming lessons he had thought about taking for so long while living in Florida. There was water everywhere, and everyone should be able to swim, his brother had told him. It wasn't that he didn't want to learn, it really wasn't. It was just...well, the timing just was never quite right. Now, he regretted it. Being able to swim would increase his chances of surviving in case he was thrown overboard like that poor guy had been earlier on the trip. At least he would be able to keep himself alive, maybe long enough for another boat to pick him up. At least he wouldn't sink like a rock. Maybe it didn't matter. Maybe he would die anyway.

Nightfall came upon them, and soon darkness surrounded the boat. It didn't make Hector less uncomfortable. A guy was sitting on the deck right outside the wheelhouse, staring at him with this creepy smile on his face. He wasn't very old, early twenties, maybe. But he had been badly beaten. His face was bruised, and so were his arms and legs. Hector could only imagine how he looked underneath his ripped T-shirt. The chill in his eyes said everything. It made Hector shiver in fear.

Raul was steering the boat when the young man later approached them. Hector's heart was racing. Hector could spot light on the horizon and with relief in his heart realized they were getting closer to the shore. Unfortunately, so did the young man. Grinning from ear to ear, he walked inside the wheelhouse.

Hector walked towards him. "No one enters the wheelhouse," he said in Spanish. "Those are the rules. Everyone stays outside. We're almost on shore. You'll be in Florida in less than an hour."

The young man stared at Hector, still smiling from ear to ear. He was missing a few teeth. Hector wondered if they had been knocked out.

"You think I'm afraid of you?" he asked.

"Go back to where you were," Hector said without answering. He knew very well this man wasn't afraid of him.

And he was right. The man grabbed Hector by the throat and lifted him into the air without as much as a groan. Hector yelled for Raul, who let go of the wheel, then rushed to his rescue. Raul hit his fist into the man's jaw, but the man barely moved. He was skinny, but he was strong. He was obviously used to taking a beating. Raul hit him again, this time in the stomach, but the man barely made a sound. He held Hector in the air, while Hector struggled for air. With the other hand, he punched Raul in the face so hard, Raul stumbled backwards, his eyes rolling back in his face. As he fell backwards, his head hit a sharp edge.

"Raul!" Hector exclaimed, gasping for air. But Raul didn't move. He was lying still on the ground, blood running from his nose and the back of his head. Hector's heart stopped. He felt a deep panic grow inside of him. He looked into the eyes of the man, while desperately holding on to his own life.

"Tell me your name," the man asked.

Hector barely had any air to speak. "Hector," he whispered, in some hope that if he told the man what he wanted to know he might let him go. "Hector Suarez."

Then he felt the man stick his hands inside of his jacket and pull out his passport and papers. The man laughed and showed Hector what he had taken from him.

"Now, I am Hector," he said, while laughing. He let go of Hector and let him fall to the ground, where he lay coughing and gasping for air for a long time. The man took the steering wheel and soon after, docked the boat. Hector lay still, hoping the man would forget about him, now that he was finally at their destination. The man left, then came back before Hector dared to get up. He smiled from ear to ear, then bent down, grabbed Hector around the throat again, and squeezed so hard everything stopped inside of him. The last thing Hector thought about before he stopped breathing, was Isabella. He was certain he could hear her voice calling for him from the dock of the Miami Harbor.

SEVENTY-EIGHT

April 1980

SHE WAS CALLING HIS NAME.

"Paaapa?"

Isabella was running from boat to boat in the harbor, asking if they had seen her father, calling his name.

"Hector Suarez?" she yelled.

A man shook his head. So did another one and another one. Isabella kept running. She had been on one of the first boats out. She and her grandparents and her uncle had all made it to safety on the very first day of the boatlift. She had managed to contact her other uncles, who now lived up north in Central Florida, but they had told her that her father and Uncle Raul had travelled to Cuba to find her.

It had crushed her heart.

They had missed each other, and now Hector and Raul were back at the island looking for her. There was no way she could contact them and let them know she was already in Miami. So, all she could do was to approach every boat that docked at the harbor and ask if anyone had seen them or heard about them. This evening, ten more boats had come to the harbor. One was harboring more refugees than the others. She wondered how many were so full they never made it to the other side, and prayed her father and uncle at least would be among those who made it back. She was certain she would be able to find them, as long as they made it.

"Hector Suarez?" she asked a flock of people, who had just jumped off an old fishing boat. There seemed to be several hundred people on this one. How had all of them been able to fit into that old boat? It was a miracle it didn't sink.

"Yes," an old man suddenly said. "Hector Suarez."

Isabella gasped. "You know him?"

The old man nodded.

"You have seen him?"

"Yes." The old man pointed to the old fishing boat in front of her. "Hector Suarez," he said again.

"Hector was on this boat?" Isabella asked.

The old man nodded. "Yes."

She wanted to kiss him. Instead, she shook his small hand. "Thank you. Thank you!"

Isabella ran to the boat, elbowing her way through the crowd, yelling her father's name. She wondered what it would be like to see him again after this many years. Would he recognize her? Would he be proud of who she had become? Would he love her?

"Hector?" she yelled. "Hector Suarez?"

The crowd coming up from the boat were all anxious to get to the shore and paid no attention to her. She was pushed backwards, but managed to fight her way back to the boat, still while yelling her father's name.

"Hector Suarez? I'm looking for Hector Suarez."

A voice suddenly broke through the air and a face appeared in front of her. "I'm Hector Suarez," the voice said.

Isabella gasped, then looked into the eyes of the person standing in front of her. He was smiling widely. Everything inside of Isabella froze when she looked into this man's eyes. The evil that emerged from them was so overwhelming it made her numb.

Isabella shook her head and took a step backwards.

"I'm sorry," she said, the feeling of disappointment eating her from the inside. "I was looking for someone else. For another Hector Suarez."

The man still smiled. Isabella felt very uncomfortable.

"Good luck finding the real one."

SEVENTY-NINE

May 2015

HECTOR FELL to the ground with a loud thud, blood gushing out from his chest. I pointed my gun at Vernon, not knowing what else to do. I didn't understand anything of what was going on.

"What the heck is going on here?" I yelled. "Explain!"

Vernon dropped the gun, then lifted both his hands in the air. "I'm sorry. I had to do it," he said.

"Why? Why did you have to shoot Hector?" I asked.

"Can I please explain later?" Vernon asked. "We need to get the boy out of there." He nodded towards the door, where the heavy banging and screaming was coming from. I realized he was right. I didn't trust Vernon one bit, but in this moment, I had to. I should have cuffed him, but wasn't carrying any cuffs.

"Stay there," I said, and pointed the gun at him while walking to the door. Vernon walked backwards both hands in the air. I grabbed the door handle and tried to open it, but it was locked.

Of course it was locked. Meanwhile, the screaming intensified behind the door. "HEEELP ME!"

"Don't worry," I said. "I'll get you out."

I looked to Vernon for help. "Try to see if he has the key on him," he said.

I bent down and went through Hector's pockets. I found a set of keys in his pants and pulled it out, then sprang for the door. I tried key after key but none worked. I cursed and tried a new one. Finally, one worked. I turned it and opened the door. A light so bright it burned my eyes hit my face and blinded me. I covered my eyes with my hand, as I felt someone throw himself in my arms. I lifted him up, turned around, and carried him away from the burning bright light. Then, I finally looked. In my arms lay Noah Kinley. He was naked and badly bruised on his small body. He was skinny and feeble and so pale. He held on to me so tightly I wasn't sure he would ever let go again.

"There's a blanket over there," I said to Vernon. "Could you grab it and wrap him in it?" I said, fighting my tears. The boy felt so skinny in my arms.

Vernon grabbed the blanket and wrapped the boy. Then, he grabbed a cup and filled it with water from the cooler in the corner. He handed it to the boy. The boy grabbed it and gulped it down.

"Easy there," I said. "I don't want you to choke."

The boy emptied the cup. Vernon fetched more for him, which he drank as greedily as the first, still while clinging to me. I held him up so he could drink again when we heard a loud crash.

Austin!

"The winds are picking up," Vernon said. "This place isn't safe."

"I have my son in the car!" I yelled, then ran out the door with Noah Kinley still tight in my arms. The adrenalin in my body was so strong, still my shoulder hurt like crazy. But I fought my way through it. I was getting all of us to safety, no matter the cost.

Vernon held the front door open for us and as I walked outside I realized what had happened...what had caused that big crashing sound.

A tree had fallen. It had fallen from across the street and blocked the road going south. Luckily, it was still open going north.

"We better hurry," Vernon said. He helped me carry Noah to the car and get him inside the back seat. Vernon jumped in with him and I took the wheel. "Are you alright Austin?" I asked.

He nodded. "Yes. Are you?"

"I will be. As soon as we get the hell out of here."

EIGHTY

May 2015

_____

"WE NEED to get him to the hospital!"

Vernon was yelling at me from the back seat. We had made it onto A1A, when Noah Kinley suddenly got worse.

"He's shaking, Daddy," Austin yelled. "His eyes look creepy!"

A wind gust grabbed the car and forced it sideways; the wheels slid on the wet asphalt. I turned hard on the steering wheel and got the car back on the road.

"Just hold on," I said and sped up. The rain was hammering on the windshield. Lightning hit somewhere close by. The thunder clap came right away. It sounded like the entire sky cracked open above us. Austin screamed. I focused on the road and staying on it. Water had overflowed the road and flooding had started.

I grabbed my cellphone to try and call Ron, but there was no service. "I think we can make it to Cape Canaveral Hospital."

The adrenalin was rushing through my veins as I passed Downtown Cocoa Beach. It was strange to see my town so vacant. All the shops and restaurants were closed up with shutters or plywood. The streets were dark and wet. Not a single car. All parking lots close to the beach that usually were swarmed with cars, even though they charged ten, sometimes fifteen dollars for parking, were empty.

I drove past the Kelly Slater statue and out of the old downtown. A tree had fallen and blocked the street on my side, so I had to drive onto the other side of the road to get past it. The wheels screeched, and I lost contact with the road as we hit the flood of water gushing across the road.

I regained control of the car and managed to continue on A1A. We passed Ron Jon's Surf shop, where the eight-foot surfboard in front of it had fallen and blocked the entrance. I turned left and made it onto 520 towards the mainland. The hospital was located on a small peninsula on the way to the bridges. We weren't far from it.

"Hurry, hurry," Vernon said. "He's cramping."

"Hold on, we're almost there," I said.

I sped up. I could see the hospital now.

"Please, stay with us," Vernon said.

I could feel the desperation in his voice. We were so close now. Just a few more yards.

"No…Vernon said. "No. Don't go. Noah…Noah…stay with us, please, don't…"

"Dad, he's dying." Austin spoke with a trembling voice.

"Almost there," I said, and turned the car into the hospital's parking lot.

"He's not breathing," Vernon said.

I raced towards the Emergency entrance and pressed the horn down. I knew the doctors and nurses would be there to keep the hospital open and sleep there for days if they had to, as a part of their hurricane preparedness training. I pressed the horn and didn't let go until I saw movement. Two nurses came running to the car as I drove up to the door. I sprang out.

I opened the door to the back and Vernon handed me the lifeless body of Noah Kinley. My heart was pounding so fast in my chest. I put him on the stretcher, and the nurses ran inside with him between them. I watched, panting, my shoulder shooting pain through my body, my stomach turning in anxiety.

Will he make it? Were we too late?

All I had was my hope.

EIGHTY-ONE

May 2015

"HE WAS MY BROTHER."

Vernon Johnson looked at me from across the room. We had been sitting in the waiting room for half an hour after I had gotten my shoulder checked and my arm put in a sling. Austin was sitting next to me and had fallen asleep in my lap. Vernon had bought coffee from the machine for the both of us. The hospital personnel had told us we were allowed to wait out the storm. They had no idea how long it would last, so they had to ration all their supplies, and that meant food and coffee as well. It was only for the patients. We decided we could live off what we could get from the vending machines.

I sipped my coffee and looked at him. "Hector Suarez was your brother?"

Vernon nodded. "Half brother. We shared the same father. Hector isn't his real name—or wasn't. He was born Alejándro Martínez back in Cuba."

"So, he changed his name when he moved to the States?" I asked. "Just like you and your mother?"

"He must have. I didn't even know he was here. As a matter of fact, I didn't even know he existed. My mother told me about him yesterday. She told me I had seen him when I was just a kid, that he had lived with us when I was younger, but I don't remember. I was too young. My mother told me Alejándro had a troubled upbringing. His mother couldn't care for him properly. Our father didn't want him…thought he was worthless. Nevertheless, he came to live with us for a time. Stayed for a year, but my mother once discovered him inside of my bedroom in the middle of the night with a pillow in his hand, and after that, they decided they couldn't keep him. He grew up at his grandmother's house and was beaten regularly by his grandfather. Got himself in a lot of trouble constantly. He came to Florida during the boatlift in 1980, according to my mother. Just like my mother and I did. I don't know how much you know about it, but back then, Castro decided to open the harbor of Mariel to let people leave if they had someone come and pick them up."

"I heard about that," I said, thinking about my time working in Miami. I remembered the stories told by my colleagues about how Miami changed around that time.

"About 125,000 refugees came to South Florida," I said. "It changed everything. The labor market, the housing market, the crime."

"Exactly," Vernon said pensively. "During this exodus, Castro decided to also open his jails, flooding Miami's streets with criminals, drug addicts, and mentally unhinged people, which contributed to Miami's skyrocketing crime rate and helped it become murder capital of the world just one year later. My brother was one of them."

"He was one of the criminals?" I asked.

Vernon nodded. "He was in prison. So was my father. I was fifteen when they took him. My mother told me they were arrested at the same time. She never told me this before yesterday. She kept everything about my brother a secret from me. My brother was only seventeen when he was put in one of Castro's prisons."

"But was released at the boatlift and sent to Florida. What about your father? Wasn't he released?" I asked.

Vernon shook his head. "He never made it. According to my mother, Alejándro came to her one day when I wasn't home a few years after we had moved to Florida. I had a good life here. But Alejándro never had any of that. He was angry when he came to see her at her apartment. He beat her badly and told her it was all her fault. It was her fault he had those scars on his body now, it was her fault her husband was gone."

"He died in prison?" I asked.

Vernon sighed. "Yes. He died inside a drawer cell. You ever heard of those? I looked them up. It's these small boxes they put the prisoners inside of and leave them without water or food for a very long time. They sometimes open the box and throw excrement at the prisoners, or ice-cold water, or they bang on the boxes, making it impossible for the prisoner to sleep. They also put them in small rooms with fluorescent lights for days, so they can't see and can't sleep. My dad died inside one of those boxes. And Alejándro listened to him call for water all night, his voice becoming smaller and smaller, until it was nothing but a hissing sound. Then, Alejándro started to call and yell for help, but no one ever came. When they realized my dad was dead, they took out Alejándro and beat him senseless, then they urinated on him and threw him inside the box instead. He spent seven years in that box. Until Castro decided to get rid of him."

I looked at Vernon and had forgotten all about my coffee. It all made sense all of a sudden. The crouched bodies, the starvation, and the bright light we found in the room where Noah was being kept. "So, Alejándro was doing the same thing to these boys as had happened to himself and to your father?"

Vernon nodded. "Yes. He kept them for years until they died of starvation."

I returned to my coffee and sipped it. It all made sense all of a sudden. Hector had told me he used to be a carpenter. My guess was, he had been working for that roofing company in Rockledge back when Jordan Turner was abducted on his way home from school. Before Hector opened the surf-shop. I wondered where he had kept the kids before he opened the shop? At his home? Maybe we would never know. At the roofing company, he had access to all kinds of wood. Even the very rare birch sort that was very durable and could sustain someone banging on it for hours, weeks and days. My skin shivered at the thought.

Austin mumbled in his sleep. I kept thinking about Noah Kinley. My stomach hurt with anxiety.

Please, let him live, God. He's been through enough. His poor parents have gone through so much. Let them have their boy back.

Vernon leaned back in his chair. He rubbed his forehead with a sigh.

"Wait, you were so young back then. Did he do it to get back at you?" I asked. "To punish you for having the life he always wanted with the dad he had longed for all his life?"

"Close," Vernon said. "He did envy me all those things. He did resent me for having all he ever wanted, especially our father's love. But there's more." Vernon emptied his coffee and cracked the cup between his hands. Then he looked at me. "It was all my fault," he said.

"What was your fault?"

Tears sprang from Vernon's eyes now. He wiped them off with a sniffle and tried hard to hide them from me. "That they ended up in prison. That they had to endure all that. That my dad died. Everything. It was all because of me."

"How so?"

"I spoke up against the regime," he said. "I was just a young kid, but that didn't matter. I assaulted an officer at my grandmother's house when they came to take her farm. She was an old lady and the farm was her entire life. I tried to tell them they had no right, that Castro was a coward for picking on old ladies. My father was in town spending time with Alejándro for the first time in years when the police came to pick him up at a public park. They told him it was his upbringing of me that had given me those ideas, that he was leading a conspiracy against Castro. He was what they called an *anti-socialist element*. In a way, they were right. My dad was a famous poet and had spoken up against the regime on several occasions. When they came to pick him up, my brother went nuts and started to fight them. So they took him as well. They decided they both were a threat to society and kept them without even a trial. My mother never even got to visit my father. She never knew what happened to him until Alejándro came to her that afternoon when I was in school. He showed her the ring, my dad's ring. That was all he had left of him. When you showed it to me, I couldn't believe my own eyes. But now I know. Alejándro must have dropped it when he took Scott. He still had it when he beat up my mother and left her bleeding on the floor." Vernon shook his head with a sigh. "I found her when I came home. She decided to keep the story a secret from me. She told me it was a robbery. I always believed that was what happened. Up until yesterday when my mom told me everything. Told me how my brother blamed me for everything bad that had ever happened to him. Everything, Detective. She also told me where to find him. She knew he had that surf shop in Cocoa Beach. She had seen his picture in *Florida Today*, the local section in the paper when he opened up the shop ten years ago. But it had been under another name. Hector Suarez. So she knew where to find him when I confronted her. When I came to him, and asked him about the boys, he told me he had done it because he wanted me to be punished. When he was released from the Cuban prison and sent to the States by boat, he was determined to find me. He was so eaten by anger over what had happened to my dad. So when he finally found me here in Florida, he wanted me to suffer in the same way he had. He kidnapped a kid and made sure I was blamed for it. He tipped off the police anonymously, and when they had a witness that identified me in a line-up and said I looked like the guy he had seen with Scott Kingston, then the case was clear to them."

"Except, it wasn't you. It was him. But back then, you looked so much alike," I said.

Vernon snapped his fingers. "Twenty-eight years of my life. Gone. Just like that. All because of one little childish mistake."

"And once your brother started torturing the kids, he couldn't stop, so once Scott was dead, he kidnapped another one, Jordan Turner, and held him captive in the back of his store for years. Till he died several years later."

"When he heard I was out, he kidnapped Noah Kinley, because he wanted me back inside. I didn't deserve the release, he told me right before I shot him. He wanted me to spend the rest of my life in jail. He knew the police would immediately suspect me."

"And he was right," I said. "We all suspected you right away."

"I shot him because I wanted him off the face of the planet. He told me you would never believe me over him. I had to get rid of him. Even if it meant I would go back to jail."

The door opened to the waiting room and a doctor entered. I stared at him, my heart beating so fast it almost hurt.

"He's stable now. Gave us quite a scare," he said. "His heart had stopped beating, so we had to revive him. Took a while before he was stabilized. I wasn't sure he would make it. He is severely dehydrated and malnourished, but I am positive he will be better soon with the right care. You brought him to us just in time. A few more minutes, and it would have been too late. You saved his life, Detective."

Epilogue

I AIN'T GOT JACK—AND I WANT MY JACK BACK

EIGHTY-TWO

May 2015

SHANNON WAS WAITING by the front door. She kept gazing out the window to see if she could spot the car down the road. But still, there was nothing. It had been four days since she left Florida with Jack's family and her own daughter, and she had missed him like crazy. He had called her from the hospital to let her know he was all right and that he would ride out the storm at the hospital with Vernon Johnson and Austin. He also told her how he had found Noah Kinley and that the case was closed.

Now he was on his way to her house in Nashville. He had texted her and told her he had landed at the airport an hour ago, and she had sent one of her drivers to pick him up. She looked at the clock on the wall, then back at the road outside.

The gate slowly opened, and she spotted the black car as it drove up.

"They're coming!" she yelled into the living room.

There were shrieks and screams, as Angela and Abigail ran out the front door. Jack's parents followed, and Shannon grabbed Emily and walked arm in arm with her outside the house. She looked at the young girl, who had been more worried about her father being alone in the storm than she would care to admit. She had been eating better over the four days she had spent at the house. Jack's mother had spoken with her, and that had seemed to help. Shannon had kept an eye on her, and she seemed to be doing better, even though she was still very skinny.

"Hi, guys!"

Jack looked radiant as he stepped out of the car. Maybe it was just because she had missed him so much. His right arm was still hurting, he had told her, but they had taken off the sling, so you could hardly tell.

She let the children get to him first. Abigail jumped into her father's arms and then continued to her brother.

"Don't you ever do that to me again," she said. "I was so scared."

The twins hugged, while Jack was greeted by his parents in a warm embrace.

577

When they let him go, Angela hugged his legs before she too continued to Austin, whom she had taken a serious liking to. Shannon had suspected them of having a little crush on one another. It was too cute.

"Hi there, sweetheart," Jack said and approached Shannon. She kissed him intensely, even though everyone was looking. He touched her stomach lightly, then turned to look at Emily. She looked a little shy. Jack smiled and opened his arms.

"How's my girl?"

"Fine, Dad."

He grabbed her and hugged her warmly. Shannon felt all mushy and her eyes got wet. It was silly how this pregnancy messed with her emotions.

"Let's go inside," she yelled and clapped her hands. "Lunch is served at the deck outside."

"Outside?" Jack asked. "But it's so cold here."

She hit him gently on the shoulder. The good one. He grabbed her around the waist and held her tight. "How's my baby doing?"

"I'm good. I stopped throwing up, finally."

"I was talking to the other one," he said with a grin.

"Jack," Shannon said.

They started to walk inside. Jack whistled when he saw the house. It was a little much. Shannon had always thought it was, but Joe couldn't get it big or pompous enough. She couldn't wait to sell it and move on.

"So, how did it go with Noah's parents?" she asked, as the door closed behind them.

"Oh, you wouldn't believe it. It was so great. As soon as the storm stopped, they were flown in from Orlando on a helicopter. The reunion with their son was heartwarming. It felt so good, you know, to be able to save at least one of those boys. It makes it all worth the effort. It is in moments like that that I really love my work."

"And it is a big part of you, Jack. I do realize that," Shannon said.

For a long time, she had tried to convince him to give up his job and just live off her money, but she was beginning to understand more and more how big a part of him his job really was. Even though she hated that he had to risk his life constantly for others. It was also very admirable and very sexy.

"I still can't believe the guy kept Noah Kinley right across the street from us all this time," she said.

Jack looked serious. "It makes me sick to think of. Noah Kinley was right there, in that shop, in the back, without any of us suspecting anything at all. I mean, all the times I have been in his shop and...I keep thinking, why didn't I hear him? Why didn't I hear him scream? But all the rooms were soundproofed. He built his own little torture chambers back there in the rooms we thought he used for shaping boards."

Shannon felt a chill and shivered. "It's creepy."

"And I even thought he was a nice guy. I surfed with him!"

Shannon nodded, thinking it showed how little you really knew about the people around you.

"And, Vernon?" she asked.

"I talked to Jacqueline Jones, and we agreed he was the real hero who saved the boy. There won't be charges pressed, even though he shot Hector Suarez. The only sad thing is, now I'll never get my new board," he said with a laugh.

"You'll live," Shannon said.

"You said you had a surprise for me?" he asked and kissed her again.

"Yes, follow me."

Shannon walked to the library and asked Jack to sit down in a leather chair, then placed a box on his lap.

"What's this?" he asked.

"Open it."

He opened the lid. Then he looked up at Shannon with a gasp. "Is this what I think it is?"

She nodded. "Yes. He kept it in the safe at the house for all these years. Probably thought he could use it against me if I ever decided to leave him, the bastard."

Jack scoffed. He looked at the gun in the wooden box. "I can't believe it. It has been here all this time. Right under your nose."

"I know. I haven't touched it. I'm turning it in tomorrow, and hopefully they'll drop the charges."

"Let's hope that happens," Jack said, and handed her the box back. "Now, let's get something to eat. I'm starving."

Shannon grabbed his hand and pulled him back. The rest of the family was already engaged in a lively discussion outside; they could hear all their voices talking over each other. It always thrilled Shannon how well their two families did together. She couldn't wait for them to all live in their dream house in Cocoa Beach. She longed for her new life to begin. Especially now, when the future looked a little brighter for her.

"I have one more surprise," she said and kissed him gently.

"There's more? I hope it's as good as the first one," Jack said.

"It's better," she said.

His face lit up.

"The scanning yesterday. How did it go?"

Shannon smiled from ear to ear. "Do you want to know?"

"Yes. I do want to know. Don't I?"

"I know."

"Then I definitely want to know."

"It's a boy."

Jack was one big smile. "A boy!! And, you're sure?"

"As sure as I can get."

"Yes!" Jack exclaimed. "No more being the underdogs around here. More manpower to the family."

Shannon laughed and put her arm around his shoulder. " I guess it evens the score a little around here." She opened the door, and they could see the entire family sitting around the table outside on the patio area. "But, we still hold the majority. Remember that."

"Like I could ever forget," he said.

THE END

What to know what happens next? The next three books in the Jack Ryder series today.
Get it here: Jack Ryder Mystery Series: Vol 4-6

Afterword

Thank you for purchasing *The Jack Ryder Series.* I hope you enjoyed it. I want to let you know that the inspiration for this story, as in many of my other books, comes from real life. There was a kid that was once abducted from her home in 1979 in Merritt Island, while she was asleep. The killer was allegedly lured in by her night-light. You can read about it here:

http://www.floridatoday.com/story/news/local/2015/04/24/torres-friends-slain-girl-connect-years-later/26307607/

Furthermore, for those of you that don't know about the Mariel Boatlift, it really happened. Castro opened the harbor briefly in 1980 and let people leave, and he sent a huge flock of criminals, drug addicts, and mentally ill people with them. Even the story about the bus driving through the embassy walls is true. Only the characters are not. I made them up.

http://www.miamibeach411.com/news/fleeing-cuba

The torture inside the prisons is not something I have made up either. The drawer-cells, the fluorescent light, the banging on the boxes, the starvation, and even them throwing excrement on them, but I thought that was too much to put in this book with the children. You can read more here:

http://www.nytimes.com/1986/06/08/books/surviving-castro-s-tortures.html

Don't forget to check out my other books as well. You can buy them by following the links below. And don't forget to leave reviews if possible. It means so much to me to hear what you think.

Take care,
Willow

To be the first to hear about new releases and bargains—from Willow Rose—sign up below to be on the VIP List. (I promise not to share your email with anyone else, and I won't clutter your inbox.)

- SIGN UP TO BE ON THE VIP LIST HERE :

http://readerlinks.com/l/415254

FOLLOW WILLOW ROSE ON BOOKBUB:
https://www.bookbub.com/authors/willow-rose

Connect with Willow Rose:
www.willow-rose.net

About the Author

The Queen of Scream, Willow Rose, is an international best-selling author. She writes Mystery/Suspense/Horror, Paranormal Romance and Fantasy. She is inspired by authors like James Patterson, Agatha Christie, Stephen King, Anne Rice, and Isabel Allende. She lives on Florida's Space Coast with her husband and two daughters. When she is not writing or reading, you'll find her surfing and watching the dolphins play in the waves of the Atlantic Ocean. She has sold more than three million books.

To be the first to hear about new releases and bargains—from Willow Rose— sign up below to be on the VIP List. (I promise not to share your email with anyone else, and I won't clutter your inbox.)

- SIGN UP TO BE ON THE VIP LIST HERE :

http://readerlinks.com/l/415254

FOLLOW WILLOW ROSE ON BOOKBUB:
https://www.bookbub.com/authors/willow-rose

Connect with Willow online:
willow-rose.net
madamewillowrose@gmail.com

Manufactured by Amazon.ca
Bolton, ON